I0667699

BLAME IT ON THE MACALLAN
Friendship, Freedom, and Enough Love

Melanie Jay

ZATORA
AUSTRALIA

ZATORA SELF-PUBLISHING

BLAME IT ON THE MACALLAN
Friendship, Freedom and Enough Love

This book you're reading is a work of fiction. Characters, events, and names are the product of this author's imagination. Consent has been granted for life characters fictionalised inclusion. Any resemblance to other events, or other persons, living or dead, is coincidental.

Copyright © 2024 Melanie Jay Books

The author reserves all rights to be recognized as the owner of this work. You may not sell or reproduce any part of this book without written consent from the copyright owner melaniejaybooks@gmail.com

First paperback edition July 2024
Book design by Zatora
ISBN Print: 978-1-7635554-2-6
ISBN Ebook: 978-1-7635554-0-2
Printed and bound by Griffin Press Australia
Published by Zatora Publishing
www.zatora.com.au

ZATORA SELF-PUBLISHING

This book is for anyone who dares to dream that
the impossible might just be possible.

Don't forget to download the Blame it on The Macallan playlist.
The QR code is also on the back cover.

Table of Contents

Dear Reader,

Thank you for purchasing my novel and thank you for your valuable time given to read it. I am forever grateful.

This story is purely a work of fiction.

It has been such an experience creating this piece of work for you to read. Features and qualities of the characters have been created from people I've met in real life or would love to meet in real life. I am the only one who knows whom and where I have created my characters from. Imaginably, I may have described the shape of someone's mouth, or the colour or style of their hair, or the intensity of their stare. Perhaps I have integrated the way I've been touched or held into the chapters. Conversation topics and words I've shared with friends and strangers may fall within the pages. Possibly even a conversation or a moment in time with *you*—but not in the same context, and not in the same space. Perhaps I've used your name and attached it to someone else's personality. You see, I can do that because it's all a fabrication of my imagination and creativity. I hope you like it and find yourself in the pages or can relate to the stories of my characters.

I have used some people's real names in my book because their real-life characters fit my time zone for this novel. But none of this actually happened.

I have sought permission for the use of significant real-life characters to be in my novel. With thanks to my beautiful friend Coco who put me in contact with Rachael from Secret Sounds. Bernard Fanning and Powderfinger have given consent for me to use their names as characters. I'm forever grateful. The story wouldn't be the same without them. Thank you Bernard, Ian, John, and Jon with no h, and Darren.

I have also mentioned the names of famous surfers from the era. They were possibly surfing in Coolangatta at the Billabong Pro at the time that my fictional characters were there.

This novel will take you back in time. Not too long ago, but it was a very different world. As you read this story, you might even feel what it was like living in the early 90s; no mobile phones, no social media to keep us connected. We used telephone booths, and made STD phone calls, we wrote letters, and we played board games and cards for entertainment. Relationships were all about face-to-face human connection and conversations were in real time and real life.

I have been writing this novel as a hobby, outside of my full-time work, so it has taken a lengthy time to complete this personal project — six years, in fact. The title of my novel has changed along the way from Have Guitar, Will Travel, to Finding You, to Found and Lost, to Take Me Back, to the final decision Blame it on The Macallan. It's perfect. The Macallan having a double meaning, related to the famous whisky and the family surname in my story.

The biggest question is, who should we blame it on? Which Macallan? I think it's all because of Frankie Macallan, but you can make up your own mind.

As a new-first-time author I am excited to connect with my readers. If you would like to connect with me, please feel free to reach out through my social media channels. I would love to know what you think. Which chapter is your favourite? Mine is Soul Surfing. What do you love, what do you hate about my novel? I want to know it all.

melaniejaybooks on Instagram.
melaniejaybooks on Facebook.
melaniejaybooks on TikTok.
www.melaniejaybooks.com
Drop me an email to melaniejaybooks@gmail.com

My ultimate goal in life is to be an author presenter at two of my favourite writing festivals of all time. The Somerset Storyfest and The Byron Bay Writers Festival. One day, someday, until then I'll just keep doing what I do best, that is being a PE teacher and finding adventure in daily life and I'll continue writing in my spare time.

I must confess that I have published another piece of work. It is called Twenty Years An Angel. It is not fiction, it was not fun to write, it was not all made up from my creative mind. It is in fact a true story of my life and the tragedy I endured, as a young person, which made me the woman I am today. It's a little book that can be purchased on amazon.com.au and zatora.com.au. It was called Bee Sting My Bali Diary, until the book trolls stole it. Buy the edited version, it's better anyway, it's updated to include annual reflections of the passing years of grief. I share my story in the hope that I will help others who endure similar tragedies and need somebody to tell them 'Hey, it's okay to get on and enjoy your life and make it the best life ever possible, as impossible as that might seem. We only get one chance at this thing called LIVING.'

I made a decision to not include page numbers. I hope you can remember where you are up to from the chapter titles. It was fun, naming each chapter. A novel with 100 chapters. Perfect!

This is Australia!

'Nooooooooooo. Please God. No!'

As he got nearer, he could smell the burning rubber from the screech of the tyres, where she had tried to stop suddenly. The enormous kangaroo lay in a heap on the road, not moving. Her car had swerved off the road and into the ditch. The front of the vehicle was facing downwards. The back tyres were lifted off the ground and were still spinning. The engine was still running, with smoke rising from the bonnet.

He couldn't move faster if he tried, but everything felt like it was happening in slow motion. He dragged her lifeless body out of the car, praying someone would come to help. Between sobs of piercing heartache, he called out to the returning silence. 'Noooooooo, come back to me, noooooo. Somebody help me, please somebody.'

He placed her lifeless body in the back seat of his car, as best he could, in a comfortable side position. Not that it mattered. She was out cold. He drove directly to the hospital with his foot to the floor, the speedo was flicking above 160km per hour. He was aware of the risk he was taking to drive at this speed, way above the quiet country road 50km per hour speed limit. But he didn't care. The rules didn't matter right now. Nothing really mattered right now.

It was very early in the morning; the sun was just coming up. The sky was pale in colour casting shades of pink and purple against a faint blue background. The dim light of the day added to the ghostly feel of his existence right now. He pulled into the emergency driveway at the front of the hospital, hoping that someone would come to help. It seemed like no-one was on duty. Not a soul in sight. He climbed out of the driver's seat and opened the back door, trying to keep calm, but feeling overwhelming, intense pain inside his chest, with the realisation that his beautiful girl was dead. He couldn't control the whimper coming from his mouth, his chin uncontrollably quivering with anguish.

He carried her lifeless body, like a dead weight in his arms into the hospital. 'Somebody, please help me. Please somebody, anybody.' He looked down at her angelic face, completely blank of expression, her slender arms and small unmoving chest behind the bright blue-butterfly T-shirt that she was wearing, her absolute favourite. It seemed so surreal that just a few hours before this moment, her whole body was alive with laughter and love. Her smile beaming with beauty and joy captivated in the moment. Now. Nothing. Nothingness. Stillness. She was gone!

In the next moment, it was like everyone that was on the dawn shift was suddenly in the hospital lobby, trying to help. It was chaos. She was placed on a stretcher and rolled into the emergency ward. Machines and cords were being attached to her motionless body with no effect, no signs of life, no beeps, no response. There was nothing anybody could do. She had suffered a massive head injury and died on impact. She was pronounced dead at 4.44 am. It was the 25th of January 1993.

The first question the detective asked him. 'Sir, I'm very sorry for your loss, but I must ask you. Have you been drinking?'

chapter one

Angourie—Noisy Ocean

Matilda Macallan grew up in Angourie, a small coastal village in the Clarence Valley region of Northern New South Wales. To Matilda, Angourie was the most beautiful little beach town on Earth. This assumption was based on her extensive travel experience as far as Ballina, one and a half hours to the north, and Coffs Harbour, the same distance to the south. Yeah, I know what you're thinking - Matilda hadn't travelled much, but she already knew she lived in the best little beach town on the planet.

Angourie was picturesque, with its laneway streets, bushwhacked tracks leading to secluded covey beaches, and rocky cliffs descending into crashing waves of small coastline bays. Matilda loved exploring Green Point, Spooky's Beach, The Green Pool and The Blue Pool, Mara Creek, and Woolooweyah Back Beach, where Matilda would hide out on a sunny day in her permanent hammock that she had hung upon the sturdy Pandanus branches. Nobody else knew the hammock in the palm tree existed because nobody ever went there except Matilda. Well, not that she knew of. A secret pathway wound through the thick beach scrub bushes to get to it.

From the palm tree hammock, she could enjoy watching a peaceful sunrise on the horizon as she listened to nature come alive, and as a young girl, she would often spend hours in the hammock, reading books and writing poetry or song lyrics.

Angourie is connected to the Yuraygir National Park, an expanse of trails, headlands, and beaches as far as the eye can see. It was peaceful, and the streets were quiet, except for the evening sounds of hopscotch rocks on the road and the soft laughter of the kids playing after-school games in the cul-de-sacs and street corners.

The best thing about this place was that hardly anyone knew this scenic, peaceful little beach town existed. Angourie was at the northern tip of the Yuraygir National Park, and there was only one way in and the same way out. Angourie, meaning 'noisy ocean,' 'the sound of the wind,' was favoured by Australian surfing enthusiasts. The town's population almost doubled when the wind and swell conditions were favourable. Angourie Point offered a smooth right-hand break on the northern side of the headland on a perfect east-north-easterly swell. If the winds were blowing directly from the north, one would catch a superb left-hand break on the southern side of the headland. For hardcore surfers, the drive to Angourie was always worth it. It was a win-win on most occasions.

To add to the excitement, when the swell and winds picked up at certain times of the year, the small-steep-sandy Angourie Bay provided dramatic circumstances to even the most experienced surfer. The rock shelf near the shoreline created a surge of power in the wave, making Angourie Point one of the most challenging surf breaks on the Eastern Australian coastline. The locals call this rock shelf *'Life or Death'* for the outcome of this break if you get it right or wrong. You didn't want to get it wrong.

Angourie had a population of two hundred and twenty-two and had been branded as a ghost town. This branding didn't quite fit with the reality of this town. A ghost town, by definition, was any town with a population of fewer than two hundred residents with a declining population. Angourie missed out by twenty-two. The description of *'ghost town'* also suggested that the once flourishing community, with economic wealth, was now deserted. Angourie had never been a flourishing community, but neither was it abandoned nor deserted. The financial wealth was not widespread, nor was the population; however, the locals who lived in the town were not ghosts and were not planning on moving anywhere else. They were lively and delighted with how their little town functioned.

The two hundred or so residents battled to maintain the characteristics of the town to keep Angourie just the way it was. Many nature enthusiasts feared the land would be re-zoned from National Parkland to Residential. This rezoning fear was an ongoing concern and a common discussion amongst the local political circles, as many of the small towns around Angourie were growing stronger in population. The natural spread was to move into Angourie. Fortunately, the southern end hosted a preserved wildlife corridor, where many endangered plant and animal species, including the swamp orchid, the grey-headed flying fox and the coastal emu called Angourie home.

The locals were the living skeletons, the souls and the spirits that bonded to keep their ghost town as it was. They adored their noisy-ocean-wildlife-loving-ghost-town.

It was the kind of town where everybody knew everybody and supported their fellow town-mates one hundred per cent, but everybody kept to themselves. The small town was full of creative geniuses who had moved to the area to find solitude, and many had found themselves a piece of paradise to live out their dreams. The small cafes were filled with local artists' paintings, sculptures, pottery, and macrame. Much of the artists' work drew inspiration from local scenes, the sunrises and sunsets of the beautiful coves, expansive beaches and secluded bays. This place, indeed, was an artists' paradise.

The nearest town was Yamba, just five minutes down the road. Yamba had a much larger population, closer to six thousand people. It was a small town also, but large enough to provide schools and employment for the Yamba locals and many feeder towns in the area. With the bustling tourist trade, local businesses in Yamba thrived in the holiday seasons. Many tourists came to explore the quiet beaches and boutique shops and to enjoy the pace of life in the beautiful beach town. The irony that struck the locals was that the beaches in Angourie were unquestionably more scenic and touristic than the Yamba beaches. Still, somehow, Angourie didn't seem to make the tourist map. For most, it was just a little insignificant surfing town.

These many things made Angourie special; the locals loved it that way.

chapter two

Jack and Laura

Matilda was a second-generation Angourie local. Her father, Jack, and mother, Laura, had fallen madly in love at a very young age, and their life paths had led them to Angourie.

In the 1960s, Jack and Laura survived an era of social hardship because of the devastating effects of the Vietnam War. Families had been torn apart during the war, and many innocent lives were lost. Jack was a man of free will and was fighting against conscription. In Australia, Jack could be called upon by law to serve in the armed forces.

Jack was very much anti-war. He was a gentle-loving peacekeeping soul, and deep in his heart, he knew he could never kill another human being, regardless of the circumstances. Something in his soul valued *peace* highly above any other core value that man could possess.

Jack was one of the Australian citizens joining the draft resistance campaign to encourage the right to refuse to fight based on non-aggressionist values. He was part of the social movement that eventually formed the conscientious objector group and the human rights movement.

As a young man in Australia, refusing service during this time of war was complex. It was only that Jack's father, a carpenter, was employed to build shelters and structures for soldiers and refugees coming home from the war that gave Jack a reason to stay in Australia. Jack joined his father with the responsibility of building community housing, hospitals, and places of refuge for soldiers returning from war. Jack was grateful to have a job back in the homeland and repeatedly appealed his conscription. It was an illegal offence, and they delivered fines. Jack paid the fines and continued to refuse service. He kept on fighting 'his peace mission.' There was another stronghold adding to his resistance to service. There was no chance in hell that Jack was leaving his beloved Laura behind, so he did whatever he could to remain in his homeland. Jack continued to be an excellent, valued, and productive worker, so he was less likely to be deployed as a soldier. As a builder, he benefited the returning soldiers and still contributed to the service. That is the way he liked to think of it. Without ever having to pull a trigger, as part of the so-called peace mission that was causing deaths by the thousands, he was still completing his mission for peace. By the war's end, the tally of casualties was close to 1.4 million; 523 Australians died in the war in Vietnam. Jack pulled different triggers: an electric drill, a welding gun, and an arrow straight into Laura's heart.

Jack and Laura had met by random chance at a community anti-war rally. Laura had finished formal schooling, but she still lived with her parents. She was a seamstress and made uniforms for the local schoolchildren. Jack fell in love with her the first moment he caught her gaze. To Jack's eyes, she was the most beautiful human being he had ever seen. When their eyes met, she looked back at him warmly and intensely, like her gaze reflected his soul. There was a challenge, though. Laura's heavily religious family was firmly against Jack and Laura's connection. When Jack and Laura met, Jack was twenty-six, and Laura was just seventeen. Jack and Laura's relationship progressed quickly, and they had an age difference that Laura's parents and community disapproved of. Laura was still young and inexperienced in making her own decisions, based on the church and family morals she had to obey whilst living with her parents.

As the dark cloud surrounding the war restrictions and depressions shifted away, the way society functioned changed entirely. People rioted for their beliefs to be heard. Many people lived their own way without allowing various societal or government controls to determine their life choices. They spoke up and rallied for individual freedoms. People also seemed to live with a sense of new life and vitality. Suddenly, people realised the value of freedom once again. Having lived through war, people were more aware that dark days had consumed their lives, and now it was time to live wild and free again.

Jack's family supported the relationship, but Laura's family disapproved. They tried everything they could to stop Laura from seeing Jack, so Jack and Laura took it upon themselves to find their chosen freedom. The only way they could do this was to rebel against Laura's family and the church's expectations. They became outcasts to the family and the church, and although it was a tough choice, they silently fled the big city in protest of their deep and genuine love for each other.

One night, just a typical Tuesday, Laura took her leave. She packed a small suitcase and her guitar and climbed out of her bedroom window, as quietly as a mouse, leaving a note on her bed telling her parents that she loved them, and Jack too, and if they would not allow her to see him, she had only one option. She scribed the note in beautiful handwritten calligraphy and placed it in an embossed envelope from the unique calligraphy set her grandmother gave her before she passed away. It read.

I'm sorry, Mum and Dad, I love you, but I also love Jack. Jack loves me, too, and we will be forever happy. I promise. I know this. Never worry about me. Trust me on this one. I'll always be OK. Jack will always take good care of me. Love Little L.

Little L, that's what her dad always called her, Little One or Little L. It was interchangeable. She loved that. She would miss that.

But now, as a rebellious teenager, Laura was asserting her independence. No one would tell Laura that she was too young to decide that she and Jack would be together forever. They both knew what they wanted in their lives, but no one else truly understood the depth and commitment of their young, innocent love. Packing up their belongings, including Jack's dog, Jezebel May (Jessie for short), they travelled north on a mission to find their "happy place." They stopped and settled temporarily in various locations along the eastern Australian coastline. Stopping for various reasons: to surf, work, make love, play music, and find adventure in their freedom away from the big city. Their smiles, inner happiness, and love for each other grew stronger every kilometre they travelled further from the structure, the rules, and the confinement of the judgments placed on them. They were young, wild, free, and madly in love with each other.

Jack first suggested that he would like to stay in Angourie. He had this gut instinct that this was their place to build a forever home. Jack was a skilled builder. Laura had no complaints and was ready to plant her feet firmly on the ground as she felt their first child's first kick of life inside her belly.

Jack and Laura had been on the road for a little over a year, exploring and finding adventure in every town they stopped in. However, they both, at the same time, had decided this was enough; this was the place for them. This place was far enough away from the big city smoke. It was closely nestled to beautiful beaches and abundant nature, and *Angourie, Noisy Ocean, The Sound of the Wind* echoed a voice to Jack and Laura. The voices of the wind that blew across the wild ocean were calling their hearts to stay. They both heard the voices. They strongly and deeply felt this was where they wanted to call home.

Jack and Laura had enough money for a deposit to buy a small piece of land in the most stunning location. It was on the headland overlooking the back beach of Angourie. It felt like home, and it felt like forever. Jack got to work and started building their beach shack with the most stunning ocean views. They caught glimpses of the sunrises to the East and the sunsets to the West.

In Angourie, the townsfolk didn't judge them. Their intense love was free to bloom. They lived as cleanly as possible, self-sufficiently from their land. They had an established vegetable garden and free-roaming chickens. They had tanks to provide clean, fresh water. When they couldn't provide for themselves, they were happy to support their local community by purchasing additional fresh produce daily in the amounts they needed for survival—nothing more, nothing less, just enough. From sunup to sundown, they worked hard to provide nutrition and shelter for themselves. Jack and Laura didn't live to work; they worked to live. They were truly living their lives, and everything they did for survival was fun and worthwhile, making them happy.

Laura did some support teaching in the local school to help the young children with their reading. Jack was the local handyman and builder. He always had plenty of work to keep him busy. Jack and Laura were talented musicians, so they also did local music gigs in town when the tourist population called out for weekend entertainment. They could get any crowd dancing and singing along to well-known cover songs and performed a few original hits. They called their acoustic duo, 'Have Guitar, Will Travel.'

They surfed, worked on their farm, made music, and made lots of love. Peace, love, and happiness surrounded and filled their home as the years passed, and their four beautiful children grew up, free to be wild, surf, play, and be creative and natural. All four children went to schools in the local area, and they were well-behaved, respectful young people in the community. Jack and Laura were supportive parents, encouraging their four children to discover and embrace their natural qualities and be unique and independent whilst maintaining the balance of being respectful to others. They encouraged them to be trusted, hold high morals, and be loyal to their small community. There was no room for error, and everyone would know about it if there was.

Angourie provided the safety, security, and freedom for this beautiful style of life that they desired. It was quiet, and there wasn't much going on for entertainment, so they made their own fun by creating wholesome friendships, finding adventure in daily outings, and exploring the local areas. The most fun was had when they were hosting dinner parties for their friends. Jack and Laura loved to entertain guests. Laura was a fantastic entertainer; she was an effortless cook. She could create the most beautiful meals out of what seemed like scraps. It was incredible.

As the children grew older, the entertainment became more focused on family-orientated evenings, as they all came together as young adults. They had the most fun when they got together for a board game night of Monopoly, 21, Checkers and Chess, Cluedo or Scrabble. Frankie and Jack played Chess, but only some of the rest of the family could get into it. Their favourite family card game was Euchre. The complex card game of Canasta became more popular as Matilda grew older and understood how to play it. When they played Canasta, they usually joined up in pairs. The usual teams were Jack and Laura versus Matilda and Frankie versus Eddie and Louis.

They had so much fun, and the family rivalry and banter were hilarious. It got competitive, at times, because they kept a running score. Louis often had to check himself to remember *it was just a game.*

chapter three

The Macallan Family

As the years rolled by, Jack and Laura consistently provided a haven as their beach shack grew to house them all. The shack that started as a one-bedroom-cosy cottage for Jack, Laura, and Jezebel was now extended with five total bedrooms, a beautiful open kitchen, large spanning decks, and the most treasured room in the house was the magnificent outdoor bathroom overlooking the Yuraygir National Park. Their family and shack grew, and their family bond grew stronger.

Most of the time, the four children got along well, and the family connection was stable. They always sat down together in the evening to share a home-cooked family meal and stories about their days. They were open about their lives wonderful and not-so-wonderful happenings, and all supported each other. The only smidgen of sibling rivalry was between Louis and Eddie, the twins, who often fought over ridiculous things. The arguments were usually over a girl they both liked, a chore they both wanted to do, a piece of clothing they both wanted to wear simultaneously or who would get to eat the last sausage. Eddie usually won most of the arguments with his calm and assertive way of solving the problem. In most of the arguments, Louis was so busy encouraging the rest of the family to take his side that he didn't even realise that Eddie had already solved the problem. The fight was soon over before it had even begun. Matilda and Frankie would watch on, not getting involved, knowing that this was just part of who they were as twin brothers. The funny thing was that aside from these silly, petty arguments that Louis and Eddie would often have, they were best mates. They loved each other immensely and would do anything for each other, spending every day side-by-side, finding adventure and fun together. They were inseparable.

Frankie, being the eldest of the four, was the responsible type. Matilda, Louis, and Eddie idolised him. He had a presence because he was tall, strong, and athletic. Frankie had a broad smile and gentle, loving, green-blue eyes like his father, Jack. He was fun and cheeky, yet sensible and kind. Frankie had a courageous nature and a heart of gold.

Because he was the oldest brother, he was always protective of his younger siblings if they ever got in danger.

One morning, when they were all relatively young, Matilda was ten, Louis and Eddie were twelve, and Frankie had just turned sixteen; they had ventured down to the beach in Angourie Cove for an early surf. Jack and Laura had stayed home for a 'lay-in.' Usually, the whole family went down together, and they had no problems. They all surfed together, sharing the waves, and having a great time. Laura would sit on the beach, under her favourite pandanus palm tree, and read a book, still part of the experience, but she wasn't keen to get in the water.

This particular morning, however, was different. Frankie promised to keep an eye on them, as he always did. He didn't notice that the storm from the night before had carved out the sand, creating a heavy undertow, and instantly, as they entered the water, all four were dramatically swept out to sea by a strong rip. Somehow, Frankie brought them all in, one by one, Matilda first, then the twins. It was quite an incredible rescue considering the circumstances, and from that day on, they all took much more notice of the dangers of the wild Angourie ocean, and Frankie was always their hero.

The Macallan kids grew up through the '70s and '80s, attending Yamba Public School and then Maclean High School, the only options in the area for a wholesome public education. They wore a strict uniform to school, which became a thing in the early '70s in Australia. Other than their school uniforms, they didn't have a lot of clothes. Life was simple. In summer, the boys lived in their surfing trunks, Matilda in her crocheted bathing suit. In winter, the boys wore corduroy flares and hand-me-downs. Laura taught Matilda all the seamstress tricks and knitting skills she had learned from her mother. It was an important life skill, and Laura liked the idea of creating her own style of clothing that differed slightly from what everyone else was wearing. She had fun with materials, colour, and mixing patterns of checks, florals, and paisleys. Laura and Matilda would stitch their own homemade floral or psychedelic patterned tunics. They all wore colourful ponchos and thick woolly knits in winter. The ponchos were Laura's favourite items of clothing to knit with big, thick, fluffy wool because the pattern was so simple, a series of squares sewn together, with a hole for the head to fit through. The poncho was versatile and could be worn over any item of clothing, providing warmth and cosy comfort in the cold winter.

Throughout their young years, the Macallan kids thrived in an era of peace and free love. As a family, they flourished in the presence of social freedom. They were free and wild, adventurous, and trusting. The world was a peaceful place to live in, especially in their beautiful hometown of Angourie. Besides the hectic, noisy ocean, there was not much to fear.

Because of their innocent and wholesome upbringing, they all sought to explore and understand the concepts of new-age spirituality. Jack and Laura had removed themselves from the solid religious bearings placed on them in their earlier years together. Rather than adhering to political or religious phases, they explored the metaphysical concepts of astrology, tarot, and crystal healing. They knew certain things about the world, not substantial things to most people, just interesting information about astronomy, the star constellations, weather patterns and cycles. They investigated and were intrigued by astrology and star signs, just out of interest. They were interested in learning about crystals and were fascinated to learn about their apparent magical powers. They understood people and personalities and the characteristics of a good-natured soul. Jack loved to read books by Howard Gardner, Wayne Payne and Reuven Bar-On as they explored the concept of multiple intelligences outside the IQ. He would lead family discussions about these topics after immersing himself in understanding the theories presented in the books he was reading. In a world revolving around intelligence and IQ scores, he strongly connected with emotional and social intelligence theories as being far more critical for humanity. The Macallans understood the importance of natural health and good living with moderation for everything. Their life motto was 'Everything in moderation—including moderation.'

Frankie was born on American Independence Day, the fourth day of July. He was a Cancer star sign, a water sign. He was a water baby with a fierce, heroic exterior and a beautiful, intuitive, emotional inner soul. His favourite crystal was Tiger's Eye, as it oozed protection qualities. After all, he was the eldest brother and the protector of the younger siblings in his family. He needed to embody all the protective qualities he could muster, especially with Matilda, as his youngest sibling. She was wild and needed protecting.

Eddie and Louis, as strange and unique as it may seem, celebrated their birthdays on the 21st of May, which placed them in the zodiac as Gemini twins, with an air sign on the cusp of Taurus, an earth sign. The personalities of both covered all characteristics of the Gemini trait. They were spontaneous, playful, and adorably erratic, more so for Louis for the latter quality. Eddie was born first, so technically, he was closer to drawing on some of the serene characteristics of the earth sign, Taurus. Laura often joked that she was sure that Eddie was born at 11.59 pm on the 20th of May and Louis was born after midnight on the 21st of May. That would have made more sense because the twins' personalities differed vastly.

At the time of their birth, no one was recording the exact moment of delivery as all hands-on-deck were focused on the safe delivery of the second baby, Louis. Laura was not due to give birth for another three weeks, so the completely unexpected-natural-home-twin-water-birth created some minor complications. Everything was okay, but in the focus on survival, no one recorded the accurate delivery time for Eddie, the firstborn. He was okay, and that was all that mattered; the focus was then on the safe delivery of baby number two. Laura did not plan a home birth or water birth; however, that was how it turned out. The nearest hospitals were Murwillumbah, Lismore, or the Gold Coast, but Eddie and Louis were born in the beach shack in Angourie.

Eddie's favourite crystal was Turquoise, a pale blue and green-coloured crystal that brought qualities of wisdom. Eddie always had a bit of insecurity about not being super intelligent, and this was only because he had a bit of a lisp when he was growing up, and he got teased about it. His teachers told him he didn't speak properly, which affected his reading results, although his reading comprehension was outstanding. As time passed, his lisp disappeared without intervention, and he had no intellectual difficulties. He was a super intelligent and creative young man, but his lure was always to wisdom. He aspired to have 'intelligence' as his childhood complex of receiving bad report cards took a while to get over. As Jack read more and more about the concept of multiple intelligences and explained these concepts to Eddie, Eddie believed he wasn't so unintelligent anymore. He had other critically important human qualities than academic mathematical, linguistic, or scientific *geniusness*.

Louis was drawn to Bloodstone, aware that he carried a feisty temper. The Bloodstone was supposedly the crystal healer for clearing emotional negativity. It was a fascinating dark green gem speckled with blood-like red infusions. Louis wore a bloodstone gem around his neck to remind him to keep calm and be more positive. It was not his natural tendency to be positive.

For the Macallans, this astrology, tarot, and crystal stuff was interesting to analyse and discuss. It wasn't right or wrong or proven. It was just fun for the Macallans to align personal characteristics with the astrological scripts and figure out the deeper qualities of each person by analysing certain astrology traits. Laura would often pull out the tarot cards if one of the family members was going through some tough stuff to put an external perspective on the potential solutions to the problem or challenge. Most of the time, it was fun and insightful and often gave a different perspective on the challenge.

Matilda was born on the 26th of January in the 1970s. This day was celebrated as Australia Day. Matilda liked that her birthday was on a particular day for celebration, as Frankie was born on the 4th of July, a specific day for American celebrations. Tilly always felt typically Australian and was proud to be. She was an Aquarius, an air sign, but often confused to be a water sign because of the word Aqua in the name. Matilda was innovative, forward-thinking, and shamelessly revolutionary. Her goal in life was to make the world a better place just by living in it and enjoying it. Matilda was drawn to Citrine, the Wonder Woman gem, possessing positivity, luck, and success qualities. It was a golden yellow gem that radiated so much energy for her. Matilda also liked Amethyst, the purple gemstone, because it had qualities she was drawn to when she needed to purify her thoughts and behaviours. Matilda was drawn to mischievous behaviours because her major priority in life was to enjoy each moment. She lived day to day without concern for the future, knowing that if she did what she loved every day, the next day would also be good. That was the plan. It caused some challenges for her because she was so carefree and impulsive.

Jack and Laura, Cancer and Taurus, were the perfect match companions, said to be the most compatible zodiac coupling. For both star signs, the core values of trust and closeness manifested into a super-connected emotional and physical partnership. The two signs are compatible because they focus on being family-oriented. Together, they create a harmonious and happy love nest, which Jack and Laura had done, regardless of a star sign prediction. Jack and Laura both loved the Rose Quartz gemstone because it symbolised love. It was a pale pink quartz gem, and it was common, but it was the one they both liked the most because of its significance in attracting and anchoring love. Their love for each other was anchored forever; there was no doubt about it.

chapter four

Trash or Treasure

The cold winter struck, bringing ice-cold winds to Angourie and claiming the life of the long-lived-town-storyteller, Bessie.

Bessie was known only by her first name; she had disconnected from her family in Perth when she was a young girl and had abandoned her full name, first and last, at the same time. That was the deep story that she shared with nobody. Not a soul knew her story. Bessie kept her story to herself, knowing she was safe only if her identity remained anonymous to the locals.

When Bessie decided as a thirteen-year-old foster child to run away from home for the tenth time, she figured Angourie was the furthest opposite place in Australia that she could get to, where she could find safety and refuge. She found security and anonymity with a single mother, who took her on as her daughter and included her as part of her little family unit. Bessie instantly had two younger sisters. Bessie didn't even tell this wonderful lady, whom she called Mum, her actual name, ever. She depended on the secrecy of living in Angourie, and she trusted no one would locate her there. Everyone in her ghost town could know her, but no one else from anywhere else would know who she was or where she was from—the perfect scenario for a desperate runaway.

When Bessie tiptoed into Angourie and into the loving arms of Ethel May, she changed her identity, and she didn't say a word of truth to anyone. Now and then, people would question her about her childhood and ask her where she was from. She made up a different story every time. It was quite a talent that she developed, hence becoming the excellent storyteller that she was. No one would ever know her genuine truth for as long as she lived and died.

On the day Bessie died, at age 66, she was still on the missing persons register as Gertrude Lancaster. The day she fled to Angourie, fifty-three years prior, she made up this new name, Bessie, with no last name. She changed her physical identity by cutting off her bum-length white-blonde hair and dyeing it in various colours throughout her lifetime. If her hair was never blonde, she was happy. Sometimes, it was brown, black, pink, blue, purple, and red. No one ever questioned it. They just thought she enjoyed colouring her hair. When she was in her late teens, her two 'half-sisters' joined in the fun, which helped the blending-in process even more. She always kept her hair short with a schoolboy cut to avoid being recognised easily. Bessie also had this thing about wearing a headpiece. She always wore a hat or a beanie, a Bandana, or a scarf on her head.

In her early twenties, Bessie found love in a man called Trevor Smythe. He had moved to the area and started his own business as a local mechanic. He became well-known in the area and was very good at his trade. Trevor had a heartbreaking story that bonded the two of them in mutual understanding, but they never spoke of each other's traumas in the company of others. Perhaps Trevor was the only person who knew Bessie's accurate tale and maybe her real name. They were both very secretive and private about their past lives. It was easy for them to love each other for the person they had met in Angourie. They left the rest of their lives behind them in foreign places, not to be brought here.

Angourie was their place of secrecy and love. Their love for each other was a beautiful story. Bessie and Trevor never married because Bessie didn't want to go through the process of registering a name for a marriage through Births, Deaths, and Marriages, as it might bring attention to her identity. She wanted to continue to fly under the radar. And she did. Trevor didn't mind. He loved her regardless of a piece of lightweight cardboard to endorse their connection. They exchanged rings in their own private ceremony at sunset on the 14th of February, Valentine's Day, in 1950 on the Angourie Headland. They vowed their love to each other forever with heartfelt words and an exchange of a passionate kiss to seal the vows. From that day onwards, people often called Bessie, Bessie Smythe. She didn't correct them, even though that wasn't her real name, neither first nor last.

Bessie and Trevor had two sons, Peter and Matthew, who grew up in Angourie and learned the mechanic trade like their father. The boys were always together and always helping their dad with everything. Meanwhile, Bessie forged a living from the shop at the front of their home. For years and years, she worked in the shop, never taking a day to rest. From sunup to sundown, the door was open for Angourie residents to buy the most needed things. If Bessie were in the back of the shop, she would close the front door, leaving a sign saying *OPEN. Please come in, I'm outback.* She always wanted to be available to her customers. The door was equipped with dangling bells so that when it opened, Bessie would hear the chimes of the dangling bells to let her know she was needed. She was always available.

Trevor had also renovated some rooms as guest rooms out the back of their home. Guests staying in the rooms at the back were a rarity because few people came to visit in Angourie, but Bessie and Trevor would always provide comfort to whoever was passing through and needed a place to rest. She called the back part of the building Bessie's B&B. Bed and Breakfast homestays had traditionally become popular after the Second World War. Medieval days of dungeon stays became more popular, and the term B&B had a new ring to it. It was an old English tradition where rooms were offered in people's homes, and guests were provided with breakfast.

Bessie liked the idea of the B&B; she enjoyed giving people a nice place to rest. All the rooms had their own bedroom and bathroom, but no kitchen. For meals, the guests would rely on Bessie's home cooking. She loved to cook for people; it fulfilled her traumatised childhood soul to know she could provide wholesome meals to random guests rather than them going hungry. Bessie knew more than anyone what it felt like to be hungry and beg for food daily. She loved the fulfilment of having a full tummy of nourishing warm food. Giving that feeling to others gave her the most joy.

Bessie and Trevor had a wonderful, long-lasting marriage until he died in a freak work accident when he was just 64. The saddest thing was that not long before he passed away, he had decided that he was going to retire from his mechanical work to help Bessie in the shop. His decision came a week too late.

Bessie passed away a few short years after losing Trevor. Some say she died of a broken heart. She had willed the run-down local corner store and B&B to her two sons to take it over, but neither of the boys had the passion or drive to continue her dream. Both of their parents had passed away within a few close years, and it was tough for them. They decided to put Bessie's Café on the market, split the profits, and get out of town. They had both outgrown Angourie and had dreams to pursue, so they took this as a chance to move away.

This provided a fantastic opportunity for Jack and Laura Macallan, as they realised the potential to create a unique lifestyle for their large family of six in their hometown.

They say, "One man's trash is another man's treasure." This was most definitely the case for Jack and Laura. They took one look at the 'for-sale' sign poked into the ground in front of the old run-down corner store. They drove straight to the bank. Jack and Laura had a vision and a dream for this Angourie treasure.

Bessie's Cafe and B&B sat on the corner of the main street, with the potential for panoramic ocean and hinterland views. However, the way Bessie's Café was structured, it didn't take full advantage of the picture-perfect-postcard-paradise opportunity. For starters, the building was just one level in height, and it desperately needed severe repair, a complete restructure, and renovation. With some modifications, taking full advantage of its fantastic location would be possible. If raised to two levels, it would catch more ocean breezes and, with expansive decking, would provide a viewpoint to watch the sunrise over the ocean to the east and capture a sunset over the hinterland ranges towards the west. The rule in real estate was always "location, location, location." Bessie's Café was in the perfect location.

Fortunately, Jack was a builder and had been in the building industry since he was seventeen. With three decades of building experience, it was the perfect time for him to take on an extensive project. Jack and Laura's children were now all grown up. They all still lived in Angourie, mostly. They would come and go as they pleased, always knowing they were welcome for a feed and a warm bed at home. The boys all ventured out and about for months, taking various jobs here and there. None of the four children had settled down with their own families yet. Matilda had moved away to the city and endured four years since leaving high school to complete her teaching degree. She had since returned home. Matilda was always getting plenty of local casual teaching work in Yamba, Maclean, and Iluka to keep her busy and some money in her pocket. She also did some music gigs around the local pubs for extra cash. Something was holding her in Angourie for now, and she didn't know exactly what it was until this. It was Bessie's Café. Like her mother and father, Matilda had always dreamed of owning her own restaurant and bar. She dreamed of an atmospheric location with a fantastic musical vibe and relaxed feel. "Bessie's Café" didn't sound like the right name for what she dreamed of, but that was an easy challenge. Creating the perfect name for their new building was the least of their worries. An important one, but Matilda knew that a fitting name would come to them as they started creating their masterpiece.

The three boys and Matilda were one hundred percent behind the decision for Jack and Laura to purchase Bessie's Café.

So, they did.

Contracts were signed, payment was exchanged within the week, and the Angourie treasure, Bessie's Café, now belonged to the Macallan family.

chapter five

Frankie Macallan

Frankie, the eldest of the four, was an avid surfer, an impressive artist, a fantastic acoustic guitarist, and a multi-talented musician. He could play any instrument by ear. It was quite an extraordinary talent he had developed through years of immersion in music and trying all kinds of instruments. He didn't restrict himself to learning one instrument; he tried them all with encouragement from his mother and father. Neither of them had the natural play-by-ear talent; this was exclusive to Frankie.

Frankie did some building work with Jack, but his major gig was travelling to local towns playing Friday and Saturday night acoustic sessions. His favourite gig was a Sunday session at the Pacific Hotel in Yamba. The vibe was alive, everyone coming in to enjoy the panoramic ocean views while listening to some good music, catching up with friends and enjoying some more free moments before the weekend was over.

He made enough money from gigs, tips, and odd-building jobs to sustain his simple life. Frankie had grown from a scruffy little lad into a handsome gentleman, with his gorgeous olive skin, honest green-blue eyes, and locks of dark curls, slightly bleached from days on end in the sun. His smile was his distinguishing characteristic; it filled his entire face and was infectious and honest, especially when coupled with his mischievous laugh.

Frankie hadn't met the girl of his dreams yet, but he had indeed tried out a few. He had broken more hearts than guitar strings. This was not his intention. He was highly likable, and it was hard for girls not to fall in love with him at first glance. He planned to settle down one day, but not just yet; he hadn't found his perfect match. After all, Frankie had grown up under the love and guidance of his relationship role models, Jack and Laura. Their love for each other was strong. They were *perfect* for each other. This was it, if there was such a thing as a *Perfect Match*, as the TV game show hosted by Greg Evans suggested. They never argued, not ever. They always supported each other, and family was number one for both. They were simply each other's person. Some called them soulmates. They liked the term, suggesting they had found the person to connect their *soul* with so deeply that they could be *mates* forever and beyond.

Frankie knew what was possible in a relationship if you were lucky enough to cross paths in life with your perfect soulmate. Jack and Laura showed a loving relationship throughout Frankie's life. They never faltered. Frankie watched in awe, realising that his parents had something special that few couples had.

Frankie grew up thinking every relationship was easy. It was not until he grew older, had dysfunctional relationships of his own and observed other relationships and partner dynamics he realised true love was a little more elusive to come by. He realised his parents had something extraordinary, and he wanted that too.

Jack and Laura had got it right from the very beginning. They met each other's needs for physical affection and loyal companionship; they spoke respectfully to each other and about each other. They supported each other through daily tasks and family responsibilities. They were romantic and thoughtful to each other, always keeping the love alive in their relationship. It was a dream-come-true connection that not every relationship could equate to. True love was hard to master.

Jack and Laura thought little about it; they just got on with loving each other the best they could, and when people complimented them on the success of their relationship, they didn't understand the fuss. They would acknowledge that they both got lucky. It was adorable. Frankie was searching for that kind of relationship for himself. Until he found it, he was content with living his simple life as a single man.

Frankie always remembered Laura's relationship advice and words of wisdom, which always stayed in his mind to protect his wild heart. Frankie had recently ended another relationship that wasn't treating him well. Although he was upset about the relationship ending, his mother had the perfect advice for him. 'When you connect with your soulmate, Frankie, you will just know. You will feel it so deep in your heart that there is no questioning whether this person is right for you. You will know, and they will feel equally the same as you do.'

Frankie hadn't found her yet; he was still searching.

So, when Jack and Laura proposed that they would love his help to rebuild Bessie's Cafe, he happily accepted their offer. For all they had done for him throughout his life, it was the least he could do. It would give him something to focus on for a while. He was contemplating travelling the world, but this was a good reason to stick around with his family a bit longer, and he knew how important it was for Jack and Laura to fulfil their dream.

chapter six

Louis and Eddie, Eddie and Louis

Louis and Eddie had grown up to look very much alike, although they were non-identical twins. They had similar features of dark curly hair that was bleached blonde from the sun and the same green-blue eyes as their father and older brother, Frankie. They had a few differing features: the shape of their faces, their difference in height and body shapes, and their personalities were quite the contrary. To make things simple for everybody else to distinguish between them, Louis regularly shaved his curly locks so neither would be confused as the other brother. Louis enjoyed looking rough and tough. It suited his personality. Eddie loved his gorgeous sun-drenched curls and thought himself the better-looking of the two.

Louis' physique was lean and muscular, more like a thoroughbred; he positioned well as 'centre' for the local basketball team. He stood about six-foot-two; his face was more angular as his jawline was clearly defined. He was more likely to get himself in a fight, possessing a bit of a loose temper and a mouth to match. Luckily, he had been brought up to resist those temptations. His father would joke and say he won his last fight by one hundred meters, suggesting that he would always choose the option to walk away rather than to take arms. He encouraged the same reaction towards aggression in his sons.

Louis often struggled with his instinct to be a man and fight, and his father's opposing voice in his head. 'Violence and hatred won't get you anywhere, son. Patience and acceptance are the way of the future. You can fight your own battles if you choose to create them. I won't be there to back you up.'

Eddie had a more rounded face, a softer jawline, and a gentle personality. It was effortless to get along with him. He was compassionate and loved animals of every kind. It was hard to get Eddie fired up. He had the temperament of a lamb: soft, gentle, friendly, and non-aggressive. Eddie was shorter than Louis, six feet tall, and had a much broader physique. He had more of a quarter-horse build. He played the guard position as a powerful defender for the local basketball team. Eddie was a fantastic three-point shooter and hardly ever missed a shot unless it was Louis defending him. Both were extremely fit from their daily surfing routine and healthy, active lifestyle. Eddie was embedded with his father's gentle genetics. He was calm and kind—a real ladies' man. The girls loved his feminine looks and his softness. He was a wonderful combination of gentleness, adventure, and common sense.

Louis and Eddie had completed school to Year 12, although this was a daily struggle. Neither cared much for the academic purpose of going to school; instead, they looked forward to the sports lessons and lunchtime with their mates, kicking a footy or shooting hoops. The major draw card that kept the twins at school was the opportunity to represent their school and the state of New South Wales in basketball and footy. They were both excellent sportsmen.

In their final school year, both received the 'Sportsman of the Year award' as a joint trophy because their accomplishments and achievements were equal and couldn't be divided. If Eddie won an award for something, Louis won the same award for some other sport the following week. They vied with each other, pushing each other to achieve impressive sports accolades.

Both joked that they couldn't decide whether they would eventually be famous as players on the Melbourne Demons Australian Rules football team, Eddie the Ruck Rover and Louis the Full Forward, or perhaps playing on the Brisbane Bullets basketball team, Eddie the Guard and Louis the Centre Forward, or maybe they would settle with playing cricket for Australia. Although they both loved cricket, they were both bored and suited more to active team sports than striking and fielding games, although they both had excellent skills, no matter what sports they attempted to play.

As middle child twins, the family dynamics were complex. Eddie and Louis both looked up to Frankie as their hero. That was positive behaviour with a matching negative because the challenge was that as much as they idolised him, they also had increasing self-doubts, as they never felt as good as him. He was the older brother. He was always more muscular, more experienced, more confident. No matter what, they couldn't change that. He just was. The twins always had to lift their game to be equal to him. Frankie was gifted and talented, and they couldn't help but idolise him. It didn't bother Eddie so much; he was easy-going, but Mr. Competitive Louis struggled with being the youngest Macallan brother. He always felt insignificant. Luckily, they had Matilda, the youngest of them all, and the best way Louis could feel important was to look after her better than anyone else did. Louis was always the chief protector of his younger sister. That made him feel important in the dynamics of the family hierarchy.

chapter seven

Wild Child

Matilda, nowadays everyone calls her Tilly, was the youngest in the family. Her three older brothers, Frankie, Eddie and Louis, all loved her, cherished her, and looked after her as if she was their child, even though she was only two years younger than the twins: Louis, the champion carer.

Like her beautiful mother, Laura, Tilly grew up to be a fantastic woman. Tilly had finished school at Maclean High School and went straight to university. She took four years away from her hometown, Angourie, and lived in Sydney while completing a teaching degree. She was also a brilliant musician and a talented surfer, artistic and creative, and she had the most euphonious singing voice. It was unique, and she was very distinctive in how she could sing in diverse tones and pronounce the lyrics of her songs. She sang very differently from how she spoke; it was almost like her singing voice didn't belong to her.

The entire Macallan family were musical geniuses; it was in their blood, and music was a massive part of their daily life.

Tilly was mainly cheerful and had a fantastic open personality. She also had her personal demons. Laura would always tell her, "Our strengths are our weaknesses, my darling." Matilda fell in love quickly and regularly found herself on the end of a broken heartstring. It was just a run-of-the-mill occurrence, and Tilly always bounced back, but in her quiet, reflective moments, she always wondered what she was doing wrong. She developed some insecurities in her relationships. Unlike Frankie, with his confidence that one day he would find his perfect soulmate and he was content to wait, it didn't occur to her that maybe she had just not met the right person yet. She was always blaming herself for relationships ending, and although that was sometimes the case, often the reality was just about wrong timing and being in the wrong location. There were no wrong people; every man she fell in love with had taught her something or shared fun moments she would never forget or regret. She wished she didn't fall in love so quickly because her heart was always on the battlefield—the place of conflict and pain.

Louis did his best to protect her from getting into the wrong situation in the first place; he prided himself on taking care of her and stepping in when needed. He did a great job as the bouncer. Eddie, the softer, gentler-natured soul of the twins, was her falling place. She would go to him for consoling discussions when she struggled with hard life stuff and broken relationships. Frankie was always busy being Frankie. Louis was the protector and equally as hard as a rock with his emotions, and he would always feel like he had to get involved, which was the last thing Tilly wanted in most situations. The Angourie Locals knew not to mess with Tilly because Louis had her back.

For this reason and to keep the peace, it was Eddie that she went to for sympathy after a relationship breakdown. Eddie would always confidently say to her, 'You'll be okay, Tilly; wild hearts can't be broken.'

She would reply, always in sobbing tears. 'Well, I must not be *wild enough* because it certainly feels like my heart is broken again.'

Eddie would laugh and say gently with a slight sarcasm while consoling her hurt. 'Well, if you weren't so *wild*, you wouldn't have another broken heart.'

They would laugh out loud together; it was always a bonding moment because it happened often. This conversation was on repeat. It was their go-to let's-have-a-laugh conversation when Tilly was broken-hearted. Somehow, it always cheered her up, as she knew she would always bounce back and share the same conversation again after the next one.

When Eddie knew Tilly was experiencing another break-up, he would ask. 'Do we need a wild-heart conversation, Tilly?' He knew her well and was always her soft place to fall.

Matilda often wondered why this happened and if she had some eternally single curse upon her. The reality was that Angourie was such a transient town; it brought temporary people, which was the nature of Angourie and the history of Tilly's relationships. She was experiencing fleeting love repeatedly. It was a pattern she had grown used to. Because she had such a kind and open heart, she carried a string of broken hearts, one after the other. She always wondered if she would ever meet someone who would want to stay and keep hold of her heart forever.

When Matilda talked to Laura about eternal singledom and mending broken hearts, her mum always had some excellent advice. 'It's important, Tilly, that you do not close your heart off from allowing new love in, even though your heart has been torn, time after time. You never know when true love will find you. And when true love finds you, all those broken-heart scars will make sense, and they will be a part of your story to get you where you got to, and your heart will be stronger because of all those scars. You'll see! Be patient, my love!'

chapter eight

Build it, and they will come!

Laura was more excited than Jack at their purchase of Bessie's Café. She had many dreams about what they could do to transform the old cafe, and her imagination was running wild with the opportunities ahead of them. She was happy to help as best she could. Laura was more the architect and the designer, as she had such great ideas and creativity. She left the heavy lifting work to the boys while she and Tilly took on the creative jobs, the painting, and the fussy details. The design structure was Tilly and Laura's responsibility, as was providing the meals and refreshments throughout the long days. It was good practice for their hospitality in the days ahead.

Laura and Tilly created their own fantasy game to make the cooking and cleaning fun. It was silly, but it was fun. They pretended they worked in a famous restaurant serving fancy millionaires, celebrities, princes and princesses, kings and queens. While being served meals and drinks, the three brothers and Jack focused on playing the game and having fun. They used Bessie's old servery bench as the dining table and found chairs from the old cafe to suit them all. Jack had the finest chair, a grand, high-backed solid wood dining chair with a padded velvet seat with the most exquisite material rich in colour and intricately patterned.

During dinner, they played a game where they pretended to invite a celebrity to their small beach town cafe and imagined how the evening would unfold. "How to Host a Celebrity" was the name they gave their fantasy game. They went to the extent of selecting the food menu and drinks they would serve. They were to choose the songs, music, and conversation topics for them. They even thought of questions they would ask the famous person if they met them. The discussions got deep.

As the family were all music lovers, most people they invited in their imaginary game were famous singers and performers from the '70s. The musicians list included Van Morrison, David Bowie, Dolly Parton, Kenny Rogers, Neil Diamond, Rod Stewart, and Billy Joel. Clint Eastwood, Barbra Streisand, and John Travolta made the celebrity list. They chose these musicians and celebrities because they had been ultimately famous just one or two decades ago and were still touring and travelling the world and known by everyone.

Frankie wanted to invite Marilyn Monroe, although she had passed away three decades prior. She was his favourite celebrity of them all.

Tilly wanted to invite James Dean. He was Laura's celebrity crush, and Tilly trailed on with the same fascination towards him. Tilly liked him even more because he was an Aquarius star sign, just like her. Laura always talked about the story of James Dean's death and how he had ironically died in a car accident when he had filmed a television advertisement about driving safety just a few months prior. He had died in 1955, long before Tilly was even thought of, but she had a special place in her heart for him. He was the ultimate "Rebel Without a Cause." He was her kind of man. He did things his own way, not by choice of rebellion, but because that was how he wanted to live his life. Tilly was much the same; she wasn't a rebellious child, and through her teenage years, she didn't need to rebel, as Jack and Laura weren't big on boundaries and restrictions. Tilly could make and learn from her mistakes, so she did. She didn't rebel; she was choosing to learn the hard way, sometimes. And she sometimes realised that what some people would consider rebellion was not at all. It was a different perspective based on personal core beliefs of right and wrong. Tilly didn't see a lot wrong with the world or people. She tried to remain non-judgmental about most things. She accepted people and their quirks and individual qualities that made them true to who they were. This created internal freedom in the way she lived her life. It also got her in trouble sometimes.

This made-up family game they called "How to Host a Celebrity" always led to an engaging discussion about musical history, the artist's favourite songs, chats about the lyrics, and general celebrity gossip. Laura always seemed to know who was who in the celebrity world. She kept up to date by reading her Women's Weekly magazine for celebrity gossip. The Rolling Stone magazine was the one magazine the family subscribed to for quarterly delivery. Jack and Laura, the passionate musicians they were, loved to keep up to date with the goings-on in the music industry. Every Rolling Stone magazine was savoured and became part of the Macallan magazine collection.

Louis was the only one in the Macallan family who thought the How To Host a Celebrity imagination game was silly. *As if any famous people would ever come here to Angourie, to their restaurant/café/bar that hadn't even been built yet.* But, because of the old saying, "If you can't beat them, join them," he went along with it, anyway.

Laura wanted to invite her ultimate idol, Stevie Nicks, from Fleetwood Mac, so that she could play "*Rhiannon*", Tilly's middle name-sake, after this song. Laura wanted to play her guitar and sing alongside Stevie. That would be so amazing.

Jack had always dreamed of strumming "*Brown-Eyed-Girl*" with Van Morrison. This was his love serenade song to Laura. She had the most beautiful brown eyes he had ever seen.

Eddie and Louis would be happy to jam with Mick Jagger, and both loved every song The Rolling Stones had ever produced. They both had matching black Rolling Stone T-shirts with the iconic red-tongue logo.

It was a tough choice when Frankie and Tilly were pushed to choose actual living celebrities, not James Dean and Marilyn Monroe. Tilly agreed she would love to host Fleetwood Mac. "*Gypsy*" was her favourite ever song.

Frankie's choice was simple. The Boss. Bruce Springsteen, although he thought that was way out of the realm of possibility. As if "The Boss," the most impressive musician in the universe, would come to Angourie for a secret retreat.

As time passed and they revisited the game often, the discussion became more serious at mealtimes when they thought this imaginary game could become a reality.

Could they get these legendary artists to come and perform at Bessie's Café and enjoy a secret retreat in their ghost town? It was up to the Macallans to make it a secretly alluring enough place to visit, and then they might be in with half a chance. It was worth dreaming about, at least.

Tilly and Laura had planned a perfect corner of the room for the stage space. It would provide good quality acoustics resonating out through the room. They wanted to create an inviting, warm, ambient venue with good sound production for a restaurant and bar full of welcome guests. They needed space for a dance floor and openness to include everyone who wanted to join the fun. The more the merrier!

They tried the room's acoustics by placing the transistor radio in the corner to see how the sound would travel. Ironically, the first song that came on was Brown-Eyed Girl by Van Morrison. They all got up to dance as the music pumped at total volume. It sounded great.

They all imagined and dreamed of the transformation happening before their eyes, by the labour of their hands, by the guidance of their hearts and imagination, as a family. Their dreams were coming true: to create a venue fit for stardom and fame. The possibilities and opportunities were endless. Jack reclaimed loudly to his family as they danced and sang around the café lounge room, famous words taken from the wise words of Noah with his ark.... "Build it, and they will come."

And they did.

chapter nine

Some things are meant to be.

Bessie's Café was dark, cluttered with pokey rooms, walls and shelving. There was so much shelving, wall-to-wall mixed and matched shelves to house the abundance of reused jars containing everything you could imagine. Back in the day, the café served its purpose, and Bessie's dream served her well. She provided daily bread, milk, and small goods to the locals. She made an exceptional milkshake for the kids who would come by after school to hang out. The extra special ingredient was Malt. You could get a normal milkshake, or a thickshake with an extra scoop of ice cream, and for an extra 20 cents, you could make it a malted milkshake, or even better, a malted thickshake. That was next level delicious. It was worth saving your extra one cent and two cent coins because the flavour was out of this world. The Macallan kids all looked forward to their malted caramel thickshake on a Friday afternoon after school. It was their end of week treat if they had been good at school all week. Sometimes Frankie would switch it up and get chocolate malted, and if he did Tilly would switch hers and get strawberry malted. Louis thought it was disgusting that Tilly would mix strawberry with malt, but Tilly kind of liked it, but most Fridays it was the usual; caramel malted thickshakes times four please. It was easier for Bessie. The Macallan kids wanted to make things easier for her.

Bessie was getting tired in her later days, and Bessie's Café had suffered dramatically from her weariness. Eventually, time took its toll, and Bessie passed peacefully in her sleep. A life well lived and loved was now at rest.

Bessie was a well-respected member of the community. When Jack and Laura had confirmed the purchase of Bessie's Café and took ownership, they invited all the locals to come and share a drink and dance in celebration of Bessie's contribution to the community. As Bessie's Café was sold, by her request, with all its contents, goods, and chattels, Jack and Laura offered the community and her two sons to take anything they wanted as part of a sharing community offering.

Jack and Laura planned to start afresh. They only wanted to keep Bessie's rocking chair perched on the front deck. This was a unique chair of great significance. Bessie often sat in her chair, knitting, reading, and drinking tea as she watched the world go by. She would also tell stories and read to the young children who would come and visit her for milkshakes and mixed lolly bags. Bessie had shelves full of lolly jars and was famous for her assorted lolly bag collections. Sometimes, the children would come to listen to a story, knowing that afterwards, if they listened carefully, they would get to choose a lolly from her special jar. Bessie was a fantastic storyteller, always telling a story with a moral message of gratitude, appreciation, kindness, or sharing. Some children learnt more about life from Bessie than they ever truly realised. The lollies were the draw card, but the impact of the stories and the messages Bessie would share was always worthwhile for these young, influential children of this small beach town. Bessie lived a hard life through war times and family trauma in an era of hardship, violence, and the "Great Depression." She had been a survivor and foraged forward in a time of widespread sadness. Bessie was inspirational. The openness and imagery she created and shared when she told her stories were genuinely captivating for any audience. Angourie was lucky to have her.

Bessie's favourite fable was the well-known story of the "Stonecutter." The story's moral is about the detrimental consequences and uselessness of greed and power. The message in the story's outcome was straightforward. Be careful about what you wish for and, more importantly, be content with life and the particular part you play in it, just the way you are. She told the story well, like she was the main character, even though she had never been a stonecutter herself, nor had she been the sun, the clouds, or a giant piece of stone in a mountain. Bessie was a special lady who filled many young minds with inspiration and joy.

Jack and Laura wanted to maintain the sense of community that Bessie had built, and in their own unique way, they were determined to keep her dream alive. With no disrespect to Bessie, they renamed Bessie's Café. The new name was simple and inclusive for the community: The Angourie Local. Their dream was to create a place that all the locals could still feel a part of, with an atmosphere of community, congeniality, and warmth.

Jack and Laura worked together with the help of their four children, Frankie, the twins Eddie and Louis, and Matilda. All the challenging work was done with passion, drive, and happiness. They worked as a team, utilising their strengths to contribute equally. Jack and Laura always believed that a family that works together as a team will always be successful. In the end, happiness was all that mattered. With a family of six, they were lucky. Many hands made light work. They had various responsibilities in the family, but there were never any arguments; everyone just got along and did their fair share, and each was grateful to the other. It was sickening for some to observe the ease with which they all got along. Most could not comprehend that a family could be functional in such a society where the commonality of dysfunction was much more accepted. As they ripped and tore, pulled apart and smashed every inch of the interior of the old café, their dreams and imaginings were coming to life. They had music playing in the background on the transistor radio. As they worked many long hours, for days and months on end, they agreed that this project would be fun. There was an unspoken pact between all the family members that at any random moment, any family member could choose to take a break whenever it felt necessary to dance, sing their favourite songs, laugh, or joke with each other. It was just as important as getting the job done because this was an enjoyable project; they were all creating together. They were all completely immersed, lost in various moments, whilst creating their amazing dream together. They built, laughed, sang, built, danced, built, ate, drank, built.

One beautiful summer afternoon, as the sun set, Jack and Laura's favourite song came on. The radio DJ had done a flashback to 1961, "Can't Help Falling In Love." It was Jack and Laura's song. It was a pleasant interlude for Jack and Laura, and they relished in the moment to hold each other in a loving embrace and dance amongst the sawdust and clutter of the demolition. They looked into each other's eyes and sang along, smiling, fully aware that "some things are meant to be." They enjoyed the more recent 80s and 90s hits on the radio and were up with the new music of their era, but when this song came on, it took them back to a time when they both dreamed of better days. Here they were, living their dream with the beautiful family they had created together. If they had ever married back in the 1960s, this would have been their song.

Jack and Laura never married; they got busy having their family, building their beach shack, and living their dream life every day. It didn't seem necessary to them then. They had no family to share their 'wedding' with. They were two soulmates on a new adventure and had already committed their hearts to each other with the love they shared daily. A piece of paper and a fancy ring with vows shared before a priest wouldn't change their relationship. They were known as "The Macallans," Jack's surname. As far as everyone was aware, they were a "married" couple. It was easier to let people think they were married, as having children out of wedlock was scandalous and unlawful for many people.

Jack came from a strong Scottish heritage and carried the characteristic Scottish genes with thick, wavy dark hair and green-blue eyes. He had a distinctive long, narrow nose and an oval face. The only disparity was that he didn't have fair skin, typically Scottish. He was blessed with an olive complexion from his mother's Spanish influence.

Laura came from Irish and English heritage. She had the same Celtic thick, wavy dark hair, with the most beautiful dark brown eyes, but her natural skin complexion was quite fair. It was only that she lived such an outdoor life that Laura had developed an olive complexion. Laura always wondered if her hidden olive genetics were part of the myth around the Spanish invasion of the Irish, leaving the family with a claim to being Black Irish. The most unique Irish of them all. It was a story passed down from generations, often discouraged because of the reality that most of the Spanish sailors were shipwrecked and passed away during the Spanish Armada of 1588. There was likely to be no Spanish connection, but she liked the story; it had held elements of mystery and historical rogue behaviour. Of course, the truth of the story possibly included torture and slavery, but Laura looked beyond that and accepted that there was perhaps some kind of mysterious cultural mix way back in her descendant history.

It was obvious in the community that Jack and Laura were together; they were rarely ever apart in all truth. There was no need to declare ownership by the marriage of either Jack or Laura to each other. They were both taken for. Their love was lavish and apparent to anyone who came to meet them. It was rare on this day to see such open and devoted love for one person. In this era of free love and wild spirits, many took advantage of society's acceptable expectations to be unattached and free. Many relationships in the '70s were casual and uncommitted, coinciding with the 'free-love revolution.' There was nothing wrong with this free-style life, but Jack and Laura were not a part of it. Jack and Laura went against the tide of the free-love revolution. Their connection to each other was a deep commitment, no matter what, and they treated each other as equals. Their love was magnificent, and their eyes sparkled for each other. They spoke to each other respectfully, shared kindness and closeness, and supported each other in every aspect of their lives. This love spread through the bond of parenthood, which was evident in how their family connected. Love, patience, and kindness were essential to their daily lives.

Jack and Laura had a vision as they transformed Bessie's Café. They were working towards creating a bustling café by day, serving the locals fresh morning coffee and beautiful hearty breakfasts made from fresh farm goods. They would provide a simple lunch menu to sustain the local surfers and give them the energy to hit the waves again for an afternoon surf. The evening vibe was the thing they were most excited about. They wanted to create a unique nightspot where various local and other musicians would come and share their music in a friendly, community-supported venue. Of course, the random tourists that popped through the town would be warmly welcome to come in and enjoy the warm hospitality that The Angourie Local would provide. The focus was, however, as the name suggested, a place for Angourie locals to hang out.

Another aspect that Jack hoped to continue was Bessie's Café B&B. Bessie had a few spare rooms out the back that she would let out as Bed and Breakfast rooms to passers-by. These rooms also needed a bit of tender loving care and creative renovations, but Jack was up for the challenge. Heck, if they wanted the likes of Mick Jagger, Stevie Nicks and Van Morrison to come and play at The Angourie Local, these rooms needed to be fit for a king and queen.

chapter ten

The Angourie Local

It took two years to complete The Angourie Local and establish a solid reputation of excellence. The Angourie Local was now a fully functioning café-bar-restaurant-local hangout for the surfers, locals and travellers by day and a fantastic nightspot for families, locals and travellers needing a place to be entertained or to stay by night.

It was an architectural masterpiece with an old-style feel, with timber and wrought-iron features, and massive panoramic decks facing east, north, and west on three sides. The interior was spacious and open, with sunlight beaming through huge windows.

The kitchen provided large bench tops and space for making fantastic meals, delivered hrough the servery window. The bar was decorated with a complete liquor range on the back wall and fridges filled with a range of wines and exotic ciders and beers.

One section of the bar stocked a full range of The Macallan whisky bottles. Jack decided as a unique feature of the Angourie Local, this would be the only whisky they would sell to promote the family name. Just to be quirky and different. He realised some patrons would prefer other types of whisky, but that was just too bad. The Macallan Whisky without the e in Whiskey, was all they would stock.

The walls were well-featured with local artworks, including paintings and various craftwork, with prices to sell should any random patron wish to purchase them. This was a constant offering, and there was a plentiful supply of new local artwork to replace the previous feature readily. The Angourie Local was also an impromptu art gallery, but the restriction was that the walls were reserved for local artists only, and the proceeds from the sale of any artwork went directly to the artist.

In the northeast corner of the room was a corner stage, a good-sized higher level of flooring to easily host a six-member band with various instruments. "Have Guitar Will Travel" expanded to include the four Macallan kids, all grown up now, along with Jack and Laura. The stage stepped down to a wooden floor, usually set with tables and chairs for dining guests; however, these were easily moved away to uncover a dance floor for nights when the vibe got a little wild and crazy.

In summer, the breezes flowed through the open windows and circulated through the spacious room onto the expansive decks. In winter, the sun beamed through during the day to warm the interior, and the Macallans would get the open fireplace cranking at night with a plentiful supply of split logs along the back wall to keep the fires burning. The ambience was sensational all year round, no matter what the season. The Macallans had combined their talents to create a brilliant renovation.

The incredible feature of The Angourie Local was its secret. As amazing as it was, the locals wanted to keep it local.

The music scene was going on, with many local talents coming to play regular gigs. Laura had also secured a few big names in a line-up of international talents to play memorable gigs at The Angourie Local. She cleverly advertised The Angourie Local to famous musicians and celebrities. She promised them a holiday in paradise, away from paparazzi and crowds, where they could be a ghost for a while, unnoticed, just blending into the shadows for the time of their stay. She had drawn up the concept of the secret agreement that the Angourie Locals had all witnessed, and she shared the idea with the musicians, celebrities, and famous guests.

The agreement suggested they could come and stay at The Angourie Local and explore Angourie and its secluded beaches without being hassled by people. The Angourie townsfolk kept this special secret well hidden. They had to keep a unique and monumental secret; otherwise, the opportunity would be lost forever. The musicians were happy to share their music with the Angourie locals and played acoustic sets on the small stage. The locals returned the favour; they shared their music and, more importantly, shared their respect, leaving the celebrity guests alone to enjoy the peace and tranquillity in their town.

The fundamental concept behind the secret agreement was that there was no advertising. The townsfolk were encouraged to enjoy the moments shared alongside the famous musicians and celebrities as memories of their minds. The agreement was to enjoy the music, feel the vibe, and be part of the celebration of freedom.

How nice would it be for "Stevie" or "Van" to hang out in Angourie for a week or more without getting hassled by anyone?

As the years passed, many famous musicians and celebrities enjoyed their *secret retreat* at The Angourie Local. The only people who knew about these celebrity visits were the locals who happened to be drinking and dining at The Angourie Local at the right time.

The alluring concept kept the locals returning to The Angourie Local. They never knew when a celebrity guest might stay in their hometown because it was never advertised.

The only glitch with the secret agreement was that if an out-of-towner was in Angourie during a celebrity or musician's secret retreat, they could go back to their community and leak the news outside of Angourie. It could ruin the "Angourie secret" forever.

Jack and Laura talked about out-of-towners in the early days. Still, with deeper consideration, they realised it didn't matter because no one ever knew who or when the following celebrities would visit. After all, that part was always a secret. The out-of-towners were usually super grateful to be part of the experience, which was as far as it went. It kept people coming back, just in case.

The Macallans family kept The Angourie Local secret strong with their pact of family secrecy about the next celebrity visitor. It stayed within the six of them. They never told a soul who or when someone was coming next. It was always a surprise, and that was the draw card. That kept the locals coming back.

Wild nights were plenty, and a new local saying emerged. After a big night at The Angourie Local, people would often say, 'I'm dusty today; I'm going to blame it on The Macallan.' The challenge was trying to work out which Macallan to blame it on. All the Macallans were spontaneous and fun and encouraged shenanigans amongst the patrons. Or perhaps the blame was on The Macallan whisky, the one and only whisky served at The Angourie Local.

Some people renamed The Angourie Local, calling it The Macallans.
It was less of a mouthful.

chapter eleven

More about Matilda, 'Tilly'

Tilly was possibly the wildest of the four children. This may have been because her three older wild and crazy brothers led her astray from a young age. Tilly grew up tagging along with the boys, doing whatever they did, which was usually something adventurous. It was mostly harmless, sensible adventures, but sometimes, their daily shenanigans had an element of risk and danger. The ocean was a risk in its own right, with their shack directly located on the headland above the so-called "Life and Death" break. The boys and Tilly surfed this break every day: morning, noon and night, if time and weather permitted.

Tilly was the female version of her three brothers, all melded into one. Her three brothers had olive skin, magnificent curls and the same green-blue eyes as their father. Many people thought Jack and Laura were brother and sister; they looked so much like each other, except for their eye colour. Laura had dark brown, almost black, eyes. Jack, the clearest green-blue eyes with dark eyelashes, it looked like he had a natural application of eyeliner along the edge of his eyes. Jack and Laura's similar features were part of their soul connection. It was like they were always part of the same spiritual mould, so it was no surprise that their four children all had very similar looks to the both of them.

Matilda, 'Tilly,' had long, dark, curly hair, brown eyes and the most beautiful, warm smile that was friendly, kind and incredibly cheeky. She was blessed with a summertime complexion. Her skin seemed to soak up every ray of sunshine and turn her skin into the colour of a golden sunrise. Tilly not only looked beautiful, but she was also strong and brave, with a calm, rational, humorous personality that many could not argue with. She was super easy to get along with; however, she had a streak of independence and authority that would put anyone in their place if they said or did anything that offended her or her family. People learned quickly that getting along with her was much easier. She was brilliantly likeable and didn't put up with disrespect, dishonesty, or rudeness. Tilly loved a laugh, and she was an engaging storyteller. And she certainly had some stories to tell. Her daily life was adventurous, wild, and fun.

Tilly was born on the 26th of January, known as Australia Day. That was her genuinely unique quality. She was indeed an Aussie girl. She was tough and challenging, yet she was soft and kind and ever so naturally beautiful.

It was lucky that she had three brothers to keep the boys away. They were all very protective of their little sister. They were very selective of whom Tilly could "hang out" with, and all three had to approve of any relationship that went past a "wink on the wave."

Tilly was very much "single." She previously had many short-lived relationships, some that her brothers knew about, some that her brothers would never know about, and some that broke her heart. She had countless one-night stands, social flings and a few 'never-to-be-spoken-of' encounters whilst working at The Angourie Local, but she had never been instantly drawn to a man quite like this. This beautiful stranger wandered into town with his surfboard under one arm and guitar under the other, looking for a place to stay and a bite to eat. Tilly was working her shift at The Angourie Local as a waitress and fill-in musician when it was quiet enough to play a song or two between serving meals and drinks. Even when many locals were out and about on a Thursday, Friday, or Saturday night, it was always quiet enough between serving meals and drinks to play a song or two. Honestly, many townsfolk came to The Angourie Local to listen to Tilly play her guitar and sing. The additional bonus was a good, hearty meal and a nice cold beer. And then, of course, the random chance of a celebrity appearance was always alluring.

Tilly worked hard to be courteous and friendly to the many folks who came to hang out. She had a way of letting them know when enough was enough, yet still made them feel special and welcomed them to dine and drink at the establishment. A handful of lovely gentlemen had passed through the town. She had her fun and a fair share of brief yet intimate relationships. She thought there could have been a few keepers across the years, but it never worked out that way, and although Tilly never liked to admit it, she had been heartbroken a few too many times. The main reason was that Tilly didn't want to move away from Angourie, so the so-called lovers let her go. More recently, she had built some walls around her heart, making it difficult for anyone to win her affection. None had affected her enough to entice her away from her wild and free single life.

chapter twelve

Dalton Jack Diaz

Tilly was clearing off a few tables on the balcony when she first saw him wandering across the road, looking almost comfortably lost, with his surfboard under one arm, his guitar case in the other hand, and a fancy-looking backpack over his shoulders. He walked up the stairs and placed his belongings in a discreet position just inside the reception area, ensuring they were not blocking any entry or exit and making sure they were well out of the way of walkways.

He noticed the sign at the front door.

> Welcome to The Angourie Local Café and B&B
> Open 8 am until the good times end.
> Eat
> Surf
> Drink
> Dance
> Sleep
> Repeat

He felt instinctively that this was a safe town, trusting to leave his stuff at the reception while he had a bite to eat, a few drinks and perhaps a place to sleep for the night. The restaurant was quite busy, and he figured it was the kind of place you would walk into and find your own table. There was no sign saying, *please wait to be seated.* So, he just walked in and headed out to the empty balcony tables.

He's possibly a pro-surfer, she thought, *but why the Bandana? Perhaps a travelling musician? That would explain the guitar.* Tilly noticed when she first saw him he was wearing a clean, white, loose-fitting shirt, light blue denim jeans that looked like they had been washed yesterday, and a nice-looking bandana holding back his curls. Tilly wasn't a bandana or a hat girl herself; she didn't own any fashion that went on her head because she thought it didn't suit her. She didn't even wear a beanie in winter; it just wasn't her thing. But this guy could wear that bandana very well. She was instantly drawn to his broad, friendly smile and sparkling green eyes. He was tall and muscular, with a naturally athletic frame.

Where did you come from, and what brought you here? The immediate thought crossed her mind. She had many questions to ask him, but she politely said, 'Good evening, sir. Can I get you something to eat or drink?'

He was instantly drawn to Tilly's deep brown eyes and her beautiful, friendly smile. He wanted to tell her she was the most beautiful woman he had ever seen, but he played it cool for now. 'I'd love a cold beer and whatever you've got on the house special.'

'House special tonight is my homemade cottage pie, with a trio potato mash, and I can do a fresh garden salad on the side, just for you.........?' Tilly paused, with her mouth finishing the word you, and tilted her head sideways in anticipation for him to offer his name in the answer.

'Dalton,' he offered Tilly his hand to shake. She returned the gesture and reached to hold his hand while trying not to take her eyes away from his. His hands were strong, and his handshake was firm, but Tilly could feel a gentle softness, and his hand felt warm. 'I would love to try the cottage pie. That sounds delicious........?' This time, he looked at her, finishing his sentence with a lingering, questioning look, with one eyebrow raised. The same look she had given him in the question of his name.

'Matilda, my name is Matilda, but no one calls me that. It sounds weird to say that, but seeing as you said, your name was Dalton, I thought I should follow you regarding my full name rather than my nickname. I guess you can't shorten the name Dalton. I work here. I do the food, the drinks and the music. Most people call me Tilly. Oh, my goodness, sorry, I'm nervously rambling. Please find a seat anywhere you like, and I'll fix you a nice cold beer and bring your meal out shortly.'

Tilly had completely lost her calm, rational self. She was like a teenager on her first date, nervous, excited, and keen to impress. This man had wandered in from who knows where. He could be anyone, for all she knew. She drew a deep, relaxing breath, adjusted her shoulder strap, which had fallen to the side, and headed out to fix Dalton a meal.

Dalton sat on the balcony at Table 26, overlooking the headland with ocean views. Unbeknownst to him, he had sat in Tilly's favourite spot, in the exact seat she would always prefer. She could see the moonlight on the waves breaking from that vantage point, which always made her feel at peace. When it was quiet, and everyone had gone home, Tilly would often sit right there with a delicate glass of red wine and do her paperwork and wages for the night, before clocking off and going home. Table 26 was so-called as that was Tilly's table; for two reasons, her birthday was on the 26th of January, and 26 was always her lucky number.

As Tilly glanced through the servery window, she couldn't keep her eyes off him; she thought it was ironic that Dalton had sat at her favourite table, of all places, and in the chair that she would usually choose to sit in. She piled up a large serving of cottage pie with plenty of mash and made a beautiful salad on the side with fresh lettuce, farm tomatoes, freshly cut beans, and carrots. She poured him an ice-cold beer and headed out to the table.

Tilly had settled her irrational nerves and was ready to ask Dalton questions. She certainly wasn't backward in coming forward. She placed his meal in front of him and, without spilling a drop, put his ice-cold beer on a coaster, gently placing his cutlery beside his plate. Dalton politely responded, 'Oh my goodness, that looks amazing; thank you, Tilly.'

Tilly grabbed a quick opportunity to ask her first question. 'So, Dalton, what brings you to The Angourie Local tonight?'

Dalton thought quickly, with a range of responses going through his mind. He told her the truth, which was always the best policy. 'I'm just on my way, heading north on a surf trip with some mates. They've stopped in Yamba for the night, but something was enticing me to check out Angourie, so I hitched a ride with a fellow I met in the surf today; his name is Frankie. He's a local surfer here, lived here all his life.'

Tilly laughed. 'Yeah, I know Frankie pretty well; he's one of my brothers.'

'You're kidding me, small world, he's an awesome dude and an outstanding surfer,' chuckled Dalton, then he added, 'I heard Angourie has some kick-ass waves at this time of year; I'm so glad I made the detour to check it out.'

Tilly was thinking; *I wonder if Frankie invited Dalton here deliberately.* He was usually trying to keep the boys away from her, but this time, it seemed that he'd sent this handsome chap her way for a reason.

'I'd best get back to the kitchen. Nice to meet you, Dalton; I'm sure glad you made the detour, too.'

As Tilly walked away, Dalton roamed his eyes all over her. She was the most naturally stunning woman he had ever seen. She had beautiful energy and a warm, friendly vibe that he liked very much.

Dalton enjoyed his meal and the peaceful ambience of this place. He thought *I could stay here a while; I like this place. I wonder if they have a vacant room I can crash in tonight or, better still, for a few days.* He was eating his meal, and his thoughts were drifting in and out as he was reminiscing about where he was in life at the moment. He was deep in thought when a beautiful sound caught his attention.

Tilly crooned into the microphone and strummed her acoustic guitar to this Fleetwood Mac classic. The sound of her voice and guitar transcended beautifully through the restaurant and out onto the deck. *'So, I'm back to the velvet .... underground, back to the floor.... that I love. . . to a room with some lace and paper flowers, back to the gypsy, that I was, to the gypsy, that I was.'*

Tilly took a moment away from the kitchen and took her position onstage to play a few songs. Gypsy, her favourite song by Fleetwood Mac, seemed the most appropriate song to play for this guy who had just wandered into her life. She could sense so much 'gypsy' in him, a free traveller, moving from place to place. He had this vibe of freedom and wildness, yet he seemed comfortable and settled in his own company. Tilly wondered, as she sang, what was his reason for travelling. Was it to escape, to explore, to engage, to eat, to surf? Tilly had met many travellers, all with different reasons for travel. He didn't seem to be escaping from anything or anyone; it was more like he was on a journey or an adventure. This was her very first instinct without even having a conversation with him. Here he was with a backpack, a surfboard and his guitar. What more could anyone need, really?

Dalton was drawn in, mesmerised, and he couldn't take his eyes off Tilly as she strummed and sang with such ease and beauty. Her dark curls hung over her shoulder, and her long arms reached around the neck of the guitar to feel for the chords, which she knew instinctively. It's like she had learned that song by heart for him, knowing he would come along and walk in the door for her one day.

Dalton enjoyed his meal and sipped on his beer, taking in the warm atmosphere in this place. Tilly played a few more songs in the set, then placed her beautiful Maton guitar back on the stand and approached him.

'Is there something else I can get for you, Dalton?' He didn't answer yet; he just smiled at Tilly. She continued talking, feeling awkward that he didn't respond to her first question, so she asked another one. 'Are you okay over here at my favourite table? Can I get you another beer?' He still didn't answer. His smile widening as Tilly stumbled through her nervous questions. 'Are you still hungry? We have some nice desserts?' Tilly smiled as she just kept on asking questions, noticing his smile widening every time she asked another one. She asked so many questions all in one string of a sentence that Dalton didn't actually have a chance to answer. Smiling was the easiest option.

He finally spoke with the sexiest laid back tone. 'Umm, I'm wonderful right now.' He paused and shifted in his seat, turning towards her. He continued, 'And I don't want you to go anywhere unless you have to serve other customers.'

Tilly looked around and saw that most guests had finished eating or were amid their hearty meals with full glasses. Louis was doing a shift with Jack and Tilly tonight, and they also had a few kitchen staff on. Louis and Jack could take care of the restaurant customers while Tilly briefly conversed with Dalton. 'I should be okay to chat for a bit. How was your meal?' Tilly questioned, knowing that he loved it or was just extremely hungry, as there was not a skerrick of food left on his plate.

'My meal was delightful; thank you. I enjoyed the music too.'

'I thought you might like a bit of Fleetwood Mac's "Gypsy" being the traveller and all that you are.'

'Yeah, well played. I have been a bit of a gypsy for a while now. I never really found a place that beckoned me to stay. I like it here, though. How long have you been here in Angourie? You live in Angourie, right?'

'Yeah, I live here now. I moved away to go to university for a few years, but I moved back last year. My parents, Jack and Laura, own the restaurant here; they moved here from Sydney in the 1960s and built a little shack on the headland. My whole family, my three brothers and I grew up here, and we still live together in the shack. Well, it's a big shack now, and we all work here at The Angourie Local to help Mum and Dad keep this place alive.'

Dalton snuck into the conversation as Tilly was eager to share so much about herself and her family. He was interested to know more. 'I love it; it's got a great vibe and busy. It is always this busy?'

Tilly looked around the room, noticing that there was quite a buzz in the room for a weeknight. 'Well, it depends; it gets busier during the tourist season, but our main customers are the locals. It's like your favourite mum's kitchen; everyone comes here for a regular feed of home-cooked meals, and we always have some music going on, whether it's the five-stack CD on shuffle with great tunes, live music, or both. We also get quite a few local bands playing here, or my family band; we all play instruments and sing, or if you're lucky, super special guests, but that's a secret. If I told you, I'd have to keep you.'

Dalton laughed again, 'Well played, nice play with words there. You are a creative, huh?'

Tilly replied, 'Well, the saying goes, "If I told you, I would have to kill you." There is no way that is happening, not tonight, anyway. I'm busy.' She winked. 'I'd rather keep you.' She laughed.

Dalton laughed. 'I see. You're beautiful, and you have a sense of humour.'

Tilly laughed again. 'Maybe I'll share the secret with you later.'

Dalton briefly snuck into the conversation, as Tilly was excited to share The Angourie Local story with her new friend. 'It sounds like your family has it all worked out: fun times, good food and ice-cold beer. What more do you need in life?!'

Tilly continued, 'It's been our family dream for a long time, and this place has an amazing history. If you want to stay here tonight, I can put you in The Rolling Stones or Stevie Nicks room. The Van Morrison room is booked out tonight.'

Dalton replied instantly. 'I'm in. Tell me more.'

'Only a few strangers to our town know about this, but I trust you enough already to let you in on a local secret. Promise me you won't tell anyone?'

'I promise. I love keeping secrets.' Dalton replied, desperate to know what this secret was.

Tilly shared openly, knowing that she could trust Dalton with the Angourie Local secret; besides, he would have no idea when another celebrity musician would play here. 'Van Morrison, Stevie Nicks and The Rolling Stones have stayed here before and performed on that stage.'

Dalton's mouth dropped open. 'Wow, really, that is very cool. I'm a huge Fleetwood Mac fan, and Mick Jagger. What the heck, that must have been an experience for you. You are fortunate; and they are lucky to have come here and enjoyed this beautiful place. I can't imagine how that even came about; how did that happen? Do you mind me asking, or is that the secret?'

Dalton's question was curious, and he didn't expect an answer, but Tilly explained anyway.

'Yes, it's special, huh? It was Mum's idea to put a dream into action, and she was the instigator of the invitations and the administration behind it all, but as a family, we came up with the idea when we were renovating this place. We used to play a fantasy game called How to Host a Celebrity, and the next thing, it was a reality. Fleetwood Mac came to stay in the early days. Stevie was gorgeous, Mum's favourite celebrity in the world. Fun fact, my middle name is Rhiannon. Do you know the song Rhiannon by Fleetwood Mac?'

Dalton nodded, 'I do.'

Tilly added. 'Did you know that Rhiannon means Goddess?'

Dalton shook his head, 'I did not, that makes sense though, suits you perfectly.'

Tilly continued explaining her full name meaning, 'Mum was very creative, my full name meaning Warrior Goddess of Scotch Whisky.' They both laughed.

Tilly paused, nodding her head. 'It's true though, Fleetwood Mac came here and stayed in Angourie for about two weeks. Baffling, right? Hard to believe?'

Dalton was dumbfounded in awe. 'Baffling and cool, if you ask me.' This was an unrealistic possibility, but he knew Tilly was telling the truth.

'Over the past few years, we have provided a secret retreat for many musicians and celebrities who want to escape their celebrity lives. You never know who might turn up in this Angourie ghost town, needing a retreat from the rest of the world.' Tilly paused and continued, 'Just like you, Dalton, I'm guessing. Somehow, you found us......with thanks to Frankie, my brother, of course.'

'To be quite honest, Tilly, how I met Frankie today was randomly coincidental. We were both surfing the same break; the waves were exceptional. We had some beautiful, long, rolling sets, and the ride was smooth. At one stage, there was a pod of dolphins surfing with us. It was so cool. Your brother is a rad surfer. We chatted between sets, and he told me I should check out Angourie Cove someday. So here I am. Today was as good as any.'

Tilly was nodding along, believing every word of his story. 'Frankie is probably the best surfer out of all of us; he's the oldest, and he's been doing it for longer. We all idolise Frankie. I like him even more now that he sent you here.'

'Well, he didn't send me *here.*' Dalton said, pointing to where he was sitting as he smiled a wide, beautiful smile at Tilly. 'He asked if I had checked out Angourie as a surf break. None of my mates were keen, but here I am.'

Tilly looked around and noticed that some of the dinner guests had departed, and Louis had started clearing tables. He gave her a bit of a look as if to question her, and without words, Tilly knew precisely what he was thinking. It was like sibling telepathy. The look was sending a clear message to her. 'Are you right over there, Tilly, having a good old chat while I'm doing all this hard work?'

If it were Frankie or Eddie on the shift, they would be okay that Tilly was taking time to chat with a stranger. She was always a hard worker, but Louis was always the most protective of her. He had been hurt in relationships before, probably because of his temper more than anything, which scared the girls away, but he didn't want to see Tilly in a relationship that might hurt her. She was all he had. She was *his* rock. Louis always went to Tilly for relationship advice, and she was the only one who could calm him down when he fired up about different things that didn't require getting fired up about.

Tilly noticed Louis' attention towards her. She whispered gently, raising her head and eyebrows to Louis as he glanced in her direction again. 'I'll give you a hand in a second.'

Dalton understood Tilly was working and probably needed to get back to help her brother. He urged, 'Please, Tilly, do what you need to do, and if you don't mind, I'd love another beer.' He tilted his head and looked her up and down. 'I'm happy just sitting here enjoying this place and this view.'

Tilly smiled shyly, accepting the compliment and blushing briefly, 'I'll be right back with your beer; this one's on me.'

She's gorgeous and cheeky. I like that, thought Dalton. He didn't know what to say out loud, as he had a million thoughts running through his head. He just smiled a cheeky smile back at her.

Tilly bought Dalton his beer and placed it on the table, gently touching the side of his shoulder with her arm as she leaned to put the beer in front of him.

'Enjoy your beer and your view, Dalton,' smiled Tilly.

Tilly went back to clearing tables and attending to customers. It was quite a busy night; it always was, to be quite honest. But Angourie's busy differed from the city's busy. Angourie busy meant you still had time to chat, talk, and enjoy your work. Everyone was glad to enjoy a slow evening, no rush, nowhere else they had to be, just enjoying an evening at The Angourie Local. In Angourie terms, it was a bustling little business, but working in the restaurant was always enjoyable. Tilly always got to meet new people. She had catered for and looked after many celebrities and had some fascinating stories about wild and crazy nights that had evolved from music sessions and open gigs. Tilly always respected the reputations and privacy of their guests. There was always something going on; it was always alive and entertaining and a great place to be, no matter the time of the day.

Throughout the rest of the evening, Tilly had brief chats with Dalton, amongst waitressing and performing. They had an instant connection and felt very comfortable with each other. Louis had kept a close eye on Tilly all night. He had eased up with how he thought about this stranger. He could see that Tilly was pleased when she was around him. She was always happy, but this guy was making her glow. Louis thought his sister was one of the most vibrant, attractive and down-to-earth women he had ever met, and knowing her personality better than anyone, he knew that one day she would find the most amazing man to share life with her. Until then, he was in full protection mode. Tilly had made some bad relationship decisions, so the older brother protection mechanism was in full force from Frankie, Eddie and Louis. Louis didn't know that Frankie had been the instigator of this new connection, bringing this stranger to Angourie with the intention that Dalton and Tilly might be good for each other.

chapter thirteen

Little Talks

It had come towards the end of the night. Tilly was finishing another music set and letting everyone know it was last-drinks and that the restaurant and bar were closing soon. Tilly called Louis over and said, 'Hey Lou, I'm happy to close tonight; you can go home a bit earlier, if you want to.'

'Thanks, Tilly, I'm tired, and the surf is supposed to be pumping in the morning. Eddie, Frankie and I will hit the surf early, around 5 am, if you want to join us?'

'Thanks, Lou. I won't make any promises, but thanks for the offer. If I'm there, I'm there. You know me.' Tilly paused and added, 'You boys need to be careful, hey? I love you.' She wrapped her arms around Louis and gave him a big, warm hug. She added, 'You know you don't have to worry about me, hey? I'm a big girl.'

Louis looked at Dalton and signalled with a raised brow, 'He seems alright, nice guy, your type, handsome and all?' Louis' voice rose higher with each describing statement, like he was questioning Tilly for her opinion.

'Yeah, he seems nice, and he's very handsome. He's super handsome, not that that's everything, but wow, he's beautiful to me. I mean, everyone has a type. He's my type of beautiful.' Tilly changed her tone and nodded slowly, assuring Louis that she was aware of the reality of her situation. 'But then, as usual, he's just passing through. Another temporary traveller, half my luck.'

Louis slipped in his brotherly advice, knowing what Tilly was like. 'Oh well, Til, it's not like you to not just have some fun while he's passing through. But for my sake, remember your heart.' He softened his words, letting Tilly know he cared for her feelings.

Tilly appreciated Louis's encouragement, but she had an opinion about this guy, different from anyone else who had passed through. 'Yeah, I know, been there, done that, plenty of times, but what if he's *the one*? Like Dad says, "When you know, you just know." I feel like, I just know, already.'

Louis queried, 'What makes you feel that?'

Tilly tried to explain. 'I don't know exactly how to explain it, but I feel like I've known him forever, and he just walked in the door three hours ago. I don't want to make a fool of myself, that's for sure, and I don't want to make the same mistakes I've always made.'

Louis continued with his encouraging wisdom. 'Til, you are the most amazing person I know, even if you are my sister. It wouldn't be possible for you to make a fool of yourself. You're no fool; just be you. That's my advice. For what it's worth, just be you!'

Tilly reached out her arms, careful not to spill the empty wine glass dregs from the glass she held onto his back. She hugged Louis. 'Thanks, Lou, will do; see you in the morrow. Love you to bits.'

Tilly cleared a few more tables, cleared the kitchen and bar area, and turned out the bright restaurant lights. She placed the 'CLOSED' sign on the door. The only customer left in the restaurant was Dalton. His backpack, guitar and surfboard were still placed unobtrusively just inside the reception area.

Angourie had gone to sleep for the night. The only lights keeping the glow in the restaurant were the beautifully scented candles placed on the tables and near the stage area.

Tilly poured herself a glass of red wine, a lovely, deep-flavoured Penfolds Grange, and headed over to join Dalton at Table 26.

'Well, Dalton, I finally get to come and hang out with you at my favourite table, seeing as you are still here in my restaurant. I would usually ask you to leave, but something is telling me a guy like you needs a place to stay tonight,' *or forever* - she thought. 'I hope this doesn't sound too forward, but you can stay here tonight. We've got plenty of vacant rooms now; it's off-peak season, and few travellers are passing through at this time of year. I'll give you a room to stay in, on one condition.'

Dalton shifted uncomfortably in his seat. As much as he would have liked to stay the night, he wasn't sure about having conditions placed upon him. The whole reason he was travelling was to get away from judgements and expectations of people. He replied with a bit of discomfort in his tone. 'I'm not usually a conditional guy, but I'm open to hearing what you offer.'

Tilly responded lightly, with a slightly serious tone. 'Well, that is good because my one condition was this. This is going a little deep, but if you stay here tonight, I want you to know that my offer remains *unconditional*. What I mean is you owe me nothing for letting you stay here. I have no expectations of you. You can stay, you can leave, you can do whatever you want to do while you are here. My offer to you has no expectations attached to it. Just be you.'

Where did this girl come from? thought Dalton. *Who thinks like that?*

After listening to her 'unconditional' conditions, Dalton felt even closer to Tilly. Dalton shook his head in polite disbelief and replied. 'Wow, this is an intense conversation, Tilly, for a woman like you who seems like such a free spirit.' Dalton tilted his head sideways and reached out his arm to gesture for her to move closer to him.

Tilly was anxious to get this off her chest. 'I know, I know, sorry. I have to say it straight up. I've met people in my life, throughout my time of living and working here, and in so many relationships that I found myself in where people placed conditions on me or claimed me, and I am guilty of doing the same thing to others. I've learned a lot recently and decided just a little while ago that I don't want to make those same mistakes anymore. I was in a vicious cycle of failed relationships, on repeat. It's embarrassing really. These days, I'm all about personal freedom.'

Dalton liked what he was hearing. 'Cheers to that, Tilly.' They both raised their glasses together and said simultaneously, 'To Freedom.'

Tilly continued her rant while Dalton listened intently. 'As time has passed, and I'm so wise now,' she winked, 'I realised none of those relationships were right for me anyway, so I should have just let go of the expectations and conditions I had placed on myself and others. I've learned that what is more important than expectations and conditions is friendship and love. My parents keep telling me that our hearts know what's best for us if we choose to follow them, and our hearts don't have conditions or expectations. They know love.'

Dalton lifted his beer towards her and prepared for another cheer. He smiled his gorgeous wide smile and clinked his glass with hers. 'Cheers, Tilly, To Freedom, Friendship and Love!'

Tilly brought her glass up to match his and looked into his eyes with a beaming smile back at him. 'Cheers Dalton, To Freedom, Friendship and Love!'

Dalton attempted to change the conversation, as it was getting quite serious. 'Where is Frankie when we need him? What would he be thinking right now?'

Tilly laughed. 'Oh, my amazing brother Frankie would be very proud of his efforts to set this up. He's a clever lad.'

Dalton replied briefly, in agreement with Tilly. 'That he is a brilliant brother you have. I can't imagine either of my brothers ever trying to set me up with a beautiful girl. I'm very grateful to your brother Tilly. Will I see him tomorrow to say thank you?'

Tilly nodded. 'Yeah, he should be around after his morning surf.'

They both took a sip from their drinks and looked into each other's eyes as they did. Tilly apologised for her rambling. 'I just have to say this. I had a few secret sips of wine tonight while working to quell my nerves. I never usually do that. I usually wait until I've finished my shift to enjoy a relaxing glass of red. But you, Dalton, have me rattled and nervous; I've never felt like this.'

Dalton replied earnestly. 'I don't mean to make you nervous. Please, just be you, Tilly; you are honestly one of the most beautiful women I have ever met. You don't need to impress me or pretend to be someone that you're not. Honestly, I love these straight-up, deep chats. It's good. I'm getting to know you quickly, although I feel like I know all this about you already.'

'Thank you, Dalton. I just felt like I was rambling, that's all. Nervous talking, I do that. Over-sharing. Too much information. It's my thing.'

'That's cool, I do too.' Dalton had a long sip of his beer and stared intensely at Tilly, taking all of her in, observing the lines and curves on her face and the shape of her lips as she continued talking.

'I can thank my Mum and Dad, Jack and Laura, for how I think. You'll get to meet them both if you are still here tomorrow.' She paused, waiting for Dalton to respond. He didn't. He took another sip from his beer and wiped his bottom lip with the side of his thumb, then tilted his head, signalling that he was ready to listen to whatever Tilly had to say. He felt she wanted to share a deep conversation with him, and he was okay with that. Dalton sat quietly, so she continued. 'I've had some deep chats with them lately about relationship stuff because I had a bit to learn. They have the most loving, enduring relationship. Somehow, they both found one another and love and support each other deeply, yet they also allow each other freedom to be themselves in their relationship. I think the thing that makes their relationship work is that they are both enough for each other. They expect no more from each other because they have a balance of respect. Jack is Jack. Laura is Laura; they don't try to change each other.

Neither thinks the other is more important; their love is equal. It's beautiful, and I have always hoped I would find my "Jack" someday, always hoping that me, being just the way I am, would be enough for someone. Most guys I have been with think they are better than me with their city money and fancy cars, or they think I'm better than them because I am a strong, independent woman. I want to find myself with someone who understands me and feels equal to me because I know just the way I am is enough.' She laughed and added, 'Maybe sometimes I'm too much.'

Dalton took a moment to process the message of what she was trying to say. He understood she didn't want to change herself again for someone; she aspired, more than anything, to be herself, and she wanted that to be enough for whomever she was in a relationship with. She wasn't prepared to change who she was for someone else. She was also highly respectful of her parents' relationship. He took another sip of his beer and was confident in replying. 'Well, as corny as this might sound, my middle name is Jack, so maybe it is Tilly that you've met your Jack.'

Tilly lifted her glass towards Dalton. 'I think that deserves another cheer, Dalton.'

As they looked into each other's eyes, they phrased together, '*To Freedom, Friendship, and Enough Love.*'

Dalton nodded, impressed with the beautiful collection of words they had put together for a unique personal cheer. It was uncanny that they had both instinctively swapped the order of words to place Enough in front of Love. It just sounded better that way. Together, they had created a cheer that wouldn't be suitable for everyone to join in because only some qualities would relate to some people and not all, but it seemed that these two could connect with an understanding of all these essential qualities. Dalton smiled his broad smile. 'Now that's a beautiful cheers collection phrase if I've ever heard one. Cheers to us.'

They both held up their glasses together. 'To us.'

Dalton was feeling a little inadequate. He was mesmerised by Tilly. She was the most intriguing, down-to-earth, beautiful and amazing woman he had ever laid his eyes upon, and there she was, sharing her heart and soul with him. Meanwhile, he held his secretive dark heart and emotional baggage deep inside. He didn't feel intriguing, down-to-earth, beautiful or amazing. Although he was feeling the weight of lifetime burdens releasing more and more as he chatted with this beautiful woman. They talked for a while about various topics, both sharing parts of themselves with each other.

Dalton leaned in towards Tilly. She could smell the beer on his breath, which she didn't mind. He smelt fresh and clean, and the beer made him relaxed and comfortable around her, so she liked the smell. He leaned closer and said to her politely and gently, 'Do you think it would be okay if I kissed you, Tilly?'

Tilly leaned in and whispered, 'I think that's a perfect idea.' She put her mouth close to his, allowing him to lean into her to connect their mouths. They kissed gently and passionately, but not for too long; it was just a little taste of what each other's mouths felt like. Dalton finished the kiss, lingering on her bottom lip before releasing his mouth from hers.

Tilly felt goose bumps rise on her arms as Dalton pulled her close for a hug. Dalton spoke gently and whispered into her ear. 'You feel so good in my arms, Tilly.' They embraced briefly, and before they released from the hug, he left a gentle lovebite kiss on the side of her neck as he moved his body away from hers. It was not rough enough to leave a mark, just enough to leave another round of goosebumps to rise through her body.

Tilly's whole body shuddered with tingles. 'Wow, just wow! What are you doing to me, Dalton? Can you see the goosebumps all over me? Oh my goodness! That's unbelievable.'

The conversation continued as they were surrounded by the ambience of the gentle flickering candles and the light of the moon over the ocean, which they could see from the deck where they were sitting. They talked about surfing, the ocean and Yamba. Dalton asked many questions about Tilly, her brothers, and her family life growing up in Angourie. Their conversations deepened as they discussed each other's families and past relationships.

Dalton shared his story with Tilly about how he had grown up in a small country town called Deniliquin, way out west; he had finished school and completed a building trade at the local technical college. He worked a few years building as an apprentice for a large building company, and he loved the work. He was a hard worker and good at it. His parents were proud of him, that he had a good trade, but they expected him to stay on and work the farm for the rest of his life, just like his two older brothers. Dalton had other plans. He had a creative, musical talent and this wild, beach-freedom need to fulfil. He wanted to play his guitar or the piano all night, rather than joining the night-shoot to hunt pigs with his father and his brothers. His brothers didn't understand that he wanted to play musical instruments. He wanted to ride a surfboard, not a rodeo bull or a bucking bronc. He wanted to feel the ocean's power underneath him and the salty sea on his skin. He wanted to breathe the fresh, clean ocean air. He respected the beauty of country life and appreciated his upbringing, family values, and morals, but country life wasn't for him. He finished his education and building trade and worked the farm for a few years, but every weekend, he would play gigs at the local pub to save some cash. Once he had saved enough money, he took his guitar and backpack and headed to the east coast. He figured he could always play some gigs for a bit of spending money, and he could figure out the rest on the way. The first thing he bought when he hit the coastline was a surfboard. He knew that his purchase would make travel a little more complicated, but he was prepared to take that risk for the enjoyment he would gain from being able to surf every day as he travelled his way north. He explained to Tilly that he had no destination in mind when he started his travels. He left out the part about why he was leaving Deniliquin. That was his dark secret for now. He wanted to tell Tilly but couldn't bring the words from his traumatic past to his mouth. So, he chose not to say anything at all. He skimmed and detoured that part of the story, and although he felt bad about it, it was like he was being untrue to Tilly, but he couldn't do it. He hadn't shared his dark secret with anyone for fear of judgement, and he wasn't ready yet because he knew his pain would return and he would have to face his grief again. He had pushed it away for a year or more, and this seemed to be his way of coping with it. He finished his story with the superficial detail that many people he had met on his travels had told him that the Gold Coast was good for girls, gigs and good surf, and he was headed that way, but he was enjoying every moment of the journey, and he had met so many interesting people so far, none quite like Matilda, though.

It was getting late; Tilly was happy to sit and chat, knowing there was no way she would get up at 5 am for a surf with her brothers if the night would go the way she was thinking. Louis would understand. Dalton had nowhere to go and nowhere to be. He didn't even know where his bed was for the night, so he was in no rush to go anywhere.

After many conversational hours had passed, Tilly asked, 'So, Dalton, what do you think? Do you want to take me up on my unconditional offer?'

Dalton replied cheekily, 'Well, I would like to take you up on your offer, but what if I have some questions? Unconditional is a big thing. I'm trying to understand what you mean by this word. It seems super important to you.'

'Yeah, it's a big one for me, and please excuse me while I go off on a tangent here. First, please understand I've recently recovered from a relationship of narcissism and control. I was attached to a strictly conditional relationship for way too long. I don't talk about it much, and I have tried to erase the relationship memory from my headspace, but I'm happy to share it with you so you can understand me better and why I am the way I am. It was just awful because I was so in love with a man who had no consideration for my needs unless it was for his personal gain. At first, everything seemed so perfect, the love bomb. But as time passed, and I was losing myself to be the person he wanted me to be, I realised everything was about him, his needs, and his reputation. I went along with it for so long, morphing myself into a completely different person from who I am because I thought that was what he wanted. He kept wanting to change things about me. In his mind, he didn't think he was trying to change me; he was "evolving" me into the best version of myself. It was absolute bullshit. I was already my best version and growing and changing every day as life moulded me, with no rules or expectations to follow. When people use the words "evolve," "strongly recommend," and "abundance," it makes me vomit in my mouth. He didn't like me because I was strong and independent, and I liked who I was, and somehow that made him feel less important. The crazy thing was that somehow he had so much control over me.'

Tilly paused, waiting for Dalton to say something, but he didn't. He was listening intently. So she continued. 'Because of this control, I kept trying to change for him and please him, to be the person he wanted me to be, and it took quite some time for me to realise what was happening to me. I'm fortunate to have my supportive family and friends to wake me up to the reality of how I was being treated. I'm embarrassed that such a strong woman like myself allowed a person to diminish my self-worth to nothing. It was hard work to recover from the relationship. I had to rebuild my self-esteem and confidence from scratch because I genuinely thought I was the words he described in his passive-abusive narrative: he called me selfish, manipulative, disorganised, over-emotional, insecure, and ungrateful. By the end of our relationship, I honestly thought I was crazy.' Tilly paused again. Dalton gave her an understanding headshake and encouraged her to continue. 'I was none of those things. I had completely lost who I was, as I kept trying to change myself to be everything he wanted me to be, but the more I changed myself, the more he kept raising the goalpost. I was strongly encouraged to learn about philosophies he believed in about wealth creation and the mind over health matters through daily affirmations. I was already super healthy. I didn't have a sick day from school in my life. I was never good enough if I didn't live exactly the way he did.' Tilly paused, realising that she had probably shared way too much and had entered a yucky state of mind. She felt yuck thinking about it, and because she hadn't talked about it, it all came out in one big, long gush of yuck. She stopped talking and took a sip of her wine.

Dalton waited, making sure she had finished talking before he spoke. 'Far out, Tilly! That's heavy. Keep going, though, please, if you can. I want to know how you got through it.'

Tilly was challenged. First, Dalton was actually interested in learning about what she had gone through, and second, she had to think about how she got through it. She had never really thought about expressing her recovery in words; she just did it. She replied with a deep and honest instant self-reflection. 'I don't know. I moved back here to Angourie, an empty shell of myself, with a heavy heart, promising myself that I would never allow myself to get into a relationship like that ever again. I started living my healthy life again, doing what I love with my family and brothers. I did heaps of beach running and surfing, and we started renovating this place, so it took my mind off everything. This place has been my saviour. This place has healed me.' She looked around the expanding space of The Angourie Local, instantly grateful for everything it was to her and her family.

'This place is amazing, that's for sure, and so are you, Tilly. You are one of the most amazing women I have ever met, and I only met you a few hours ago. But keep going; I feel like there is more that you want to tell me. I'm listening and understanding.' Dalton supported allowing Tilly to talk and encouraged her to say more if needed.

Tilly continued, adoring this moment to share herself so openly with this beautiful stranger, realising that she had never really opened up to anyone like this, other than her family. 'I learned a lot in the healing process, and I think my heart has fully recovered. The only trigger I'm still trying to heal from is the inner fear of being cast aside for no reason. Basically, for him, I was never exactly what he wanted or needed in his life, so it was easy for him to say, it's all your fault; I don't want this anymore, and goodbye. I was discarded without a second thought as he moved on to his next victim.'

Dalton was trying to give some friendly advice while understanding where Tilly was coming from based on the previous relationship she had been in. He had never been in a relationship like that, so he tried to understand it. 'Yeah, that's hard. I guess you need to trust your instincts. If you keep your heart too guarded, and you keep feeding that inner fear, you might miss out on letting the right person in.'

Tilly adored his response. It was like something her mum or dad would say. 'Yeah, you're so right. It's hard, though.'

They both sat in silence for a moment, deep in their internal thoughts.

Dalton hesitated to bring up his dark secret because he didn't want Tilly to think he was one-upping her with a better story. He was happy to settle with this conversation being dark enough for one night. He would save his story for another time.

Tilly had said a lot, and she hoped that she hadn't scared Dalton away with her intensity in communication. He didn't seem to be bothered, more reflective than anything. Tilly continued, taking the conversation back to where this gush of yuck had started. 'Getting back to where this conversation started and relating this to you and me. Because of what I've been through, it's better for me if you have no expectations or conditions in your communication. I feel way more comfortable with that.'

Dalton wanted to understand exactly what she was saying. 'Can you give me an example?'

Tilly wanted to give an example, but she knew also that the conversation had gone very deep. She wanted to lighten the mood of the conversation again. It was a heavy topic, and she didn't really have an example, because it was hard to explain how someone could control everything you did, and when you did it, they could still leave you feeling like you did the wrong thing. 'Okay, for example, if you say, "I'm only going to stay the night if you stay in my bed with me," that is conditional and expectational, and it is a complete turnoff to me. I'll be straight out that door. However, if you say, "I would love to stay the night, and you are most welcome to spend the night in my bed with me." That would be non-expectational and unconditional. You give me freedom to choose, and I get to choose my freedom.' Tilly gave Dalton an example, and she was clever in the way she hinted she might like to spend the night with him, as she did.

'Yeah, I get it. I like it. No conditions, no expectations. Freedom.' Dalton giggled, picking up on Tilly's suggestive hint. 'So, are you saying you might like to spend the night with me?'

'I would love to if that's okay with you. Let's sort out a room key,' suggested Tilly. 'The biggest decision is......which room?' she paused. 'Do you want to stay in our Fleetwood Mac suite of lace and paper flowers or the Rolling Stones' suite? We're pretty fancy here.'

Dalton had a big decision to make. He equally loved the Rolling Stones and Fleetwood Mac. 'I think I'm going to go with the Fleetwood Mac lace and paper flowers room, if it means I get to hear you sing that Gypsy song again, Tilly. That was beautiful, you know?'

'Thank you, but it's nothing special; my whole family are musical; you wait until we all get up there on that stage. The family band is called "Have Guitar, Will Travel." We play in town sometimes, but we mostly do regular gigs here. I'm sure you'll get to check us out.'

'Hmm, that sounds like my middle name, laughed Dalton. Dalton Jack, Have Guitar, and surfboard, Will Travel, Diaz.'

Tilly laughed. 'Is that your last name, Diaz? Dalton Jack Diaz? Well, THAT is a very cool last name for a country boy from Deniliquin. Look at you all fancy pants. You definitely belong in the lace and paper flowers suite.'

Dalton questioned. 'What is so fancy about Diaz?'

'Are you kidding? It's just fancy, Dalton Jack Diaz. You sound like a rockstar already.'

'Really? I'm just Dalton Jack Diaz from Deniliquin. Nothing rockstar about me, I promise. I'm not here for your secret retreat, although if I were a famous rockstar, that would be something I would do, for sure. It sounds fantastic.'

'Well, here is an idea for you. Perhaps you could jam with us all and show us your rockstar talents. Any new talent is so exciting for this town. You could draw a bit of a crowd for us with your country-boy-finds-beach-freedom look. You got it going on. I'd pay to watch you play,' winked Tilly.

'It's a deal for sure. I'll have a jam with your family. You let me know when. Sounds fun.' Dalton was excited at the invitation.

'Deal.' Tilly secured the offer. Tilly offered her hand to shake, but rather than simply accepting a handshake, Dalton leaned in and gave Tilly another lingering kiss, his lips covering her full mouth this time as he breathed in her soft breath. Tilly spoke softly as their lips parted gently, holding Dalton's hand in hers. 'Wow! You're giving me butterflies and goosebumps all at once. Perhaps I can show you the Fleetwood Mac suite?'

chapter fourteen

The Gypsy Room

They both stood up and grabbed the last few remaining glasses off the table. Dalton blew out the candle and pushed in the chairs. Tilly walked ahead, blowing the last few tealight candles out on the random tables they were still burning on. The large, scented candles were still burning, so Dalton and Tilly walked around, gently blowing them out and ensuring no fire hazard remained after they had closed the restaurant for the night.

Dalton wandered around in awe of the natural beauty of the building. 'This place is something special, Tilly. You and your family have done a great job renovating this place, and I can only imagine how much fun you've had over the years.'

Tilly replied, 'Yeah, it's been an amazing journey; this place has kept us together as a family and provided some wonderful memories along the way. We are fortunate.'

They walked through the bar and into the galley kitchen area to place the glasses on the sink, with no intention of washing them up. 'That job can wait until tomorrow,' said Tilly as she placed the glasses in the dishwasher. Dalton watched as she leaned over to put a few remaining dishes on the rack. *Geez, she has a nice butt*, he thought, still not saying anything out loud for fear of sounding like a sleaze.

And then, he couldn't resist, trying to keep it a little more PG. 'So, Tilly, has anyone ever wanted you so badly that they couldn't wait to get their "gypsy" room key?'

Tilly turned around to face him, offering her mouth to his again. He gently kissed her mouth and held her in his strong arms so she didn't fall. They had both had a few drinks, and he didn't want to fall all over her if she lost her balance. He pushed gently against her on the kitchen bench and lifted her leg to the top of his thigh, holding beneath her knee with his hand. Tilly melted into his stronghold.

Aromatic fragrances from beautiful home-cooked meals drifted around the restaurant kitchen, and it was still warm from the industrial ovens, fryers, and dishwashers that had been working all night. Still, the steel bench was cold against Tilly's back. Dalton did his best to hold her weight in his arms, so she didn't have to lean against the cold bench.

He started kissing down her neck and into the cleavage of her loose top before removing it altogether as Tilly lifted her arms to give permission. His kisses were so intense, yet gentle and passionate. She wondered if she was going to be covered in love bites on the back of her neck and the soft parts of her breasts, but it didn't bother her too much; it was all feeling so good, like nothing she'd ever felt before. *She didn't want it to stop, but she knew also that they could find a much more comfortable place to make love for the first time, but then that would be a boring story to tell*, she thought and giggled to herself. There were many scattered and random thoughts in her mind, but the main thought she kept returning to was, *oh my goodness, this guy is totally gorgeous, and he's right here in my restaurant kitchen.*

'Where did you come from?' she whispered.

'Where have you been?' he whispered back.

Meanwhile, Dalton was focused on exploring her beautiful body; he had removed her top and lacy bra and worked his way down to her stomach. Tilly had a solid, athletic body from surfing and living an active life. It was natural, curvaceous, and womanly, with a healthy amount of flesh to grab hold of. She had a natural tan from a lifetime in the Angourie outdoors.

Tilly adored the feel of Dalton's hard body. He was taller than her, and his skin was as smooth as silk. Their bodies fit well together. Dalton was still fully clothed, but Tilly felt warmth and strength through his soft shirt. She was trying very hard to let him lead the way and not distract him from everything he did to her.

They heard a noise; it sounded like someone was trying to get in the restaurant's front door, so they both paused and listened carefully for what it was.

Tilly realised quickly that it was her dad, Jack, at the front door. She didn't exactly need him walking in, investigating a noise in the kitchen right now. She whispered, holding her finger up to Dalton's mouth to hush him. 'It's probably just Dad checking I've locked up properly; he does that sometimes. He will be on his way once he realises I have locked up. He still thinks I'm an irresponsible teenager.'

Dalton whispered back, keeping his deep whisper as quiet as he could. 'Well, Tilly, I'm not sure about you, but I feel like an irresponsible teenager right now, and I love it!'

'Me too,' laughed Tilly, raising her shoulders with a snigger.

'Shall we get the "gypsy room" key and finish what we've started in there? It might be a little bit more respectable. Are you okay with that, Tilly?' proposed Dalton.

'I'm totally okay with that, Gypsy Boy,' flirted Tilly.

They pulled themselves apart from each other, and Tilly dressed herself.

They ensured the coast was clear and went to the reception area, checking that Tilly's dad wasn't still hanging around. Tilly identified the "gypsy" room key, as Dalton called it, by its keyring, dangled with lace ribbons and an intricate jar full of origami paper flowers. Laura was very creative; she had made fancy keyrings for all the fancy guest rooms based on celebrity guests staying at The Angourie Local.

Tilly had one more thing to do. The Angourie Local tradition was always to *Blame It on The Macallan*. A good night at the Angourie Local usually ended with The Macallan nightcap. Dalton hadn't been introduced to her favourite family named Whisky yet, so she tiptoed back into the bar and grabbed a half-empty bottle for her and Dalton to take back to the gypsy room.

Tilly and Dalton made their way along the garden pathway to the room, kissing, giggling, and laughing, trying not to make too much noise to interrupt the guest staying in the Van Morrison suite.

Once they got into the room, Tilly suggested she needed to use the bathroom. Dalton took a moment to have a look around the room. It was a very funky-styled room. It felt very Fleetwood, very 70s. There were signed posters on the walls and merchandise that the band had donated to The Angourie Local. The wallpaper was a Fleetwood Mac album cover in black and white, on repeat, all over the walls. It was very cool. Other than the themed décor, the rest of the room was kept simple, fresh, and clean.

Dalton wondered why they didn't do more promotions to get more guests to stay. Then he remembered The Angourie Local secret, understanding that publicity would ruin the whole concept of privacy and retreat, and there were only three rooms. The element of surprise was ongoing to the community, which was the best part. They never knew who might rock up to The Angourie Local. This whole idea relied on a community of trust and spontaneity. Tilly was the queen of spontaneity. It must have run in the family genes. Hence why she was right here, right now, in this gypsy room with Dalton.

Dalton heard the shower start up and waited to give Tilly some privacy. All he wanted to do was go in there and join her in the shower. He glanced at himself in the dresser mirror, placing the keys and the bottle of whisky on the dresser top. He noticed the notepad on the dresser with the cute little design logo at the top of the page saying *The Angourie Local.* Then he saw the name of the whisky. The Macallan. He had never heard of that whisky before. He was at The Angourie Local in the Gypsy Room with Matilda Rhiannon Macallan and a bottle of The Macallan Whisky. Even more ironic was that the clock radio was turned on and playing a Fleetwood Mac song, *Rhiannon.* Dalton felt for a moment like he was dreaming. He already had quite a few beers and he was feeling fantastic. Everything in this moment made him feel like it was precisely where he was meant to be. He hadn't felt like this for quite some time. He held up the bottle, taking more notice of the label.

The Macallan.
Highland Single Malt Scotch Whisky.
1990
Product of Scotland

He took a large swig of The Macallan's Whisky for a bit of Scotch courage. *Wow, that's damn heavy stuff, but smooth*, he thought, as he shook his head, blowing out his cheeks from the warm taste of the whisky as it slid down his throat and warmed down to his belly.

The dresser mirror was flattering; he was looking good. He looked relaxed and happy. He removed his Bandana. His hair had gone a little crazy curly after his surf today, but he could do nothing about that. He didn't want to disturb Tilly in the bathroom just yet, so he slid open the door, which led outside to a big open garden. He was desperate to go to the toilet, so he discretely relieved himself in the thick bushes. Living on the farm, he learned at a very young age that there was nothing wrong with urinating in the bushes discretely. It was natural body waste, and nature's bathroom was always much more beautiful than four close walls and a septic system leading to the ocean, eventually.

Dalton returned to the room and removed his clothing, placing his shirt and jeans on the side arm of the large suede-covered armchair. He kept his boxer shorts on, for now.

He knocked first and then opened the bathroom door after hearing Tilly respond to welcome him. 'Come in.' Tilly was washing her hair in the shower, and the smell was delicious. The guest room had scented soaps, shampoo, and conditioner sachets that smelled so good. As Dalton entered the bathroom, Tilly gestured, as she opened the shower door slightly, 'You're welcome to join me in here if you want to; there is plenty of room.'

Dalton removed his Calvin Klein boxer shorts, placing them on the bath ledge. He pulled the door open and stepped into the giant-sized shower. It was a decent shower. The water pressure was powerful, with plenty of room for two people. A quirky little sign on the shower door read *SAVE WATER, SHOWER WITH A FRIEND.*

'I've been waiting for you; where have you been?' smirked Tilly.

'I've just been checking out this cool "Gypsy Room." I love all the lace doyleys and the crystal bowl of paper flowers; now that's cute. Who made those?'

Tilly replied, delighted that Dalton loved the origami paper flowers bowl. 'I did. It's really easy. I'll show you someday.'

'I like the big native garden outside as well. I wasn't expecting that when I opened the door. I thought it was just going to be the road.'

Tilly took a moment to explain about the garden. 'Yeah, it is special. Mum and Dad planted that garden years ago; it was one of the first things we did when we bought this place. I'm surprised at how quickly it has grown. All the plants are natives, so they don't require much attention. It's the best garden to have and attracts the birds too.'

'Your Macallan family have done a great job creating this amazing place. I can imagine the other rooms are amazing too, but I like this one the best. We made an excellent choice.' Dalton realised he had side-tracked their conversation away from the flirtatious banter they had going on previously, so he took a moment to bring back their mood they were sharing before they entered the room.

Dalton grabbed the fresh cake of Palmolive Gold soap and slid the bar out of the packet. He started washing his body, creating a soapy scented lather. As he did, his eyes roamed up and down over Tilly's glistening brown body. 'Damn, girl, where have you been hiding?'

'Where have I been? Where have YOU been? Wasn't that my question to you?' replied Tilly with a reflective and humorous tone.

Dalton replied, 'I'm pretty sure you asked me, where did I come from, and I said, where have you been?'

Tilly thought about it and realised he was right; this cute little thing they said to each other was pretty cute. It didn't matter which way they said it to each other. They were happy to have found each other; wherever they were from or wherever they had been, it didn't matter. Here they were.

They talked, laughed, and washed each other's bodies, enjoying the warm water refreshing them and sobering them a little from the few drinks they had both had over the evening. Neither were drunk, but they could both feel the relaxing and inhibiting effects of the alcohol. They both wanted to feel everything with full sensation as they explored each other for the first time.

Dalton started kissing Tilly again, first on her mouth and then onto her neck and then all over her body, and this time, he kept moving down below her waist and started kissing between her legs. The water was warm, and Dalton's tongue was smooth and wet, making Till feel so many sensations throughout her body. She had to stop herself from feeling this way, just yet, so she stopped him and returned the favour. She kissed his mouth as she started handling him, feeling him growing harder in her hands. She took a moment to kiss him with more intensity and passion, as she continued to play with his beautiful hardness. Then she moved her way down his body and started gently kissing and sucking on him, using her hands, tongue, and entire mouth to make him feel so good, but not too good. Not yet. Dalton had to stop her because the intensity was too much for him. He wasn't ready yet.

They explored each other's bodies, in between mouth kissing and washing and massaging, then teasing and kissing and caressing, with their hands and mouth and tongue to where neither could handle it anymore. Still, neither would let the other feel the sensation of a full orgasm. Not yet. It was like perfect torture. They had already figured out how to bring each other to the point of ecstasy, and then they would retreat just in time. They both intended to make this first love-making session last for hours.

They moved out of the shower and into the bedroom. Dalton ripped the top sheet and doona off the bed, so they had complete freedom to move around on the giant king-size waterbed. It was so 70s. So Fleetwood. They continued to play and pleasure each other throughout the night. Neither was too concerned about the lack of sleep they were getting; they were more interested in thoroughly enjoying the moment they were in. Dalton was strong and physical with Tilly, moving her body into different positions, but the way he moved her was gentle and consenting, and he seemed to know the exact position to place her in, which felt equally good for her. If it was feeling good for her, it was feeling good for him, and vice versa. Her moans and groans of pleasure turned him on even more, as he felt so capable of pleasing her. That was always good for a man's ego, not that his ego needed any boost. He was confident and sure of himself, as he had enjoyed plenty of sexual experiences with women. He knew exactly what he was doing and he loved that she loved every minute.

Tilly was giving her fair share of sexual confidence and experience back to Dalton; it was quite a night of equally shared erotic pleasure.

They eventually fell asleep in the early morning hours as they both went into a deep, euphoric slumber for a few hours. They were both physically exhausted and satisfied from their adventurous, love-making session, so the sleep was deep and restful.

Tilly woke up first, her whole body entwined with Dalton in the same position as how they had fallen asleep. She woke with a brief thought of, *where am I?* And then instantly felt the most comforting sense as she realised she was in Dalton's arms, with his beautiful body wrapped around hers. Their legs entwined with each other, Tilly's back against his warm, strong, solid chest. His arms were firm and heavy on her, but she liked the weighted feeling. It comforted her.

Tilly remembered that her brothers were going for a surf and wondered if Dalton might want to join them, but she didn't want to wake him up. Or did she? If she would wake him up, it certainly wasn't to ask if he wanted to go for a surf with her brothers. Tilly moved Dalton's arms from around her shoulder as she turned around and slid down the bed and started kissing around Dalton's navel. She moved a little lower and placed her warm mouth around him, and she could feel his delight immediately as he hardened inside her mouth. He made a deep but gentle groaning noise and whispered to her. 'Morning gorgeous, that feels so damn good.'

Tilly paused briefly at what she was doing and whispered back. 'Morning, gorgeous.' She kept kissing him with her warm mouth, bringing him to the most amazing orgasm.

'Oh my god, Tilly, you are so good at that, thank you.'

She slid out of the bed and smiled over her shoulder at him as she walked naked to the bathroom. His eyes were roaming all over her beautiful body. He had never seen a woman with so much natural and confident beauty. She was perfect for him.

Tilly ran the shower, and Dalton joined her as they washed each other whilst chatting and laughing about the evening's shenanigans. They were reminiscing at how crazy the whole night was, that he had just wandered in here for a drink and meal, and now, here he was with her; how they were lucky not to get caught in the kitchen; how they hadn't got much sleep; and how Tilly was about to do the walk of shame.

It was a Thursday morning, and Tilly had to be in the restaurant, serving breakfast to hungry customers soon. As she washed Daltons back, Tilly explained that they always had the regular locals who would pop in for their after-surf morning coffee and the breakfast special, usually toast, bacon, tomatoes, and eggs; however, the customer would like them. She had to go home after her shower to get a change of clothes, and she laughed at how she might feel like a dirty stop-out, walking down the street in her clothes from the night before. Before long, the whole town would have it figured out. They both laughed because neither of them cared what anyone else would think. They had both enjoyed a special night together, and neither would have changed a thing.

They agreed to catch up later in the day. Dalton decided he might try to get a bit more sleep. Tilly gave Dalton a departing kiss and headed home to get dressed for the workday. It was just a short walk of shame down the road.

As Tilly was walking home, she thought *as if this is a walk of shame. It's more like a walk of joy. I have no shame in my choices about sharing the night with Dalton last night, only joy.*

chapter fifteen

When You Know, You Just Know

When Tilly arrived home, Jack and Laura sat on the deck overlooking the Angourie headland, enjoying the coffee together. They had the most amazing view, and the sun lifted over the ocean as the new day began. They were sitting close together. Their love for each other was so clear as they sat chatting about the beauty of the day and their plans to enjoy it. The boys had all got up early to go for their surf.

Laura gave Tilly a cheeky smile and questioned, with no expectation of a detailed answer, 'Hey Tilly, how was your night?'

'It was beautiful Mum, thanks.'

Laura wouldn't let Tilly get away that easily without some deeper questioning. 'Louis said you might have made a new friend last night?'

Jack sat quietly, sipping his coffee, listening but not commenting.

Tilly laughed gently. 'Did he now? Well, we can blame Frankie for this one. Frankie brought him here. He might be the one.'

Jack and Laura saw Tilly was very relaxed and happy about her night. She wasn't anxious, nervous, or secretive about talking about her night with Dalton.

'Why don't you make a coffee and come and join us? We want to hear everything about him.'

Tilly went into the kitchen to make a coffee while Jack and Laura continued chatting on the deck.

'This could be the one. When you know, you just know,' said Laura quietly. Laura was such a romantic, and she always hoped for the best for Tilly. In her experience, she had fallen for her first real love, Jack, and it was easy for her. Jack was perfect for her from day one; their relationship was not complex. She wanted the same for Tilly. She always carried her philosophy about love on her sleeve. She believed strongly that *when you know, you just know*. There is no doubt, and there are no questions or second guesses. You just know. You feel it deep in your heart, and it's the most simple and beautiful thing in life.

Jack replied light-heartedly. 'He could be the one, Laura, just don't put any pressure on her. She's young, she's got her whole beautiful life ahead of her. Just because we were together from such a young age doesn't mean it works out that way for everyone. The youth these days seem to take longer. But I agree with you; I've always been a believer that *when you know, you just know.* She seemed happy, and Louis said it was like they had known each other forever, the way they talked.'

Tilly emerged onto the deck with a warm mug of coffee, the steam rising from the top. 'So, tell me what you two know already. You seem to have this all worked out.' Tilly questioned with a curious smile.

Jack responded first, 'Not at all, Tilly, we don't have anything worked out. All we know is that Frankie was surfing with your new friend Dalton and his mates yesterday, and he got chatting to him in the surf. Frankie asked if he'd surfed Angourie, and when he said he hadn't, Frankie was devastated and wanted to share our "noisy ocean" with him. That's when Frankie invited him here to Angourie. He said Dalton was travelling with no vehicle, so he hitched a ride with Frankie, and you know the rest. Frankie said he seemed like an extraordinary guy. He is a down-to-earth country lad who likes to surf, and he loves music and sounds perfect for you, so he brought him here.' Jack put his hands out to the side and made a face, suggesting what else should Frankie have done? They all laughed in unison.

Laura added, 'Then little Louis came home excited last night; not only did you let him come home from his shift early, but he was rattling on that you and this guy were getting along well. He kept a close eye on you and seemed to think you were both very comfortable with each other. He felt very safe leaving you with Dalton, knowing you were enjoying your time with him. He said he's never seen you like that before.'

Tilly was interested that they already knew so much about Dalton and she hadn't even said a word about him yet. 'Oh, Louis, he's the sweetest. I think he was protective and worried at first, but then he seemed to ease up a little. Our dear little Louis; he worries about me.' Tilly took a long sip of her coffee, looking at the ocean where the boys surfed.

Laura continued, 'So Tilly, what do you want to tell us about him?'

'Well, as you know, he's from the country; he grew up in a tiny town out west. His two brothers and his parents are all farmers, which is what he was supposed to do. But it just wasn't his thing. He finished school, did a building trade, and then went off travelling. He plays guitar and likes to surf, so he's just making his way up the East Coast, having fun playing gigs to make money and surfing. Honestly, I do not know his plans; we just had a really fun night together.' Tilly paused and looked at her dad. 'I feel like I've known him forever and only met him yesterday. Is that weird?'

Jack replied instantly as he stood up and made his way towards the kitchen. 'Well, you know what I think about all that fate and soulmate stuff? We are already connected to certain people; we know and feel it. If you find someone like that, you're fortunate. Hold on to that one if you can. Your mum and I found each other, and from the day we met, we just knew, and we still know, don't we love?' He clarified and questioned Laura, giving her a wink, not expecting an answer; the question was rhetorical.

'We do, Jack, we got lucky!' Laura responded as she watched Jack enter the kitchen, wondering where he was going in the middle of the conversation. 'There is no need to rush though, love; just enjoy each day with him.' Laura continued the discussion with Tilly.

'Well, Mum, I don't even know if he's going to stay here; he's just passing through. I can offer him a room, and he can play gigs here and do some café and bar work. What do you think?'

Laura raised her voice so Jack would hear from the kitchen, 'Can we afford another staff member at this time of the year, Jack?'

Jack said, 'Sure we can, let's just play it by ear like your mum said. No need to rush, love.' Jack was rinsing out his coffee cup in the sink and had things to do; he was a busy man and always had something to occupy his time; who knows what he was up to today. Perhaps he was going to tinker on his car, go for a beach walk or do some fishing; maybe he was planning on doing some work at the café. Whatever he was up to, he was off. Laura just went along with it; she had a plan and was easily entertained with her artwork and painting. She loved to look after the garden and her vegetable patch. She might also spend some time at the café during some part of the day.

Tilly figured she would get ready for work at the café. She had to open at 8 am, seeing as the boys were all out surfing. They could probably do with another staff member to do the early shift during the week when the surf was good. Usually, one of the boys would do the early coffee and breakfast shift, but not today; they were all out catching some beautiful Angourie waves.

'Thanks for the chat, Mum, and for always being so understanding. Big Love.' Tilly reached out her arms, wrapped them around Laura, and gave her a big, warm hug.

'Big Love, Tilly. You know all I want is for you to be happy. You do whatever you think is right in your heart, my love.'

Laura and Tilly embraced momentarily, then picked up their coffee mugs and headed to the kitchen to offload their crockery and get on with their day.

'Have a beautiful day, Mum. See you later at the café.'

'You too, darlin', have a great day. Do you think I'll get to meet this man today?'

'Sure, Mum, if he's still hanging around, I might have scared him off; he might have disappeared already. And you know, the weird thing is, I have no way of contacting him if he leaves. He has no fixed address and no phone number. All I know is his name is Dalton Jack Diaz from Deniliquin.'

'Well, let's hope he's hanging around a little longer; for your sake, Tilly, he sounds like a keeper.'

Tilly went to her room. She showered and washed her hair, and dressed for the day, recapturing certain moments of the night before that played over in her mind. She envisioned Dalton's beautiful face, gorgeous body, deep green eyes, and messy curly hair. She had never seen anyone so naturally good-looking. He was attractive to her soul. He was her kind of beautiful. She could look at him all day and never get bored. She could hear his sexy voice in her head, and his cheeky laugh kept resounding. Deep down, she had no doubts or fears that Dalton might disappear, but who knows? She didn't know him; she'd only just met him.

Tilly dressed quickly, slipping on a comfortable, beachy-looking dress; it was a bit of a hippie style but not too lax. It accentuated her curves and showed off her long brown legs without being too revealing or making her look like she was trying too hard. Tilly didn't have to try too hard at all. Tilly made sure the neckline of her dress covered up the love bites on her chest. She combed her curly locks and left her hair to dry naturally, as she always did. Her curls were best left untamed, and she didn't need any products to give her any more bounce. Tilly looked in the mirror, happy with what she saw; she felt good, looked good, and smelled good. She had experienced the most amazing night; she was happy in her soul, and her inner happiness radiated through her entire presence.

Tilly grabbed her shoulder bag and headed back to the café to open shop for the morning trade.

chapter sixteen

Gypsy Boy

When Tilly arrived back at the café, the first person she saw was Dalton. He was sitting on the front deck stairs, dressed in the same outfit he wore the night before. He was strumming away on his guitar in his own creative world. This was such a turn-on for Tilly.

Tilly interrupted. 'Hey Gypsy Boy, how are you doing?'

'Hey Gypsy Girl, I was wondering when I might get the pleasure of bumping into you again,' Dalton smirked with a cheeky double-meaning grin.

'Watcha playin'?' Tilly asked as she removed her bag from her shoulder and sat beside him.

'Hmmmm.' He paused as he collected an idea to have a teasing conversation with Tilly. 'Well, I met this amazing girl last night and had this little song pop in my head. Do you wanna hear it?'

Tilly played his little conversational teasing game back. 'Sure, I'd love to hear it. I'm jealous, though. Who is this amazing girl you met?'

As he strummed his guitar, finding the song's rhythm, he replied, 'Well, I met this girl last night, and she was amazing. We had the best night together. We talked for hours about everything. She was damn hot too, but then this morning, she just got up and left, and I'm hoping I'll see her again.' He smiled sideways, knowing that Tilly was playing along with this game, and he wondered what her response would be.

She could either be a real tease and crush his ego or play along with the game and tell him everything she liked about him in this fun game of "reveals."

'Well, why would she want to see a guy like you again?' Tilly questioned cheekily.

Dalton was quick-witted in his response and replied, 'Because I've written a song for her.'

'Oh well, that's cute. I guess you could play me the song, and we can decide whether she'd like it or not.'

He started to strum and sing the lyrics...

If it was just one night, one night, one night, one night with you.
Can you imagine the things I, things you, things we could do?
I'd tell you my story from the start; you'd tell me about your broken heart,
We'd talk about places that we've been and all the crazy things we've seen in that one night.

Oh.... in that one night.

He stopped and paused, and said, 'That's it.'

Tilly was blown away; what a cute little song and his voice and the way he played the guitar. Wow! She replied, 'Dalton, if this girl has any common sense, she won't spend just one night with you; that's a beautiful start to a song.'

Again, Dalton replied with humour and quick wit. 'Well, that's all I've got so far because you came along and distracted me.'

They both laughed. Tilly wrapped her arms awkwardly around Dalton, trying not to squash his guitar. They gave each other a beautiful, long, warm kiss. Just the feeling of his mouth on hers stirred emotions inside Tilly again. She could have taken him back to that gypsy room right then and there if she didn't have to open the café five minutes ago.

Tilly sat back and looked at Dalton as they sat on the stairs beside each other. 'Can you tell me again, where did you come from?'

Dalton replied, to continued with their banter, 'And can you just tell me again, where have you been?'

Tilly replied as she stood up to open the café. They could see their first customer for the day walking across the road. 'I've been here, mostly right here,' as she spread her arms, claiming the expanse of Angourie, 'pretty much all my life. I'm so glad you found me.'

Dalton moved across to the side of the steps so the customer could walk past, and then he stood up, packing up his guitar and belongings to follow them in. As the customer moved past Dalton, he tipped his head forward and said, 'Top of the morning to ya!'

The customer didn't reply with a vocal to Dalton; he just tipped his head back in reply. Dan was a regular customer and a local Angourie surfer. As Tilly fiddled in her bag to find her keys to unlock the door, Dan questioned her. 'I see you have a new friend, Tilly. How are you this morning, love?'

'Morning, Dan. Yeah, that's Dalton. Frankie dragged him here yesterday; you might need to fight him off your waves; apparently, he likes a good surfing location and hasn't been to Angourie before.'

'Well, once he gets a taste, he won't go far.' Dan suggested to Tilly.

Dan turned to Dalton, who was now standing just behind them both. 'Welcome to heaven on earth, mate. I've been here for thirty years; there is no better place than right here, and it helps that Tilly can make a splendid brew.'

'Oh, thanks, Dan,' smiled Tilly.

'I'll just have my regular coffee and the breakfast special. Thanks Tilly.'

'No worries, take a seat, and I'll bring it out.'

Dalton placed his guitar in the reception area again, which was out of the way of customers and thoroughfares. Tilly went inside with Dan. Dalton stood on the deck near Table 26, admiring the morning ocean views. It was even more beautiful in the daylight than the evening view. The beaches were secluded and peaceful. Only a few surfers were out in the water, catching some beautiful, long, rolling sets. Dalton thought it was most likely to be Frankie, Eddie, and Louis.

'Oi, Dalton, come and give me a hand, will you please?' called Tilly from the kitchen.

Tilly had come into the kitchen from the bar area where she had turned on the coffee machine. It was making a churring noise as it warmed up and did its job of crushing the fresh coffee beans. It smelt good. The smell of fresh coffee in the morning took Dalton back to his childhood. Fresh coffee and freshly cut grass were two of his favourite smells he associated fondly with his childhood. It reminded him of Sunday mornings waking up on the farm when his dad would go out and mow the house yard while his mum brewed the coffee pot. The kids would get dressed to help Dad on the farm for the day with their little *Blundstone* boots and *Akubra* cowboy hats. Lately, Dalton had exchanged his Akubra cowboy hat for a blue Bandana; however, he had stayed faithful to always wear a pair of Blundstone boots unless he was getting around in a pair of comfortable, well-worn thongs or barefoot most of the time if he was anywhere near the beach. Dalton fitted the description as a beach cowboy. Although he was born in the country, his natural environment and where he felt most content and happy was the beach, even though he had only been exploring the east coast of Australia for only $1/24^{th}$ of his life. He was comfortable in his boardies when he wasn't wearing his jeans, boots and Bandana. Most of the time, he didn't wear a shirt at all, but when he made the effort to throw a shirt on, he filled it well. Today was one of those days. He wore his jeans and the same white shirt he had on the night before, but he was relaxed and beachy and wearing his comfortable thongs rather than being barefoot. His curly hair was out of control, so he tied it up in a messy, tucked-up ponytail and covered it with his Bandana—an easy fix.

Dalton noticed Dan was out of sight, and there was no one around as he walked into the kitchen, sweeping Tilly into his arms and kissing her mouth. It felt the same as the night before, so passionate, yet gentle, leaving Tilly yearning for more.

Tilly returned the kiss and then quickly readjusted her focus.

'So, Gypsy Boy, how do you like your coffee?' Tilly asked as she pulled slightly away from Dalton. Not that she wanted to, but she had to make Dan's coffee and breakfast for him.

'I'm easy, Tilly, you know me,' and he laughed. 'I'd love some sugar and some milk; other than that, however, it comes will be just fine.' Dalton felt uncomfortable just standing around, so he offered some help to Tilly. 'Can I help? I *can* cook, you know?' Dalton wasn't asking a question but letting Tilly know he could cook and didn't mind helping.

Tilly accepted the offer graciously. 'If you don't mind, please grab the bacon and eggs from the cold room, and I'll get this grill going. You can grab some extra eggs and bacon for us as well if you're hungry. I don't know about you, but I'm starved.'

As Dalton walked over to the cold room, Tilly couldn't take her eyes off him. He was wearing a pair of thongs, which probably wasn't particularly good kitchen etiquette, but this was Angourie, who was going to mind. Dan was out in the restaurant and wearing his beach thongs, too, so he surely wouldn't complain.

Tilly shook her head in disbelief at the situation as she tried to focus. He was just so damn attractive, and here he was in The Angourie Local Café, helping her cook breakfast. She struck up the gas, and it started heating the hotplate immediately.

'We're cooking with gas.' Tilly accented the word gas in an American twang.

'This is a great set-up you've got here, Tilly. You've got the breakfast set up; then, flowing on to your easy lunch menu and bar and restaurant gigs at night. Dalton questioned seriously, trying to understand how they sustained the extended opening hours that The Angourie Local required as a family. Do you tire of it?'

Tilly replied, 'Not really; we all share the load a fair bit; there are six of us in the family, so it just works out. Mum and Dad used to work many more hours, but they've slowed down now. The boys and I do most of the morning and daytime work. We all usually help at night, especially on the weekends when it's busy. We've also got our regular chefs, who do most of the cooking.'

'Sounds like you've got it all worked out,' replied Dalton.

'It's just you and me this morning, Gypsy Boy, and I don't know about you, but I'm ravenous. Somebody I know kept me up very late. As she winked at Dalton, and come to think of it, I didn't even have any dinner last night. I was too busy talking to a gorgeous random stranger.' Tilly looked Dalton up and down, her eyes all over him.

They both laughed.

'Well, let's get this cranking. Do you want me to do the hot stuff?' Dalton moved in to place the bacon and eggs on the hotplate.

'You *are* the hot stuff, Dalton.' They both laughed as Tilly went to get some fresh bread from the pantry.

Tilly went out into the bar area to put on some morning music. She placed her easy-listening CDs in the five-stack player. Suzanne Vega to start the day. *Tom's Diner.* It's such a coffee shop in the morning song. She finished the coffee and delivered Dan a fresh 'brew,' as he called it.

'Thanks, Tilly.' Dan acknowledged as Tilly placed the coffee in front of him with a bowl of sugar and extra milk on the side, as he liked it.

'So, is that the boys down there surfing Tilly?' questioned Dan.

'I think it is. Frankie has been talking about those long rolling sets for days. He's got a new Mal that he wanted to try out, so he'll love it down there this morning. Have you been surfing much, Dan?'

Tilly was a wonderful conversationalist, and she always listened to the customers' stories and conversations, not to be nosey at all, but so she could keep in touch with their lives as part of being a connected, small community. Just like the background and history of Bessie's Café, The Angourie Local was more than just a café. It was a community gathering place, and it was comfortable, so many locals would come and chat with any of The Macallans.

Dan replied. 'You know me, Tilly, I surf, and I fish. I try not to do anything else. So, yes, I have been surfing *a lot.* I love it; it's what keeps me sane. It helps that we live in the best surfing location in the *fuckin'* universe. Excuse my cuss; you're a lady. I'm doing a few competitions this year, so that should be rad. Should keep me focused, *so I'm not thinking about what might have been between you and me.'* Dan thought, but didn't say it out loud.

'You know me, Dan. I have three brothers, so I hear some pretty rad language. It doesn't bother me; it's just words. Surely, I don't come across as the verbally sensitive type. It's all good,' reassured Tilly.

Tilly felt like Dan was flirting a bit to make Dalton feel uncomfortable in case he was looking on. She was reserved in not returning the flirtatious comments. Dan was a good friend, and a valued customer. Tilly and Dan had some history together; they had shared one drunken night back a few years ago before Tilly went to university, but their relationship went no further. Dan was a bit older than Tilly, and the chemistry wasn't there for her, although she felt maybe Dan felt differently. Tilly wondered if Dan had come in for coffee and breakfast to keep a closer eye on this new handsome fellow in town.

'Let me get your breakfast, and I'll be back.' Tilly smiled and headed back into the kitchen.

Dalton was cooking up a storm; he had helped himself to the fresh tomatoes and mushrooms and was making this whole breakfast look so much better than it was before. He had also found the avocadoes and had three plates ready to be served. It was looking like a breakfast feast.

Tilly was surprised by what she saw as she walked back into the kitchen. How could this guy be super gorgeous, good in bed and a superb cook, amongst many other qualities she was discovering?

'I hope you don't mind Tilly. I've helped myself to some more stuff to make a *special* breakfast this morning.'

'Sure thing, what's the *special* occasion, Dalton?' Tilly baited Dalton, hoping for a quirky response about their shared night.

'Well, as I told you before when we were outside on the steps, I've met this most amazing girl, and I need to impress her, so I thought I might show off my cooking skills, even if it is just breakfast.'

'Aaahah,' Tilly nodded, biting her lip, and giving a cheeky smile to show her approval.

'Do you think your mate Dan will like the little extras?' questioned Dalton.

'Sure, he will; I'll just tell him you're trying to impress him so he will let you share his Angourie waves.'

'Sounds like a plan. Shall we eat?'

Tilly took out Dan's plated breakfast, and Dalton carried the other two plates for Tilly and himself.

As Tilly walked towards Dan's table and placed his meal down in front of him, Dan noticed Dalton was not far behind her, carrying two plates out towards another table, so Dan quickly offered, 'Hey, you guys are welcome to join me here if you like, I feel like a bit of a loner.'

'Sure, we can do that, as long as you don't mind,' Dalton replied as he looked at Dan and then at Tilly for her approval.

They all joined for breakfast. Tilly was back and forth to the kitchen a few times to get the salt and pepper and some water and juice for the table. She also brought out the coffee she had made for herself and Dalton. Once everything was in place, they had a friendly, long, comfortable chat over breakfast.

Tilly thought it might be awkward, and she thought Dan might be intrusive, asking Dalton many questions, figuring out who this guy was that had come along, and was making moves on Tilly. Not that Dan had any claim over her; he was protective because he had known her for a long time. Other than the one night they had shared, which made things a little awkward, they were just friends, and Dan knew that, although if he had his choice, things would be different. Tilly had made it clear how she felt and wanted to keep their relationship as 'friends only.'

As it turned out, Dalton asked Dan a lot of questions about the Angourie reef and the danger spots, as he had heard that Angourie wasn't a place for beginner surfers, not that Dalton was a beginner surfer. Still, it was good to know the relevant information firsthand from a local.

Dan asked where Dalton had come from, and Dalton explained his story, from the country to the beach and how his travel adventures had landed him here, for now. Tilly listened again, picking up more details about his life that he explained to Dan. He explained more detail about his building trade and surfing passion, perhaps because Dan seemed interested in those aspects of his life. It was interesting for Dan to understand how a country boy could be so passionate about surfing when it was such a distant goal for anyone growing up on the land, ten hours from any beach. Perhaps it was the fact that it was such an unlikely possibility that Dalton could be a surfer that made him want to make it part of his life even more. It was a challenge. Most things he tried doing for the first time, he picked up quickly, and surfing was just another one of those things. It was the same with his building and handyman skills and his natural ability to play the guitar.

He was a natural at many things, thought Tilly.

Just as they finished their breakfast, Laura arrived and came over to say hello. Laura hadn't met Dalton yet; she had only heard about him from Louis, Frankie, and Tilly. She liked what she was seeing, as all three were chatting comfortably. Everything seemed to be very natural. Laura had a soft spot for Dan. He was a nice guy, salt of the earth, and she always thought that he and Tilly might end up together, but she also understood that there was no chemistry for Tilly. She could see it now; she could see the physical chemistry between Dalton and Tilly. It was apparent that there was a strong connection going on between them. They were sitting side by side, and Dalton rested his hand on Tilly's leg. Now and then, he would give her leg a little rub and a squeeze to let her know he was thinking about her during the conversation.

'Morning, everyone; how are we all today?' Laura jollied, not expecting a response from everyone; she was just being polite.

'Dalton, this is my mum, Laura.' Tilly tilted her head towards her mum and then, 'Mum, this is Dalton,' tilting her head back towards Dalton.

'Nice to meet you, Dalton.' Laura put her hand out to shake Dalton's hand. Dalton stood up and gestured towards a hug rather than a handshake.

'Nice to meet you too, Laura.' Dalton warmly embraced Laura, and she immediately understood what Tilly was feeling. He had a friendly personality, and he was relaxed and easy-going. He didn't seem to have any barriers, expectations, or reservations other than just to be himself.

Dan stood up to hug Laura, too. 'Morning, Mrs Macallan, good to see you again. It's been a while.'

Laura replied, 'Yeah, I haven't been around a lot. Lately, it's been quiet, so I've been working in the garden at home while the kids and Jack look after this place.'

'Sounds good,' replied Dan with nothing more to add.

Dalton conveyed more interest in continuing the conversation. 'What have you been doing in your garden, Laura?'

Laura was excited to reply. 'Oh! We've just got a lot of fresh vegetables and fruits; most of the food here comes from our garden, the basics, you know; lettuces and all the green stuff, tomatoes, the pumpkins, and sweet potatoes are going wild. We've got chickens for fresh eggs and lots of basic herbs- parsley, basil, oregano, and mint—the simple stuff. We also have a few nice trees: avocadoes, fresh lemons, limes, and oranges.

The other stuff we buy locally to support our local farmers. We've been doing this for years, so it's just ongoing maintenance to keep it free of bugs and weeds. Jack set up all the vegetable runs when we moved here many years ago, and we've been mostly self-sustained since then.'

Dalton loved that Jack and Laura were mostly self-sufficient from the land. 'That's great that you can do that, Laura. I love food so much, and it's always better when it's fresh or even better when it's from your garden. I grew up on a farm out west, and my mum and dad had a vegetable patch. Probably not as amazing as yours. We had cows for meat and dairy. It's a lot of work, but nothing is better than fresh farm produce.'

Dan edged into the conversation, directing his question towards Dalton. 'Do you miss the farm, mate? Do you think you'll ever go back?' He was trying to determine Dalton's purpose here in Angourie and wondering how long he planned to stay.

Dalton replied without too much detail, the same story he told Tilly last night. The farm life wasn't for him; he had creative outlets to fulfil, and the ocean drew him to freedom. He kept the story simple and finished with, 'I guess I'm just here to have a bit of fun and see where life takes me, and I'd love to surf with you someday, if that's okay?'

Dan was a little taken aback by Dalton's confidence and friendly manner. Dan was being a little abrasive, but Dalton didn't pick up on it.

Dalton had drifted deep into the dark recesses of his mind, and his thoughts were not about anything he wanted to share right here and right now, at this breakfast table. He hadn't shared his dark secret with anyone since leaving Deniliquin, and this certainly wasn't the time or place.

He tried to shift his thoughts, as he had not been in that headspace for quite some time. His stomach felt nauseous, and he swallowed hard, taking a sip of juice to wash down the lump in his throat.

Dalton wondered why this breakfast conversation had brought up these intense feelings. All he could work out was that he felt guilty that he was hiding the truth from Tilly, and he felt like she could feel it. He wanted to tell her everything, but it just wasn't the right time, just now.

Dan's probing questions had him skimming the true story of why he left Deniliquin again. As he dodged and weaved and answered Dan's questions with superficial details, he watched Tilly looking at him inquisitively, knowing that she felt that there was something he was leaving out.

In this moment Dalton regretted not sharing his darkness with Tilly when they were having deep chats the night before, but at the time it didn't seem like the right moment. But then again, when would be the right moment to share his deepest, darkest guilt.

chapter seventeen

Dalton's Dark Secret

The part that Dalton had left out and the details he was holding close to his heart were too painful to share with anyone. Few knew about this brief, traumatic piece of his life.

While Dalton was gigging in local pubs in Deniliquin, his hometown out west, he was always meeting lots of girls and had a few on the run, at the same time, most of the time. But there was one girl he had fallen deeply in love with. Her name was Chelsea.

Dalton was twenty-three. Chelsea was just seventeen, still in high school, and their relationship was kept secret from most people. Small towns gossiped and Dalton and Chelsea didn't aspire to be gossiped about, so only a few close friends knew they were a serious thing. Dalton's family and a few of his friends knew about the closeness of their friendship. Only two of Chelsea's friends were aware of their bond. The main reason that nobody knew about how close they were was because Chelsea's parents disapproved of the association. They had strong morals, and they were not supportive of the age difference between Dalton and Chelsea, feeling that Chelsea would be lured into a physical relationship before she was ready. What they didn't know was that Dalton was respectful to Chelsea, and he was happy to wait for her until she was ready to advance the relationship to include a sexual connection.

When Dalton started seeing Chelsea, early in the spring as she was nearing the end of her final school year, he cleaned up his act. He told other girls that he was casually dating, when it suited him, that he was in a serious relationship and that he couldn't see them anymore. Hearts were shattered all over the place, but to his credit, the girls that he was dating knew that he was a player, and the relationships he was in were nothing serious. There were no hard feelings, just a few little soft heartbreaks. Dalton was always honest, and he did always tell his "girlfriends" that the relationship could be nothing serious. He was just having fun until Chelsea came along.

She was different; she was innocent and beautiful, and yet, she had this creative, quirky wild side that brought out his mischievous nature. Chelsea had a way of inspiring Dalton's creativity. Together, they were like wildflowers. When they were together, they would ooze joy and happiness, and their vibe was energetic and free. Their relationship was beautiful.

There was, however, this one massive complication with their relationship. Chelsea's parents. The only way they could see each other was for Chelsea to sneak out and meet Dalton in random places, which made their relationship challenging, but even more exciting. Chelsea would sometimes sneak out through her bedroom window in the middle of the night and go over to Dalton's and stay for a few hours, always making sure she was home by the morning to get ready for school. Chelsea's parents never even knew she was gone, even though the only way to get to Dalton's was to drive. She always parked her car across the road so they wouldn't hear her drive away, and she always made sure they had gone to bed before she left. She had to be so careful. If they ever found out what she was doing, they would have forbidden her to see Dalton. For Chelsea, it was a risk worth taking. She was madly in love, crazy in love, head over heels in love.

Dalton and Chelsea had been together for a few months, and their feelings for each other were getting more serious, although Dalton had never pushed the boundaries. One night, in the middle of summer; it was a beautiful warm summer night; they met down by the river for a moonlight picnic; they brought drinks and snacks to share, and they toasted marshmallows on the fire that they made. They confessed their true love for each other and made love for the first time under the full moon and stars. Dalton admitted he loved Chelsea with all his heart, and he wanted to make her "his girl" forever. Chelsea decided she was going to tell her parents about the seriousness of her relationship with Dalton so that she could see him and stop feeling guilty. Chelsea was too young to get married, but as soon as she was old enough, that is what she wanted to do. Chelsea wanted more than anything to be Dalton's "girl" forever.

They had spent a beautiful night together; the moon and the stars had faded, and the slow dawn was rising. It was time to go home. Dalton had made Chelsea a mixed tape of love songs recorded from the radio, but there was also a special surprise. He had also written a song for her, called "my girl" and it was the first song on the cassette. Dalton gave the cassette to Chelsea and explained carefully, 'I want you to listen to this anytime you're feeling lonely and know that I'm thinking of you.' They both embraced with a long, loving kiss and shared their departing words, as always, "I'll see you when I'm looking at you."

They climbed into their separate cars to drive home. Chelsea popped the cassette into the music player to listen to the song Dalton had recorded for her. They drove in convoy down the dusty road until it turned to tar. They were getting closer to the town now. Dalton lived close to the river, on his farm, and Chelsea lived closer to town. Dalton turned off down his laneway to his farm and looked back in his rear-view mirror. *Damn, she's beautiful.* He wound his window down and blew her a kiss out of the window as she passed him on the turnoff.

Her window was rolled down, too, as she blew a kiss back and called out, 'Thank you for the song; it's beautiful.'

Dalton pulled into his driveway, parked in his usual spot and climbed out of the car, reaching across to grab the picnic blanket and food basket from the passenger seat. It was then that he heard a piercing screeching noise and then a loud metallic bang.

'No, what was that?!'

Dalton had a rush of goosebumps fill over his whole body as he imagined what the sound might have been. He'd heard that sound before. A car, hitting a kangaroo. It was all too common on the country roads, especially on the dawn. The kangaroos would come out to the streets to eat, and for whatever reason, they would decide to cross the road when a car was coming. Roadkill was common; cars were written off often. The only possible saviour was to have a roo-bar attached to the front of the car. Most of the farm trucks and utes had these roo-bars in place. Dalton had a roo-bar on his car for that exact reason.

Dalton climbed back in his car and paved his way back out of the driveway, dust billowing behind him, and onto the road heading back into town, in the direction Chelsea was heading.

He didn't have to drive very far before he caught sight of the wreckage.

'Noooooooooooo, not Chelsea, please God, no!'

As Dalton got nearer, he could smell the burning rubber from the screech of the tyres where Chelsea had tried to stop suddenly. The enormous roo lay in a heap on the road, not moving. Chelsea's car had swerved off the road, and into the ditch, the front of the vehicle was facing downwards. The back tyres were lifted off the ground and were still spinning. The engine was still running, with smoke rising from the bonnet.

Dalton couldn't move faster if he tried, but everything seemed like it was in slow motion. He dragged Chelsea's lifeless body out of the car, praying someone would come to help.

'Nooooooooo, Chelsea, come back to me, noooooo, somebody help, please somebody.'

Dalton placed Chelsea in the back seat of his car, as best he could, in a comfortable side position. Not that it mattered. She was out cold. He drove directly to the hospital.

It was very early in the morning; the sun was just coming up, so it seemed like a ghost town. He pulled into the emergency driveway at the front of the hospital, hoping that someone would come to help. It didn't seem like anyone was on duty. Dalton climbed out of the front seat and opened the back door, trying to keep calm, but feeling overwhelming, intense pain inside his chest, with the realisation that his beautiful girl was dead.

Dalton carried Chelsea's lifeless body, like a dead weight in his arms into the hospital. 'Somebody, please help me. This girl has been in a car accident. Please somebody, anybody.' Dalton looked down at her angelic face, completely blank of expression, her slender arms and small unmoving chest behind the bright blue-butterfly T-shirt that she was wearing, her absolute favourite. It seemed so surreal that just a few hours before this moment, her whole body was alive with laughter and love and freedom. Her smile was beaming with vibrancy and beauty. Now. Nothing. Nothingness. Stillness.

The next moment, it was like everyone that was on the dawn shift was suddenly in the hospital lobby, trying to help. Chelsea was placed on a stretcher and rolled into the emergency ward. Machines and cords were being attached to her motionless body with no effect, no signs of life, no beeps, no response. There was nothing anybody could do.

Chelsea had suffered a massive head injury and died on impact. Chelsea was pronounced dead, at 4.44 am, it was the 25th of January 1993.

The next few months were living hell for Dalton. The worst part was when he had to explain to Chelsea's parents that she was with him the night she died, and even though he could never bring her back, he wanted them to know that he loved her more than anything he had ever loved, and he wanted them to know that she loved him as well. Chelsea's parents expressed no sympathy or understanding. They didn't care. They had loads of questions entwined with bitterness and they were unforgiving. They wanted to lay charges on Dalton. There was so much blame placed on Dalton for the accident. Chelsea's father wanted to charge Dalton for manslaughter. Saying that he was lying, and that he was driving the car recklessly and he caused the accident. It was all untrue, but this was Chelsea's father's perspective. He wanted to blame someone for Chelsea's death, not a kangaroo. The kangaroo was dead as well. There was no revenge or reconcile in blaming a kangaroo.

Dalton understood how upset they were, and he understood their immense grief. It was something he had trouble living with for himself, let alone how her parents must have felt. He kept on reliving his last special moments with her, seeing her beautiful face in the rear vision mirror and hearing her voice.

'I'll see you when I'm looking at you.' 'Thanks for the song, it's beautiful.'

Dalton played Chelsea's song for her at her funeral, and it may have been the one saving grace that allowed everyone to understand their young love. It was obvious how deeply he loved her, and close friends of hers had explained how happy Chelsea was with Dalton, although their love was kept mostly secret.

There were so many things Dalton couldn't get past in his months of grief following Chelsea's death.

He couldn't get past her parents' anguish and tragic loss. It broke his heart. Chelsea was their only daughter, and she was everything in their lives. Nothing he could do could bring her back for them, and he felt so much to blame for that. Nothing could take away their pain and heartache, and it was his fault. If he hadn't been with Chelsea, she would still be here.

He couldn't get past the fact that he had to drive past the location of the accident every day. There was no other road to his house, so if he went into town, he would pass the accident site. Many people had placed flowers where the accident had happened. Most days, he wouldn't leave the house because he couldn't face the accident scene recurring in his mind. It was debilitating, and he felt trapped and condemned. He retreated into a deep depression. He hated himself for what had happened. In Dalton's darkest moments of grief, he considered taking his own life, so that he could be with Chelsea.

He kept on receiving hate letters in the mail from Chelsea's "friends," the ones that didn't know her or understand her intense love for him. They blamed him for being in a relationship with someone way too young for him, and if it weren't for him, she would still be here.

Chelsea had a few close friends that understood and reached out to Dalton, now and then, to check he was okay. He wasn't okay.

Early one morning, just at dawn, about the same time that Chelsea had passed away, a few months earlier, Dalton woke up from yet another sleepless night. *Was this nightmare ever going to end?* He didn't think so. Not while he stayed here, staring at the same four walls, in the same bed that he had shared with her, feeling the same grief and depression day after day. One more hate letter in the mailbox could almost drive him crazy and cause him to take his own life. The only thing Dalton could do was to leave Deniliquin, and never come back. He packed a backpack; he grabbed his guitar, and he left a note for his family.

Dear Mum, Dad, Timmy and Johnno,

I'm so sorry, but I'm out. I can't do this anymore. I'm okay and please don't worry about me, but I need to leave this town.

I hope you understand; I can't stay here anymore in this grief. It's taking every ounce of my energy to fight to stay alive, and I believe if I stay here, my grief will kill me. I'm doing what I must do for myself and you all. Without me here, you can get on with your lives without me dragging you all down with me.

I'm going to the East Coast. I need to leave my demons behind me.

Thank you for loving me and understanding that this is what I need to do.

I'll see you when I'm looking at you.

Your loving son and most awesome brother,

Dalton x

chapter eighteen

Dan

Dan could see that Dalton had drifted off into his thoughts, so he didn't delve any deeper. Instead, he replied with, 'Sure we can have a surf mate, and fair enough mate, having a bit of fun has never hurt anyone. Sounds like a good enough reason for me. How long do you plan on staying around here for?'

You do not know, how untrue that is, was the exact thought that crossed Dalton's mind but instead he replied with, 'I haven't figured that out yet, I was on my way northbound, with some mates I've recently met up with. We're all stopped here in Yamba and Angourie, for a bit, while it's the quiet season, not too many surfers in the water, but the swell is good.' Dalton had avoided a direct answer about how long he was planning on staying, but his response to Dan seemed to suffice, for now.

'It's always good here, mate; you just gotta choose which side of the headland you want to surf. If it's no good here, we can make a trip into Yamba or take a four-wheel drive and head down to Sandon. Mate, that's heaven on earth down there, a little hard to get to but totally worth the hustle, mate.'

'Let me know if you want to make a day trip, and I'll come with you. That sounds like an offer too good to refuse,' replied Dalton excitedly.

As the boys continued chatting about surfing, Laura and Tilly started clearing the plates from the table as new customers had arrived.

Tilly had noticed a few customers at the entry of the café, deciding it was a good time to take her leave from the table. 'I'm going to leave you, boys, to chat and plot your surfing tour, while I get on and earn my keep. I'll catch up with you later, Dalton. Nice to see you again, Dan. You're looking well.'

Laura left the boys to chat as well as she wanted to give Tilly a hand in the kitchen. 'Have a great day, lads.'

The boys both gave their straightforward gratitude words as the plates, mugs, and glasses were removed from in front of them.

'Thanks Tilly, Thanks Laura,' replied Dan.

'Thanks Tilly, thank you Mrs Macallan,' added Dalton.

Dan and Dalton chatted for a while and decided they would go for an afternoon surf together, meeting at 3 pm at the top carpark. Dan had noticed Dalton's surfboard in the reception office, noticing that it was a short board. Dan didn't miss a beat if it was anything to do with surfing. He offered to bring Dalton a spare longboard to surf on, as the waves were more suited for a longboard today. Dan headed off to do whatever he was doing for the day. He was a chilled-out kind of dude. He lived for surfing and fishing and a good laugh, and he didn't take life too seriously. If the waves were good, he was happy. If rookie surfers made him angry on his waves, he wasn't happy. Dan's life was as simple as that.

chapter nineteen

Where did you come from?

After Dan left, Dalton went into the kitchen to see if Tilly needed a hand with anything. The café had filled up with crowds of people, and it was just Laura and Tilly making food and drinks and catering to everyone's needs.

Dalton offered to help. 'Is it usually this busy?' He queried.

'It can be, but we weren't expecting this today.' replied Tilly. 'Word must have got out that there was a new kid in town.' Tilly winked at Dalton as she handed him a pile of dirty plates. Dalton jumped in to help. He did some more dishes that were piling up and helped Laura and Tilly with the breakfast orders. It was too easy; they all got along well and worked well together.

After the rush was over, Laura was out clearing a few more tables, and Tilly and Dalton both stopped for a moment and looked at each other.

'Where did you come from?' Tilly questioned Dalton, giggling and shaking her head as she spoke these words again, and they both burst into fits of laughter.

Dalton felt a pang of emotion as he had delved into some deep thoughts in his mind, with Dan's questions at breakfast. None of these thoughts or feelings were shared out loud, but he felt them strongly. Dalton had relived the whole reason, in his mind, why he was here in Angourie, and he felt guilty that he was falling in love with Tilly.

He was worried about whether he could handle falling in love again, and he felt guilty to Chelsea that he could allow himself to love someone else. It hadn't even been a year since she passed away. And then his thoughts went deeper. It wasn't so much the falling in love he was worried about. The falling in love part was something he couldn't really help. It was out of his control. Love was love. The thing he was worried most about was losing someone he loved again. That part, he didn't think he could handle, and that part was never something he could control.

Dalton shrugged off his feelings and tried to lighten his dark mood that he was slipping into.

He replied forcing himself back into a good mood, 'I'm here Tilly, and that's all that matters right now. I'm here with you, and I'm loving every minute. I wish I could take you back into that "gypsy room" right now.' Dalton suggested with a tilt of his head towards the door, as he pulled her in close and kissed her again.

Tilly laughed. 'Now, let me just clear this up with you. I didn't have the heart to tell you last night, but that room is called the "Fleetwood Studio," but I love you how you call it the "gypsy room," so I think we should call it the "gypsy room" from now on.'

'Well, whatever it's called, when you get a break from here, that's where I'll be. You are more than welcome to join me.' Dalton was so cheeky and so hard to say no to.

Tilly was honest in her reply. 'The boys should be back from their surf to do the lunch shift, and I'll have some time to chill with you. Until then, I'll just keep helping Mum here, and you can get some beauty sleep.'

'That's cool Tilly, I can help for longer?' offered Dalton.

'No, it's all good. Mum and I can do the rest. It's quiet now.'

'I've promised Dan I'll go for a surf this arvo, and if you want me to, I can come back and do a gig here for you tonight. Earn my keep, you know?' Dalton offered.

'Really? Would you do that? I'd love to hear you play. That's a deal for sure.' Tilly lifted, firstly feeling a little jealous that Dalton was going for a surf with Dan, but then she quickly changed her mood. Dalton wanted to play a gig here tonight.

'What time do you want me to set up?' Dalton questioned with quite a serious and professional tone.

'We usually play our first set at 6 pm. It can get busy on a Thursday night, so you can play a few sets until closing at 10 pm or 11 pm, depending on the crowd.'

'Sounds perfect. I'll get some beauty sleep, but when you are done here, and your brothers arrive to help, promise me you'll come and see me in the gypsy room?' Dalton pleaded in a confident yet cheeky way, remembering that Tilly didn't like being told what to do. Was asking her to promise him she'll come and see him a little too much? He added, 'Only if you want to, not putting any expectation on you.'

As he started walking out, Tilly tuned into the song playing through the speakers, The Pretenders' classic, Brass in Pocket. She mouthed the lyrics to him.

'*I'm gonna make you see, there is nobody else here, no one like me, I'm special, so special, I've gotta have some of your attention. Give it to me.*'

Dalton gave her a big wide smile, saying 'You sure are Tilly, so special,' as he kept on walking.

chapter twenty

The Lunch Crowd

Frankie, Eddie, and Louis arrived just as the lunch crowd started moving in. The three boys were all showered and fresh after their surf, dressed in casual beach attire, but it was tasteful, collared funky shirts and nice dressy board shorts. They were all such handsome-looking boys. Part of the reason the café was so successful was that people would come to the café just to interact and connect with the Macallans. They all had such spunk and having conversations with them was always interesting. The boys were all cheeky and fun and very chilled out. They were always good for a surf report, which the locals and tourists were always interested in hearing about. It was only Louis who lost his cool, sometimes, if he got stressed out, and that was always moderately entertaining. The Macallans were a successful team, and they worked brilliantly together.

When the boys first arrived, they made themselves a good meal. They were all excellent cooks; they had to be. It was their job to cook any items on the menu, although The Angourie Local Café also employed a team of chefs.

Frankie was on kitchen duty and made all the brothers Club Sandwiches with bacon, tomato, lettuce, cheese and a nice chutney sauce that Laura had made fresh that morning.

Eddie and Louis started taking lunch orders and Tilly finally had a chance to disappear. She had done her morning shift and would be back in the evening, but right now she had a Gypsy Boy to hang out with for a few hours.

Laura had gone back home after the breakfast clean-up, and was planning on spending the afternoon and early evening with Jack. They planned to have a nice beach walk and share a nice bottle of wine with some platter snacks for their anniversary, before coming back to help for a busy evening. The restaurant was almost fully booked for the night. Jack and Laura had a special date to celebrate the first day they met, back at the rally. As they had never married, this was always their special date to celebrate the anniversary of true love.

Frankie and the boys took over the music selection to get the venue rocking with a fantastic collection of upbeat background music. They took Tilly's chill morning music selection of CDs out of the five-stacker and replaced it with the boys' shared collection. The five CD stacker was set on random. Frankie's music taste was broad, he mostly liked a bit of 90s rock; Pearl Jam, Red Hot Chili Peppers, Guns N Roses, LIVE, Aerosmith, Nirvana, Smashing Pumpkins and Metallica. Eddie was more into the softer rock classics like Crowded House, R. E. M, Counting Crows, Hunters and Collectors and Hoodoo Gurus. His favourite band of all time was INXS, he couldn't get enough of listening to their music and his favourite INXS song of all time was The Stairs, a song that not many people knew of. It wasn't their most popular song. Eddie also had a thing for the more alternative sound of Depeche Mode and The Cure. Louis' favourites were Stone Temple Pilots and Hootie & The Blowfish. He also had a thing for Tom Petty and Alice Cooper if he felt like listening to some heavy rock music. All three agreed no one could ever get sick of any songs from U2, Bruce Springsteen—the Boss, and John Cougar Mellencamp. There was no limit to good music on constant play at The Angourie Local. Lucky for the boys - Jack, Laura and Tilly enjoyed the collective music taste. Tilly liked to add a bit of Sophie B. Hawkins, Sheryl Crow, Toni Childs, Tracy Chapman, Suzanne Vega and Wendy Matthews when she was the DJ, just to even up the women's vocals. Her favourite rock song was I Remember You by Skid Row, she had a serious celebrity crush on Sebastian Bach.

Although the boys wouldn't openly admit it, they didn't mind a few talented female artists thrown into the mix for the softer morning café vibes. Tilly would catch Louis singing along to Sophie B. Hawkins, and she would tease him about Sophie B., saying he was secretly in love with her. She would say 'For such a tough fella Louis, you sound so lovely crooning *Damn, I wish I was your lover!* She would sing the lyrics to him, of course.

They had an outstanding collection of music in the office with wall-to-wall CD racks, to create the daily vibes at The Angourie Local. Music was important, it was the only reason most of the Angourie locals came to The Angourie Local. Well, the music, and the food, and drinks, and the people, and The Macallans' and The Macallan.

chapter twenty-one

Housekeeping

Tilly finished her breakfast shift and helped the boys set up for lunch. It was about midday, and she wasn't due back to the café until the evening shift at 5 pm. She contemplated going back home to get some rest, but Dalton *had* invited her to his room. She figured she had a window of alone time to spend with Dalton because he had mentioned that he was going for a surf with Dan at 3 pm. Tilly started work again at 5 pm.

Tilly weighed up her options. Sleep? Dalton? Sleep? Dalton?

Who needed sleep, thought Tilly, *life's too short?*

Dalton had been resting for about an hour or two when he heard a knock at the door.

He woke from the deepest slumber, and it took him a moment to realise where he was. That's right, he was in the gypsy room. He had showered when he came back from breakfast and afterwards had fallen into the most beautiful, deepest sleep in this comfortable bed. He was completely naked when he got up to open the door, so he quickly wrapped a towel around his waist.

'Housekeeping.' Tilly knocked again and spoke softly in a playful accent.

Dalton recognised her gorgeous voice and opened the door rubbing his eyes and smiling. 'Hey Tilly, come in, I've been waiting for you.'

'No, you haven't, you've been asleep.' Tilly mocked, giggling.

'You're right, I have been in the deepest sleep, but I feel wonderful now, especially since you are here. You must be tired though?' Dalton was feeling great but acknowledged that Tilly must have been tired since she hadn't had as much sleep as he did.

Tilly had so much energy from the good feelings she got when she was around Dalton. 'I'm okay, I'm functioning on a love drug right now. I wouldn't need to sleep for days if you wanted to keep me awake.' She wasn't tired at all. Tilly was quite an energetic soul, and she felt that sleep was quite overrated. She could easily function on six to seven hours of sleep a night and she always had unlimited energy. Although she didn't require a lot of sleep to feel excellent, she loved a nana-nap, especially if she had someone to entwine with.

'So, what do you want to do, Tilly? We've got a few hours to fill in before I'm go for my surf with Dan?'

Tilly noticed the bottle of The Macallan on the dresser. It was half empty, but there was certainly enough for a nice afternoon buzz if Dalton and Tilly shared a few glasses together. She had a thought and walked over to the little bar fridge in the room's corner to check if there was ice in the trays. They usually made sure they were filled for the guests. As Tilly pulled the ice tray out of the small freezer, she said to Dalton. 'It's not that I need to be drunk with you, not at all. I'd rather not be, but I feel like we should share a Macallan whisky moment this afternoon. What do you think?'

Dalton reached for the bottle of The Macallan. He had already had a swig when he came back to the room, and it put him straight into a deep slumber. 'To be honest with you Tilly, I already had a swig this afternoon before I went into the deepest sleep, so why not? A Macallan moment with my favourite Macallan will be fun.'

'A little swig, hey? Let me teach you then, the only way to drink The Macallan.' Tilly filled two glasses with ice and poured The Macallan directly over the ice cubes filling the glasses. She picked up both glasses and gave them both a swirl, handing one to Dalton. As she did, she wondered if he would remember their cheers from last night. As she lifted her glass to his, they said in unison, looking into each other's eyes, 'To Freedom, Friendship and Enough Love.'

Dalton was sitting on the edge of the bed with a towel wrapped around him, as Tilly sat in the big armchair in her beach dress. They sipped on the ice-cold whisky and shared some more stories with each other. Tilly told Dalton the story about her and Dan so he wouldn't feel awkward trying to work out their weird connection. Dalton had already picked up on something going on between them, but he couldn't work out exactly what it was. He was happy that Tilly had come forth and shared the brief history of their relationship, especially since he was about to go surfing with this adventurous stranger in just a few short hours.

A few drinks later and they were feeling The Macallan buzz. As they were talking, Tilly was trying to stay focused on the conversation, but she kept getting distracted by Dalton's physique. His body was naturally formed. He was a musician and a farm boy, and for the past year, he travelled, and he surfed. He had no routine to sculpt his body, and it was easy to tell that he didn't go to the gym. For her, his body was natural perfection. She felt like she already knew where every crease, crevice and freckle were placed on his shoulders, neck and torso. She had observed the strength and masculinity of his forearms, chest, and torso. She hadn't studied his legs much yet, but she had already noticed their shape and their strength. She had yet to learn more about his legs. She sat opposite him and shook her head in awe of his beauty in front of her, realising that everyone had their idea of what was attractive to them. She knew that not everyone would have the same attraction to him as she did, but in her mind, she could not fault the design of his body. Looking through her eyes, it was like he had been created from a magical dream or manufactured from a cast of human perfection.

Tilly stood up and started removing her clothes and headed into the bathroom. 'Well, Gypsy Boy, I smell like four hours of bacon and eggs, so I reckon I might start with a shower and see what happens. You're more than welcome to join me.'

Once again, they explored different things about each other. Their physical chemistry was so strong. Dalton couldn't believe he had met a girl who had so much energy to match his physical desires. Dalton had only ever been in one serious relationship, and that was something he didn't talk about. He couldn't talk about it. Dalton's other experiences with women were short-lived flings, one-night stands, friends-with-benefits, nothing like this. With Tilly, everything was different. She was on another level of freedom and confidence, and she was so desirable to him. There was no innocence with Tilly. She came with experience and sass, and being with her was a very different experience for Dalton. He was used to being independent and a little arrogant and always in control of his emotions. Tilly had him spinning. He was falling for her, quickly, like most men did. Most of the time it was Tilly that ended the relationship or the fling, and sent them on their way, when she realised the relationship wasn't quite what she wanted. However, she wouldn't deny that there were a few decent heartbreaks along the way, and the most recent one that she didn't ever talk about, which made Tilly even more determined to know what she wanted, because she didn't enjoy being hurt. Some people would say she was fussy, but she wasn't. She was really easy-going. She just knew what she wanted, and it didn't take her long to figure out if something was not quite right about the relationship. She knew exactly what she wanted, and she knew exactly what she didn't want. And she didn't want to waste any time on something that wasn't going anywhere. She had been there, done that, too many times.

It was different with Dalton. She wanted this to go somewhere. She was a little scared about how close they had become, physically, so quickly, but for Tilly, the physical connection was one of the most important things in a relationship. Jack and Laura had always encouraged that, saying that without the physical attraction and closeness with each other, you might as well just be friends forever. And some people were content with that. However, Tilly knew it was possible to have a long-lasting relationship that was more than friendship. If you found the right person, it was promising to have a strong physical connection, a deep soul connectedness, and a relaxed and trusted friendship that would last forever. That was the magic.

When Tilly was with Dalton, she felt that strong and passionate physical connection. Their sexual chemistry was beautiful, as they melted into each other with intense body touching and exploring, their tongues twirling and their muscular bodies moving and grinding in sync with each other. Their lovemaking was mesmerising and satisfying for both.

They got along well as friends. Tilly felt like she had known Dalton forever, knowing that their friendship would grow stronger.

There was something deeper that Tilly couldn't quite explain, though. She had this deep feeling in her soul when she connected with Dalton that he had some deep hurts, deep down in his soul, that she felt he was hiding. She wanted to find out more about him, so he could open his soul to hers, but they'd only just met. She kept her feelings about that to herself for now, trusting that when Dalton was ready, he might open up to her.

It seemed complicated that he had left his family and he was travelling alone in search of freedom. What freedom was he searching for? Tilly felt that there was something else he was escaping from, but she couldn't work it out and he wasn't sharing this part of himself with her just yet.

Tilly and Dalton made love all afternoon, warmed by The Macallan buzz. Just as they were drifting off to sleep wrapped around each other, Dalton whispered into Tilly's ear. 'I'm not sure if you're still awake beautiful girl, but I want to ask you a crazy question.'

Tilly replied with gentle inquisition as she was almost asleep, 'Ah huh! Ask away.'

Dalton spoke in a whisper. 'Will you marry me?'

Tilly replied in a non-enthusiastic tone, 'Don't be silly Gypsy Boy, we've only just met, why don't you ask me when you're sober?'

Tilly felt so protected as she morphed into his chest, his heavy arm wrapped across her body and his fingers entwined with hers. Their legs twisted in a comfortable knot. Dalton matched his breathing with Tilly's as they both fell into a deeply euphoric sleep.

chapter twenty-two

Dreams

It was 2.45 pm. Dalton had set an alarm on the clock radio for 2.30 pm, but it didn't go off. He noticed the clock radio was playing music softly, so he must have clicked the wrong button when he was trying to set the alarm. He tuned into the song that was playing and realised it was *Dreams* by Fleetwood Mac. *That is ironic*, he thought. Yesterday *Rhiannon* by Fleetwood Mac was the song on the radio when he entered the Gypsy Room. He made a mental note to himself. *I must tell Tilly about that because that's just a weird coincidence. It's just the local radio station, but somehow, it's tuned into The Angourie Local guest rooms, and it's playing Fleetwood Mac songs for me while I'm in the Gypsy Room.*

The reality was simple. Fleetwood Mac had released a new song, so they were getting a lot of airplay on the radio. It was purely a coincidence, but Dalton liked it. He often noticed things like that, little coincidences, and chance occurrences, and it always made him feel connected to a part of something bigger than himself.

He had to get to the top carpark to meet Dan at 3 pm, so he quietly slid out of the bed and climbed into his boardies. Tilly was sound asleep, so he kissed her gently on the forehead and said, 'I'll see you when I'm looking at you, beautiful girl.' He went to grab his surfboard and then remembered that Dan was bringing him a spare longboard. Instead, he grabbed the empty bottle of The Macallan whisky that he and Tilly had finished drinking, and a notepad and pen from the dresser. He headed out the door, running down the hotel pathway and onto the road toward the beach. The top carpark wasn't far. It was just four hundred metres down the road, so Dalton made it in plenty of time, but he had a look about him that said, '*I've been shagging all afternoon, don't mind me.*' His hair was a mess, and he had a sleepy, satisfied look all over his face. The reason he was carrying an empty whisky bottle and a notepad and pen was anybody's guess.

chapter twenty-three

Sunset Surf

Dan was there already, waiting for Dalton to arrive, with two longboards waxed and ready to ride. He was sitting up on the lookout ledge checking out the sets slowly rolling in. It was the most beautiful day. The sun was sparkling on the crystal-clear water and the longboard riders were in surfing heaven.

'Hey mate,' said Dalton, coming up from behind Dan.

'Hey bud, how are you doing?' replied Dan, not looking around or expecting a reply. 'Let's get amongst it,' added Dan, as he passed Dalton the spare board.

Dalton went to take the board and had to reposition the items he was holding into his other hand. 'Thanks, mate, nice board.'

'What have you got there?' queried Dan. 'Did you need a stiff drink on the way, mate, to calm the nerves?' he added.

'Ahhhh, don't even ask, let's go get amongst it.'

They trekked off down the bush pathway and onto the beach. It was a bit of a walk down amongst the scrubby ferns and beach wattles. Angourie was well known for its natural environment, and the locals did the best they could to keep it both natural and functional. The pathway that Dan and Dalton took was the only way down to the beach, and if you weren't local, it wasn't easy to find. There were no signs guiding tourists to beach access. Dalton was glad Dan was with him for his first surf at Angourie, and Dalton was feeling lucky to be surfing with an Angourie legend, so to speak.

Dalton placed the few items he was carrying on a large log of petrified wood that sat high on the beach.

There were quite a few surfers out the back, and Dan and Dalton paddled their way out past them. For the first time since Dalton had surfed the East Coast, he started feeling a little insecure. He didn't know this break, but he had been warned of the rock-shelf underlying. He trusted Dan wouldn't put him in danger, but was he putting Dalton to a test of manhood? Dalton had sensed a bit of underlying jealousy going on at the breakfast table, and although Dan had mentioned nothing, it was obvious there was some history between Dan and Tilly. Tilly had filled Dalton in on the basics of their confusing friendship, but Dan didn't know that part. Dalton cleared his head of his irrational thoughts as he took a massive turtle roll and felt the calming strength and cleansing power of the ocean. He was feeling okay because the waves were quite mallow today, and the longboard riders were out in full force. Had it been any other day, he might have felt a little more threatened by Dan's bravado to get way out the back for the biggest, longest waves.

They surfed for a few hours, catching some fantastic long rides. They were both cutting some classic moves, "hang five," "hang ten," "floater," "front to back," "cha-cha," "360." Dalton hadn't done a lot of Mal riding, but as with most things, he picked it up easily, and he was a classic show-off towards the end of the day.

Dan and Dalton were having a great time. They both had a few wipe-outs; it was all part of the fun.

chapter twenty-four

Message In A Bottle

It was around five o'clock, and Dalton started paddling in towards the beach, signalling his time was up. They had a good few hours catching some classic waves. He signalled for Dan to stay out a while longer. It was getting dark, and Dalton had promised Tilly he would be set up and start performing his first set at 6 pm. He was a man of his word, and there was just this one other thing Dalton had to do. He placed his board on the sand and perched himself on the log where he had placed the empty Macallan whisky bottle, The Angourie Local notepad, and the complimentary pen. He had a plan to put some closure to his Chelsea grief, and he had decided he would write her a message in a bottle to let her know he had found new love. Writing the message was important for him to acknowledge that it was okay to let go.

At the top of the notepad was the insignia "The Angourie Local," with a picture of a rolling wave cresting over a beach-shack café. *How fitting that is*, he thought.

He wrote:

Chelsea, my girl, my angel,
It's been a while now since the last time I saw your beautiful face. I think of you every day.
I hope that one day I can forgive myself for what happened to you. To us! Our plans, our dreams, our aspirations. I'm so sorry.
I need to tell you something, and I hope you are okay with this, but I've met another woman. She's beautiful, strong, and amazing, and I want to love her with every piece of my heart, completely and forever.
I will always hold you and the memories we shared forever in my soul.
One day, I know I'll see you again in a beautiful place called heaven.
I'll see you when I'm looking at you.
Your spunkrat always,
Dalton x

Dalton rolled the note into a scroll, so it was small enough to squeeze into the bottleneck, and he screwed the lid tightly on top. He walked along the beach and found himself on a well-worn sandy track that led to the most easterly point of the headland. It was a beautiful spot, and he sat and took in some deep breaths of nature's beauty as the last shimmers of sun gleamed upon the ocean. Dalton placed the bottle into the water's edge and made a wish. 'I wish that the release of this bottle allows me freedom, friendship, and enough love with Tilly. I also wish that Chelsea knows I will always love her forever.'

The bottle spun and rolled away in the rush out of the waves, back and forthing for a while, and then drifting out to sea on the current.

Somehow, this simple act had given Dalton a feeling of closure and respect for his love for Chelsea.

It was a strange thing, grief.

chapter twenty-five

Big Talks

Dalton sat for a while admiring the beauty of the ocean, the headland, and the surroundings of Angourie. He could see Yamba, the larger beach town to the north with its scattered beach houses on the hills and the denser population of the houses packed into the small town beneath. *I could make this my home forever*, he thought.

He looked over into the Angourie Bay, and he could see Dan paddling into the shore. He knew he had little time, as he was about to start his gig soon.

Walking up the beach together, they chatted about the classic waves they caught. Dan acknowledged Dalton was a bit of a natural surfer, being a country boy and all. Dalton accepted the compliment and returned the generosity of his compliment in acknowledging that Dan had some superb skills. They gave each other a high five, and both decided they should catch some waves together again sometime.

Dalton followed Dan as they hiked back up the bush trail. They made small talk on the way, as it was quite a challenge through the bush with the heavy boards.

Once they got to the top, they loaded the two longboards onto the roof of Dan's car.

Dalton explained he was gigging at The Angourie Local for the Macallans tonight. He invited Dan to come along if he wasn't too busy.

'That'd be great, thanks,' replied Dan. 'I'll duck home and clean these boards off and shower up and head on back; what time do you start?'

'After 6 pm, mate, I'll be playing some sets through the night until late, so no rush. Just come on over when you get hungry. They do some good quality meals there, huh?'

Dan agreed, nodding, and replied, 'It's an outstanding set-up. I don't know anywhere like it in the world, mate. Not that I've travelled much, but it's a unique place, and they get some fantastic gigs. I don't know if you know this already, but they've had Stevie Nicks, Van Morrison, Mick Jagger, Annie Lennox, and quite a few ultimate celebrities who come to escape from the rest of the world.'

'Is that right?' queried Dalton, having heard a bit of the story from Tilly already but just going along with it and interested in what Dan had to say.

'The special thing about The Angourie Local is that The Macallans tell no one about the gigs that are coming; otherwise, it would ruin the allure of the place. People are drawn to the unexpected spontaneity that they have created. And if you don't get a random secret performance from a celebrity, they also get some sensational local bands and travelling artists passing through, like yourself.'

'Thanks for the compliment, but I wouldn't exactly call myself sensational, perhaps just a travelling artist. I just love to play music. I hope everyone enjoys my style; it's a blend of country, folk, pop ballads and a lot of broken heart songs.' Dalton laughed light-heartedly at his own description of his music.

'I'm sure you'll fit right in, mate, and maybe your heartbreak will be over if you stick around here longer. I'm always here if you want to chat, or not.'

Dalton tightened the strap down over the surfboards and said, 'Thanks, mate. I moved away to leave all of that behind, so I might try to keep it that way.'

'All good. I hope you stick around, mate. I enjoyed surfing with you today. It's nice to have a new surfing buddy for a change. I usually surf alone or with the Macallan boys and Tilly if she's keen. She's usually busy working, or that's what she tells me anyhow.'

Dalton changed the subject, feeling a little uncomfortable talking about Tilly. 'So, what's the go with The Angourie Local? Will it get much of a crowd tonight?' asked Dalton, keen for some local advice.

Dan replied. 'Mate, if word has got around that a good-looking rooster like yourself is in town, you'll have every man and his daughter there, especially on a Thursday night.' Dan kept talking as he adjusted the position of the boards and did a final check of the straps. 'Most Thursday nights, if they don't have an outsider, the Macallan family takes turns to get the crowd dancing. They call themselves "Have Guitar, Will Travel." Weird name, I know, considering The Macallan family are not really the biggest travellers, but they are damn good. The whole family gets up there, including the three boys and Tilly, and they play some classic covers, and they have a few original songs as well. They are all super talented.'

'Well, that makes me nervous because I'm not super talented. My expertise is simply entertaining drunk crowds of cowboys and pig farmers at a few small local pubs in Deni.'

'You'll be right! Do you want a lift back into town with me?' offered Dan.

'Sure thing, that would be great,' said Dalton as he climbed down from the tyre on the other side, where he was checking the boards were secure. 'I guess if all goes wrong, The Macallans can back me up, right?'

Dan queried, 'Are you talking about The Macallan whisky or the Macallan family?'

Dalton laughed, 'Well, I was talking about the family, but the whisky could help too.'

Dan added. 'I don't know if you've heard our local saying here. After a big night at The Angourie Local, we like to blame it on The Macallan.'

Dan took their conversation a little deeper. 'I don't know if you've heard Tilly sing; she's got the voice of an angel. She's a catch that woman if anyone can hold her down for long enough. I'll be honest with you. I tried to lure her into my web, but she was out of my league. I think you're more in her atmosphere though, mate. I can see a bit of chemistry between the two of you. If you get the chance with her, don't let her go. She's an amazing woman; she just hasn't met her perfect match yet, and she's got some demons. Perhaps, lucky for you! Perhaps she's been waiting for you to come along,' encouraged Dan.

Dalton softened. 'I don't know if I'm any match for her, mate; I've got a fair few of my own demons holding me back. I'm my worst enemy, and I'm worried about getting into any relationship. I'm too scared I'll lose them again. I'm just here to have some fun. I probably won't stick around for long. I like to keep moving; that way, I can't be hurting anybody or upsetting anyone.'

Suddenly, Dan felt defensive for Tilly. He had seen the way she looked at Dalton, and if this guy was going to be another one to hurt her, he wouldn't be happy. He said something just in case it was any help to his beautiful friend Tilly. 'You're only hurting yourself, mate, if you keep running away from people that want to get close to you. Why don't you try it with Tilly?' Dan pushed again, trying to encourage Dalton to stick around and get to know Tilly better. Dan could see that these two were a match for each other, even though he would hate to admit it. Dan would have done anything to have Tilly for himself, but that would never happen. He could instinctively feel that Dalton was a decent guy, and he could see that he would treat Tilly well. 'Anyway, that's none of my business. I would just hate to see you let a beautiful thing slip away because of your fears and hang-ups from the past. Let it all go, mate, and allow yourself to love again. Tilly's worth it, I'm telling you, she is.'

Dalton confided in Dan as Dan moved closer, feeling their discussion was becoming more personal. Dan walked around to Dalton's side of the car to unlock the door. They were standing face to face. 'Thanks for the advice, Dan; I'm trying. I carry a lot of guilt for what happened in the past. That's what I need to move on from, more than anything. That was part of the whole weird message-bottle ceremony you witnessed just now and allowed me to keep to myself. Thank you.'

Dan questioned Dalton wholeheartedly and with deep wisdom. 'Dalton, I don't know what happened in your past, mate, but the past is in the past; you can't change it, and you can't relive it. What you can do is make the most of what's here in your life right now. Don't you see it? For some reason, you met Frankie in the surf, and you ended up here in Angourie; surely that means something to you. Do you believe in fate?'

Dalton replied. 'I believe everything happens for a reason, but sometimes it can take me a while to figure out the reason,' replied Dalton.

'Well, I know I met you for a reason, mate ... to tell you to have a good hard look at yourself, and if Tilly shows any signs of attraction towards you, you ought to grab her sexy arse and never let her go.' Dan laughed, bringing some humour to the seriousness of their conversation.

Dalton laughed as they both climbed into the car. 'You're right, mate; she's a beautiful and very sexy woman. I've never known anyone quite like her.'

Dan started the car up. It took a few clicks to get it going, but what a sound it made once it got purring. The old Holden EH Premier sedan; a classic car. It was still in mint condition of its 1964 vintage, with the rare rear Venetians, exterior sun visor, chrome front mudguard, and the diamond dot picnic radio. It was painted in its original Theatre-Grey metallic body colour and the Atherton-Ivory white roof. The interior décor, the leather, the wood panelling, and the vinyl all match the striking two-tone red and ivory combination of Astoria and Waldorf red. The exterior paint job was cracking because of the salty coastal air and the scorching sun, as Dan had nowhere to park this classic car out of the elements. Dan loved his car very much. It was the only thing he had ever actually owned in his life, other than his surfboard collection. This car, he called THE PIE, because of its number plate, 732 PIE, was his pride in possession. It had been his mother's car, and he had purchased it from her when he turned seventeen, under one condition: he could never sell it. His mother made him promise that if he didn't want the car anymore, he had to pay-it-forward, as an ongoing gift to someone else. He loved the idea and promised with his whole heart that he would do that. He just hadn't decided who would be his pay-it-forward recipient if ever the time came that he would have to choose. He didn't really like many people.

'Nice car!' commented Dalton, as he tapped on the front dash. The dot diamond radio ironically started playing Start Me Up, by the Rolling Stones.

Dan replied, as he nodded along to the beat of the song. 'Thanks, I love it. It was my mum's car. I bought it from her when I first got my licence, and I've promised her I'll never sell it. The sad thing is that my beautiful mum passed away a few years back, and I have no other close relatives.'

'I'm sorry to hear that,' consoled Dalton.

'Believe it or not, and this might surprise you after everything we've talked about. I will sound like a hypocrite after I've been here preaching to you to let things go. This is hard to explain, but I couldn't let things go. I was too hurt. So, for me to let things go. I had to let my family go. Something had to give. I am a rebel to my family, and I never wish to go back into the past to heal any relationships. It's taken me a while, but I have no guilt feelings whatsoever about that. My mother and I were close, but nowadays, I have no contact with my father or my brothers. I have had to force myself to let go and to move forward on my journey. There was too much hurt for me to carry, so I left it all behind. Guilt-free.' Dan was so easy talking about his past with no guilt connection; this was a different perspective for Dalton to hear. From where Dalton was from, family was the most important thing, and he carried a lot of guilt from leaving his family behind.

Dalton wanted to know more. 'That surprises me, but it makes sense now why you are so adamant in telling me to let my past go. It obviously works for you.'

'It's just me now. My father and my brothers wouldn't even know where to find me, especially here in Angourie. Dan made a magical twinkling action with his hands and changed his voice to a secretive tone, *the elusive and most secretive location in the universe.'*

'See, it's different for me,' added Dalton. 'I'm not rebelling. I just can't go back, ever. I have too much guilt for what happened, and coming from such a small-town, many people will never forgive me. If I continued to live in that town, I would be forced to carry guilt around on my shoulders every day. It was horrible.'

Dan asked with intense sincerity and warmth in the way he asked the question. 'Do you want to tell me what happened? It might help you let go?'

Dalton took an enormous sigh. 'In a long story short, without too much emotion, it goes something like this. I was in love with the most beautiful girl I've ever met in my life. Her name was Chelsea; she was younger than me, just sweet sixteen when we met, still in high school, and her family forbade our relationship. I was twenty-three, and, of course, being a "wild young musician", I wasn't the most acceptable person with whom a heavily religious family would want their only daughter to be hanging out with.'

Dan questioned, seriously. 'Don't tell me you got her pregnant?'

'No, it's much worse, actually,' responded Dalton, trying to swallow the enormous lump that was forming in his throat. He took a deep breath and sighed, blowing a deep breath of emotion out before he went on.

'We were out on a special date one night, down by the river, and I asked Chels to marry me when she was of age, of course. She said yes! We had the most beautiful, romantic night and made love under the stars. My entire world was complete. I could look into her eyes and see my whole future ahead of me: our children, our farm, our life together. It was going to be so perfect; we had everything planned out, other than how to tell her parents, as they did not approve. Anyway, on the way home that night, Chelsea was involved in a fatal car accident. She hit a kangaroo just outside my farm. She wasn't supposed to be out with me; she had snuck out the window because her parents had banned her from seeing me. I had to be the one to tell her parents that Chelsea, their only child, was dead. I keep reliving that moment repeatedly in my mind. The guilt inside me gets all a bit too much, and I think if I had stayed in that stinking asshole of a town, I would have taken my own life. My parents still struggle daily, still living in the town, with the ripple effect of our family name, because of me, if you are a Diaz, you might as well be on death row.'

Dan sighed. 'Far out Dalton, that's heavy, man. You've done well to keep that close to your belt. I think I need another surf after hearing that.'

Dalton started shaking his head and sobbing as Dan stopped the car about fifty meters from the front of The Angourie Local, to allow Dalton some more time to talk. 'Yeah, it's pretty shit. The feeling of carrying Chelsea's dead-weighted body into that hospital haunts me in my dreams. Her beautiful lifeless body, her soul departed, and there was nothing I could do, there was nothing anyone could do.'

Dan paused as he digested the thought of how Dalton must feel. Then he continued with his wisdom. 'Man, I can understand how you must feel. That's so sad for you and for Chelsea's parents, but it wasn't your fault, and you must forgive yourself for that. Let it go, man! Allow yourself to fall in love again. You are worthy of that. You have so much to offer this world.' Dan paused and tried to lighten the conversation again. 'I will tell you something else, and don't take this the wrong way, but Tilly is a strong woman; it would take more than a roo to take her down. I don't think you have to worry about losing her anytime soon, if that is what you are worried about.'

Dalton held his head in his hands, rubbing his temples to clear the images that had re-entered his consciousness. 'Thanks for listening, man, I haven't talked about this stuff to anyone since I left Deniliquin. Not even Tilly. She does not know about Chelsea, and I'm not sure that I really want to tell her. And yes, you are right; the thing I'm worried about more than anything is letting myself fall in love with someone and losing them again. I don't know if my heart could handle that. I'm still grieving for Chels. I think about her every day. I keep thinking I see her, walking down the street or whatever, I see her everywhere, and I have to remind myself, she's dead.'

Dan offered his advice again to help Dalton. 'Tilly is a strong woman; she can help you get through it; she can love you and heal you, but you have to let her in. Too often, she's been left behind because the situation wasn't right for whoever the idiot was that walked away from her. I've seen it time and time again. I've seen her go through heartbreak, and she has got some walls that might need breaking down. She can be a stubborn hardass if she thinks she's going to get hurt again. If she lets you in, you must tell her how you feel about her.'

'So, do you think I should talk to Tilly about what happened to Chelsea?' questioned Dalton.

'Honesty is the key, man. Eventually, the truth must come out. If you care about Tilly and you think you might have a future with her, I think you *have* to tell her, sooner than later. Something that has affected your life so dramatically has to be shared. She needs to understand your past, to love you the way you need to be loved. Just like you need to understand her past. The few things I can tell you about Tilly are that she's experienced and accepted so many guys who just wanted to use her for a one-night stand and move on. Other times, she's been the one to fall in love so deeply, but it wasn't reciprocated. I'm not sure what happened with the most recent one. She returned from Sydney after she finished her university degree, a completely broken woman, lifeless and vacant. It took her a while to get back to herself, but she did it. She'll put up her barriers if she thinks you are going to hurt her; trust me, I've seen it happen. It's like the flick of a switch. Otherwise, she's the most open, easy, free-loving woman I've ever known.'

Dalton wasn't sure if Dan knew that he and Tilly had spent a wild night together already; there was no guarantee that Tilly didn't think of Dalton as just another one-night stand. It didn't feel that way for Dalton, but who knew? Dalton questioned, 'How do I even know what Tilly thinks of me, anyway?'

Dan replied, 'Man, you can feel it, can't you? I can see it, just watching you both together. You two have magnetic energy with each other. It's beautiful. You need to embrace that. That is rare.'

Dalton laughed. 'Thanks, man.' Dalton patted Dan on the shoulder and changed the subject. 'And thanks for the surf today, I loved it. Let me know if you feel like a buddy next time you're going for a paddle. I might not keep up with you; you're a legend, but I'm happy to watch you and I love being in the water. It feels so good.'

Dan put his thumb up. 'Cool, man, let's do it again sometime.'

Dalton jumped out of the car. He tapped the top of the roof as he signalled goodbye. 'See you tonight, and hey, thanks a million!'

Dan smiled and gave a wink to Dalton. 'See you tonight, fella, looking forward to it. I'll go home and spruce myself up. I might get lucky too if I hang around you as a lucky charm.'

Dalton laughed again and shook his head. 'Yeah, funny! I like your sense of humour. See you later, Dan!'

chapter twenty-six

Dalton's Request

It was just on dusk, Dalton was supposed to be ready to play his gig at 6 pm, which didn't give him much time to get showered and "spruced up," as Dan called it. Dalton wondered if Tilly was already here, wondering where he was. He quickly made his way back into the "gypsy room" where he showered, washed his messy post-surf hair, had a shave, and got dressed in some nice jeans and a nice, collared shirt. He put on some deodorant and splashed on some aftershave. He had a bottle of his favourite Joop. It was almost finished, so he applied a few quick sprays around his neck. He loved to smell good.

Tilly loved that he smelled good, too; she had told him that on the first night they had met.

He was ready. Tonight was going to be special; he could feel it. Dalton loved to play his guitar; it was his comfort zone, and he had the confidence to play his music to any crowd. This is what he had been doing for years now since he was fifteen, so he had a trusted set of songs he could play, depending on the crowd. And he was looking forward to hanging out with Tilly, doing what he loved, and she loved, together. Dan had made him feel nervous, saying how amazing the Macallans were. He hoped he could get the crowd going as well.

He grabbed his favourite pick from his wallet, making a mental note to himself that he also had one of Tilly's guitar picks in his wallet. She had left it on one table near the stage last night, and he had grabbed it when he was blowing out the candle. He wanted to surprise her with it when she realised she had lost it, because he could see that it was a sentimental guitar pick.

Dalton's guitar pick was special, too. It was a marble-coloured Clayton pick with an image of a mermaid on it. It was his lucky pick. He was playing with it for the first time when he met Chelsea. As he peeled the pick out of the slip in his wallet, he flashed back to the night he met Chelsea. It was at a fundraising gig for the local high school. It wasn't his intention to fall in love with her; it just happened, as love does.

He took a deep breath and sighed as he tried to push away his thoughts, and said to himself, *Let go, Dalton, let her go.* He closed his eyes and clasped the pick in his hands in a prayer position as he signalled to heaven, placing his hands to rest on his chest. At that moment, he had an overwhelming feeling like Chelsea was in the room with him. He felt an icy breeze on the back of his neck. An image of her came into his mind, and she said, *'It's okay Dalton, I'm happy for you; let me go, you can be with her, she's perfect for you. Don't you realise I sent you here because I want you to be happy? I'm okay. I'm watching over you; you are safe and loved, and I want the best for you. I love you forever. One day, I'll see you again. In the meantime, be free, my love.'*

Then she was gone.

Dalton felt weird. Moments like this had happened to him three times since Chelsea had passed away. He always believed in something afterlife, but this was more than anything he had experienced before, and he hadn't even been drinking.

He felt comforted by these moments rather than fearful. It was special. He took meaning to them as a sign to move forward, and that was exactly what he needed to do right now. He was about to spend a beautiful evening with Tilly and her family, and the last thing he needed was fear, doubt and backward thinking right now. He was grateful for the chat with Dan.

Dalton grabbed his guitar and walked out the door, heading to the restaurant. He was feeling refreshed after his surf and big talks with Dan, and he was ready to play some great tunes to The Angourie Local crowd. Entertaining a new crowd was always much easier than trying to reinvent yourself week after week to the same people who always wanted more and more.

As he walked in the back door to The Angourie Local, the first person he saw was beautiful Tilly. She looked amazing, simply beautiful, in a pair of light denim jeans and a loose tank top. He could see Jack and Laura were there, too, behind the bar. It was family night, after all.

Dalton's mind took him back to that afternoon, a couple of hours earlier when they had been tangled around each other in a euphoric sleep from an afternoon of lovemaking. She was the most beautiful woman alive. It was hard for him to have that thought, feeling guilty for Chelsea, but this was true: Tilly was gorgeous. She was talking to some guests, her wide smile beaming, her soul shining happiness and joy in a radiance of energy around her. She looked at him and smiled. He smiled back, and he hoped she could feel the warmth he felt for her through his genuine smile and sincere thoughts of *Wow, it's so good to see you again.*

Tilly walked over and gave him a gentle hug, not giving too much else away as guests were looking on. She whispered in his ear, 'Oh my god, you look and smell amazing. I want to take you back to the gypsy room right now.'

Dalton laughed as he tried to shrug off her comment because if he had his way right now, that is exactly what he would do. 'You're funny, Tilly; we've got some work to do tonight. We are going to get The Angourie Local rocking,' and then he whispered back in her ear, 'and then you can do whatever you want to me in that gypsy room.'

'Oh my god, yes, please,' whispered Tilly.

Dalton put on a serious face as best he could and changed the subject and his tone completely. 'Alright, Matilda, so let's be serious now. Shall I get set up? Do you want me to start with some chill dinner music?'

'Matilda? Well, that is very serious of you. Am I in trouble?'

'You could be,' Dalton winked.

Tilly replied, returning to the serious tone that they were flipping back and forth between, as she was in a bit of a rush. 'I'd love it if you get set up. I'm going to take some dinner orders while you get started. I can join you later when I'm on my break and we can try a bit of a jam together.'

'Any requests?' pushed Dalton.

'Nope. You do you. The good thing here is no one really cares; they are happy to listen to any kind of music. Just play whatever you think the mood is. Frankie and the boys will be over soon, and they can jam with you too.' Tilly was very encouraging and wanted to let Dalton know that the vibe was relaxed and easy-going, with no stress. 'Can I get you a drink?' added Tilly.

'I'd love a whisky on ice to get me started,' suggested Dalton.

Tilly teased as she questioned. 'Are you up for The Macallan after this afternoon's shenanigans? I thought you'd be back to beer?'

'The Macallan sounds absolutely perfect, thanks Tilly,' Dalton smiled with a thumbs up. A quick flash of his mind went to the bobbing Macallan whisky bottle that he had set out to the ocean.

Dalton headed over to the stage area, in the corner, and looked at the set-up. All he had to do was plug in his guitar to the amp, everything else was ready to go. He did a quick microphone test. 'Testing one, two, one, two,' and strummed a few chords on his cherished and dramatically eye-catching Maton guitar, which had been given to him by his beloved grandfather. The sound of the guitar strum through the guitar microphone was crystal clear and the combination of voice and instrument blended through the speakers to fill the room with musical clarity and a brilliant vibe. What an amazing set-up they had here. It was pretty much plug-and-play for any travelling musician.

Hmm, Dalton thought, *what should I play first?* He had a few songs in mind, but he wanted it to be something special, something memorable. This was a memorable moment in the making.

He strummed the chords G, followed by a melodic C, and then D. It sounded good. He sang.

'Hey, where did we go, days when the rain came, down in the hollow, playing a new game, laughing and a running, hey, hey, skipping and a jumping, in the misty, morning fog, with our hearts a thumpin' and you, my brown-eyed girl. You......, my brown-eyed girl.'

Tilly looked over with the biggest smile on her face, with a handful of questions running through her mind. *Why that song? How did he know that was a special song? That was Jack's song to Laura. Had Dalton been talking to Jack? Did he request that?*

Jack and Laura stopped working for a moment and came onto the dance floor and held each other for a dance together. Jack looked over to Dalton and gave him a reassuring smile of 'you're alright.'

The rest of the night was absolutely perfect. Dalton played a set of songs that everybody loved, many couples got up for a dance during the early evening whilst dinner was happening and as the night went on more tables were moved away so the dance floor could grow, as everyone loosened up for a party night.

'Have Guitar Will Travel' joined Dalton, or Dalton joined 'Have Guitar Will Travel' and the combination was perfect. They had the dance floor rocking. Who would have even thought a little local bar in a secluded beach town, on the edge of Australia, could fathom the idea of providing so much fun and freedom on a Thursday night? This was perfect!

Dalton was loving the vibe; Tilly was loving Dalton. They were all having so much fun. Even Louis had a smile on his face for the entire night.

This was one of those nights that Tilly realised that this was why she had returned to Angourie. Why would she want to be anywhere else than right here? She hoped Dalton felt the same.

Dan was dancing with a girl, so that was a good thing. Tilly always felt bad that she couldn't be the girl for Dan, as she knew he wanted to be with her. For Tilly, something was missing. She couldn't quite put her finger on it. He was a legendary surfer, the best she had ever witnessed; he was funny, he was a badass, and he would do anything for Tilly, but she just didn't have that 'thing' with him. He was more of a friend to her, that she could talk to for hours, but that is all it was, and she loved that. She didn't have the magical physical connection with him. There was no spark whatsoever. She tried to work it out and explain it to him, but it just wasn't there.

Dalton was happy for Dan also, after their conversations today. He knew Dan adored Tilly, and he knew Dan knew how Tilly felt about him. Dalton felt a little guilty that he was so close to Tilly when they had only just met, but he wasn't going to put any barriers up to stop that, and he knew Dan was on his side. In everything that they had talked about, Dan was encouraging Dalton to pursue his closeness with Tilly. So, seeing Dan with a girl made both Tilly and Dalton extremely happy, and she was beautiful. Tilly wondered where she had come from. She hadn't seen her in Angourie before.

It was coming close to the end of the night. The crowd had simmered. Dalton put down his guitar and requested a song for the rest of the band to play. He asked if they would mind if he took Tilly for a dance. They all agreed that that would be totally okay. 'Gypsy by Fleetwood Mac, please,' was Dalton's request.

Dalton went over to Tilly, who was in the bar cleaning glasses. He grabbed her hand and pleaded with Tilly to take a moment away from her work, as he guided her to the dancefloor. 'I've asked your beautiful family to play a special song for us. Please have this dance with me?'

Tilly let her hand melt into his as she felt such warmth and good energy coming from him. 'I'd love to dance with you, Dalton.'

Dalton replied with a cheeky smile, as he gave her no option but to dance with him. 'I'll help you in the kitchen later.'

Laura did an amazing version of the Fleetwood Mac song. Tilly loved it, such a brilliant choice of song for her Gypsy Boy.

As the song finished, Laura announced they would play one last song, and it was last drinks and closing time. The last song was always American Pie, by Don McLean. Louis played the piano for this one. Jack, Frankie, and Eddie did a superb mix of the lyrics. Laura and Tilly usually took to the dance floor to mix with the crowd, and it was no different tonight other than that Tilly and Dalton were dancing together rather than Tilly roaming the room, dancing with friends and strangers. Laura did her best to share herself around.

What a wonderful night it had been. Everyone was having such a great time. It was always hard to make the call for the last drinks. Sometimes they partied on until the wee hours. Tonight was a smaller, vibrant crowd. Laura could feel that most of the patrons were paired and probably happy to head home with their loved ones. Even Dan had a new friend. They were happy to end the night with this one.

The Macallans packed up their instruments and helped with the clean-up of the kitchen and bar area. It was a team effort. The kitchen had closed much earlier, so it was just the drinks and glassware to clean up. The industrial dishwasher was loaded, and the clean-up was done.

Tilly and Dalton had offered to close again. The Macallans were heading out the door and all saying goodbye.

Dalton was so grateful for the fun night that he enjoyed with the Macallans. 'Night, everyone, thanks for an awesome night.'

'Good night you two.' Laura gave Dalton and Tilly a hug and thanked them for a fantastic night.

Jack added, 'You're welcome to join our band anytime, Dalton. That was a successful night tonight.'

Frankie had made a new friend throughout the night, and he introduced her quickly to the family. 'Hey everyone, this is Chelsea. She's new in town, moved in just down the road, yesterday and she's already found us. I'm just going to walk her home quickly, and I'll be back to help lock up tonight.' Then he added, patting Dalton on the back as he did. 'I think the Angourie locals liked having you here man, especially the ladies. They usually give me a hard time, but tonight it was all about you, thank goodness.' Dalton laughed but was also having a quiet reflective thought to himself, as he heard the name Chelsea. *What a strange coincidence*, he thought.

Tilly waited until Frankie had finished talking to Dalton, then she offered to Frankie. 'It's okay Frankie, take all the time you need walking Chelsea home. Dalton and I can close up here.'

Louis, as hard as he was and a man of few words, gave Dalton a pat on the back, 'Thanks man, a good night!'

Eddie, with a little more heart, 'You make my sister happy!'

The Macallans left, everything was in order, and it was just Dalton and Tilly left to lock up.

chapter twenty-seven

But...

Dalton and Tilly looked at each other, so happy that it was just the two of them together now. Everyone had gone home happy, and they had the rest of the night to share with each other. All Tilly had to do was lock the door as everyone departed.

Dalton said to Tilly, 'So what do you think we should do now?'

Tilly leaned in and pushed herself against him, as close as she could.

'What I really want to do is get as close to you as I can,' urged Tilly. She had a few drinks and was feeling very free, on an energetic high from the evening they had shared.

'Is that right Tilly?' Dalton questioned with a tone of seriousness.

Dalton had been preparing himself for this all night. He had made a promise to himself that before things went any further with Tilly, he needed to share his dark past with her. As he responded abruptly to her warmth and flirtatiousness, he came across as a bit stand-offish and cold. He was acting differently from how he was the night before, and from how he had been throughout the entire night, while on stage. He changed, suddenly.

'Are you okay Dalton?' questioned Tilly. 'Did I do something wrong?'

'All good Tilly, I just need to talk to you about something that's been on my mind. Can we sit here and chat for a bit?' Dalton tried to appease Tilly as she was being so forward and he really wanted to slow things down, just for a moment, to share this important stuff with her, so he could give himself to her fully. It was important to him, right now, that she understood his past.

He tried to continue the conversation, pulling a chair back from the table and taking a step backwards from Tilly. 'Tilly, please listen to me. You're an amazing woman and I'd love to stay here and be with you forever, that's the truth, *but...*'

Before he could express what he was trying to say, Tilly had pulled far away from him. She became instantly defensive, thinking he had changed his mind about her. This had happened to her so many times, she had lost count. Her walls came flying up around her like a blockade. The *flick of a switch* that Dan was talking about. She took another step back and put one hand up, signalling to stop. 'It's okay Dalton, I get it. You don't need to explain anything to me. I'm used to it. I've heard it all before. So many times.

Go. Just go... No. I'll go. It's better that way. Then it's my choice. If it's not meant to be, it's not meant to be. It's okay. It's fine.' And she left.

Dalton was left standing in the middle of the room, shaking his head. That was not the outcome he was hoping for.

'Tilly, please come back. Let me explain. Tilly, please, let me finish what I was saying.' She just kept on walking. 'Tilly, please don't do this, please come back.'

'Go, just go!' she signalled with a wave of her hand above her head as she walked out the door, not even looking back.

Tilly walked, half ran, half stumbled down the road, past her house and followed the well-beaten bush track down to the beach, in sobbing tears, just like she always did when something had upset her. It was usually after yet another break-up, another boy visiting that she had fallen madly in love with, while in Angourie on holidays, leaving at the end of a week, and she knew she'd never get to see them again. Sometimes she saw them again, and it was always a pleasant surprise when the next summer rolled around, and the families would return to Yamba for their annual Christmas vacation. But none ever stayed. As relationships got more serious as she got older, and she thought she had found '*the one*' on many occasions. She was always '*the one*' left behind.

The noisy Angourie ocean was her soulitude, her grounding space, fresh air, the sky full of stars, the moon in its constantly changing phases, the rolling waves that reminded her of her freedom and strength. Her mother always reminded her how strong she was, and how she could do anything she set her heart to. Tilly didn't always believe that, as she had her heart broken over and over again. She didn't realise how strong a little heart could be, but she always bounced back.

This time was different. It felt a million-fold worse. She really thought Dalton was '*the one.*' She'd never felt like she did with him, with anyone. Never. But there he was doing the same thing every other boy, man, she had ever fallen in love with, had done to her. The old cliché line, 'You're an amazing woman, Tilly, but....'

She walked along the beach, her footprints staggering behind her as she walked heavily in the sand. Her heart was aching inside her chest, and she felt like she was going to explode. It was twisting in a knot of pain to the point where she couldn't take another step. She knelt on the ground and pounded her fists into the sand. Not again.... why me? Not you Dalton, please! You're not like the others. Why?

She stayed there on the beach for quite a while, maybe an hour, sobbing, aching, thinking. Even though it was a warm night, she could feel the cold sand through her jeans. The sand seemed to capture the temperature of the ocean as it surged closer, edging nearer and nearer towards her. The moon was bright, lighting up the crests of the waves, just before they crashed heavily and rolled onto shore. She sat and watched the waves, the moon, and the beautiful stars. She felt the cool night air close in on her. She lifted her head and looked up at the stars.

She didn't believe in God, she didn't not believe in God, she believed in something bigger than humanity. Talking to the universe seemed like the right thing to do right now.

She said out loud, 'Universe, soul stars, can you hear me? What should I do? What is wrong with me?'

Of course, there was no answer-back, no guardian angel from heaven to guide her way, but suddenly she had this instinct that maybe she needed to leave Angourie for a while, for everything to make sense. She needed a new perspective.

She said out loud, as if speaking back to the universe, 'You know what? You're right, I should get away from here for a while. Maybe there is more to life than this noisy ocean.'

She stood up, dusted the cold sand off her jeans, and made her way back to the house.

As she started walking back along the beach, a lone wave came thundering into shore, almost reaching, and covering Tilly's footprints, that were traced high along the water's edge. Tilly thought she saw something flash in the water, like a fish jumping. She didn't think much of it, other than *gee that fish is close to shore*. She kept walking, nudging higher up the beach so her feet wouldn't get wet by the waves.

It wasn't a fish; it was the bottle that Dalton had placed in the ocean earlier that afternoon. It had made its way to the shoreline, and it was trying its best to get to her, but she didn't notice it.

That's what I'll do. I'll get away for a while. I'll be the one to leave this time. Tilly had decided. Her thoughts were clear. She would get out of Angourie for a while. She didn't need much, a backpack and her guitar. In the morning she would have a surf and a run and then get on the road. She hoped that by then Dalton would have left. Perhaps he'd hitch a ride with Dan to continue his travels northbound, or he would head back to his mates in Yamba. She did care, and she wondered if she was making the wrong decision, but she had decided. She had convinced herself Dalton was gone or going anyway, like they all did. She wasn't prepared to have her heart broken again. If he had doubts now, it would never be quite right.

Dalton was hoping she might come back later in the evening and knock on his door in the gypsy room, but she didn't.

chapter twenty-eight

The Letters

Dalton woke early and packed up his stuff. He wanted to catch Dan for a lift before he had set off for his sunrise surf.

Using The Angourie Local notepad and pen, Dalton scribed two brief notes, and as he left, he placed them on the front counter. Wrapped inside one of the folded notes, he placed a respectful amount of cash to pay for his accommodation, meals, and drinks over the past few nights.

One note had *To My Gypsy Girl* scripted in beautiful cursive writing across the front.

Inside it read ...

> *My Beautiful Gypsy Girl,*
> *I think I love you Tilly. I hope we can be together again someday. Some things take time. I'm sorry for what happened last night, and I hate myself for the way my words came out so wrong. I just wanted to share my past with you so I could love you completely and forever because I think I can do this with you. You're strong ENOUGH. I want to hold you forever in my arms and in my heart. Until then, you'll be on my mind.*
> *To Freedom, Friendship, and Enough Love.*
>
> *Your Gypsy Boy*

The other was addressed to *The Macallans.*

Inside it read....

To the Macallan family,
Thank you all for your wonderful hospitality and friendship. I've honestly felt
more love and kindness, here in Angourie, over the past few days than I've felt in a
very long time. It's hard to explain, and this brief note is not the place for me to tell
you my dark secret of the past. I tried to share this with Tilly last night, but things
didn't quite go as I planned. Tilly has asked me to go. I'm doing as she wishes. I'm
so sorry for the trouble I've caused. It wasn't my intention. Please find the cash to
pay for the expenses that I have incurred for your family.
Dalton

Dalton hadn't felt this way for quite some time now, but in an instant, when Tilly reacted the way she did, he felt just the same as he did, when he was leaving Deniliquin. He felt that the best thing he could do for everyone was to leave and never come back. People in this town would hate him for how he made Tilly feel. He was a bad omen wherever he went.

Dalton grabbed his surfboard, guitar, and backpack and walked across the road and down to the intersection where Dan had explained that his house was. As soon as Dalton saw The PIE parked out the front, he knew he was at the right house. He knocked gently on the door, and asked shyly, and politely, for a favour. He asked if Dan would give him a lift to the highway, so he could hitch a ride north. Dalton felt terrible the moment that he realised Dan had company. The girl that Dan had met had stayed over and they had shared a long night together. Maybe they hadn't been to sleep yet. There was music playing in the lounge room and the kettle was on.

Dan replied instantly, 'Of course I can. Just give me a minute. I don't want to lose this girl. She's a keeper. It seems you were my lucky charm.'

'At least I'm good for something,' replied Dalton. 'I wish I was a lucky charm for myself, although maybe it's quite the opposite.'

Dan disappeared for a moment to talk to his new girl, telling her he would be back soon and not to go anywhere, please.

Dan returned to the front door with the car keys. He didn't ask questions and respected Dalton's privacy. He was deeply concerned about what had happened between Dalton and Tilly. Everything seemed to be okay at The Angourie Local the night before.

Dalton didn't want to talk about it, he just wanted to leave, and Dan respected his wishes. The drive to the highway was awkward. Dalton explained he wasn't leaving any details, he didn't have a phone number or fixed address to contact; he was off travelling again, and he didn't know if or when he would be back.

As the drive continued, Dan became more concerned. He hoped Dalton would open up to him. It wasn't right to ask what happened, but he wanted to know. He was intrigued by how something that seemed so right, could go so wrong.

'Mate, I can see how much you're hurting. Did you talk to Tilly about everything? Did she not like what happened in your past? I don't understand, mate, what happened?' Dan tried to dig for some more information, but Dalton was speechless. 'Look, I'm always here for you. If you ever change your mind, you can always crash at mine.' These were Dan's parting words.

Dan knew that nothing he could say was going to get Dalton to change his mind. He was on autopilot, plagued by demons mode.

As Dalton stepped out of the car, he gave Dan a soft, forced smile. 'I'm okay mate, and hey thanks for everything.' He tapped the side of the open window with his free hand and they both said in unison with the same hopeful yet not promising anything 'See you, man.'

Dalton wasn't waiting on the side of the road for long before he was picked up by another gypsy surfer, heading North. He was wearing a black Akubra hat, very similar to the hat Dalton used to wear religiously. Somehow, Dalton had got lucky enough that the car had room for all his stuff. He placed his surfboard, guitar, and backpack in the back, and they were off.

Dalton had never been further north than right here where he stood, so wherever they were headed was going to be an adventure. New sights, unfamiliar sounds, new people, fresh waves. He was excited to be on the road again, and although his heart was broken into a thousand pieces, he was trying to play it cool.

Why did she react that way? Why didn't she stay to hear me out? The night was going so well and then she just changed on me.... or maybe it was me who changed on her. I can't blame her. It was me. I was the one who went cold when she was just being her beautiful free self. Damn it, what have I done? Why didn't I go after her and explain? Why did she tell me to go, just go? Dalton kept drifting back to his analytical thoughts, still trying to figure out how everything had gone so wrong. Miscommunication at its absolute finest.

It was too late now. Dalton was in the passenger seat of this cool, rusty red and white, two-tone VW Kombi and they were heading north.

chapter twenty-nine

Tilly's Morning Surf

Tilly woke up early and grabbed her favourite longboard from the surfboard racks beside the house. The noisy ocean was looking perfect this morning. It was flat, with some nice, long rolling waves drifting onto the shoreline. The sun was rising on the horizon, with spans of orange and pink covering the entire sky, only slightly imperfect by the placement of a few white, wispy clouds.

Wow, it's so beautiful, I love this place, thought Tilly. It was all she knew, other than her few brief years at university, in the city, which was nothing to write home about. Literally, Tilly would send a letter home at the end of every semester to tell her family about her academic results from examinations and assignments, about the friends she was partying with and some boys she'd met. They were always way too city, with their fancy cars and polished shoes. Tilly was always too wild and free to fit into their 9 am to 5 pm routine lifestyle. It just wasn't her. On the other end of the spectrum, there were drunken lads she'd picked up for a wild night, after dancing at the bars until 3 am. These one-night things, flings, were never more than a bit of fun before Tilly realised these 'lads' had no dreams or aspirations in life. This happened way too many times to even keep a count of.

Then there was Jesse, and she would rather not bring thoughts about him back to her mind, as she had worked so hard to move away and recover from the heartbreak he caused her. By the end of the four years at university, Tilly was convinced that the only place where she would find someone worth holding onto would be back in her hometown of Angourie.

The only time she called her family in the four years, while she was away studying, was when it was any of her family member's birthdays, and it was from a public telephone booth, outside of her university apartment complex. There was always a line a mile long to use the phone and everyone waiting would listen in to the conversation, so it was much easier and more personal to send her interesting and sometimes wild-life details in a letter.

As Tilly strolled along the beach, with her board under her arm, she wondered why she was having these thoughts and then quickly realised that it was because she was about to travel, and again the only way to contact her family would be by mail or a phone call from a dodgy phone booth. She wasn't looking forward to that.

Tilly pushed her board into the water and waded in beside it. The water was fresh, not too cold, but certainly invigorating for the soul. The only way to get in was to charge and get fully wet. Trying to edge in slowly was always the wrong decision. It was a bit like ripping off a bikini wax strip after a winter of wearing a full steamer wetsuit. When it was time to get back in the bikini, it just had to be done. One, two, three, go!

Off she went, the wave breaking over her face and onto her back as she pushed through the crest of the wave. She shook her head and pushed her long hair back out of her face, taking a big breath of fresh freedom. She had to paddle quite far out, into the depths, as the waves were streaming in from almost back at the headland point, providing a beautiful long ride to shore. She kept on pushing through the set of waves until she reached the clearing out the back.

The next moment Tilly was paddling and up on a decent-sized wave. This one was going to take her all the way in.

That was pretty good for my first wave, thought Tilly as she paddled out again.

Tilly surfed for quite a while and caught some beautiful waves, none as spectacular as the first one, and then she headed in and went for a brief jog. This was always her ritual whenever she had time by herself. The surf cooled her down; the jog warmed her up. It was always a perfect balance.

She unleashed her leg rope and placed her board upside-down under her favourite shady tree, so the wax wouldn't melt. Then she set off for her run. Some mornings she would make it all the way over the headland and continue all the way to the end of Woolooweyah beach. It was quite a decent beach run, probably ten kilometres in total. Today, she decided she would go all the way. Who knew when she would be back to do this again? She was going to make the most of it.

She passed a few of the locals who were out for their morning walk. Many elderly couples had moved to Angourie, for this exact reason. They were walking hand in hand, enjoying the beautiful nature of the place and each other's secluded company. There weren't many people in this town, which made it ideally romantic and peaceful. Tilly often made a comment to the couples that she passed at how lovely it was to see such closeness.

This morning Tilly was on a mission. With many scattered thoughts in her mind, she still acknowledged the walkers she passed by, and said good morning with a beautiful smile, if she knew the walkers or not.

Tilly had almost reached the end of the beach, to the turnaround point, when she saw something just ahead of her in the sand. It looked like a turtle's head poking out of the sand, but as she got closer, she realised it was a glass bottle. At first, she thought, *bloody tourists. If they want to get drunk on our beautiful beaches, they can at least take away their rubbish afterwards.* The locals wouldn't dare leave rubbish on their beautiful beaches.

She grabbed the bottle to remove it from the sand, deciding she would take it back and place it in the bin. As soon as she grabbed the lid, she realised it was a Macallan's whisky bottle. '*Hey, that's our whisky,*' she said out loud.

As she pulled the bottle further out of the sand and wiped it clean, she realised there was a note inside. *A message in a Macallan's bottle. Well, that's the coolest thing I've ever seen, but who would do that?* Tilly had a thousand thoughts racing through her head.

She opened the lid and tried to reach in to get the note out, but as she did, she accidentally pushed the note to the bottom of the bottle. It had been scrolled and then scrunched lightly in the middle to squeeze it into the bottle, no doubt. It had been placed ever so gently, just clasping inside the neck of the bottle, but she had accidentally pushed the note in further. Her fingers were too wide to reach deep inside, even her little finger. She had to find a way to get the note out. She walked up to a nearby dune and found a thin stick lying in the sand. *That might work if I can jimmy the note up to the surface somehow, and then drag it out with the pointy stick.*

This procedure took some time, but it worked, and she released the note from the bottle without damaging it at all. As she unravelled it, she couldn't believe her eyes. The first thing she noticed was the "The Angourie Local" logo on the header of the notepaper.

What is this? She looked around to see if someone was watching, playing some kind of trick on her.

As she unravelled the note even further, she noticed the beautiful handwriting. Someone had put quite a lot of thought into this, she imagined. It wasn't some kind of children's game.

She started reading out loud:

Chelsea, my girl, my angel,
It's been a while now since the last time I saw your beautiful face. I think of you every day.
I hope that one day I can forgive myself for what happened to you. To us! Our plans, our dreams, our aspirations. I'm so sorry.
I need to tell you something, and I hope you are okay with this, but I've met another woman. She's beautiful, strong, and amazing, and I want to love her with every piece of my heart, completely and forever.
I will always hold you and the memories we shared forever in my soul.
One day, I know I'll see you again in a beautiful place called heaven.
I'll see you when I'm looking at you.
Your spunkrat always,
Dalton x

Tilly sunk down, onto her knees in the sand, while she tried to process her thoughts in what she was reading.

Dalton, Dalton.... could that be my Dalton?
Chelsea, who is Chelsea?
Was that the name of the girl that Frankie met last night? I think so, but it seemed that she and Dalton didn't know each other at all. And this Chelsea is in heaven. I'm so confused. Could there be another Dalton? Not that I know and not one who stayed at The Angourie Local and drank The Macallan whisky.
She read the lines again, blinking through tears....
Could that be me, the woman he's talking about, who he wants to give every piece of his heart to, completely and forever....
Oh my god, what have I done? Is this what he was trying to tell me last night?
I must go. I must get to him. I must stop him from leaving...
Tilly's body had turned to jelly. She couldn't believe this was happening. She started running, but her legs wouldn't work; it was like she was dreaming. She stumbled and

dropped the bottle and the note on the sand. She fell hard on her wrist in the process but gave it a quick rub and scavenged up the note and the bottle and ran as constantly as she could all the way back to the headland. Her breathing was laboured, and she could hardly get any air into her lungs, not because she was unfit, but because all of her emotions had piled into her core; from her stomach, crowding her chest and moving to gather in her throat.

The repeated thought that kept going through her mind was, *I'm so stupid, I'm so sorry. Please don't leave, Dalton, don't go, please don't go. Please wait for me!*

Tilly reached the tree where she had placed her surfboard. She thought for an instant that she should grab it, but then on second thoughts, it was just a board, and everyone was honest around here. She could come and get it later as soon as she'd stopped Dalton from leaving. That is all that mattered right now. And this note could be the most important thing she'd ever found in her life. She couldn't run as fast as she could and carry the longboard and the bottle, and the note all at once.

Tilly left the board where it was, and she ran as fast as she could up through the bush track and onto the road and back to The Angourie Local. Her feet were toughened, so running on the road wasn't too much of an issue, nor did she care right now about anything other than stopping Dalton from leaving. She ran straight through the reception area and up the garden path to the gypsy room. The door was closed. As she arrived, she stood just outside the doorway to catch her breath. She could hear two voices coming from inside the room. A male and a female voice. Her heart sank, and she wasn't sure what to think, for a moment, and then she realised it was the familiar voices of Jack and Laura. Her mum and dad were doing the checkout and cleaning rounds this morning.

It was too late; he'd already packed and gone.

~

Tilly knocked on the door and Laura replied, 'Who is it?'

'It's me. Mum, Dad, what have I done?' Tilly clambered into the room; she was a mess. She was out of breath, she was crying, tears burning down her hot flushed face as she grasped the bottle and the crumpled note. She sank down on the end of the bed. 'I found this.... on the beach. It's from Dalton to Chelsea.'

'Who is Chelsea?' questioned Jack. 'Is she the girl that Frankie met last night? The new girl in town?'

'Well, yes that is Chelsea, but this is a different Chelsea just to make things more confusing, Dad. There is a Dalton and a Chelsea.'

Jack squeezed his brow together. 'Can someone please tell me what is going on here? I'm so confused. Everything was going so well last night and today, as they say in the classics, everything has turned to custard.'

'Dad, please, now is not the time to be funny. I love you, but not now, please. No silly Dad jokes. This is serious.' Tilly spoke intently and forcefully, but with the respect that her father so deserved. He was only trying to understand what was going on, and to be quite honest, Tilly was only just figuring it all out herself.

Laura calmed Tilly down and gave her a warm hug. 'Mum, Dad, let me try to explain.' Tilly continued on as she ended the embrace with Laura.

'I'm in love with Dalton and I know now that he's in love with me, too. I know, crazy, we just met. But last night, after you all went home, he went cold on me, after we had just had the greatest night together. He was trying to tell me something important, but he started to tell me saying, *Tilly, you're the most amazing woman, but..* and you know me, I've heard that line, so many times. I reacted irrationally and impulsively, as I do. I told him I didn't want to hear what he had to say, and I told him to go.' Tilly broke down in tears. 'And he's gone...'

Jack piped in, 'I'm still not understanding. It's a bit like jelly and custard to me right now, with a dash of Macallan's,' as he gestured towards the empty bottle that Tilly had thrown on the bed. Jack half-joked, trying to be serious. It was just his sense of humour, knowing that Tilly wouldn't find it funny at all.

She completely ignored her father's attempt at humour as she continued with what she was trying to explain. 'I wanted to be the one to leave this time, so I packed my bags this morning. I went for a last hoorah surf, and I did my favourite beach run, and this is what I found, way at the end of the beach.' Tilly tried to hold in her tears as she passed Laura the note. Laura read it out loud to Jack.

Laura explained to Jack while he looked utterly confused. 'It's a message that was in the bottle, Jack. Tilly found the bottle while she was running this morning.'

'I'm with you, I'm with you,' nodded Jack.

Laura read the note slowly and clearly.

> *Chelsea, my girl, my angel,*
> *It's been a while now since the last time I saw your beautiful face. I think of you every day.*
> *I hope that one day I can forgive myself for what happened to you. To us! Our plans, our dreams, our aspirations. I'm so sorry.*
> *I need to tell you something, and I hope you are okay with this, but I've met another woman. She's beautiful, strong, and amazing, and I want to love her with every piece of my heart, completely and forever.*
> *I will always hold you and the memories we shared forever in my soul.*
> *One day, I know I'll see you again in a beautiful place called heaven.*
> *I'll see you when I'm looking at you.*
> *Your spunkrat always,*
> *Dalton x*

After she finished reading, they all just stayed in a moment of silence, processing the whole thing.

Jack was scratching his head. 'That's our notepad paper. Did Dalton write that note, and put it in the bottle for you to find?' He processed his words slowly, still trying to put two and two together.

'Yes Dad, Dalton wrote the note. Who knows why, who knows what happened to Chelsea? I do not know about any of that, but what I hope, is that I think the woman that he loves might be me.... Do you think? Am I just making that up in my head?' Tilly paused, waiting for a response from Jack and Laura. Neither of them replied. They were both deep in thought, processing the note. 'And I told him to go....' Tilly burst into floods of tears again.

I have to find him.

chapter thirty

Big Love

Jack and Laura had agreed that Tilly should try to find him. Jack also reminded her of his wisdom, that everything happens for a reason, and that the breaks and bends of life are important for discovering who you really are on this journey of life.

Tilly went back to the house and finished packing her bag. The Macallans had closed the café briefly between breakfast and lunch and they all had time to attend to this family crisis to say goodbye to Tilly for whatever amount of time she needed to take to find Dalton. She didn't have much time, right now, if she wanted to have any kind of chance of finding her Gypsy Boy.

She got showered and dressed, and as the family all gathered to say goodbye, she told Louis, Eddie and Frankie about the message in the bottle. All three brothers were of the firm and supportive agreement that Dalton was worth finding. Louis wanted to go with her until Eddie reminded him that his basketball grand final was this weekend, and the team wouldn't win without him.

Finally, Tilly was ready, and she announced boldly, 'When we were talking the other night, Dalton mentioned the Gold Coast. I think that's where I'm going to head to. Frankie, can you please drive me to the highway so I can hitch a ride?'

Jack and Laura had a brief meltdown about Tilly hitch-hiking, until Frankie reminded them that Tilly was a grown woman, and extremely capable of looking after herself on her own.

Frankie enforced, 'She's about to travel to the end of the world to find this Gypsy Boy. You won't stop her until she does. You know what she's like. She's your daughter.'

Tilly joined in with the discussion about her. 'I'm standing right here, Frankie.'

'It's true Tilly, I'm on your side. These two were identical to you when they were younger. What are they even worried about?'

Jack and Laura looked at each other, knowing their history and what they both did for each other in the name of love. Nothing was going to hold them apart. So why would they place those restrictions that were placed on them, on their own daughter?

Jack was the first one to give the farewell words of wisdom. 'Go, my baby girl. I hope it works out for you.' Jack squeezed her tightly in a warm bear hug. As he let her go from his hold, he asked her to close her eyes and open her hand. She did. He placed in her hand, one of her special guitar picks. On one side it had engraved 'Have Guitar,

Will Travel.' On the other side it had the family initials J. L. F. E. L. T. 'We will all be with you Tilly, keep us close.'

Tilly kissed the guitar pick and placed it tightly in her jeans pocket. 'Thanks, Dad, I love your hugs. I'll miss you.'

Laura was next to share some words with Tilly. 'You know you can do anything you set your heart to, my beautiful, strong, amazing girl.' Laura held Tilly so closely, ending the embrace with a kiss on her forehead, and their saying to each other, 'Big Love, baby girl.'

'Big Love, Mum.' Tilly loved this little saying they had. A song by Fleetwood Mac inspired this, and Tilly couldn't remember exactly when it started; they just always said it to each other.

Eddie and Louis both gave Tilly a hug. The last time Tilly left was to go to university, and she didn't return for four years, only for brief Christmas vacations.

Tilly had started crying again with Louis' extra-long hug. She was emotional, and it was causing the whole family to feel unsettled as well. 'Let's go, Frankie, before I change my mind.'

Frankie agreed to take Tilly on one condition.

'Can we talk about the condition later, Frankie? Whatever it is, I'll do it. I promise. Even though you know I don't like conditions. Let's just go.' Tilly pressed some urgency in trying to get away quickly, so she had half a chance of finding Dalton.

They had driven a fair way down the road with no words spoken. It was an awkward silence and Tilly was burning up inside. Her heart was pounding, her mind was racing, tears streaming down her cheeks. She was a mess, again. She was heartbroken, and she was also feeling stupid that she didn't give Dalton a chance to explain what he wanted to tell her. But if it was that he didn't want to be with her, she didn't want to hear it. That was how she felt. She couldn't take it again. Not this time. Not from Dalton.

Frankie broke the silence. 'Tilly, promise me this.'

Tilly interrupted. It was something she heard often. Promise me this, promise me that. Always so many promises. 'So many promises Frankie, why do you do this to me?'

Frankie replied, 'Because it's important and I want you to commit to something for me. If I ask you to promise me there is more of a chance that you will, don't you think?'

Tilly replied, 'I guess so. Go ahead, give me the promise request.'

Frankie readjusted his hands and placed them in the ten and two positions on the steering wheel. As he talked, he used hand gestures to accentuate particular aspects of what he was saying. 'I want you to promise me that while you're out searching for Dalton, you will take some time to realise your worth. You are so worthy to be loved. The men that have come in and out of your life so far were not meant for you, but you need to leave those relationships in the past and not treat the new relationships you come into now in the same way. Us men, we are all different. Just think about me and Eddie and Louis, the same genetics, and none of us are the same. So, my advice is, don't treat men like they are all the same. They are not. How is that for a challenge? You like a challenge? Promise me you won't treat Dalton a certain way because of your past. This is exactly why you are in this situation right now. These are harsh words Tilly, I know, but you have to stop assuming that your next relationship will be like any other you've been in. You've always been my strong, amazing, do-anything girl. I love you, my baby sister. I still don't even really know exactly what happened last night, but you'll figure it out. You know what Dad says. If it's meant to be, so it will be.'

Tilly just sat there deep in her own thoughts, thinking about her conversation with Dalton last night, when it all went so wrong. Self-doubt started creeping into her thoughts. *Why did he say that to me, that we needed to talk about something that's been on his mind? Why did he put it on me after such a great night together? Why did he say it to me the way he did? Maybe I'm not the woman he loves. Maybe the woman in the bottle note, isn't me and this is all just a big waste of time. The night was going so well and then he just changed on me.... or maybe it was me who changed on him. I can't blame him. It was me. I was the one who went cold when he was just trying to tell me something. Damn it, what have I done?*

Tilly shook her head and zoned back into the conversation Frankie was trying to have with her. 'Sure Frankie, so you want me to promise you I'll find my worth and stop treating men like they are all the same? I'll try. Pinkie promise.' She reached across and joined her pinkie with Frankie.

They drove a little more, still not talking much, over the river crossing, which always gave Tilly chills up her spine. The road was so close to the flowing water and there was no edge on the side of the bridge. It felt like you could just fall off and no one would ever know where you had gone. That was Tilly's worst fear, drowning in a car or being burned alive. Apparently, drowning was the best way to die. Tilly zoned back into the conversation with Frankie.

'By the way, I'm not driving you to the Gold Coast. I haven't got enough petrol for that. I'm dropping you at the highway and you're on your own from there. This is what you wanted to do, remember.' Frankie was strong with his words, letting Tilly know that she was deciding to get out of town and to find Dalton. This was her destiny. He was only helping her as far as the highway.

'I know, I know Frankie and thank you,' Tilly responded, still trying to keep the tears from rolling down her cheeks.

There was silence again as Tilly racked around in her mind trying to convince herself that this was the right decision to make. She was doing this. The silence lasted a few minutes. Frankie didn't soften. He had to be strong with her, because he could see that she made an impulsive and irrational decision and she needed to learn that this wasn't the best way to approach a new worthwhile relationship. She had messed up. If Tilly would listen to any of The Macallans, it would most likely be Frankie. He was her strong, down-to-earth hero after-all. No bullshit. No drama. He wouldn't put up with it. All of that was a waste of time.

Frankie broke the silence with, 'So what do you think Tilly, what's your plans? Do you have a plan?'

'No Frankie, I don't have a plan. If I had things the way I planned, I'd be hanging out with Dalton right now, but I stuffed that all up. I really thought he was "the one" Frankie, and then just like I've heard a thousand times before....' Tilly changed the tone of her voice to a deep male tone. 'You're an amazing woman Tilly, and I would love to stay here forever with you *but........*'

Frankie replied, 'Did Dalton say that to you last night? As far as I knew, he was keen to stay on for a bit and work in the Local and do some gigs and surf with Dan and all of us.'

'Yeah, well, his words didn't come out that way. That's how the sentence started, and I didn't give him a chance to finish. Dad always said, when someone throws in a *but* mid-sentence you might as well forget about any words precluding but. He didn't get a chance. I didn't want to hear him say it, I couldn't stand it if he did, so I was the one to leave. I walked out before he could finish his sentence. I told him to go, and you know the rest.'

'Wow Tilly, big, brave move. You don't even know what he was going to say to you. From what I could tell in our brief chats in the surf and on the way back to Angourie, the guy has had a tough life. So, you think now, after finding the message in the bottle, that maybe he just wanted to tell you something deep about himself? You know us blokes are a different breed to you women.' Frankie tried to encourage Tilly to think differently, that maybe Dalton just had something important to tell her.

Tilly had convinced herself that the conversation was one to end the relationship or slow things down and then end the relationship. She replied, 'Maybe you're right, but it didn't feel like a pleasant conversation was coming up. He completely went cold on me, after we had enjoyed the best night ever.'

Frankie encouraged Tilly with his words of wisdom as he pulled over on the side of the highway. 'Oh Tilly, I don't know the whole story. There are so many things I'm still not understanding, but this is your decision and I know everything happens for a reason. Whatever this is, whatever path you're on, this is your destiny, and you have something big to learn from this. Just do what you've gotta do and know that I love you so much. I'm always here for you.' They had reached the destination for Tilly to jump out and hitch a ride.

'Thanks, Frankie. I love you to the end of the world.' Tilly had streams of tears down her cheeks, but she wiped them away with a big, beautiful smile. 'I'm good, Frankie. I'm good.'

'Do you want me to stay for a bit until you catch a ride?' questioned Frankie, slightly worried about his little sister heading out into the world with no way to contact her. She had no fixed address and no phone to call. She could phone them, but would she? She could send postcards and letters that would at least keep some kind of track on where she had been, but that's about it. Tilly was always a free spirit, so he needed to trust that she would be okay.

'I'm good, Frankie, I'm good.' Tilly said this again, nodding her head. She gave Frankie a huge hug, kissed him on the forehead and as she walked off in front of the car, she gave him a thumbs-up signal as she walked to a nice clearing on the side of the road where she could place her backpack and her guitar. As Frankie drove away, he shouted out the window, 'I love you to the end of the world Tilly.' That was the thing they said to each other, for good night wishes or sentimental farewells. Tilly and Frankie had always kept a strong bond with each other, even when she had moved away for four years. They wrote letters to each other. Always signing off with, *I love you to the end of the world*. Frankie would do anything for her, and Tilly adored her biggest brother. He was hard on her sometimes, but always honest and grounded.

Frankie had to do a bit of a highway drive north to get back onto the eastern road heading back to Angourie. When he came back to the turnoff, only five minutes later he could see that Tilly was jumping into an old Chevrolet, much like Dan's car's vintage.

Tilly couldn't quite believe her luck. A hitched ride in a Chevrolet. It was such a cool-looking car, aqua blue with a white embellishment down the side fattening out at the boot. Its tyres were matching whitewall and aqua trim. Wow!

From what Frankie could see, it looked like a bunch of girls in the car, perhaps out for a girls' road trip. He was happy with that and felt right about it. *Tilly. She always lands on her feet that girl, sometimes she just can't see it though.* Frankie muttered to himself and shook his head.

On the short drive home, Frankie wondered how Tilly would go. He wondered if and how she might possibly find Dalton. *Neither of them had a contact number and Dalton had no fixed address. He was travelling. If Dalton kept in touch with The Macallans he could locate Tilly, but that would only be finding out where she had been and where she was possibly heading next. Would he even contact them? Tilly had given him clear orders to go, just go! Did she even know his last name? Not that it really mattered. It's not like she could look him up in the phonebook. He was on his own adventure.* These were Frankie's driving thoughts. *Ah well, an adventure it would be, and a good story to tell, whatever the outcome.* Frankie got lost in his thoughts as he drove the same familiar road he had always driven. Frankie had a slight twitch himself tempting him to travel again, but right now he was hanging out in Angourie to help Jack and Laura, and he'd actually met a nice girl himself on the Thursday night, *which all turned to custard,* in Jack's terms. Frankie hadn't told anyone much about this girl yet. He didn't know much about her, other than that she had moved to Angourie, from Sydney. He was keen to get to know more about her. She had only stopped in briefly with her parents at The Angourie Local on the Thursday night, for dinner and drinks, and she was obviously very new to the town. He walked her home. She still dressed in Sydney style, and she had a bit of a city up-tightness about her. That wouldn't take long to drift away after a few days, weeks, and years in Angourie. Her parents had made the drive up, from the big smoke, to settle her in and see her new home, and they were leaving town the coming Monday. Frankie was hopeful of catching up with her again in the coming days. Her name was Chelsea, just to make things even more confusing. She was a writer, a novelist, and she had come to Angourie to find some peace to immerse herself in her writing.

When Frankie had first heard about the message in the bottle to this Chelsea girl, he immediately thought the worst and thought that maybe Dalton was mixed up somehow with this new girl in town, but as he understood more about the message, he realised that the Chelsea in the message in the bottle had passed away. There was no connection between the two. It was just an unusual circumstance of an uncommon name that was suddenly a common name in this small town.

Frankie was deep in his thoughts as he was driving. It had turned out to be a very unexpected chain of events for the morning, and it was still earlyish, about 11 am Frankie wondered if he would see Chelsea again today. They had made no plans to meet up. He didn't even know if she was slightly interested in meeting up with him.

Frankie had travelled and explored a bit of the east coast of Australia, and it was in his heart to travel again, but just now it was Tilly's turn. He hoped she would be okay.

Frankie arrived back home to the shack, made himself a cup of coffee, and sat on the deck. He pulled out his guitar, and he started to strum. He hadn't written a song for a long time but suddenly a melody and lyrics started to flow. This Chelsea girl had stirred some emotions in his heart.

chapter thirty-one

Travis

Travis' welcoming comment to Dalton was about his Bandana.

'Hey, Bandana boy, you look like you and your surfboard need a lift?' He added that the only reason he stopped to pick him up was because he looked like Axl Rose, and being the hard-core surfer he was, he mostly felt sorry for Dalton, that his surfboard wax might melt, and his guitar might get wrecked if he was left waiting in the sun too long. He also mentioned that he was heading straight to Byron Bay, with no detours. Dalton jumped in, happy to accept the ride.

As it turned out, the fella, Travis, that Dalton had hitched a ride with, was heading to Byron Bay. This pleased Dalton very much, and he couldn't quite believe his luck, as he always wanted to surf and busk at Byron. He had heard about Byron Bay so many times, in surf storytelling conversations. Pretty much every surfer he'd ever met that lived around the North Coast of New South Wales had surfed and raved about 'The Pass.'

Travis quickly filled Dalton in on the Byron Bay fun facts, as he knew them. The most amazing thing about Byron Bay was that it was the most easterly point in Australia. The local Arakwal Aboriginal people's name for the area is *Cavvanbah*, meaning *the meeting place*. It was Lieutenant James Cook, who named Cape Byron after Royal Navy officer John Byron. The cool thing was that if you got the timing right, you could be the first person in Australia to see the sunrise at the beginning of every new year. Of course, New Zealand was more easterly and those waking up in East Cape, north of Gisborne, could claim to catch the first world sunrise of every new year, but Byron Bay, Australia, was next in line behind the Pacific islands. The other cool thing about Byron Bay was that from the lighthouse, you could watch a beautiful sunset over the back of the hills, taking in views of Mt Warning in Wollumbin National Park. Its crested peaks reach high, shadowing the orange and pink dusky skies in the distance beyond. Mt Warning was on Dalton's to-do list, as he was quite an adventurer, however, he had recently learned that Wollumbin, which means 'cloud catcher' is a traditional place of cultural law, initiation, and spiritual education for the people of the Bundjalung Nation, so it was more respectful to consider not climbing the summit. Dalton's travels were in the hands of fate anyhow, as he had no transport of his own. He was relying on the generosity of others to transport him to his next adventure. He had no plans at all. He had enough money to keep him going for a while. He had no bills to pay, just a belly to feed, and he needed a place to stay each night. He wasn't fussy about the accommodation either, he just needed a bed to get some sleep and he figured if he needed to make some more money he would get some jobs gigging and doing bar work in various towns he ended up in. He could also do any kind of handyman or labour jobs with his extensive building experience behind him.

These were more serious and grounding thoughts in Dalton's mind as they headed north with great tunes pumping on the radio. Dalton started laughing out loud, for the first time in quite a while, since this inner turmoil started with thoughts about sharing his dark secret with Tilly. It was the simple things that could bring so much joy. Travis had switched the radio station over because a bunch of advertisements had come on to spoil the mood of fun music. It was perfect timing, because as he switched radio stations, the sweet sound of Greg Ham's flute solo from Men at Work—Down Under was just starting. This brought a giggle to Travis and Dalton when the lyrics kicked in and they sang along.

'Travelling in a fried-out Kombi, on a hippie trail, head full of zombie, I met a strange lady; she made me nervous; she took me in and gave me breakfast, and she said....'

Dalton made a mental note of another little ironic song moment. The lyrics were fitting to this moment right now, and he thought it was uncanny how this kept happening. He noticed things like that. Like little signs from above that he was where he was meant to be.

Dalton couldn't quite believe that today was the day he was going to surf at the most easterly point of Australia, and apparently, there was always heaps of marine life to keep you company. Dalton had seen photos of surfers longboarding surrounded by pods of dolphins, and there was one story re-occurring where this guy was out surfing, and a shark started circling. He thought he was toast; it was an oversized Great White and it seemed to be hungry. As the story goes, a pod of dolphins came and surrounded him as he made his way to the shore. This was all hearsay, but believable and comforting, all the same.

It was about 8 am as they pulled into 'The Pass' carpark. It was perfect timing for an early morning surf. The sun was warming the water as the dolphins, just as Dalton had heard about, splashed and played amongst the waves. Travis and Dalton observed the surfers already out on the water, as they watched the rolling sets continually forming beautiful strong curved waves. It wasn't overcrowded but a comforting amount of people for a virgin Byron surf.

'Let's hit it,' announced Travis.

As Travis spoke, these three brief words, Dalton realised that Travis had a slight accent of some kind. Dalton couldn't work out if his accent was Kiwi, South African or English. He also realised at this moment that they hadn't spoken a lot during the journey, a little bit of get-to-know-you stuff when Dalton first got in the car. Dalton realised he was caught up in his deep thoughts and suddenly he felt a bit rude. He thought he should apologise but Travis didn't seem too bothered. He had been listening to some good music and singing along so Dalton decided to let it go. He didn't need to explain his whole life story to this guy, who was clearly happy to get in the water, as soon as he possibly could.

Dalton had learned through intermittent conversation that Travis was from Wooli, a very small beach town about two hours south of Yamba. He often did long weekend trips to Byron, leaving Wooli very early on a Friday morning and heading back on a Monday afternoon, especially when the swell was good. This was one of those weekends. Starting now, Travis planned to surf from sunup to sundown only stopping to eat and find some fun after dark. Byron was a tourist town and he always met interesting people who were travelling, usually surfers like himself appreciating the beauty of Byron's bays. There were plenty of different bays to surf in, depending on the wind direction. Wategos' Bay was ideal for longboards on a northerly swell. Tallows beach was often choppy and erratic but if you wanted a challenge surf it would certainly provide that opportunity. The Pass is a very popular surf break so it could get overcrowded, that was the only problem. Clarkes, Main Beach and The Wreck were always optional too. Travis was the eldest of three brothers, much like Dalton, he was hugely independent. He had his own successful business making surfboards and renovating old cars, hence the souped-up VW Kombi looking immaculate. He was an unusually attractive rooster, with a chilled-out attitude and a free spirit, not unlike Dalton. Travis had grown up riding freestyle BMX flips and tricks and spins. He had suffered a few minor injuries deciding to give it away and find his adrenaline hit in the ocean. The landing on the water was usually much softer than hard concrete. The main difference between Dalton and Travis was that Travis was quite content living and working and surfing along the eastern coastline of Australia. Dalton was still feeling like he had to run a bit further from the troubles he had left in his wake. Byron wasn't quite far enough away from Deniliquin, or Angourie, but this would be okay for now.

They grabbed their boards and headed onto the sand.

chapter thirty-two

Adeline, Georgia and Jacqui

As Tilly piled into the Chevrolet, the first thing she noticed was that it smelled like Armoral and various overpowering scents of perfume: musk and sweet marshmallow, and the smell of opium, the perfume her mother used to wear when she was younger. The leather seats were polished; the dash was glimmer clean. These girls were obviously on a road trip in what she assumed was someone's daddy's fancy car.

Tilly smiled as she climbed into the spare seat in the back after placing her backpack and guitar in the oversized boot. There were three suitcases fitted in as well, so it was a tight squeeze, but it worked. 'Hey!'

'Hey, what you up to, girl? Where are you going?' said one girl with an American accent.

'Hey, good question. Let's just say I'm on an adventure heading wherever you girls are going. I just need to get away for a little while, you know how it is, *and trying to find the one that got away,*' she whispered under her breath. Then, loudly, as the car moved forward, and the engine roared. 'Thanks for stopping. I really appreciate it.'

'No worries, lucky for you, we are on a little getaway weekend too,' said the driver. 'My name is Adeline.' She flicked on the indicator and started concentrating on her driving as she made her way back onto the highway. Although it was the main road from Sydney to Brisbane, this part of the highway was always quiet and traffic-free. The next major town north was Coolangatta, and south was Newcastle. In between were scattered small beach towns and regional country towns, none heavily populated and certainly none that would draw heavy traffic.

The flamboyant blonde in the front passenger seat offered her name next. 'I'm Georgia, and I'm from Georgia,' she laughed, throwing her head back, in familiarity with the joke she shared whenever she shared her name with people outside of America. The old cliché line that never went astray. 'I'm here visiting my two dear friends, Adeline and Jacqui. We met on summer vacation last year when I visited Australia with my family.' She said Austraaaalia with a long drawl. 'My father is well known in America; his name is Charlie Daniels. Have you heard of him?'

'I have Georgia. I think your family might have stayed at my parents' hotel in Angourie last year. I think we met. In case you don't remember, my name is Tilly.' Tilly instantly felt a sense of relief that, somehow, she had hitched a ride from total strangers who possibly weren't *"total"* strangers.

Tilly was just another face to Georgia. She had met lots of people while travelling with her father and his band. It was glaringly obvious from the first impressions of meeting Georgia that she was more interested in herself than anyone else around her. Stunningly beautiful as she was, she had a distinct arrogance about her, which was quite off-putting. Tilly gave her the benefit of the doubt, however, knowing that people aren't always as superficial as they might seem at first impression.

Jacqui tried to introduce herself, with Georgia talking over the top of her. 'Hi, I'm...' was all she managed to get out before Georgia chimed in with, 'Oh, of course, you're that girl from the local pub. What's the name of that place?'

'The Angourie Local,' replied Tilly, you may know it as The Macallan's. That's the family name.'

'Yeah, I remember now, we had a great night at your Angourie Local,' the way she pronounced Angourie made it sound like a deserted ghost town in the Midwest of America with deserted streets, padded bars on the windows and rolling tumbleweed down the main street. Which probably wasn't far from reality, other than the fact that Angourie was the most beautiful little beach town in Australia. 'I remember thinking your brother Frankie was quite a catch; we had a fun night. Well, *I* did.' She paused and laughed, waiting for Tilly to laugh with her, but Tilly didn't. She was waiting for the punchline of the supposed joke about why Georgia had a fun night, and perhaps Frankie didn't. 'He was okay for an Aussie boy, but I think he had a bit of growing up to do, didn't even own his own car if I recall correctly.'

Man, this girl has no filter, thought Tilly. *She thinks it's totally okay to criticise my brother to my face.* Georgia hadn't made the best first impression on Tilly, but there was not much Tilly could do about that. Tilly was the one getting a free ride here. Perhaps at least it was better that she said it to her face than gossiping behind her back. Tilly could only imagine what Georgia would have to say about Tilly if given the opportunity to describe her to someone. *Some random hitchhiker they picked up on the side of the road.* And to be quite honest, that's all that Tilly was right now, *a random hitchhiker..., on a little getaway in search of Dalton. The one that got away.*

Jacqui finally got to speak, and with light humour but complete sincerity, she said, 'Georgia, that's a little rude to speak of Tilly's brother like that, we generally have a few more manners here in Australia, in case you hadn't noticed,' as she swigged a mouthful from her beer can, and burped. Jacqui forced the burp to make a joke out of the situation. It clearly wasn't something Jacqui would usually do. Jacqui laughed to lighten the seriousness of what she had just said, but she hoped Georgia took the cue to apologise. 'I'm Jacqui, I'm Adeline's younger sister, and Georgia's filter.' She laughed again and Tilly laughed also, as she thought this was quite clever how she pulled Georgia up on her ignorance by making a joke about the situation.

I like this girl, Jacqui, thought Tilly. *She's a good one.*

Tilly was by nature an excellent judge of character, simply from being around people, a lot, many people. She got to meet and interact with various people from different cultures and countries, including celebrities who thought the world owed them a living at a click of their fingers, others who were down to earth and extremely talented, just trying to get away from the fame and fortune of celebrity life; then there were the minority who were escaping their celebrity world lost in a mirage of drugs and dependencies. Some just wanted to play their music and have fun. People came in all shapes and sizes, that was for sure. Along with the musicians, she had met all kinds of locals, the ones who had been born and bred in Angourie, the mad surfers and artists and creative geniuses, the ones who had moved from the hustling, bustling cities to escape the madness, the ones who came to Angourie to retire, the young wealthy investors who saw the potential of the town, and then there were the few lonely souls who came to the bar to drink away their sorrows at the end of each day. Those were usually the ones who had lost love, destroyed love or were still looking for love. Tilly had certainly met all walks of life. She was quick to figure out people. With this thought in her mind, she drifted back to thinking about Dalton and wondered how she had gone so wrong and how she had allowed him to get away without even giving him a chance to explain himself or what he was about to say. Tilly felt so stupid. She was usually so strong, confident, and knowing, but this time, she had completely stuffed up. Dalton was gone.

Georgia apologised to Tilly, taking Jacqui's cue. 'I'm sorry, that was very rude of me. I'm sure there is a perfectly good reason your brother didn't have a car.'

Tilly accepted the apology with a brief, 'That's okay,' as she recollected that the only time Frankie didn't have a car, from when he bought his own baby poo yellow Fiat 128 Sports Coupe at age 17, was when Eddie and Louis had borrowed it to take a drive to Sydney for the State Basketball Finals. Frankie must have used that loophole of a white lie in conversation to steer Georgia away from liking him too much. She wasn't Frankie's kind of girl, just a smidge too materialistic, and Frankie would have smelt that from a mile away. That is what Tilly had worked out in this brief interaction so far.

Tilly was happy to let Georgia think whatever she wanted to think about Frankie, knowing that it wasn't anywhere near the truth. It didn't matter. Tilly was grateful for the lift, and keeping the peace was more important just now. There was no way Tilly wanted to try to explain that Frankie had lied to Georgia because she was downright rude, and Frankie would have seen right through her.

Georgia, Adeline, Jacqui, and Tilly chatted around and around in various conversation topics, in that rank order of dominance of the conversation, as they continued the drive north to Byron Bay. Georgia seemed to know everything about everything. She seemed to know more than Jacqui about calf wrangling because she had been to a rodeo or two and dated a few outback cowboys, although Jacqui had spent a year mustering and working a farm over in the west, in The Kimberleys, the year after she graduated from high school. Georgia had probably never worn a pair of Blundstone boots in her life. She was much more comfortable in a pair of stilettos or platform wedge heels, but oh! she knew everything. She knew more than Adeline about history and the arts because she had travelled to many countries and did a lot of cultural tours, and she also dated her fair share of soldiers, although Adeline had spent four years studying the Arts with a High Distinction record and a major in Modern History and Society.

Adeline and Jacqui were close sisters, so they complimented each other in sharing stories of wild and crazy moments of their lives, amongst the studious days when they both spent years at university gaining their tertiary qualifications. Tilly felt quite insignificant, having completed a modest teaching degree but finding the passion of her life in playing music and entertaining guests at the family-owned Angourie Local. Tilly sat quietly, taking it all in. It was quite unlike her. She was usually the outgoing, talkative type swooning amongst the guests at The Angourie local, but today she was happy to sit quietly and listen and observe stories of these three young women, who she figured were just a few years older than her. Tilly realised quickly that she had lived quite a sheltered life, however, she was contently grateful of the close family connection she had with her parents and her brothers. This thought made her feel instantly nostalgic, and she had a moment of thought. *What am I doing, leaving my beautiful family?* Nothing was going to stop her from finding Dalton.

Adeline was driving, so she didn't partake, but the other girls shared the six-pack of cold beer from the esky behind the driver's seat. They had all agreed that beer in a can wasn't usually the preferred choice of beverage, but it was much easier to consume as a *roadie* than swigging from a bottle of wine or, heavens above, trying to sip on some bubbly champagne.

As Tilly twisted her arm to swig on her beer, she realised that the intense pain was back in her right wrist, since she had fallen over at the beach yesterday morning. She had paid little attention to it since that moment, but again it was sending a throbbing burn up her arm and her arm felt distinctly heavy. Tilly had broken the same wrist badly when she was on a Year Seven school excursion in Coffs Harbour. It turned out roller-skating wasn't quite her thing. She decided, after that day, that surfing crazy Angourie waves with her brothers was a much safer sport. The break required a few pins to join it all back together. Lucky for Tilly, the surgery went well, and it healed perfectly. She had no issues with it, even in all the years of rough and tumble with her brothers and surfing in rough waters. The injury never affected her ability to strum the guitar or move her hands up and down the keyboard. She was a lucky girl.

As Tilly finally found herself in a quiet moment, sitting still in the back, behind the passenger seat, she realised she had perhaps broken her wrist again. She said to Adeline as the driver, 'Hey Adeline, I don't mean to interrupt your stories, but do you know if there is a local hospital anywhere nearby, where we are heading, that I can get my wrist looked over? I think it may be broken. It's a long story and I will spare you the details, but I was running on the beach, and I fell over in the hard sand.' Tilly spared no more details about Dalton, or the message in the bottle that she had tucked safely in her bag. The girls knew Tilly was getting away from something, but they did not know the reason she was leaving Angourie or that she might have a broken wrist.

Jacqui offered that she knew that there were hospitals in Lismore, Murwillumbah and further north in Brisbane or the Gold Coast, which was another few hours north, but there was nothing around here. Byron Bay was very much a chilled-out-surfers-artist-paradise-hangout where the locals were often known to be '*higher*' than the lighthouse lookout that pillared the coastal town. Jacqui suggested Tilly could catch a train from the Byron Bay train station. She didn't know how regular the trains were and how reliable they were, only that there was a train line, and she only knew that because she frequented the Railway Hotel whenever they made a trip into Byron. She had met a guy once who was from Queensland and she remembered vaguely that he said something about coming to Byron Bay via bus and rail.

Catching a train from Byron. It was worth a try, thought Tilly. She considered that she *could* put up with the pain for a while longer and spend some more time with these girls, that she had just met, however she also knew that she needed to get her arm looked at, if she wanted to spend the next few weeks, months, however long it would take to find Dalton, doing some gigs to earn a living. Having a good, strong strum-arm was kind of important, and besides, she didn't know how much longer she could put up with Georgia's overt flamboyance, arrogance, and criticisms. She had never met anyone quite like her. It didn't even matter that she was as stunningly gorgeous as she was; she was quite unlikeable.

chapter thirty-three

Girls Just Wanna Have Fun!

Adeline and Jacqui had been to Byron Bay frequently for fun getaway weekends with friends or just with each other. They always had a good time and would, on most occasions, hook up with some random men for a weekend romance. They both had some good gossip stories to share. Georgia, on the other hand, had never been to Byron Bay. Tilly thought quietly to herself that it would be interesting to be a fly on the wall to watch the weekend of Georgia from Georgia, in Byron-land-of-the-hippies-Bay, transpire. Tilly was sure that it would be an eye-opening experience for Georgia, as Tilly was certain that none of the fun-loving-down-to-earth-locals would put up with her arrogant mannerisms.

Adeline took the girls on a scenic Byron Bay beach tour, passing by all the beach bays: Wategos, The Pass and Tallows, then up to the lighthouse to catch the sunset. The music on the car radio was blaring as they were having a great time checking out the local scene.

'Cool Kombi,' said Adeline, about the souped-up rusty red Kombi parked up by the beach. 'If I didn't have this cool Chevy of Dad's to drive, that would be my choice of car. You could go anywhere in that.' None of the girls heard her comment as they were all singing along to the music. 'Girls Just Wanna Have Fun' was blaring as they passed through some of the quiet beaches. Georgia sure did a good impression of Cyndi Lauper with her blonde hair blowing about and her chest pushed out for full effect as they passed crowds of people along the beaches and carparks. Jacqui and Adeline chimed in with the chorus. Tilly just watched and laughed along. She was trying to have some fun and lift her spirit, but she just couldn't get into it, no matter how hard she tried.

After they had completed a full Byron Bay beaches tour, Adeline suggested they head to the Byron Beach Hotel for dinner a little later on, but it was still early. She suggested they could check out the Railway Hotel and see if there was any chance for Tilly to get on a train to get to a hospital. Adeline parked the car as close as she could to the entrance of the Railway Hotel, where keeping an eye on the car would be possible from the outdoor beer garden, where they planned to sit. It was Daddy's car, and the order was given that the car was to be looked after; or else.

Freedom and Friendship

The hours passed as the day turned into afternoon and early evening. Travis and Dalton had surfed every decent wave of The Pass and Clarkes Beach. The sun was moving towards the mountains. Travis gave Dalton the signal to head in. Dalton was happy to follow the call, as he'd started to feel a bit like shark bait. There was something about the ocean at night that made it seem like a whole new planet. It was a fear that Dalton was trying to overcome, as it made no sense, but just being in the dark ocean and not able to see shadows beneath gave him the heebie-jeebies. He tried to convince himself that the marine life didn't care if it was day or night, if they were hungry, they were hungry, but that didn't have any positive impact either.

They headed into town to find a bite to eat. The local pub would do. Travis suggested they do good burgers and beers on a Friday night. They freshened up under the beach shower, making an effort to wash, put on some deodorant, brush their teeth, and put on some fresh clothes from their backpacks. Both were looking high class for surf bums.

Dalton was wearing his good luck jeans and a nice T-shirt. It fitted nicely over his muscular chest and after a day of sun and surf, his arms were looking masculine and strong. Dalton's curls were out in full force.

Travis had more of a relaxed-country-beach look. He had a nicely shaped beard and a good head of hair to match. His hair was a sandy colour. It was thick and a little wavy and he had it cut into a nice natural look. It wasn't short, but it wasn't long. It looked like it took no effort to style because it didn't. A perfect beach-hairdo. He wore a pair of jeans, black suede country-surfy looking boots called "Rollers", and a checked shirt with the sleeves rolled up.

For a moment, Dalton thought Travis would put on his Akubra hat, but he didn't. It was almost night-time, after all. It was obvious that he was a country boy, even without the hat. Dalton had a quiet laugh to himself and thought *man, this guy is more country than me, yet he lives on the beach.* Travis liked to make a point of difference when he did his weekend trips to Byron. He wanted people to know that he wasn't a local. He found it was more of a talking point for the ladies if he didn't look like he was from around here. It seemed to work. From the way he was talking, he often got lucky.

Dalton listened intently to his stories and humoured Travis and his shenanigans. It reminded Dalton that Travis' life was the kind of life he was living before he met Chelsea and the time in between Chelsea and Tilly when he was northbound from Ulladulla to Yamba. He had stayed in and around Sydney for quite some time, living a free life while he was healing. He was gigging and working some contracted building jobs. He had stayed there for almost a year before moving on again. He had saved up heaps of money for his onward journey, and he had not found love or any reason to stay. He had never got close enough to anyone to take any relationship to more than a one-night stand or a brief fling. This free life, however, was Travis' permanent status, or so it seemed. He was happy being wild and free, and he had no intention of having any encounters with women past one night. He had his Kombi for accommodation, and he could literally do whatever he wanted to do. Dalton had a back-of-mind envy of that permanent-single-life status that Travis was embracing. However, for Dalton, this lifestyle didn't work. He had tried it out for a while, but it always left him feeling empty. He was at a stage in his life now where he realised he was looking for someone to be his forever girl. He had found that contented feeling with Chelsea and, momentarily again, with Tilly. Other girls he had met along the way were easy to come and go, and he didn't mind. He enjoyed the come-and-go phase, and the single life was fun, but since he met Tilly, he couldn't imagine being madly in love with anyone else; she was perfect for him. If only she knew that.

The boys packed up their boards and climbed into the Kombi. Travis turned the radio on and up. It was Cyndi Lauper. The boys sang along with their deep country voices as they took one last moment to watch the waves roll onto shore.

Just as Travis was about to reverse out, a car roared past behind them, with a bunch of girls yahooing out the window. 'Sounds like someone else is having some fun this weekend, too.' *Girls just wanna have fun,* blaring out of the speakers.

'Let's go eat. I could eat a horse,' announced Dalton.

Travis laughed and replied, referring to the idiom that Dalton had made. 'Who says that, other than a country boy from Deniliquin? I could eat a horse?'

Dalton replied, 'You can take the boy out of the country, but you can't take the country out of the boy.' They both laughed again.

They found a park in the Main Beach carpark, just near the local top pub. It was a place where Travis could park his car for the night, and he could wake up with ocean views. They could have a few drinks, and Travis wouldn't have to drive anywhere. That is, if Dalton wanted to share the Kombi with Travis and if Travis didn't kick him out, if he found better company. Dalton wasn't too worried, there was a camping ground with cheap cabins right across the road, or there was always the backpackers' accommodation further down in the main street, or even better, the local pub had some cheap overnight rooms available.

Dalton had a bit of a think and opted for the pub accommodation. He grabbed his backpack, guitar and his surfboard and decided he would leave Travis to do his thing for the night. They would still enjoy dinner company together and then part ways for the night.

Travis and Dalton were enjoying each other's company, but Dalton was very aware not to invade Travis' free space. They could still hang out together, but both regained their independence. Dalton was extremely grateful for Travis giving him a ride, and his journey from now on would be richer for having met Travis.

They walked across the road to the pub. Dalton left his gear just to the side of the entrance, inside the main door. The publican didn't mind and suggested he leave it there out of the way while they ordered a cold beer at the bar. Dalton insisted he was buying the first round; it was the least he could do to thank Travis for his company today.

The beer tasted good, and it was thirst quenching after a day in the hot sun, surfing. Dalton's thoughts drifted again to Tilly and the important qualities she liked to acknowledge in her cheers. He thought about his cheers with Travis. If there was one thing Travis had taught Dalton, it was that it was important to have 'freedom.' The 'friendship' fitted in right here, too.

Dalton raised his glass to Travis. 'Mate, this won't make any sense to you, but here's cheers to freedom and friendship.'

'I'll go with that!' agreed Travis, it sounds good, 'To freedom and friendship.'

Dalton and Travis enjoyed their beer together, sharing yarns about their day of surfing. They talked about their favourite waves, their preferred location of the two breaks they surfed, the beautiful pod of dolphins that they surfed with, and the wipe-out Travis had taken whilst trying to be a big showoff.

As they finished their first beer together, Dalton interrupted the conversation. 'So, mate, I've decided, and thanks for the offer, but I will not cramp your style tonight, I've organised a room here in the pub, I'll go now and check in and dump my stuff in the room. That way, I know it's safe and out of the doorway. I'll be back. I won't be long. Promise me you won't leave town without having another beer with me tonight.' Dalton ensured Travis understood there were no hard feelings, and he was grateful for the offer to share the Kombi if needed, but he was happy to give Travis his independence back, too.

Travis replied as he took another long sip to finish his beer, 'I'll be right here, mate. I'll see you when you get yourself sorted, man.'

Travis went to the bar to order another beer, only to find that Dalton had already paid for it for him, and the bartender had poured it for him as he walked to the bar.

'This is for you, mate, from your buddy.' The bartender handed Travis a cold beer.

'Thanks, mate, he's a legend.' Travis sat back down at the same table he and Dalton had claimed, overlooking the park and the beach across the road, happy to relax and people-watch for a while. There was nowhere else he needed to be right now.

chapter thirty-five

The Railway Hotel

The girls tucked away all their belongings into the boot of the car, and two by two they walked into the hotel, heading straight towards the bar. Georgia and Adeline walked ahead, Georgia commenting that this place was 'quite nice considering it was beside a railway line,' and shortly after commenting loudly, 'I wonder, though, why would someone build a hotel beside a railway line?' Adeline replied that 'it probably made sense for all the railway workers to have a place to stay when they were working far away from home, and it made sense that they would probably enjoy a cold beer after a hard day's work on the railway line.' Adeline was thinking to herself that Georgia probably didn't know what it was like to work a day of hard labour. She was pretty sure that Georgia had already made an impression on anyone who had heard their conversation that this opinionated young lady wasn't from around here.

Jacqui and Tilly were following close behind, caught up in conversation about what Tilly should do about her wrist. There was not an eye within Cooee that wasn't fixated on the four girls walking into the bar. All four girls were attractive, and other than Tilly, who was dressed casually in a pair of light denim jeans and a T-shirt, the three girls had made an effort to dress in a style that screamed '*hey, look at us, we're here for some fun tonight.*'

Georgia announced to the bartender that she would like a bottle of their finest champagne and four *chilled* glasses.

'You have to admit,' said Jacqui out the side of her mouth to Tilly, 'this girl sure has style.'

'And she sure knows how to get everyone's attention,' replied Tilly, with the same discreet whisper.

Georgia placed a wad of cash on the bar and said, 'This should fix the bill for a few rounds, and keep the change for yourself, you cutie!'

The bartender went bright red from the bottom of his cheeks to his forehead. He was a young chap, probably just 18, and it was more than likely to be his first bar job. He looked nervous and was possibly a traveller from England passing through. His fair skin was not yet blessed by the Byron Bay sunshine.

'We'll find a place in the beer garden, thank you, cutie!' Georgia added as she signalled to the girls to follow her, flashing a flirtatious smile to the bartender.

Georgia wasn't waiting around for the bartender to prepare the drinks; it was expected that he would leave his post in the bar and bring the drinks over to the girls. Georgia walked off with a toss of her head and expected the girls to follow her, which they did, while Tilly felt a flood of arrogance by association wash over her. She wanted to wait at the bar until the ice bucket and champagne were placed on the counter for her to collect. Tilly hesitated to follow Georgia, and the bartender felt her awkwardness.

'It's okay, I'll bring the drinks over,' assured the young barman, as he gave Tilly the nod of approval to follow the leader of the pack. The girls followed Georgia to a nice table in the beer garden.

A small stage was set up for a live performance, which excited Tilly immensely. She loved to be entertained by any live music performance, even if it wasn't amazing talent. She appreciated the music connection and the passion from whomever was performing. Music was part of her soul.

It was early in the evening and the sun was just going down as the girls settled into their first bottle of champagne for the night. As Tilly felt a shooting pain dart through her wrist as she twisted her glass to her mouth, she hadn't forgotten that the reason they had come to the Railway Hotel was for her to find out if she could make her way somehow to the most convenient hospital.

Tilly excused herself from the table and wandered back to the bar. The young barman was the only staff member on duty, and she wondered if being so shy and young, and cute, that he might not even have the information she needed. Tilly had a few drinks under her belt, and she knew how to work a room. Although Georgia was confident and loud and look at me, without even needing to be anything other than herself, Tilly had her own attractive appeal going on, and she had the room watching her every move.

'Hey barman, sorry to call you that, but I didn't catch your name. I'm sorry that this might be a tricky question, but I need to get to a hospital. I heard I could catch a train from here, is that right?' stumbled Tilly. She was trying to ask her question with limited details she wanted to share and not share at the same time. It might have seemed quite dramatic that she needed a hospital, and she didn't want to be dramatic at all.

The barman was very helpful and replied with, 'I think there is a timetable on the noticeboard over there,' as he pointed near the exit, 'and I think from memory the evening train comes at around 6 pm, which is soon. Do you have a ticket?'

'I don't have a ticket. No, how do I do that?' questioned Tilly with some urgency, looking at the time and realising it was almost 6 pm. She needed to get her backpack and guitar from Adeline's car, and she needed to say her farewells to the girls. She also needed to decide if this was what she wanted to do. The decision she was making was to either jump on a train bound for the hospital or hang out here in Byron Bay with her new friends for the weekend. In the back of her mind was sitting the possibility that Dalton might be here in Byron Bay. The other, more likely, possibility was that he had made his way to the Gold Coast, where he would have heaps of opportunities to surf and gig and stay for a while. That was Tilly's plan too, other than finding Dalton. Tilly had never been to the Gold Coast. Murwillumbah was apparently on the way, although she had never heard of it. What she really needed was a hospital to cast her broken arm. And soon.

The bartender replied with an additional thought. 'Hmm. There is an excellent hospital in Lismore, which is on this train line too. You need to decide which one you want to go to.'

Tilly had a quick think and decided that the hospital option was the best plan, as tempted as she was to stay the night and party with her new friends.

Tilly went back to the table where the girls were sitting. They had drawn a bit of a crowd of "friends." A few gentlemen had joined the table, and the girls were laughing and chatting freely to them. Tilly was tempted, for a moment, to stay with the girls and see where the night ended up, but she also knew that it was really important that she got her arm checked out by a doctor. Tilly also reminded herself that she wasn't here for a good time, she was searching for Dalton. In the past, Tilly had always moved on from broken relationships by quickly finding a replacement body, heart, personality, whatever it was she was looking for. It was different this time. She didn't want the relationship with Dalton to be broken, and it was her fault, so she had to be the one to go out and find him and make amends.

'Hey ladies, I just wanted to let you know I'm about to jump on the train and get myself to a hospital. I think I'm headed to Lismore on the next train.' She didn't spare any other details, as she didn't have time, and the girls were all busy chatting with their new friends. 'I'll need to grab my backpack and my guitar from the car if that's okay, Adeline, but before I go, let's have a *cheer* to celebrate today.' Tilly held up her champagne glass to the middle of the table and placed her glass upwards in the air. 'To freedom and friendship' was all that she could put together for these girls. There was not enough love, yet, to celebrate between them in this new cheers custom that Dalton and Tilly had created with each other.

'I like that,' smiled Jacqui. She replied, clinking her glass with Tilly. 'To freedom and friendship.'

'Cheers, Tilly,' joined Adeline.

'To a fantastic night ahead,' added Georgia. 'Are you sure you won't stay and party with us, girl?' questioned and encouraged Georgia.

'I'd really love to, but I need to get my arm looked at. It's quite painful. I'm sure we will cross paths again some other time.' Tilly was convinced that her plan was what she needed to do.

'How will we find you again, Tilly?' questioned Jacqui.

'Good question,' replied Tilly. 'I guess the only way to keep in touch is through my parents and family at The Angourie Local. They are the only ones who will know where I have been and where I am possibly headed. All I can tell you now is that starting with getting my wrist fixed up, I have my guitar and my backpack, and I will be travelling. Who knows where I'll end up? I'm on a bit of a mission.'

The band had started up in the corner, and the guitarist strummed a familiar riff as the drummer tapped lightly in time. The singer leaned into the microphone with her soft, husky voice and sang the words, *'I have climbed the highest mountains, I have run through the fields, only to be with you, only to be with you.'* This was one of Tilly's favourite-ever U2 songs.

Tilly tuned into the lyrics, thinking, *is that a sign or what?* She would do anything to find Dalton, and that was her plan. She politely asked Adeline for the keys and headed out to the car to get her stuff, as she sang along. *But I still haven't found what I'm looking for........*

chapter thirty-six

Matty, Joel and Axl

As Tilly left the table, one gentleman commented. 'Well, she didn't stick around long, did she? Didn't even introduce herself or want to know who we were. A little rude, but she seems in a rush, so fair enough, what's her story?'

Jacqui waited to see if the other girls were going to answer. Neither of them did, so she explained what she knew about Tilly. 'We picked her up on the highway today, just down south at the Yamba turnoff. She was hitching a ride and said she was on a little getaway or something. She has her guitar and a backpack, and she didn't tell us much other than that she is getting away from The Angourie Local for a while. Her family owns the restaurant down there. I may be wrong, but from some of the things she was saying, I think she's searching for "*the one that got away.*" Apparently, she fell while she was jogging on the beach and hurt her wrist. She was a little secretive about the whole thing, but I don't know her, so I didn't ask. She's on a mission to get to the Lismore hospital to get her arm looked at so she can play her guitar again.'

'Well, she's a good-lookin' sort, lucky guy whoever she's chasin',' said the tall, long-haired lad. He was as Byron as they come, with a tie-died shirt and loose cotton pants. His hair was dreaded halfway down his back, and he smelt like Nag-Champa and tea-tree oil. After complimenting Tilly, he complimented the three girls at the table, too. 'You're all good sorts, just sayin',' as he took a sip of his Bacardi and coke and laughed, nodding his head to the beat of the U2 song playing in the background.

Adeline lifted her drink for a cheer with Matty. Not Matt, not Matthew, as he'd introduced himself earlier.

Georgia was deep in conversation with the other tall, dark-haired friend called Joel. He looked like he had just got out of the surf, with his messy beach-styled hair. Not quite dreaded, it was curly and untamed, but not in dreadlocks.

Jacqui was chatting with another lad who seemed a little older than the other two. He was very tall, about six foot four, with a sun-kissed complexion. His skin looked smooth under his loose tank top, with his Aries ram tattoo out for show on his left deltoid. Jacqui noticed two other things about him that interested her. His blue eyes were bloodshot, either from a long day in the surf, or the cigarette he was holding onto wasn't just tobacco. Jacqui could smell marijuana, but this was just normal for Byron. Jacqui's mind started wandering as she thought she wouldn't mind having a joint. This wasn't something she did often, so a smoke now and then with a stranger in Byron was always fun. Jacqui also noticed that this tall, bald guy had big hands and wondered what else might match if his body was in good proportion. He claimed to be a better surfer than the other two put-together, and although he didn't have charming looks; he had a charismatic and extremely charming personality with a Clint Eastwood smile. His name was Axl. He claimed he couldn't grow his mane like Matty and Joel, the other two lads, and he wasn't as controversial as Axl from Guns n Roses, but he could perform a good karaoke version of *Sweet Child O Mine.* Jacqui liked his sense of humour. He seemed to know that he was the black sheep of these three lads, but he was used to it, and used his charm and charisma to make up for what he lacked in dreadlocks and curls.

Tilly came back to the table to return the keys to Adeline. She had her backpack over her shoulders, looking ready for an adventure. Her guitar was, in its hard case, draped over her left shoulder. She said her farewells and gave the three girls a warm hug each. With a little help from the barman, she had scribbled "Tilly" and the phone number of her parents' house onto the back of a Railway Hotel coaster, times three. She pulled the coasters out of her back pocket and handed them out to the girls. Axl commented, 'Where is mine?' He laughed with the sentiment of friendliness like he had known Tilly forever, and she had seriously hurt his feelings. Of course, he was only joking, and Tilly laughed too.

They heard the squeal of train wheels on the track and a loud whistle as the train pulled into the station just outside the Railway Hotel. 'I must go, the train is here. I hope you all have a fantastic night and I'll see you sometime. Thanks so much for the lift, Adeline.'

'All the best Tilly, see ya!' There was a range of waves and bye's and see ya's and nods and cheers, as they all farewelled Tilly as she moved away from the table. Tilly ran to get onto the platform and handed her ticket to the conductor as she boarded the train.

Joel made a comment, but no one really acknowledged it. Everyone was busy chatting over the top of the music. 'I think that might be the Murwillumbah train. I hope your friend knows where she is going.'

The three girls enjoyed the evening chatting with their three new friends as they listened to the live music and consumed another bottle of the finest champagne between them all.

The next song that the band played was *Paint It Black* by The Rolling Stones, another classic. They all sang along and drifted with the vibe of the afternoon.

As time ticked on, the girls realised they needed to get going if they wanted to get to the Byron Bay Beach Hotel for dinner. They were enjoying the company of these three lads, but it was the fantastic burgers that Jacqui and Adeline had promised Georgia that instigated the move.

The girls politely invited the lads to join them, but they were quite settled in for the night. They were mates of the band members and promised they would support the gig for the night. It was also just a short stroll home after a few drinks, so that was their plan. The Railway Hotel was their local.

As Georgia announced they were leaving, Matty suggested, as more of a question, that if the Byron Beach Hotel wasn't pumping, they might see them back here later? He added the band was kicking on until about 11 pm.

'No worries. We might do that,' said Adeline.

'Nice to meet you Matty, Joel and Axl,' said Jacqui.

'Thanks for the fun, y'all,' said Georgia.

chapter thirty-seven

House Rules

Travis ordered another round for Dalton and their new friend, Myles, who had joined their table. He had wandered into the beer garden area of the Beach Hotel for a drink after an epic day of surfing, hoping to find some new friends to chat with. Myles was new to Byron. He had recently moved up from Sydney, a banker who had enough of suits and ties and formality. He had heard that Byron was the place to let it all hang out. Myles had only been in Byron for a few weeks. He had been sharing himself around, renting rooms in various pubs and backpackers, just to make sure this was the place he wanted to settle into for a while. He had seen Travis and Dalton at The Pass earlier and thought he might strike up a conversation to hang with some new friends.

There was a band playing some classic acoustic rock, getting everyone in the mood for some Friday night fun. The Beach Hotel in Byron was the place to be. Most of the other pubs had a midnight license, but the Beach Hotel was the one place in Byron that kicked on until the wee hours of the morning. This was a bit of an inconvenience for anyone staying at the pub overnight. They had no choice other than to party on, which is what Myles had done tonight. He had booked his room and dumped his bag, and he was starting his night with a round of drinks with Travis and Dalton.

Dalton had booked a room also, and Travis was content with staying in his Kombi, so none of the boys had any worries about counting their drinks. They were free to party.

Dalton had enjoyed a great day with Travis, although he still had Tilly on his mind. There was not much he could do about the whole situation. He contemplated sharing his story with his new friends but didn't see the point of dampening the vibe.

As Travis came back to the table, he was excited to mention that three good-looking sorts had wandered into the bar. They had headed out to the pool table area with their drinks. Travis suggested that Dalton and Myles join him and perhaps have a game of pool. Dalton and Myles had no reason to argue, so they followed Travis out to the pool table bar. Travis had already set his sights on a freestanding and empty high table and crossed the room with a confident swagger, with Dalton and Myles following behind. Myles and Dalton were in a conversation about how good the music was, and neither was too concerned about these 'good-looking sorts' until they got into the pool bar area and realised exactly what Travis was talking about. It wasn't every day you saw girls like this. Perhaps they had their beer goggles on, or perhaps it was their lucky night. These three stunning-looking ladies were beaming a vibe of good energy, and they were all easy on the eye.

Myles was instantly drawn to the tall blonde, who had a massive wide smile and a cheeky laugh. Georgia was rummaging through her handbag to find some coins to slot into the table. She was having a joke with Adeline, saying that she wasn't sure what she might find in the depths of her handbag, and then when she looked up, she saw the three boys heading over towards the spare table. She pulled out a handful of coins and lined them up on the table.

'Who's in for a game of doubles?' Georgia queried the room, which was currently filled with a few old blokes having a chinwag in the corner, quietly drinking their beer. They didn't look terribly keen for a game just yet, but Georgia was certain that either, or both, were pool sharks, just hanging to watch and wait to enjoy a night of free pool. The general pub rules were that if you were winning, whoever challenged you paid for the next game. If you were a shark, you could end up with a very cheap, entertaining night.

There was another young couple on a lounge seat in the corner. They were too wrapped up in each other to worry about anyone else in the room. Then, there were two older, attractive women at another high table. They looked like they were two great friends solving the world's problems, deep in conversation with each other and not interested, now, in a game of pool.

Then, of course, there was Georgia, Adeline and Jacqui and the three boys Dalton, Travis and Myles.

Georgia had already analysed the room and was confident these three boys would join in a pool game and have some fun.

Myles was the first to respond with a cheeky line. 'If you are my partner, pretty girl, I'll play.'

Georgia responded with, 'Why the hell not, and thank you, that's an offer I won't refuse,' as she did her best head throwback laugh and her best southern drawl accented 'refuuuuuse.'

Adeline joined in, 'Which one of you boys wants to join forces with me and take these two flirts down?'

Dalton kept quiet, as he wasn't particularly feeling like being a big flirt tonight. He had saved all of those moves up for Tilly, and he was feeling the effects of where that landed him right now, and it wasn't good.

Travis looked at Dalton, and Dalton gave him the nod. 'It's cool, man, you play. I'm rusty with my pool skills, anyway. It's been a while.' This was a bit of a half-truth. In all the years Dalton spent playing gigs in bars until late at night, he would often be the last man standing. In country pubs, the stayers, towards the end of the night, always ended up at the pool table. Dalton had some pretty good pool skills, but it had been a while since he played. He recalled that the last time he played was in his local pub in Deniliquin, the night he met Chelsea.

Dalton pushed his dark thoughts into the back of his mind and decided he would enjoy his night here in Byron Bay. He went to the bar to get another round of beers for the boys, acknowledging that the girls had already had their drinks sorted.

The pool table was nice. It was mahogany wood with beautifully thick carved legs, and maroon felt. Most of the pool tables you'd see at pubs were the standard green or blue small-size tables. This table was oversized and very well looked after. Georgia pushed the coins into the table, and the pool balls all came rolling out with a loud, tumbling rumble into the end cavity of the pool table.

Travis found two decent cues for them to play with. They still had complete pool cue tips, and they were relatively straight. They just needed a bit of chalk on the tips, and they were good to go. Travis liked a heavier cue, so he chalked it up and passed his preferred selection to Adeline, his playing partner, and he passed the lightweight cue to Georgia and questioned, with a hint of double-meaning flirtatiousness, 'Who wants to break tonight?'

Georgia replied, 'I think Myles should break. Show us your skills, city boy.' In the brief conversation that Georgia and Myles had shared, she had worked out that he wasn't from around here and had come up from the big city, Sydney. Georgia liked that about Myles. She believed that the city boys were more materialistic than the country boys or the surfer types. She wasn't shy about announcing that she had expensive taste and only the best of everything was good enough for her.

Myles swaggered over and positioned himself in the centre of the table. He rested his left hand on the table to make a bridge to position the cue, and then he gave the white ball a powerful push into the triangle of coloured balls. None of the balls went into the pockets, but it was certainly a good, strong break. The balls were spread evenly across the table. 'So, I have a question for you, *Miss America*.' Myles had already worked out in their brief conversation that Georgia was from Georgia in the USA. 'What do you call the balls? We call them *bigs* and *smalls* here in *Australia*.' He said *Australia* with a strong Aussie accent.

'We call them solids and stripes,' replied Georgia so matter-of-factly, in a way that suggested as if you would call them anything else.

'Ok, so let's go with that tonight, solids and stripes,' suggested Myles as he moved closer to Georgia and handed her the pool cue as she was taking the next shot for their team.

Travis leaned over and started with an easy shot on a set-up stripe. 'I like the big ones,' he said as he pushed the green number nine into the corner pocket. Travis worked his way around the table, sinking a couple of easier stripes. He couldn't quite get the red eleven in, so he decided he would do a nice setup for Adeline and place it just near the middle pocket for her next shot. Then he passed the cue onto Adeline, giving her a sneaky little, non-threatening kiss as he did. 'Good luck, partner, we've got this, a good start anyway.'

Adeline didn't refuse the kiss. It was gentle. Travis was quite an easy, non-threatening kind of guy to take a random kiss from. Adeline had no problem with it at all; in fact, she liked his confidence, and his soft lips felt nice on hers. He smelt good too. There was a refreshing aftershave scent left lingering around her as he moved to her side to watch Georgia take her shot.

The boys were impressed with their teammates. Georgia knew what she was doing with a pool cue, and Myles was quite excited by that. This was going to be a fun night. Adeline took her turn next and sunk three balls in a row. Travis had set up the first one for her, and she followed on with a few nice clean shots into the corner pockets.

As the game continued, the banter and acceptable level of sexual innuendo continued. They were all enjoying each other's company, and the flirt was innocent and fun. The two older lads in the corner decided they wanted to play and give these young punks a run for their money. It was Tank who introduced himself first and put a coin on the table. 'Hey, my name's Thomas, but you can call me Tank. Me and my mate Robbo over here challenge the winner for the next game. Cool?'

'Cool,' replied Travis, 'you want to play, you pay. That's the *house rules*, I believe.'

Travis and Adeline were victorious in the first game by quite a margin. Myles and Georgia had sunk only three balls between them. They were too busy trying too hard to impress each other with their cool moves. It was quite entertaining to watch, though. They were quite a match for each other, both loud and extroverted, and having a lot of fun together.

Dalton and Jacqui were happily chatting together at the table and quite entertained by the whole sideshow that was going on at the pool table. There was laughter and jokes and flirting and some seriously good pool skills being performed. Dalton was excited to have a game later and test out his repertoire of skills, or lack thereof, as it had been quite some time; however, he was enjoying his night and was quite content to sit and wait like a true pool shark. There seemed to be quite a lot of sharks in the room tonight, with Travis and Myles obviously having some decent pool skills. Tank and Robbo were yet to step up, and Dalton quietly knew he could sink a ball or two or eight if he focused on what he was doing.

Tank plugged his coins into the table, and the balls came rumbling down again. 'Let's go.' Extremely confident in their skills, Robbo placed a row of coins on the table, knowing the next couple of games would end quickly.

'We challenge you to a best of three.' Robbo lifted his chin with an air of confidence. 'I'll leave these coins here for the next couple of games, huh?'

'Mugs away!' said Travis to Tank as Tank and Robbo stepped up to the table, finding themselves a cue on the rack.

"Mugs away!" was a common term for "Losers to start!" Although technically Tank and Robbo hadn't played yet, and they were not losers yet, Travis and Adeline were the current winners on the table. That's how it worked; these were the *house rules.*

The pub band had resumed their positions on the stage to play their third music set for the night, and they kicked it off with 'Listen to The Music' by the Doobie Brothers and then Fleetwood Mac's 'Dreams.' It was uncanny how similar the singer sounded to Stevie Nicks. She made a good impression, that was for sure. For a moment, Dalton thought Stevie was here. It wouldn't be impossible, as he knew that Fleetwood Mac had travelled to Angourie various times for gigs at The Angourie Local. Byron Bay was just a short distance to travel, but the anonymity of their visit would not exist here. A few of the locals got up to drift and sway to the music, all expressing their peaceful minds and flowing vibes of freedom. Of course, Dalton's mind was jolted back to the gypsy room and visions of Tilly. He tuned into the lyrics, '*Now here you go again, you say you want your freedom, well who am I to keep you down? It's only right that you should play the way you feel, but listen carefully to the sound of your loneliness. Like a heartbeat, drives you mad, in the stillness of remembering what you had, and what you lost, and what you had and what you lost.'* Dalton had to snap himself back to his conversation with Jacqui, as she was saying to him, 'Dalton.... Dalton.... do you want to challenge these old fellas with me, and we can win the table back?'

Dalton replied, 'sure, sounds good.'

Jacqui reached into her pocket to find a coin, but all she could find was the coaster from the Railway Hotel, with Tilly's name scribbled on it, and The Angourie Local phone number. She pulled it out and placed it on the table for a moment as she emptied all her pockets to find coins. The coaster lay rested on the table with Tilly's name and number facing upwards. 'I better not lose that,' she said as she picked it up and placed it back in her pocket.

Dalton didn't notice the exact words or numbers on the card. All he noticed was that it was a scribbled word and a phone number.

'Collecting numbers tonight, are we, Jacq? I should be so lucky that you are here playing pool with me,' softened Dalton.

'It's not what you think, Dalton. It's actually a girl... friend, if you really must know.' Jacqui replied defensively, making sure Dalton understood she was not collecting numbers as he assumed.

'It's all good, Jacq. You're a free woman; you don't need to explain anything to me. Let's get this game underway.' Dalton eased Jacqui's unnecessary need to explain as he reached into his jeans pocket and pulled out two one-dollar coins.

Tank and Robbo had defeated Travis and Adeline in three extremely challenging games, but not by much, so Dalton and Jacqui had a challenge on their hands to win back the table. Jacqui grabbed some chalk to dust up her cue as she caught a glimpse of Myles and Georgia, with their mouths interlocked in a cheeky kiss over at the high bar table. They were getting along well and had been flirting hard-core during the pool games, Georgia pretending she needed Myles' help to steady her cue while she did her best to shoot a combo. They were a pretty good match, both with their high-class arrogance and extroverted confidence. *Each to their own,* she thought.

Travis and Adeline were also getting along well.

It's funny how the night had worked out. The girls had a fun time at the Railway Hotel, and the boys they had met there were fun, too. Matty, Joel, and Axl would have been keen to hang out with the girls a little longer, but Adeline had promised Georgia she would take her up to The Beach Hotel. Adeline wanted to relax and enjoy the night as well, so being the designated driver, she wanted to get to The Beach Hotel and park her car up for the night, where it was secure and enjoy a few drinks with the girls. Matty, Joel and Axl were welcome to join them, but the boys had been drinking all afternoon and had no transport to get them up to The Beach Hotel, so the girls said their farewells, and they parted ways.

These three new friends were fun as well. Jacqui was still trying to work out how they all knew each other, and she hadn't pieced it together yet, and she hadn't asked yet either, but she was happy to go with the flow of the night. What she could work out was that Travis and Dalton had both been surfing for the day, and Myles had joined them for a random drink after meeting them in the surf, but she couldn't work out where any of them were from or how they had met.

Jacqui was happy chatting with Dalton, and he was quiet but engaging all the same. He just seemed a little lost in his thoughts, and Jacqui was considering asking him if everything was okay, but right now, she was enjoying getting to know him. They had much in common with Jacqui's experience on the station mustering. She knew a bit of country stuff, and they were sharing some good stories with each other. Dalton had not shared any deep stuff about Chelsea or why he was travelling, and he had mentioned nothing about The Angourie Local and Tilly. There was no reason for him to mention it. What was Jacqui going to do about it, anyway? She was a nice girl, and Dalton enjoyed getting to know her, too.

Tank sank the black eight ball to win the game, and without a moment of hesitation, he gave a nod to Dalton and signalled, 'Mugs away, young lad. The name is Tank, and this is Robbo.' They all shook hands. 'Are you playing with her?' Tank signalled with a point of his chin and a raised eyebrow to Jacqui. Tank didn't speak to Jacqui, only to Dalton. Perhaps he was shy, or perhaps this was his generational way of being respectful to women. Jacqui was beautiful, and Dalton understood how her looks could be intimidating.

'I believe I am,' replied Dalton. With a gentlemanly tone, he asked, 'Jacqui, would you like to break, or would you like me to?' Dalton was thinking, I get it now; this is what Tilly was going on about finding someone who is your equal. At this point in time, that quality of 'equalness' would have made the situation much more comfortable for Tank to feel equal to Jacqui and be able to speak with her without feeling intimidated by her. The way he spoke only to Dalton showed a lack of respect for Dalton's generation, but that wasn't Tank's intention.

For his generation, he was showing respect by only talking to Dalton. Dalton didn't dwell on it; it was just a quick thought. Everyone was brought up differently, and people had their own way of communicating, depending on their upbringing. He was sure if he took the time to understand it, there would be a good reason why Tank spoke to him rather than to Jacqui.

Jacqui replied, 'You can give them a good shake-up, Dalton. Show them what you got.'

Dalton positioned himself at the head of the table, with his feet centred and balanced and his head lowered to determine the centre of the white ball. He stretched his arms out and placed his large hand on the table to provide a bridge for the pool cue to rest on. Jacqui was a little taken aback by what she was observing. She had noticed his good looks and his friendly personality, but what she hadn't noticed was that this guy was well put together. His stance was confident, not arrogant, just comfortable and sexy. Jacqui was a sucker for a good body. He wasn't giving her much of a "come on" vibe. In fact, he was quite standoffish, but he was friendly enough, and she was looking forward to having some fun playing a game of pool with him. And those hands. Jacqui had a thing for big hands.

Dalton sent the white ball into the triangle of coloured balls, creating an impact that sent them all hurtling around the table. Two "striped" balls went into the corner and middle pocket simultaneously. They were off to a good start. Next, he sunk another two balls, again into the middle pockets, and not wanting to be too much of a show-off, he set up another ball on the corner edge of the top pocket for Jacqui to sink on her next shot. He also snookered Tank, giving him no option but to strike his own ball first, giving Jacqui two shots to play her first move. Jacqui was smart. She had played a bit of pool in her time, so she went for a more difficult shot first to set up a shot for Dalton and then took her second shot to sink the easy ball that Dalton had positioned for her. She missed the next shot, but it didn't matter; they were five balls ahead of Tank and Robbo. Robbo powered in and played three good shots to even up the game a little. Then it was Dalton's turn again. Dalton finished the game off with three classic shots and not even a chance of missing. Myles stood on watching, quite in awe of the performance he had seen. It certainly didn't look like a fluke. This Dalton fella knew how to play pool. He was the Tiger Shark amongst the crowd tonight.

As Myles swaggered over to the table, he announced that he had played pool amongst many sharks in his lifetime, but he'd never seen such a performance as that. 'Dalton, I think I have a nickname for you. I'm going to call you Tiger.'

Dalton laughed out loud. 'Tiger, I like it. My last nickname was "Gypsy Boy," so I guess we are keeping in with the wandering free spirit theme.'

Jacqui explained. 'I think he means "tiger" as in "the tiger shark" Dalton. She crinkled her nose and made a scratching tiger paws signal with her hands, not Tiger like a free-spirited Tiger.

'Who says that a Tiger Shark isn't free-spirited Jacq?' Dalton laughed as he smacked Jacqui gently on the bum with his pool cue.

Myles had already placed some coins on the table and was ready for another game; this time, it was Myles and Georgia against Dalton and Jacqui.

Travis was returning from the bar with a tray full of drinks. He had bought another round of drinks for the boys and the girls, and he had shouted Tank and Robbo a beer each as well. As Travis came to deliver the drinks, he realised that the game was already over. Myles was resetting the balls on the table. 'What happened there? Did someone foul the black?'

'Nah, mate, Dalton's a friggin Tiger Shark. Took these two fellas down in two sequences with a little help from Jacqui,' winked Myles.

'Geez mate, is there anything you can't do?' humoured Travis to Dalton.

Dalton laughed as he passed the cue to Jacqui, 'I'll stack 'em, you rack 'em.

The night continued with humorous and flirtatious banter over many games of pool as the three boys and the three girls got to know each other. They were instantly drawn to their likewise better match, which could have been a social experiment worth documenting. How did they meet and feel attraction instantly to the most suited partner for each, with no discussion or introduction? It just kind of happened, and now Georgia and Myles were enjoying each other's loud and provocative personalities, both arguing over who was going to buy the next round of drinks because they both wanted to share their wealth with their new friends. Travis and Adeline were deep in a discussion about the value of vintage cars and how they took so much pride in driving a vehicle with character, so much more than these modern-day cars that all looked the same. Dalton and Jacqui were in a discussion about country people and hard work ethic, and both were heavily distracted by the band, both taking moments to join in and sing along with the music.

As the night travelled on, the discussions progressed, figuring out sleeping arrangements for the night. Myles was planning on smuggling Georgia into his Byron Beach Hotel Room for the night. Travis had already asked Adeline if she wanted to check out his Kombi later. It was Dalton and Jacqui who had made no plans, neither were making the first move. Dalton had booked his room for the night at the Beach Hotel, but he didn't plan on sharing it with anyone; however, as it worked out, Jacqui didn't have anywhere to stay other than in the car, which had no roof. She hadn't booked a room anywhere and was just going with the flow of the evening. It certainly wasn't her plan for the girls to meet up with three handsome men, but she would stay with Dalton if he offered.

chapter thirty-eight

Train to Nowhere

Tilly jumped on board the train just in time. It didn't stop at the Railway Hotel Station for long. Just long enough to drop off the travellers coming up from Sydney or Newcastle for the weekend and then loading on the few travellers and local workers heading north for the weekend. It was a Friday night, so most of the travellers were coming into Byron Bay, not leaving.

Tilly found a seat and placed her guitar and backpack in the luggage section of the carriage. All she had with her in her shoulder bag was her wallet and a book she was planning on reading. It was a novel by Paulo Coelho called The Alchemist. She had read it many years ago and felt that she needed to read it again to remind her of this adventure quest she was on. Every time she read the book she gained different meanings from it, at different stages in her life, when her personal journey was seeking something new.

She sat down and took a moment to gather her thoughts as the train pulled out of the station with a swooshing, long-sounding horn.

What a day it had been. Meeting the girls was fun, and she had really enjoyed their company, wishing she could still be there partying with them right now, but her wrist was growing ever more painful by the minute. Tilly felt bad for not leaving personal contact details, but she didn't know where she was headed, so it was no point. All she knew was that she had to get to the hospital and get her arm looked at, and then she had to find Dalton somehow. She had a feeling that he might have been headed for the Gold Coast. The only other chance would be that Dalton was in Byron if he had hitched a ride there. Being the mad keen surfer that Dalton was, Tilly would almost place a bet that if Dalton had the choice, he would have opted for next-stop-Byron, but that would mean that whoever picked him up hitch-hiking, if that was his mode of transport, and that was most likely, would have to be headed to Byron too. That was unlikely.

Tilly put a gamble on Dalton being at the Gold Coast, and that was where she was headed after the hospital stop in Murwillumbah. She would have to figure out how to get from Murwillumbah Hospital to the Gold Coast, but that was the least of her worries right now. Not that it really mattered, but she realised she had accidentally told the girls she was going to Lismore Hospital. Not intentionally, she just got confused, as she wasn't aware of these towns where she was headed.

The train was moving quickly, and Tilly was quite surprised. She hadn't travelled by train before. Her trips to Sydney were always sharing some road trip fun with her brothers or her parents. Her travels north to Ballina and south to Coffs were with school trips on a bus full of smelly teenagers. This was different. Train travel was enjoyable. It felt safe; there was no other traffic to worry about. The train was spacious; there was plenty of room to get up and walk around. It even had a bathroom carriage and a restaurant carriage.

Tilly noticed people were getting up and heading to the restaurant carriage, so she thought she might do the same. She looked around, observing the passengers on the train. There was another lady sitting across from where Tilly had placed her luggage. She looked honest enough, deeply immersed in her book, The Giver. *She's probably a daily traveller*, thought Tilly. Tilly went for a wander through the train, as she felt the train slowly picking up speed as it moved out of the station. Tilly had a brief inkling of concern for her stuff, then realised that was a silly idea. With this honest lady sitting here and the fact that they were on a fast-moving train, she quickly realised her stuff was perfectly safe. The thing she worried most about was her treasured guitar, but everyone had just left their stuff where it was and nobody seemed to worry, so she thought she would do the same. Tilly felt instinctively that her luggage was safe. I mean, what was someone going to do, run off with her guitar and jump off a moving train? Probably not. Not tonight, anyway. It seemed like quite a chilled-out, fun crowd on board the train.

A few of the guests had brought their guitars into the restaurant carriage to have a bit of a carriage jam. It was like a public carriage for socialising, whereas the other carriages were quiet. Some people were sleeping, reading, or just staring out of the window. Tilly wanted to join the fun crowd. She stepped into the restaurant carriage and could see people gathering around some people with instruments. She half thought about going back to get her guitar, to join them, but then realised there was quite a lot of talent here already. She joined in the spontaneous fun and sang along with them. They had started with a classic from Rod Stewart with the lyrics, 'W*ake up Maggie, I think I've got something to say to you.*'

Tilly went to the bar first and bought herself a West Coast Cooler and a packet of plain salted potato chips. The West Coast Cooler in a bottle seemed like the easiest thing to do rather than hold on to a glass of wine on a rattling train.

Tilly sat down and introduced herself to some of the crowd of people who had gathered in the lounge section of the carriage. *How fun!* thought Tilly. *I wish my arm wasn't so sore. I don't think I could even strum a guitar right now.* The next thing she knew, she was singing along as they played many classic songs that everyone could sing along to. They had a repertoire of Aussie classics: Mystify by INXS, What's My Scene by The Hoodoo Gurus, To Her Door by Paul Kelly, I'm Still On Your Side by Jimmy Barnes, and The Road to Nowhere by Talking Heads. Everyone was singing along to these well-known classic radio hits.

Tilly felt like these guys might be a little more than random passengers having a jam. They were a well-coordinated band, without the drums, of course. It was just two guys with guitars; the other three were singing and tapping along. One had a harmonica, and they had other shakers and rattlers that they had shared with the gathered people.

The train ride went quickly; it seemed like they had just sung a few songs, and the conductor was already announcing that the train would arrive at Murwillumbah Station in five minutes. Most of the crowd that had gathered had moved away to collect their belongings to disembark the train. Tilly stood up to go back to collect her luggage when the guitarist stopped strumming and said, 'Hey, thanks for joining us; where are you off to?'

'I'm on the *train to nowhere*,' she laughed, making the connection to the song they had just finished playing.

'Ha, ha, you've got a sense of humour too,' said the man who had been doing most of the singing.

'I'm doing my best to be funny. I'm actually stopping off at Murwillumbah to go to the hospital. Long story. Broken arm, I think.'

'Why don't you continue on the connecting bus with us to the Gold Coast? There is an excellent hospital there. We jump on a bus from Murwillumbah Station, and it gets us into the city tonight in time for an enjoyable meal somewhere. You're very welcome to join us, or do you have to go to Murwillumbah Hospital?'

'Nah, no hospital in particular. I just think I need to get it looked at. It's sore.'

'Come on, enjoy the ride.' Have you ever been to the Gold Coast?

The other people were all encouraging Tilly to stay as well.

It was tempting. Tilly did plan to get to the Gold Coast eventually, but all she could think about right now was her arm. It was throbbing in pain, and it was feeling very heavy. The fact that it felt heavy indicated to Tilly that it was broken, not just sprained. She had sprained her arm many times, but the two breaks she had before felt just like this one. Tilly thought ahead; it was already 7 pm. By the time she got her arm looked at in Murwillumbah; it was likely to be 10 or 11 pm, and then she would need to find accommodation somewhere. It was also likely that they would take an x-ray, bandage it, and say come back tomorrow. Either way, she would have to find somewhere to stay, which got her nowhere closer to the Gold Coast and where Dalton was likely to be. Murwillumbah was a small country town; most likely, everyone would be asleep by 8 pm. This was one thing Tilly loved about small country towns: the peace, quietness, and tranquillity of life, but right now, some fun with this "band," as it seemed they were, could be fun.

'Look, my name is Bernard Fanning. Our band here is called Powderfinger. We are heading back to Brisbane eventually via the Gold Coast. We feel we owe it to our local fans to do a bit of a hometown tour for our new album, and you are very welcome to come and hang out with us. Heck, you've got a magnificent voice. You can do some stage harmonies with us if you're up for that. And if you're worried about your arm, we can get you to the Gold Coast hospital tomorrow. We've booked a couple of rooms at this cool hotel where we are staying. I'm sure we can get a room sorted for you as well. It'll be my shout. I know that all sounds like I'm totally up myself, but I'm sure it also sounds like too good an offer to refuse, huh?' He was so confident and encouraging, yet so easy-going.

Tilly was a little embarrassed. She thought this guy looked familiar, and realised they were all very talented, but she didn't realise she stumbled upon a random free train gig by one of Australia's newest leading talents. These guys were from Brisbane and were just doing some national tours. She had heard of them. She liked the band's name. She had so many questions to ask ... first, why were they on this train? Tilly was a little out of the loop in her Angourie bubble in keeping up with the new Aussie music scene. Unless the songs were being played on Rage on a Saturday morning, she hadn't heard of them.

Tilly thought about Bernard's offer for a moment and made a quick decision. *Why the hell not?* 'Do I need to get another ticket for the bus, and how? This coach-rail thing is a whole new experience for me.' Tilly questioned, yet also answered his request, by the question she asked him.

'So, you're going to join us, I'm guessing? That's great! I'm sure the conductor can sort you out with an extra onward journey ticket.'

Tilly replied, 'I guess this one of those why not moments. Instead of asking yourself why, ask why not. Sure thing, I'll follow along to the Gold Coast, thanks for the invite.'

'May I introduce you to my friends? This is John, Ian, Jon, with no h, just to confuse you, and Darren.' As Bernard announced their names, Tilly smiled and shook their hands individually.

'You guys are pretty good, I must say. I play in a band with my family; we do small gigs at our local hotel in Angourie. You guys have an excellent sound. I can only imagine the full scene when you're plugged in with the acoustic and electric guitars, drum kit and the whole shebang. Can I ask you something?'

'Of course, but first, tell us your name?' Bernard replied with a cheeky grin.

'Ha! My name is Matilda Macallan, but people call me Tilly.'

'Welcome to the band, Tilly. Your question is?'

'My question is, what are you guys doing on this train? Would it not be quicker for you to fly to your next destination?'

'We are just on our way back from Sydney. We had to pick up some new gear for our tour, and we promised our mate we'd play at his pub in Byron. It was easier to take the train, and to be honest, it's much more fun for us to travel this way. We can load all our cargo in a carriage with us, and we get to enjoy the ride and meet interesting people like you.' He gestured to Tilly and glanced around the train, noticing the people moving about to collect their belongings as the train ride ended. 'We also like doing this, playing a free gig for the train passengers; it's a good way for us to get in some practice and promote our music. If we were on a plane, we wouldn't get to do this, and we would sit around in terminals for hours, waiting for connecting flights. Many of the gigs we are doing are in rural and remote areas. The only way to get there is by train or bus, anyway.' Tilly was enjoying this conversation with Bernard. He was charismatic and charming, and Tilly was a sucker for a talented musician, that was for sure.

As Tilly and Bernard were chatting, the conductor came by to check their tickets. Tilly spoke to him and he advised her she needed to book her onward bus ticket at the ticket window on the platform at the Murwillumbah train station.

As the train pulled into the station, Tilly quickly dashed to the ticket window. Fumbling in her pocket for some extra change, she accidentally dropped her sentimental guitar pick on the platform floor. She didn't notice, as she was in such a rush.

'Hey, good evening, just a one-way ticket to the Gold Coast, please.' Tilly asked politely to the lady behind the glass window. She had to speak loudly over the noise of the people on the platform and the train engine. Tilly had lost her voice a little from singing, so it was husky as she tried to speak louder.

'Well, well, well nice to see someone has manners tonight. I haven't heard a please, let alone a thank you all day.' The lady printed the ticket and placed it in an envelope. It was like she was on remote control, a busy lady indeed, but very organised and good at her job.

Tilly thought she would pay her a compliment in return. 'Well, it's easy to say please or thank you. I like your funky glasses; where did you get them from?'

'Oh, these old things. I call them my Dame Edna's. I got them from the local chemist in Murwillumbah; they've got magnification lenses, so I can see what I'm doing. I literally turned fifty and went blind overnight. Before that, I had perfect vision.'

'Really. Wow, that's crazy. I guess that's something I've got to look forward to.' Tilly replied gently and with a light sense of humour.

'Losing your voice and your sight might make things difficult.' She replied.

'Oh, yeah, I always have a bit of a husky voice, but I've been singing on the train, and I'm tired, so it's completely gone. Might need some ginger and honey. Isn't that what the famous people do?' Tilly replied, reconnecting with the lady about the glasses. 'Dame Edna would know!' They both laughed.

'Here is your ticket. You just need to wait now for the bus to arrive and then you'll be on your way to the city. Take care.' The lady passed the envelope through the window and gave Tilly a friendly smile.

Tilly followed on with the other passengers and the band as they offloaded all the gear to the bus shelter and waited for the connecting bus to arrive. Tilly had enough trouble carrying her own gear, let alone trying to help the band, but she apologised she would usually be much more helpful if not for her broken wrist.

As Tilly grabbed her gear, she said thank you to the lady, who was still quietly sitting, reading.

'Hey, I'm so sorry to interrupt. I just wanted to say thanks for looking after my gear.'

'Oh, no worries. I did nothing, just sat here reading, as I always do, but I could hear your lovely voice from the next carriage. That was you singing, was it not?'

'Yes, it was fun. What a great band. Powderfinger, have you heard of them? New Aussie talent. You should check them out sometime.'

'I keep to myself these days. I've got a few health complications and mostly a broken heart, but I appreciate some good Australian music. I'll keep an eye out for them.'

'Oh, I'm sorry to hear, I hope you're okay.' Tilly felt so much compassion for this lady; she had a beautiful, warm energy, and Tilly felt like she could talk to her for hours, even though they had only exchanged a few sentences.

'I'm okay. I spend a lot of time on the train, meeting different people, not all as lovely as you.'

'Well, thank you. I don't feel so lovely right now. I think I've got a broken wrist, I'm losing my voice, and I've probably broken someone's heart, making them feel like you do right now, and there is nothing I can do about it. I hate to think that I've caused someone heartache, and I didn't mean to. I'm just a little impatient and impulsive. My biggest flaws.'

'I don't know about that; my way of thinking is that everything works out as it should, you'll see.'

Tilly got goosebumps all over. This lady had a mystery about her. It was a good feeling, and Tilly took her advice on board. She repeated back to the lady. 'Everything works out as it should. I like that.'

The lady said her farewell as a question. 'Take care. It was nice to meet you ....?'

'Tilly, my name is Tilly; it was nice to meet you .....?' Tilly repeated her method to exchange names, thinking, that's funny. That's exactly the way Dalton and I introduced ourselves and our names to each other. Tilly kept her thoughts to herself but felt quite a sense of déjà vu with this lady. It was like they had met before.

'Lee. Just Lee.' The lady answered briefly, offering her first name only. Nothing more, just like Tilly had done.

Tilly loaded her belongings in the way she had figured out was least destructive to her arm. She placed her backpack on first, bounced it up to her hips and latched the thick band around her waist to clip together at the front. This meant the weight of her backpack was not on her shoulders but supported by her strong and muscular legs. She lifted her guitar case with her undamaged hand. She didn't have to walk too far to the bus shelter, where everyone was gathering. As she stepped off the train, she waved back with her free arm, 'See ya, Lee.'

'See ya, Tilly.'

Lee was catching the bus to the Gold Coast as well. She was a regular commuter and knowing there was still some time to wait before the bus arrived; she continued reading her book on the train as it sat motionless at the station.

She thought it was best to leave Tilly to continue with her new friends.

chapter thirty-nine

Bus Chats

Tilly felt like a school kid again, heading towards the back of the bus with the naughty kids. They had placed all of their gear underneath, so there was no opportunity for musical instrument distractions, just good old bus chats. The band and Tilly dominated the last three rows, all spreading out in a double seat each, but close enough to talk together without interrupting other people on the bus. Bernard and Tilly ended up in the back seat, both leaning back against the opposite windows and putting their feet up towards the middle of the seat and the aisle. They had all enjoyed a few drinks on the train, so the conversation was free-flowing and merry.

Tilly had brief chats with all her new Powderfinger friends, asking where they were from, and they all shared their basic life stories. Ian was interested in reading Tilly's book, which he noticed was sitting on top of her backpack at the bus station. She passed it over to him, and he got started straight away. It was an easy read, not a lengthy book, but an amazing journey entailed.

Bernard sat back and waited until the conversation had ended and Tilly had finished her conversation with the others. He could see that Tilly was trying to avoid questions about herself, so he decided it was her turn to share some more of her story. *Who was this mysterious, beautiful girl they had met randomly on this train?* Bernard started the conversation with full intent on finding out more about her. 'So Tilly, you kinda know all of us now, and we know nothing about you. What's your plan? You said you were on the train to nowhere; now you're on the road to nowhere with some random musicians. What brought you here?'

Tilly thought for a moment. How much time did she have to tell her entire life story, and what would Bernard, an almost famous musician, find vaguely interesting about Tilly's sheltered small-town life? She was more interested in finding out more about all these new people she had met, so she kept her story brief.

'Well, to keep a long dramatic story brief, I grew up in a small town on the beach, just near Yamba, called Angourie. Have you heard of it?'

'No, I haven't heard of Angourie, but I have been to Yamba a few times and a place called Iluka. It's beautiful there.'

'Yeah, funny that everyone has heard of Yamba and Iluka, but no one has ever been to or heard of Angourie. I kind of like it that way, anyway. My family all live there. Mum and Dad, my three older brothers and me. We own a local café, restaurant, and bar down there. It's called The Angourie Local; some people call it The Macallans. You should come and play a gig there. We've had some decent talent stay and play with us: Fleetwood Mac, Van Morrison, and The Rolling Stones. We keep it secret, just for the locals. If you come and visit and stay with us when you're super famous, we won't tell anyone you're coming.'

Bernard replied with absolute disbelief. 'Are you serious? How do you get away with that without everyone knowing about it?'

Tilly replied, 'I know it's crazy, huh! I guess for us, it's not about making money; it's about giving the artists some solitude away from the rest of the world, so it's not advertised, and no one knows about it. If you turn up at The Angourie Local, you might just get lucky. It's our local secret. The beaches are secluded, and they can escape the rest of the world. The idea started with my mum and a silly game we used to play while renovating. Then, it was my twin brother's wild idea because they are both obsessed with The Rolling Stones. Mick Jagger, wild as he is, said yes to an invitation letter from my brothers as a comedown after their Aussie tour a few years ago, and the rest is history.'

'So, you're telling me you've hung out with Mick Jagger, Van Morrison and Stevie Nicks, in Angourie?'

'And the rest, yep!' Tilly laughed. 'Maybe I'll add your name to the "Angourie Local Legends List" someday. We have a special wall of fame, photos, autographed merchandise and stuff. The proof is all there if you don't believe me!'

Bernard replied, backtracking, but still in disbelief. 'Oh, I believe you, but that's the coolest, almost unbelievable idea I've ever heard. My biggest fear with our growing population of fans, and this again sounds like I'm completely on myself, is that I'll lose myself and my freedom. We haven't even started our tours yet, and I'm already feeling the squeeze of popularity. As nice as that is that people appreciate our music, it's suffocating at times. I can imagine being able to go somewhere like that would be so refreshing to those hugely famous artists.'

'Yeah, they always have a great time and appreciate being left alone.'

There was a moment of stillness and awkward quiet, and Tilly wondered if Bernard believed her or not. Regardless, it didn't matter; it was the truth. He could believe it or not.

Tilly tried to avert the attention away from herself and back to Bernard, as she wasn't sure how much more she wanted to share about her situation. The conversation was superficial for a little while, about things around them, the weather, people on the street, and the amount of traffic on the roads, and then Tilly diverted the conversation back to Bernard again. 'What about you? What's your plan?'

'Me, my story is much more boring. I grew up in inner-city Brisbane, no secluded beaches there, and went to school at St Joey's. Mum made me learn piano when I was young, which I hated at the time, but somehow, as a bit of a loner at high school, I discovered I had a bit of a talent for writing my own songs. They were mostly about my sad teenage heart from all the girls I scared away.' He laughed.

Tilly butted in with, 'Yeah, right, you're really scary.' She laughed, too. Then added, 'Then what?'

'When I finished school, I just wanted to play music, but my mum encouraged me to go to university until I got a decent job. That was the deal. So, I started a journalism degree at the University of Queensland. All I wanted to do was jam with my mates, so it wasn't long before I quit university and joined my mate Ian,' patting Ian on the back as he was sitting directly in front of Bernard, 'in the band he had already formed, called Powderfinger. Never thought I'd be a lead singer, but that's where I ended up. We have just been doing a few little gigs here and there, and mostly playing at friends' parties and weddings and stuff, but we have got a few dates lined up for a bit of a tour on the Gold Coast and Brisbane. We're keeping it local for now until we can figure out what we are doing. That's my life in a nutshell. Who knows what the future holds, just having fun for now?'

Tilly listened and was interested in Bernard's young life and how his path was different to hers, but music was still the dominant theme. It always interested Tilly how music connected people and was such a huge part of her soul. When Bernard finished talking, she said, 'Sounds like a plan. It seems like everything is working out for you so far.'

Bernard shrugged his shoulders and replied. 'Yeah, maybe. We'll see!'

Tilly and Bernard realised that the other band members had all drifted off to sleep, realising after some time that Tilly and Bernard were in quite a deep two-way chat and leaving them to continue their conversation. There was no doubt these fellas were tired. The life of a musician on tour required late nights and little rest.

Bernard looked around at his sleeping friends and then back to Tilly, quite aware that she had more of a story to share. He started, gently encouraging her, 'So, tell me more. Your family owns this great little bar in a secluded beach town, but for some reason, you're running away with a broken arm. There must be more to this story.'

'Yeah!' Tilly nodded, looking out the window as she noticed the roads were busier; they were moving closer to the city areas, more traffic, sirens, and many people out and about. 'I'm not sure what you want to know about me. I grew up in Angourie and never really travelled much, only to Sydney to go to university for a couple of years, then back to Angourie again. I finished my degree, though, as a qualified teacher. But like you, music is my passion. Umm, what else do you want to know?'

Bernard got straight to the point. 'Relationships? You're a beautiful girl; surely you've broken a few hearts.'

'Too right. I've been on both ends of heartbreaks. Never really met someone who I truly thought could be *the one* until recently, and I messed it up. A complete sabotage. Well, and truly. I threw in my hand too soon. Didn't listen to what he was trying to say to me. I told him to go, so he did. Now I'm trying to find him.' Tilly stopped talking and looked out the window, trying to stop her tears.

Bernard replied calmly, 'I'm sure there is more of a story to that. May I ask if the broken arm has anything to do with it?'

Tilly held up her arm and rubbed it, realising again that it was painful. 'Well, yes, but no, if that's what you think. Nothing violent. No way! Quite the contrary, it was completely romantic. My arm....' She paused. 'I tripped on a message in a bottle in the sand. That's how I know I fucked it up.' Tilly started getting a little more emotional as she was explaining what had happened.

Bernard shook his head. 'Clear as mud. All good, Tilly, no need to get upset. Is there anything I can do to help?' Bernard responded with a little sadness, as he was really enjoying his first conversation with Tilly; she was easy to get along with. He was enjoying her company and hoped that they might spend some more time getting to know each other. His reply suggested an understanding that he would not question anymore, just accepting that Tilly was on a mission to find her one.

Tilly replied, 'Not sure if you can help. The problem is, he's travelling, and I have no way of contacting him, and he can't contact me. I only hope to run into him somewhere if it's meant to be. I do feel like he's headed up this way. He's a surfer and a musician, so he'll try to get to a city where he can get some gigs.'

Bernard replied, sharing his own experience. 'I'm not sure how he'll go as a solo artist, but I know the pub band scene is good here on the Gold Coast. We've got a gig next weekend at the Surfers Paradise Surf Club. If he's keen and motivated as a soloist, I'm sure he will have no trouble getting into the pubs or bars for a Sunday Session. Fisherman's Wharf has a great music scene, and so does the Surfers Beer Garden. I guess the hardest thing is that he's the new kid in town. He'll have to get a bit of a name for himself.'

'He's a talented musician, but has a bit more of a country sound. Do you think that would go against him, here in the big city smoke?' Tilly questioned, trusting that Bernard would have a good feel of the music scene on the Gold Coast.

Bernard replied after thinking for a moment. 'I don't think so; it depends on what kind of cover music he can play. People just appreciate a nice bit of background music to create a bit of a vibe. What kind of music does he play?'

Tilly replied. 'Well, when he did a gig at our local, he played a bit of everything: Paul Kelly, Van Morrison, Fleetwood Mac, Cold Chisel. He can do some good Aussie covers or whatever people want. He's one of those guys who can just pick up the guitar, listen to the song and play along. It's like he can play by ear.'

Bernard replied. 'Lucky him, that's talent, and a lot of practice, I imagine.'

Tilly replied, 'I know, right, I'm not that talented. I need to see the chords there in front of me. On the piano, I can feel my way, and with singing, I can collect lyrics from a thousand songs, and they stay in my mind. But for me, guitar was always a bit more of a challenge. I love it, but it just makes no sense.'

Bernard replied, 'Is that so? Here you are wandering around Australia with a Maton guitar, and you are telling me guitars make no sense.' Bernard commented she had a quality guitar in her belongings. He was impressed.

Tilly added, trying to explain what she meant. 'I know, go figure! I love to play the guitar, and I adore my Maton. It's my favourite instrument, but yeah, it makes no sense to me whatsoever. There is no consistent pattern to the chords.'

Bernard changed the conversation again, realising that Tilly had done well to divert the conversation away from the topic of her messed up relationship. 'So, Tilly, it sounds to me you like have come all the way here to the Gold Coast on a wish that if you wander in and out of enough bars and clubs, you might eventually find your man?'

Tilly hadn't forgotten, for one moment, about the throbbing pain in her wrist. She replied, 'Something like that after I get my arm fixed.'

Bernard replied. 'Well, I reckon if you get up in the morning and head to the Gold Coast Hospital, you'll have it sorted by lunchtime, ready to busk with us somewhere tomorrow night. What do you think?' Bernard came up with a quick plan to appease

Tilly's concern about her arm and to suggest that she was very much welcome to hang out with them a little longer.

Tilly smiled, 'thank you, Bernard, that sounds like a radical idea. Busking with you all sounds super fun. I'd love that. I might give the guitaring a bit of a miss for a while, but I can sing with you.'

Bernard questioned with a kind and sincere heart. 'Promise you won't run away?'

'I promise. Not yet. You haven't scared me away yet. And when you do, you must promise you'll write me a song.' Tilly laughed, and so did Bernard.

'If I am supposed to be any help in finding this man for you, then I probably need to know a little more about him. How will we know when we find him?'

'Well, for one, he will be the only man wearing a blue Bandana and Blundstone boots on the Gold Coast. I'm sure of that. Looking around, I don't see anyone that slightly resembles him at all.'

Bernard questioned, 'Do you mean like Axl Rose's Bandana?'

Tilly nodded. 'Yep, exactly, but it's blue.'

Bernard clarified, 'A blue paisley Bandana and Blundstone boots. Okay then, that makes things simple, I think.'

Tilly added, 'Yep, and damn, it looks good on him.'

'I'm sure it does,' agreed Bernard. 'So, what's the name of this guy?'

'His name is Dalton. Dalton Diaz,' replied Tilly.

'Cool name, too. Tilly and Dalton, Dalton and Tilly, sounds good together.' Bernard was trying to be engaged in the excitement that Tilly shared as she talked about Dalton.

'You know what's funny,' added Tilly.

What's that?

Tilly replied as she stared blankly out of the window. 'Dalton looks a bit like you. He's got the shoulder-length curls and the ocean eyes. He's lean and tall like you, too.' She looked back at Bernard as he shifted in his seat, thinking of a humorous reply.

'Is that right? Sounds like you have good taste in men then, Tilly.' They both laughed again. Bernard felt he could be a little flirtatious still, knowing that Tilly had no interest in him at all, but it was fun all the same.

Tilly went along with it, too; she was enjoying Bernard's company, and it felt awkward talking about Dalton, but this was her staying true to herself. As much as she was intrigued by this conversation with her new friend, she was on a mission. One, get her arm fixed. Two, find Dalton.

Tilly made room in the conversation for a change of topic, but Bernard pursued the questions a little more.

'So, I don't know the complete story, but does Dalton know you are trying to find him?'

'Nope, don't think so,' Tilly replied sharply. 'The last conversation we had together, I told him to go. I really thought he was about to confess that I wasn't his type of girl, and I had already fallen head over heels for him. I lost it. I was completely irrational and told him to go, just go. I walked off, not giving him a chance to explain. The next morning, I went for a run on the beach and found the bottle with the message. That's another story. Hard to believe I know. You must think I'm full of make-believe stories. But that's how I know I fucked up. I went back to apologise, but he was gone. He must have left early that morning. So, I told my family I was leaving Angourie to find him. The only people that know I am looking for him are my family, so unless he has phoned

The Angourie Local, and why would he? He would have no idea that I'm trying to find him.'

'Have you told anyone else about him?' Bernard questioned for clarity.

Tilly thought about this question for a moment and answered. 'No, not really, just you. I talked to a lady on the train but didn't tell her this entire story, so no one else knows. You, my family and me.'

'Ok, so we've got a bit of a mission ahead of us, don't we?' Bernard was keen to help Tilly.

chapter forty

Party Hard

The bus driver's cheery voice came through the bus speakers, jolting the rest of the band members awake. 'Hey everybody, we are here at Surfers Paradise Transit Centre. All passengers departing us here at Surfers Paradise, I wish you all a wonderful stay. Party hard! Please do travel with us again.'

Bernard had booked the band in for a week-long stay at The Islander, a popular hotel offering affordable and comfortable accommodation in a great location, opposite the Surfers Paradise Beer Garden and a short walk to Cavill Ave, the beach and a lot of funky nightclubs. The best thing was that it was just a minute's stroll from the transit centre. This was important, as they had quite a bit of gear to move. Most of it was in wheelie suitcases and transport trolleys, which made it much easier to move, but it was a mission, regardless. And Tilly was no help whatsoever. Lugging her own gear was hard enough a task. Bernard offered to put her guitar and backpack on top of the suitcase trolley, which made things a lot easier for Tilly.

Bernard made it very clear again that Tilly was welcome to stay with no pressure, of course. 'You know that there is plenty of room at the hotel, Tilly. We've even got a few spare beds because there are only five of us and we've booked four rooms. That's eight beds for all of us to share. Most of the rooms have two beds or a queen, so if you play your cards right, you might even have your own queen-size bed. They always treat us well here; it's not a problem.'

'Thanks, Bernard, and thanks to you all. That's really nice of you.'

Ian added, 'Well, you might need to get up and sing a few songs with us sometime this week; that would only be fair payment.'

'Seriously, I'd be honoured to.' Tilly smiled.

'We have booked this hotel for a week, so you can stay as little or as long as you want. I guess it'll depend on how long it takes to find D Man, or if I scare you away any sooner.' Bernard picked up the large trolley and pointed toward the hotel. 'This way.'

chapter forty-one

Popularity is my Paycheck!

Bernard and the band, and Tilly had all checked in the gear and made their room choices. Tilly ended up getting her own room, additional to what Bernard had already booked. A spare room was available on the same floor as the boys, next door to Bernard's room. Bernard didn't mind paying for the extra room, but Tilly insisted she would. She felt more comfortable doing that. She preferred being independent.

After all, they were staying here for a full week, ahead of their gig at the Surfers Paradise Surf Club, the following weekend.

They all freshened up after their long day of travel and met back in the lobby, deciding they would head out into town, as it was already quite a late part of the evening. Jon suggested they head over to the Surfers Paradise Beergarden for a feed, some drinks and a few games of pool. He loved to play pool almost as much as he loved playing the drums. They all agreed that sounded like a fantastic idea.

They made their way into the main entrance unnoticed. The boys headed over to claim a large empty table near the pool table area, while Bernard and Tilly headed straight to the bar to order the first round of drinks. It was Bernard's shout. He bought the boys a beer and Tilly a house cocktail. Tilly suggested they grab the food menu and order their meals as well, as it was getting late for the kitchen. She grabbed some menus to bring back to the table where the boys were all sitting. They had grabbed a nice tall table near the pool tables. It was a perfect place to eat and drink and be immersed in the games. Jon was thrilled.

'Nice table choice, boys.' Tilly complimented them on their choice as she and Bernard passed around the beers and menus from the trays.

Tilly noticed the squeeze of popularity that Bernard had talked about on the bus. She could feel people's eyes focusing on the band, particularly on Bernard. Being the lead singer, he was always noticed first in the crowd.

It was a weird feeling to Tilly because although people didn't come and invade their space; they were more likely to point and stare and whisper. Tilly wasn't even part of the band, but because she was with them, it was assumed that they had a forcefield around them, that no one should say hello or start a conversation. It was a lonely, segregated feeling, although they had done nothing to invite the segregation. They would, quite the contrary, be very open to chat with whomever came over to have a conversation.

Tilly asked Bernard, 'Does it feel weird to you that people just look and stare?'

Bernard smiled and replied, 'I knew you were going to ask me that. It is a weird feeling, huh? I guess at first it felt strange to be recognised by complete strangers, but now I kind of like it because it means that our music is becoming known to the public. When more and more people recognise us, that means we get more big gigs, and that means we make more money. Sounds materialistic, I know, but I'm a musician. Popularity is my paycheck.'

Tilly reached into her pocket to pull out some coins for the pool table. She didn't mind a game of pool, and she wasn't too bad with a cue. She had spent many years at the university in the student lounge, in what seemed like wasted hours of Wednesday night pool comps. Suddenly, Tilly was happy that she had spent many hours playing pool, as she might have a slight chance of giving some competition to Bernard and his friends, and at best, she wouldn't look like a complete idiot.

It was a well-known assumption that musos were good pool players. They hung out in pubs and clubs and dingy bars until all hours of the morning, so it was a given. Bernard and the band were keen to play while they enjoyed a delightful meal and some drinks. They had been here a few times, and they always enjoyed a good night. It took a little while until people would be brave enough to come and have a game of pool with them, but once they did, it was the icebreaker, and it always turned into a fun night. That was if Jon didn't get too competitive. He didn't need to; he was a shark from way back. Spent his youth playing pool while touring with his dad's band. He was either playing drums or playing pool.

Tilly emptied her pocket into her hand to gather some coins for the first game. The entire contents fell out.

Oh no, she thought, as she dug her hand in deeper until the pocket was empty. She turned it inside out. *Where is my lucky guitar pick? It must have fallen out somewhere.* She thought back over her day. The only thing she thought of was when she was buying her bus ticket. She was rushing to get the coins out of her pocket. *It must have fallen out then. Damn it, that was my favourite guitar pick.* The only family heirloom she carried. Tilly remembered back to the day that her dad had bought the set of picks for the family Christmas present. It was kind of knick-knacky, but so thoughtful. The simplest and most thoughtful gift she had ever received. The family band name on one side, Have Guitar Will Travel, and all their first initials, ordered by date of birth, on the flip side, J.L.F.E.L.T. Each family member had a pair of picks, presented in a cute little wooden box. They all had different colours: red, green, blue, yellow, black and white. Tilly's white one was her favourite. It was marble white with black lettering, Frankie's was cool as well. It was the opposite, marble black with white lettering. The picks weren't anything particularly special, yes custom-made, but nothing fancy. It was more the gesture of the family item, and everyone had their own piece of the collection to bond them all together. They all looked after them carefully, and Tilly had looked after hers especially well. In all the years and the many gigs she had played, she had never lost her pick, not even misplaced it once, until now.

Bernard questioned again, a little louder this time, 'You okay, Tilly?'

Tilly shook herself out of her little trance. 'Yeah, yeah, I'm okay just getting some coins for the table, and I realised I've lost my lucky guitar pick. It's fallen out of my pocket sometime today, maybe when we were at the train station, and I was buying my ticket. That's all I can think.'

'What kind of pick was it? Metal, wood, plastic? We have plenty of picks that you can choose from.' Bernard consoled Tilly with a kind offer to give her one of his picks, but what he didn't really understand was the sentimental value of the pick she had lost. It couldn't be replaced. It was part of a family set.

'It's not just any pick, it's my special one from our Macallan family pick collection. Dad had a whole family set of marbled guitar picks custom-made, back a few years ago when we first decided that we had a family band.' She laughed. 'You gotta love my dad. He's one of a kind. You should have seen how excited he was to deliver them to us. It was like a ceremony of the gods.' She laughed again. 'It's all good. It's just a pick. There are worse things you could lose, I guess.' Her mind, of course, went straight to thoughts of losing Dalton, but she said nothing, keeping her deep thoughts to herself.

Bernard could see that Tilly was being light-hearted about it, but he could also tell that deep down she was devastated. He could sense that her family was very special to her. He could tell already by the brief conversations they had shared that she adored her brothers and had a very close connection to her parents. He liked that about her. It was an admirable quality and not common to a lot of families. It was rare that you would see a family of six living, working morning, day and night together and still enjoying each other's company in a small town. It was a rarity. 'True. Maybe we could ring the train station tomorrow and see if anyone had handed it in. I mean, if someone found that, they would realise it was special, huh?'

'Yeah, maybe. Good idea. I'll do that. That's the only place I can think of where it may have fallen out.' Tilly was annoyed at herself, but there was nothing she could do right now. Waiting until tomorrow and calling the train station was a great idea. It was worth a shot.

'Cool! For now, let's enjoy the night and play some pool. Will you be my pool partner? You and me, against John and Darren.' Bernard placed the coins in the slot and the balls came rumbling out under the table.

'Sure, but what about Ian and Jon?' Tilly was concerned about leaving Bernard's friend out.

'It's all good Tilly, they can play the winners. House Rules, right? Winners keep the table. The losers pay for the next game. Jon, our little drummer boy, is bloody good with a stick in his hand, so don't worry too much. I'd be more worried about us getting left out. After this first game, we might have to pay our way for the rest of the night. Lucky you've got a pile of coins stacked up, Tilly.' Bernard laughed.

Tilly laughed too, but in the back of her mind, she was confident that they would be okay if Bernard could play a little. She was pretty good, for an Angourie girl. 'Are you doubting my pool-playing abilities Bernard, and we haven't even started the game yet?' Tilly's smile was beaming with confidence.

'Well, to be brutally honest Tilly, you have got a broken arm.' Bernard laughed again, trying to keep the humour going with Tilly.

Tilly had forgotten about that minor detail. She burst out laughing. 'True that, yes, I do have a bloody broken arm. I think those three shots of Midori, Cointreau and Vodka in my Illusion shaker made me forget.' Bernard had bought Tilly an Illusion shaker from the cocktail specials menu.

'Well, let's just play and see how it feels. The alcohol might numb some of the pain, but you need to be careful. If it's too painful, I'm happy to sit and chat with you while the others play. No doubt other people in the bar will come and challenge us for the table.' Bernard made the first break, and the game was on.

Bernard was right. As soon as the meals arrived at the table and they paused the game, to eat, a young couple came to ask if they could have a game. Tilly was intrigued at how shyly and politely they asked, obviously realising that these guys were new celebrities. If it were anyone else at the table, they would just come along and put their coins in without the polite questioning, but Tilly realised it was just their way to start the conversation. Bernard was quick to reply and joked with them saying 'Oh, look you'll have to ask the lady, she's the boss,' pointing to Tilly. 'See that pile of coins there on the table? She's the beholder.'

The young couple didn't know what to say, so Tilly eased the awkwardness. 'Of course you guys can play. We will give you a challenge after we've finished eating. Cool?'

'Yeah, that'd be cool,' replied the young man. 'Hey, um, are you guys Powderfinger?' He was so nervous but couldn't resist asking.

Bernard replied again with his wicked sense of humour. 'Well, yes we are, except for the beholder of coins here. She's our finance lady, paying for our entertainment tonight.' He laughed and slapped Tilly gently on the leg.

'Ha ha! Very funny.' Tilly shook her head and laughed along with him.

The young man continued, not sure what to say to Tilly, so he continued to address his words to all the band members. 'Well, I just want to say that I love your music. I've been to a few of your gigs in Brisbane, and I think you have a long future ahead. You have a unique sound. My brother plays in a band called Grinspoon. They are from Lismore, not sure if you've heard of them, but they have got some good music coming out too. Just another new Aussie band.'

Darren replied this time. 'Yeah, man, yeah, of course. Grinspoon is great. Talented musicians. We are hoping to do some gigs with them in the future. We are just starting our own tours at the moment. That's keeping us busy.'

Ian joined the conversation. 'If you're keen to support us, we are playing a gig next Saturday at Surfers Paradise Surf Club.'

Bernard was quiet. He was feeling a little ashamed about his comment to Tilly. He didn't mean to be derogatory, but he felt it may have seemed that way.

The young man replied again, this time including his girlfriend. 'Yeah. We've got nothing on next weekend; we will come and have a listen.' He looked at his girlfriend as he spoke, checking for reassurance of what he was offering.

The young girl finished the conversation as she felt rude as it was very clear that the band had stopped playing pool to eat their dinner, and here they were, interrupting them.

'Look, we will leave you to eat your dinner in peace, but we look forward to a challenge afterwards. We will just have a bit of practice while we wait.'

Bernard replied politely, 'Sure, no worries.'

The young couple set up their game and played a quick game of pool. They were quite good. Tilly realised it might be a bit of a challenge to win the table back, but so far, Bernard and Tilly were undefeated. They finished their meals and joined the young couple to play.

Meanwhile, the bartender had bought over another round of drinks announcing, 'This round is on the house, fellas, and for the beautiful lady, another Illusion Shaker for you.'

He's very charming, thought Tilly. She was enjoying the cocktails very much, and she knew they were quite heavy on the alcohol, especially following her day of drinking on the train. Tilly was a good drinker. She could handle a fair amount of alcohol in her system before it would have any effect on her, but she was feeling the buzz, that was for sure.

The barman came over to Tilly to pass her the special cocktail in the fancy silver shaker. 'Thank you, bartender.'

'I hope you're not driving anywhere tonight, young lady?' He said this as a statement, but also as a question.

Tilly answered, 'Nope, I'm staying with the band tonight, right across the road.' Tilly noticed he smelt good too. *What is with these Gold Coast men? They all smell so good.* She took a big breath through her nose to inhale his scent. Tilly was a sucker for a nice cologne.

'Well, you enjoy your night then.' The bartender gave Tilly a friendly smile and then made his way back to the table to collect the empty glasses.

As Bernard and Tilly started their game of pool against the young couple, Tilly cast her eyes around the room, noticing different crowds of people. It was a very different vibe to The Angourie Local. The Gold Coast crowd seemed to take much more pride in their appearances. The men were still the beach-loving surfy crowd, relaxed and all. After all, they were in Surfers Paradise, but there was more class in the way they dressed and in their appearance. They dressed similarly to her brothers, surfy, but classy. Clean-shaven, neat haircuts and there were lots of unfamiliar scents of aftershave. Tilly was keeping her nose out for the smell of Dalton's Joop.

The women seemed a little less classy somehow, beautiful but somehow lacking grace, as there was not a lot of clothing being worn. Short skirts, short dresses and long heels. There was no elegance, no long dresses or long skirts, no tailored pants, and not a pair of jeans or boots in sight. The room was full of these Gold Coast girls, and they were all beautiful, and then there was Tilly. She felt that they probably thought she had no class. Tilly didn't think too much about it. It was a matter of perspective. Tilly had showered and changed at the hotel, but she was still wearing her favourite blue denim jeans and a clean white tank top. Tilly wore her favourite black ankle boots. She had a simple, easy-going look. Bernard had dressed almost the same, except he had a dark grey T-shirt, blue denim jeans and black roller desert boots. He was clean-shaven, and he had washed his hair of messy curls. He had taken little time or given much effort, but he looked good. He had a charismatic, confident, not cocky, but comfortable ease in the way he carried himself.

Bernard was immersed in a conversation with the young couple. They were talking about the best nightclubs to go to in Surfers Paradise. When Tilly finished her turn, she had sunk three balls in a row and was cleaning up the table, she came over to give the cue back to Bernard for his turn next. The young girl disconnected from the conversation to have her shot, so Tilly interrupted the conversation between Bernard and the young man. It was the first time that Bernard noticed Tilly was a bit slurry and the question was left of centre.

Tilly asked mid-sentence. 'Can I ask you guys something?'

Bernard and the young man stopped talking. They were in the middle of a discussion about whether Cocktails and Dreams or The Esplanade was their favourite nightclub.

Bernard stopped talking and responded, noticing that Tilly was a little affected by the Illusion shakers. 'Sure Tilly, what's on your mind?'

'Can I ask what cologne you are wearing?' She realised this was out of the blue, so she added, 'I think you have the same cologne as the bartender.' She pointed over toward the bar.

The young man answered first, 'I'll have to check with her,' pointing to his girlfriend, 'she pays attention to that stuff. I think it's Armani, something.'

'What about you, Bernard?' Tilly wasn't particularly interested in the young man's answer, but she went along with it, anyway. She was more interested in finding out the name of Bernard's cologne.

Bernard had bought the new cologne in Sydney, where it was all the rage. He liked the strong, spicey, recognisable scent. 'Umm, it's Obsession for Men by Calvin Klein. Do you like it?'

'I do, it's really nice.' Tilly responded politely and then realised she had rudely interrupted their conversation and she realised she was feeling a little drunk as that wasn't something she would normally do. She reminded herself that she had to be careful not to give any hints of a forward invitation to Bernard. He had made it quite clear a few times he thought Tilly was a really nice girl. Tilly could sense that he wished she wasn't looking for Dalton, as he was enjoying her company more and more, and she was enjoying his company as well. They got along well together. She was enjoying her night, and she was feeling quite flattered that she was hanging out with Powderfinger. As the night went on, many people made a big deal about their presence, which made her feel even more privileged that they had asked her to stay with them for the week and sing with them the following weekend at their gig.

Tilly thought back to the bus chats. Bernard had asked her about her relationship status, and she had told Bernard all about Dalton and the mess she was in, but she hadn't yet asked Bernard about his love life. She had consumed a few more drinks now, and she was feeling a little more carefree about asking some deeper questions other than what cologne he was wearing.

Tilly and Bernard won another game of pool against the young couple, and this time, they challenged Jon and Ian. Jon hadn't played yet, so this was the test. Bernard knew as soon as Jon picked up a pool cue, their time on the table would be over. He was ready to sit and chat with Tilly anyhow, so he played the game as best he could. Jon and Ian took over the table, and consequently, they also took over the role of being responsible for *"celebrity chats"* with random people who challenged them to a game of pool for the rest of the night. Tilly's wrist was numb and heavy. It started to throb again, so she was happy to sit and chat.

Tilly poured another glass of her Illusion Shaker for herself, and the rest she poured into a spare glass for Bernard. 'Here you go. Help me drink this. It's so good that it's so bad. I just feel like I'm drinking pineapple juice until I try to walk a straight line. No more for me. I'll just drink water for the rest of the night.'

'Good idea, Tilly, that stuff can make you do crazy things.' Bernard agreed that water would be good for the rest of the night. The bartender had brought over a jug and six glasses, so he poured a glass of water for himself and for Tilly.

Bernard continued to have a joke with Tilly as light-hearted as he could be, and hopeful that Tilly wouldn't take his comments too personally.

'I've heard too many Illusion Shakers can make you *delusional.*' Bernard played around with the name of the drink to have a humorous effect and a bit of a flirt. 'I've heard it can make completely normal people think that I'm amazing.' He laughed a big, head throwback laugh. Tilly joined in the laughter and then consoled Bernard, saying. 'Oh Bernard, a completely normal person wouldn't need to be delusional to think you're amazing. I think you're a great guy, and I've only known you for half a day. I can't wait to see you guys performing on the weekend. If the train ride gig was anything to go by, then I'm guessing it's going to be an entertaining show. Do you guys play mostly original songs, or do you do covers, like you did on the train?'

'I'm glad you asked that question because it's something me and the boys always talk about. Because we are not popular just yet, it's important that we get our original songs out there, but being such a new band, many people don't know our songs yet, so we find that balance. We want to give an entertaining show with our songs, so they get known, but we also want to make sure we give the crowd something to sing and dance along with.' Bernard was explaining this to Tilly and, as he was talking, he couldn't help but notice how beautiful her face was. He said nothing though, as he was being respectful of Tilly's situation and the fact that she was searching for this Dalton fellow. He kept on talking as Tilly listened carefully. 'We probably do sixty per cent originals, forty per cent covers show for now. We do a bit of Bowie, The Doors, The Beatles, Led Zeppelin. Of course, as we get more of a following and people can recognise and sing and dance along to our songs, those stats will change.' Bernard realised he was talking a lot, so he paused for a moment. Tilly jumped in to speak as she was keeping up with his conversation and she was interested to know his thoughts on the topic.

'I agree with you. I mean, in my family band, we do ninety-nine percent covers and now and then we throw in something that we have created. My brother Frankie comes up with some good stuff, and I have written a couple of broken heart songs, and a couple of fuck you songs, excuse my Angourie slang. But I think it's always super fun when big bands throw in a cover song here or there. Sometimes the cover can be better than the original. I think my favourite cover song is *Counting Crows–Big Yellow Taxi.* Such a great version of *Joni Mitchell's* already amazing song.'

'Yeah, well, hopefully as we continue to get some more gigs around the place, we can get some of our songs on the charts. One of my personal goals is to hit Number One in the Australian charts. Just once, that would be cool. My mum might be proud of me then.' Bernard was a little melancholy, as he always felt that his mum wanted him to achieve more in his life than being in a band.

'I'm sure she's proud of you already. Don't you think she deliberately made you take piano lessons so you could be famous?' Tilly spoke calmly and with kindness, but she was quite serious with her question.

'Yeah, maybe. I *love* my mum. She's awesome and I hope she's proud of me someday.' Bernard accented the word *love* to give full meaning and respect to his mother, who had done so much to encourage him with his music when he was younger.

'Cheers to *Love* Bernard.' Tilly lifted her glass to his.

'Cheers to *Love* Tilly.' Bernard clicked his glass with hers and winked a big smile at her.

Bernard continued talking. 'Cheers to Love, that's a cute thing to say.'

'It's just a weird thing I do. I like to cheer on my four favourite things. Friendship, Freedom and Enough Love. It's hard to find all four things with everybody. I think certain people can give and be some of those things to us. All four are a rarity. Being *enough* for someone for the long haul is the toughest one.'

Bernard replied with great depth to his thoughts. 'I would say all those things, in their truest form, are equally hard to find with one person unless you find yourself "cheering" with the right person for you.'

Tilly had the same thoughts. She acknowledged this by nodding and smiling. 'So true, Bernard.' Tilly continued, explaining why she had used the love for her cheers, just to be sure Bernard knew what she was talking about. She didn't want him to get the wrong idea. 'I can hear how much you love your mum, the way you speak about her, so I thought she deserved a cheer.'

'Well, I think we deserve a cheer for each other, Tilly. How about we start with Friendship and Freedom? I'm feeling free and friendly tonight.' Bernard laughed his wide-mouthed laugh again, and Tilly joined him. They both held up their glasses again and said together, 'To Friendship and Freedom.'

Bernard turned around to his mates and asked them if they needed another round. They all nodded in agreement. Bernard looked at the barman and signalled, 'Another round, please.' He then pointed his hand above Tilly's head and signalled no more for her, with his hand signalling a cut-off, then lifted the jug of water. The barman gave a thumbs up and pulled a downward face, suggesting he knew exactly what Bernard was talking about.

The bar was getting more and more crowded as the night went on. They had some good music playing through the speakers. Some people were up dancing on a *that'll-do* for a dancefloor near their tables. The vibe was fun and energetic. Meanwhile, the rest of the band continued to play pool, talking and chatting to people, doing some spontaneous advertising for their gig the following weekend.

Tilly and Bernard's conversation was getting a little more serious. Tilly starting with the big question. 'So, Bernard, I've told you all about my love life disaster; what about yours?'

'My love life disaster? I don't have a love life disaster?' replied Bernard.

'You know what I mean. Tell me about your love life. I've told you about my love life disaster.' Tilly responded, trying to make sense of what she was asking.

'Well, my love life is just great. Because I don't have one. I'm a free bird now, which suits me just fine.'

'Are you sure about that?' Tilly questioned further.

'I am absolutely sure. I'm never in one place for long enough to be good to anyone. I'm just having fun, meeting new people and travelling a lot. I need to fall in love someday, and I need to have my heart broken someday, and I need to feel loss and grief someday. That's how the best song writers say they create the best songs, from full emotions. I can't say I've ever truly been in love. And love is not in my life at the moment.' Bernard spilled his true feelings to Tilly as she listened.

'But you're happy, right?' Tilly questioned for clarification and understanding.

'I'm totally happy. Honestly, I love having no commitments to anyone, just to my band and my freedom.'

'But what about, you know, what about fulfilling your physical desires? What if you meet someone special on your travels? I'm sure you've met plenty of beautiful girls.'

'Yep, all the time. I have a lot of good friends from different places we've been, but they all know the story. I can't be tied down to anyone now. I need my freedom. If they can understand that and be happy with a spontaneous night, or maybe a week together hanging out, I'm all good for that. I don't let myself get attached. It's quite heartless.'

Tilly replied with an understanding nod. 'It is, yes. But that's okay. If you are honest from the start and it's just a bit of fun, then no one gets hurt.'

Bernard was nodding too. 'Yeah, that's the way I think about it. And I don't care what people think about me, it's my choice what I do. I know that comes across as quite arrogant, but people must understand my life is not in one place. I don't have that stability now. I'm like a rolling stone.'

'Ha, nice pun.' Tilly could hear The Rolling Stones, *Start Me Up* playing through the speakers. 'Do you want to dance?'

'Sure thing, why not? I love this song.'

Tilly and Bernard started dancing in a bit of cleared space towards the bar. It looked like a good place for a dance floor. A few others joined them. They were having such a great time. Bernard couldn't quite believe it when *What's My Scene* by the Hoodoo Gurus kicked in. By now the dancefloor, they had started, was full. For the next few hours, they passed time dancing, talking, playing some more pool, and Tilly had another Illusion Shaker.

It was getting close to midnight. Bernard had nowhere to be, other than here right now, nor did Tilly, other than to get to the hospital the next day. The rest of the band members said their farewells to Tilly and Bernard and wished them well for the night.

Tilly and Bernard took a walk along the beachfront. It was a beautiful night. There was a cool, gentle, salty breeze. It wasn't hot; it wasn't cold. It was like a nothingness kind of temperature. Not cool enough to need a jacket or warmer clothing, but not hot enough to feel uncomfortable in jeans. It was the perfect night for a stroll.

As Tilly and Bernard walked and talked, they came up with a plan for the week. Tilly would go to the hospital in the morning to get her arm looked at. That was the priority. Bernard offered to go with her as he knew his way around the Gold Coast. Bernard thought he might hire a car for the week so they could do some exploring around the Hinterland. If he hired the car in the morning, that could be the best way for them to get to the hospital, and then they would have some freedom to go wherever they wanted. Tilly always wanted to go to a place called The Natural Arch and to Mt. Tamborine, so they decided that was on their to-do list. The theme parks didn't interest Tilly at all, especially with her broken wrist. Bernard suggested they have a bit of a practice, playing some gigs at The Islander throughout the week. They didn't expect much of a crowd as it wasn't advertised. They would just do some poolside evening acoustic sessions. Tilly agreed that would be super fun. Then, on the weekend, Powderfinger would play their gig at Surfers Paradise Surf Club. Bernard invited Tilly to go on stage with them again if she wanted to and if she felt comfortable after their practice through the week. Tilly was keen.

Tilly could feel the Illusion taking effect again. 'I'm feeling a little tipsy, that is for sure, but it's been a great night. It was so much fun dancing and playing pool with you all. You have some great friends. It's nice that you all get along; otherwise, it would be tough hanging out together so much if you didn't.'

'Yeah, they are good mates, as well as my workmates. But my work isn't work. That's the best thing about being a singer-songwriter. My work is my passion and my hobby. I'm so lucky.'

'You are lucky, and I'm lucky to hang out with you tonight. Thanks for the invitation.' Tilly was slurring again but was sincere with what she was saying.

'We are both lucky to hang out with each other, Tilly. It's equal. I've had a great night, and I'm looking forward to doing some exploring and adventures with you this week.'

'That's nice. All I can think of right now is that my bed will be an adventure tonight. I'm pretty sure it's going to be spinning. Those Illusions have made me delusional; I think you're amazing, Bernard.'

Bernard laughed as he wrapped his arm around Tilly to hold her upright. 'Let's get you back to the hotel.'

'Yes, let's do that.' Tilly leaned into Bernard, feeling safe, wrapped in his arms.

Tilly and Bernard made their way back to the hotel, talking and laughing along the way. When they reached the hallway, Tilly turned to Bernard and asked shyly. 'Is it okay if I stay in your room tonight?'

'If that's what you want to do, you're very welcome to stay in my room, but are you sure?' Bernard was a little concerned about Tilly having too much to drink. He thought it would be a good idea to stay close to her for the night, but he didn't want her to make a decision that she would regret, either.

'Yes, I think that would be nice.' Tilly was a little worried that she might be sick and might need some help through the night.

'All good. Do you need anything from your room?' Tilly's room was just next door.

'Yeah, I'll just grab my toiletry bag with my toothbrush.'

'Good idea.' Bernard walked Tilly to her room while she grabbed her stuff.

Tilly was thinking ahead for what would be best for her to feel okay in the morning. 'I might need some more water, lots of water, I think.'

Bernard replied, 'There is a jug of cold water in the fridge in my room. Let's get that into you.'

Tilly grabbed her stuff as quickly as she could, looking at herself in the mirror as she grabbed her toiletry bag. She looked tired, and she looked drunk. It had been a very long day. 'You need to get a good sleep.' She whispered to her drunken self in the mirror. As she made her way back out into the hallway, she pulled the door shut behind her to lock her hotel room, keeping her few treasured possessions safe. The most important things were her Maton guitar and the message in a bottle from Dalton to Chelsea. Tilly's only other important possession was her sentimental guitar pick, which she remembered she had lost. She made a mental note to herself to remember to call the train station in the morning. She was sure that was where her pick would be, if anywhere, on the platform, and the only luck that she had on her side was that

Murwillumbah Train Station was a quiet country railway station. Someone may have picked it up and handed it in, realising it was perhaps quite special.

To anyone else, it was just a guitar pick. To her, it symbolised family connection and the importance of the little things.

Her father had always said to her, 'If you take care of the little things, the big things will always just fall into place.'

Of course, he wasn't talking about her guitar pick. He was talking about the big concepts of life: relationships, friendships, study and work, family, and the environment. If every person did their bit to take care of the little important things, then everything else would work out just fine.

Jack had many words of wisdom that he would share and model in how he lived his life. He was a gentle, kind, good person. He was considerate and hardworking, and he loved his family.

Tilly felt so bad that she had lost her guitar pick.

chapter forty-two

Finding You

The barman called "last drinks," and requested that the pool-players make it their last game. Myles and Georgia were back in the game and were duelling with Travis and Adeline.

Jacqui ended up being the brave one to ask Dalton what his sleeping arrangements were for the night. It was getting late, and he was not putting out any offers to her. 'So Dalton, where are you sleeping tonight? Are you crashing in the Kombi with Travis, or what?' Jacqui had to ask, because he was being so uninviting.

'Nah Jacq, I've booked a room here at The Beach Hotel. I booked a room earlier and dumped my stuff in there. I've got a nice comfy bed to crash in.' He still offered nothing to Jacqui. Dalton was playing very hard to get.

Travis overheard their conversation as he came around to the head of the table to take a tough shot. 'Dalton, man, you need to chill out and feel the Byron hippie vibe.' He added with a slow, drawling tone, 'Peace, happiness, free love.' As he lined the cue up slowly to take his shot, he suggested to Dalton. 'You should invite Jacqui to stay in your room for the night. She doesn't look like a crazy vampire or anything to me. You never know, you two might have a fun night. It looks like you're having fun so far.'

The bartender announced again, 'last drinks.' Most of the pub guests had finished up for the night and everyone was heading home. It was getting close to 11 pm. The band had played their last song, the classic by Rick Springsteen, 'Jessies Girl' and quite a few had taken to the dancefloor for one last dance. Tank and Robbo had left about two games of pool ago when they had lost the table to Dalton and Jacqui for the third time. It was just the three couples left in the pool table room. Travis sunk the eight ball and announced that he declared him and Adeline the winners of the night, because they were the final winners of the last game.

Myles cheekily responded, 'Does that mean you get to shout the last round of drinks then, Travis?'

Travis responded easily, 'Sure man, you've been shouting us all night. Is everyone keen for one more round? What about you ladies?'

Georgia quickly responded, 'I think a nice celebratory couple of bottles of Moèt would go down smoothly right now. And it's my shout. I haven't paid for a drink since we walked into this pub.' She was already walking to the bar before anyone could even try to argue with her, waving a $100 note that she had pulled out of her back pocket.

Myles called out, 'What are we celebrating Georgia?'

'Finding you!' she replied.

Georgia returned from the bar, with the barman following her, carrying a large fancy ice bucket containing two bottles of Moet, placed elegantly in the ice. Georgia carefully held three champagne glasses in each hand, their long stems placed carefully between her elegant fingers.

The other five had moved to a large table where they could all sit together and talk and enjoy this celebratory drink that Georgia had felt necessary to finish the evening with.

The bartender poured the champagne delicately into each glass, carefully tipping each glass onto the side and slowly raising it up to meet the bubbles, causing no overflow. The Moet wasn't to be wasted, not a drop. As the barman poured the drinks, he politely reminded the group that there would be no more drink sales, however it was totally okay for them to continue to enjoy the night while the staff cleaned up, up to midnight, which was the planned closing time for this evening. It was a quiet night, other than this rowdy lot, so the manager had ordered the bar be closed in an hour.

As all six had their glasses filled, Dalton was the first to start the cheers. His favourite thing. A special cheer. What was it going to be? To friendship, yep. To freedom, yep. To enough love? Not yet. Not with these six very different people.

Dalton raised his glass and announced, 'To friendship and freedom.'

Everyone joined in, clinking their glasses together in the middle of the table, reflecting Dalton's cheers. 'To Friendship and Freedom.'

'I like that,' said Jacqui. She looked at Dalton with a curious smile, feeling a little more depth to his personality. He was playing so hard-to-get-to-know. Jacqui drifted back in her mind to her cheers with Tilly at the Railway Hotel. I think that's what she said, 'to freedom and friendship, to friendship and freedom.' That's strange! I've never heard that 'cheer' before and now I've heard it twice, with these two complete strangers, in one day. Jacqui almost considered mentioning the oddity to the group, but knowing that only Georgia and Adeline would understand, she let it go. She noticed that Georgia and Adeline had put the pattern together too, as they clinked their glasses together, both giving Dalton an inquisitive look, and thinking, *where have I heard that cheer before?* None of the girls mentioned Tilly's cheer, they just got on with the conversations that were around them.

The six chatted and laughed about the proceedings of the night as they slowly sipped the delicious champagne. Dalton announced he had never tasted Moet before. Looking at the label, he announced he could easily be convinced to travel to Epernay in France.

'Nice drop,' he announced as he lifted his glass to Georgia.

Travis piped in with, 'I hate to be a negative Nancy, but I don't think that part of France is anywhere near the beach, mate. San Sebastian though, now that is the place to be. I travelled there a few years ago, it's my favourite place in the world. It's right on the border of France and Spain, on the west coast. It snows on the beach in winter. How crazy is that?' Travis got excited to share his travel story, and his favourite place in the world, with the group.

Myles and Georgia were interlocked in a kiss when Travis asked the group about their favourite travel destinations. Jacqui was the first to answer, 'Dalton and I have had a bit of a chat about this earlier, but I'd have to say, The Kimberleys. I worked on a cattle station out there as a Jillaroo for a few years, and it was the most beautiful, peaceful place I've ever been. There was so much space and freedom, and the fresh country air was divine. The night skies are so clear and beautiful, filled with blankets of stars, like layers of the universe spread on top of each other. You have to see it to believe it. My favourite thing was when we went on full moon trail rides. There is nothing quite like it.'

Dalton replied, 'That sounds amazing, Jacqui.' Everyone was quiet in reflection of their favourite places.

Travis encouraged an answer. 'What about you, Dalton? What's your favourite place you've ever been?'

Dalton searched within for an answer. 'I haven't travelled far in my life, to be quite honest. I grew up in Deniliquin, in the country, and the furthest I travelled was to the Edward River for magical moments, or to the various pubs on weekends to play gigs. When I left Deni, I made a beeline and travelled straight towards the East Coast, through Albury, Goulburn and my first surf ever was in a place called Wollongong. Have you heard of it?'

'Yeah, mate I have,' replied Travis, 'I used to play basketball, and that is where the State competition games were often played.'

'That's cool,' continued Dalton. 'I stayed there for a little while and did some gigs all round the place. I used to go to the basketball stadium a lot and shoot hoops with a mate of mine. Small world, huh!'

'So how did you end up, up here?' queried Adeline to Dalton.

'Well, after my car died. It didn't survive the winter. I moved on from Wollongong in search of warmer water to surf, so I hitched a ride north and ended up in Sydney. I spent a bit of time in Sydney as the gig scene was good for me. I had reliable and regular well-paid gigs, almost every night, and it helped me to save a bit of cash. The public transport was good, which made it easy for me to get around, but it wasn't my favourite place to be. I couldn't get out of there fast enough. To be honest, it was way too busy for my liking. Too much traffic and city stress, my country boy pace was far too slow. Then once I moved on, again, I just had to rely on spontaneous travel opportunities. I met up with some lads who were on a surfing holiday up the coast, so I joined them for a few months over the summer. We surfed Nelson Bay, Seal Rocks and Forster. It's nice there. Then we made our way up through Crescent and Hat Head and we spent a few weeks solid at South West Rocks, while the swell was good. It was awesome. There were some nice beaches not too far south of here actually, but because they were so isolated, it was hard to find any work. I loved Nambucca Heads and Sawtell, and there was a funky village, inland from Sawtell called Bellingen. There was a place called Promiseland, it was amazing. It was like a Peter Pan forest of fresh water holes and undiscovered rainforests. It was magical. Wooli and Minnie Water were absolutely beautiful, but again, no work for me, unfortunately, so I had to keep moving on. The last placed I stopped was Yamba and Angourie, and to be quite honest it was beautiful there, that would probably be my favourite place I've ever been on the east coast. The boys I was travelling with are still in Yamba, I think. I just had a bit of a situation and I had to leave, hence me sticking my thumb out on the highway and hitching a ride with Travis.'

Adeline interrupted the conversation. 'Ah, so that's how you two met. I was wondering about the connection of all of you.'

Dalton was glad for the diversion from Adeline's question, so he didn't have to explain what had happened. Jacqui wanted to question Dalton a little more about his "situation" and what had happened, but she just left it alone and let the conversation flow.

Travis jumped in, saying, 'Well, I couldn't just leave him standing there in the blistering sun. His surfboard wax would have melted.' They all laughed at Travis' hard-core-surfer sense of humour. With Travis, everything was about surfing. 'Well, to me, he looked pretty harmless, with his guitar under one arm and his surfboard under the other. And he was wearing a blue Bandana with country boy boots. He had to be an okay fella. I was keen to find a new surfing buddy for the weekend. It worked out well for the both of us because now we've ended up somehow in your lovely ladies' company. As for Myles, we just met him here at the pub, about an hour before we bumped into you three beautiful ladies.' Travis winked and gave a special smile to Adeline, making sure she knew she was the *extra special one* out of the three girls.

What about you, Adeline? queried Travis. Myles and Georgia were still immersed in each other's mouths, in between sips of Moet, so Travis left them alone, for now.

Adeline had been thinking about her reply. 'To be quite honest, right here in Byron Bay is probably my favourite place in the world. I haven't been to a lot of places, really, to compare it to. I've spent most of my adult youth inside textbooks and university lecture halls and tutorials. I've had the most fun coming here for spontaneous weekends with Jacqui, and we usually have a good time. Tonight is extra special, though. Meeting you boys has been fun.'

'Aww, thanks Adeline,' replied Travis as he glanced over again to see if he could yet invite Myles and Georgia to join the conversation.

'I think it's time you two got a room.'

Myles finally took a breath to reply. 'I was just thinking the same thing. You must have read my mind, Trav. I do have a room booked here at the pub for the night. I'm not sure what *y'all* all have planned, he gave a cute little smile to Georgia as he imitated her southern American accent, but I've been planning my night since you beautiful girls walked in. I'm hoping Georgia will keep me company tonight, in my room?'

Myles had somehow asked Georgia to stay with him, without actually asking her to stay with him for the night. It was brilliant and very cute, and there was no way Georgia could deny his request.

Myles was extremely grateful for the little encouragement from Travis, as it gave him a way to ask Georgia back to his room in an easy, non-persuasive manner.

Travis had already invited Adeline to stay in his Kombi for the night. That had happened much earlier in the night, after they won their second game of pool.

The only mystery was with Dalton and Jacqui. Dalton was playing so hard-to-get and he was being so nonchalant, it was very hard to tell what he was thinking. Jacqui took the matter into her own hands.

'So, Dalton, everyone is going to bed now and I don't have a place to lay my head. Would it be okay if I came and shared your room with you? I promise I won't touch you.' She paused. 'If you don't want me to touch you?' Jacqui pleaded with Dalton to let her come and stay in his room, and she let him know it was all on his terms.

As they were all decided now and had started to get up and make a move and leave the table, the barman came over to let them know it was closing time.

'All good,' said Travis. We are all headed out now. Thanks for a great night, man! He gave the barman a solid handshake, followed by an upper arm tap. The barman was well built, and Travis commented, 'Man, do you surf, bro?'

'I do. It's the whole reason I moved here from Spain last year.' He replied with a gorgeous Spanish accent that was to die for. Adeline looked him up and down and thought to herself, *this is why I love Byron Bay,* as she squeezed Travis' hand a little more tightly to appease his feeling of inadequacy, right now. Funny thing was, Travis wasn't feeling compared at all. He had the confidence of a lion, because he knew he had much more to offer Adeline than what she had experienced just yet.

Myles and Georgia were in a deep conversation and were both fixated on each other. It was obvious they were staying together for the night in Myles' hotel room.

Jacqui was enjoying Dalton's company and was hoping he would offer her a place to stay in his room, but she was also half thinking that she wouldn't mind going home with the Spanish barman if Dalton wasn't playing the game. He was her type of gorgeous.

Dalton finally made a plan for Jacqui, as she had nowhere else to stay.

'Jacqui, you are welcome to come and keep me company tonight. It's really not a problem. There are actually two beds in my hotel room. I love your company. It's just that I'm pretty tired, so I don't know that I'll be a lot of fun, that's all.'

'Dalton, you are overthinking this whole thing. Let's just go back to your room and we can work it out from there. I just need a place to sleep. I would sleep on the floor if I had to.' Jacqui responded with a sense of calm and confidence that made Dalton feel very much at ease.

The barman was clearing glasses, and he was half tempted to offer Jacqui a place to stay at his apartment, but it seemed to be all sorted out, so he let the offer go. By the time he grabbed the last glass from the table, the six guests were all ready to head back to their rooms for the night. The barman gave Jacqui a knowing look, and somehow with the look of his eyes and a suggestive shoulder shrug, without saying a word, he shared body language to say, 'maybe another time you can stay with me.'

Jacqui somehow knew exactly what he was *saying.*

Travis and Adeline were the first ones heading out the door. Travis shouted back, 'Let's catch up for breakfast back here in the morning. They do an amazing Surfer Scrambled Eggs, and oh my goodness, the Salmon Eggs Benedict is beautiful.'

Myles responded confidently. 'Sure Travis, sounds good, but not too early huh, we might be tired in the morning,' as he winked at Georgia.

'Let's make it a 10 am breakfast. I'm pretty sure the kitchen closes by 11 am for breakfast orders. We don't want to miss out.' Travis put his arm around Adeline, guiding her towards the door as they exited.

Jacqui followed Dalton as he led the way towards the hotel rooms in the back of the pub. He reached back to grab her hand, but it was quite obviously an after-thought. He was attempting to enjoy the night, and he *was* enjoying the night, but his heart wasn't in it.

chapter forty-three

Myles and Georgia—We're in the Dolphin Room Baby!

Dalton, Jacqui, Myles and Georgia headed in the other direction, towards the back door, which led to a hallway of hotel rooms. Dalton and Myles had both checked their bags in earlier in the evening, and both had a key to their rooms. Myles was in Room 3, and Dalton was further along in Room 9.

Dalton made a comment about the room key. 'Is your keyring tag a funky surfboard, too, Myles?'

'Nah man, mine has a dolphin,' replied Myles with a look of surprise, taking notice for the first time. 'What a cool idea that is.' Myles smiled his big, wide smile towards Georgia as he held her hand and pulled her to the side of the hallway, towards room number 3. 'We're in the dolphin room, baby!' He said this like he was singing the lyrics to Guns N Roses, *We're In The Jungle, Baby!* What was even more exciting was that there was a dolphin plaque, just the same as the keyring, on the door.

Dalton and Jacqui continued along the hallway to the surfboard room, number 9, taking notice of the other room plaques along the way. There was a shark, a whale, a turtle, a wave and a lighthouse. Jacqui commented that all the room themes were significant totems of Byron Bay and that someone was very clever to develop an idea like that. Dalton instantly drifted his thoughts back to The Angourie Local and the themed guest rooms. It was a creative idea, that is for sure.

Before Dalton could even get his key in the door, they could hear Myles and Georgia laughing and knocking things over in the room as they were in the throes of passion, feeling the intensity and excitement of being alone in each other's company for the first time. Jacqui and Dalton quietly entered Room 9.

Georgia was dolled up in a black shimmery slip-on dress and slip-off heels. Underneath, she wore matching black Playboy lingerie. Myles was hustling to remove her clothes as he kissed her passionately and thrust his body close to hers as he peeled her dress overhead and unclipped her bra. There wasn't much to remove, but Myles enjoyed every moment of sliding his hands all over her voluptuous body as he undressed her. He was very careful not to put her hair out of place as he lifted the dress over her head. It looked like she had spent some time on the hairdo.

'My goodness, you are beautiful,' commented Myles as he glanced over Georgia's porcelain, curvaceous body while she stood before him with just the lingerie remaining, her front clasping bra already undone. 'I must say, I love your beautiful underwear, but I will have to remove it all if that's okay with you. I need to feel your beautiful body next to mine, skin on skin. Is that okay?'

Georgia replied, in between breaths, as she kissed his mouth. 'That's. Totally. Fine. With me. I would love to be skin-on-skin with you.'

Georgia's nipples became hard as he kissed her gently on each breast, as he peeled back each strap separately and allowed her bra to fall to the floor. Georgia was still standing, and she looked down at his beautiful mane of hair as he kissed her breasts. After he had removed her bra, he moved downwards to her belly button, kissing her sides as he did. She grabbed hold of his hair gently and pulled his head back up so she could kiss his mouth again. This time, she slid her tongue into his mouth and gently played with his tongue. By doing this, she showed him exactly what she wanted him to do to her when he moved back to her body to remove her bikini underwear. Myles understood the suggestion clearly, so as he moved back down to remove her underwear, he didn't waste any time to slide his tongue into her and play with her, just the way she had played with his tongue in the kiss. Georgia let out a loud groan, and then she quickly realised where she was and quietened her expression of pleasure. Myles knew what he was doing. He had the pleasure of experiencing many women, and he always attempted to make the experience all about them because that made the experience more enjoyable for him. He was keen to learn what women wanted, knowing they were all different in what turned them on. Myles eased Georgia back towards the bed as if in a choreographed dance. Their bodies moved together, attached, as Myles' arm held strongly around Georgia's back. He lay her down gently on the bed.

'Tell me what you like, Georgia?' asked Myles.

Georgia wasn't giving any secrets away just yet. 'I like everything you are doing to me, Myles. But what I really want is to do that back to you. How can I be laying here completely naked, and you are still half-dressed?'

Georgia sat herself up on the bed even though Myles was leaning heavily against her. She pushed him back, so his feet were back on the floor, and he was back in a standing position next to the bed. He was very tall, so as she sat on the side of the bed, her head was aligned with his ribcage. She couldn't quite reach to kiss his nipples, nor could she kiss his mouth, but she felt she would have easy access to his manhood if she could gain some access, so she undid his belt. She didn't feel the need to remove the belt completely from its buckles. She simply needed access to loosen his pants and slide them down to his feet. He had already removed his shoes as they stumbled through the door, making things a little easier. Myles helped with the process, and his jeans fell to the floor. He used his feet to remove them completely, sliding his Calvin Klein underwear all the way down and piled them on top of his jeans.

Now, they were equal. Both were completely naked. Myles was wearing only a shark tooth leather necklace and a leather wristband. Georgia was wearing only a fancy necklace, earrings, and a couple of gold bracelets around her wrist. Now they were ready for some fun. Two exposed, naked bodies, ready for a night of exploration and adventure. Georgia suggested they both have a shower together, and Myles agreed that was a great idea.

chapter forty-four

Dalton and Jacqui - Everything happens for a reason

Dalton opened the surfboard door to Room 9, and Jacqui and Dalton entered quietly, trying not to wake up the guests in the next room. They were sure Myles and Georgia had that task already assigned to them as their night duty. Dalton had not really checked out the room yet; all he had done was dump his bag, his surfboard and his guitar on the spare bed when he checked in, then went back to the hotel bar to meet again with Travis.

As they entered the room, Dalton apologised for having his stuff on the bed as he moved it to the corner of the room. There wasn't a lot of spare room to put anything, but he cleared off the bed for Jacqui as if to suggest politely that the spare bed was where she was sleeping tonight.

Jacqui had nothing with her, it was just her. Her bags and belongings were all still in the boot of Adeline's car. She was a free spirit, just herself and what she was wearing, and the night ahead of her. The only plan she had in front of her was breakfast at 10 am.

'Do you mind if I have a shower, Dalton?' asked Jacqui.

'Not at all. Go for it,' replied Dalton.

He was being so uninviting and not warming to any suggestive cues to get intimate with Jacqui, but Jacqui didn't mind. She just went along with it. She could sense he was holding onto something that he had not shared with her yet. The night was young.

Jacqui went into the bathroom and had a nice, warm shower. She felt clean and warm and fresh as she walked back out into the room with only her hotel-standard-white towel wrapped around her. As Jacqui made her way over to the spare bed, she deliberately announced, as she placed her towel on the back of the chair, 'I hope you don't mind if I sleep naked tonight. I don't have any bedclothes with me.'

Dalton was searching for something to wear to bed in his backpack. He usually slept naked, so he had nothing that even resembled a likeness to boxer shorts. He had so many pairs of surfing board shorts, but he didn't want to sleep in those. He decided he would just have his shower and do the same thing, climb into bed naked without her seeing him. He replied saying, 'That's okay Jacqui, no worries, make yourself comfortable, I'm just going to have a nice shower too.' He ran his eyes over Jacqui, admiring her bronzed summer body. He only saw a glimpse as she climbed under the sheets. This was her way of teasing him, just enough to show him what was here for him, if he wanted it, but not being too suggestive, as he was being so hard to get.

While he was in the shower, thoughts of Tilly were rushing through his mind. The shower in the gypsy room, the amazing night they spent together. He wanted her so badly right now, and all he could think of was, *she told me to go. Just Go!*

Dalton had enjoyed quite a few drinks, an afternoon full of cold beers with Travis, and the Moet to finish the night, so his head was not thinking clearly. He wanted more than anything to be with Tilly, right now, but that was not a rational thought. He might as well enjoy this night with Jacqui. She was a nice girl. He reminded her a lot of Chelsea. The country girl into horses, and the simple life. He just didn't have that "thing" with her, that "you-just-know feeling" that he had with Chelsea and, again, with Tilly. Dalton was so in love with Chelsea, with all his heart, and she was gone, just gone. There was nothing he could do about that. And then, he met Tilly, although it felt wrong to meet her so soon after losing Chelsea, he felt Tilly could be the "one." There was something about her that made his heart pound and his soul ignite. Tilly was freedom, friendship, and love. Tilly had mentioned this thing about 'being enough.' Dalton didn't feel that he was enough for Tilly. Just yet. Deep down, he felt that he still had some personal healing and letting go to do. In contrast, there was Tilly. She was a free spirit, ready to share her wild heart completely. For Dalton to feel like he was enough for Tilly and to feel like her equal, he needed to find that inner strength of acceptance that would allow him to be completely free to give his heart to her. He thought he had found that in scripting the message in the bottle to Chelsea. From his perspective, his heart was free, and this is what he was trying to tell Tilly about on that fateful night. The other way around, for Dalton and Tilly to find 'equalness' of their souls, in feeling like they were equally enough for each other, was for Tilly to be dragged to a place of understanding where Dalton had been and experience what he had gone through, and nobody would wish that kind of grief on anyone.

From his perspective, for him and Tilly to be equal, he needed to let go of his past completely. He needed to allow himself to love, to be free, to be wild, and he needed to say, "I love you" and mean it with all his heart, feeling no guilt.

Although Tilly had told him to go, he realised it was completely his fault for not being strong enough to explain that he was ready. He was her equal. He was good enough for her, and she was good enough for him. He was ready to give his heart completely to her. There were so many levels of equality and being enough for each other between Tilly and Dalton. *Maybe she already felt that. Why did she tell him to go?*

These were Dalton's shower thoughts. He always had deep and meaningful thoughts in the shower and had some of his best creative ideas there, but didn't everyone? Dalton took his time in the shower, letting the hot water run over his back. It had been a long day, after all. He had left Angourie in the wee hours of the morning, and the day had turned out to be an amazing adventure, meeting Travis, surfing the various breaks of Byron and meeting the girls for the night of the pool table and Moet shenanigans. He had seriously had the greatest day. The only thing missing was Tilly. She would have loved today with Dalton. It was everything she loved. Adventure, friendship, freedom, fun. Dalton was deep in thought, letting the water run over his face to sober him up. These three girls are the kind of girls Tilly would hang out with. She was very different to them. In fact, they were all very different from each other, but they had the same spontaneous-fun-life-loving personalities.

Dalton came out of the bathroom just wearing a hotel-standard-white towel wrapped around his body. 'Damn good shower for a cheap pub hotel, huh?'

Jacqui tried hard to pretend she was asleep. She was blinking through her eye sockets because she couldn't believe what she was looking at. Was this guy for real? His body was to die for. How could she resist?

Dalton turned off the bright room light, so the only light was the dim bedside table lamp, giving a nice soft glow to the room. He placed his towel on the other chair next to Jacqui's and climbed into bed, half trying to cover himself and half not caring at all. 'I hope you don't mind if I sleep naked tonight. I don't have any bedclothes with me.'

They both started laughing, as it was blatantly obvious that Dalton had remembered and repeated word-for-word what Jacqui had said to him. He was teasing her, just as she had done to him.

There was a long pause of silence.

'How is your bed, Jacqui? Is it comfortable?' queried Dalton as he snuggled down under his doona and nestled his pillow under his head. He was lying on his side, facing Jacqui, her bed only about a metre away from his. The room was small, so both beds were close together.

Jacqui had to think quickly about her response, as her mind was on the end goal of somehow ending up climbing into bed with Dalton. Whatever he was holding onto wasn't her issue. She was just happy for a fun night with a stranger. It was usually the Byron tradition to end up sharing a bed with someone she had never met before.

'Um, actually, my bed is really uncomfortable. I'm not sure that I can sleep here.' Jacqui laughed, hoping that Dalton would grasp her humour and invite her into his bed.

Dalton lifted his doona and said, 'Come on, come and sleep in here with me. I'll try not to sleep talk, and I promise I won't touch you if you don't touch me.'

'I can't guarantee that,' said Jacqui, 'sometimes I *sleep-touch*.'

'Very funny. I'm sure you do,' said Dalton.

They both laughed as Jacqui climbed out of her bed and into Dalton's. Their bodies were both clean, warm, and smooth on each other's skin.

It was Jacqui that made the first move, and she didn't waste any time. As soon as she climbed into the bed, she rolled Dalton straight onto his back and straddled her legs over him. She leaned down towards his face to kiss him, pausing briefly to say, 'I'm so sorry, Dalton, but as if I could be in a bed with you and not touch your beautiful body.'

'Thank you, Jacqui, you've got a gorgeous body of your own to *sleep* with!' He was still trying to play hard to get, suggesting that he had invited Jacqui into his bed to sleep with him.

Jacqui replied with a very cheeky and flirtatious, 'Yeah, but it's much more fun to *sleep* with you, and I'm going to use the word *sleep* lightly. I'm not sure if we will get much *sleep* tonight.'

'Is that right, Jacqui?' replied Dalton. 'I thought you might have already been asleep to be *sleep-touching* like that.'

'You know, I always thought it was a weird thing to say when people would say, "Did you two sleep together?" meaning, did you two make love? Fuck? Get it on? Whatever? I'm thinking if two people did make love, fuck, get it on, whatever, they probably didn't "sleep" together at all. Is that just me, or have you thought the same thing?'

'To be honest, Jacqui, I've never really thought about it, but you have a good point for a deep and thoughtful discussion about how "they" came up with that saying. Did you sleep with him?' Dalton paused and waited for Jacqui to respond. When he realised she would say nothing because his response was probably way too deep a thought, he continued, '...but I think I've had way too much Moet to figure any of that out right now. Let's just agree that "sleeping together" means no sleep.' They both laughed again.

Jacqui got back to kissing Dalton. She figured that if they talked much longer, he might talk himself out of *sleeping* with her because he was obviously quite taken by the Moet. Jacqui leaned forward and put the weight of her small but ample breasts on his chest. He loved the way it felt, although he was still feeling a little guilty, that he had another woman in his bed when he had decided only five minutes prior that Tilly was "the one." She still was "the one," but she wasn't here right now, and she might never be. Dalton didn't even know where Tilly was right now. He was pretty sure she was back at The Angourie Local. It was the weekend, so it was highly likely that she was waiting for the next tourist to walk in for a meal and a drink at the bar with his surfboard and his guitar and make love to her in the gypsy room. He wasn't the first. She had told him that.

Jacqui started kissing Dalton's mouth again, this time with more passion and aggression. Jacqui had to take control here because Dalton was still playing so hard to get. He was a good kisser. He knew what he was doing, but he wasn't yet giving her his full attention. She could feel that his mind was elsewhere, so she had to work harder to get him to be in the moment. She straddled her legs wider and moved her body lower so that she was moving closer to his hardness. It didn't matter what his mind was thinking; his body liked what Jacqui was doing to him, and Jacqui loved his body and his perfect hardness. She moved further down and put him inside her mouth. For the first time, Dalton showed some enjoyment in what Jacqui was doing to him. Jacqui had figured out his weakness. He loved oral sex. Not only did he enjoy receiving it, but he enjoyed giving it too.

Dalton and Jacqui didn't sleep much at all. They explored each other's bodies and enjoyed a beautiful night of uninhibited sex together.

Dalton was responsible and used a condom when he entered her. He had been travelling for a while and had a few encounters with random women along the way. He realised very early on that it was better to be safe than sorry. There was no way he was putting himself into a situation where he could get a stranger pregnant. That would not be a good outcome, for the sake of a fun night. There was also such a powerful media and social acceptance for safe sex. HIV/AIDS was rampant across the world, and everyone living in this era was fearful of the dangers of unprotected sex. Everyone was taught in schools about how to use condoms and lubrication to enjoy sex while still enjoying the pleasure of multiple partners. Following decades of free love, this was the new norm. Protected sex could still be fun. It was so easy.

Dalton and Jacqui were good together. They enjoyed each other's bodies for many hours, and then finally, in the early hours of the morning, they curled around each other and eventually fell into a beautiful, deep sleep.

When Dalton woke up, Jacqui was lying on the pillow beside him, staring at him. The sun was beaming through the crack in the curtain, shining on the corner of the room where Dalton had placed his belongings. It was well and truly daylight.

Dalton spoke in a soft, husky, sexy morning voice. 'Hey Jacq, you look beautiful this morning.'

'So do you, Tiger. I can't stop looking at you.' She laughed at the reference to calling him Tiger, which he had probably completely forgotten about. She had forgotten about Myles' nickname for Dalton also until just now.

Dalton laughed also and then softened the tone again, saying, 'Last night was amazing, thank you.'

'No, thank you and thank you and thank you,' replied Jacqui with cheeky flirtation about how many orgasms he had given her. He knew exactly what she was suggesting.

Dalton replied with a compliment to Jacqui. 'You were an easy lover; it was fun pleasing you. I'm glad you liked it.'

'Liked it. I loved every minute of last night, even though you were playing so hard to get all night. It was totally worth the challenge.' Jacqui had to remind Dalton of how much effort she had to make for him to let her climb into his bed, then she added, 'I wish I could put you in Adeline's car and take you home with me?'

I'm not sure how we would fit my guitar, surfboard, and me in that car with all of you girls and Georgia's five suitcases for the long drive back to where? Where did you say you were from?

Jacqui replied as she pointed south. 'Don't laugh at the name of my town. It's actually a really beautiful little town. It's called Nana Glen, it's down near Coffs Harbour.'

'That's right, I remember now, we had this conversation last night, didn't we?' Dalton recalled the conversation about where she was from, how she ended up being a jillaroo for a while, and that she had grown up in a small country town.

'We did. We talked about lots of things, but don't you try to change the conversation here. I'm sure we could fit you in our car for the return trip. There is good surfing in Woolgoolga and Coffs Harbour; you might like it there for a while. We picked up this girl today on the highway near Yamba. We fitted her in somehow, and she had a backpack and a guitar. I'm unsure about your surfboard, as we have no roof on Adeline's car, but we could make it work somehow. Where there is a will, there is a way.' Jacqui continued talking, but Dalton had already tuned off from the last part of what she was saying. He was focusing on the first part of the sentence, where Jacqui had mentioned picking up a girl on the highway near Yamba with a backpack and a guitar. Jacqui paused, noticing that Dalton's facial expression had become quite intense. She continued talking. 'She reminded me a lot of you, actually. She was travelling from Angourie as well.'

Dalton felt a rush of blood rise through his body. 'Huh? Tell me more.' Dalton was intrigued and instantly sobered. He felt like this was too coincidental not to be Tilly that she was talking about. A girl, a backpack and a guitar, hitching a ride near Yamba from Angourie, just like he was. But why would Tilly have been hitching?

'Did we not tell you about Tilly?' queried Jacqui.

Dalton replied with a questioning tone, 'I don't believe so?' He felt a wave of nausea rise to his throat when Jacqui mentioned her name.

'Oh! No big deal, really. When we were driving here today, we picked up this girl; her name was Tilly. She was hitching on the highway, with her guitar and backpack, just like you, on the side of the highway near the Yamba turnoff. We gave her a lift into Byron and had a few drinks with her at the Railway Hotel. That was earlier in the night before me, and Georgia and Adeline came here to this pub.'

Dalton questioned, wanting to know everything but keeping it simple for now. 'Why didn't she come with you?'

'She had hurt her wrist somehow. She thought it might be broken. She said she fell while she was running on the beach. She tripped on something, so she was getting on the next train to get herself to the Lismore Hospital. She was a gorgeous girl, so fun and easy to get along with, but there was something mysterious about her. It was like she was running from someone or on a mission to find someone.'

With these words, Dalton felt a shiver up and down his spine. 'Oh my god, I can't believe you are telling me this now, Jacqui. How did this not come up in conversation last night? She may have been trying to find me.' Dalton put his head in his hands and started shaking his head. 'I mean, that sounds really conceited, but how many girls called Tilly from Angourie can there be?'

'I'm not sure what you are talking about, Dalton. You might need to explain, but how do you know that girl was trying to find you? Why was she trying to find you? How do you even know her?' Jacqui encouraged Dalton to talk some more to clarify what he was talking about. This entire conversation had taken a very weird tangent suddenly.

'Oh my god, where do I even start?' Dalton sat up against the bedhead, placing a pillow behind his head, and sat upright. He put another pillow behind his back as a backrest. Jacqui leaned up with a pillow under her chest, propping her hands under her chin, with her fingers neatly interlocked, ready to listen to this story she was about to hear. She could tell already that it was a story she probably didn't want to hear, but there was not much she could do about that. It was too late.

'I'll try to keep it brief, as I'm sure you don't need all the details. Just a few days ago, I was surfing in Yamba with my mates whom I had met while travelling up the East Coast. I met Tilly's brother, Frankie, in the surf, and he invited me to come and stay in Angourie for a few days and check out the surf there. So, I did. I just wandered into The Angourie Local for a meal, a drink, and a place to stay, and I met Matilda, Tilly. We hit it off well. Like you said. I reminded you of her. She reminds me of me, too. We were really getting on well, like really well. When I met her, I felt like I'd known her forever. I think I fell in love with her the first time I saw her. But stupid me, I fucked it all up.'

'What do you mean, you only just met her?' Jacqui interrupted, not quite understanding what had happened yet.

'It's so hard to explain. I've been grieving the loss of my first love, Chelsea. She passed away not even a year ago, and the reason I left Deniliquin was to get away from my grief. When I met Tilly, I realised if I were to let my heart fall in love again, I had to let go of Chelsea and move on. So, I wrote a letter to Chelsea, placed it in a bottle and let it go into the ocean in Angourie. This was my strange way of letting go, saying goodbye and asking for forgiveness.'

'Wow. Dalton, I'm so sorry. No wonder you've been keeping yourself locked in. Please tell me more. I'm listening.' Jacqui was all ears to Dalton; she didn't really know what to say, so she encouraged him to keep on talking to explain the situation.

'Anyway, I had been for a surf with one of the Angourie surfers, Dan, "Badman." He knows Tilly well, same hometown and stuff, grew up together, all that. He told me I should make a move on Tilly if I liked her before someone else did. I decided to pour my heart out to her, tell her I love her and want to be with her forever, even though it might have seemed crazy because we had only just met, but my words came out all wrong. I stupidly started the conversation by saying something like, "I really like you, Tilly, but...." She didn't let me say what I needed to say, and she told me to go. Just go! She told me she had heard it all before, blah, blah, blah. She was so mad at me, I've never seen anyone react like that.'

Jacqui was frustrated that this had happened to Dalton. 'Oh no, didn't you try to explain?'

'Honestly, I don't know what happened at that moment. She just completely switched. It's like the same thing had happened to her for her whole life, and I was just another one, like all the rest. It certainly wasn't the conversation I thought it would be.' Dalton paused, deep in thought.

'So, what did you do?' Jacqui needed to know more.

'I waited, hoping that she might return to the room later that night, after she calmed down, to talk about things, but she didn't. So, I did what she told me to do: I left. Early the next morning, I got a lift with Dan to the highway, and that is when I met Travis. He picked me up and gave me a lift to Byron, and we surfed all day together. I came back here, checked in here for the night, and went to get something to eat with Travis, and that's when you girls came into the picture.'

Jacqui nodded, 'Go on.'

Dalton continued telling the story to Jacqui as she entered the story. He looked her in the eyes as he said. 'I met this gorgeous girl, Jacqui, who is lovely, and I had a great night with her. She's a gorgeous girl.' Dalton leaned down and kissed Jacqui on the forehead.

Jacqui felt terrible. 'Oh Dalton, I'm so sorry. No wonder you were playing so hard to get. It all makes sense to me now.'

Dalton shook his head in disbelief at the whole situation. 'I can't explain this, but I feel awkward and torn right now because I am in love with Tilly, and now you tell me she might be trying to find me, and here I am in a bed, naked with you.'

Jacqui tried to ease Dalton's guilty thoughts. 'And I'm so glad that you are. I have no regrets, but I'm sorry for how you must feel. Don't feel too bad about it. It was just some fun.'

'I have no regrets, Jacqui, but I hope you understand. I need to find her. I need to find Tilly.' Dalton felt anxious and irritated about what he had now discovered.

Jacqui had listened intently as Dalton shared his story. She only had two more questions that were playing on her mind as she was piecing this all together. 'Do you think it's definitely the same Tilly? Do you think she realised she made a mistake telling you to go, and now she's trying to find you?'

Dalton's mind was racing. 'I think so. Maybe. I mean, it has to be the same Tilly. Can I ask, what did she look like?'

Jacqui replied with a soft, understanding grin, feeling the anguish Dalton was feeling. She now understood why he had been so stand-offish and distant all night. 'She had dark curly hair, dark eyes and a gorgeous smile. She was probably the most beautiful girl I've ever seen. And I'm not into girls, but she was beautiful, so naturally beautiful.'

Dalton replied confidently. 'Yep, that's her. Was her guitar a Maton?'

Jacqui replied, 'I don't know, I don't play an instrument. It was in a hard, black case just like yours, but I wouldn't know what kind of guitar it was.' As Jacqui said this, she realised how perfectly matched Tilly and Dalton were for each other and how she was lucky to enjoy a night with Dalton for the night that it was. He and Tilly were most likely perfect for each other. Jacqui had met Tilly before at The Angourie Local, and she knew she was a beautiful musician and a surfer. Looking at Dalton here with his guitar and surfboard, she had no doubts that their love was meant to be. Jacqui added, to ease Dalton's guilt that she felt exuding from his core, 'Hey Dalton, don't feel bad. I've got a thing for foreign men anyhow. You're way too much of an Aussie country boy for me. I would feel like I was dating myself.' She laughed out loud and then finished saying, 'I'm happy with the night we shared; it was beautiful. Thank you. I'll be fine. Honestly, you need to find your girl.'

'So, what do we do now?' asked Dalton.

'You have to go and find her.' Jacqui replied, as she added, 'After you have breakfast with all of us. We can plan to help you.'

'Did she leave you any address or contact details?' Dalton questioned Jacqui, hoping she might have a way to contact Tilly.

'Well, funny that you ask. Remember last night when we played pool, and I had that coaster in my back pocket? That was from Tilly. Do you remember when you were teasing me about collecting phone numbers?'

'Yes, yes, I do! Is that from Tilly?' Dalton couldn't believe what he was hearing.

'Yep. She gave one to each of us girls before she jumped on the train. It's her parents' number at The Angourie Local, but she said she was travelling and she didn't know where she was going or for how long. You could give The Angourie Local a call.' This was Jacqui's only suggestion, but that was useless because Tilly was on the road.

'That's an idea, but if she doesn't know where she is headed, how will they know?' Dalton questioned the logic of Jacqui's suggestion.

'True.' Jacqui shrugged her shoulders, knowing that was all she could offer as a suggestion.

Dalton wasn't sure what to do but wanted to get moving. 'Let's get packed up and go to breakfast. It's almost 10 am.'

Jacqui was happy to go with the flow. She felt content in her heart that last night was just a one-night thing with Dalton, and she was happy to enjoy it for what it was. She was excited for Dalton to know that Tilly was looking for him, and Jacqui realised that perhaps the whole reason for them meeting and "sleeping" together was for this serendipitous moment to occur. If Jacqui and Dalton hadn't met and spent the night together, Dalton would be none the wiser to know that Tilly was searching for him. If she, in fact, was. *Everything happens for a reason*, she thought.

Dalton shook his head again as he consoled himself with the idiom. *Everything happens for a reason.*

Jacqui had only herself to worry about. She had no belongings to pack, so she had a quick shower to freshen up while Dalton packed his stuff. Dalton jumped into the shower after her. He didn't know where his next hotel room would be, so he was making the most of the good shower while he could. He washed his gorgeous curls and freshened himself up with deodorant and a good-smelling aftershave. He was almost at the bottom of his bottle of Joop! It smelled good, sweet but sexy, almost feminine, which he liked because women always said he smelt delicious.

Jacqui hurried him along as she helped him stack up his belongings. 'Let's go, Tiger. You've got yourself a roaming tigress to find. Such a wild story you have unknowingly created.'

chapter forty-five

Travis & Adeline—Making Love

Travis and Adeline had woken early and "made love" again. They had little sleep. After leaving the pub, they returned to the Kombi, grabbed a picnic rug and headed down to the beach for a moonlight beach walk, which turned into stargazing and beach love. They kissed and made love under the stars for a few hours before returning to the Kombi for a cosy night's sleep. Adeline was surprised at how comfortable the mattress in the Kombi was. They both had a restful sleep and awoke as the sun came beaming in through the windows.

They were calling it "making love" with each other because of the way their bodies collided. It was soft, gentle, and passionate. Although Travis had a hardcore extroverted personality, with sex, he had a tender, loving, hippie soul. He was carefree and kind, and his main goal in life was to surf awesome waves, have wild fun and be free to wander the world. His favourite thing was kissing, so he and Adeline had spent most of the night with their mouths entangled, exploring each other's tongues and soft lips. Of course, this deep, passionate kissing led to beautiful lovemaking.

When they woke up, they couldn't resist having each other again and again. The only problem for Travis and Adeline to get on with their day and get to breakfast was that they didn't have the luxury of a hot hotel shower. Travis had parked his Kombi near a beach shower, so that was sufficient. Adeline stepped outside the Kombi, wearing only her simple underwear. She figured that no one in Byron really gave much of a worry about what anyone was wearing or not wearing. She had a quick refreshing shower and got dressed back in the clothes she had worn the night before. Adeline's bag was back in the car's boot. It was a bit of a further walk, so she decided not to worry about changing her clothes for now. She was happy to go to breakfast in what she was wearing.

chapter forty-six

Tapestry of Life

Tilly awoke wrapped in Bernard's arms. They had shared a beautiful night, wrapped closely with each other, after Tilly could finally lay her head down without spinning and needing to be sick. Tilly instantly felt a brief pang of guilt, thinking *what have I done, staying here in Bernard's room for the night?* These thoughts were mixed with thoughts of, *oh no, I lost my guitar pick yesterday.* As Tilly's thoughts wandered to the negative, wondering how she could have allowed herself to sleep in a room, with Bernard, when she was so deeply in love with Dalton, she readjusted her thought pattern, to the more positive, *Tilly, you had some guilt-free-fun, a few too many drinks, and someone to look after you for the night, and yes you may have lost your pick.* Tilly vaguely remembered her conversation with Bernard. They had talked about respect and freedom towards each other in deciding to share the night together in the same room. There was nothing strange about it and there were to be no weird feelings towards each other afterwards. Bernard looked after Tilly, and eventually, she fell asleep in his arms.

The first thing Bernard said when Tilly opened her eyes and turned towards him was 'Hey, while I think of it, remind me to ring the Murwillumbah Train Station to ask about your guitar pick.'

Tilly laughed. 'Yeah, we need to do that today. I was just thinking about that, among other things. How did you read my thoughts?' Tilly was seriously shocked at how Bernard was thinking the same thing.

'I was just thinking back over yesterday and last night, and I saw how devastated you were when you realised you had lost it. I'm guessing it's the only sentimental thing you have with you?'

'Yes, I'd say it's the only sentimental thing. I've got a few other really important belongings, though. My Maton guitar and a very special message in a bottle.'

'You're full of surprises, Tilly. What is this message in a bottle you keep talking about?'

'That's the missing piece of the puzzle and the reason that I realised I fucked it up with Dalton.'

'This whole Dalton situation sounds like a true love story, and the message in a bottle, a good song lyric.' Bernard joked, then took a more serious tone. 'I hope last night hasn't ruined it for you. You know it's okay that you stayed here in my bed with me last night. No hard feelings?'

'No hard feelings; last night was fun, the drinks, the dancing, the beach walk, the conversations and thanks for looking after me. I haven't been sick like that in quite some time. I'm usually a good drinker, but those Illusions really hit me. I'm looking forward to spending this week with you and singing with you on the weekend. Life is what it is, and everything happens for a reason. I don't have any regrets about last night, do you?' Tilly was confident in what she was saying, but deep down, she felt untrue to her feelings for Dalton.

Bernard thought for a little while longer as Tilly awaited his response. 'I don't have any regrets, but I feel more concern for you as you've explained to me how much you love this Dalton fella. That's up to you and your conscience, I guess. What happens if you find him? Do you tell him about spending the night with me?'

'This whole thing with Dalton is a mystery; if I find him, it will be a miracle, and then I have a lot of explaining to do. I'll be lucky if he took me back after the way I treated him. He must think I'm crazy anyway.' Tilly was getting worked up.

Bernard took over the conversation, calming Tilly down. 'Look, the way I see it is this. You've left everything behind you: your job, your family, your friends. You are on a mission to find this man. You've got a broken arm, a message in a bottle, and a journey ahead of you to find your way back to his heart. You've both got some explaining to do, by the sounds of it. I haven't seen the message, but it sounds like he's got a bit of baggage to overcome and to share with you. If you truly love each other, everything will be okay. If it's not meant to be, then none of this was meant to be. It's what it is, the tapestry of life.'

Tilly hugged Bernard. 'That's lovely, Bernard, and I hope you're right. No hard feelings?'

'No hard feelings, oh and one more thing.' Bernard kept on talking. 'I wouldn't change a thing about what happened yesterday and last night. Meeting you, and spending time with you, has been such a joy in my life. You know Tilly, sometimes life's not all about you. It's about the joy you bring to others as well.'

'Thanks Bernard, I've really enjoyed your company too, and I hope we can stay friends forever, even when you're super famous.'

Bernard laughed. 'Of course.'

'So, I've got three important things to do today. One, make a phone call about that guitar pick. Two, get to the hospital, get this bloody arm plastered, and three, find Dalton. Can you please help me with all those things?'

Bernard gave Tilly a warm hug and a kiss on the forehead. 'Sure, I can help you do all those things. I can't promise we will find Dalton today, but let's make it part of our plan.'

chapter forty-seven

'Lovers' Breakfast

As Dalton and Jacqui walked down the hallway and past the dolphin room where Myles and Georgia had stayed, they could hear voices coming from inside the room. Dalton banged gently on the door and called out, 'See you at breakfast, lovers.'

Myles called back. 'We will be there soon. Go on ahead, we will catch up.'

As Dalton and Jacqui walked out into the restaurant, they caught sight of Travis and Adeline. Travis was sitting at the end of the table. Adeline was very close by, sitting in the adjacent corner. They had pulled their chairs near to each other so they could sit as close as possible to chat. Adeline was staring intensely into Travis' eyes as he talked about something interesting, using his hands expressively to explain the details of their conversation. Adeline didn't break her gaze from his eyes, and you could feel from their closeness and the relaxed vibe that they had enjoyed a beautiful night together.

'Hey lovers,' Dalton dragged out the word loverrrs, as he smiled widely towards Travis and Adeline. He pulled a chair out for Jacqui to sit down, and they all joined together at the large table for six. 'The other two lovers are on the way. We just walked past their room, and they are coming shortly. How was your night? Looks like you two are still getting along well?' Dalton queried, already feeling the vibe strongly that these two had enjoyed each other's company very much.

'We're good. We had a *beautiful* night, thanks, Dalton.' Travis answered first, as he smiled and reached to squeeze Adeline's hand for emphasis on the word beautiful.

Adeline added her response. 'Yes, we had a great night. Thank you. How about you two lovers?' Adeline thought she might throw in the assumption, as Dalton had already done to them. "Lovers" seemed to be the catchphrase of the morning.

Jacqui jumped in first to answer, knowing that Dalton might get carried away to tell his story about finding out about Tilly. He was quite fixated on it since he had discovered that Tilly might be trying to find him. Jacqui was okay with this fixation. She wasn't jealous. There was no reason to be. She and Dalton had only just met the night before. Jacqui also wanted to make sure that the breakfast catch-up was enjoyed by this newly formed group of friends. It was a unique occurrence that three guys and three girls could meet up and all enjoy each other's company for a few hours and then magically partner up for the night to all enjoy a great night as "paired lovers." The plan to meet again in the morning was the best idea, and Jacqui was trying to remember whose idea it was. She could feel Dalton's enthusiastic vibe to get moving and to find Tilly. She answered Adeline with, 'Ummm, let's just say we had a wonderful night and a very interesting, let's say, serendipitous morning.'

'Hmmm, sounds like there is a story in that. Do you want to share?' encouraged Adeline.

'Sure, maybe later. I'd love to hear how your night was. How was it sleeping in the Kombi?'

'It was surprisingly comfortable.' Adeline looked at Travis to see if he would agree with her. Travis was nodding his head in agreement.

'It's not bad,' added Travis, nodding as he lifted his eyebrows, acknowledging the pride he had in his beautiful Kombi machine.

Adeline couldn't resist and hoped that Travis didn't mind her sharing their secret rendezvous story. 'We enjoyed a bit of a moonlight beach walk first and wow, the stars were beautiful. I'm usually spoilt with the beauty of blanket skies of country stars, from where I live, but beach stars are pretty good too, especially where we were, at The Pass.'

Travis was gazing as she retold her version of the night. He was mesmerised by the softness and beauty of her face. Adeline could feel Travis' gaze upon her, but he didn't interrupt, so she just kept on talking. 'It's secluded and dark down there, quite spooky, really. There were no bright streetlights to interrupt the darkness of the night.'

Travis added his bit to say, 'We had an unforgettable beach picnic rug adventure for a few hours, and then we came back and slept in the Kombi. Waking up to the sound of the waves was special. It was fun.' Adeline jumped back in to finish their story. 'I had a really beautiful night, thanks to this guy.' She squeezed Travis' hand and leaned towards him to kiss him on the mouth. He leaned in and returned her kiss.

'Aww, you two are cute!' Dalton smiled, as it was nice to see Travis happy with a girl. Not that he needed a girl to make his life complete, he was a free soul enjoying his freedom in life to travel and surf with no connections or commitments anywhere. He was a great guy, and it was lovely to see him enjoying this moment with Adeline. She was a beautiful girl. Her face was angelic, with porcelain skin and soft pink cheeks. She had light freckles and a strong but well-proportioned nose. She had a warm voice tone when she spoke through her natural pouty lips with a small yet noticeable scar. Her personality was oozing intelligence and gentleness. Dalton hadn't realised last night, with his Tilly blinkers on, how beautiful Adeline was. But as they sat closely at the table, in the clear light of day, and she told her story of how her night with Travis went, Dalton took notice of her natural beauty. She spoke with kindness, enthusiasm, and gratitude. As they all sat chatting easily with each other, Dalton's mind drifted back to the day before, when he had met Travis by fate and then, how they also by random chance met three most beautiful girls and had a fantastic night in enjoyable company. He was pretty sure Myles and Georgia had shared a memorable night as well. They were yet to find out.

Dalton felt an intense pang of guilt towards how Jacqui might feel towards him, after their discovery and his instant distancing from her. How convenient it would have been that these six new friends could hang out longer for the weekend and who knows where the direction of their lives would take them? They were all fancy-free, enjoying their adult youth, and somehow, by chance, they had all ended up in Byron for this fateful night.

The most significant fated moment for Dalton was held in the brief conversation when Jacqui mentioned they had met a 'Tilly,' who was hitching from the highway near Yamba, and that she seemed to search for someone or something.

It was all too coincidental, and Dalton had to act upon it, although he felt terrible about leaving his new group of friends. He kept on thinking. Imagine if Jacqui said nothing about this hitchhiker, Tilly. He would never have known that Tilly was possibly searching for him.

Just as he was thinking this, fate stepped in again. The Spanish bartender, who had been working the night shift, came over to take their breakfast order. He was standing at the other end of the table from where Travis was sitting. He leaned in near Jacqui to place the menus on the table. 'Morning, my new friends. How are you all feeling this morning? Or should I say, how is the Moet feeling this morning?' He spoke with a strong, beautiful, recognisable Spanish accent. Jacqui almost fell off her chair as she spun around to look at him.

Jacqui spoke first. 'Wow, you are here early, after a late-night shift. We kept you up late last night. It is so nice to see you again.'

'You too, my friends. Can I get you some water for the table while you review the menu? Are your other two friends joining you as well?'

Dalton replied this time. 'Yes, thank you. Some water would be great. We will need six glasses, as I'm pretty sure Myles and Georgia will join us soon.'

Jacqui added, 'May we ask your name?'

'Of course you can. My name is Juan, it's pronounced Yoowan, but you can call me John if that is easier for you. Juan is just like John, in your language, a very common Spanish name.'

'No, we can call you Juan. That's much more exciting than John,' announced Adeline, as she was also fascinated by this gorgeous-looking man. Adeline didn't take her hand off Travis' leg, making sure he understood her attachment to him, even though she was having a bit of a flirt with Juan.

'Why thank you!' Juan accepted the compliment and felt a little awkward as the girls were giving him a lot of attention, and the boys sat quietly. 'I'll bring the menus for you, times six, my friends.'

'Thanks, mate. I'm super hungry,' replied Travis.

As Juan left the table to collect the menus, Myles and Georgia came into the restaurant, both with the biggest grins on their faces. They had enjoyed a wild, fun night together. Adeline noticed that even though Georgia was still flamboyant, she was a little quieter than usual. She liked this version of Georgia. It was much easier to be around her at 10 am after the night they had all shared. Georgia was probably a little hungover, thought Adeline.

Myles pulled out a chair for Georgia, and she thanked him as she sat down next to Adeline. Myles sat at the other end of the table, in between Jacqui and Georgia. 'How are we all feeling this morning?' queried Myles with a slight brow raised, suggesting he was a little worse for wear.

As Myles sat down, Juan returned with two jugs of water and six glasses.

'Here is some water for you all. Just give me a wave when you are ready to order. I can highly recommend the Surfers Scrambled Eggs. They are delicious and will give you guys plenty of energy for your surf today. I hear the surf is going to be spectacular this afternoon. We have an east-northeast swell combined with a southeast wind. The best conditions for The Pass.' Jacqui couldn't stop staring at him, and she loved that he was including the guys in the conversation, so they felt just as important as the girls that he was naturally charming, simply by his presence.

Juan returned behind the bar and fiddled with the sound system to put on some breakfast chill music to add to the ambience of the Byron Hotel for a Saturday morning. The playlist started with '*Bette Davis Eyes*' by Kim Carnes. It was a good start, followed by music from Chicago, Stevie Nicks, Tom Petty, The Bangles, The Cars and Foreigner. It seemed to be the Best of the 80s collection, perhaps a double-length CD.

The three guys had decided they would keep breakfast simple and go with the Surfers Scrambled Eggs with a side of bacon, as recommended by Juan. The Eggs Benedict tempted Georgia. Jacqui and Adeline had decided on the stack of pancakes with banana, bacon, and maple syrup.

They all enjoyed friendly banter about the previous evening's shenanigans as their breakfast arrived. Dalton was distracted, but also enjoying the company and the conversation. When it eventually seemed that everyone had stopped talking and sharing stories, Dalton decided he might like to question Georgia and Adeline to investigate whether they knew any more about this mysterious girl, Tilly. He was just about to start the conversation, but he wasn't sure how to approach the topic without being disrespectful to Jacqui or sounding self-important. Adeline felt the tension between Jacqui and Dalton, but she wasn't sure exactly what the feeling was all about. She miraculously helped Dalton out by saying, 'Jacqui, I hope you don't mind me bringing this up with all of us here now. I mean, we're all friends anyway, but you mentioned before that you and Dalton had a wonderful night and an interesting, serendipitous morning. Do you mind sharing with us what may have been so interesting to you both while the rest of us were sleeping?'

Jacqui finished her mouthful of pancakes, bananas, and bacon. 'Sure, we can share. Can we, Dalton?'

Dalton replied with an inviting, 'Sure, how do we explain? You go first.'

Jacqui had everyone's attention as she wove together the story of Tilly and Dalton, the circumstances that led up to their interesting morning, and how she figured out that Tilly might be looking for Dalton. 'This won't make any sense to you, Travis, and Myles, but yesterday we picked up a hitchhiker just on the highway near Yamba, likely in the same place, Travis, where you picked up Dalton. Her name was Tilly. She came with us to Byron and hung out with us at The Railway Hotel before catching a train to Lismore Hospital.'

Myles asked for clarification, 'Why did she go to the hospital? What was wrong with her?'

Jacqui continued. 'She had hurt her arm and wanted to get it checked out. Tilly thought it might have been broken, and this was a problem for her, as just the same as Dalton, she is a musician: a guitarist, singer, and songwriter. She was travelling with a backpack and a guitar, just like Dalton. No surfboard, though. Obviously, she's not as hardcore as you fellas.' They all laughed.

'Oh, she's an amazing surfer. Let me just say,' added Dalton. 'She's from Angourie, say no more.'

Travis encouraged Jacqui to share more information. 'I'm not following yet. Dalton, how do you know this girl, Tilly?'

Dalton carried on with the story, trying to make it all make sense because it was so confusing.

'As you know, Travis, I was surfing in Angourie for a bit, and I met this girl Tilly at The Angourie Local. We hit it off. She is the most beautiful girl I've ever seen. I fell in love with her instantly. Like, instantly.'

The girls all nodded in agreement. Tilly was a stunning woman.

Dalton added. 'You girls are all next in line equally. You are all gorgeous girls, just saying.'

'Awww, thanks Dalton, but tell us more. If she is the most beautiful girl you've ever seen, and you fell in love with her instantly, then why are you here, and why is she on a train to Lismore Hospital?' Adeline was trying to make sense of the story.

'So, the next part is hard to explain. Let's just say that we had a stupid miscommunication, and Tilly told me to go. So here I am. Now, she may be looking for me. Maybe. I know that sounds conceited. I left a message in a bottle declaring my love for her, and I think maybe, just maybe, she found it and has realised our mistake, and now she is trying to find me. Of course, this is all hypothetical; she may not be looking for me at all. She may just be getting away from it all and travelling for a while. But if she is looking for me, I want her to find me.'

Travis, the ultimate romantic, added. 'Or even better, you can find her again. That makes a much more romantic story.'

'What if she's not looking for me, and what if she doesn't want me to find her?' Dalton queried the group.

Travis responded. 'You've gotta back yourself, man. What's the worst-case scenario? She tells you to go again. I bet that if you find her again, she'll ask you to stay.' Travis continued with his supportive words. He had only known Dalton since Friday, but he could tell that he was a decent guy and could feel the torment of his broken heart. When he met Dalton, he was acutely aware that they didn't talk about their personal lives. Without words being spoken, Travis could tell that Dalton was dealing with anguish. Now he knew what it was, and everything was making sense.

'How do I find her?' Dalton asked again for any advice from the group.

Georgia popped into the conversation with a big question for Dalton and Jacqui. 'Hold on, hold on, hold on, can we just back up a bit? I'm still trying to figure out how you two had a beautiful night together, and now all I'm hearing about is this Tilly and how she's looking for you. Shouldn't we have figured that out before you two enjoyed a beautiful night together?'

Jacqui agreed. 'Yes, we probably should have, and now I think about it, there were so many signs. I was actually thinking about it in the shower this morning. None of us picked up on the cues last night, probably thanks to the cloud of Moet lingering over all of us.'

Georgia queried. 'What signs? What cues did we miss Jacqui?'

'First, I remember so clearly now, driving past Travis' Kombi when we were doing a drive around the bays. I recall thinking that's a cool-looking Kombi. Not that we girls knew Dalton and Tilly knew each other, but in a different circumstance, or if Dalton was standing on the road or near the car, they may have spotted each other. And that would have changed everything.'

Jacqui continued, with her thoughts out loud. 'Then there was the "freedom and friendship" cheer thing. I mean, who does that? Was that odd to anyone else, or just me?'

Adeline added. 'Yes, I thought it was a coincidence that Dalton's *"Cheers"* was the same as Tilly's *"Cheers,"* but honestly, I thought nothing of it.'

Georgia added, 'Oh, that, yeah, I noticed that, but I just thought it was some kind of Australian thing that I hadn't heard about yet. That happens a lot to me. You Australians have lots of weird sayings that make no sense to me.'

Jacqui continued. 'Then there was Tilly's contact name and phone number on my coaster in my back pocket. It fell on the table when I was getting coins out of my pocket, when we were playing pool. Dalton saw the coaster and teased me about collecting phone numbers of strangers, but we never put two and two together with that either.'

Dalton added here, 'Was that Tilly's name on the coaster? I didn't see the name; I just saw letters and numbers.'

Jacqui continued. 'The universe did its best to help us figure it out, but we didn't. None of us put two and two together until this morning when I noticed Dalton's backpack and guitar, and I mentioned that we had picked up a hitchhiker named Tilly from Angourie with a backpack and the same guitar case. How many Tilly's from Angourie are there?'

Dalton replied, 'That's the whole stupid thing though. I don't know that she's looking for me. When I left her, she was back at The Angourie Local. It was only by random chance Jacqui woke up this morning, after an awesome night, mind you,' as he squeezed Jacqui's hand on the table, 'and told me I reminded her of this girl Tilly that you ladies had met yesterday. Tilly is not a common name, so I am just clutching at straws. If her name was Sarah or Amanda, I might not be feeling the way I am feeling right now. You girls all have beautiful names, too. Jacqui, Adeline, and Georgia. I would search for you all as well.' They all laughed.

Jacqui didn't want to interrupt Dalton's flow, but she couldn't resist teasing him. 'Swoon. You're such a swoon.'

Dalton continued on talking, and as he did, he was making sense of the situation. 'I can only come up with three options. One: It's my Tilly, and she's trying to find me, knowing I was heading up the east coast to surf. I mentioned the Gold Coast to her, as I think I could sustain an income there, so that is where she may be heading to find me. Two: It's my Tilly, and she's not trying to find me at all. She's just decided she's heading out for an adventure to get away for a while. Three: It's not my Tilly at all; it's just some random girl, who is the fifth most beautiful girl in the world travelling with her guitar.' Dalton made a pointed gesture to the three girls at the table, silently counting Tilly as Number One. They all laughed again.

As they had all finished their breakfast, Juan cleared their plates.

'So, my friends, do you have plans for today?' Jacqui almost melted in her seat.

Jacqui was quick to answer, surreptitiously letting Juan know she was a free woman, assuming that Juan would think she was paired with Dalton. 'We are just making plans now. Dalton is on a mission to find the one that got away.'

'Oh, I thought you two were together; it's none of my business, though, my apologies.' Juan felt rude now that he had asked.

'It's okay, and I'm glad you asked.' Jacqui replied, thrilled that Juan was curious as to their connection.

Travis jumped in, keen to add another surfer to their tribe. 'We need to get Dalton to Lismore, somehow, and the rest of us will hit the beach. The Pass sounds like the place to be this afternoon. You are welcome to join us for a surf, man!' Travis knew the others wouldn't mind if he invited Juan, feeling the vibe that everyone, especially Jacqui, would be okay with that. Juan was a cool guy.

Juan was excited to accept Travis' offer. 'If you don't mind, I would love to join you. My shift here finishes at 1 pm, and then I start again at 5 pm, I have a split shift today. So, I have just four hours to play with you.' Again, Jacqui was melting in her chair; just the thought of Juan "playing" with them had sent her mind to places it shouldn't go just yet. Of course, her thoughts were more personal, including only her and Juan, but she was looking forward to hanging with him at the beach. Suddenly Jacqui wished she could surf.

Travis suggested Juan meet them at The Pass after his shift finished. 'We will see you there, man!'

Myles and Georgia moved closer to each other. Myles leaned in to give Georgia a quick little teasing kiss. This was their way of letting each other know they couldn't get enough of each other. Myles quickly took a break away from Georgia's mouth to add to the plans. 'We might catch up with you guys later. I think we both need some more sleep.' Myles and Georgia had said little during the conversation. He and Georgia had no sleep at all. Both were feeling the effects of their many shared bottles of Moet. After the pub closed, they took another bottle back to their room and finished it in the early hours of the morning. Myles had his room booked until the end of the week, so he was in no rush to leave. He was happy to take Georgia back to his room to catch up on a bit more *sleep.*

Georgia joined in the conversation. 'I'll meet you at the beach later this afternoon. Don't leave town without me, Adeline.' Adeline, Georgia and Jacqui had planned to drive back down south that Sunday afternoon, as all three had commitments the following day. Their fun Byron weekend would be over soon, but they all wanted to make the most of the rest of the day with their new friends.

Juan was still clearing plates as he suggested to Dalton that the train to Lismore usually departed from The Railway Hotel at around 4 pm Dalton felt a wash of dismay move over his body. 4 pm seemed like an eternity away. He wondered if there was another way to get to the hospital. He could get bitten by a shark, but that was a tad dramatic. He could fake an asthma attack, dramatic as well. He could hitch a ride, or he could be patient and wait to catch the train. His concern was that by the time he got to the hospital, Tilly would most likely be gone.

'It looks like you're stuck with us for a few more hours,' said Travis with secret delight as he enjoyed Dalton's company.

'I don't think I can wait until 4 pm. I'm wondering if there is another way. I'm happy to make my own way, just figuring out the best way.' Dalton explained with some frustration.

Travis added. 'The challenge will be finding your way to Lismore. Most people heading out of Byron Bay are headed straight to the Gold Coast or south on the highway. Lismore is a bit off the track.'

Dalton was thinking carefully to track her moves. 'I'm thinking by the time I get to Lismore, she might already be on her way to the Gold Coast.'

Jacqui was trying to brainstorm with Dalton. She knew Adeline would prefer to spend the day with Travis, and Georgia would want to spend the day with Myles, so asking them for a lift was useless. Jacqui could offer to drive Dalton to Lismore, but she selfishly wanted to spend the day hanging out with Juan. Dalton was adamant that he was happy to go on his own. This was his mission. He spoke his thoughts out loud. 'If she caught the train last night at 4 pm, she would have arrived at the hospital late, but I imagine they would have put a cast on her arm fairly quickly and despatched her.'

There was a pause as everyone was in their own thoughts, trying to think about the possibilities of Tilly's location.

Dalton continued talking out loud as he tried to figure it out. 'If she arrived late in Lismore, then where would she stay?' Dalton was lost at this point. He did not know about Lismore or any towns further north than Byron Bay.

'Maybe she has friends there?' Jacqui suggested.

'I don't know, maybe.' Dalton was unsure. He had never heard Tilly talk about Lismore, and the only reason she was going there was to go to the hospital.

Jacqui felt worried thinking of the possibilities. 'If she's hitchhiking, she might not have a choice other than to stay in Lismore somewhere. I can't imagine she would want to hitch a ride in the middle of the night. Especially with the news of that balaclava rapist and murderer roaming the Tweed Heads area.'

Dalton wasn't worried about Tilly hitching; he was more concerned about where she would be. 'She's a strong woman, and she's smart. She'll be fine, but I'm just trying to figure out her whereabouts.'

Jacqui suddenly felt a genuine sense of urgency for Dalton to get to Lismore. This was really important to him. If Tilly had stayed in Lismore for the night, perhaps she was still there. She checked her watch. It was only 11 am. The drive to Lismore was roughly an hour, perhaps just a little more, so Jacqui worked out that if they left now, she could be back in time to meet up at the beach with Juan and the others.

Travis and Adeline were deep in their own conversation when Jacqui interrupted. 'Hey Adeline, do you mind if I drive Dalton to Lismore? Do you have the keys?' Jacqui was sure Adeline wouldn't mind, and it seemed like the only option to get Dalton to Lismore before it was too late.

Adeline agreed it was a good idea, reaching to grab the keys out of her handbag. 'Sure thing, babe, you might need to put some more petrol in it. I think we've used up the full tank getting here.'

Travis was disappointed, but he understood Dalton's dilemma. 'Mate, we wish you could stay, but we understand you gotta do what you gotta do. How can we keep in touch?'

'I'm not sure how we can keep in touch. I don't have any fixed address or phone number. Perhaps it's easier if I get your contact number and address to keep in touch with you.' Dalton suggested this as a better option, as Travis had a fixed address and phone number.

Travis grabbed a coaster from the table as Adeline grabbed a pen from her handbag. They scribbled names, phone numbers, and addresses on both sides and handed it to Dalton. 'Please keep in touch, mate. We want to know how this story ends.'

'Come on, Dalton. Let's go!' Jacqui was keen to get going for Dalton's sake and for her plans as well to get back to the beach with Juan and the gang.

'I'll just go grab my stuff and check out, and I'll meet you out the front. Is that okay?' Dalton was already standing up at the table and heading towards the back of the hotel to return to his hotel room to collect his bag, which was already packed, his surfboard and his guitar.

'See you guys, it was so wonderful meeting you all. I'll keep in touch, I promise.' Dalton had Adeline's and Travis' contacts so that would keep him in touch with the gang, as he trusted they would all exchange contact details at the end of the weekend when they all departed each other's company and returned to their daily lives.

chapter forty-eight

Change of Plans

Dalton returned to Room 9, the surfboard room, to collect his stuff and checked out at the hotel reception area. All he had to do was hand in his key. He had already paid the account the night before, just in case he wanted to get up and depart early for a sunrise surf. That never happened, as the evening took another turn. As Dalton collected his stuff, he had flashbacks of the night before trolling through his mind. It had been an enjoyable night for him and Jacqui. It wasn't the magic that he had with Tilly, and in the cold light of day and sobered, he felt shallow and guilty about the whole thing, but he had just to let it go. That one random decision to share the night with Jacqui might have been the catalyst to change the rest of his life. Who knows, really? Stuff like that played on Dalton's mind. In life, there were so many interwoven interactions, discussions and chance occurrences, it was hard to understand how this wasn't all part of the bigger picture of life. The events of the morning were even more clear in Dalton's mind. When Jacqui mentioned the name Tilly, he just knew it was part of the bigger picture of what was meant to be. The most ironic situation was that Jacqui was now about to drive Dalton to Lismore to find Tilly.

The other weird thing was that Jacqui was totally okay with it. She was not attached to Dalton. He was gorgeous and all, but he was so shut down the night before it was hard to get to know his actual personality, anyway. Jacqui had many one-night stand flings in Byron. It was just the usual thing for her. She was searching for her Mr Right and having fun along the way. Dalton wasn't all that Mr Right for her. Juan, on the other hand, now that was something worth pursuing. Dalton reassured himself, realising that maybe his whole reason for being with Jacqui wasn't about him at all; maybe the whole reason was that she would get to meet Juan. He liked that idea of serendipity so much better and didn't feel so guilty anymore.

Jacqui had parked off to the side of the road, at the front of the hotel, so they could load up the car with all of Dalton's stuff.

'Wow, this is quite a fancy vehicle you've got here, Jacqui.' Dalton was impressed.

'Yeah, it's cool. It's Dad's car. He lets us drive it, provided we look after it and pay for our own fuel. Adeline is a way better driver than me, so she is usually the chauffeur.'

'I'm more than happy to pay for a tank of petrol, Jacqui,' offered Dalton. 'It's the least I can do.' He added as he climbed into the passenger seat. 'Do you want me to drive?'

'Nah, it's cool; it's probably best if I do. Dad would prefer it if just Adeline and I drove. We are in the insurance policy. Anyway, you've got way too much on your mind.' Jacqui was happy to drive; she enjoyed driving her dad's car.

Just as they were about to depart, the car was loaded up with the surfboard lying across the back seat beside Dalton's guitar and backpack. Juan came running out of the hotel. He was waving his arms for them to stop with a genuine panic of expression.

'I'm sorry to bother you, and I don't mean to be rude, but I was listening to your conversation, and something is not making sense. Did you say this girl Tilly, you say her name is, you say she caught the train at 6 pm?' Juan struggled to get his words in the right order.

Jacqui replied, 'Yeah, 6 pm from the Railway Hotel.'

Juan explained his understanding of the train timetable. 'The 6 pm train is northbound to Murwillumbah, not to Lismore. I hate to say this, but I don't think your girl is in Lismore right now. I'm very sorry, but this I know. There are only two trains per day. The 4 pm goes to Lismore, and the 6 pm goes north to Murwillumbah. If, as you say, she got on the 6 pm train; she is headed north to Murwillumbah. I don't know what to say.'

Dalton looked enquiringly at Jacqui. 'Are you sure she got on that 6 pm train? Do you think she was lying to you about saying she was going to Lismore Hospital, or do you think she just had a change of plans and didn't tell you?'

'Yeah, I think she may have headed north to the Murwillumbah Hospital. She doesn't seem like the type of person who would be untrue. She's as down to earth and trustworthy as they come, for as much as I know, in our brief conversations. When she departed, she said she was going to Lismore Hospital, but she boarded the 6 pm train. She was in such a rush to get on before it departed.'

Dalton interjected. 'Okay, she might have said she was going to the Lismore Hospital, meaning that she was going to the Murwillumbah Hospital, but she boarded the 6 pm train?'

Jacqui continued to explain. 'Yep, we were all busy when she was saying goodbye, and the train was about to pull into the station, so she didn't really have time to explain anything. It was quite a rushed decision, actually. She was adamant she would get her arm looked at, and she wasn't sticking around Byron to party with us because her arm was too painful.'

Dalton simply replied, deep in thought. 'Okay.'

Jacqui added, 'Damn, in that moment, if she had known half an hour later, we would bump into you, our lives would be very different right now.' Jacqui spoke her thoughts out loud as she was trying to piece it all together for Dalton. 'Okay, so let's think this through.'

Dalton talked his thoughts out loud again as he was trying to figure out her whereabouts. 'We know she got on the 6 pm train to the Murwillumbah Hospital. Let's narrow that down as a pretty confident fact.'

'Yep, I'll go with that as a fact. For sure, she was on that 6 pm train.' Jacqui confirmed Dalton's first piece of the puzzle.

'If she got on the northbound train, she would have gone to Murwillumbah Hospital last night, do you think?' Dalton queried Jacqui, thinking she might know more about the hospital procedures than he did.

Jacqui had a go at thinking about this next part out loud. 'She would have arrived in Murwillumbah at around 7 pm and checked in through Emergency to get her arm looked at. That's after-hours, so she would have either been done and despatched or, more than likely, she would have had to book a room somewhere near the hospital to go back and get it cast in the morning.'

Dalton added, 'If it's a small country hospital, and anything like Deniliquin, I can't imagine it's heavily staffed to deal with a minor broken arm after hours. They would probably send her away with some bandaging and Panadol and tell her to come back in the morning.'

Jacqui nodded and then shook her head. 'I think you're right.' She did not know where Tilly might be, so rather than try to give advice, she asked a question. 'So then, if that's the case, where would she be today?'

Dalton was even more confused. He didn't know the geography or names of places of towns in this part of the country, so he couldn't even visualise where she might be going. He had a feeling that she would end up on the Gold Coast. That was his eventual plan, and Tilly was aware of that. Maybe he was best to just head to the Gold Coast and try to find her there, rather than chasing a day behind her.

Just as he was thinking this, Jacqui confirmed his thoughts. 'I remember vaguely, from when I was a kid, catching a train from somewhere near Lismore. We ended up in Murwillumbah and then we had to get the bus to the Gold Coast. Perhaps that's where she's headed.'

So now Dalton had a decision to make, should he wait for the 6 pm train to Murwillumbah and then make his way to the Gold Coast, or should he head out to the highway and hitch a ride. It would be easy to get a hitch from the highway to the Gold Coast as it was the next major city, there were only small towns in between, so other than local drivers coming in and out of Byron, every car could be an option for a lift.

Just as he was thinking this, Dalton had a thought. If Tilly had spent the night in Murwillumbah, she would have to wait on the daily connection to the Gold Coast. Only problem was Dalton did not know what the train and bus schedule was from Murwillumbah to the Gold Coast.

chapter forty-nine

Murwillumbah Train Station.

How can I help you?

'I have an idea, Jacqui. Let me call through to the Murwillumbah train station and ask about the northbound timetable.' There was a phone booth right on the corner of the street, so Dalton ran down to it, flipped through the phonebook, found the number to call the Murwillumbah Train Station, popped his twenty-cent coin and his ten-cent coin into the slot at the top of the phone, and dialled the numbers.

'Good morning, Murwillumbah Train Station. How can I help you?' came the dull and grungy voice at the end of the line. It sounded like this lady had already answered the phone at least one thousand times this morning. There was no enthusiasm or friendliness in her tone, but that was okay. Dalton just needed some advice on the connecting bus schedule.

'Ah, good morning. How are you?' Dalton queried in a friendly tone.

'I'm good. How can I help you, sir?' The response remained dull and monotone.

'Um, I'm just wondering when the bus departs today, heading northbound?'

'It might help me if you tell me what bus you want to catch.' There was no nicety or friendliness in the response. It was very much business and over and done.

'Oh, sorry, I guess I'd like to know if there is a bus that heads to the Gold Coast. Northbound?' Dalton felt he was being an inconvenience but called to get some information, so he asked anyway.

'Bus leaves twice daily at 9 am and 7.15 pm to the Gold Coast and Brisbane. The same bus goes to the Gold Coast and then onto Brisbane. Is that all?' Again, she was very dismissive, trying to end the conversation as soon as possible.

'Ah, just one more thing. If I depart on the train here from Byron Bay at 6 pm, will I be able to make the connecting bus to the Gold Coast this evening?'

'That's the plan mate. Do you want me to hold you a ticket? It'll cost you seven dollars one way. Twelve dollars for a return ticket. You can reserve a ticket, or just get your ticket when you get here.'

'Um, no thank you. I just need to work a few things out, but thank you for your help. I might see you tonight.'

'Ah, no, you won't. I clock off at 5 pm, not a second after.'

'Do you mind if I ask one more question, ma'am?' Dalton used the polite manners that he had learned as a young man. It was a common courtesy to call someone sir or ma'am if you couldn't address them by another preferred name.

'One more question. I have a busy day here!' This was the unfriendly reply that Dalton expected.

He had to be very careful about asking one more question because he didn't feel that this lady aspired to be helpful. 'I'm wondering if, by any chance, you saw a very beautiful, dark-haired girl arrive on the train last night with a backpack and a guitar, and if so, did she disembark in Murwillumbah?'

'Who do you think I am, a dating service?' Came the reply.

'No ma'am, it's quite a long story, and I'll spare you the details, as I can tell that you are a very busy lady, but I am trying to locate my beautiful friend. We got separated, and she is looking for me, I think, and I'm looking for her. If you had any information, that would be very helpful.' Dalton pleaded, knowing that he would probably not get any help from this lady, but it was worth a try.

'Mate, I see people come and go all the time. A bunch of travellers got off the train last night from Byron. Your girl might have been amongst that crowd, I would have no idea. I just answer the phone and sell the tickets from the booth here. The weekend trains are always busy. I sold a pretty, dark-haired girl a ticket to the Gold Coast last night. She had come from Byron, I'm guessing. I only noticed this girl because she got off the train, bought the bus ticket and got back on again. I didn't see her after that. Might have changed her mind or something. Don't know if that helps. She didn't have a guitar, and no backpack either.' Dalton was surprised that she shared this information with him. He was glad he asked. The fact that she had no guitar or backpack meant nothing. If this, by chance, was Tilly, she might have left them on the train while she jumped off to buy the ticket. Dalton was trying to piece all this information together.

'You've been very helpful. Thank you so much.' Dalton continued to use his best manners.

'Mate, good luck finding your girl. Personally, I think you've got Buckley's chance. It's a big country. If you've got nothing else you need from me, goodbye, you've wasted enough of my time.'

'Oh! Well, enjoy the rest of your day then, and thanks again.' Dalton was quite taken aback by her abrupt tone, but he didn't bother responding to it; it wasn't worth it, and she had been extremely helpful.

She didn't respond. She just hung up, leaving Dalton with a loud beeping tone in his ear.

Dalton hung up the phone onto the hook with a loud clunk.

'How did you go?' asked Jacqui as Dalton walked back towards her, while she waited at the car, with all his stuff piled up, the surfboard hanging over the back seat.

Dalton regathered his thoughts and answered. 'Um, that was an interesting conversation. From what I can tell, I can catch the train from here at 6 pm. It will get me into Murwillumbah in time to connect with the northbound bus to the Gold Coast and Brisbane. I'm not sure that helps me to find Tilly, but I know that if she stayed in Murwillumbah last night, she might catch that bus too. It's the only evening bus headed north. So, unless she was up early this morning to catch the 9 am, then I might have a chance. However, the *very helpful* lady thinks that Tilly might have headed north already on last night's bus. She said a pretty, dark-haired girl bought a ticket to the Gold Coast last night. I know that's a wild chance, but I feel like it might have been Tilly. Either way, I think I'm best to catch the 6 pm train from here to Murwillumbah, and if she stayed in Murwillumbah, then hopefully, she might be at the station waiting to catch the northbound bus to the Gold Coast tonight. Otherwise, she's already gone, and I'm a day behind her. Dang it. I don't know how I'll find her on the Gold Coast. It's a big city. Anyway, the good thing is, Jacq, I get to hang out with all of you for the day. It's a win-win, really.'

'Sounds good to me.' Jacqui was happy that Dalton might find Tilly reasonably easily if luck was on his side, and she went to Murwillumbah Hospital. There was a little more of a concern if she had gone to the Gold Coast. She would be a lot harder to find once she hits the city.

'Don't worry, I won't cramp your style with Juan.' Dalton spun his head around in a small circle and dragged out the letters of his name, Yooowaan, in a friendly teasing manner. *At least he still had a sense of humour,* thought Jacqui.

chapter fifty

A Little Worse for Wear

Tilly and Bernard, both feeling a little worse for wear, gave breakfast a miss for the time being. They showered and dressed in their rooms separately and met in the hotel lobby.

Tilly always had deep thoughts in the shower. Most often, this was when her most creative thoughts and ideas came to her. She always planned her day with undisrupted thoughts productively. All she could think about for today was getting to the hospital and wondering what Dalton was doing. Did he even know that she was looking for him? Most likely not. He could be anywhere. As far as she knew, he could be back in Deniliquin with his family, but instinctively she could feel him heading north. He was determined to follow the waves and his freedom and get to a suitable place to make money playing his music. For this reason alone, she kept thinking she was in the right place. Where, north of Angourie, would he go better than the Gold Coast to get some gigs? Byron Bay was the closest bet. It was a cultural town, good for live music and supporting raw talent, but it was off the highway, so the chance of him being there would depend on who gave him a lift. Tilly assumed he was hitching. That's all she knew; that's how he arrived in Angourie.

Bernard did the same, planning his day in the shower and thinking about Tilly. He remembered Tilly talking about the Hinterland, Natural Arch and Mt Tamborine. *That could be fun*, he thought. He had never been there before, so an adventure of the unknown was always good. The shower felt good, washing away the cobwebs from a heavy night with many beers. Bernard never kept count; he drank the number of beers required for a good time. It could be one or twenty, depending on the company and the vibe. He was feeling last night was about a ten. Ten out of ten. He had a great night and looked forward to spending more time with Tilly. He was completely aware that their newly established relationship was platonic. Warmly and deeply platonic. He felt okay about it, and he hoped she did too. From their conversations, they were on an equal level of understanding. Bernard felt comfortable enjoying Tilly's company in the essence of freedom and friendship, just like in her cheers.

Bernard and Tilly met in the lobby, giving each other a gentle hug to restart their day. The rest of the band were there as well. As far as anyone else knew, Bernard and Tilly had spent the night in separate rooms. No one knew they had shared a bed.

Bernard's friends were heading out for breakfast, followed by a swim at the beach.

They all parted ways, Tilly and Bernard heading off together. The first stop was the hire car yard, just a few hundred metres down the street. The conversation was fun as they dreamed up which hire car they would choose.

Would Bernard choose a conservative compact car? Fuel-efficient and economical? 'That would be boring,' encouraged Tilly. 'What about a bright yellow convertible VW beetle? That's much more Gold Coast,' she laughed.

'I think that's a radical idea, Tilly. The only problem is, how do we fit our gig gear in it for Saturday night?' Bernard was thinking ahead to the weekend.

'True, that's true. That is a good point, but so sensible, so unlike you, Bernard,' joked Tilly.

'Well, how about a compromise then? We get the VW for our adventure today, and then we get sensible for the rest of the week?' Bernard suggested this option, hoping Tilly would agree, as he had to think about the gigs and transporting the gear for the band.

'That sounds more like you, Bernard. Good plan, let's do that.' Tilly agreed excitedly. Then added, 'Do you think they will have a yellow VW beetle convertible?'

'Of course they will. We are in Surfers Paradise.' Bernard was confident he had seen yellow VW convertibles sporting AVIS rent-a-car logos on many visits to the Gold Coast.

'True that.' Tilly was hoping he was right.

chapter fifty-one

Let's Hit The Beach

'Let's hit the beach then, Tiger. Any chance you could give me a surfing lesson so I can impress Juan this afternoon with my gnarly skills?' Jacqui made a quick-thinking decision to ask if perhaps Dalton could give her a very short, sharp surfing lesson so she could impress Juan with a basic level of surfing competency. Jacqui was a quick learner, and she was a natural sportswoman. However, she had never taken the opportunity to learn to surf, being more of a country girl.

'Sure can. Let's do it. You know I'm only new to surfing myself, so I may not be the finest instructor. Are you sure you would not prefer this to be a bonding thing you could do with Juan?' queried Dalton.

'Nah, I think I'd rather at least have a bit of a go, and then I can pretend later that I'm a total beginner, and it'll be that much more of a turn-on when I can stand up the first time and pull off a few cut-backs.' She threw her head back, laughing, knowing there was absolutely no chance of that happening.

Dalton threw his arm around Jacqui's shoulder and gave her a friendly side hug. 'Let's just go to the beach; what else will we do, anyway?'

Jacqui melted into him. It felt so lovely, although she knew it was just a friend hug. 'We might as well enjoy this beautiful day together. If you weren't trying to find the love of your life, we might have realised we have even more of a connection than we had last night. But hey, that's okay, I get it. She's a special girl for you. You'll find her, Dalton; I know you will.'

Jacqui was happy to spend the day with Dalton. She loved hanging out with him, and she thought he was super gorgeous, but he was back to giving off the "I'm taken" vibes he gave when they first met last night. Tilly had won his heart for sure; he was a goner!

Jacqui started the humming engine of the Chevrolet; it was all loaded up with Dalton's stuff. They slowly rolled into the carpark, just around the corner from the Beach Hotel, where Travis had parked his Kombi. Jacqui pulled up alongside the

Kombi. Dalton climbed out to check if Travis and Adeline wanted to join them for a surf.

Dalton called out as he walked towards the Kombi, just loud enough for Travis and Adeline to hear. 'If the Kombi is rocking, don't come knocking.' The curtains were all pulled together, and the doors and windows were all closed. He could hear faint music coming from inside the Kombi. Adeline pushed open the back door and poked her head out first to say, 'Hey, what's going on? Are you heading to Lismore to find your girl, or what?' Travis climbed out as well.

Dalton replied with a confusing, 'It's a long story, but Tilly is probably in Murwillumbah, not Lismore, so I'm catching the train tonight at 6 pm to see if I can find her there, and if not, I'll be rolling on to the Gold Coast.'

'Gold Coast?' questioned Travis.

Dalton replied. 'Yep. I hear there are some great surfing beaches on the Goldy. If Tilly is not in Murwillumbah, that may be where she is headed.'

'Sounds like a plan,' replied Travis, unconcerned about asking questions. He was so confused already.

'Solid plan,' replied Dalton, as he shook his head, contradicting his words. 'I have no idea where she could be, but I can only try to figure it out as I go.' Dalton had no solid plan at all. It was just a matter of going with the flow and trying to trace Tilly's footsteps. There was a slim chance that he could get to Murwillumbah, and she would be boarding the bus he planned to get on. That was an exciting possibility, and he wouldn't miss that opportunity. That was the one thing he was holding onto right now.

'Let's hit the waves, man.' Travis climbed out the back of the Kombi and grabbed his surfboard, which was leaning up against it, placing it in through the back door to slide into the custom-made surfboard gap as Adeline stepped out of the other side, grabbing the portable radio, to turn off the music. Mr Jones from the Counting Crows was blasting through the little radio speaker. It was a bit crackly, but it was still a vibe.

'Good song.' Jacqui commented. 'What radio station are you on, Adeline?'

'Triple M babe,' replied Adeline as she walked around to climb into the front seat. As Travis started the engine, she fiddled with the radio to tune it into Mr Jones. Jacqui did the same in the Chevrolet, parked beside the Kombi. They were rocking, ready to convoy, *in stereo*.

Dalton and Jacqui in the Chevrolet followed behind Travis and Adeline in the Kombi in search of some nice rolling waves. The boys were happy to go with the flow. Just being in the water was going to feel good. They were all carrying heavy heads from the night before, so they weren't searching for a hard-core surf. No one was sure if Georgia and Myles would join them. They knew where to find the other couples at one of the many surfing locations if they wanted to. It wouldn't be hard. The whole Byron Bay district didn't cover too much ground. A quick drive-by of the beaches would locate the Chev and the Kombi. Myles was driving a fancy BMW. It didn't quite fit into the Byron Bay vibe, but Georgia was impressed, and that was all that mattered.

They pulled into The Pass carpark, and Travis jumped out to do a quick surf check to see if there were some easy-going waves for the girls. It looked perfect. The water was aqua-blue and almost like a lake. There were a couple of nice rolling sets coming in, with a bit of whitewash after the crash of the wave. Nothing too heavy or strong, and they could paddle out easily in the stillness section.

Travis left the music playing from his car as they unloaded the boards. One classic hit to the next. It was The Rolling Stones, Start Me Up. Travis danced, Mick Jagger style, and everyone started laughing. 'Are you still drunk from last night, Travis?' questioned Jacqui.

'Nah, Jacq, I'm just high on life. Did I mention that The Rolling Stones are my favourite-ever-ever band? It would be against my religion to turn this song off without letting it play until the end.'

Jacqui and Adeline took a quick chance to have a girly chat about the night before while the boys sorted out the boards with wax. Jacqui loved the smell of the board wax; it smelt like an endless summer rolled into a packet.

'So, Adeline, what's going on with you and Travis? Will you see him again? Is he a keeper?'

Adeline replied, making sure that Travis was immersed in the music rather than listening to their conversation. 'Yeah. I hope so. He likes his freedom, but we will keep in touch and see what happens. Nothing too serious, you know me, young and free. I like these wild weekends with you way too much to give any of that up, but for the right one, you know I would, in a heartbeat. What about you, Jacqui? What happened with you and Dalton? None of us know exactly what happened last night. We just know what happened this morning.'

Jacqui smiled shyly. 'Do you really want to know?'

'Of course I do.' Adeline replied with disbelief. 'Since when don't we tell each other EVERYTHING?'

Jacqui made sure Dalton wasn't listening before she answered. 'It's just that I feel bad for Dalton because I'm sure, as things have turned out, he's probably carrying some regret this morning about what happened with me last night.'

'Yeah, and so.' Adeline pushed for more details.

'We had a great night and all, you know me, I put the hard moves on him because he was playing so hard to get. My seduction moves worked, as usual, and damn, it was good too. He's beautiful. Then, this morning, I woke up and saw his guitar. It was the same as Tilly's. I mentioned Tilly and Angourie, and the whole world turned upside down. He realised she might be looking for him. Until this morning, he obviously did not know she was possibly trying to find him. The irony of the situation is that he's trying to find her, and he would have known nothing about her if he hadn't spent the night with me. Just imagine if I didn't say anything about the guitar. Weird, huh!'

'Far out, what a crazy coincidence that of all the people we met and the places we could have gone, we ended up where we did last night, and one thing led to another to bring those two back together, maybe. I guess we may never know. That will be their story to tell.' Adeline was such a hopeless romantic, so she was completely spellbound by the situation.

Travis locked the car and placed his key in the safe lock on the tow bar. 'Come on girls, let's hit the beach. Are you ready?' Travis grabbed the board, wrapping the leg rope around the fin and tying the Velcro so it wouldn't come undone on the walk down to the beach. Dalton had his board as well, waxed up and ready to go.

'Ready as I'll ever be,' replied Adeline, grabbing her towel that was hanging over the car door. Jacqui and Adeline had placed all the valuables in the boot of the Chevrolet, so everything was safe while they went for a surf.

chapter fifty-two

Relax, Let's Have an Adventure!

It had only taken Bernard and Tilly half an hour to get organised with transport for the week. They were lucky to find exactly what they wanted. For their Hinterland adventure, a white VW convertible beetle. The yellow ones were all taken. And a red 8-seater Toyota Tarago people mover with plenty of storage room to transport the gear.

They set out on their adventure, deciding the first stop would be the Gold Coast Hospital. It didn't seem very adventurous, but it was important for Tilly to get her arm looked at. Bernard had promised these things to Tilly. One, to ring the train station about her lost guitar pick; two, to get her arm looked at; three, to help find Dalton.

Surprisingly, on a Saturday morning, the emergency department was not busy at all. Tilly was straight through the triage nurse and into the doctor's room within about half an hour of their arrival. The doctor assumed a break and sent her straight in for an X-ray. The outcome was a minor fracture in the radius, as Tilly suspected. The hospital staff were brilliant. Within two hours, Tilly was despatched with a beautiful white cast on her wrist. Bernard had asked for a permanent marker while in the hospital waiting room as they prepared Tilly's paperwork. He was the first to sign it. Special friends forever and always, even when I'm super famous. Love Bernard F, with a xx. The doctor had recommended that Tilly keep the cast on for a month to six weeks, depending on the strength gains as it healed. As she had already broken her wrist before, the pins gave some extra strength, which was good.

It was just after midday by the time they started heading into the Hinterland, with a brief stop on the way to collect a picnic basket and plenty of food and drinks for a feast.

Tilly and Bernard had picked the perfect day, or the perfect day had chosen them. The sun was shining, with clear blue skies, not a cloud in sight. There was a gentle breeze to freshen the stillness of the air. They cruised along the country roads with the rooftop down, their hair blowing, and the radio set on loud.

Frankie Goes To Hollywood—*Relax* was the theme song of their day. Good beats. Controversial lyrics. They both tapped and sang along to this classic 80s song. Tilly and

Bernard loved to talk about the meanings of the songs that came on the radio. They spoke about the influence of music, the sentimentality of some songs, and how it reminded them of various times in their lives.

As they adventured and talked about everything, their comfort level grew. They had discovered another level of a very comfortable friendship. It wasn't a strong physical connection that either of them felt for each other. Not the way Tilly felt about Dalton. It was a respectful level of understanding, kindness, and trust; they had many things in common. In the lengthy conversations, Tilly expressed again that she hoped they could keep their friendship as Bernard moved on with his passionate music career. They talked about how that could work by writing letters and informing each other if their address changed. The problem with Tilly was that she had no fixed address right now. She told Bernard he could always send mail to The Angourie Local, and she could always collect it from there whenever she returned home. This would be an easy way if they kept each other up to date. Bernard used fax often for his gig bookings, but this wouldn't work for Tilly. They had heard about this thing called email, but neither of them had a computer to send an electronic mail from.

They talked about international travel and places they would love to visit overseas.

They talked about family and childhood memories and the influences in their lives that had made them who they were.

They talked about Dalton a lot. Tilly was trying to take her mind away from thinking about him, but everything she talked about created a link to how much she regretted what she had done to him and how much she wanted to find him and tell him how sorry she was. Bernard listened and consoled Tilly and told her again if it's meant to be, it'll be. Everything always works out as it should. He reminded her it was important to enjoy today in the meantime. That today is a gift.

They had no plan for their day other than to relax and see where the road would take them. Neither Tilly nor Bernard had explored this part of the Hinterland, so everywhere was new and everywhere was an adventure.

They discovered rainforests, waterfalls, and bush tracks leading to rock pools and spectacular mountain lookouts. They discovered an abundance of wildlife, birds and harmless reptiles, bugs and butterflies. The Natural Bridge cave in Springbrook National Park was the last place they ended up, where they set up their picnic rug and shared a bottle of wine. As darkness set in, they watched the glow worms come to life.

chapter fifty-three

Pay It Forward!

Byron Bay was the kind of place where you could trust most people, but it still wasn't worth the risk of being lazy. Dalton had stowed his backpack and guitar in the Kombi while they all went for a surf. It was easier to fit them in there than to squeeze them into the Chevy boot with all the girls' bags.

Travis led the way down the narrow path. Dalton, Adeline, and then Jacqui followed along behind. Travis knew these beaches and bush tracks like the back of his hand.

They hit the sand and placed their stuff under a beautiful shady tree overhanging the beach.

Travis had taken over the role of surfing instructor with Dalton's approval. He started with the lesson. 'Okay, girls, you ready for your surf lesson with *Trav.*' He said Trav with such an attitude, like he was the number one surf instructor in the universe. The girls both laughed. He waited until they had finished giggling and continued talking, ensuring they were listening. 'I probably should have warned you before we started that my fees for the surfing lesson are not monetary, but rather, intimate favours in return. I'm not sure where that leaves you, Jacqui. Perhaps I'll let you *pay it forward* to someone of your choosing.'

Jacqui looked at Dalton, shaking her head and rolling her eyes to let him know she wouldn't do that to him.

'Oh, is that right, Mr Jagger?' Adeline mimicked the way Travis was acting so cool.

She walked over to where Travis had laid the boards near each other on the sand. She placed one leg on either side of the surfboard to mirror the same way he was standing. She held Travis' face in her hands and kissed him, then gently placing the tip of her tongue inside his mouth, licked his face from the inside of his mouth all the way up to his eyebrow. She put on her sexiest voice, saying, 'How much of the surf lesson does that get me, Trav?' Then she pulled her mouth into a provocative pout and lifted her eyebrows.

Jacqui and Dalton looked at each other and laughed, enjoying the banter and the humour shared between these two new lovebirds.

'That'll get you everywhere, Adeline.' Travis laughed. 'You're such a cool chick. I'm so glad I met you.' He leaned forward, pulling her towards him to kiss her mouth. He moaned as if to suggest he would love to continue kissing her, but instead, he pulled away, aware that they were not in secluded company.

'Save it.' Adeline grinned.

'All right, girls, serious now. You need to lay face downwards in the sand for me. On the count of three, you're going to push up onto your feet naturally. Don't overthink it. Just put one foot in front of the other.'

Jacqui and Adeline did as they were instructed.

'Ready one, two, three, up!'

They both did it perfectly.

'Alright, let's go, that's all you gotta know.' Travis pointed to the water. The waves are calm enough today. We can teach you the rest out there on the water.

The four set out into the water, starting closer to shore. Travis and Dalton were standing in the water waist-deep with the girls beside them on the boards. They gave the girls a little push, and off they went, and up they stood, side by side. Both had a natural balance, and the waves were perfect for beginners. Adeline let out a cheer. 'Woo-hoo, I'm surfing.' Jacqui joined in, 'Yeeee ha!'

Almost two hours passed, and it was getting close to 1 pm. Travis wondered if Myles, Georgia and Juan would join them soon. Adeline and Jacqui enjoyed an excellent surf and were catching some nice long rides. Dalton and Travis were extremely patient, treading water out deeper and helping the girls to get started on the wave. Now and then, the boys would catch a wave and show the girls some tricks.... Hang ten, walk the plank....

It was the most beautiful day, and the atmosphere of the aqua-blue water reflecting off the cloudless sky was helping to create such a beautiful moment for these four to put to memory. Adeline and Travis were being playful, flirty, and fun with each other.

Dalton and Jacqui were having fun, too. They had a comfortable chemistry, but all Dalton could think about was finding Tilly. He kept checking his watch to keep an eye on the time, although there was no need to. He couldn't leave Byron Bay until the scheduled train departure time at 6 pm. He kept drifting into deep thoughts about everything. He had an amazing night with Jacqui. She kept letting him know she thought he was amazing, but she knew his heart was for Tilly, so she understood how he felt and respected his decision. Dalton liked Jacqui. She was the kind of girl that could keep a guy happy. She was playful and fun. She was energetic, easygoing, gentle, and kind. They had both enjoyed a nice night together with a good physical connection. But there was something magical about Tilly; it was like nothing he had ever felt with anyone. She was different. He was mesmerised by her beauty in his heart, mind, body, and soul. It was like those aspects of him immediately joined to her, and from the moment he met her, he knew she was the one he was supposed to spend forever with. Everything in his life up to that point made sense. His childhood and the way he grew up, his musical passion, loving and losing Chelsea, his move away from Deni and his family, and finally, his east-coast adventure that led him to surf in Yamba at that precise moment in time to meet Frankie, and then follow an instinct to go to Angourie. And there she was.

Dalton was so annoyed with himself that in that one moment, he had said the one thing Tilly had heard on repeat for her whole life... "You're an amazing woman, Tilly, and I'd love to stay here and be with you forever, *but......*"

He dived under the water, took a deep breath and sat on the bottom of the ocean floor, watching the waves roll overhead, thinking, *I know I'm going to find her; I will, somehow.*

Dalton noticed a dark shadow in the water beside Jacqui as he surfaced.

She had seen it, too, and was quietly panicking. Jacqui's heart was pounding, her ears were ringing, and her blood had turned ice cold as it pumped through her veins. She was screaming on the inside but spoke softly, almost in a whisper, because she was petrified. 'Um, guys, is that a dolphin?'

Adeline did not like what she was seeing. She stayed perfectly still on her board.

Travis hadn't determined yet if the shadow was a dolphin or a shark. He climbed on the board behind Adeline, placing his chest on top of her bottom and his hips between her legs. He paddled them into the shallow water.

Dalton swam towards Jacqui and her surfboard. All he could think to do was to get to the board and paddle him and Jacqui in towards the shoreline to safety. Just as he got to the board to climb on, the creature surfaced, rounding its body and letting out a blowhole of chuff, right in front of Jacqui's board. It was a divine dolphin coming to play. The chuff from the explosive blow was all over Jacqui's face. Dalton continued to climb on the board with Jacqui to calm her. She was panicked even though she now realised it was a friendly dolphin.

By the time Dalton got himself balanced and safe on the board with Jacqui, she was laughing hysterically. It was a laugh of relief that she was still alive. It's funny how the body reacts to various situations. For Jacqui, the intense feeling of sheer panic was replaced immediately with laughter as she sat there with dolphin blowhole water all over her face. They were having some fun today, that was for sure, scaring the life out of poor Jacqui.

'I'm proud of you, Jacqui,' said Dalton. 'The best thing you could do was lay quietly on your board and let him pass by, just like you did. But far out, was that the coolest thing? He's come to show off right in front of you, giving you a big wash of "hello, baby."

Jacqui was still shaking, adrenaline coursing through her body. 'Yeah, not the "hello baby" I was looking for. Scared the life out of me.'

Dalton calmed Jacqui, assuring her she was okay, as he paddled slowly and gently towards the shoreline. He had himself positioned the same way Travis did with Adeline. His chest rested on her butt cheeks as her legs allowed his body to fit behind her on the board. Jacqui was enjoying the feeling of Dalton rescuing her. She felt protected by his firm, muscular body.

Just as they were about to hit the shallows, Jacqui heard Georgia shout out from the beach. 'Oh my god, are you guys okay? That shark was so close to you.'

Travis and Adeline had already hit the edge of the water. Travis was carrying the board a little further up the beach to place it on the sand. He hadn't finished surfing yet, but he wanted to be social for a bit, as their other friends had now arrived. Juan must have caught a lift with Myles and Georgia, or they had just arrived simultaneously. It was Travis who replied to Georgia's shriek. 'We are all good, Georgia. It was just a friendly dolphin popping up to say hello all over Jacqui.'

'How do you know it was a dolphin?' queried Georgia.

Travis explained calmly and clearly, as Georgia seemed quite distressed. 'Sharks and dolphins are very different in the way they move. They are completely opposite to each other, to make it simple. The best way to explain it is that shark tail fins are vertical, so they move side to side. Dolphin tail fins are horizontal, so they move their bodies up and down. You can tell when they surface if they round their bodies or swim side-to-side. Travis gave some hand signals to make the distinction between the two visually clearer for Georgia. My dad used to have a saying. He was pro-dolphin, of course. Up and down, no need to frown; side-to-side, it's time to ride. That's what my dad taught me when I was about five. The problem is when they are a dark shadow under the water, and you can't see their motion, it can be quite scary. I grew up surfing in a little town in New South Wales called Wooli. It's an unprotected, free ocean, and some wild creatures roam close to our shoreline. We get large stingrays, big sea turtles, dolphins, sharks and even whales close to the shore at different times of the year. It's beautiful. Truly, we are the lucky ones, blessed to share the ocean with them. Every day we surf, we put ourselves in their hometown, and it's always a risk. I don't think they ever deliberately want to hurt us. To them, it's a survival mechanism.'

'Don't you get scared?' asked Georgia.

'Not really; I always keep an eye out around me, but to be quite honest, they move so fast, by the time you realise you are in danger, it would be too late.' Travis justified he didn't feel scared and admitted to the lack of reason to worry anyway.

'Wow, I think you surfers are quite crazy.' Georgia blatantly shared her opinion.

Meanwhile, Myles was waxing his board and zipping up his wet suit. 'So, does that mean you will not come and have a surf lesson with me, Georgia?' Myles teased, knowing the answer already.

'No, Myles, I'm just going to stay on the sand and catch some UV rays.'

Adeline and Jacqui came up to say hi to their new friends, who had now arrived. Jacqui had calmed down somewhat, and she was now quite exhilarated by what she had seen. That was a once-in-a-lifetime experience for sure.

Juan walked over to Jacqui and reached his arms out to hug her. She wasn't quite expecting such a warm, friendly welcome. It was nice. 'Are you okay, Jacqui?' queried Juan in his gentle Spanish slur. Jacqui leaned in, receiving the hug inside his muscular, warm chest.

'Yeah, I'm okay, now!' Jacqui responded, laughing with double meaning; she had gotten over the shock of the dolphin incident and that she was totally okay inside Juan's embrace.

Dalton and Travis headed back out for a surf with Myles as they left the girls to catch up and chat with their new friend, Juan.

Juan had also brought his surfboard, but he signalled to the boys that he would catch up soon for a surf.

The three girls and Juan sat side by side on the beach, chatting and observing the boys at play. The swell had picked up a little as the tide was moving out. They were all catching and sharing some great long and gentle rides. The waves were perfect for some Malibu tricks. It was entertaining. Travis had obviously been surfing for a long time. Without being an absolute show-off, he was leading the boys with some tricks to try. Dalton and Myles were doing their best to learn these new Wooli moves. They were all laughing and having such a great time.

Jacqui encouraged Juan, 'Why don't you go out there and show these boys some Spanish surf moves? I'm sure you could show them a thing or two?'

'I don't know about that, Jacqui.' He said Jacqui with such a distinguished tone, emphasising the 'Ja' and the 'qui' with pouted lips so that this truly Aussie-sounding name sounded French. 'The Aussie surfers are the best in the world; I have nothing compared to their talents.' Juan grabbed his surfboard and wrapped the leg rope around the end to make it easy to carry to the water's edge.

He smiled back as he walked to the water. 'I'll see you again soon. You are not going anywhere, no?'

'We will be right here watching you, Juan. Have some fun,' Jacqui replied calmly, although her heart fluttered like a butterfly inside her chest.

Juan splashed through the waves, his thick black hair flicking sideways each time as he pushed through the waves to get out the back to where the other three were surfing.

These four were the only surfers occupying the waves this afternoon, and they were pleased about that.

chapter fifty-four

Beach Chats

The three girls sat on the beach, watching the four boys at play. They had spent quite some time now sharing stories about how their nights had gone with the gorgeous boys they had met, laughing and giggling together about how the previous afternoon and evening had turned out and sharing gossipy, girly details about the intimacy of their nights.

Quite a bit of time had passed, and Jacqui was the first to say it, but they were all thinking simultaneously. 'Imagine if Tilly was here right now, all four of us perfectly matched with our dream men. Poor Dalton must feel like the odd one out right now.'

'I hope he can find her,' replied Adeline as she drew a love heart in the sand, scribbling Adeline loves Travis, with a love heart and an s. Georgia copied and did the same, scribing Georgia loves Myles with the same love heart symbol and an s. Jacqui also copied saying, 'It's early days, and I don't even know the guy, but I can dream, can't I?' She wrote Jacqui loves Juan with a love heart and an s. Then, beside it, she drew another love-heart and wrote Dalton Loves Tilly inside it, with a capital L.

'How weird is it that we picked up Tilly yesterday and ended up at the pub where Dalton was, in all the places in this country? I can only think that somehow this was all meant to be.' Jacqui had this on her mind all day, and she couldn't quite shake it; the serendipitous moments of the past few days had her bewildered. She hoped that speaking her thoughts out loud would help it all make more sense, but she kept coming up with nothing.

Adeline added to Jacqui's thoughts. 'But don't you think Jacq, if it were all meant to be, wouldn't Tilly have somehow ended up with us at the pub rather than getting on that train? What help is it that she's on a train to who knows where, and Dalton is here with us?'

'I don't know the answer to that, Adeline. Maybe so I got to enjoy a romantic night with him? It's about time I had some lucky stars shine on me.'

'How do you think Tilly would feel if she knew he had spent the night with you? How would you feel if you were her and found that out?' Georgia joined in the conversation, asking the difficult question everyone was thinking about but didn't want to ask. She didn't have a lot of tact; she was very matter-of-fact and straight to the point, which was good in a way, but she often came across as extremely rude and somewhat arrogant.

'Yeah, I've thought about that, Georgia, since I found out about this whole Tilly-Dalton connection this morning. The moment I realised it was Tilly he was being weird about, I had a wave of guilt rush over me, but I consoled myself with the fact that if I had not spent the night with Dalton, he would be none the wiser that Tilly may even be looking for him. I guess the guilt is more for him to carry if he chooses to carry that.'

Georgia replied with a softer tone, 'Yeah, true that. How were you to know anything about the two of them?'

'Well, I didn't until this morning.' Jacqui stated again.

Adeline joined in the conversation to try to ease the little bit of tension. 'I guess you just put it down to life and something that happened. The fact that you two shared a fun night together doesn't have to mean anything if you can both accept that it played an important part in your lives. Just because you slept together doesn't mean that you are committed to each other in any way. I think society, in general, puts way too much emphasis on people sleeping with people. Can't sex just be a fun thing for people to do together, and then it's the end? If nobody gets a sexually transmitted disease or gets pregnant. Sex is supposed to be fun, right? Be responsible, use protection, have fun, the end.'

Jacqui was nodding as Adeline spoke. 'I agree if it's a two-way understanding. Someone always gets hurt if emotions get involved. It's a difficult balance to allow someone that deep level of intimacy to make the encounter worthwhile without feeling any emotions. I can guarantee you Dalton and I had a fun night. I'd relive the night again in a heartbeat. I wouldn't change a thing. I'm not sure Dalton would feel the same.'

Georgia joined in again with a tone of judgement that eased as she spoke. 'I was brought up in a family that believed that if you want to have sex with someone, you have to be married to them. I believed that for a long time until I visited you girls here in Australia. You girls are wild. Myles sure doesn't believe in the whole married-before-sex thing, either. Damn, we had fun last night. He's mighty fine. My family would disown me if they knew the *shenanigans* - is that the word y'all use? - that we got up to last night.'

Jacqui clarified, 'Yes, we do use the word shenanigans, in a slang way of implying mischievous activity, non-serious fun and no one gets hurt. That's shenanigans.'

Adeline added to the serious part of the conversation. 'Yeah, it's not just your family, Georgia. A lot of people *think* that way, but a lot of people don't *act* that way. I think large sections of society might follow that rule of "no sex before marriage", but these days it's more and more uncommon. I guess it depends on who you talk to. Every person is rightful to their own beliefs for their own body.'

Jacqui broke out in raucous laughter to try to ease the tension of this whole discussion. 'If Dalton told me last night he didn't believe in sex before marriage, I still would have tried to jump his bones. Damn, that boy was on fire.'

Adeline laughed as well. 'Yeah, Travis would have had to call triple zero to stop me from having my way with him.' They all laughed again.

Jacqui's mind skipped forward as she had a random thought. 'This is going to sound like a strange question, but you are my friends, so I can ask you anything, right?'

Georgia and Adeline responded simultaneously. 'Of course you can.'

'Do you think Juan would be okay with sex before marriage, or do you think his culture would be stricter than us wild Aussies?'

Adeline replied first. 'I don't know anything about Spanish culture, but the accent sounds like it is all about love, sensuality, and seduction. From what I can tell, Juan seems like an easy-going soul.'

Georgia added, 'Do you honestly think someone with that body and that accent would be against seduction? It's like he been created just for that purpose.'

Jacqui replied hastily as she noticed that the boys were starting to paddle in, perhaps finishing their surf for the afternoon, or just having a break. 'That is not really something I want to think about. I wonder if he would let me seduce him. I just don't know how that works when we are heading back home this afternoon, dang it.'

Adeline replied confidently. 'I guess you exchange phone numbers and addresses and keep in touch. We can drive up again in a few weeks for a visit if Dad doesn't need the car. I'm keen to see Travis again, but he's in Wooli, not as far away from Nana Glen as Byron. Travis said he does like to come here for weekends to surf. We can arrange another Byron trip. That's easy. Georgia might want to come with us again, if Myles is still hanging here in Byron as well?'

Georgia replied excitedly. 'I would love that, and yes, I think Myles plans to stay around here for a while. He said he has no desire to go back to the city.'

Jacqui replied with a suggestion and a tinge of judgement. 'That is good, I guess, considering Myles seems like such a city boy, perhaps that's just taking a while to wash off. His natural Byron hippie vibe will start to ooze out of him in no time. Next time you visit him, I bet he will be growing that thick hair into a beautiful mane of dreadlocks, and he will smell like tea tree and incense, like Matty from the Railway Hotel. Damn, he smelt so good. I liked that he didn't have a body odour. I'm all for the natural, clean, earthy smell, and every philosophy behind living a clean hippie life, but I can't do the BO thing.'

Georgia agreed. 'Me either. Makes me want to gag.' She made a gagging gesture, then added. 'Do you really think Myles will change that much about himself while living here?'

Adeline answered this time. 'Most likely. Most visitors that turn locals do. It's just the local Byron look, the Byron way, and Myles' personality seems to be craving the Byron way of life.'

'We'll see, I guess. Time will tell, but you girls are probably right. I'd be okay with that. I wouldn't mind growing some dreadlocks myself.' Georgia was quite okay with Jacqui's suggestion that Myles was much more of a Byron boy than a city slicker.

Adeline couldn't quite believe what she was hearing from Georgia. 'You, with dreadlocks. I'd like to see that.' She noticed that Georgia was a little insulted, so she softened and said, 'I guess you could still wrap your hair up in your silky scarves.'

The conversation ended abruptly, as the four boys placed their boards face down, side by side, in the sand, so the wax wouldn't melt, a couple of metres just in front of the girls.

It was quite a scene, these four young gentlemen, fit, strong and healthy. Their bodies glistening with saltwater and sunshine.

Jacqui was the first to ask. 'How was it?'

The boys were all lightly breathing from their energetic surf and the walk back up the beach. They all undid their ankle straps and placed the long ropes on top of the boards. Travis, the cheeky one, shaking water from his hair all over Adeline, as he came to sit beside her. He was the first one to reply to Jacqui. 'It was good, nice, calm, clean waves. Playful and fun. Did you see Juan's record longest ride? He almost caught the wave back to the pub?'

'I did see that long ride,' replied Jacqui. 'You guys were all getting some decent long rides and plenty of tricks on show, as well.'

Juan asked a question. 'Do you girls want to have a surf on top of the waves?' Jacqui melted, the way he asked the question like that. It was just the translation of English that made the question come out like that.

Jacqui replied, 'Thanks, but no thanks. I am all good. I've dried off now, so I'm happy to just watch you guys surf some more.' Jacqui was still recovering from her dolphin scare and didn't want to go back in the water, but she didn't make a big deal about it.

Adeline added to Jacqui's response. 'No, thanks, I'm all good. I had some fun earlier, and it's getting more around shark feeding time as the sun sets, right?' She finished the sentence with a questioning tone.

Travis replied. 'I think sharks feed at any time of the day or night, but mostly on large fish, of course, but it is scarier as the water gets darker, that's for sure.' He said this nicely to ease Adeline's concern and take away the pressure that she might feel to go for another surf. He was happy to sit on the beach with her and relax.

Georgia added her response, 'I don't surf, I never have. I'm not sure if I ever will, but I'm happy to sit here and watch you all.'

Myles sat himself down behind Georgia, with his chest against her back and placing his legs around her, trying his best not to wet her, as he knew she wouldn't like it if he did.

Juan sat next to Jacqui, as she inconspicuously rubbed out the Jacqui loves Juan, and Dalton loves Tilly love hearts in the sand. Jacqui couldn't stop staring at him, as he flicked his hair and shook his head gently to the side, to get the water out of his ears. 'Wow, that was a fun surf, thanks for inviting me, you guys and girls.' Juan said this to everyone, but it was only Jacqui that was really listening, as the others were in their own little conversations with each other.

Travis realised Juan was talking to them all and responded. 'All good man, anytime we come back up this way, we will pop into the pub and let you know we are in town. You are always welcome to join us.'

'That would be cool. How often do you make a trip to the Byron Bay?' Juan was interested to have some more surf mates come to visit him in his new hometown.

Again, Travis responded, 'I come up at least once a month. It all depends on the surf conditions. If it's gnarly conditions, I just make the trip. It's always worth it. For me, it's just a two-and-a-half-hour drive or so, depending on the weekend Byron traffic. It's no big deal. I just sleep in the Kombi, so it's always a nice easy weekend away for me, especially if I meet someone like Adeline here. She kept me warm last night. That's always a bonus.'

Adeline gently punched Travis in the arm, for making her sound like she was just another one of his girls that he meets randomly. Adeline wasn't too offended, though; she was guilty herself of making Byron trips just to have a fun random hook-up weekend. They were both as bad as each other. The truth was, though, they both really liked each other, probably more than a random hook-up, but neither had expressed that to the other. They were just enjoying each other's company.

Myles added to the conversation, 'I'm here to stay in Byron, for the next little while. I've got no plans of going anywhere else. I might even see if I can find myself a job. But honestly Juan, I'm always up for a surf, mate, if you're keen. I've just got to figure out a way I can convince Georgia to come and stay and grow some dreadlocks with me.' Myles crooned his neck around to look at her as he ruffled her hair that was bunched on top of her head in a massive bun. 'That's what I was hearing, right?' Myles looked inquisitively at Georgia as he raised his eyebrows with a questioning grin.

Georgia smiled back at him. 'Well then, Myles, you can be the one to tell my parents that I'm moving to Byron Bay to grow dreadlocks and learn how to surf with some random guy that I met at the pub who doesn't even have a job.' There was that blatantly honest, tactless Georgia coming out in full throttle. The strange thing was, Myles didn't even mind that was she was so blunt and tactless. It was the truth.

Myles replied unnerved, not offended at all. 'I can do that, then that will be their problem to deal with, as I have no problem with any of that at all.'

Dalton had found himself a place to sit down, feeling a little left out on his own with all of these loved up couples surrounding him. He finally joined in the conversation. 'Well. It sounds like you guys have got it all sorted out. Jacqui and Adeline will be making regular trips up from Nana Glen to Byron to visit Travis and Juan for their surfing rendezvous. Hopefully, that dolphin didn't scare you off, Jacq, and you feel okay to get back in the water again someday. You'll all be staying with Georgia and Myles, because he'll be managing the local bank to afford to pay for Georgia's hairdressing appointments, to have her dreadlocks styled into a beehive. It sounds perfect. Who would have thought a random Saturday night at the pub would turn out like this?' He laughed at his wildly creative future vision of them all.

Jacqui was the first to reply. 'I loved surfing today. It was so fun, and I think I'll be okay to get back in the water again someday. I just got a little fright, that's all.' She had more to add, but Georgia had something to say over the top of Jacqui.

'I think it's all just perfect. I'm so happy to have had this weekend with you all. Thanks for inviting me, Jacqui and Adeline.' No one quite expected these words to come out of Georgia's mouth. She had changed her tone and softened. She had no retaliatory comment about Dalton's dreadlock-beehive tease. She just let it go straight over her head. Possibly because it was close to her truth of what she might expect to happen. Myles couldn't resist giving her a big squeeze from behind her. He pressed his warm back against her, and as she turned her head around towards him, he kissed her on the cheek. It was lucky that he had dried off a bit, otherwise, she wouldn't have been so receptive to his hug.

Jacqui continued with her trail of thought but acknowledged Georgia's comment first. 'I'm so happy for you, Georgia. You're always welcome to join us. I was going to say, Dalton, it's just you that we need to get sorted out now, you need to find your beautiful Tilly.'

Travis had an idea. 'Can I make a suggestion?'

Adeline responded. 'Of course.'

Everyone was listening and waiting for this brilliant idea. Dalton was half expecting Travis, the hard-core surfer, to suggest one more surf for the boys. But his suggestion was unexpected. 'I say we all head up and get beach showered and half clean and dressed, and then let's convoy to The Railway Hotel, where we can have a few more drinks together and see Dalton get on that train at 6 pm, what do you all say?'

Everyone thought it was a great idea. They all started to gather their belongings and headed up the beach, chatting and talking with each other.

Juan hadn't drifted far from Jacqui's side. They had a lot of catching up to do, as these two knew nothing about each other. Juan explained to Jacqui that he had to go back to work at 5 pm, but he would love to join them for a while. Juan had driven his own car, so he had the ability to leave when he needed to. He was not relying on anyone else to depart the group, to have to drive him anywhere. Jacqui loved that he already had his own car and independence. Although he hadn't been in Australia for very long, he had a regular job, his own apartment, and his own car to get him around. She was impressed. And that accent, and those eyes, and that mouth and that smooth brown skin.

chapter fifty-five

Convoy!

The convoy was on!

Travis and Adeline climbed into the Kombi; Dalton's stuff was still in the back.

Jacqui was in the driver's seat of the Chevrolet, offering Dalton the passenger seat. Myles and Georgia nestled in the back seat. They had grabbed a lift to the beach with Juan. Myles thought he might still be over the limit from the amount of alcohol that he had consumed, so he played it safe, leaving the BMW back at the Beach Hotel. He was grateful for the lift back into town in the Chevy. He had never been in a Chevrolet before.

Juan jumped into his Datsun 120Y alone, ready to follow the others to The Railway Hotel.

They were all packed up and ready to roll.

The Chevrolet and The Kombi already had the radios in sync with Triple M. Jacqui turned up the radio as she listened to the songs start. Georgia couldn't believe it when she heard the unmistakable chords for Tom Petty, Free Fallin, one of her favourite songs ever. She started singing, 'She's a good girl, loves her mama, loves Jesus and America too, she's a good girl, crazy about Elvis, loves horses and her boyfriend too.'

Dalton and Myles started singing to the next verse, '*It's a long day living in Reseda, there's a freeway running through the yard, I'm a bad boy, cause I don't even miss her, I'm a bad boy for breaking her heart.*'

Dalton felt a pang of guilt for being a *bad boy* with Jacqui last night, but he quickly put that aside and continued to enjoy the moment.

They all sang together. '*And I'm free, Free Fallin, Yeah I'm free, Free Fallin.*'

Dalton and Jacqui continued singing the following verse in harmony, '*Now all the vampires are walkin' through the valley, move west down Ventura Boulevard.*'

Myles couldn't resist moving in close to Georgia. It was easy with the big, long leather bench seat in the back. There were no seatbelts or rules about wearing them, so Myles took advantage to get as close as he could to Georgia as the music created the scene for him. Myles leaned in and gently sunk his teeth and mouth into Georgia's neck, like a vampire, leaving a love bite to remind her again of the mischief they had gotten up to the night before. Georgia was certain she would have love bites and various indentations from Myles' tough love with her, all over her body from last night. She didn't mind, though; Georgia loved the intensity of his passion towards her. Georgia let out a playful squeal as Myles squeezed her tightly as the Chevy launched forward while Jacqui tried to find the clutch balance.

Jacqui laughed as she explained, 'This is exactly why Adeline is usually the designated driver. I'm a dreadful Chevy driver. Dalton, do you want to drive? Please say you will?' She was already applying the handbrake and climbing out of the driver's seat by the time she finished asking the question.

Dalton replied excitedly, 'I'd love to, if you don't mind. I always wanted to drive a Chevy.' Dalton and Jacqui both walked around the front of the car to swap positions. They raised their right hands for a walk-by high-five as they passed each other. Dalton slapped Jacqui gently on the bum as his hand swung back around and lowered back down. Jacqui turned around and gave him a cheeky smile. 'What's that for?' She questioned.

'Just because.' He paused until he was seated. 'You might have a sexy butt, but you do not know how to drive a Chevy. Let me show you how it's done.'

Jacqui laughed. 'I'm more than happy to ride shotgun, Tiger. You be the boss.'

Dalton climbed in and re-adjusted the mirrors to his height. As he did, he caught a glimpse of Myles and Georgia in the rear-view mirror. They were attached by the mouth again, in the back seat. 'Oh my goodness, you two! I might have already said this last night, but I'll say it again. Get a room!'

Myles and Georgia pulled themselves away from each other, smiling at each other, as the convoy rolled out en route to The Railway Hotel.

Dalton had full control of the Chevy. He had no problem finding the balance point of the clutch, and they rolled out in style, behind Travis in his cool-as Kombi and Juan in his baby-poo yellow Datsun 120Y. The music was pumping, and the good vibes flowed freely from these seven vibrant young souls, enjoying a moment in time with each other.

'Convoy!' shouted Georgia, her hair blowing wild and free in the wind.

chapter fifty-six

The Railway Hotel

They parked all three cars side by side: the Kombi, the Chevy, and the Datsun.

Here they were again. The girls were back exactly where they started their Byron getaway the day before. Only this time, they were walking in with a few extra passengers.

Dalton handed the Chevy keys to Adeline and made a joke. 'I think you should hold on to these. Jacqui said you are the designated driver, and she showed us why. Nice car, huh? Your dad has done a marvellous job keeping it in perfect condition, and you girls are so lucky that he trusts you enough to drive it. It'd be worth a motza.'

Adeline replied. 'Our lives wouldn't be worth living if something happened to that car, so we do our best to look after it.'

'I guess so,' replied Dalton to Adeline. Then he spoke loudly as he started walking towards Travis. Travis was around the driver's side of the Kombi. He was just about to lock it up. 'Hey Trav, do you mind if I grab my stuff? I'll take it with me now so we can all drink and chill. When the train arrives, I can jump on without bothering you again. I feel like I've bothered you enough over the past few days, and I am extremely grateful. Thanks for everything, man! It's been great.'

'Seriously, man, no worries. You haven't been a bother; it's been an awesome weekend. Good times, man!' Travis opened the back of the Kombi, and Dalton reached in to grab his surfboard, guitar, and backpack.

'On the road again,' whistled Dalton.

Jacqui and Juan had already headed inside with Myles and Georgia. They were headed out to the beer garden where the Sunday session was fully underway, the band playing a Hoodoo Gurus classic, *1000 Miles Away*. The band was a male and female duo, and they were doing some magical harmonies with the classic Aussie song.

Travis and Adeline headed straight to the bar, as they had already agreed to buy the first shout. Both as designated drivers, they were shouting themselves a non-alcoholic drink in the first round, and then they could decide to sit in or out of the shouts for the rest of the evening. With their full tray of drinks each in hand, they headed out to the beer garden with the rest of the group.

Dalton was finding a place to put his gear out of the way to enjoy a few drinks before parting from his new friends. At the bar, he asked about a train ticket. The irony here was that Tilly had the same conversation, in this exact location, with this same bartender exactly twenty-four hours prior. He was the young foreign bartender, fresh in town and learning the ropes of this Aussie pub. Neither Tilly, Dalton nor the bartender knew there was any connection or irony to this situation. Until Dalton threw in the random question, just in case this fellow might know anything. Dalton knew for a fact that Tilly had been here yesterday afternoon. The rest of the details were shady, but just by chance, this guy might know something; he thought he'd give it a shot.

Dalton asked uncomfortably, 'Hey, man, this will sound like a weird stalkerish question, but I'm looking for a friend. I lost her somehow and am trying to find her again, but I have no way of contacting her. I'll spare you the details, but we can put together that she left on a train here yesterday, and she's possibly headed to a hospital. Is any of this ringing a bell?'

'Ah, yeah, man! This, may I say, beautiful girl, was here yesterday with those girls who just walked out to the beer garden. They made quite an entrance and were a crowd-pleaser until they left quite early in the night.' Dalton was working hard to make clear what the bartender was saying through his thick accent. 'The local boys, Matty, Joel and Axl, were quite upset when they left. They will be happy to see the girls again, only not with the extra guests. I can see they have all made new friends in town.'

This fellow was on for quite a chat, so Dalton pressed on more to ask specific questions to get some information about Tilly. Possibly, any information would help to determine where Tilly might be going. 'Yeah, that's her. She was with those girls and left to get on a train, but they weren't sure where she was going. Do you know exactly which train she got on?'

'Yeah, I do; she got on the 6 pm train because she was determined to get to a hospital. It looked like she had hurt her arm, the way she was carrying all her luggage. She had a guitar and a backpack, so she was pretty loaded up.' The barman was sharing some good information freely, and Dalton was most grateful for that.

Dalton interrupted and said, 'Yep, that's gotta be her. Did you catch her name by any chance?'

'I did, man. She asked me for a pen, and I helped her write her name on a couple of bar coasters for her friends because she had hurt her arm and couldn't write properly and was in a rush to get on the train. Her name was Tilly. Tilly Macallan. She said her name was Matilda, but nobody called her that. I thought it was cute, Matilda Macallan. I only remember Macallan because she said it was like the Scottish whisky, The Macallan. We sell it here, it's popular. She just wrote Tilly and a phone number, times three, for the girls she was with. I hoped she would write an extra one for me, but she was probably way out of my league. I'm not sure I would be enough for her. She was a special lady.'

'Good on you, lad,' said Dalton. Dalton liked this fellow's honesty and sense of humour. He was a young-looking chap, maybe just out of high school, and he was here in Australia doing his gap year thing. 'I wish she gave you a coaster with her contacts. It might be helpful to me right now. But I guess I can get that off one of the girls, so it's all good. Jacqui has the exact coaster you are talking about in her back pocket, and to be honest, it's not any help because the phone number is Tilly's parents' hotel back in Angourie. And we know that she's not heading that way soon. That's where I've come from and where we parted ways.'

The barman shared some more information, hoping it was helpful. 'She boarded the 6 pm train to Murwillumbah. She may have also travelled on to the Gold Coast because I told her she could catch the connecting bus to the Gold Coast. Her ticket was only to Murwillumbah, so if she changed her mind, she would have had to get off somewhere and buy another ticket to the Gold Coast. That's all I can tell you. I hope that helps. Oh! And yes, she was beautiful; she had a nice energy. I can see why you are trying to find her. I can see you two would be good friends. Are you guys in a band together, if you don't mind me asking?'

Dalton wasn't sure what to say; it was too long a story, so he replied, 'Umm, no, not really. I mean, we could be. That's a great idea, but no, we just got lost from each other, somehow. I'll spare you from the stupid story. It's embarrassing, really.'

'Mm, okay,' said the barman and paused for a long moment, thinking about what else he wanted to say. He didn't want to say something that might mess up this whole situation that he seemed to be an integral part of. Any information he could give Dalton right now would be extremely helpful or not. He thought about what he wanted to say, then added, 'This might sound weird to say, and I don't want to say the wrong thing to confuse you, but other than trying to find a hospital, it seemed to me like she was on a bigger search than that. Do you think she knows you are trying to find her? Is she also trying to find you? I mean, did she know you were here in Byron? Is that why she came here?'

Dalton was getting increasingly confused the more the barman asked questions. 'You know what? There is so much I don't know. I wish I knew the answers to those questions. I know I'm trying to find my way back to her, but I don't think she knows I'm looking for her. How would she know? Aargh! It's just a big mess. I wish I could go back in time and fix the whole stupid thing. Never in my whole life have I regretted saying one simple word... One simple word has caused this whole big mess.' Dalton was getting a little worked up, so he bought his train ticket from the barman and headed out to the beer garden to enjoy some music and drinks for a little while.

'May I ask the word?' queried the barman, keeping Dalton in the conversation a little longer. He was intrigued by what this one extremely powerful word could be.

'But...The stupid word was "but." I think you're amazing, Tilly, "but"......'

'Aargh, I see,' said the barman, 'And let me guess, she didn't want to hear whatever else you had to say after the word, but?'

'Nope. That's the last word I said to her.' Dalton looked out through the windows towards the train platform.

The barman asked. 'What could possibly be the "but" with that girl? How is she amazing, but?'

'That's the whole thing. It wasn't about anything wrong with her. It was me. I wanted to tell her she was amazing, but I also needed to tell her something important about me that I hadn't shared yet. I regret not telling her sooner. I just didn't. I couldn't. I should have been honest with her straight up because I wanted her to understand me and my dreaded past. I wasn't ready to face it myself yet.'

'Oh, dang it, sounds like you fucked up, man. I hope you can find her somewhere out there. It's a big world these days.' The barman sympathised with Dalton as he had to end the conversation as new patrons had come to the bar for drinks.

Dalton was grateful for the chat and the information the young barman shared. Tilly Macallan was on that train. At least he knew that for real.

Dalton thought about scribbling his details on a coaster for his new friends, just like Tilly had done, but what contact number would he even put down? His parent's number in Deniliquin? They did not know where he was, and he didn't regularly keep in touch with them. If he gave his parent's number to his friends, that would mean he would have to explain this whole situation to his mum, dad, and brothers in case anyone called to find out his whereabouts, and that was not something he was ready to do. Admitting to his family that he had, yet again, messed up another beautiful girl's life wasn't something Dalton was prepared to do. His parents wouldn't understand any of this. It was complex enough for him to understand what was going on.

Dalton had a bit more of a think. He wrote his parent's contact number on six coasters for his new friends. It was the only way anyone could contact him, and these six new friends were possibly the only people other than the barman, who might have any chance of helping Dalton find Tilly again. He had to be contactable somehow.

He wrote:

Dalton Diaz
Deni 0358469970
Friendship & Freedom 4 EVA.

Dalton joined the table of his friends in the beer garden, and Myles started the tease, saying he had no choice but to drink Dalton's drink before it got too hot, as he was chatting up the barman for too long. Luckily, Dalton had already bought himself a beer, as he didn't know that Travis and Adeline had already bought him a drink. Myles headed to the bar to buy another round of drinks, giving Dalton a chance to explain to the others that he wasn't chatting up the barman, and he had some information that Tilly Macallan was definitely on that train to Murwillumbah last night. Dalton pulled out the six coasters and handed them to his friends as he clearly and thoughtfully explained his decision.

'Now. I've thought long and hard about this. I don't want to lose touch with you all, but I have no way for you to contact me other than through my parent's home number in Deniliquin. They do not know about Tilly or that I'm even here with you all in Byron. I haven't spoken to them for a few months. And to be quite honest, I don't want to tell them about this whole shemozzle. They won't understand. So, if any of you find Tilly before I do, please leave a message and a contact number with my parents saying one of your friends from Byron called to say the surf's up. They don't need to know the whole dramatic story.'

It was like his new friends already knew what he was coming back to say, and they had already planned this all along, as Travis started the cheers. 'Cheers, Dalton,' then they all joined their glasses, 'To Friendship and Freedom.'

Jacqui put her arm around Dalton and roughened him up to shake off his seriousness. 'Lighten up, Tiger. You'll find her. Or she'll find you. Everything is going to be okay.'

'Yeah, maybe you're right, Jacqui. Once I get on that train, I know I'm heading in the right direction.' Dalton took a long sip of his ice-cold beer, and they all started singing along with the band on cue, to Me and Bobby McGee. It was like the band had been listening to their conversation and knew the perfect song to play.

'*Busted flat in Baton Rouge, waiting for a train, when I was feeling near as faded as my jeans.*' Travis wasn't much of a singer in public unless it was The Rolling Stones, but he was digging this song and getting right into it. Adeline joined in with him as they swayed in each other's arms, knowing that the evening together was ending soon.

'*Windshield wipers slapping time, I was holding Bobby's hand in mine, we sang every song that driver knew.*'

The whole beer garden of patrons seemed to join in with the chorus. '*Freedom's just another word for nothing left to lose, nothing, don't mean nothing honey, if it ain't free, no no........good enough for me and Bobby McGee.*'

Myles returned from the bar to restock everyone's drinks. The evening was closing in, and the vibe was feeling good, but Jacqui, Adeline and Georgia were consciously aware that they had to depart their friends soon and get on the road. Juan was leaving soon to return to the Byron Hotel to start his 5 pm work shift. Myles had planned to catch a lift back with him, as he was staying in the Byron Hotel for another night. Myles and Juan's inevitable departure seemed appropriate for the others to separate.

All these little lovebirds had planned to see each other again, so they sadly drifted away from each other as the weekend ended.

Myles and Georgia disappeared behind Travis' Kombi for a last kiss. They didn't want anyone giving them a hard time, so they made out with a bit of privacy. This way, they could relish each other and the passion they had created between each other over the past twenty-four hours.

Travis and Adeline had already had a quick little goodbye kiss in the beer garden, and Travis stayed in the bar to keep Dalton company. Adeline took her time while the others said their goodbyes to warm the car up and reset the mirrors back to her height.

Jacqui and Juan were having their special moment beside Juan's car. They exchanged numbers and decided they would like to see each other again. As Jacqui went to walk away, Juan said politely, 'Is it okay, Jacqui, if I give you a kiss to remember me by?'

Jacqui almost fell over to get back into his arms. He closed his arms around her and lifted her gently to reach her mouth with his. Jacqui didn't realise how tall Juan was until now. She had never felt a kiss quite like his. It was so many feelings all in one: passionate, gentle, intense, and desperate, and it tasted delicious. Jacqui was trying to keep her heart from racing as she tried to be calm. Meanwhile, she was quietly losing her mind. She wished they didn't have to go back home right now, but there was no time left to play with. All three girls had work at 8 am the following morning, and more of the worry was that their dad was expecting the car home by 10 pm. It was the Sunday night Chevy curfew. At this stage, they would go close to breaking the rules, which might mean no more Byron Bay weekends.

Adeline beeped the horn to remind the girls that time was up. It was one of those fancy horns: *barp, bedda, barp, barp, barp, barp,* and as it made its song, it added some humour to the seriousness of the goodbyes. Adeline reversed the car into the open carpark space so the girls could quickly get in without banging the car doors on nearby parked cars.

Adeline turned the radio on. It was Elton John, Tiny Dancer.

Come on, girls, we've got Elton in here to drive us home.

Jacqui and Georgia reluctantly climbed into the Chevy, accepting that their weekend was over. Myles and Juan walked over to where the Datsun was parked, waving as the girls drove off. Juan had forgotten that his car was in stereo with the girls. He started the engine with Elton blaring as well. '*Hold me closer, tiny dancer, count the headlights on the highway, lay me down in sheets of linen; you had a busy day today.*'

chapter fifty-seven

One More Hour

Meanwhile, back in the beer garden, Travis and Dalton enjoyed one more hour of each other's company. Travis was in no rush and was happy to spend more time with his new mate, trying to figure out a plan to help Dalton find his girl.

The music was good. Dalton appreciated the duo and thought he and Tilly could do that for a while, doing music gigs and travelling together. He just had to find her first.

He finally shared his past with Travis, making the story about how he lost Tilly much easier to understand. Until now, Travis could only piece together a few details, and now it all made sense. A total misunderstanding, mixed with a few drinks on a Thursday night at The Angourie Local, and it had turned into a simple mess.

Travis and Dalton had worked out that Tilly was in Murwillumbah after getting to the hospital yesterday, or she was already at the Gold Coast. That part they had no idea about. The linking detail that the helpful-not-friendly-but-helpful train lady had given was quite significant. She had told Dalton that a dark-haired girl had got off the train in Murwillumbah to buy another ticket to the Gold Coast. By coincidence, that could have very well been Tilly, but there were a lot of dark-haired girls in the world, so it wasn't anything unusual. It could have been anyone. By instinct, though, Dalton felt it was Tilly. The timing and the way the world worked in mysterious ways. He knew that the grumpy lady had answered the phone for a reason, which was all in his favour. In her unhelpful way, she was trying to let Dalton know that the girl he was looking for was on her way to the Gold Coast.

With Travis' help, Dalton had planned to get to Murwillumbah Train Station and jump off to check the platform. Dalton strongly felt that Tilly wouldn't hang around Murwillumbah for long because it probably wasn't where Dalton would be going. It was too far inland from the beach. He had to think like Tilly to determine her logic and movements.

If she had disembarked in Murwillumbah to go to the hospital and get her arm checked out, it would be likely she was getting on the bus northbound tonight. Dalton would do his checks and then get on the bus.

The only suggestion Travis could make was that Dalton go to places where he and Tilly would hang out. Also, to do things he loved to do, surf and gig. If he was doing what he loved, it was likely that Tilly might find him.

Dalton ordered one last drink at the bar, as it was nearly time for the train to arrive—a Macallan's Scotch Whisky on ice for the memories of Tilly. The taste of it on his lips took him straight back to the gypsy room and the sweet taste of Tilly. He was craving her so badly. His heart ached to feel her beside him again, but she felt a thousand miles away right now.

Travis asked Dalton to grab him a strong iced water as he was driving back to Wooli as soon as he saw Dalton step foot on that train. He had enjoyed a couple of slow beers over the afternoon, but nothing that would put him over the limit to drive. Travis wouldn't risk losing his license. It was his freedom and independence, and Wooli was too isolated a town to get stuck in.

The bartender announced through the PA system. 'Testing one, two, testing one, two. The northbound train to Murwillumbah is arriving in ten minutes. All passengers, please make your way to Platform 1 with your tickets at the ready for boarding. Thank you.'

Dalton and Travis had a mate's embrace, and Dalton sculled the last few dregs of his ice-cold whisky. He set off to grab his gear and gave Travis a wave as he exited through the back door onto the platform. Travis exited through the front door.

As Dalton boarded the train, he had a strange feeling and was trying to figure out what it was. Part of it was a weird feeling that he knew that somehow, for some reason, he was supposed to meet Travis. He couldn't believe it was less than thirty-six hours since they met. In the past hour, it felt like their conversation had brought them to know each other so well, like they had known each other forever. The second feeling was that Dalton could feel where Tilly had been already. It was the weirdest feeling, like he knew where she had sat. Of course, he didn't know if he was right, but it felt like something was guiding him to follow her steps.

Dalton leaned his backpack, guitar, and surfboard behind the divider wall, separating the seated section from the departure area of the carriage. This way, it wasn't in the way of any other passengers, but it was easy to access for his exit at Murwillumbah. He planned to jump off and look along the platform for Tilly. If he didn't see her, he was going directly to the ticket booth to buy a bus ticket to continue travelling straight on to the Gold Coast. He didn't know that that was precisely what Tilly had done twenty-four hours prior. Her reason to continue was different, as she had made some new friends, inviting her to continue the journey with them. Dalton knew none of these details; he could feel her.

As Travis walked to his car, he had the same strange feeling that his by-chance meeting with Dalton was more important than just a one-off random hitchhiker friendship. He had yet to work all that out in the future of life, but right now, he was content with their friendship and the random acts that had set Dalton on a trail of adventure to reconnect with Tilly. All Travis could nail it down to was that if he hadn't picked up Dalton, Dalton wouldn't have met Jacqui, and if he hadn't met Jacqui, he wouldn't have known Tilly was looking for him, and if he didn't know Tilly was looking for him, who knows, but the outcome would differ greatly from what was happening right now. It was all just strangely meant to be. And aside from all that, Travis had enjoyed an awesome weekend in great company. He liked Adeline, and he hoped to see her again. They had exchanged contact details and agreed that this weekend wouldn't be a one-night stand. They both had deeper feelings for each other.

Travis unlocked the Kombi and repositioned the gear in the boot to ensure everything was secure, since surfboards and bags were floating around, not tied down to anything. He was happy for them all to just stay in the back. There was no need to tie them to the roof. It was just him, on his own, travelling back to Wooli. He neatly positioned everything in place and climbed in for the return journey to his own bed. As Travis leaned over to put his wallet in the glove box, he caught the scent of Adeline still lingering. It was sweet and musky and beautiful. He breathed it in, having a flashback to their last kiss. Adeline was soft and gentle, and he loved her kindred spirit. Just then, as he pushed the glovebox closed, he noticed Adeline's cardigan on the floor of the passenger seat. That's what he could smell. He lifted it to his face and breathed her in again. Travis' thoughts wandered. *Oh well, that means I must see her again to give her back this cardigan. I'm pretty sure she said it was one of her favourites. I can't believe she left it there. Hmm, maybe that was deliberate—cheeky, intelligent, beautiful girl.*

chapter fifty-eight

Dalton, The Detective

Dalton made his way into the dining carriage and bought himself a packet of sea salt chips and a West Coast Cooler. There wasn't much to choose from, just a small range of alcoholic and non-alcoholic beverages and a few chip packet choices, including Burger Rings and Twisties, which he wasn't much of a fan of, not when he was drinking, anyway. He didn't feel like a beer and had consumed enough whisky and champagne over the past few days. A West Coast Cooler was sweet, light and refreshing.

Dalton took his chances to ask the bar attendant if she had seen Tilly the day before. Chances were that she did the same shift every day, and what did he have to lose? He paid for his items and sat on the barstool, fixed into the carriage for safety. He swung it around to get in and then turned himself back into position, facing the bar attendant.

'Sorry to bother you, and this might seem a little strange, but may I ask you a question?'

'Sure, said the lady, blushing a little, turning her mouth up and then straightening it, not sure what Dalton would ask her.'

'Were you working this same shift yesterday?'

'Umm, yes, yes, I was. Why?' Trish answered curiously, wondering why Dalton was asking her this question.

'I'm wondering if, by any chance, you noticed a very beautiful girl with dark, curly hair on the train yesterday?'

'Yes. Yes, I did. We had a fantastic afternoon yesterday. This carriage was alive. You would have loved it; a lot more going on yesterday than today.'

'What do you mean?'

'We had a travelling band on the train yesterday, and they did a carriage gig for the passengers. I noticed the dark-haired girl had a guitar on the train with her, but she didn't play it and wasn't sitting with the band. I'm not sure what connection she had with the band, but she was singing with them and had a lovely voice.'

'Oh! That sounds like fun. I wish I were here yesterday. Do you, by any chance, know what the band's name was?'

'Oh, I'm not good at paying attention to that stuff. I'm sorry. I think they were a Brisbane band; they've been travelling down south. I'm guessing they played a gig in Byron. Heading back home again, I'd say. They had a lot of gear with them. If it helps, I remember the lead guy's name because it did not suit a young man. It was Bernard.'

'Bernard Fanning?' Dalton questioned.

'Yeah, I think so.' The lady agreed because she did not know what his last name was.

'Was the band called Powderfinger?' Dalton was hopeful she might know the answer because this would definitely help if Dalton were to find Tilly if she was still hanging out with the band. And knowing what Tilly was like, that was highly likely.

'Yeah, I think that was it. I was going to say it was some double-whammy name all in one. Powderfinger, Bernard Fanning, that's ringing a bell now that you've put it all together.' The lady still wasn't certain, but this seemed to be correct. *I mean, how many musicians called Bernard could there be?*

Dalton sat for a moment quietly as the lady served other customers. He was trying to think what other questions he could ask her without being too invasive, yet something that would help him find out where Tilly might go and if it was her hanging out with the band and why.

As the customers moved away, the lady asked a question first. 'So, may I ask, are you a detective or something? And why are you looking for that girl? Is she in trouble?'

Dalton replied with a gentle, honest smile. The one that crossed his whole face, the one that Tilly had instantly fallen in love with. 'No, I'm not a detective at all.' He shook his head, thinking it was funny that this lady could think that Dalton could hold such a prestigious, law-abiding position. 'No. It's much more confusing than that. You see, I met this beautiful girl in Angourie just a little while ago. The dark-haired girl whom I think you saw on the train yesterday. I fell in love with her, and I think she was in love with me. Strange, I know.' Dalton smiled again, lifted both hands and parted them to the side, signalling uncertainty. He took a sip of his drink. 'We had a miscommunication and somehow ended up going separate ways. It's stupid, and I won't go into all the details, but I messed up. Anyway, I'm trying to find her, and as strange as it seems, she might be trying to find me too.'

The lady replied quickly as another customer lined up to be served at the bar. 'Clear as mud.' She took a moment to serve the next customer as Dalton waited patiently.

Once she finished serving, she returned to where Dalton was perched on the barstool. 'So, I guess I should ask your name?'

'Dalton Diaz, I'm from down in Deniliquin. It's nice to meet you....?' He left the word *you* lingering as his reply became a question, just like when he met Tilly.

'My name is Patricia, but people call me Trish.'

'May I ask Trish, did you catch the dark-haired girl's name?' Dalton thought this might be a vital question to ensure they were talking about Tilly here.

'I meet many people on this train, but I think I can remember. Just give me a second to think.' She scratched her head as she recalled the vision in her mind from the day before. 'So, from what I can remember, her name was a double letter first and last like yours, Dalton Diaz, starting with M. I don't remember her first name, but I remember her last name was the same as the whisky we sell here on board the train. The Macallan.

She said another name that she got called that started with T because I remember thinking that's like me, Patricia, to Trish. Whatever her name was got shortened to Tippy, Tibby, or something like that.' Suddenly, she remembered. 'Matilda to Tilly, that was it. I remember now.'

'Good work, Trish!' Dalton was super excited; this was good information that he was on the right track. 'If I were a detective, Trish, I'd ask the Railways Commissioner to give you a pay rise. You've been extremely helpful.'

'Happy to help. Would you like another drink? It's a pity drink on me,' she added. 'We call it a drink "on the train" because it's "on the house." I'm shouting you the drink, but it's "on the train." Do you get it?' Dalton took a moment to catch onto Trish's comedy line. Once he got the joke, he thought about it, and it was pretty funny.

'Yes, I get it. That's a good one. I'd love another West Coast Cooler "on the train," thank you, Trish.' Dalton laughed gently at her sideways sense of humour.

Trish felt sorry for Dalton because what he didn't know, and what Trish had observed yesterday, was that Tilly was getting on well with Bernard. There was a lot of flirting going on that Trish could sense and an easy connection between them. She didn't want to say anything to Dalton because she could see how desperately he was in love with her and how important it was for him to find this girl. She also did not know what the outcome would be, so it was none of her business. She just felt sorry for Dalton.

As Dalton accepted the kind gesture of another drink 'on the train,' Trish added another piece of exciting information to this puzzle. Nothing revolutionary, but just cute and interesting. 'Dalton, this probably won't surprise you, but this Tilly girl you are talking about, you know she bought herself a West Coast Cooler and a packet of plain salted chips, just like you? I only remember this because she asked me if I could undo the lid for her because she had hurt her arm, and she couldn't get enough strength to twist the bottle top and hold her chips simultaneously.'

'Interesting. Yes, I heard from some new friends of mine that she had hurt her arm somehow.' Dalton was sure this was his Tilly now, not a doubt in his mind.

'She told me she tripped on a bottle on the beach while running and fell on her wrist. We didn't get to chat for long because it got busy at the bar, but that's the brief rundown she shared with me. She was going to the hospital because she had hurt her arm from tripping on a bottle. She was a lovely girl, friendly and easy to talk to. She made quite an impression on the band. I think.' Trish stopped herself there because she didn't want to say anything that might hurt Dalton's feelings or give him a reason to worry about her.

'Is that right?' Dalton pushed for a little more, but Trish didn't give anymore. New customers came to the bar again, so the conversation ended, and when they got back to it, Trish guided it to take another direction. She really felt sorry for Dalton. He was such a likeable young lad. Dalton reminded Trish of her own son, whom she had lost connection with. Sadly, Trish's son had taken a pathway of alcohol addiction and ruined his life at sixteen. Trish could do nothing other than watch him self-destruct, landing himself in a community support mission at age eighteen.

By that time, the alcohol had turned into a full-blown heroin addiction, and he almost lost his life if it weren't for some really good mates to get him professional help before it was too late. Sadly, Trish and her son never regained their close connection, and she always blamed herself for always working away from home and doing the long-haul return passenger train trips from Brisbane to Sydney. She would often be gone for ten days at a time, and her son was left to fend for himself. He was old enough to do so, but rather than discover the beauty of independence; he took the pity route. He wanted everyone to feel sorry for him. Trish didn't see the signs until it was too late. She had grown up differently, with her parents controlling her every move, so she thought giving her son freedom would be what he wanted. But that's not the way he saw it. He viewed her time away from him while she was working as abandonment. This caused substantial mental health issues for her son that he couldn't get past. She explained that her only way forward was to keep sharing her expression of love with her son through many love languages, hoping he would return to her when he was ready. Although he was distant from her, she always let him know in different ways that she loved him. She would write him letters to tell him how much she loved him. She would send him gifts in the mail when she hadn't spent time with him because he would rarely come to visit. When he came to visit, she would do things for him that made him feel at home, his washing, cooking meals for him, and pampering to his every need. And she was open in her expression of words, telling him and affirming how much she loved her son. The one thing missing was the quality time, that time, she and he could never get back. And quality time was her son's love language.

Trish shared this story with Dalton in between customer service interruptions. It was a sad story, and Dalton could feel how much guilt Trish was carrying for what had happened to her son. He felt similar in his guilt for what had happened to Chelsea. Trish and Dalton both had pity feelings for each other and questioned if they had given enough love before the grief. For Dalton, the grief he carried was guilt and permanent loss of love. For Trish, the grief she carried was guilt and unnecessary loss. Dalton decided he wanted to do a special "Cheer" with Trish.

'Get yourself a drink, Trish. I need to do a special "Cheers" with you,' requested Dalton.

Trish opened herself a bottle of West Coast Cooler, intending to take only one sip; the rest she would keep until the end of her shift.

'Cheers, Dalton,' she raised the bottle to his.

Say this with me, 'To Friendship and Enough Love' claimed Dalton.

They both said it together, 'To Friendship and Enough Love.'

Dalton explained the reason behind his "Cheers." 'I'm saying this, Trish, because I am enjoying our little Friendship here, and I can feel you've had a tough time. I want you to know that you did give your son Enough Love. One day, he will realise you were doing your best.'

As Dalton finished his West Coast Cooler, he could hear the conductor announce the train was soon to be arriving at the Murwillumbah Train Station. 'Next stop, Murwillumbah Train Station.'

Dalton said his farewell to Trish and gave her a friendly hug. 'Thank you, Trish, you've been super helpful. I will jump out here and see if I can see Tilly if she stayed in Murwillumbah last night.'

'Oh, I'm pretty certain she kept going onwards with the band to the Gold Coast. The bus trip is not part of my journey tonight. My night usually ends here. I live here, so I don't know for sure. I'm sorry.'

'Thanks, Trish, you're a gem!' Dalton waved as he returned to the carriage, where his gear was safely stowed.

'Good luck finding her, Dalton. I'm sure you will. You two will be great together.' Trish waved and blew Dalton a kiss.

Why did everyone say that? You two would be great together? Dalton thought a little more about it. Maybe they just had that kind of "couples who suit each other" look. Their personalities were similar, that was for sure. Their hobbies and interests were common with each other. They both had vibrant, friendly energy and a positive attitude. They also had both made a foolish mistake to lose each other.

The train pulled into the station. Dalton felt confident that leaving his stuff on the train was safe while he grabbed his onward bus ticket. From what he understood, the train wasn't going anywhere for a while.

He asked a nearby passenger, who was contently reading her book, to keep an eye on his stuff if she didn't mind.

'Sure thing, I'm just waiting to transfer to the bus. I can mind your stuff. We usually have a half-hour wait until they ask us to transfer to the bus. I usually just wait here on the train, reading; it's quiet.'

She paused, and Dalton quietly said, 'Thank you.'

She continued. 'This train isn't going anywhere until the bus arrives to deliver the passengers on the southbound journey.'

The passenger delivered her entire response without glancing away from her book. *She must have eyes in the back of her head*, thought Dalton, considering he was standing behind her, and he wondered how she knew he was even talking to her. She was completely aware of everything around her, although she seemed completely immersed in the pages. *A well-travelled train patron,* thought Dalton. *She possibly does the journey every day. A Gold Coast-Byron commuter, perhaps. If that were the case, she would know the regulars and the newcomers. Interesting,* he thought. *I must see if she knows anything about yesterday's journey when I return to the train.*

As the doors jammed open with a loud clack, Dalton peered out, noticing that it was helpful that he was up high, above the small crowd of people boarding the train. He looked through the crowd to see if he could spot Tilly, just in case, but there was no one even close to her characteristics. Many older people were carrying bags of groceries, possibly in Murwillumbah, for their weekly shopping from small towns like Mooball, Crabbes Creek and Burringbar. The other passengers had lots of luggage in large suitcases, possibly en route to more fabulous adventures. The train journeys around Australia were epic from Roma St in Brisbane. Travel agents promoted overland train travel as the best way to view Australia's vast countryside, and because of its comfort and affordability, many people were jumping on board. The most popular route was on a train known as The Sunlander. The journey was part of the Queensland Rail network. The Sunlander travelled from Brisbane to Cairns. It was high-class train travel, decked out with sleeping berths for first-class and second-class passengers. It also had seated-only carriages for those who couldn't afford the luxury but still wanted to take part in the long journey. The most popular section of the journey was the passage through the Glasshouse Mountains and the cane fields of North Queensland. The passengers here in Murwillumbah were more likely starting their southern journeys to Sydney.

Dalton marched over to the ticket booth, where a small line of passengers had made the same decision as him: to continue on further north. He almost fell over when he heard the familiar monotone voice of the *very helpful lady* he had spoken to on the phone yesterday in the ticket booth. He briefly considered introducing himself to her as the "pest on the phone" yesterday, but the line behind him was growing, and he knew people had little time to re-board the train. There was no time for a *friendly* discussion. He simply said, 'Good evening, Ma'am. Can I please have one one-way bus ticket to the Gold Coast?'

'Ma'am,' she said. 'The last time somebody called me Ma'am was yesterday from some young chap on the phone, calling me, thinking I could sort his ruined love life out for him. He thought he was going to find some girl that got away. I told him he had Buckley's chance of finding her. It's a big country. These trains go all the way around this country these days. She could be anywhere or missing. Lots of young girls go missing these days. Did you hear about that Ivan Malat creep?' She didn't wait for an answer. She continued doing what she was doing and talking. 'Murdering young girls, picking up hitchhikers and tourists, and they are never to be seen again. There was also that Balaclava creep, just up the road here in Tweed Heads, raping women while their boyfriends watched. What a creep! They never caught him, you know. It's one of those unsolved mysteries. I watched a show on it, on the idiot box, last night. Horrific.' She shared all this information as she multi-tasked, not stopping for a moment while she inputted the ticket information, printed it and placed it in a neat little flap envelope for Dalton, sliding it under the glass screen as they exchanged the ticket for cash.

'Well, ah, thanks for sharing that news, Ma'am. It's quite distressing. Our society is quite sad.' Dalton didn't even try to talk her through what she had shared with him; he just let her vent and understood that she wasn't having the best day. She seemed to be one of those people who liked to view the world as all parts of bad and evil and no in-between. There wasn't much Dalton could do about that, not right now. He had a short amount of time to buy his bus ticket and remove his belongings from the train. He waited as she passed him his ticket and his change, wondering if she would recognise his voice as clearly as he recognised hers. She said nothing that hinted that she recognised him.

She was obviously running out of five- and ten-dollar bank notes for change. She piled ten one-dollar coins in change in front of him. Just as he was about to walk off, he changed his mind. He couldn't resist. He wanted to thank her somehow, as she had been the catalyst for figuring out Tilly's whereabouts. He simply said, 'Hey, by the way, I just wanted to thank you for your help yesterday. You were really helpful, and I think that because of you, I may have more than Buckley's chance of finding my girl.'

The very helpful lady instantly changed her tone and started laughing. 'I knew it was you, young chap.' She gave him a cheeky smile and started pointing at Dalton with her hand beside her face as she leaned forward, pulling a face at him. 'There are no young blokes with half as many manners as you. I was just stirring you up, you know, with all that horror news. You're a good lad. You'll find her. I know you will. That's if she doesn't find you first.' She winked and gave Dalton a semi-warm smile.

He couldn't believe that she had taken so much time to wind him up, the hitchhiker murderer stuff and all that whole big story, and all along she knew it was him. He shook his head with humorous disbelief, laughed and thanked her again as he walked away. He felt bad because he had already taken up too much of everyone's time, and they were all giving him dirty looks from the line-up behind him. Hopefully, she was in a better mood to serve the rest of the customers, since she had given Dalton a hard time. As a last thought, he wondered why she was still here. It was way past 5 pm. No wonder she was cranky.

Dalton checked around again, checking the platform for any signs of Tilly. He placed the ticket envelope into his wallet, grabbed the pile of one-dollar coins, and shoved them into his pocket. One coin caught the side of his jeans pocket and fell onto the ground. As he stooped to pick it up, he noticed a shiny white guitar pick on the ground. He couldn't believe his eyes. Engraved with tiny black letters, 'Have Guitar, Will Travel' on one side, and on the other, the letters were scribed in a row diagonally across the middle of the pick, J. L. F. E. L. T.

Dalton couldn't believe his eyes. Those letters stood for Jack, Laura, Frankie, Eddie, Louis, and Tilly. This was Tilly's guitar pick. He looked around to see if this was some kind of joke. He half expected to see Tilly standing before him, but this was just a wish. It confirmed that everything he had thought about was correct. She had been here. Possibly, just like he was. She may have fumbled through her pockets for extra cash to buy the onward bus journey ticket and rushed back to collect her belongings. Somehow, amongst all that commotion, she had dropped her pick.

Of all the places, he could have dropped his one-dollar coin. This was another sign that he was on the right track to find Tilly. There were so many pieces of this puzzle that he was trying to connect. The weird thing was it was always after the fact that he realised the signs were there all along. He wanted to tune himself into being more aware of things that might guide him to her. There was a word for this occurrence— synchronicity. Meaningful occurrences that seem to have no cause but are destined to happen in our life journey to put us exactly where we are meant to be or guide us to a new journey.

chapter fifty-nine

Meeting Lee

Dalton looked around from the higher vantage point on the train ledge, observing every aspect of his three-hundred-and-sixty-degree view. He looked at every person standing beneath him on the platform, quickly noticing their features and moving on if they didn't slightly resemble Tilly. He only had time for quick observations of the crowd of people. He would know Tilly from a mile away by how she moved, her dark features, her way. He couldn't feel her here. Instinctively, he knew she had boarded the bus from the information he had learned from Trish and the "very helpful" ticket lady. Dalton re-boarded the train and gathered his gear together. He had quite a load.

He approached the lovely lady who had been minding his bags.

'Hey, thanks for looking after my stuff. Much appreciated.' said Dalton to the lady. She took a moment to glance away from her book towards the voice, then realising it was the man with the guitar, surfboard and backpack, she placed the bookmark inside, closing her book on her lap, all the meanwhile keeping her eyes fixed on him.

'No worries, my name is Lee-Anne. People call me Lee or Leeroy, depending on how many drinks I've had.' She laughed, a beautiful, contagious, friendly laugh that instantly eased any tension or distance a stranger would feel towards someone they had never met. 'And you are?'

'Dalton, my apologies for being so rude and distracted. My name is Dalton. People call me Dalton; no matter how many drinks I've had, it's one of those names you can't shorten. My mum chose my name on purpose, after my brothers, Timothy and Johnathon. These were two official names deliberately chosen because Mum loved the full name, only to be devastated that my brothers were nicknamed Timmy and Johnno. She must have thought she would be safe with Dalton. I was also lucky that my childhood best mate's name was Del with an e, so that somehow saved it. I just stayed Dalton. Anyway, enough about me and my name. I must sound like a total self-important goofball. Thanks for looking after my stuff. I wasn't sure what I was doing.

I've decided to catch a bus to the Gold Coast.' Dalton was talking a lot, but he wasn't making much sense. He had a long day and a few drinks along the way.

Lee spoke calmly, instantly soothing the rush Dalton was in. 'Can I ask you something? Is everything okay? You seem a little on edge. Can I help with something?' Lee fired questions at Dalton, trying to figure out his story as she could sense his nervousness and unease.

'Me? No, I'm okay, thank you. I'm trying to find someone very special who ran away from me. It was my fault. It's all very confusing. I'll spare you the details. She was on this train yesterday, I believe.'

Lee tilted her head with a clue that she may instantly be part of Dalton's puzzle. 'Was she now?'

'Yeah, I'm fairly certain, if that's such a quantifiable thing, that she boarded the train in Byron, then disembarked here and bought a bus ticket, heading to the Gold Coast. She made friends with the band who were on board the train yesterday. I do not know her whereabouts after she arrives at the Gold Coast, but I am sure that's where she's going.'

'There was a pretty girl on the train yesterday who sounds like the girl you're describing. She had a guitar and a backpack, just like you, and she looked a little lost, too. I catch this train every day. I see many people come and go. I know the locals, and I know the travellers. There was something about that girl. She was definitely on a journey. If you ask me what I think, I will say she didn't have a plan. She looked like she was living her best "gypsy" life. I've been there, done that myself, and I learned a lot about people.'

'You do not know the coincidence of how you have described Tilly. That's my girl, that's my Tilly.' Dalton was shaking his head at the irony of what this stranger had identified about Tilly.

Lee and Dalton chatted on the stationary train until the bus arrived and was ready for boarding. Lee helped Dalton to transfer all of his stuff to the low hold underneath the bus. As they boarded the bus, they sat near each other close to the front, with plenty of room to take up a seat each and continue their conversation. Most of the passengers had moved to the back of the bus.

They talked about various things, from music to travel to dogs. Lee had travelled the world to thirty different countries, so they didn't run out of things to talk about. Lee did most of the talking as Dalton listened and followed along, intrigued by her stories. Dalton had never left Australia. He had so many questions about each country Lee had travelled to. She talked about adventures through Africa, Vietnam and South America. There was something mysterious and spiritual about her. It was like she was a psychic or a medium or something like that. Not that Dalton had ever met a medium or a psychic. After losing Chelsea, he thought about it once to see if he could reconnect with her, but he decided not to go because he didn't want to be disappointed. This lady, Lee, seemed to know everything about Dalton, even though he hardly spoke, and they had only just met.

Just as Lee was about to reach her destination, she grabbed a piece of notepaper from her bag, scribbling a phone number and the words, *I hope you find what you're looking for. When your heart finds Friendship, Enough Love, and Freedom in one person, let it rest there and call me. I might have a surprise for you both. Take care, nice to meet you.* She signed it *Lee (the bus and train lady)* with a smiley face topped with an angel halo. Not allowing Dalton to see yet what she had written, she folded the note in half and then in half again and placed it into Dalton's hand.

Dalton could sense that there was something that Lee wasn't telling him, some dark secret, possibly some kind of story of grief or loss like his. She was such a vibrant, enthusiastic, warm person, but there was some deep, dark sadness that she seemed to hide. There was also this strange sense of déjà vu. It was like they had met before; she could read Dalton's past and perhaps his future. *Weird,* he thought.

As Lee stepped off the bus, Dalton waved goodbye, saying, 'Take care. It was nice to meet you.'

Lee replied, 'Keep in touch. You've got my number.' She pointed to the piece of paper in his hand.

Dalton sat back comfortably in his seat, this time just behind the driver, as the bus driver scribbled some notes into his logbook. Dalton was waiting until he had finished writing, so he wasn't interrupting, to ask if he could let him know when they had arrived at the Gold Coast.

Meanwhile, Dalton unfolded the note and couldn't quite believe what he was reading. He hadn't spoken to Lee about friendship, enough love, and freedom. How did she know this sentiment of special words that only Dalton and Tilly shared with each other? The other uncanny thing was that she had finished her brief note with the sign-off, "Take care. It was nice to meet you." Yes, a common phrase for a farewell, but that was exactly what Dalton had said to her no more than thirty seconds prior as she stepped off the bus. But he hadn't seen the note she had written. He quickly glanced out the window to see if he could still see her. She was gone, nowhere to be seen. It was like she had just vanished.

Dalton sat, shaking his head at the circumstances of what had just occurred. 'That was bizarre.' He muttered to himself. 'How could someone possibly know what I'm going to say before I even say it?'

He thought about the note a little longer. *A surprise! What on earth does that mean?* Dalton took out his gig folder and placed the note inside the front cover's plastic sleeve. That was all he had now, a keepsake of this brief encounter with this mysterious woman. Who would believe him if he tried to explain this? All he had now was a piece of paper, a phone number, some words of curiosity, and a smiley face with a halo attached to a first name only. They had only met briefly, but somehow Dalton felt significant importance from this connection. Dalton went deep into his thoughts. *How would she know that phrasing? Maybe she met Tilly yesterday, but why wouldn't she have told me that if she did?*

Dalton stared out the window at nothing in particular, vaguely intrigued by the vast land stretching across the horizon. He reflected again on the serendipity of interactions with people over the past few days, strangers he didn't know, who were guiding him to find Tilly and plotting his future life. Little tiny instants that seemed insignificant at the time, just a part of the day, were suddenly tremendously important moments in the big scheme of life. Everything that was happening was vital to his quest to find Tilly.

chapter sixty

Surfers Paradise

Dalton caught a reflection of himself in the window and noticed heavy dark circles under his eyes. Then, he realised he hadn't slept much over the past few days. He closed his eyes for a moment to rest them. It seemed like an instant when he was suddenly jolted awake with a voice announcing that the bus was arriving at Coolangatta.

'Coolangatta.' Then louder, 'Coolangatta, hey Bandana boy, are you getting off here?'

Dalton responded wearily. 'Are we at the Gold Coast already?'

The bus driver responded. 'We are. Just. Coolangatta is the border town. If you want to get to the heart of the Gold Coast, stay on until we get to Surfers Paradise. I've just gotta wait until the departure time, but it won't be long until we get moving again.'

Dalton wearily replied again, 'How far is that?'

'It's about another hour from here. We have quite a few stops on the way.'

'Do you think it's got a bit more nightlife for me to get some gigs in Surfers Paradise?'

'Hell yeah, Surfers is the party town. It has such a great history, too.' The over-excited bus driver talked at great lengths about Surfers Paradise. Dalton did his best to keep his eyes open and listen carefully while he did.

'Is that right?' Dalton tried to share his interest, but he was so tired. 'Is that right?' was all he could muster.

'Back in the day, in 1917, there was a land auction to sell subdivided blocks in Elston as the Surfers Paradise Estate. The auction failed because the blocks were too hard to get access to, but the name Surfers Paradise stuck around, and no one called it Elston anymore. Because of the name Surfers Paradise, it became a huge tourism mecca for Australians and international tourists. It took sixteen years for the name to change from Elston to Surfers Paradise officially. And now it just gets called Surfers. It's a great place to visit. Beautiful beaches, plenty of nightlife, and Meter Maids for miles. That's another story. Have you heard about the Meter Maids?'

Dalton was trying hard to listen. He was interested, but still sleepy. 'No mate, I have never heard of Meter Maids.'

The bus driver continued with his narrative that he shared a lot. He had his storyline perfected. 'Apparently, Surfers was one of the first places to relax swimsuit laws. You might not believe this; it shocked me, but back in the day, there was a law that women had to wear neck-to-thigh bathing suits. In Surfers, the laws were relaxed, allowing the women to follow the Melbourne fashion, a one-piece suit. Then get this: in the 1950s, a local designer here in Surfers, Paula Stafford, held a fashion parade with six models wearing two-piece French swimsuits. It was all over the world news and attracted much attention to Surfers. Audrey Hepburn visited, intrigued by the relaxed dress standards. Pretty cool, huh!'

'That is a cool story. I've never even heard of Surfers Paradise, to be honest. I've heard that the Gold Coast is the place to be, but not about any particular suburbs. That is a nice history to be proud of. Anything that encourages freedom gets my vote.' Dalton tried to engage, as this guy worked hard to be an excellent touristy bus driver. His job was driving, entertaining, and promoting the locations on his bus route. He was doing a brilliant job.

'I almost forgot to tell you about the Meter Maids. This is my favourite part. The beaches became so popular with the young free crowd. Hundreds of thousands of tax dollars were spent on building the Surfers Paradise Surf Club, and they employed full-time lifeguards to watch over the crowds flocking to the beach. The Meter Maids were the do-gooders for the tourists because the council had to put in parking meters as a measure of crowd control. The Meter Maids would walk around in their high-fashion skimpy swimwear, feeding coins into council parking meters to attract more tourists and to keep the locals happy. It worked. The Meter Maids are still roaming the streets today, although there was quite a conspiracy when two maids appeared in Penthouse magazine. There is some big lawsuit going on, still to this day. Regardless, it's a cool place to hang out for a while, especially if you're a musician and a surfer. I can't believe you haven't been there before or even heard about it.'

'Where I'm from, mate, there is no such thing as a parking meter, let alone a Meter Maid. But Surfers Paradise sounds like the place to be. I'll get off the bus there. Does my ticket count?' Dalton had never heard of these things; it sounded interesting, that was for sure.

'Sure mate, this Greyhound will get you there. Let's make a deal: I'll give you a free longer ride. You give me a free ticket to your gig.'

'Well, that seems presumptuous. I don't know what I'm doing once I get there, let alone if I can muster up a crowd for a gig.'

'Mate, you'll get some gigs here. A new kid in town with some talent is just what this place needs.' The bus driver provided some confident assurance to Dalton.

He continued. 'I've lived here my whole life. I have a house just out of Surfers Paradise in Broadbeach. What I know is that we desperately need some new music in the pub scene. I don't know what you'll get paid as a solo artist, but I guess you'll have fun and meet new people. I can guarantee plenty of nightlife—possibly the best nightclubs, restaurants, and bar scene in Australia. And because of the climate and the crowds drawn to this place, the women around here leave little to the imagination. If you know what I mean.'

'Okay, cool.' Dalton was trying not to be rude, and he was interested in the tourist stories, but he was exhausted. Obviously, the bus driver had many more tour guide stories to share with his new country passenger, so Dalton decided he might cut him off and ask for some reprieve. 'Mate. I'm loving these stories. Knowing all those little details is interesting, but I'm exhausted. I can't even think straight. I hope you don't mind if I catch a bit more sleep on the way.'

'No worries, I'll wake you when we get to Surfers Paradise Transit Centre.' The bus driver waited as the rest of the passengers collected their belongings and exited. He hurried through the bus to check that no one had left anything in the backs of the seat pockets, underneath the seats, or in the overhead cargo racks. It was surprising how much lost property was collected and never claimed, so he checked at every main bus depot. He stepped off the bus to check the cargo latch was secure and was swiftly back on to continue the journey. He was a cheery fellow, waving and farewelling the passengers and wishing them safe onward travels. It was clear that he loved his job.

The bus made a screeching noise and a swoosh as the bus driver indicated and slowly manoeuvred his way back into the main flow of traffic.

Dalton was already asleep before the bus had even got moving again.

chapter sixty-one

Take Me Back

Tilly and Bernard arrived back at the hotel at around 9 pm, completely revitalised, refreshed and relaxed after a great day immersed in nature. They said goodnight and gave each other a warm, friendly hug. Tilly was hoping Bernard wouldn't ask him to stay in her room. Although she didn't regret the previous night staying in his bed, she didn't want to ruin their friendship with a complicated closeness, especially when she knew deep down the only person in the world she ever wanted to make love to, ever again, was Dalton.

Bernard could feel Tilly's ease with their friendship, and he understood her desire to find and reconnect with Dalton. He certainly didn't want to ruin anything, so he just left Tilly to make her own decisions for sleeping arrangements. However, he wouldn't have minded at all if Tilly snuggled with him again, with no expectation of anything sexual.

They retreated to their own rooms, showered, and nestled into their own large beds for the night.

Tilly had a shower, her thoughts fixed on Dalton and wondering again where he was. She felt like she could feel him nearer. It was weird; it was like a sixth sense, a seventh sense, or maybe just a longing to find him. She dressed in her pyjamas and sat on the bed, reading the message he had placed in the bottle. She thought by reading the letter over and over again, she could figure out more about him. She knew he had lost a very close love, was sad and sorry, and had feelings for a new person he had met. Tilly was hoping this was her. In her deep gut instincts, she knew this letter was about her, and she wished so much that she could go back in time and listen to what he had to say rather than cursing him and walking away.

Tilly cursed herself. *I'm a stubborn idiot. Why didn't I listen to what he had to say? Why did I just walk away? Perhaps I've been pushed aside too many times. I know I'm a good person for the right person. When I find him, I can only hope he will take me back.*

chapter sixty-two

Party Hard!

A voice came through the bus speakers, jolting Dalton awake. "Hey everybody, we are here at Surfers Paradise Transit Centre. All passengers departing us here at Surfers, I wish you all a wonderful stay. Party hard! Please do travel with us again.'

Dalton waited patiently as the other passengers moved abruptly through the aisle. He was in no rush and needed to get his gear from beneath. After the aisle was clear, he stood up slowly and made his way towards the exit door. As he passed the driver, he tipped his head forward. 'Thank you, sir! You've been so kind. Do you mind if I grab my stuff from underneath the bus?'

'Sir, I haven't been called Sir in a decade; must be your country gentleman manners. You are from the country, y'all?' The bus driver offered to know information about Dalton based on his appearance.

'How did you know?' Dalton laughed as it was obvious he was a country boy, just arriving in the Gold Coast city.

The bus driver laughed and pointed towards Dalton's feet. 'The boots give it away. Bandana almost confused me, but only a country boy wears Blundstone boots.'

The bus driver stood up and followed Dalton down the steps, close behind him. As they stepped onto the footpath, the bus driver tapped Dalton on the shoulder and offered his hand to Dalton. 'My name is Glenn, and my last name is Gaffer. Gaffer by name, Gaffer by nature. They call me Mr GG. Easy to remember that way.' He reached into his top pocket, pulled out a packet of cigarettes, and placed a cigarette on the edge of his mouth as he offered the packet to Dalton.

Dalton stepped back a little. 'Oh, thanks for the offer, but no thanks, man. I don't smoke. That stuff kills you, you know?'

'You've gotta die of something.' Glenn threw his head back with an evil laugh and then corrected himself. 'Yeah, you're right, though. I really should pack it in. I used to do a bit of hiking in my spare time to keep in shape, but I've been slack these days. I don't get out and about much anymore. I keep myself busy working and doing my hobbies, you know.'

'Is that right?' Dalton didn't ask anymore, but Glenn offered more information anyway, whether Dalton was interested or not.

Glenn was on for a chat. 'I like to make stuff out of glass, you know, glass animals and things. That's what Gaffer means, you know, Master Glass Blower. It was our family trade. My dad was a gaffer, and so was my grandad. He was one of the best in the country. I like to combine my hobbies; woodcarving, glassblowing and a few other things.' He did a weird snigger and sniffed his nose. 'Hourglasses are my speciality though. I can make you one if you like, and I can wrap it up and send it to you in a fragile post-pack. You'll need to give me your address before you go.'

Dalton replied briefly and politely. 'I don't have an address, man. I'm a free traveller at the moment.' He hoped this answer would suffice to politely let the bus driver know he wasn't particularly interested in his hourglasses. Dalton hoped this might end the conversation and was not interested in giving out his address to anyone, let alone a random bus driver called Glenn Gaffer.

The bus driver was persistent in getting Dalton's phone number. 'Before you go, can I get your number? I'll write it down?'

There was no way Dalton was giving more strangers his parent's phone number, so he replied again, with avoidance. 'Ah, good question. I don't have a contact number and am unsure where I'm headed. I'm just winging it, so why don't you give me your number, and I can call you? I'll write it here in my gig folder so I won't forget. If I get a gig, I'll call you to tell you the good news.' Dalton opened his folder and wrote down the bus driver's name and phone number.

Glenn was persistent in questioning Dalton about his whereabouts. 'So, you're telling me no one really knows where you are now? That's a nice way to be.' Glenn said this with a little too much interest, making Dalton feel really uncomfortable.

'Well. No. Loads of people know where I am, but they don't know where I'm going next because I haven't planned that yet.' Suddenly, Dalton felt extremely vulnerable and was very glad he had not offered his contact details to this man, who initially seemed super friendly but was getting creepier by the minute.

Just as Dalton thought he was free to leave, Glenn spoke again. *Man, this guy likes a chat more than I do.* It was usually Dalton who was making friends and conversations with strangers. He was tired, so he wasn't making much effort, but he appreciated that Glenn, Mr. GG, was only trying to be helpful.

Glenn spoke again. 'I have a, let's call it a cottage, down in Sandon in New South Wales, and another house close to here in Broadbeach. I can hook you up if you need a place to stay for a while. I'm often away doing long bus trips up north and out west. It's a big house, plenty of room. I have a few roommates and always keep a spare room for guests. My cat would love the extra company, and the garden could do with a caretaker if you need work. The frangipani tree is out of control this time of year. Just saying! I'll leave the offer there.'

He paused for a moment. Dalton didn't reply, as he was taking in all the information.

Glenn sensed Dalton's apprehension and backed off. 'Call me if you get stuck. You seem like a sensible, down-to-earth fella.'

'Thanks, mate, that's really nice.' Dalton was still half asleep from his short but deep catatonic nap. 'I think I will go to the Surfers Paradise Surf Club for a feed. It's just up the road, I believe. I'll take it day by day from there, but thanks for the offer.' He reached under the bus to collect his belongings, ensuring he had all three items: his guitar, backpack, and surfboard.

Dalton was in Queensland, on the Gold Coast. He'd never been this far north before. The first thing he noticed was the smell of salt in the air. The stickiness as the ocean breeze touched his skin. It felt moderately warmer, even though he was just a few hours north. The traffic was noisier than in places he had been recently, reminding him of his time spent in Sydney. There was a hustle and bustle feel of a city, more activity and people out and about. By now, it was late in the evening, and he hoped he could find somewhere to get a feed. The beach towns in Australia were renowned for the local surf club as the go-to. Surf clubs provided the general services of good meals and a bar, usually a pokies room, and they claimed some of the best real estate in the country, with spectacular ocean views.

Dalton made his way to the Surfers Paradise Surf Club, asking directions from people on the way. It turned out to be just up the road from where the bus had dropped him off, so he didn't have far to carry his stuff. There he was, loaded up again, the gypsy that he was, with his backpack, surfboard and guitar, walking into a completely new place that he had never been before, hoping to find some good food, a cold beer and he was hoping they could give him advice for a cheap place to stay for a little while. His mind tripped back to the last time he had felt like this, not too long ago when he had wandered into The Angourie Local and met Tilly. Again, he felt regretful, getting angry at himself for being so careless with his words. Concise communication was never his strong point. He was always good for a chat, but sometimes he took the long way around to get to the point of what he was trying to say. In this circumstance, it had cost him the girl of his dreams. Dalton tried to clear his thoughts away and took a deep breath. The salty, warm air felt nice in his lungs, and it also made him thirsty.

It was late in the evening, so he wasted no time heading to the bar to ask if he could get a feed and a cold beer. This was not a problem for the blonde, chilled-out barman. Dalton instantly felt a friendly vibe from this place: a relaxed, party atmosphere and friendly young people. It's just what he needed in his life right now.

The barman was interested to know if Dalton was a musician, playing a local gig somewhere. Dalton laughed and said, 'I wish. I'm just a blow-in from out west, but I'd love to get a gig somewhere if I can. I've literally just stepped off the bus five minutes ago, and all I can think about right now is some food.'

The barman guided Dalton to the hallway to place his belongings out of the way. After a brief chat about Dalton's reason for visiting Surfers Paradise with his guitar and surfboard, he recommended Dalton head straight to the kitchen to order his meal, as the chef would take the last orders soon.

The barman suggested that the Surf Club had some gigs coming up soon, and he should check out the gig guide at the reception. Dalton agreed he would do that.

Dalton ordered a tropical chicken parmigiana. It suited how he felt now, like he was on a tropical island holiday. He found a place to sit on the balcony to take in the full view of the beach and street scene. The footpath along the beachfront was lit with night lights, bustling with people on their evening walk, many on roller skates: young lovers and families, and the odd elderly couple strolling hand in hand.

Dalton sipped his cold beer and reflected on his past few hectic days. His mind was in turmoil. He didn't know exactly where Tilly was, but he didn't need to worry because he knew she was here somewhere, and if he kept his senses switched on for signs, he would soon find her.

He finished his meal and asked the barman for some advice on the best place to stay that was close by.

The barman was happy to help. 'I would recommend The Beachcomber Hotel. It's just a short walk back towards the bus station.'

Dalton had noticed The Beachcomber Hotel entrance as he walked past but thought it might be fancy and overpriced. 'I was thinking more of a backpacker-type place to stay for a bit.'

The barman was careful to give his advice. 'I probably wouldn't recommend the backpackers to you only because it's full at this time of year, because of all the young people coming in from interstate to party before they all go to university. It's a bit of flow-on from schoolies, and it happens every year. Unless you want to get caught up with all the drunken teens partying their socks off, I can't imagine it's really what you are here for.'

'Uh. No, not at all. That doesn't sound like my thing. Thanks for the heads up.' The last time Dalton got mixed up with a teenager, it didn't turn out so well. He had a flashback to Chelsea and all her young friends hating him and the reason why he left Deniliquin. He quickly pushed the thought aside, deciding The Beachcomber Hotel would be a good option, and it was just nearby so he could continue enjoying his Surf Club meals.

The barman added, 'I hear that the original owner of the Beachcomber, Bernie Elsey, was quite the controversial entrepreneur, and the hotel's mission was to remain that way in his honour. He died about a decade ago but created a legacy that remains. If you want to add to the good vibes of the place, I'm sure the management would support you and maybe give you a free room for a few free live music gigs. You might have seen the publicity around this guy. He's sure got a reputation for himself. He was the original ideas man to host wild pyjama parties, Hawaiian theme parties, and crazy pool parties. He's a legend if you ask me. He's done a lot to put Surfers Paradise on the world tourism map.'

'Is that right? It sounds like he was ahead of his time. What a legend. I'm not sure my style of music would be wild enough.' Dalton was interested, however, lacked confidence in himself as a country boy in this big city.

'No harm in asking. What have you got to lose?' the barman added, giving Dalton a few more words of encouragement.

'Thanks, Man.'

chapter sixty-three

Breakfast Platter for Two!

Tilly awoke and realised she was ravenous. Bernard and Tilly had a tremendous day of exercise the day before, and, as she came to think of it, they hadn't eaten that much. They bought heaps of food for their picnic, but it was all back in Bernard's fridge, in his room, because they didn't eat it all. She hoped he didn't mind if she knocked on his door to ask if she could get some food. They had fresh berries and fruit and an assortment of yummy cheeses, meats, and crackers. This platter of food was exactly what she felt like eating. She was craving it from the moment she opened her eyes.

She walked along the hallway to Bernard's room in her pyjamas still, her eyes puffy from the few tears she had shed the evening before, thinking about her silly actions in losing Dalton. She didn't mind; who would care about what Tilly looked like right now? She just needed food and some morning company. She felt flat, lost for purpose and hopeless in her venture to find Dalton.

She could hear Bernard talking on the phone inside, and she listened to the mention of her name. He sounded happy. She didn't want to cause any problems, so she knocked gently on the door, saying "room service," just for a joke, but also to ensure that whoever he was talking to didn't need to worry about a knock on the door and a woman's voice entering the room.

Bernard replied instantly and joyfully, 'Come in, Tilly, I'm just talking to Mum, telling her about our day yesterday.'

Tilly walked into the room, smiled and said loudly, 'Hi, Bernard's mum; I'm going to steal some food from your son's fridge, if he doesn't mind. I'm starving.'

Bernard said, 'Help yourself, Tilly,' followed by, 'I'll let you go, Mum. I just wanted to make sure you and Dad are okay, and you know I should be home for a visit next week. We've got a gig here in Surfers Paradise this weekend, and then I'm heading home for a little break. We've been on the road for a while now.'

Tilly didn't hear the conversation replies from Bernard's mum, but there were a series of farewells and heartfelt I love yous. The general feeling was a lovely connection between Bernard and his mother.

Bernard was naked and sitting on his bed, covered by his sheets. He unravelled the phone cord from around his arm and hung up the phone, placing the earpiece back in the cradle. He went to stand up to help Tilly with the food. It was then that he realised it would be quite a surprise if he stood up and walked to the kitchenette in his current butt-naked state. Not that Tilly would mind, and not that Bernard would care if Tilly saw him naked, but it just felt a little bit strange since they had agreed on this whole plutonic, comfortable, friendship-relationship thing. Rather than making things awkward, Bernard asked Tilly to pass him a towel from the bathroom as an easy solution.

Tilly went to the bathroom and returned with a towel, saying. 'Thanks, Bernard, that is very respectful of you.' She then continued, with no humour or light-hearted, general conversation around it. 'Are you hungry? I'm on a mission today. I need food.'

She was abrupt, but Bernard took no offence. Tilly knew what she needed and wanted, and Bernard understood that. He was happy that she had chosen to come and join him for breakfast because there was no way he would be bothered to set out the platter the same way she was setting it out with so much creativity. All this beautiful food would get wasted. Just then, Bernard remembered Tilly had worked in a restaurant for most of her adult life, a self-learned chef and food presenter. It came naturally to her. Who would have known that strawberries, bananas, blueberries, kiwi fruit and oranges could look so good on a plate with salami, crackers and cheese? Tilly served a breakfast platter of perfection for two within minutes. She had also whipped up two warm instant coffees that looked roasted, milky, and delicious.

'Wow, Tilly, what you have created here in this hotel kitchenette is amazing. Thank you for going to all that trouble.' Bernard was grateful and wanted to let Tilly know he appreciated what she had done for him, even though she was abrupt and humourless.

Tilly replied, still in her serious and sensible mood. 'No worries, Bernard, let's eat.'

'Let's!' replied Bernard.

They ate and chatted about reflections of the previous day. It was a lovely morning conversation, and they enjoyed each other's company. Bernard suggested he would make his first job of the day to return the VW beetle and swap it for the Tarago. They had a gig tonight at the hotel, so at some stage, he would get together with the boys to create the playlist and have a bit of a jam. They wanted to try some new acoustic cover songs for a romantic dinner set and practise their latest original songs to blend in with the mix. Bernard invited Tilly to the practice and asked if she wanted to do some duets or harmonies with them. Tilly agreed she would love to do that, and they decided they would meet in the hotel foyer at 2 pm.

After asking her to join them for the practice, Bernard queried Tilly. 'So, Little Miss I'm Hungry and Busy, what's this mission you're on today?'

Tilly took a big, long sip of her coffee and replied with a sigh. 'Oh, I don't know. My mission is to find Dalton somehow. I don't even know how, I just feel like I need to be everywhere he might be, and hope we bump into each other. It's not like I can call him up or send him a fax. Perhaps a message in a bottle thrown into an ocean might be more realistic. It worked for him; that's how I know I need to find him.'

'Well, Tilly, that all sounds very romantic, and I think we should add that song to our cover song playlist tonight. "Message In A Bottle," by The Police. What do you think?' Bernard was trying to get Tilly to think a little bit further than her past. He hoped that getting her mind set on thinking about today might drag her out of the dark and abrupt mood that she was in.

'Yeah, sounds good Bernard, it's a good song.' Tilly was grateful that Bernard was trying to lift her mood, but she couldn't find any joy today.

Bernard added, 'So, Tilly, where do you think Dalton would hang out if he were in Surfer's Paradise? Do you know that he's even here?'

'No, I don't know where he is, and it sounds weird, I know, but I can feel that he is here somewhere. He loves to surf and play music, so north of Angourie, he could be in Byron Bay or somewhere on the Gold Coast. He's probably short on cash, as he's been surfing and gigging for a while now, so I'm guessing he would try to get somewhere he can stick around for a while and earn some money. He's a qualified builder and would have many job opportunities here.'

Bernard lifted his eyebrows; he had been interested in the whole Tilly and Dalton story, this surfer/musician she was madly in love with, but he hadn't taken notice of that detail, that Dalton was a builder as well. 'Well, that's the first I've heard of that. You could be right. This is the place to be if he has a good head on his shoulders and trade skills. This place is booming.'

'He seems to be an intelligent man, so that's what I'm thinking.' Tilly was deep in thought. In her mind, she was planning her day, knowing that she needed to be back at the hotel for the 2 pm practice with Bernard and the boys.

'So, what's your plan then?' Bernard was curious of Tilly's plan about how she would find Dalton. He also knew that he shouldn't offer to help, as she had made it clear that this was her mission for the day. Although Bernard was happy to help, he felt the vibe of independence oozing out of Tilly.

Tilly had already decided on the first part of her plan. 'First, I'm going to call the train station to see if they found that bloody guitar pick of mine. We forgot yesterday, all caught up in our Hinterland adventure. I also think they might know something about Dalton if he has ended up on public transport. Maybe they keep a log of traveller's names or something.'

'That's a great idea, Tilly. I'm so sorry we forgot to make that call yesterday.' Bernard felt terrible that he had forgotten all about the guitar pick.

'All good. I'll give my parents a call too. They must be wondering where I am and what is going on,' replied Tilly.

'Good idea. You know you can call from the hotel room, but I think it's expensive.'

'Yeah, I'll just go to the phone booth on the corner and throw in my thirty cents.'

'It might be a long-distance STD phone call because you are calling interstate.'

'Oh yeah, true that.' Tilly hadn't thought about that. He was right.

'I've got a bunch of coins in the side pocket of my guitar bag if you want to grab a handful.' Bernard wanted to be helpful somehow; that was the least he could do.

'Thanks, Bernard, that would be great. If Dad is on for a chat, I'll call him back on 1800 REVERSE. That way, he can pay for the phone call. He won't mind, though. He will be happy to hear from me, as long as I don't tell him about my lost guitar pick. Maybe he will be at work. I'll catch my mum at home; that is probably a safer option.'

'I'm truly sorry we forgot to call the train station yesterday. I feel dreadful about that.' Bernard was honestly sorry, as he knew the sentiment of this lost guitar pick. Tilly walked over to clean up the plates from breakfast. Bernard stood up, realising what she was doing, and gently took the plates out of her hand. 'I can do this; you go and do your thing. You've got a big day ahead of you.'

Tilly smiled, grateful for his kindness. 'Thanks, Bernard. I appreciate everything you have done for me. I'll see you at 2 pm.'

Bernard quickly placed the dishes on the table, turned around, and hugged Tilly. 'You're an amazing woman, Tilly. I also appreciate everything you have done for me. I've loved our long chats and our time together over the past few days. I really hope you can find Dalton. Good luck today.'

Tilly smiled and said, 'See you soon,' as she walked out, closing the door behind her, thinking to herself. That's the first time I've ever heard, "You're an amazing woman, Tilly," without a, but....

She returned to her room, showered, and dressed in a summer dress. It felt like the day was heating up, and it was only 9 am. She put on her favourite summer scent, Sunflowers, by Elizabeth Arden. As soon as she sprayed the perfume on her neck, she drifted back to thoughts of Dalton. The scent of both together. Their sweetness of scents combined. Tilly wore 'Sunflowers.' The bottle was almost empty as it had been a gift from her brother, Frankie, at the previous Christmas, and she had worn it every day for more than a year. Dalton wore Joop!. Joop! Homme, which was also a sweet-scented cologne. The two of them combined smelt like a summer garden of fresh flowers.

Tilly took a deep breath and filled her lungs with the sweet scent as she looked at herself in the mirror. The warm shower had relieved her puffy eyes, but she still looked tired. She felt fresh, clean, and ready for a great day exploring Surfers Paradise. She had no idea what today would bring. But she felt like she was in the right place.

chapter sixty-four

No Pretty Strangers

Dalton enjoyed a long, restful sleep. At first, he didn't know where he was—another strange bed in an empty hotel room. There was a spare, empty bed beside him. He was delighted to see his guitar, surfboard and backpack leaning against the wall and happy that he had woken up alone. *No pretty strangers* had taken advantage of him. He remembered he was in Surfers Paradise in Queensland, a place he had never been before. He was excited because he had some exploring to do. He had a mission to arrange work, possibly some odd building jobs. A gig here or there would be great, and he was eager to get into the ocean and have a surf. He was also hoping that somehow, he might find Tilly, although he didn't realise how populated the Gold Coast was. It might be more of a mission than he had at first thought. Surfers Paradise wasn't quite like Angourie or Deniliquin.

He showered and dressed in his board shorts and a nice clean T-shirt. He tied his Bandana around his head, grabbed his wallet, and headed out into the street and across the road to the Surf Club, where he had enjoyed his meal the evening before. He had noticed a big sign outside the front entrance advertising The Big Breakfast, and he was hoping it was still available, as it was just after 10 am. He could smell the bacon and eggs, and it was making him hungry. He was also craving a nice coffee.

The waitress greeted him with a friendly smile. 'How can I help you, sir?'

Dalton asked. 'Would it be too late to bother the chef to make me The Big Breakfast?'

'Not a problem at all. We do "All Day Big Breakfast" here. Where would you like to sit?' replied the young waitress. She looked like she had just got out of the surf, with messy blonde curls and brown skin from days of sunshine.

'I'd love to sit on the balcony if there is a table for one.'

'Sure, I can set up a spot for you.' She replied eagerly to help Dalton.

'Thank you.' Dalton made himself comfortable in a perfect spot where he could see people surfing and enjoying their day. Lots of people were out walking and enjoying the Queensland sunshine.

The waitress returned with cutlery and a jug of cold water. That is just what Dalton felt like. He also asked if he could order a coffee, a caramel latte.

As Dalton waited for his coffee, he observed the beach action. Crowds had already claimed their sand with elaborate umbrellas and beach tent set-ups. Music was playing through a loudspeaker. It sounded like a radio station playing the latest hits. At the hour, the music would pause, and an announcement said, 'It's time to turn over.'

A bronzed man was spraying the line-up of locals and tourists with a shiny liquid. Dalton felt this wasn't sunscreen; it was like a bronzing oil, as everyone seemed so darkly suntanned. This was an experience that Dalton had only ever observed in Surfers Paradise. Perhaps they hadn't heard of *Slip, Slop, Slap*, although Dalton was aware of this campaign since a young lad. Everyone in Deniliquin knew about *Slip, Slop, Slap. Slip on a shirt, Slop on sunscreen, and Slap on a hat. Slip, Slop, Slap.* The slogan sang in his mind.

As Dalton enjoyed his Big Breakfast, he continued to observe the beach shenanigans. He observed that all the swimmers were being safely guarded between a set of red and yellow flags. The surf lifesaving guards sat in a tall tower to watch the ocean. *Interesting*, thought Dalton as he sipped on his coffee. *If someone goes outside of the flags, do they get rescued too?* Dalton had not seen this kind of elaborate surf lifesaving set-up before and had to remind himself he was in Surfers Paradise. This is the place if there was ever the need for an elaborate surf lifesaving tower. It was tourist central. Many tourists came to Australia without understanding the power and strength of the waves along the coastline of wide-open beaches.

Surfers and bodyboarders were taking over a section of the larger waves outside the flags, but they were still part of the watch. There was a jet ski on the beach at the ready. There was a surf boat equipped with life rafts and yellow lifesaving buoys. Dalton wondered how the boat would get out through the waves if a situation occurred. Many people were on the beach sunbaking, enjoying a swim and body surfing the waves. Some had drifted out past the breakers and were having a relaxing loll, rolling over the waves as they rolled in, and had not formed into crested waves yet.

Some days, the ocean was like a lake, calm and gentle, with small rolling waves lapping quietly on the shoreline. Other days, it was a tumultuous washing machine of strong, powerful, dumping waves that would devour you and spit you out on the bottom of the ocean floor before you realised you hadn't taken a breath. There were the in-between days as well. Those were the days when everyone would flock to the water and enjoy the playfulness of nature. Today was one of those days. Crowds of people were laughing and playing, enjoying the sun's warmth and the salty water's fresh coldness on their skin. The ocean was always rejuvenating and exhilarating, even for those who spent most of their days in the water. Dalton felt compelled to go to the beach for a swim. It was still mid-morning, but it was already a hot day. He wasn't looking forward to dealing with the crowds of people, but it seemed like the thing to do.

He had heard Coolangatta had some surf beaches, not as crowded as Surfers Paradise, and better surfing conditions, even for the pro-surfers. Some boys he had surfed with down south in Yamba had recommended that he try out Kirra, Greenmount, Snapper Rocks and Duranbah, and apparently, the Rainbow Bay Surf Club had the best surf club meal and great views. Dan, from Angourie, had discussed entering a Kirra surf competition. Dalton wondered if that was the same competition he had seen on the poster, The Billabong Pro, the event in Kirra on the coming weekend.

Dan was a legendary surfer in Angourie, and Dalton was pretty sure Dan could perform against the international rankings as an "almost local." The poster listed iconic names among the rankings, including Munga, Grant Frost, Tom Carroll, Donavon Frankenreiter, Kelly Slater, Rob Machado, Rabbit and Sunny Garcia. Dan was as local as any Australian, and although Angourie was across the border, it was not that far away. Dan hadn't surfed much in Queensland; he stayed close to home surfing the North Coast beaches of Yamba, Iluka, Brooms Head, Evans Head and The Sandon. He made some trips to Minnie Water and Wooli for a change and when the seasons brought a decent swell to those areas. But mostly, he stayed at his home break. He was the Angourie gatekeeper.

The more Dalton thought about it, the more he felt that this must be the competition Dan was talking about entering, but he wondered why Dan hadn't mentioned that it was so soon. Possibly because it was irrelevant to Dalton, Dan didn't speak a lot about himself, and bragging about entering a surf competition would be the last thing he would do. Besides, he wouldn't have known that Dalton would be on the Gold Coast. All he knew from their previous interaction was that Dalton was leaving Angourie as fast as he could.

Dalton had booked his room at The Beachcomber Hotel and was on a flexible arrangement. He could stay for longer or leave when he wanted to. He hoped to stay there for the next month, giving him the stability of sorting out some work and earning money. He had yet to talk to the owner about playing some gigs there, but if he could, that might save him some money and earn him some money if he could get to know some more of the local hotel owners and publicans. He was happy to be in accommodation close to the Surf Club as the best location for good food, drinks and meeting people. It was a buzz from morning until late at night. Dalton thought he might even ask for a bar job if nothing else came up around town regarding building or gigs.

He was keen to explore the area, but with no private transport, he would have to rely on hitching a ride or jumping on a bus to get him here and there. He thought about hiring or buying a cheap car to allow him some freedom, but that decision was based on what kind of work he found for himself.

The more he thought about it, the more he wanted to find some local regular gigs, as this meant he was free to continue travelling as opportunities presented to him. Finding some casual handyman work would also be great, but he didn't want to be contracted to a company for months or years. Some people liked that security and stability for their families. Dalton was at this stage of life, still finding out where he wanted to be. The Gold Coast was full of opportunities, and it seemed like a lot was happening, but Dalton was more of a relaxed soul. He would be happy here for the time being, but it was not the place he wanted to settle down and live for a long time. Dalton reflected on the past few months, where he had been, and where he was going.

As he sat still for a moment on his own, he realised he was agitated and frustrated. The thing that kept moving Dalton forward at a fast pace was that he was still running from his guilt over Chelsea's accident, and this was something he hadn't yet come to terms with. It caused him to have nightmares, episodes of inconsolable tears, and a heavy heart full of regret and pain. His grief was evident in everything he did. In certain aspects of his life, he would feel himself healing in random moments, conversations with people, lyrics he wrote, or songs he would play, expressing other people's loss or grief. These quiet, reflective moments all helped move him forward. He wasn't open about what had happened with him and Chelsea. He didn't share his story with anyone. Only Dan, so far. It wasn't a story he wanted to share with strangers or even new friends. It was something he kept close to his heart. Deciding to write the message in the bottle to Chelsea as a way of announcing his grief and then deciding that he would share his story with Tilly was one of the most significant decisions he had made. Tilly had not allowed him to go ahead with what he needed to say when his words came out wrong. This had caused him to become even more protective of his grief, to hold on to it even tighter, and that wasn't healthy.

Meeting Tilly had somehow eased that pain, and he felt that being with her would fill the void in his heart, but he had no influence over that. Tilly had her barriers and her own battles to overcome, and as far as Dalton knew, she was on her own adventure, possibly here on the Gold Coast, just like he was. He wondered, when he found her, how she would react. He was carrying some guilt about his night with Jacqui, which was playing on his mind. If he reconnected with Tilly, and she ever knew about that, would she even take him back? He knew from his conversations with Jacqui that Tilly was heading north on some kind of mission, hopefully to find him, but he wasn't confident about her reason. He thought Tilly might have found the message in the bottle from his conversation with Trish. She could be confused by that message, but surely, she would know it was about her. He was sure Tilly had ventured to the Gold Coast on the bus and train, just like he did from Byron Bay. He also knew that she might be hanging out with Powderfinger, and they were due to perform on the Gold Coast in the coming week. That was his best chance of finding her; it was just a week away.

Dalton finished his coffee, got up from his seat and headed towards the cashier's counter to hop in the queue to pay for his meal. As he moved closer in the line, he noticed a series of posters advertising local events on the walls. He stopped abruptly; the man standing behind him in the line almost bumped into him.

'Oh, sorry, sir!' Dalton apologised to the man.

'No worries, young man. I see something caught your eye.'

'It sure did.' Dalton was looking at a poster that said, "Powderfinger, Surfers Paradise Surf Club this Saturday night from 7 pm til late. $10 admission. For ticket sales, see reception."

As Dalton got to the cashier counter, he told the lady, his table number 26, to pay for his meal. As he said it out loud, 'Table 26 on the balcony, I had the coffee and The Big Breakfast, thank you,' he shook his head at the irony of what he had just said. Table 26. Was this another sign of fate, or was it just a weird, uncanny coincidence? Synchronicity?

He thought he might ask the lady if he could buy the ticket here. 'Sorry to bother you, Ma'am, but do you also sell the Powderfinger concert tickets, or shall I get them from reception?'

'Yes, sorry, sir, you must go downstairs and buy them from reception; we don't have any tickets up here. This is just the restaurant payment section.'

'Oh, no worries at all. I can stop there on my way out. You've been very helpful, thank you.'

The lady gave him the change and wished him well.

Dalton walked downstairs to the reception counter and bought himself a ticket, reserving another three extras, just in case. The lady was abrupt, explaining that she didn't usually put a hold on tickets for an expected sell-out show. She said that she would need to sell the reserved tickets if the show became a sell-out, and he hadn't paid for them and picked them up before Thursday at 5 pm. Dalton agreed that was no problem.

He didn't even know exactly who he was reserving the tickets for. He planned to call Dan and see if he was coming up for the surf comp, but otherwise, he hoped he might meet some people in the week ahead. Ten dollars for a ticket to support a great Aussie band wasn't the worst thing he could spend his money on. He considered paying for the extra three tickets but decided it might be best to wait and see if Dan was coming up. He needed to get to the bank and withdraw some more cash, as he was running low on cash in his wallet. There were still a couple of days ahead.

Even though he was inside the building, Dalton felt a strong, cool breeze on the back of his neck. It gave him goosebumps all over. This often happened when he felt Chelsea's angelic presence around him. He couldn't help but think that Chelsea was part of this whole tapestry of life that he was living.

What would be the chances that Powderfinger would play right here, at this Surf Club? Is that a sign of fate? He thought. *Synchronicity, again?* If Powderfinger were playing here, Tilly might be around somewhere. Based on the conversation he had with Trish on the train. Apparently, Tilly had connected with the band on the train. Perhaps she had already met Bernard and the band previously, perhaps in Angourie, before the train trip. Maybe they already knew each other. Tilly had never mentioned meeting Powderfinger or having them perform at The Angourie Local, but Dalton didn't know for sure. If that was the case, and the kind of person Tilly was who loved to support Australian music, she would come to the concert for sure. Dalton suddenly felt nervous, excited, and worried. It was less than a week away, and he might find Tilly.

Dalton decided he would go back to the hotel, grab his board, and head out for a surf to get himself moving for the day. He grabbed some coins from his backpack to give Dan a quick call from the phone booth. He wanted to check if he was coming up for the Billabong Pro at Kirra. Dalton wanted to offer Dan the option of sharing the room with him at the Beachcomber Hotel if he needed a place to stay. The room had two double beds. This was Dalton's way of returning the favour for everything Dan had done to help him during his stay in Angourie. Dan was the only person whom Dalton had talked with, about Chelsea, since leaving Deniliquin. Somehow, he felt an important connection of friendship and trust. Dan was as down to earth as they come, a decent bloke, and a fantastic surfer.

In the excitement of seeing the Powderfinger poster and heading back to his hotel to collect his board, Dalton didn't notice the loud siren from the surf tower across the road, beckoning the swimmers at the beach to exit the water. A helicopter circled overhead, suggesting a shark sighting. Dalton was oblivious to all this happening.

chapter sixty-five

The Phone Booth

Tilly walked out of the hotel and onto the busy street and instantly felt the warm summer breeze. She looked around to orientate herself and tried to locate a nearby phone booth. She remembered seeing a few in the streets the night she and Bernard had gone for their evening stroll along the boardwalk.

Walking towards the beach, she could smell the breakfast aromas oozing from the many cafés along the street. It seemed like every second shop was a funky café, bakery, restaurant or gimmicky tourist shop selling stuffed koalas, kangaroos and Australian flags. The nightspots were now closed as the morning-shift shops took over the trade. It was a busy place. It seemed like no matter what business you opened here, you would be successful.

Many people were wandering around, mostly tourists, in their summer clothes and fancy beach hats, carrying their beach bags and umbrellas. Everyone was in a beeline towards the beach. Tilly followed the crowd, glad she had filled her belly with a yummy breakfast platter. She was tempted to stop in and get The Big Breakfast at the Surfers Paradise Surf Club. It advertised beach views from the balcony. The sign outside at the entry was tempting. Everything she loved; bacon, eggs, tomatoes, avocado, mushrooms; just the way Dalton made the big breakfast for her on that beautiful morning. If she hadn't just eaten, she would have tried it. *Maybe tomorrow morning, I'll do that for breakfast. That would fill me up for the whole day,* she thought.

Tilly noticed that the phone booth across the road from the Surf Club was empty. *Perfect, I'll call the train station and home, and then I might check out the beach.* She was glad that she had put her togs on underneath her dress. She didn't have a beach towel, though. That would have taken up way too much room in her backpack. She could buy one here. The surf shops were a dime a dozen. This was Surfers Paradise.

Tilly opened the door and stepped inside the phone booth, with the door closing tightly behind her. Phone booths were small and quite claustrophobic for anyone who didn't like confined spaces. It didn't worry Tilly much, but she wondered how most people could fit in comfortably. Tilly also wondered how Wonder Woman ever did her miraculous costume change inside one. She laughed as she imagined Diana spinning around and turning into Wonder Woman on the television shows she watched as a kid. Wonder Woman was always her favourite superhero. She was strong and pretty. As

Tilly got older, she realised that Wonder Woman was probably even more unique, a little kinky and wild, with her fascination with the golden lasso and ropes and her thigh-high boots, but ultimately, she acted from a place of love and peace. Everything she did was about goodness and love, like most other superheroes fighting the baddies. The evil characters were all about power, control and money.

Tilly wasn't a large person, and she wasn't small. She was voluptuous, rumpy, and quite tall, but she could only fit in, and it was a squeeze for her. She reached under the phone to the little shelf where she could see two large phone books: yellow and white. The Yellow Pages was a business contacts phone book full of business numbers and advertisements. The White Pages was a thinner phonebook listing personal phone numbers. It was the Yellow Pages that Tilly required to search for the Murwillumbah Train Station phone number. As she tried to hold the phone book open and dial the numbers at the same time, she rested the handle of the phone into the cradle of her neck, resting her head to one side to hold it in place with her ear.

She dialled the number awkwardly and waited patiently until it connected. As it did, she placed the phone book back on the shelf, allowing her hand free to hold the earpiece again. She preferred the earpiece to her right ear, so she swapped hands, feeling awkward as she did because of the cast on her arm, getting tangled in the phone cord.

'Good morning, Murwillumbah Train Station. How can I help you?' The grungy voice came through the earpiece, and Tilly instantly recognised the lady's voice who had sold her the bus ticket a few days earlier.

'Oh, hello, my name is Tilly. How are you today?' Tilly used her polite manners and was hoping the lady might remember her.

'I'm very well, thank you; how can I help you? And just so you know, I'm busy. No need for the small talk.' The reply was abrupt, as Tilly had expected. This lady was very busy. She was probably doing five things at once, so Tilly asked her question.

'Um, I have a query for you, and I'm hoping you can help?' Tilly asked politely.

'Oh! Here we go, another one of these. Yesterday, some fellow wanted me to solve his missing person's case.'

'Oh, I'm sorry to hear that. Nothing like that from me. I was travelling through Murwillumbah the day before yesterday on the train to the bus here to the Gold Coast. I bought my ticket from you, but you wouldn't remember, you were very busy. I understand you are a busy lady. Anyway, I seem to have lost a sentimental object, and I wonder if anyone has handed it in?'

'Lady, I've got no idea who you are. What have you lost?'

Wow, she is so rude. I've never met anyone quite like her. I wonder if I should mention the Dame Edna glasses; she might remember me. Tilly cleared her throat as she held back her true feelings and said, 'I've lost a sentimental guitar pick on the platform, and I'm wondering if anyone has handed it in?'

'Nope, not to me. I feel sorry for you, love. That would be like trying to find a needle in a haystack. You've got Buckley's chance. And that's exactly what I said to that fellow yesterday when he asked me about his missing girl. She could be anywhere. It's a big world.'

Tilly's mind raced as she questioned herself: *could that have been Dalton asking about my whereabouts and if she'd seen a girl fitting my description? Am I the missing person? Surely not. It couldn't be that small a world.* Tilly thought she would ask one more question quickly and then leave the lady alone to get back to her five things at once.

'Can I please ask you one more thing?' Tilly asked nicely.

'Please do, and then I must go. I've got a line up here,' hurried the lady.

'The fellow looking for his missing girl. Was he wearing a blue Bandana and country boots?' That was the one thing that would give it away, so she thought it was worth asking.

'Yes, yes, he was. He was very polite. Must be from the country, I thought, out west somewhere. I rarely have the pleasure of serving people with manners. He bought a bus ticket to the Gold Coast, just like you did.' She had recognised Tilly's husky voice and decided instantly that she should be a little more helpful, as she was piecing things together.

'Do you remember me now?' replied Tilly excitedly.

'I do. You're the girl that said my glasses were like Dame Edna, and we chatted about you losing your sight and your voice.' The lady relayed their conversation topics, acknowledging that she remembered the conversation with Tilly.

'Yes, yes, we did. Well, there is nothing new to report. I've still got my husky voice and my sight, but I've lost my favourite guitar pick, and I still haven't found my missing piece, that well-mannered man, in the blue Bandana.'

'Oh. I wish I could help you. All I can tell you, and I don't know if it's any help, but he's looking for you as well. He asked me if I'd seen anyone fitting your description: a beautiful girl with long, dark, curly hair with a guitar and a backpack. Is that you?'

'Yep, that's me.' Tilly was shocked at the information she had just received from this lady. Dalton was looking for her. And he was on the Gold Coast.

I knew it. I could feel him here. She didn't say it out loud, but she felt strongly that she knew he was there. Her sixth sense was spot on.

'Well, I can't help you any more than that. It's up to you to find each other now.' The lady was keen to finish the conversation.

'You do not know how helpful you have been. I owe you this small world. Seriously. Thank you so much. You deserve a thousand thankyou's today.' Tilly couldn't quite explain how grateful she was. All the lady said was that Dalton had bought a ticket to the Gold Coast, and he was looking for a girl with long, dark, curly hair. That was enough!

The lady continued. 'Is there anything else I can do for you?'

Tilly gathered her thoughts again and replied. 'Well, yes, I rang because of my guitar pick. If anyone hands it in, please keep it safe for me. It's marble white, and it has engraving on both sides. It's part of a family set. My dad would be devastated if he knew I lost it.'

'Yes, I'll keep it safe.'

Tilly had another idea. 'If you find it, can you possibly wrap it safely and send it to The Angourie Local?'

'Can do!'

'Thank you!' Tilly was ever so grateful.

'Goodbye now and good luck. I'd love to know the outcome of your story. Make sure you write to me.' The lady hung up just as Tilly was finishing what she had to say.

'I will, I promise. Thank you.' Tilly hadn't even finished the sentence, and she heard a loud clunk in her ear.

As she hung up the earpiece, Tilly started dancing inside the phone booth, running on the spot. *Oh, my goodness! Dalton is trying to find me, and I'm trying to find him. That's unbelievable. I wonder how he knows that I'm here on the Gold Coast. He must be a good detective because I haven't told anyone from home yet where I am. How would he know I was here? Or maybe he doesn't know I'm here. He's looking for me, but he's on a wild goose chase; just like me, just guessing this is where I am, looking for him.*

Tilly looked around outside the phone booth, thinking she might see Dalton. He might be right here, in Surfers Paradise. He could be anywhere. From now on, her eyes would be wide open to everyone around her.

She grabbed more coins from her back pocket, reminding her that the phone call she had just made was originally about her guitar pick. She was so glad that she made the phone call because, although she had been unsuccessful in that circumstance, part of her mission today was also to find Dalton. She was one step closer, knowing he was here.

Tilly slotted some more coins into the coin slot and dialled the familiar numbers of her parents' home phone. It was mid-morning, so chances were that her mum or dad would still be at home. One of them would be at The Angourie Local, supervising breakfast, and the boys would also be in the restaurant. She thought she'd try home first, and if there were no luck, she would call The Angourie Local.

Her mum answered the phone almost straight away.

There were a series of beeps and then, 'Hello, this is Laura speaking.'

'Hey Mum, it's me.'

'Hey darling, how are you? I've been thinking of you.'

'I'm good, Mumma. I'm up here in sunny Surfers Paradise!'

'Oh, that's good. That sounds like a nice place to be.'

'Yes, it is. I'm having a great time. It's been a whirlwind couple of days, and I've met some great people. You'd be happy to know I've been to the hospital about my arm. I had a little break in my wrist, so they've put it in a cast for me, and I'm hoping it will heal nicely. I can't play my guitar for a while, but I might have a bit of a singing gig with a new band called Powderfinger this weekend coming.' Tilly had a lot to share, and it all flew out in a jumble of sentences.

Laura replied calmly, taking all the details in but not asking anymore. She was just happy to hear Tilly's voice. 'Oh, that sounds lovely, darling. How exciting for you.'

Tilly realised she had been talking only about herself. She felt rude, changing the focus of the conversation to her family. 'How are you guys? Are you all okay?'

'Same old, same old. You know how it is. Everyone around here is asking about you, saying where is Tilly? What happened to the country boy? Otherwise, it's business as usual. The boys are great, you know. And dad, he's wonderful. Missing his girl, of course, but he's good. He's been worried about you and your arm, so he will be happy to know you've got it in a cast.'

'I love you, mum, miss you all.'

'We miss you too, darling.' She paused. 'Any news on Dalton?'

'No, not yet. I'm still searching, but I believe he might also be here on the Gold Coast.'

'Well, that's interesting. Did you know we found some letters that he left here, on the counter after you left? One to you and one to us as a family, thanking us for having him here, and he also left some cash. What a lovely boy! He has true feelings for you, Tilly. You made a big mistake, you know that?'

'Yeah, I know, Mum. What did the letter say?'

'I didn't read it. It's addressed to you, my darling.'

'Do you have it? Can you read it to me? I don't mind if you do.'

'I have it on the kitchen table. Just give me a minute.'

Tilly's arm was itching inside her cast, and it was only the second day. The heat of the day wasn't helping, and inside this phone booth, it felt like forty degrees. While waiting for her mum to return to the phone, she placed the earpiece in the crook of her neck again so she could free up her arm to stick a pencil from her shoulder bag down inside her cast to give her arm a scratch.

'Are you there, Tilly?'

'Yes. I'm here, Mum. I'm inside a stinking hot phone booth. I'm not going anywhere,' she laughed.

'This is what it says darling,' as she read out loud;

"My Beautiful Gypsy Girl,
I think I love you Tilly. I hope we can be together again someday. Some things take time. I'm sorry for what happened last night, and I hate myself for the way my words came out so wrong. I just wanted to share my past with you so I could love you completely and forever because I think I can do this with you. You're strong ENOUGH. I want to hold you forever in my arms and in my heart. Until then, you'll be on my mind.
To Freedom, Friendship, and Enough Love.
Your Gypsy Boy"

'Thanks, Mum, yeah, I really messed up, didn't I? Do you think he'll take me back? I'm such a loser?'

'If he loves you, Tilly, he will take you back. Nothing can stop true love. You just need to find each other and start again, maybe slowing things down a bit this time.' Laura always had the best advice.

'Yeah, I hope you are right, Mum. We'll see! I have to find him first, or maybe he will find me. If, for some reason, he calls you, please tell him I'm staying at The Islander Hotel in Surfers Paradise.'

'Let me just write that down, darling.' Laura grabbed a pen and scribbled the hotel's name on a notepad near the phone.

'Thanks, Mum, I love you. Give my love to Dad and the boys.'

'I love you darling, have fun, keep in touch, we miss you.'

'Miss you too, Mum! Bye! Big love!'

'Big love, my baby girl.' Laura finished the conversation, and they both hung up. Tilly loved this little saying they always said to each other. It made her feel so close to her mum, even though she was so far away.

Tilly grabbed her shoulder bag from where she had put it on the small bench. She moved out of the phone booth as quickly as she could. It was hot in such a confined space.

chapter sixty-six

It's Time To Turn Over

Tilly had no plans for the rest of the day other than to gig with Bernard at 2 pm. She had ticked her two big jobs off the list. She had called about her guitar pick and was on track to finding Dalton, knowing he was on the Gold Coast somewhere. That didn't mean he was in Surfers Paradise. The Gold Coast was a big place, but she was as close as she could be to possibly bumping into him.

Tilly walked across the road, observing the crowds of people gathering on the beach. Music was playing, and a dark-tanned man was spraying people with oil. There were so many people baking in the sun. She had never seen anything like it. Tilly decided she would first buy a towel and join them. She turned left and headed down the street, where she saw a big sign advertising huge beach towels for $10.

Tilly was a sucker for a sale; she ended up walking out of the shop with a beach towel, a large striped beach umbrella, a big-shady-full-brimmed beach hat, and a new pair of sunglasses. She was ready to join the tourist crowds. *This is fun*, she thought. Although she was an Aussie through and through, she was a tourist to Surfers Paradise.

She bought herself a fresh juice and headed across the road to join the crowds of bronze on the beach. She found a space to lay her towel on the edge of the crowds. Finding a place to put yourself without invading other people's space was quite a procedure. It was like everyone was within a few meters of each other, which felt strange to Tilly. She was used to her empty Angourie beaches. Twenty people in the middle of summer were considered a crowd. That was nothing compared to this. So many people. *I guess it's an excellent way to meet people.* If you fancied getting to know someone, just lay your towel beside them and wait for the announcement, "It's time to turn over," to start a conversation.

Tilly wasn't planning on meeting anyone. She wanted to have a swim, as it was getting hot, but otherwise, she was happy to read her book and chill for a while. The sun felt nice.

Tilly set herself up: the umbrella, the towel, the hat, the sunnies. She removed her sundress, fixing her bikini as she did. She grabbed her book from her bag and realised she hadn't even started reading it yet. She had read it before a few years ago and was inspired to reread it as she was on her new life adventure. *The Alchemist* was one book Tilly could read over and over again, taking new life messages every time she did. She had been carrying the book around with her, but she had a few very busy days with no downtime. This was finally her moment.

She opened the book and reacquainted herself with the shepherd boy, who believed his sheep could understand what he said. *Well, of course they can*, she thought.

Tilly had only read a few pages when a loud siren sounded, alerting the swimmers to get out of the water. A voice came through the loudspeaker, warning the swimmers to evacuate the water calmly. A shark had been spotted, and it was unsafe for swimmers. The announcement continued. 'Please evacuate for your own safety. We will let you know when it is safe to return to the water. There is no need to panic. We have a full helicopter view of the shark moving through the area.'

It was amazing how quickly everyone got out of the water and stood on the shoreline, observing the helicopter circling above.

Tilly was glad she had waited a moment to warm up in the sun before going for a swim. That would not have been a pleasant introduction to her first swim in Surfers Paradise. It's not such a surfers' paradise, really, at all.

This was nothing out of the ordinary. Tilly would see lots of ocean wildlife while surfing, which never worried her. If she saw a shark fin, she would usually paddle into shore and wait until it had moved on before getting back in the water. From the Angourie headland, you could see the shadows moving through the water. It wasn't worth the risk; after all, it was her in their territory, and they had every right to swim in their ocean. Her brothers were a little braver. They would often just keep on surfing. No harm ever came their way.

Tilly watched the action and waited. Younger children were screaming and running to their parents; it was quite a scene. Some surfers just stayed out there, perhaps not hearing the siren or not caring at all.

After an hour or so, the lifesavers announced it was safe to return to the water. The shark had moved on, heading down south. Tilly wondered what the process was, guessing that the chief surf lifeguard would call the surf towers down south to warn them of the passerby. The helicopter was on spotters' duty, so he would have also played a significant role in keeping people safe.

Tilly drifted her thoughts to Angourie and thought about how lucky they were to have never had a shark attack. With unpatrolled and wide-open beaches, it was quite surprising. Possibly, just the fact that there was not such a heavy population of swimmers and surfers lowered the chances. It was always a possibility and a daily risk.

Everyone started to relax and head back into the water, but no one ventured past the breakers, keeping a safe distance from the shoreline. Tilly waded into the shallow breakers, keeping her casted arm out of the water. It felt nice to be in the water, although it was crowded. She much preferred her empty, noisy ocean.

After a few hours of sunbaking with the bronzing oil, reading, swimming, turning over, sunbaking, reading, swimming, on repeat, she headed back to the hotel at about 1 pm to give herself some time to shower and freshen up before the gig practice with Bernard and the boys.

chapter sixty-seven

Sunflowers

Dalton had a plan; with a pocketful of coins, surf wax in his other pocket, and his surfboard under his arm, he bounced down the stairs and out into the street. His first job was to make a quick phone call to Dan to see if he was coming up for the weekend to surf the Billabong Pro or just to watch the competition with Dalton. He was sure that was something that Dan would be interested in—the best surfers from around the world here at Kirra on the Gold Coast.

Dalton noticed earlier that a phone booth was directly across the road from the Surf Club while street-watching and eating his Big Breakfast. As he walked towards the beach, where the phone booth was, he could see from a distance that someone was already in the phone booth, so he took a quick moment to duck into the little convenience store and grab himself two large bottles of cold water. He had quite a few drinks yesterday by the time he added up the Railway Hotel drinks with Travis, the train drinks with Trish, and the few quiet beers at the Surf Club. He was feeling a little worse for wear and needed to rehydrate.

Walking towards the booth now, just a minute later, he saw it was empty. *Perfect, I'll give Dan a quick call.* He quickly sculled a bottle of water and put the empty bottle in the rubbish bin on the corner of the street.

Dalton leaned his board against the phone booth as he squeezed himself inside. '*Geez, these booths are squishy,*' he thought, reaching into his pocket and grabbing the coins and the piece of paper on which he had scribbled Dan's phone number. The piece of paper had nestled itself right into the bottom of his pocket, so he had to use both hands to hold his boardies down and carefully pull it out. While he did so, he rested the earpiece under his chin. He sniffed and sniffed again, squinting his eyes. He could smell something that reminded him of Tilly. The phone smelt like Sunflowers, the perfume that she wore.

That's weird. How does a phone smell like Tilly? he thought.

Dalton dialled Dan's phone number, realising that he might need extra coins because it was an STD call. The phone rang out and then clicked over to the message bank. 'Hey, this is Dan. I'm surfing. Leave me a message, and I'll call you back.'

Dalton had already put the coins in, so he thought he might as well leave a detailed message, as he was paying for the call anyway.

Damn, he must be surfing, or fishing, or hanging out with his new girl, thought Dalton. Dalton started talking to the message bank like he was chatting with Dan. 'Hey Dan, it's Dalton, man. I'm just calling to let you know I'm hanging out in Surfer's Paradise. The Billabong Pro is on this weekend, and I'm wondering if you are coming up for it. Call me if you need a place to stay. My room has a spare double bed for you and your friend. Call The Beachcomber Hotel and leave me a message. I'd love to see you and surf some Gold Coast surf breaks with you. Call me, man. See you!'

As Dalton was about to hang up, Dan's voice came through the earpiece. 'Hey, D man, it's me. Sorry, man, I was just on the loo when I heard the message come through. I thought I was going to miss you. Lucky you're a good talker. What were you doing, leaving me an essay to listen to?'

Dalton started laughing. 'Yeah, I'm just in a phone booth, man, paying for the call anyway, so I didn't want to hang up without leaving you a message. I thought you might be surfing or busy with your new girl. How is that going?'

'All good, man. She's a keeper. I'm smitten. I'm looking at her beautiful face right now. We haven't left each other's sides since Thursday night. She surfs too, man, she's amazing. I don't know where she came from, but I'm keeping her.' He laughed, smiling at Ariiel, who was standing beside him, making them both a coffee, wearing only his Billabong T-shirt.

'Oh, that's so cool, man. Good on you.' Dalton was happy for Dan. He sounded so happy.

'So, what were you asking me? Am I coming up for the Billabong Pro this weekend?' Dan queried Dalton.

'Yeah, I thought you might be a starter. It starts on Friday and goes all weekend, with heats and different categories, and then finals on Sunday. The surf looks like it will be cranking; it's such a good swell coming in for the weekend.' Dalton was excited to explain all of this to Dan.

'Look, D-man, I hadn't thought about it, to be honest. I've been doing mostly New South Wales competitions. I haven't entered, but I'd love to give it a crack as a wildcard. I wonder if they are still taking wildcard entries?' Dan was interested but unsure about the process, so he asked this as a question.

'I'm not sure, but I can find out for you. Someone around here would let me know where to go to ask some questions for you. I might need to head down to Kirra Surf Club and have a talk to someone down there. Leave it with me. I'll call you later in the week. If you decide to come up, you only need yourself, your board and your girl. You are welcome to stay with me if you want to. I have a room at The Beachcomber Hotel.'

'Cool, man, sounds like a plan.' Dan was excited.

Dalton also asked if Dan knew anything about Tilly's whereabouts. 'Have you heard from Tilly at all? I hear she has headed up this way, too.'

'I was going to ask you the same question, man. Me and Ariiel had dinner at The Angourie Local last night. Frankie was filling us in on what happened. You two are the talk of the town. Tilly left here a few hours after you did, apparently looking for you.

She found a message in a bottle and then took off looking for you, and nobody has heard from her since.' Dan explained everything he knew about Tilly.

Dalton was surprised; this confirmed that she had found the message in a bottle. 'Wow, Tilly found my message in a bottle. Okay. That message was to Chelsea, not Tilly, but okay. And she's definitely looking for me?' He questioned Dan a little more, in case he had more information.

'Yeah, that's what Frankie said.' Dan had no other information to share.

'Okay, that is good to know. Thanks, man!' Dalton didn't know what else to say. He was thinking about finding Tilly and what it would be like to hold her again.

'Call me if you find out any information about the surf comp. I'll make some phone calls from here, too. I've got some mates that are probably entering the comp.' He paused.

Dalton thought the phone had been timed out and disconnected. 'Are you still there, Dan?'

'Yeah, I'm here, just thinking. Look, leave it with me. I'll call my mate, Rabbit. He's probably organising the damn thing.' Dan was good mates with Wayne Bartholomew. He was super famous in the surfing world. Everyone called him Rabbit. Dan thought Dalton may have heard of him, but then realised Dalton was only new to surfing and was a country boy. Dalton didn't flinch at the drop of his name, so Dan let it go, thinking he would make the call himself because if anyone knew what was going on with wildcard entries for the Billabong Pro, Rabbit would be the man to talk to about it.

'Are you sure? I'm going to head down to Kirra for a surf, anyway. I'll see what I can find out.' Dalton didn't mind helping Dan out. It's the least he could do.

'Yeah, it's all good. I'll call Rabbit later today. But hey, at least I know where you are now, so I can keep in touch with you. So, you said The Beachcomber Hotel?' Dan sipped the coffee that Ariiel had passed to him, then gave her a silent kiss on the forehead.

'Yep. I'll be out and about, looking for work and Tilly, but leave a message at reception, and I'll keep checking in there.' That was all Dalton could suggest for keeping contact with Dan.

'Cool man! Hey, and thanks for thinking of me.'

'No worries, man. Surfers Paradise would be lucky to have you.'

'Ha ha! Thanks, man.' Dan laughed at Dalton's kind humour. Then he continued, 'Hey, I'm just thinking now the coffee has kicked in. If I do come up, I'll bring Ariiel for the trip, so we might stay somewhere fancy, make a weekend of it.' Dan winked at Ariiel as he came up with this fantastic idea.

'Good idea. A cool Aussie band is playing here this weekend at the Surfers Paradise Surf Club. They are a new Brisbane band called Powderfinger. You can book a room here at The Beachcomber Hotel. It's nice and reasonably priced. Fancy pool too! Apparently, they have wild pool parties here. That's what I've been told.'

'Oh really! Well, that's very tempting, that's my kind of party. I could just come as myself, in my boardies.'

'Yeah, that's what I was thinking. It's right up your alley.'

The phone started beeping as Dalton's credit was running out. 'I'll say goodbye, man, but keep in touch. Call me if you're coming up. I'll make sure I get the tickets for the band for you. Could be a fun night.'

'See ya buddy, nice talkin' to you. Thanks for the call.'

'See ya, Badman.' Dalton usually called Dan, Dan, but he had heard that his nickname was Badman, so he thought he would throw that one in for a change and a pun.

They both laughed and hung up the phone simultaneously.

As Dan put the phone back on the hook, he couldn't help but mention to Ariiel how nice it was that Dalton had kept in touch. He didn't have a mate quite like him, wondering if it was just his generation, because he was from the country, or just because he was a nice guy.

Ariiel had only met Dalton briefly, the night he was playing a gig at The Angourie Local, so she couldn't comment. She thought it was nice that he had invited them up to the Gold Coast for the weekend.

Dalton felt the heat in the phone booth, but he had some more important phone calls to make. He reached into his pocket to grab more coins, again getting the scent of Tilly's perfume on the phone's earpiece as he placed it on his neck to hold it with his chin while he grabbed the coins.

He reached under the shelf to grab the Yellow Pages and searched for The Angourie Local. As he dialled the numbers, he felt extremely nervous. He hoped maybe Tilly had phoned to let her family know her whereabouts, and if she had done that, the next part of finding Tilly would be easy.

The phone rang for a while before a voice came through the earpiece.

'You've called The Angourie Local. This is Frankie. How can I help you?'

'Oh. Hi Frankie, it's Dalton. How are you, man?'

'Dalton, good to hear from you. I'm good. How are you?'

'Um, I'm not bad. I'm up in sunny Surfers Paradise trying to find your sister.'

'Oh. Okay. I won't ask you how Tilly is if you're not together. She left here a few hours after you did, on a mission to find you. We haven't heard from her since she left. We assumed she was with you. My last conversation with her was a bit of tough brotherly love, but it would be nice to hear from her.' Frankie was a little concerned that Dalton and Tilly were not together yet, and they hadn't heard from Tilly, but it was consoling that somehow Dalton knew Tilly was looking for him.

'Well, this might sound confusing, but from what I have pieced together, I know she is here on The Gold Coast trying to find me, and I'm trying to find her. So, if she calls home, please tell her I'm staying at The Beachcomber Hotel in Surfers Paradise.'

'Okay, man. Will do.' The Angourie Local was full of customers, so Frankie didn't have time to chat.

The phone started beeping again. Dalton's credit was running out, so they said their quick goodbyes and hung up. Dalton could understand that Frankie was busy; otherwise, he would have put more coins in for a longer chat.

chapter sixty-eight

Nothing Else Matters

Dalton had one more phone call to make to his parents in Deniliquin. After hearing the concern from Frankie about not knowing Tilly's whereabouts, he realised that his parents probably felt the same way. The last time he talked to them was when he was leaving Southwest Rocks quite some time ago. He had sent them a postcard from Yamba to let them know he was making his way north and safe, but he hadn't talked to them for a few weeks. Dalton's mum answered the phone almost instantly, like she was waiting patiently for the phone to ring.

'Hey, Ma!'

'Hey Dalton, how are you?'

'I'm pretty good. I won't talk long. It's an STD call, but I just wanted to let you know that I'm up in Queensland, in Surfers Paradise.'

'Oh, that must be lovely. Are there lots of people there?'

'Yes, it's busy, Ma. I don't think you would like it very much.'

'You know me, I dislike big cities very much.'

'Surfers Paradise is not such a big city. It's not like Sydney or Brisbane, but it's more crowded than Deni. I will stay here just a little while, Mum, until I get some money behind me. I might do some building here, or maybe some gigs, or some bar work. I'm not sure yet.' As soon as Dalton said that out loud, he regretted it. The last thing his mum wanted him to do was gigging or bar work. To her, that was just asking for trouble. He waited patiently for the response and reminded himself not to react.

'Well, I think you should get some building work, son. That bar work and gigging is not good for you, just getting drunk every night and wasting your money.' She got worked up and then stopped herself because she was happy that Dalton had called and didn't want to argue with him over the phone.

'Well, it's not quite like that, Ma, but a building job might be okay. There is plenty of opportunity here, that is for sure. There are lots of building projects going on, mostly demolitions of small unit complexes, being replaced with massive high-rises.'

'Oh, well, you don't want to do that sort of building. You might fall off the scaffold.' She realised she was being negative again and tried to resist making negative comments about everything Dalton was suggesting.

Dalton sighed quietly to himself, 'Yes, Ma. I guess what will be, will be.' He made a mental note that this was why he didn't call home often. Pretty much everything he suggested was going to get him locked up or killed. He often wondered if his mum knew the good and responsible person he was.

The beeps on the phone kicked in again, indicating that credit was running out. 'Look, Ma, I have to go. Please give my love to Dad, Timmy, Johnno, and the dogs. I just wanted to let you know that I'm okay. I'm safe. I'm happy. I'll call again soon. Bye Ma.'

'Bye, son, I love you.' She started crying as she hung up the phone.

I wish she wouldn't do that, criticise me and then cry when I say goodbye. The last time Dalton called, it was the same; only she was criticising him because his car had broken down and he didn't have a good job because he was doing gigs and travelling. She only said these things because she wanted the best for her son. She had a different perspective on life than he did. For Dalton, how she cared so much only made him feel he was useless in everything he did because she disapproved of his passion for music and his adventurous soul. She was a different person, a homebody. More than anything, she loved her family together, and she couldn't think of anything worse than being away from her own kitchen for more than one day. Dalton had contemplated these things, and he realised, after quite some time and a lot of soul searching, that if she really loved him, she would understand the things that made him happy and encourage him to do those things. Knowing they came from her dissimilar heart, he had learned to shrug off her comments and criticisms. If he had acted upon her criticisms and followed her advice, he would never have done the things he loved. He hoped that one day she would understand. In the meantime, he wasn't changing. He was who he was. He knew that the in-between of birth and death was his life. He could only choose what made him happy. Otherwise, what was the point of life?

As he walked across the road to the beach with his surfboard under one arm, guzzling his water with the other, he reflected on his conversation with his mum. There is no way he would have told her about what happened with Tilly anyway, because he would have been criticised even more than he already had been. The best thing to do was to leave everything unsaid. Nothing else mattered as long as his mum knew the basics, where he was, and that he was safe and well.

chapter sixty-nine

Gone, Out of Sight

The first thing Dalton noticed was the smell of coconut oil mixed with the salty ocean air. It felt and smelt like a summer holiday, reminding him of Tilly. Dalton had only recently decided that summer was his favourite season since travelling the East Coast. He never used to like the summer living out west. It was always too hot, too dry, or too wet, or it was a summer they just wanted to be over. There were years of droughts, bushfires and flooding rains, and the intensity of those natural disasters always occurred in the summer. Working on the farm was tough. The heat was intense. The animals were covered in flies and itch, and the mosquitoes were giant after the rains and brought different illnesses and fevers. There was no escape until the summer was over. It was a waiting game of endurance and patience. They would get up early in the morning to get the farm work done, and the middle of the day was just a waste of waiting until the sun's bite dropped with the sunset so they could work late into the night.

Sometimes, even the early mornings and the evening temperatures were unbearable, but they had to continue to finish the work. The only reprise and the fun memory that Dalton had was that sometimes the family would meet up with friends and go water-skiing on the Edward River. Those summer days and nights, camping out under the stars, were some of Dalton's most incredible memories from growing up in Deniliquin. Summer was good for something, and now, since he had discovered surfing, it was such an easy, perfect-for-summer sport. Boardies, surfboard, done! No need for cumbersome wetsuits. The fresh, cool water on hot skin was divine, making you feel revitalised and crisp. Suddenly, summer was okay.

People were nervously beginning to re-enter the water as discussions flowed around the shark alarm and whether it was safe. Dalton assumed it was reasonably safe to enter the water with a helicopter overhead, as the lifeguards had assured the beach crowd the shark had moved on.

Dalton pushed his board into the water, feeling the fresh rush of the ocean over his back. He liked that he was in a protected area, observed by the surf-life savers, at this moment, and he also liked that many other surfers and swimmers weren't game to enter the water yet, as he had an ocean of waves to choose from, all for himself. Wave after wave after wave, he practised the new moves he had learned from the boys in Byron. As he was resting on his board, out the back, waiting for the next set to come through, he thought over the past few days about surfing with Dan in Angourie, surfing with Travis, Myles, Juan and the girls in Byron, Jacqui's dolphin scare, and now here he was in Surfer's Paradise.

A couple of hours went by, and he was tired. His Big Breakfast was wearing off, and he thought about what he might like to have for a late lunch or dinner.

As he paddled in for his last ride, he surveyed the coastline, admiring the long stretches of sand all the way down to Coolangatta. The Gold Coast was beautiful. He scanned the closer beach scene. So many people gathered under beach tents and umbrellas, laying on their large colourful beach towels, listening to the music through the public announcement speakers. *What a great day! What a great place for a holiday! I wonder if Tilly is here in Surfer's Paradise?* Just as he was thinking this, he caught a glimpse of a girl with a beach umbrella walking off the beach. She looked similar to Tilly, just the way she walked, except the girl was wearing a big beach hat. Tilly didn't ever wear a hat. Dalton remembered in one of their conversations Tilly mentioning that she wasn't a hat girl, didn't own one, never did, but she was carrying a shoulder bag, just like Tilly did. *Could that be Tilly?*

Dalton paddled a little faster and was steady to catch the wave as it picked him up gently for an enjoyable ride into the shore. He didn't stand up. He just lay on his board and let the power of the wave carry him in as he focused on the girl.

By the time he reached the shoreline, she was gone, out of sight.

Frankie and Chelsea

Frankie was excited to finish his lunch shift at The Angourie Local, as he had plans to meet Chelsea. He farewelled his brothers and Jack. They closed the restaurant for a few hours before reopening at 5 pm for the night shift. After grabbing his car keys and a bottle of Lindemann's Shiraz from the bar, Frankie headed out the door. 'See ya, I might not be home until late tonight. Don't wait up.' He winked.

Jack called back, 'Enjoy your night off, Frankie.'

Louis was the first one to comment. 'Lucky you've still got us here to help you, Dad. Tilly's off again in the world, trying to find Dalton and then who knows where she will be? Now Frankie's heart is in a flutter with this Chelsea girl.'

Eddie replied, 'Yeah, but she's moved here to Angourie, so that's a good thing; at least Frankie will stick around.'

Jack replied to Eddie and Louis, 'Well boys, you will also find love at some stage, and who knows where that will take you. I guess we just keep going with the flow, and we'll work things out as life goes on. This place is well established now; it's just a matter of keeping the good vibes going, and people will always keep coming back.'

Eddie nodded and replied, 'True that.'

Louis also agreed, adding, 'Can I just say something that's been on my mind?'

Jack urged, 'Of course, Louis, go ahead.'

'This Chelsea girl that Frankie has met. Has she got anything to do with that message in a bottle from Dalton? I'm still so confused about all of that.'

Jack replied, 'Good question, Louis, but I don't think so. It's just a coincidence that they have the same name. From what I can put together, Dalton had a girlfriend or someone close to him called Chelsea, and she passed away, and it's his fault somehow. I'm unsure of any details, but it doesn't sound good.'

Louis replied, 'Oh!'

Jack added, 'I don't think there was foul play, but he's guilty about it all, and he was struggling to tell Tilly about it.'

Louis continued to clarify, 'So this Chelsea girl that Frankie has met has nothing to do with Dalton and Tilly going their separate ways?'

Jack replied confidently, 'Nope!'

Louis responded, still a little confused. 'Okay, that's cool, confusing but cool.'

Eddie joined the conversation, saying, 'Yeah, I think it's weird that Dalton and Chelsea have both arrived in Angourie around the same time, and that message in the bottle was addressed to Chelsea also, but Frankie's Chelsea came here with her parents. She's an author, writes books and poetry and stuff, and Dalton was travelling with his surfing mates and met Frankie in Yamba. It's just weird. This whole thing is just weird.'

Louis added, 'And good old Tilly, Little Miss I'm So Strong, and I Won't Get Hurt Again, goes and throws away a good thing because she's too stubborn and headstrong to listen to what he had to say.'

Eddie added to this reflection on his little sister. 'Like you always say, Dad, our strengths are our weaknesses. Yes, she's strong-willed and protective of her heart, and that's a good thing, but damn, if she wasn't so strong-willed and protective of her heart, that might have been a good thing in that situation.'

Jack nodded. 'I agree, but who could ever tell her that? She's strong-willed and protective of her heart.'

They all laughed.

Eddie added, 'That's our Matilda, and we love her for that.'

Jack continued. 'Tilly and Dalton are the only ones who know the whole situation, and it's up to them to work it out. Tilly just has to find him and actually listen to what he has to say and decide if it's something she can handle. I imagine that this has been a big life lesson for her.'

Eddie grabbed the keys from the counter as they headed out the door. 'Do you wanna come for a surf with me, Lou?'

Louis replied, 'Sure, bro!' And then. 'Do you wanna come for a surf, Dad?'

Jack had a quick think and responded, 'No, I won't, but thanks for the offer. You boys go and have some fun. It's a sensational afternoon. Don't rush back. Mum and I will look after the restaurant this evening. I feel like it will be a quiet night tonight. There are no bookings yet. We might even get the night off.'

Frankie ducked home for a super quick shower and was on the road within about ten minutes. He thought he might see his mum quickly to tell her his plans, but she wasn't home. She must have been out for her walk, so he left a note on the kitchen table, saying, 'I'm heading out for dinner with Chelsea. Don't wait up, I love you, Mum.'

Frankie had planned to pick up Chelsea at her new home and take her to Yamba for a dinner date. The biggest decision for Frankie was to decide where he should take her. He thought it might be nice to get some food from Coles and set up a picnic blanket at the lighthouse hill to watch the sunset, so he threw in his picnic basket in the back seat of the car and grabbed the picnic blanket and a couple of big beach towels from the garage shelves. His other idea was to go to the Pacific Hotel for a nice meal. The views overlooking the ocean were divine; if Chelsea hadn't been there before, that could be special. The other option was to head out to Yamba Shores Tavern on the riverside. They had a nice restaurant deck overlooking the water and delicious food.

The more Frankie thought about these options and what Chelsea might prefer, the more he concluded the picnic would be best. After all, Chelsea had moved up from Sydney only a few days prior. Frankie was confident that she would have been spoiled with restaurant choices in Sydney, so the local pubs and restaurants here probably wouldn't be entirely up to the standard of what Chelsea would be used to.

She seemed to be very down to earth and a creative soul, so Frankie was guessing the picnic might be more her style. He wasn't trying to impress her, just getting to know her.

Frankie had written a song for Chelsea. It was back in his room, in his notebook beside his bed. He ripped the scribbled-on pages out of the notebook, folded them and put them in his back pocket. He grabbed his guitar, capo, and his lucky guitar pick, his family pick. Frankie's was a marbled black colour, the same as Tilly's, engraved on both sides.

As Frankie settled into his car on the way to pick up Chelsea, he tuned into the local radio station and sang along as the harmonious voice of Bruce Springsteen's, *I'm On Fire*, started crooning through the speakers. *Such a great song*, he thought.

Frankie wasn't far down the road when he suddenly remembered, *Oh no, I must tell my family that Dalton called today to say he was on the Gold Coast, and he wondered if we had heard from Tilly.* He had totally forgotten about the phone call. They had a busy lunch shift, and Frankie's spare thoughts were all about Chelsea. Frankie was a little concerned that Dalton and Tilly were not together, and he didn't want to panic Jack and Laura, but instinctively, he knew she would be okay. Perhaps it didn't matter if he didn't tell the family. It might cause less worry, and surely Tilly would call home soon.

As Frankie pulled into Chelsea's driveway, he spotted her straight away. She was sitting up on the balcony with her mother and father. It looked like they were all having a few drinks in the afternoon sun, an empty bottle of wine on the balcony table and a glass in each hand.

As Frankie stepped out of the car, Chelsea called out. 'Hey Frankie.'

'Hey, up there!' Frankie called back.

Her parents called back too, 'Hello, and Hi.'

Frankie spoke loudly so they could all hear what he was saying. 'It looks like you're having a delightful afternoon. I feel cruel stealing Chelsea away.'

Chelsea's father called back, 'She's all yours, Frankie. Otherwise, we won't have any wine left.'

Chelsea took the last sip of her wine and gave both of her parents a quick hug. Her parents and Frankie continued conversing from the balcony to ground level as she went downstairs.

Frankie called upwards, 'This is a great place you have found here. Let me tell you, it's hard to find any property for sale in Angourie these days. You got lucky with this gem.'

Chelsea's father replied, 'We did nothing. It's all Chels. She did it all on her own, found this place, and decided this was where she wanted to be. We were lucky to get the invite to come and check it out. She's Little Miss Independent Author these days. Knows what she wants.'

Chelsea's mother added, 'When I was her age, I had no idea what I wanted to do with my life, let alone buy a house in a place I'd never been before.'

Chelsea's father added more to the conversation, 'That's our Chelsea. Does what she wants.' They both had a lot to say, and Frankie was listening carefully.

Frankie wasn't sure what to say because her father sounded proud of her but also a little lost and sarcastic about her independent decision, so Frankie was careful with his response. 'I guess when you know, you just know.'

Chelsea's mother spoke next to fill Frankie in on their plans, hoping to ease some of the tension she felt from Chelsea's father. 'We are heading back to Sydney tomorrow. I'm sure we will see you again the next time we come up for a visit. It is lovely here.'

'I'm glad you have enjoyed it here; it is a beautiful little town. In my biased opinion, Chelsea has made a good decision moving here.' Frankie replied.

'Thanks for looking after Chelsea for us and showing her around. That's lovely of you.' Chelsea's mother responded, trying to get a word in before her husband again.

'It's my pleasure,' replied Frankie.

Chelsea had already popped through the front door, ready to go, with a bottle of red wine, a picnic blanket under her arm, a shopping bag and her shoulder bag. She gave Frankie a quick hug and a kiss on the cheek. He did the same. She called back, 'See you, Mum and Dad. Don't wait up. I'll see you in the morning before you leave.'

'Have fun, you two!' called Chelsea's father.

As Chelsea opened the car's back door to place her belongings out of the way, she smiled when she saw the picnic basket and the guitar on the back seat. 'Ah, it looks like you've got the same idea as me, Frankie. A picnic, and some music. That's just what I was thinking, too.'

Frankie replied, 'Oh, it's not just the picnic idea we've jinxed on. If you look inside the picnic basket, you'll see that we have selected the same bottle of red wine.' Frankie giggled at the uncanny connection they already had with each other, as they had not discussed any plans other than to meet and have dinner somewhere together.

'Cute, we're cute,' announced Chelsea, nodding and climbing into the front seat beside Frankie.

They both looked at each other and smiled. 'I'm thinking lighthouse.' They both said this at exactly the same time and after giving each other a curious look, suggesting, *how did you know I was going to say that?* They both burst into fits of laughter.

chapter seventy-one

The Girl With The Beach Umbrella

Dalton searched the nearby streets for about an hour, hoping to catch sight of the girl with the beach umbrella. It was like she just vanished. He couldn't tell from such a distance if it was Tilly. She had the same walk, but the rest, he couldn't tell. The girl was wearing a big beach hat, which wasn't a hat Dalton recognised and he couldn't see any other distinguishing features. Tilly didn't usually wear a hat, so that was a reason for him to think that maybe it wasn't her. It was just a girl with an umbrella and a walk similar to Tilly.

Dalton rushed back to his hotel room to drop off his surfboard and shower quickly to wash off the ocean salt. Dalton tried to stop thinking about the girl, as he could do nothing about it. Instead, he grabbed his wallet and guitar, in its case, and decided to catch a bus to Coolangatta for the afternoon and evening. He thought it might be a nice way to spend the evening trying some busking and getting a feed in Cooly. There was a chance that Tilly was in Coolangatta as that was almost where he got off the bus, if not for Glenn, Mr GG, the creepy bus driver, encouraging him to stay on to party in Surfer's Paradise.

He walked down to the bus transit station, passing The Islander Hotel on the way. He noticed a blackboard sign out the front saying Poolside Live Music, Happy Hour, 5 to 6 pm. Free Drink upon entry. He almost changed his plans; that sounded fun, but he had decided he would do some busking to play his own live music, and he had also promised Dan he would go to Kirra and get some information about the Billabong Pro. The bus was leaving in ten minutes.

As Dalton sat on the bus, he tried to take notice of the different towns he was passing through: Broadbeach, Mermaid Waters, Miami, Burleigh Heads, Palm Beach, Currumbin, Tugun, Kirra and finally he arrived at Coolangatta. Broadbeach looked busy, not as busy as Surfers Paradise or Coolangatta, but it looked like another location for work. There was so much construction going on. It was hard to figure out where one town ended and the other began. This was very different to where Dalton had grown up. The distance between one town and another would be at least twenty deserted minutes on a long stretch of country road. Sometimes, there was not a house, not even a worn-out shack in sight, between towns.

chapter seventy-two

Meant To Be

Tilly covered her cast in a plastic bag and showered. The shower had good pressure. It was nice and warm and quite spacious for a small hotel room.

Having a cast proved to be quite an inconvenience, and she hoped her arm would heal quickly. Her shower thoughts were scattered, reflecting on her day at the beach, firstly about the suntan oil man and how very 'Surfers Paradise' the concept was to spray people with coconut oil. Then her thoughts drifted to the shark alarm as she wondered how often that happened, and then her mind flowed to her purchases of the day: the umbrella, the beach towel, and her new beach hat. It was all cumbersome if she were to continue travelling. She thought about her phone call to the train lady and how excited she was that Dalton was more than likely here, somewhere on the Gold Coast. She didn't know where, and the Gold Coast was a big place. She thought about her conversation with her mum, and she was grateful for the relationship they had with each other. She missed her family and would have loved to be sharing a meal and serving customers at The Angourie Local, but this is where she was right now. She was about to have a practice gig with Powderfinger.

Tilly was dressed in some comfortable jeans and a loose tank top. This was her go-to outfit for most casual occasions. She put on basic makeup: eyeliner, mascara and her favourite Clinique Black Honey lipstick. Tilly's hair was wild after her swim at the beach, so she had washed it and combed through the knots. Her natural curls were bouncing with no product required. She was lucky like that.

As Tilly grabbed the hotel key and her shoulder bag, she considered taking her guitar with her and then had second thoughts. She should allow her arm to rest a few more days in the new cast.

Bernard was already waiting for her as she arrived at the hotel foyer.

'Hey Tilly, how are you gorgeous?' Bernard stepped forward and gave Tilly a gentle hug and a kiss on the cheek.

Tilly returned the hug and received the kiss, giving Bernard a big smile. 'Hey Bernard, how are you? How's your day been?'

Bernard replied, hoping Tilly would catch his compliment. 'Yeah, pretty good. A beautiful girl came into my room this morning and made me breakfast, which was a delightful start to the day.'

Tilly laughed, enjoying his sense of humour, realising he was talking about her. It reminded her of Dalton's little game he played with her when they first met, and he wrote a song for her. She quickly let her thoughts go and refocused on the conversation with Bernard. 'Did she now? Lucky you!'

'I was very lucky. After that, I went back to sleep for a little while, and then I went and lay by the pool and had a few refreshing swims until about an hour ago.'

'Nice. That sounds fun.'

Bernard was keen to hear about Tilly's day and if she had any news after her phone calls. He replied. 'It *was* fun, bloody hot today. What about you? Any news on the guitar pick?'

'No news on the guitar pick, but I got other news.' Tilly paused, feeling that she needed to be careful about how she shared the news about Dalton with Bernard. 'The lady I spoke to on the phone said a fella with a blue Bandana fitting Dalton's description bought a northbound bus ticket to the Gold Coast, and she had a feeling that he was looking for me. He asked about a dark-haired girl travelling north.'

'That's cool, Tilly. Right? The Gold Coast is a big city, and it will still be hard to find him, but at least you know you are on the right track and in the right area. So, he's looking for you, but does he know you're also looking for him?'

'No, I don't think so. How would Dalton know I was looking for him?'

'Well, I mean, you know that he's looking for you because of information from a complete stranger. It might be the same for him. Is there anyone you've talked to whom Dalton may have talked to and told them you're looking for him, other than me?'

'Ummm, no, only my family. I have told no one other than you. The girls I hitched a car ride with to Byron Bay had an idea I was heading up this way, but they knew nothing about Dalton and me. Anyway, as you said. "What will be, will be? If it's meant to be. It's meant to be." Thank you for trying to figure all this out with me.' Tilly tried to put closure on the conversation, aware that Bernard was on a schedule to meet with his band for practice.

Bernard encouraged a little more information from Tilly to ensure she was okay. 'Did you have time to call your family as well?'

'Yeah, I talked to Mum, so that was nice. I've told her I'm staying here at The Islander Hotel and having a little sing-a-long with you guys. She doesn't know who Powderfinger are, but she is happy for me.'

'Well, that's cool then. If Dalton calls back to your home, they can tell him where you are so he can find you.'

'Yeah, true that. Anyway, enough about all of that.'

'Well, you know what I think, Tilly, if it is meant to be, it will all work out, you'll see.' Bernard was concerned about Tilly, but there was nothing they could do.

Tilly changed the topic. 'So, what's the plans for this afternoon? I'm keen for a sing-a-long.'

'Well, I hope you're okay with this. You don't get to practice. You just get to straight out, wing it, and perform with us. We were going to have a practice in the function room upstairs, but they've got something going on up there, and it's all booked until 10 pm. They asked us to set up by the pool and play poolside music this afternoon and into the night for happy hour and dinner. The bonus is we get paid. What do you think?'

'Hell, that sounds fun. Why not?'

'Cool, I thought you'd be okay with it. You perform all the time, right?'

'Yeah, all the time. Sometimes improvisation works better, anyway; it's more natural that way, and if I'm not playing my guitar, just singing, that's one less thing to worry about.'

'Let's do it then. The boys are already out there setting up.' Bernard encouraged as he pointed toward the pool.

'Am I okay just wearing this?' Tilly queried as she felt a little pang of nerves.

'Of course, you look beautiful, just as you are. It's just poolside tunes. Nothing fancy.' Bernard complimented Tilly, ensuring she felt no pressure about the evening.

'Okay, let's do it!' Tilly walked beside Bernard as he led the way to the poolside stage they had set up.

chapter seventy-three

Meeting The Lads

Dalton stepped off the bus in Coolangatta and headed straight to the Coolangatta Hotel. He felt like a nice cold beer and hoped to ask the locals some questions about the Billabong Pro. It looked like the whole town was ready for it, with signs posted everywhere and scaffold seating on the beach for the crowds.

He ordered a beer at the bar and headed to the tables out the front, where he could do some people-watching and feel the vibes of this place. He had to consider putting his guitar somewhere out of the way, so he leaned it up in the corner beside him, where he could keep an eye on it.

As soon as he sat down, a few young local surfy-looking lads headed over to the table and asked if they could join him. 'Hey man, mind if we join you?'

'Sure, you can,' replied Dalton. 'I hoped someone might come and join me.'

'Haven't seen you around before. What brings you here?' asked the tall, skinny, bronzed lad.

'Umm, that's an excellent question. I wanted to ask some questions about the Billabong Pro for my mate, and I plan on sitting out in the park across the road later, playing my guitar to get some beer money. I'm just here for a good night, basically.'

'Cool!' replied the tall lad. He was happy with that answer, but the shorter lad wanted to know a little more.

'Where are you from?'

'Well, I've come here on a bus from Surfers Paradise. I'm travelling for a little while, but I am originally from a little town way down south and west called Deniliquin.'

'Cool!' said that tall lad.

'What do you want to know about the Billabong Pro?' asked the shorter lad.

'My mate, Dan from Angourie, is a legend surfer, and I reckon he should enter the comp, but he thinks it might be too late.'

'How old is he?' asked the shorter lad.

Dalton shifted his head sideways. 'I don't know, maybe in his thirties or early forties. I'm not good at picking ages. Do they have strict age categories?'

The shorter lad again replied. 'Not for the Open event. It kind of depends on your ranking. He might enter as a Wild Card.'

Dalton replied. 'Cool, I'll let him know.'

The shorter lad was keen to ask more questions about Dalton. 'So, what kind of music do you play? I'm guessing country.'

'Did the Blundstone boots and Bandana give it away?' Dalton tipped his head.

'I've never seen someone wearing a Bandana and Blundstones. It's like Axl Rose had a love child with James Blundell.' The taller lad commented, coming back into the conversation. 'That's not a criticism, man. I love Guns' n' Roses and don't mind a bit of country music.

'All good, mate. The Blundstone boots probably give it away. I'm as Australian as they come. Yes, I play a bit of country, but mostly just covers of great bands I love. I can play any song you ask me to play, but it might sound countrified when I do. I've been playing for years; it's just a hobby, and sometimes, I play gigs in local pubs for cash. It's great. That's my plan for a while.'

'You should ask the Manager here. Talk to Shawn; he will give you a gig on a quiet weeknight, and if it sounds good, he might ask you back to rock a Sunday session.'

'Sounds cool.' Dalton liked the idea.

'Cool,' said the tall lad. That seemed to be his answer to everything.

The shorter lad added, 'If I see him, I'll call him over. He's usually here most days. It's a busy pub, especially now with everyone coming into town for the comp on the weekend. Good for business, and if you're half as good as you say you are, that's just what this place needs.'

'Cool!' replied Dalton, raising his glass for a cheer. 'Nice to meet you, lads. Cheers.' They hadn't exchanged names or deep secrets. Just a "Cheers" would suffice.

An hour or more passed, and the lads and Dalton chatted about surfing and travelling the East Coast. The lads, Tom and Richie, were best mates from high school, living to surf, drink, meet girls, and chat with strangers. Nothing else mattered. They were interesting fellas, with lots of stories of shenanigans and mischief. They lived for sunrises and the best swells. If they could afford food, drinks, and surf wax, everything was okay in the world. They shared a cheap backyard den, beside the tall lad, Tom's granny's house. She lived in the perfect location across the road from the beach, and all she asked was that Tom and Richie were forthcoming with their rent and would help her with the gardening and handyman tasks she could not do herself. She was independent and always out and about in the community, attending various groups and activities, but there were some things that she needed a strong hand for. The lads were good for that, always. She spent most of her days watching trash TV: Days of Our Lives, The Bold and the Beautiful. She would record shows on the other channels to watch later while she was busy attending community events. She maintained a bit of balance to keep herself healthy, going for a very long beach walk every morning and consuming two glasses of Chardonnay every evening. In Coolangatta, Agnes was well known as the daily beach walk lady, but few people knew her by name. She was close to eighty years of age, but she would walk at least five kilometres daily without fail. The lads paid her a small rent, and they paid for their water and electricity. She was just as happy as they were with the arrangement. She had two strong lads to help her with whatever she needed whenever she needed it, and they had a cheap place to stay across the road from one of the best surfing locations in the world, Snapper Rocks. It was the perfect combination.

Dalton was enjoying their stories, and the pub was getting more crowded. The lads had noticed that there were a lot of unknown faces in town, not the usual crowd. The Billabong Pro surfing competition was international, bringing some of the best surfers from all over the world. The population of the Gold Coast, especially Coolangatta, was expanding for just this week as the competition brought not only the surfers but also their families, friends, supporters, sponsors, and surfing enthusiasts to the area.

Dalton had picked a perfect time to visit the Gold Coast. It was humming. Richie decided to buy the next round and invited Dalton to join in. He went to the bar to buy the beers and returned with the publican, Shawn, introducing Dalton to him as a musician from the far-out-west. Dalton laughed as he shook Shawn's hand. 'My name is Dalton Diaz. I'm from Deniliquin, just passing through the Gold Coast on a surfing and gigging tour.'

Shawn wasted no time suggesting that Dalton was most welcome if he wanted to plug into the PA and play some tunes. They were not expecting a busy crowd this early in the week, and they could do with some live music.

Dalton thought about this offer for half a second and replied. 'Why not? That's an offer I can't refuse. Do you have any preferred music you want me to play?'

Shawn responded, 'Mate, anything to keep this crowd humming would be great. We will have quite a few international tourists here following the surfing tour, so if you can share some of our Aussie-flavoured hits, that would be perfect.'

'Can do. No worries. I'll finish this beer and start playing.' Dalton gave Shawn the thumbs up and took a swig from his beer.

'Look. I'll swing you some cash later. I need to get back behind the bar. Thanks heaps, man!' Shawn was grateful that Dalton was keen to play and trusted that he might be half-decent. Otherwise, he figured he wouldn't have gone along with the request at such short notice and with such a busy crowd.

Dalton was slightly nervous and happy to have another relaxing beer before he started. He had played for many country-pub crowds, more than he could remember. As he made his way north, he had played at a few small beachy pubs. He had played a few larger gigs in Sydney, which was fine, but this was a buzzing, mixed crowd, and the wrong mood could be detrimental to the afternoon vibe.

As he finished his beer, he created a set list in his head. He also asked the lads for some advice on what the locals liked. They were not particularly helpful, with no genuine passion for listening to good music. Music wasn't surfing, swell, eating, drinking or girls. They suggested, like Shawn did, that Aussie covers would be best. Mental as Anything, The Choirboys, Hoodoo Gurus, Midnight Oil, Cold Chisel, INXS. *That's a good start*, thought Dalton.

It was time to plug in and play; no need to busk in the park for a few coins tonight.

chapter seventy-four

Nothing Fancy

Bernard, the band, and Tilly were all set up and ready to entertain the hotel guests for an afternoon and evening poolside session. They hadn't planned or publicised the gig, thinking it might be more appropriate and memorable as a quiet, relaxed session with the hotel guests. Still, word had somehow spread that Powderfinger was playing a free gig at The Islander Hotel, so the crowds were already gathering. As much as they had tried to keep it on the down low, the hardcore fans were not missing out. It wasn't long before the tables were full; the bar was busy, and the vibe was fancy. People were dressed to the nines. The women here on the Gold Coast were out to make an impression amongst the crowd gathering for this new Aussie talent.

Tilly looked at Bernard and said, 'I've got a bone to pick with you, Bernard Fanning. You said it was nothing fancy. I thought we were having a private practice in some hotel function room, but here I am, sitting on this stage with you as the rich and famous crowds gather. Everyone is so dressed up. I didn't even put proper make-up on. This moment could be my biggest claim to fame ever in my life, and here I am in my jeans and thongs and an empty face.'

Bernard acknowledged how Tilly felt but also let her know it didn't matter what she was wearing. He simply smiled and replied. 'That's even better, Matilda Macallan, as you realise our original connection was always authentic. It's about how amazing you are as a natural, beautiful person. You don't need make-up to be beautiful, to me or anyone. No matter how fancy they are dressed, other than you, I'm not impressed by anyone right now. I'm impressed with your bravery to get up here and sing with us.'

'Thank you, Bernard, that's really lovely, but I still wish I had some make-up on and maybe a nice dress or something *a little more fancy.*'

'What song should we play first?' Bernard asked Tilly, as he was keen to get the gig started. The other guys were ready to begin when Bernard and Tilly were ready.

'Can we do a cover to start with? Can we do Fleetwood Mac? Gypsy? It's probably the song I feel most comfortable singing when I'm this nervous.' Tilly's heart was pounding. It made no sense because she had played many live gigs with her family and rarely got nervous, but this was different. These guys were super-talented musicians.

As soon as they played the beginning chords, Tilly relaxed, trusting in their musical genius that this would be a fun evening. Tilly was only joining in for a couple of songs, and for the rest of the night, she could chill with the crowd and enjoy the performance.

As the song finished, Tilly looked around. The crowd was giving them a big clap. Bernard announced, 'Thank you, thank you all so much. Please put your hands together for Matilda Macallan, joining us from Angourie in NSW.' The crowd clapped louder. 'We're Powderfinger, from Brisbane, via Sydney, and a few other places in between.' As Bernard announced Brisbane, there were a few loud cheers from the crowd, and then on Sydney, another few cheers. There was quite a gathering of tourists to Surfers Paradise. 'We are glad you could make it here to The Islander Hotel for our "secret" gig tonight. We hope you enjoy the next few hours with us. We are going to play some original songs and some covers. Please pop over and request a song if there is something you want us to play. We are here for you for the next few hours or so.' The crowd clapped again.

As Tilly got up to walk off the stage and get to the bar for a nervous drink, Bernard announced again. 'Let's give Tilly another clap, so hopefully she returns to the stage a little later.' The crowd gave an enormous cheer and another clap for Tilly as she headed to the bar to grab a drink.

Tilly hadn't made it all the way to the bar before a young man walked over to her with a West Coast Cooler. 'This is for you,' he said as he passed Tilly a bottle of West Coast.

'Oh, that's nice of you.' Tilly recognised this man from somewhere but couldn't quite remember where. It was more his voice that she remembered.

'You don't remember me, do you? My name is Glenn. Mr GG, remember, I'm the bus driver. I dropped you all here at the bus station the other night, and Bernard said you were doing a gig here this week. I saw the sign while driving past and thought I would stop in for a few bevvies.' Glenn was right up in Tilly's face, and she took a step backwards, trying not to be rude, but she felt uncomfortable with his closeness.

'Oh, that's right. That's where I remember you from. Yeah, cool.' Tilly felt a little awkward and hesitant to take the drink from him, but it seemed like a nice enough gesture. He was a very talkative and lively chap who seemed to know everything about Surfers Paradise. *She thought he couldn't be too harmful, but she didn't want to get caught up in a long conversation with him, as she wanted to mingle and meet some people.* She said, 'Glenn, thanks for the drink. I don't want to be rude, but I'm keen to get around and talk to some people if that's okay. If I have this drink with you, I feel obligated to stay with you and return the favour. I hope you don't mind.' Tilly felt very uncomfortable. She had been in situations like this before, and she had learned some hard lessons by being too friendly and too kind. She wanted to enjoy her night and mingle. She also had a bit of a gut instinct that this guy was a bit of a cling-on. If she accepted the drink, he would take that as an invitation to hang around her for the night. She didn't want to babysit. She wanted to be the social butterfly that she was.

Glenn replied, 'Hey, it's totally okay. You can have the drink; it doesn't mean we're besties, and I don't expect you to buy me back. Just buying you a drink to say *cheers, big ears, no contract.*'

Tilly was feeling more and more uncomfortable. She couldn't explain it. There was just a weird vibe this guy was giving her, so she made an excuse for a quick exit. 'Look, I'm just going to the loo. Thanks anyway, I'll catch you later.' She left the drink on the nearby table and walked away and into the hotel foyer, where there was a bathroom. At first, she thought of going to her room to use her own bathroom and putting on some make-up, but on second thoughts, she was worried that Glenn might follow her. She didn't know why she felt this instinct of over-friendliness that was also creepy. It felt weird to her, and she was going with her gut.

Tilly went to the bathroom in the foyer and returned to the bar to buy her own drink and a round of drinks for the Powderfinger boys. When she returned to the poolside area, Glenn was gone. She could see the full West Coast Cooler that he had bought her and an empty beer bottle that he had been drinking, sitting on the table near where he had bumped into her and offered her the drink. She thought *that's weird, but I'm glad he's gone.*

Tilly didn't want to overthink it, trying to focus on another song the boys might play for her to sing along with them. The atmosphere was relaxed and chilled out, so some easy-listening music now would be good to keep the afternoon's mood cruising along. She wondered if the boys could play "*Time After Time*" by Cyndi Lauper.

chapter seventy-five

Plug and Play

Dalton plugged in his guitar and did a quick tune-up. He was 'testing one, two, testing one, two, two, two,' on the microphone. It sounded sharp. He was happy. The set-up was like what The Macallans had at The Angourie Local. It was an acoustic guitarist's dream, just plug in and play.

He started with Fleetwood Mac—Gypsy because it was his favourite song for Tilly, and it would put him in the right mood. Everyone loved Fleetwood Mac.

Over the next few hours, he entertained the ongoing flow of guests at The Coolangatta Hotel. Most of the crowd was there to mingle and talk; others came to enjoy a pub meal, and others to dance and listen to the spontaneous live music that Dalton was performing.

The lads, Tom and Richie, were Dalton's biggest supporters, giving him a massive cheer every time they liked a song he played. They were easy to please as long as he played classic Aussie rock music. Dalton was doing alright. The lads were happy.

There seemed to be a lot of international tourists around, which added to the flavour of the vibe. Dalton could hear people talking. Many had different accents, and everyone was in a holiday mood.

As the night rolled on, people came to dance on the dancefloor in front of the stage. The lads were asking some of the international guests for a dance, and they were grateful for the performance Dalton was putting on to keep everyone in a happy, easy-going mood.

The lads kept a constant flow of beers coming to Dalton throughout the evening. He was happy to continue playing for a couple of hours. He was okay as long as he didn't run out of song ideas. The crowd kept asking for requests, which made the choice easy. As time was rolling on, approaching midnight, Shawn gave Dalton the signal to wrap it up soon. It would take an absence of atmosphere to clear the guests out of the pub; otherwise, they would all be keen to party into the early hours. The Coolangatta Hotel only had a midweek license to midnight, so Shawn knew he needed to wind down the atmosphere and move people on. Dalton played one last song, *Love Shack*, by the

B-52's. The crowd wanted more, but Shawn was adamant that Dalton pack up. Shawn played background music through the speakers as the dancefloor cleared, and the call was out for closing time.

Dalton packed his guitar back in its case and returned to the tables, where Tom and Richie had gathered a crowd of energetic young people. They were all having a fun night, talking loudly and getting to know each other. Richie was the first to notice that Dalton had re-joined the table, so he attempted to introduce Dalton to the gathered new friends. He spoke loudly as he wrapped his arm around Dalton's shoulder. 'Hey everybody, this is our new friend Dalton, he's from far-out-west.'

There was a round of hey, hello, and aloha's going on as the table of friends invited Dalton to join in.

Shawn came over to the table and handed Dalton some cash. Dalton didn't look at the amount Shawn had given him, not at that moment; he was happy to accept the payment, whatever it was. Shawn said, 'Thanks, man! You saved me tonight, you did a great gig, and we would love to have you back sometime if you would like to come and play.'

Dalton replied eagerly. 'I'd love to play here again; that would be tops.'

Shawn was in a bit of a rush to get the pub closed for the night, so he didn't have time to chat. 'I can't talk now, but can I get your contact number?'

Dalton replied, 'Mate, I don't have a home base at the moment, but you can call and leave a message at the Beachcomber Hotel in Surfers Paradise.'

Shawn handed Dalton a business card and said, 'Well, here are our contact details. Call me and check in later in the week. We might need you this weekend. By the look of the crowds coming into Coolangatta for this Billabong Pro, we might need a weekend of bands on call. Honestly, I didn't think we would be this busy.'

'Sounds good, man! I'll call you on Thursday evening or Friday morning. What's best?'

'Yeah, call me Friday morning. I should have a plan sorted out by then. I might get you in for a Saturday or Sunday lunch session. We've got another band sorted for Saturday night already. It's going to be a huge night.'

Dalton quickly remembered that Dan and Ariiel were a maybe to come up for the Powderfinger concert on Saturday night. 'Mate, I've just remembered that I have plans for Saturday in Surfers Paradise, but count me in for Sunday, for sure.'

'Look mate, as you are hard to get hold of, let's just lock that in. If you turn up around midday on Sunday, we can kick on into the afternoon.'

'Sounds good to me,' agreed Dalton. They shook hands. Dalton lifted the beer he had been carrying and held it up for a cheer to Shawn. 'Oh, and cheers for the beers, mate!'

Shawn pointed to Tom and Richie. 'You can thank the lads for the beer train. Nothing to do with me.'

'Cool. I guess I'll see you Sunday, around midday.' Dalton confirmed their arrangement. Shawn disappeared back into the bar.

Dalton thanked Tom and Richie for the beers they had kept flowing all night while Dalton was busy performing. 'Hey, thanks, lads, for the beers.'

'Cool,' was Tom's reply.

Richie was a little more eloquent in adding to the conversation. 'That's the least we could do to shout you a few beers. We are over here having the night of our lives with our new friend Sunny and the girls while you entertained us on the stage. Mate, the music was all class. Did you see it? This place was going off.'

'Oh, thanks, man. I'm glad you enjoyed it,' replied Dalton.

'I hear Shawn has you returning to do a Sunday session. That's cool, man. You won't even need to busk out in the park. Surely a paid gig is better money than busking?'

'Sure is. It depends on the night, though. Sometimes, on a successful busking night, I can make a few hundred bucks.'

Tom returned to the conversation, keen to encourage Dalton to party with them a little longer. 'So, what are your plans tonight? Are you heading back to Surfers Paradise?'

'I'm not sure, going with the flow just now. It depends on the bus schedule this late at night, or I'll be hitching a ride or hailing a cab.'

'You can crash at ours, and Richie can drive you back in the morning, or you can jump on a bus. They are pretty regular along the beachfront stretch during the day.' Tom was keen for Dalton to hang out with them a little longer.

'You know what? That would be great. I'd love to do that.' It took little convincing to encourage Dalton to party on. He wished he had brought his surfboard for a morning surf with the lads, but he was not aware that the night would turn out the way it had. Perhaps they would have a spare board he could borrow if an early morning surf eventuated after their night of many beers.

'Cool,' said Tom—his response to most things.

Again, Richie added, 'Let's get another round, my shout.'

The vibe was loud and happy. Different people were talking and laughing and having a great night. There was a vibrant mix of people here for a fun week with the Billabong Pro on the calendar for many tourists. Dalton could hear the different accents of men and women blended with the standard Aussie tones. The people that had joined the table were from Hawaii. Sunny, one of the Billabong Pro contestants, had a harem of followers—three beautiful girls on holiday in Australia to cheer on their favourite hometown, Hawaii boy.

A few groups of people cleared out as Shawn issued another call. 'We're closing soon.' Other groups merged closer, leaving just the stayers, including Dalton, Tom, Richie, and a few other lads and women they had been talking with throughout the night.

Tom and Richie had already put out the word for an after-party at their house. These last few stayers were keen to party on. As they awaited the call from Shawn for the last drinks, they continued drinking, talking, and getting to know each other.

Richie returned with a single, round tray supporting eight flaming shot glasses. 'Who's up for a Flaming Lamborghini?' Flaming Lamborghini was the technical name for Baileys, Kahlua, Sambuca and Blue Curacao, set on fire in a shot glass.

Richie placed the tray carefully on the table and encouraged everyone to get in and grab one, or the flames would go out. All the people gathered reached in to grab a shot glass each.

Richie held his glass up and declared, 'Cheers, big ears!'

Tom returned the cheers. 'Same goes, big nose.'

Everyone laughed and threw their heads back, swallowing the shots in sync. All were returning their glasses to the tray with various sound effects of 'pheeeeew,' 'man, that stuff is heavy,' 'ooh, that is hot,' and 'damn, that's fire all right.'

Cody, the tall, dark-haired stranger who had joined the table only recently, didn't say a word. It was like it didn't have any effect on him.

Dalton was the first to make the circle wider to welcome their new friend to the group. This tall, seemingly arrogant stranger confidently introduced himself to be part of the gathered friends without hesitation. 'Hey, my name's Cody. The soul-surfer. I'm here to watch the professional surfers do their thing this week, but in the meantime, do you mind if I join you guys and girls?'

Dalton was familiar with the term soul-surfer. He had shared brief discussions about the concept with his surfing mates, mostly self-classified as soul-surfers. They didn't surf to compete. They surfed for the passion, the sheer pleasure of surfing, and the adrenaline, not the accolades of a title.

Cody was the same, and even though they had just met, he was adamant about expressing his opinion at the forefront of their introductions to clarify that surfing was not meant to be judged. Surfing was intended to be a free and wild connection with the ocean and the nature within it, not a performance to the crowds of people on a beach and the sponsors. Although he was here in Coolangatta t/o watch the Billabong Pro, his attitude was typically negative towards these surfing professionals getting paid to perform with nature. To him, it was criminal.

Sunny was quiet and kept out of the conversation, as this soul-surfer forcibly expressed his point of view. Sunny was hoping to blend into the crowd, and for this moment, he hoped Cody didn't realise that Sunny was one of the contestants in this devilish sport.

Cody looked like a modern-day Tarzan, with longish, untamed, sun-bleached hair and a full dark beard. He was muscular but lean, like he had just walked out of the jungle. He didn't smile much and seemed shy, but when he spoke, he had a deep, husky voice and spoke simple words; few, but carefully decided to say what he needed.

When he spoke and said, 'Does anyone care to join me for another "fancy car on fire," or is the bar closed?'

Richie laughed. 'Oh, you do have a sense of humour? And there I was thinking you were just a completely rude, arrogant stranger.'

Cody nodded and pulled a downward smirk, agreeing that he probably appeared rude and arrogant as he was making sure he let everyone know about his opinion.

Richie continued. 'If you walk to the bar and order another round of Flaming Lamborghinis, no one will say no. Trust me. Who would say no to Tarzan, dude?'

Cody laughed. He was often likened to the actor Christopher Lambert, who played Tarzan in Greystoke, Legend of Tarzan. He picked up the tray of empty glasses and walked to the bar. He had a presence that cleared the path before him as he walked. There was no problem in ordering another round. He just signalled, with his large, muscular hand, "another round" and pointed to the empty glasses. The bartender gave a hesitant look to Shawn, who nodded okay, and the bartender instantly completed his request. Shawn knew Tom and Richie well, and he knew they would slow down the drinks soon, and he would gently herd them all out into the street.

They were harmless, local larrikins, and they caused no trouble. The after-parties usually ended up at Tom and Richie's place, a short walk from the venue.

chapter seventy-six

Time After Time

Tilly made her way back to the stage with a tray of drinks. There was no sign of Glenn. He seemed to have vanished, making her feel a little more at ease, but still uncomfortable. Where did he go? Tilly was always pretty good at gut instinct feels. There was just something about him that was odd. Tilly thought of mentioning something to Bernard about him, but then she decided it was probably over-the-top dramatic. Glenn had innocently bought her a West Coast Cooler, that's all, and he came to watch the gig, that's all. Tilly let it go. She was being over-cautious.

Bernard and the boys were finishing a set. Bernard announced, as the crowd was clapping for more, that they would take a quick break.

Tilly held out the tray of drinks and was ready for the balancing act as the boys took turns to grab their beers. They were all very grateful to Tilly and said "thanks" as they grabbed them individually and carefully off the tray. Tilly responded with humorous gratitude. 'Are you serious? I don't deserve thanks; you are letting me ruin your show. It's the least I can do to buy you a beer for the pleasure of doing so.'

They all laughed, and then Bernard replied, 'There is no way you are ruining the show, Tilly; you are adding to it. All the lucky men in the audience get to listen to the voice of a beautiful woman, and they get to look at you while their lady's goo and gaa over us.' They all tapped their drinks together for cheers.

Bernard stepped off the stage and came around to the table, just in front of the stage, that was reserved for the band. He reached out and pulled Tilly close, hugging her and speaking gently in her ear. He said, 'I need to hug you, Tilly. Your version of Gypsy was amazing, you know. Thank you for being up on stage with us; that was incredible. It was a memorable moment for me, thank you.'

'Thanks, Bernard, it's a special song for me. It's one of my all-time favourites. It's probably the only song I feel comfortable playing anywhere, anytime. I know it off by heart. It's a Macallan thing. My mum loves Stevie Nicks. You know my middle name is Rhiannon, right? Did I ever tell you that? It's because of the Fleetwood Mac song? So embarrassing, really. Matilda Rhiannon Macallan. It's such a mouthful, Matilda, so old-fashioned, Rhiannon, so 80s, and Macallan, so Scottish. I love that people just know me as Tilly. It makes life so much easier.'

Bernard and Tilly sat at the table together as Bernard took a long, thirst-quenching sip of his beer. The other band members sat down, too, enjoying a quick break.

Bernard couldn't help but say something that had been on his mind. 'Sorry to change the conversation, Matilda Rhiannon Macallan. This might seem completely off-tangent and weird, but I must tell you this.'

Tilly replied, intrigued by what Bernard might say. 'Go ahead, what's up?'

'I don't want to change the vibe of the conversation here, and for that reason, I wasn't sure if I should say something, but that bus driver guy, Glenn, did he seem a little strange to you?' Tilly turned her head and lifted one eyebrow, showing that she was reflecting on her feelings about this Glenn guy. Bernard continued as he tried to explain what he was feeling. 'I couldn't put my finger on it. He was just a little creepy somehow, too friendly, or something? Did you feel that too?'

Tilly tilted her head sideways in the other direction with a deep questioning look, not just a reflection, but more of a deeper thought this time. 'I got a bit of an ick. There was something strange about him, but I couldn't put my finger on it either.'

Bernard continued to add to the conversation. 'I noticed he bought you a drink.'

Tilly was amazed that Bernard had paid attention to what was happening in the audience while working hard on stage. 'Yeah, did you see that? He bought me a drink, and I didn't drink it. I'm glad you said something because I thought it was just me being unfriendly. There is something not right about him. He was stalkerish or murderish or something.'

Bernard continued, 'I mean, he might just be really friendly, but I saw him watching you, and then he came over to you with the drink. It was just a little creepy. When you left the room, I saw him put something in your drink.'

'Really?' Tilly was shocked because she was such a trusting person. She wouldn't think something like that would happen.

'Yep, I don't know for sure. I watched the whole thing when he came and talked to you, and he was in your face. I'm certain he put something in your drink as you walked away.'

'It's still sitting there on the table. I should get it and put it in the bin before someone drinks it.' Suddenly, Tilly was concerned. She got up immediately and walked to the table where the West Coast Cooler was still placed near the empty beer bottle. She looked around, expecting to see Glenn watching to see if anyone had drunk the deserted drink. She couldn't see him anywhere. She thought about saying something to the people behind the bar, but she didn't have the time for that. They were about to start their second set on stage. Instead, Tilly poured the total amount of liquid into a big pot plant and returned the empty bottle to the bar. She returned to the table where Bernard was sitting.

A few random guests had come over to say hello and were getting autographs from the band members. Even though they weren't "famous," they were on the way to being a bit more than just a local pub band. Bernard was delightful to his fans, and Tilly gave him space to interact with them. The rest of the band members were also getting their fair share of attention. It was nice, a friendly interaction of people appreciating musical talent and wanting to be part of the experience for whatever reasons they had. Some were into the bass guitarist and his unique skills. Some were into the drummer. He was highly talented. Some were into the lead guitarist; he was a cutie, and some were all about Bernard and his unique, genuine Aussie way. The fans wanted to acknowledge the band's early fame because these guys had talent. Powderfinger, this new Aussie band from Brisbane, was going places.

The band had spent some time interacting with the fans and then excused themselves to get back on stage for the next set.

As Bernard stood up to make his way to the stage, he looked back as Tilly was still sitting at the table. He said to her, 'Come on, girl, you're up.'

Tilly smiled and replied, 'I am?'

Bernard reached out his hand and signalled for her to hold it as he encouraged her back on stage. 'You are.'

Tilly had already thought about the song she wanted to sing with them. 'I have a song in mind if you guys can cover it.'

Bernard questioned, 'We can do our best; what is it?'

As Tilly and Bernard stepped onto the stage, they manoeuvred around the instruments carefully placed on their stands. Bernard was still holding her hand. 'I would love to sing Cyndi Lauper's Time After Time. Can you play it?'

'Hell, yes, we can! Good choice, Tilly. It's a beautiful song, and your voice will nail it.' Bernard let go of Tilly's hand as she stepped towards the microphone, and Bernard stepped away to grab hold of his guitar. 'Do you want me to back you up, or do you want to sing solo?' Bernard questioned, allowing Tilly to sing alone or duet with him.

Tilly was nervous and excited at the same time. She had performed this song so many times, but always alone. 'I would love it if you would sing with me. Let's wing it and see how it turns out.' She trusted Bernard could match and harmonise with her vocals. He was talented like that.

Bernard turned to the band members and said, 'We can do Time After Time, right? C, G, D, Em.'

John gave a confident reply. 'Yep, we got this.' Ian nodded, and Jon gave a thumbs up. Darren adjusted the shoulder strap on his guitar and gently strummed the song's rhythm. The crowd instantly gave a cheer. They could recognise the song straight away. Everyone knew this beautiful, heartfelt song. It had been around for a decade, and it was one of those songs that everyone knew all the words to.

Tilly announced nervously through the microphone, 'Oh, you know this one, do you? Sing along with us. We've never played this song together, so we might need your help.'

Bernard joined in on the lead guitar, keeping in time with the rhythm that Darren had set. He allowed Tilly to sing the first verse, adoring and admiring her beauty as she crooned into the microphone, making eye contact with a few lucky people in the crowd as she did so.

'*Lying in my bed, I hear the clock tick and think of you.*'

Her voice sounded beautiful as she put her unique style of vocals heavily into the lyrics. She curled her tongue in the back of her throat as she gently rolled the words out of her mouth in a slightly higher pitch to the guitar melody.

chapter seventy-seven

Agnes

The fun vibe continued as Dalton, Tom, Richie, Cody, Sunny, and the three American/Hawaiian girls had more drinks, listened to music, and talked until Shawn finally closed the bar at midnight and asked them to be on their way.

It wasn't much of a walk to Tom and Richie's. They were ready for the after-party. The only consideration was that they needed to be respectful to Agnes. Their backyard den was separate from the house where Agnes slept, so they often had an after-party, but they were always aware that they needed to keep the music down. As long as they played some chilled-out music and her favourite song, '*Shine On You Crazy Diamond*,' by Pink Floyd, Agnes never complained. She was a peace-loving soul with a youthful heart.

Tom and Richie felt Agnes was probably inside the house partying alone, enjoying the modern music, but not interfering with their fun. She would leave them to party on, just as they should be. She never complained, not once. Agnes could always catch up on her sleep at any time of the day, with a veranda siesta in her rocking chair.

She didn't want an invitation to the parties; that would just be weird, but it didn't bother her that the boys had after-parties. Her entire philosophy of life was about living and enjoying moments. She loved that Tom and Richie would sometimes invite people to their den and have some fun in their lives. They were both young and single, and she wanted them to find their person someday. It didn't seem right to her that two men would live together and spend their entire young adult lives looking for waves. Back in her day, they would have been married off by now, working and supporting their own family. She understood it, though; life was different these days. Very different. She respected that.

Agnes had her own life story and grew up in a different generation with a vastly different way of life. She had grown up during the war. She married young, and her husband was absent, always off fighting to serve the country. They had three children, and she was pretty much a single parent, although her husband was a dedicated financial provider. He sent her money for her to look after the family adequately. She was the nurturer. She didn't work. Keeping the household and raising her three boys was a full-time job. Most of the society functioned this way. The men went off to war, and the women were the home-keepers. That's the way it was.

As time moved on, Agnes' sons all married young and moved out of home, leaving her in an empty nest. Agnes' husband, Harry, was killed in the war in Vietnam. Agnes had stayed in the same house all the boys had grown up in. She had some memories there. The house was home to her three sons, who would still visit on random occasions to make sure she was happy. She was quite an independent soul, and did most things herself, other than Tom and Richie giving her a hand with heavy things now and then. She was extremely capable of looking after herself. She didn't plan to move anywhere else and was happy having the company of Tom and Richie, who had shared the den in the backyard for a few years now.

She loved having the lads, Tom and Richie, living there more than she was ever bothered by some late-night music.

chapter seventy-eight

Just For Fun

As Tilly finished the song, repeating, *Time After Time, Time After Time, Time After Time, It's okay, Time After Time.* The crowd clapped and cheered, and she took a shallow bow, saying, 'Thank you, thank you so much.'

Bernard lifted his hands to clap them high above his guitar. 'Let's give it up for Tilly Macallan. She's come all the way from Angourie, in New South Wales. We are so blessed to have her here joining us on stage tonight.'

Tilly blushed as the crowd cheered and clapped. Bernard was in awe of her relaxed and natural beauty, as she was so humble and grateful for the crowd's appreciation.

Bernard added as the crowd continued to clap. 'Isn't she beautiful?'

Tilly wasn't sure what to do next, and Bernard could feel her nervous tension. To save her from feeling awkward, he suggested they perform another cover, and he asked Tilly if she would stay on stage to help him out. 'Can you please help me out with this one, Tilly?' Bernard turned towards the band. 'Can we do Crowded House, Distant Sun?' This time, it was a popular Crowded House song, another soft and gentle song everyone could sing along to.

Bernard strummed, and Tilly instantly felt nervous, as she wasn't sure if she even knew the chorus, let alone the verse lyrics. She gave a worried look to Bernard, and he nodded at her and lifted his brow and chin as if to say silently, *it's okay; you'll know it.*

He started with the first line, and as he sang, he directed the lyrics to Tilly. She smiled at him as he sang. *'Tell me all the things you would change; I don't pretend to know what you want.'*

Tilly relaxed into the moment, admiring Bernard and the boys do their stuff. It was brilliant. These boys were all individually talented, and their skills combined magnificently. She didn't need to be the main character here; she was the backup, and there was no pressure for her to sing at all. She could add some 'oohs and aahs' if she wanted to or just sit and enjoy the music being performed beside her. The crowd sang along when the chorus came in, and the lyrics came to Tilly like a slow volcano.

As the song finished, Tilly stepped down from the stage and sat at the reserved table at the very front. Tilly wanted to give the boys the room to perform their own music with its unique sound. She wasn't part of this. She had never heard these songs, as the band was beginning their music career. Tilly knew Bernard would ask if he wanted her to join them on stage again. He knew her well enough now to know what songs she liked and knew. The day they had spent together exploring the Gold Coast Hinterland was all about them sharing their music preferences. Bernard also knew Tilly's lyrical style now, and he knew what songs would match her unique voice.

The crowd continued to give joy and appreciation throughout the evening, and the band gave gratitude at every opportunity to thank the audience. The room was filled with brilliant energy. As the night continued, the volume level of the crowd chatter increased as people consumed more alcohol. The social inhibition diminished, and suddenly, everyone was friends with everyone. The music sent a vibration of harmony and good feels throughout the crowd. Once the band had finished their third set, they kept the energy flowing by directing a playlist of rock songs through the PA system. Bernard had made a special CD for this exact moment, as he felt it was important that the music didn't just stop once they had stopped performing. The band packed up, leaving the music playing until the crowd had dispersed and moved on.

They were in Surfers Paradise, and the young crowd moved into Cavill Avenue, where the nightclubs played dance music until 3 am.

After the band had packed up, Tilly and the boys sat and chatted, enjoying a quiet drink and discussing how they thought the night went. An informal reflection of what songs worked with the crowd and what songs they felt didn't go so well. The favourite for all of them was 'Time After Time.'

The band were all grateful for Tilly's contribution as the only girl on stage, which had created a different dynamic from what they were used to. Bernard asked again. 'Tilly, I hope you will come and sing with us on stage for our big show at the Surfers Paradise Surf Club on Saturday night. Even if just for one song, as a special guest. We would really love it if you would.' The boys all nodded in agreement.

Tilly held up her glass and announced a new cheer. 'Just for fun.' They all joined in, repeating her words. 'Just for fun.'

chapter seventy-nine

The After-Party

The gang arrived at the den, and Tom took charge of the music. He put five CDs in the stacker and pressed shuffle. Oasis, REM, Pearl Jam, Nirvana, and Pink Floyd for Agnes. They had purchased a few roadies before leaving the Coolangatta Hotel, and Richie had a stash of Lemon Ruskis and Woodstock Bourbon in the fridge.

The boys had set up an old pool table with old couches and a bar in their lounge room. It was the perfect set-up for some after-party fun. There was lots of random chatter between the boys and the girls, and the pool table was the centre of attention. They played a game of Kelly Pool, which meant everyone was involved. The rules were simple. Every player was given a number that indicated their corresponding ball. The idea of the game was to sink your own ball before anyone else did. If you could sink your own ball, you won the game. If someone else sunk your ball, you were out of the game. As soon as a player sunk their own ball, the game was over, but the trick was not to let anyone else know the identity of your ball; otherwise, they would try to sink that ball to get you out of the game. It was fun, and it included everyone, up to fifteen players.

Dalton was still in fine form; it hadn't been too long since his last few pool games at the Byron Bay Beach Hotel just a few nights ago. On his second turn with the cue, he potted five balls, including his own, to win the game. Many other balls had already been pocketed, but he cleared the rest of the table, and they began a new game. This time Dalton sat out, choosing instead to chat with Cody, who wasn't interested in the game too much. He was more interested in the collection of CDs in the three full racks lined up along the wall, and he was picking out some of his favourites to place in the stacker. Dalton was interested in hearing more about Cody's soul-surfing philosophy. Cody was an experienced and passionate surfer, and it was a massive part of his daily life. It was almost like he lived and breathed surfing for the pure enjoyment of it. He had no intention of making money from his skills, and he would never enter a competition like the Billabong Pro. That went against every moral that he adopted. Dalton had to be the peacemaker a few times as Sunny and Cody were getting into heated discussions about surfing, and Dalton was trying to maintain the party's vibe.

Tom, Richie and the girls continued to play Kelly Pool, and Tom was keen to give them all some professional lessons about the topspin, backspin, and angles of the pool table. Richie played it cool, singing and chatting to the girls and trying to keep Sunny out of the conversation with Cody. The last thing they wanted was any kind of alcohol-induced arguments from taking place to ruin the night.

Cody had been through the entire CD collection and placed a bunch of CDs beside the player in a collection for playing next. He had taken on the role of a DJ for the night and was doing a great job. Everyone was happy with the music that he was playing—one classic hit after another, the best of the best.

Time was ticking on into the early hours of the morning. Dalton and Cody shared many stories about their lives and music interests, and they spontaneously decided to go for a very early morning surf. The sun wasn't even rising yet. It was 3 am. It was more of a night surf and even more dangerous. Cody was keen to share his surfing passion with Dalton and show him first-hand what soul surfing felt like. Dalton had never been for a night surf before, so it was a first-time experience. Cody had explained that the philosophy of soul-surfing was all about the intimate connection with nature—the desire to be out of your comfort zone but completely trusting your soul with the powerful force of the ocean. Cody had surfed in this area frequently. He knew the layout of the rock shelf of Snapper and the perfect location to catch a long ride from Rainbow Bay all the way around to Greenmount. This part of the coastline was his favourite stretch on the entire east coast of Australia. He had surfed in Bells Beach, way down south, almost as far south as you can go in Australia and across the Bass Strait from Tasmania. Bells Beach was a favoured location for all surfers if they ever got the chance to visit.

There was something special about the stretch of surf breaks from Duranbah to Greenmount. It provided various conditions for all levels of surfer, from amateur to pro. Cody had surfed all the breaks many times; he knew the danger spots, so he wasn't concerned about taking Dalton, a confident beginner, for a night surf.

Dalton and Cody tried to convince Tom, Richie, Sunny and the three girls to come along as well, but they all rejected the offer, deciding to catch up on a few hours of "sleep."

In the den, Tom and Richie had their own bedroom. There was also a spare room and a few sofa beds for friends to crash out on. The sleeping arrangements were very loose.

By the time Dalton and Cody had borrowed some wetsuits and a surfboard each from Tom and Richie's extensive collection in the garage, it seemed that loose sleeping arrangements had been made. Tom and Richie had decided they might share the love for the night, and Sunny had matched up with one of the Hawaiian girls and disappeared into the spare room. They left the house with the music on shuffle and repeat to muffle any bedroom noises. Everyone was happy with how the night had panned out.

Dalton and Cody, strangers to each other and strangers to Tom and Richie were trotting across the road with a surfboard each, eager to experience the beginning of this brand-new day together.

chapter eighty

Soul Surfing

Dalton and Cody were sneaking out across the road with a surfboard each tucked under their arms. They borrowed the boards from Tom and Richie's quiver. Cody was on a mission, knowing exactly where he would hit the water at Snapper Rocks just in front of the Rainbow Bay Surf Club. He had surfed this particular break many times over the past few years. It was a well-known surf break and the beginning section of the man-made Superbank, which extended from Snapper Rocks Point through Rainbow Bay, Greenmount Point, Coolangatta Beach and Kirra. The entire bank extended over two kilometres, and it was possible to catch extremely long rides with optimal swell and wind conditions in your favour. Snapper was always a challenging yet very popular surf break. It wasn't very popular right now, though. There was not a soul in sight. It was still dark. The moon was high in the sky, drifting across the ocean towards the west. The waves were crashing loudly, but there was no other noise around, no traffic, no people, no early morning bird noises, yet. The world was still asleep. The night silence made the sound of the crashing waves seem tenfold louder. The light of the moon glinting on the crest of the waves was magical, giving the white water a fluorescent glow.

Cody made a comment to explain his ocean philosophy to Dalton. 'The ocean is inviting us in, man. Do you feel it? The waves get lonely at night, and they crave our company. Can you feel the ocean pulling you in closer?'

Dalton thought it was quite a strange thing to say, but he also appreciated Cody's alternative way of thinking. It could be true that the ocean came to play with us, craving our company and energy, just as humans craved the ocean for the feeling of cleansing and revitalising our bodies' energies. 'I've never thought about the ocean like that, but maybe you are right, man. I do feel like I'm being pulled in, that is for sure.' He laughed gently, not trying to be sarcastic because Cody was deadly serious, but he felt they were in a rip and being pulled out by the outgoing tide.

Cody also felt the rip in an undertow on his lower body. 'We can use this rip to take us out the back, man. It'll save us a lot of duck diving, and then we will have more energy to pick and choose our waves. Are you okay with that?' Cody ensured Dalton felt okay with a bit of risk, making the adventure easier.

Dalton wasn't as experienced in the surf as Cody, the soul surfer, but he understood Cody had heaps of experience in this location and wouldn't put Dalton in unnecessary danger. Dalton replied with some hesitation, 'Yeah, I'm okay with that. We often use the rip to help us get out the back quicker. I trust you, man; you know this ocean, right?'

Cody called back, raising an arm above his head as the ocean dragged him away. 'Like the back of my hand, Dalton.' Cody reassured Dalton that they were safe by confidently responding. He held his hand above his head and then pointed out the back. As he placed his hand back into the water, he paddled out through the breakers.

Dalton followed as closely as he could.

It was a beautiful night. The waves were powerful and surging enough to give a long ride, but gentle and inviting for a smooth entrance onto the wave, with no need for extensive paddling.

They both duck-dived through a set of messy breakers. Some were probably smooth enough to catch, but the time between the waves was not long enough to give Cody or Dalton a suitable position to paddle onto the crest. It took a bit of an effort to get further out the back, and there they were, now in the perfect spot for some waves to emerge for them. It was just a matter of choosing the right one. They patiently waited and talked. They could see in the distance a large, smooth set rolling in. This was going to be good.

A few waves crashed overhead as they duck-dived into the first few of the set. Dalton emerged from under the wave break to see Cody paddling onto an epic crested wave. He was off. The moonlight glistened as Cody carved back and forth on the front surface of the wave as he made his way to shore. Dalton felt a little intimidated out in the deep, dark ocean all by himself. He calmed himself down, taking a few deep, relaxing breaths, as he saw a perfect wave growing as it rolled towards him. The wave was ready to break in the perfect spot where he had started paddling. The next moment, he felt a surge from underneath him as he pushed himself up to stand on his board. He had never surfed on a board like this before. It felt amazing. He was balanced, and his legs felt strong as the wave picked him up and took him for the longest ride he had ever experienced, all the way to shore. Yep, this was an invigorating feeling. He let out a loud 'Yeeeeew!' And Cody echoed back with a shrill 'Yeeeeew!' And then, 'Yeyah Brother! You're soul-surfing.'

Cody waited on the shoreline for Dalton to come all the way to shore. They walked back together along the beach. The soft light of the sun was emerging on the horizon. The stars were still glimmering, and the atmosphere was magical. Dalton adjusted the leg strap of his board into a more comfortable position around his ankle and then looked up ahead of him, along the stretch of beach, heading back towards Snapper Rocks. He realised just how amazing the scene was in front of him, and he was taking it all in with all his senses. The sound of the waves crashing and rolling into the shore, the smell of the salty air, the harsh feel of the cold ocean on his skin, the taste of the saltwater in his mouth. He said to Cody, 'Wow, I've never realised how amazing this time of the day is, and the sad thing is that few people ever experience this. I mean, most of the world is asleep right now.'

Cody replied, 'So you get me now? The ocean and mother nature should be appreciated and respected. I feel the connection deep in my soul. Surfing should not be something that people become wealthy from. It doesn't seem right to me. Other than purchasing our boards, we don't pay for the experiences that nature provides us every single day, so the way I think about it is this. We don't have a right to be paid to surf because how can we pay back Mother Nature and the ocean for the experience she provides us?'

Dalton created footsteps along the water's edge as he thought about Cody's deep philosophy. 'I get it, man. It's not something I've ever really thought about because I surf, just because I love the freedom of the ocean and the feeling of adrenaline when I ride the waves. I've never thought so deeply about the commercialisation of such a free sport, but you have a valid point. I guess for me, I'm a natural soul surfer because I'm not talented enough to get paid to surf.' He laughed out loud.

Cody laughed, too. 'You've got some talent, man, considering you've only been surfing for a little while. You are a natural, that is for sure.'

'Well, honestly, it's been a little over a year now. When I left Deniliquin, I headed straight to the East Coast. I lived around Sydney and the North Shore for about a year and then started surfing my way North. It's all a blur to me now; surfing, playing music, and grieving is what I did as I fucked up my way through a tough time in my life. I was on a destructive path, to be honest, until I ended up somehow in a little place called Angourie, about three hours south of here. Ever heard of it? Oh, and then I fucked it up again.'

'Angourie? No mate, I can't say I have heard of it. But I'm hearing you. Surfing, grieving, playing music and fucking your way through life. I can relate to all that, except I don't play an instrument. I always wish I had learned to play the guitar, to sit around a campfire and keep myself company. I am a bit of a loner, to be honest. A wild, untamed lion, wild and free and adventurous. The king of my jungle. I have a reason, though. I lost my very first true love in a stupid car accident, and ever since, I've been kind of reckless, with no respect for life, really. I ride motorbikes without the respect they deserve. I surf without giving the ocean the respect it deserves, and I most definitely don't treat women with the respect they deserve.'

Dalton didn't know what to say. Cody had joined their group late in the evening and was a man of very few words, so Dalton knew little about Cody besides that he looked like Tarzan, loved to surf, and had great taste in music. At this moment, everything made sense about why he was the way he was. Quiet, melancholy, yet hard and wild. 'Wow, man. I'm so sorry to hear that. We have a lot in common, it seems.'

'True, man? I'm sorry for you too.' Cody was trying to figure out which part Dalton referred to as "a lot in common." Other than the surfing and fucking, he could only assume that Dalton had also lost a girlfriend in a car accident, as he wasn't brave enough to ask for details.

'It is what it is, man.' Dalton replied with a brief response. He didn't delve any deeper into their conversation just yet, as they had reached the section of beach where Cody and Dalton would enter the water again to catch the rip out past the breakers.

'True, it is what it is.' Cody also kept his response brief as they re-entered the water, ready to take on the incoming waves.

Dalton and Cody talked and surfed over the next few hours, slowly watching the sunrise on the horizon. It was magical. First, the gentle sunlight brought a pink and orange haze over the ocean. As the sun rose, a circular crescent appeared slowly, way out on the divisional line of the horizon, dissecting the ocean and the sky. The orange light increased intensely as the sun moved upwards, so much so that it was hard to look at without glinting. Somehow, it looked like the sun was burning the ocean, like a rising fire. The hues of orange and gold scattered the sky as the ocean turned to a shimmer of silver and gold.

It seemed like a well-planned symphony of nature. As the sun rose steadily, creating a backdrop on the ocean, the bird noises increased, coinciding with the hum of early morning traffic. The waves seemed to quieten, allowing the other noises of nature and humanity to have their turn for the day.

The morning surfers entered the water to start their daily rituals, all sharing a brief hello, a wave, or a head nod as they shared the ocean. Cody called it, and Dalton was happy to follow his lead. 'I'm catching the next one and calling it a morning. Have you had enough, Dalton?'

Dalton replied in agreement. 'Yeah, man. I'm completely satisfied. I'm happy to call it a day.'

They laughed together as Cody paddled solid and hard to catch the surge of the incoming wave now right upon them. Dalton did the same, and they surfed in together. Dalton made sure he didn't get in Cody's line.

'A nice party wave for two. Good call, Dalton.' shouted Cody. Cody was impressed with Dalton's control over his board, not to snake him out.

As they reached the shallows, they unleashed their ankle straps to make walking the short distance back to the den easier.

Cody pointed out some celebrity surfers who must have been here for the Billabong Pro. They were most likely having a bit of practice before the big day, testing the waters, and adjusting to the Australian conditions. The comp was just a few days ahead. Dalton suggested they sit and watch the newly arriving surfers for a while.

Cody recognised Munga, Donovan, Tom Carroll, and Grant Frost. Kelly Slater had arrived, too, and was just entering the water. There was a lot of talk about Kelly Slater. He had won the event in 1992 and was the favourite to take out the championship again for the 1994 Billabong Pro.

As the lads sat and talked, most of the conversation was about analysing the styles and techniques of the pros. Cody was adamant that he was opposed to making money from surfing, but he admired the skills of the professional surfers all the same. They sat and watched and analysed, with just a few words spoken, for quite a while.

Dalton finally edged in with a question he had wanted to ask for some time now. 'Hey man, I've been dying to ask if you're okay to talk about it; if not, that's okay too, but you mentioned before that you had lost your girl in a car accident. Do you want to talk about it?'

'Yeah, we can talk about it. I tend to keep it all bottled up and close to my heart, but you said you thought we had something in common.' Cody was ready to share, but he wanted to know more about Dalton's story before sharing his dark secret that he didn't talk about with anyone. Cody asked with a softness in his deep voice. 'Did you lose your girl in a car accident, too?'

Dalton could feel a huge lump rise instantly in his throat. 'I did, just over a year ago.'

Cody replied softly. 'Ah, sorry to hear that. Well, I can tell you it doesn't get any easier. My beautiful girl, Louisa, passed away four years ago. It was horrific. She was driving home from work; she was always working. She was such a good person. She was everything: smart, funny, kind, and she had a banging body and the most beautiful angelic face I've ever dreamed of.'

Dalton nodded, raising an eyebrow at the depth and detail that Cody was sharing.

Cody continued. 'She was driving home from work one night, she had been working late, some drunken idiot ran a red light and took her out, cleaned her up, directly into a telegraph pole. The car was unrecognisable, and I guess as horrible as it sounds, she was unrecognisable as well. She died on impact, they say. It's supposed to make me feel better to know that she didn't suffer any pain.'

Dalton spoke softly and deeply as he shrugged his shoulders and shook involuntarily. 'Wow, that gives me chills down my spine. I'm so sorry for the loss of your beautiful woman. She sounds amazing.'

Cody wasn't finished yet; he had more to say, and Dalton encouraged him to continue, listening intently as Cody spoke. 'I think about her every day: when I wake up, surf, go to sleep, in my dreams, when I hear certain songs. She loved music. She would have loved watching you play your guitar, man. She's with me everywhere I go. She's in my heart. No one in this world could be anything like her. She was everything to me. She was my special one.' Cody realised he was rambling, and he stopped himself. 'Yeah, anyway, that's my story, man. What about you?'

'I'm so sorry, Cody, that's a horrific trauma that you have to carry with you. It seems we are very much alike, as my story is similar to yours. Perhaps not as traumatic.' Dalton paused, wondering whether he should share his story and how much detail he should give, not wanting to take away from Cody's emotion at that moment.

Cody urged him to continue. 'Please, Dalton, I'd love to hear your story if you don't mind sharing it with me.'

Dalton tripped back in his mind, creating images of his dark secret. He wanted to share his story without getting too emotional. 'Sure, I'd love to share with you. It's quite ironic that our stories are closely matched. My very first true love, Chelsea, and I were both so in love with each other. She was a few years younger than me and still in high school, her senior year. Smalltown gossip and all that, apparently, I wasn't enough for her, "just a musician."' He raised his hands in the air, giving quotation mark signs with his fingers, on both hands, around the words "just a musician." 'Chelsea's parents forbid her to see me. It was tough. That might seem enough of a story to say our relationship ended, but that's not how it happened. Our relationship didn't end like that.' Cody narrowed his brow, wondering what more had gone wrong for Dalton.

'Like Romeo and Juliet, being in a forbidden love relationship would be horrible, but please go on, there was a car accident?' enquired Cody.

'Yeah!' Dalton took a deep breath. 'As rebellious youths in love, we went behind Chelsea's parents' backs and continued seeing each other as much as we could, which was rarely. They had her under lock and key. Chelsea snuck out one night. She met me by the river, and we had a romantic picnic. I asked her to marry me when she was old enough. She said yes.' Dalton paused, taking a moment to breathe, before he continued with the story.

Cody didn't take his eyes off Dalton, listening to the emotion and the love in his heart that was being expressed as he spoke about this beautiful girl with whom he was so in love. 'Are you okay? Please tell me more.'

Dalton nodded. 'We had a magical night and made love under the stars for the first time. I was her first. She wasn't mine; I'd been with other girls, but she was my special one. Making love was so beautiful with her. Anyway, on her way home, driving along the dusty country road just past my driveway, she hit a kangaroo. I heard the crash and went straight to the scene. She was killed instantly, just like your Louisa was. I know this because I was the first person on the scene to find her. She was gone!' Dalton was holding back tears that welled up in his eyes. A few tears escaped, rolling down his cheeks, and he wiped them away with the side of his finger across his cheekbone. He continued talking softly as Cody listened, shaking his head in disbelief. 'And yes, they say, it's supposed to make me feel better to know that she died instantly. Like you, man, I'm sure you feel the same. It doesn't make a shit of difference. Gone is gone. The pain is the same for us left here to remember them. I still feel her around me, and she's in my heart forever.'

There was a long silence between the two lads as they listened to the world momentarily, processing the deep conversation they had just shared. They both tuned in to the sounds of crashing waves and the birds chirping in the trees, welcoming the new day. Dalton and Cody turned towards each other simultaneously and gave each other a knowing look. They both nodded at each other with a held-trauma smile.

Cody reflected on their conversation, feeling more connected to his new friend. 'Wow, man, thanks for sharing. That's tough.'

As they both paused again, they momentarily looked out to the ocean as two dolphins arched in synchronicity through the waves in an uncanny moment. They both said out loud at the same time. 'Did you see that?'

They both looked at each other, shaking their heads, and laughed.

Cody, the man of few words, spoke again with such wisdom. 'Nature, huh! We are all so connected. What a beautiful fuckin' world.'

Dalton could feel the connection, too. 'Man, if I had a beer right now, I'd make a special Cheers with you, To Freedom, Friendship and Enough Love to Last Forever.'

Cody replied, leaning in to give Dalton a manly hug. 'Thanks for sharing this moment with me, man.'

Dalton replied. 'Same to you. It's been an amazing night and morning. I'm not tired at all. I'm just appreciating this moment right now. We only live once, huh!'

'We sure fuckin' do. Excuse my disgusting French. Some people don't get life, huh? I've realised in losing Louisa that sometimes it takes death to make someone truly appreciate life. Seems ironic, huh?'

Dalton replied, agreeing with Cody. 'I know, I know, just look around at this beautiful world; as much as it can be so tough, it's also beautiful if you let it be.'

Cody nodded as he got up, wiping the sand from his hands before grabbing his surfboard. 'Those dolphins, man? That was unbelievable, huh?'

Dalton also stood up while continuing the deep conversation. 'Synchronicity, that's what I call it. It's such a beautiful and powerful concept, and it's all around us all the time, but as humans, we have to look for it and notice the signs. Everything in life is a flow, and everything and everyone is connected. The directions we take depend on our strength to be resilient, matched with our softness to keep moving forward, not allowing the world to harden us. That's what I believe. That's my "soul surfing" philosophy.'

Cody smiled his cheeky soul surfer smile, and Dalton knew, before he spoke, that he would say something humorous and light-hearted. 'Let's see if we can find a breaky beer back at the den, for that Cheers to Freedom, Friendship, and Enough Love to Last Forever.'

Dalton smiled back. 'That sounds like a perfect soul surfer kind of plan.'

chapter eighty-one

The Waitress—Maddi

Tilly woke early and headed down to the beach for a morning swim and to get herself some breakfast somewhere. She enjoyed a beach walk and finished with a splash in the shallows. She couldn't get fully in for a swim because of her arm cast.

She had seen the sign for the Big Breakfast at the Surfers Paradise Surf Club, and she thought it might be an opportunity to check out the venue to imagine where she might perform on stage on the weekend. Tilly was a visual thinker, and it helped her visualise herself on stage to remove some of her nervousness about being on stage with Powderfinger. She rarely got nervous about performances, but this was slightly different. These guys were talented; she was just a small, insignificant, beach-town musician.

In the discussion about Tilly performing on stage with them, they had decided they would just call her up from the audience and get her to sing one song, "Gypsy", of course. They would make it very impromptu, so the audience felt like they were a part of the act and connected. Tilly would have to be in the front row to get called on stage. Security would be there to help her through the stage barriers. It would not be a wild gig; it was general admission and standing only. She was only worried about her arm getting bumped, but it was in a cast and protected, so it should be okay. Tilly didn't need a guitar; they would be the musicians. She couldn't strum anyway with her broken arm. She would just sing. Easy.

She made her way up the Surf Club stairs and found an empty table on the balcony. She couldn't quite believe her luck when the only empty table was Table 26. A young couple had just finished breakfast and were walking out as a young waitress cleaned the table. Tilly asked the waitress politely. 'Hello, should I just sit down or wait to be seated? No one was at the entry, so I just walked in.'

The young waitress replied as she filled her arms with plates and cutlery. 'Sure, you can sit here; you're all good, no stress. I'll just clean up the rest of the table for you and get you a menu.'

Tilly quickly replied, as she could see the girl was very busy. 'Um, no menu needed. I know exactly what I want.'

The waitress nodded. 'I'll be back in a jiffy to take your order. Just let me get this mess back to the kitchen.'

'No rush, I'm in no rush.' Tilly looked around the restaurant, feeling a bit like she was at home in her Angourie café. The venue was nothing like the Angourie Local, but it was the noise of people eating and chatting, some gentle music in the background, and an ocean breeze. This ocean view was a little different from Angourie. There were crowds on the beach, traffic on the road below the balcony, and people everywhere. *This place must make a killing of an income.* Tilly observed that every table was full, and people were still walking in, off the street; it was only 8 am.

Tilly enjoyed her Big Breakfast, Caramel Latte and the complimentary jug of ice-cold water. It was just what she needed after days and nights of social drinks.

Once she had finished her meal and an hour of people-watching, Tilly asked the waitress who she could talk to about having a quick look at their entertainment venue where the bands performed.

The waitress was very helpful in giving Tilly simple instructions. 'If you go downstairs to the ticketing area, our events coordinator will help you. Her name is Rhonda. If you get her in a good mood, she's delightful, and she'll be on for a chat like she's known you forever. Otherwise, um, look out.'

Tilly laughed and queried. 'Oh, okay, thanks for the tip. How do I know if she's in a good mood?'

The waitress shrugged her shoulders, saying, 'Ummm, it's just luck, really.' She laughed.

'Okay, wish me luck then.' Tilly smiled.

'Nah, she's usually okay. She's just one of those people you don't want to catch in a bad mood, especially if she's hangry. That's why she likes me, because I bring her food.' The waitress laughed again.

'Okay, thanks for the heads up, and thank you so much. The food was amazing. Delicious! Compliments to the chef.' Tilly moved aside so the waitress could clear the empty plates and cutlery.

The waitress smiled. 'I'll let the chef know.' The waitress added, 'Can I ask a nosy question?'

Tilly tilted her head, wondering what the nosy question could be. 'Sure, go ahead.'

The waitress asked, still holding the dirty plate, cutlery and empty jug, making sure the serviette didn't fall off as it was near the edge of the plate. 'Why do you want to see the entertainment venue? Are you a performer?'

Tilly humbly answered. 'Well, I am, but not from here. I perform local small-town gigs in New South Wales, but Powderfinger has invited me to perform a song with them; they are playing here on Saturday night.'

The waitress felt rude to ask, but she was being honest. 'I saw the sign for them, but I've never heard of them. Are they good?'

Tilly replied with a gentle smile. 'Well. I had never heard of them either until about a week ago. I met them on the train on the way up here. They are actually really, really talented and down to earth. I guess they are not super famous.' Tilly paused, then added. 'Yet.'

The waitress was excited to hear about them. 'Well, I am working in the bar during the concert on Saturday night. I guess I'll see them perform, and I'll see you then.'

'I guess you will.' Tilly reached out her hand to introduce herself, then realised the girl was balancing plates and an empty jug.

'Oh, sorry, you've got your hands full. Anyway, my name is Matilda. People call me Tilly, and it's really nice to meet you.'

'Hmm, my name is Madison, but people call me Maddi. Nice to meet you, too. I should get back to work; otherwise, the boss will get me in trouble. I always get side-tracked talking to people.'

'Nothing wrong with that; if the customers are happy, they will always return. I appreciate the small-town vibes in the big towns. It's nice to not just feel like a number. I'll see you Saturday when I order a stiff drink at your bar to settle my nerves. Make sure you make it a strong one.'

'Ha ha! I'm sure you will be fine; see you then.'

Tilly grabbed her shoulder bag and headed downstairs to find the lovely Rhonda.

chapter eighty-two

Big Breakfast at the Den

Dalton and Cody were still a couple of hundred meters from the den when they caught the wafting smell of bacon and eggs for breakfast.

Cody commented first. 'Can you smell that?'

Dalton quickly replied, 'Oh my goodness, yumm! Bacon and eggs for breakfast.'

Cody replied. 'Who on earth is up this early cooking bacon and eggs?'

Much to their surprise, as they got closer to the den, they realised Tom and Richie were cooking a big breakfast in the front yard on their flat plate BBQ.

Tom and Richie were possibly still drinking, hadn't slept yet, and were still on a high from the previous evening's shenanigans.

Dalton and Cody smiled at each other as they neared the den. Cody started a jig-jog across the road towards them, excited that Tom and Richie were up and about.

Richie first caught the glimpse out of the corner of his eye, noticing Dalton and Cody crossing the road and heading towards them with their surfboards tucked under their arms. Richie called out, not too loud, aware that the neighbours were still likely sleeping. It was just 6 am. 'Top of the morning to you, fellas.'

They both replied in a duet. 'Top of the morning to you, fellas.'

Cody added. 'What's going on, boys? A BBQ breaky, work up a bit of hunger, did we?' He winked, smiled, and finished with a nod towards the girls lying on a spread of beach towels on the front lawn, soaking up the morning sunshine.

Richie replied. 'We had an awesome night. How about you two? How was the surf?'

Dalton replied first. 'It was spectacular. I will go out on a limb and say it was the best surf ever.'

Cody added. 'The sunrise and the company were second to none.'

Tom spoke for the first time in the conversation. 'That's cool.'

The girls all sat up with interest to see these two strong specimens walking closer with their boards, their bodies still pumped from the surf.

Cody and Dalton leaned their boards up against the garage. Cody asked, 'Is there a hose to rinse these boards off?'

Richie replied, as Tom was busy looking after the food on the BBQ. 'There is a hose just at the back of the den, thanks, man!'

Cody and Dalton looked after the boards straight away, giving them a hose down and returning them to the garage, back to the racks where they had borrowed them from.

Cody commented to Dalton. 'It's such a cool setup, hey? Imagine living across the road from Australia's Superbank, with this many surfboards to choose from. These boys have got it made.'

Dalton added, nodding his head. 'They sure are living their best life.'

Cody threw in a line of judgment. 'The girl thing doesn't interest me. I'd rather be alone and just surf, but that's just me. It gives me the ick to think about how many girls they have brought back here. I wonder what Tom and Richie's body count is?'

Dalton smiled, trying to be non-judgemental because he had been there before. His body count was pretty high, and he didn't want to criticise his new friends, not knowing their whole story. 'To be honest, man, I don't think they keep count. They are just having fun, and good on them, I guess, as long as they are using protection, who cares?'

Cody nodded. 'Yeah, true, each to their own.'

The boys returned to the front lawn, where Tom and Richie served up plates of bacon, eggs, tomatoes, mushrooms, and sausages. It was a total feast.

Tom handed Dalton a full plate. 'Oh, thanks, man, that's exactly what I needed, thank you.' Dalton was so grateful for his new friends, how the night had turned out, and this massive plate of food.

Cody accepted his plateful as well, giving immense gratitude to the boys. 'Thanks, guys, this is amazing, and thanks for an awesome night and the loan of the boards, much appreciated.'

Richie replied, 'No worries, fellas. I'm happy to share the good times with you.'
Tom replied with a mouthful of food. 'That's cool, anytime.'

The girls were quiet, a little sheepish after their night of shenanigans with the boys. They were all very quiet, giggling now and then and grateful for the fantastic breakfast served to them.

Dalton decided he would catch a bus back to Surfers Paradise, as that way he wasn't an inconvenience to anyone. He only had to carry his guitar a short distance back into town, and he knew where the bus station was, as he had already been there when he first arrived on the Gold Coast.

The lads and Cody gave Dalton their contact phone numbers and urged him to keep in contact. As Dalton left, he reminded them he was playing a gig at the Coolangatta Hotel on Sunday and would love to see them all again if they were around.

They all agreed that they would be there, except for Cody. Cody was a little more undecided. 'I might see you, man. I just do my thing, no promises.'

Dalton walked away, giving a smile and a wave. 'Cool, see you all, and thanks so much for the memories.'

chapter eighty-three

The Perfect Plan

'Hey Rhonda, my name is Tilly. I'm sorry to bother you today. I have a strange request.'

Rhonda was not smiling yet, more intrigued by what Tilly would ask. 'How can I help you?'

Tilly asked politely. 'I'm performing with the band Powderfinger. They are playing a gig here on Saturday night, and I know it's an extraordinary request, but would it be okay if I could see the stage area?'

Rhonda pulled her eyebrows together and tilted her head at the question. 'Can I ask why?'

Tilly explained her reason as best she could. 'Well. I don't have anxiety, or I've never had a reason to have anxiety, but I'm feeling extremely nervous already about the weekend.'

Rhonda appeased Tilly. 'It's okay. You don't have to hide your emotions from me. I have full spectrum autism, so I might understand a little about how you feel.'

Tilly tried to explain. 'Well. I'm feeling more nervous than I ever have been in my entire life, and I think it will help me visualise myself in the situation before I'm actually there. I'm super nervous because these guys are really talented, and I don't want to mess it up for them.'

Rhonda was lovely in her reply. 'That is not such a strange request. I've heard far stranger things. Of course, I can show you the stage area. Let me just grab the keys.'

Rhonda and Tilly chatted and walked along the hallway to the backstage entrance.

'I'll take you in this way because it's quicker.' Rhonda opened the backstage door into the darkened room. 'Do you want to come up onto the stage? Is that what you need?'

'That would be awesome. I just wanted to feel the venue and the room's size and feel myself on the stage.' Tilly and Rhonda walked up the stairs and onto the wooden stage.

Rhonda explained a few things as Tilly looked around. Tilly had never performed at a venue like this before. All her performances were at smaller venues or The Angourie Local. She was used to her stage being more simplified. A chair, and a speaker set up in the corner of a busy restaurant or a noisy pub. This venue was a little different. There were spotlights up on the roof and black duct tape on the floor with an X here and an X there. Rhonda stepped onto the central marked X on the stage floor. 'So, depending on how the band wants to set up the stage, this is where you'll be.' She spread her arms wide, gestured to a massive crowd, and said, 'With a full house of fans singing with you.'

Tilly was lost for words.

Rhonda continued. 'We have almost sold out of tickets. There are just a handful of tickets left, and we will have a full house. That's rare for a venue like this. We've never had a sell-out.'

Tilly was excited. 'I had best buy my ticket then.'

'Yep, you better. If you wait much longer, there won't be any left. I've got a few tickets on hold, but I've told the fellow I will sell them if he doesn't pick them up by Thursday afternoon. People can't seem to make a firm decision about anything these days. It does my head in.' Tilly saw the other side of Rhonda coming out gently, not in full force, but she could see she wasn't the type of person who would be a pushover. This was the other side of Rhonda that Maddi was warning Tilly about. Tilly had no idea, of course, that Rhonda was talking about Dalton. He had reserved three extra tickets for Dan, Ariiel, and whoever else needed one, but he hadn't purchased them yet. Indecisive, for a good reason. Dalton did not know what he was doing from one day to the next.

Tilly replied, agreeing with Rhonda. 'I'm sure it is annoying when you are trying to arrange events and people leave their bookings until the last minute. That would be frustrating.'

'It is. I'm pretty sure some people think the universe revolves around them.' Rhonda was getting worked up. This was obviously a trigger for her frustrations at work as an event manager.

Tilly was eager to let Rhonda get back to her ticket booth. 'Well, thank you, Rhonda. I won't take up any more of your time. Thank you for showing me the venue. I'm looking forward to Saturday night.'

Rhonda was smiling but also pushing Tilly hard. 'Why don't you come back with me now, and we can get your ticket sorted out? Otherwise, my girl, you won't be singing on any stage.'

Tilly smiled back. 'Sounds like a perfect plan, Rhonda.'

Tilly and Rhonda went directly back to the reception and ticket sales area. On the way back, Tilly took notice of the posters on the walls this time, as she wasn't in such a nervous headspace. She felt much more at ease about the performance on Saturday night, having seen the venue and the stage where she would be performing. The Powderfinger poster looked good; the boys all looked rock-starish, and Bernard looked exceptionally handsome. She wondered if they employed someone to do the marketing and promotion for them or if they did it all themselves. She hadn't heard them talk about a marketing team, so she figured it was all self-promotion. They had done an excellent job, and she was impressed.

Tilly handed over her last $10 note and made a mental note to herself. *I must get to the bank today. I'm out of cash.* She had a few loose coins in her shoulder bag pockets, but she had spent all her other cash over the past few days on food, drinks, and fun.

Tilly had a full belly from breakfast, and she had quelled her nerves by seeing the stage where she would perform on the weekend. She checked in her wallet and saw that she had her bank card with her. She headed out the front glass swinging door of the Surf Club and took a sharp left to turn down the laneway that would take her to the bank. She had passed it on her way to breakfast and had made a mental note to herself to get cash later in the day. Now that she had paid for breakfast and bought her Powderfinger ticket, she was out of cash. She had no choice but to stop in and replenish her supply of notes for the next few days. She didn't like carrying a lot of cash around, but sometimes, finding an ATM compatible with her independent bank was hard. The bank in Yamba didn't have an ATM yet, so she was used to going into the bank. The bank clerks knew the customers, and it was always a personal experience to catch up with the clerks. Tilly had become close friends with one girl at the Yamba bank. They had gone to high school together and often hung out together, surfing or enjoying beach days on their days off. No matter which ATM she went to, they all charged transaction fees for withdrawals. It was easier to be organised and go into the bank every few days when she needed more cash. Tilly had some decent savings as she had been doing a lot of casual teaching work and a lot of work at the Angourie Local since returning from university. She didn't have a lot of things to spend her money on in Angourie, so it was easy to save up. Tilly was saving for her first car, but there was no rush. She had her license, so she could always borrow a car from Frankie, the twins, or her parents, but she didn't go to many places other than to work here or there.

Tilly opened the bank door, noticing how cool the air-conditioning was and realising again that it was warm outside. This Queensland weather was steamier than her tiny beach town. She liked it; it made her want to go for another swim. She wished she didn't have this silly cast on her arm.

chapter eighty-four

Mr Music

Dalton purchased his bus ticket, a one-way ticket to Surfers Paradise. The bus was due to arrive at 8 am. He found a nice grassy spot under a shady tree while he waited for the bus to arrive. He only needed to wait for twenty minutes. He had timed it perfectly without even knowing the schedule. The lads had informed Dalton that the buses were regular along the east coast strip from Coolangatta to Southport. They were right. The buses were due on the hour; some would make all stops to Southport, and some were going to Brisbane with only a few stops in Broadbeach and Surfers Paradise, the same bus Dalton had caught a few days prior. It didn't matter which bus Dalton caught, as they were all making a stop at the popular Surfers Paradise bus station.

Dalton opened his guitar case, one brass buckle at a time. He wedged it gently open, sliding out his Maton guitar from the caramel-coloured velvet lining, and did a quick manual tune-up. He placed the capo on the third fret and strummed to the tune that reminded him of his favourite girl. He wondered where she could be and if she knew he was looking for her. He knew she was looking for him, maybe, but that didn't help the situation. How would she find him, or how would he find her? Either way, they were both searching for each other. He had a feeling she was in Surfers Paradise somewhere, but exactly where he had no idea, and with a population of thousands, he didn't even have a place to start. The words rolled out of his mouth as he strummed a melodic D chord. *So, I'm back to the velvet underground, back to the floor, that I love. To a room with some lace and paper flowers, back to the gypsy that I was, to the gypsy that I was.*

Dalton played a few songs to fill in some time as he waited for the bus. Just as he was about to pack his guitar away, he remembered he had written a song for Tilly after the first night they spent together. He reflected on the amazing night they shared in the gypsy room, and he started to strum and sing.

"*If it was just (A) one night, one night, one night, with (D) you.*
(A) Can you imagine the things you, things I, things we could (D) do?

(Em) I'd tell you my story from the start, you'd tell me (G) about your broken heart,
(Em) We'd talk about places that we've been and all the (G) crazy things we've seen
in that one (A)night.
(A) Oh..... in that one (D) night. "

Dalton could see a big yellow Surfside Buslines bus coming closer. The bus window panel read Surfers Paradise, bus number 26. He thought, *Of course, it would be Bus 26, Tilly's favourite number. Surely, that's a sign I'm heading in the right direction to find her.*

Dalton boarded the bus, carrying his guitar with him, as there didn't seem to be any other people boarding the bus, and it was empty of passengers. It was still early. Dalton figured he would save the bus driver the trouble of stowing it underneath. He could just prop it up on the seat beside him. The bus driver was busy with his head in some paperwork and didn't seem to mind that Dalton was carrying his guitar onto the bus. He said nothing until Dalton reached the top step.

Without looking up, the bus driver said. 'Good morning, Sir Dalton. No blue Bandana today, Mr. Music?'

Then, Dalton realised this was Glenn, Mr GG, the same bus driver from his last Coolangatta to Surfers trip. The last time he travelled this route, he was half asleep and not in the mood for talking. He felt the same this time, making him aware that he had created a pattern of late nights and not much sleep over the past little while. He didn't want to mention this to the bus driver. He kept his internal thoughts to himself, but decided he should probably make more of an effort to chat with the friendly driver this time. 'Good morning, Glenn, was it? Glenn Gaffer? Mr GG?' Dalton questioned, raising his voice with each name and asking if he had the name right. It was a little hard to forget because Dalton remembered thinking Glenn Gaffer, Mr GG, was creepy. At first, he didn't know what Gaffer meant, but Glenn explained it. Being a Gaffer, a master glassblower sounded like a beautiful, creative occupation, but Glenn made it sound haunting somehow.

'You remember me, Bandana Boy. That's me, Mr GG, Gaffer by name, Gaffer by nature. Double N in Glenn, double F in Gaffer. N for No, F for Fear, like the clothing brand, do you know it? No Fear?'

Dalton replied, taking it all in and feeling ultimately creeped out. 'Yes, I do.'

Glenn smiled a shifty sideways smile, with his thin lips. Dalton half-smiled back, thinking, *What an odd thing to say! I wonder if he says that to everyone.* Glenn stood up, welcoming Dalton to the bus. He climbed out of his driving cubicle and stepped down onto the footpath, immediately removing a crumpled pack of cigarettes from his top shirt pocket and lighting a cigarette. This was his quick five-minute break, and he took the chance to have quick drags, consuming two cigarettes in rapid succession. As he did, he attempted to ask around and check if any other passengers were boarding the bus to Surfers Paradise.

It was just Glenn and Dalton for the ride so far.

Dalton placed his guitar securely for travel, stowed between the seat and the front steps divider plastic panel. He looked around, noticing no other passengers were on board, and felt slightly uncomfortable. He thought he should probably sit up the front and chat with the driver, although there was something not right about this man. Dalton couldn't pick it; he had a weird, off-putting, over-friendly presence, and the whole

Gaffer, No Fear comment was creeping him out. He eased his thoughts with the fact that this man was a responsible bus driver. Yes, it was a little creepy, but no harm would come to Dalton, not today. He wasn't in the mood for weird creeps. His day had started brilliantly with a soul-surfing experience, and he was on his way to find his girl in Surfers Paradise. That was the plan.

Dalton sat and chatted with Mr GG, but he was adamant about keeping the details of the conversation very impersonal. Usually, he took time to get to know people and loved to ask questions and share life stories with them, but this was different. He wasn't sharing anything more about himself with this man.

Glenn was the first to ask Dalton a question. 'So, how was the infamous Coolangatta? Did you have a wild night? Did you play a gig somewhere?'

Dalton considered his response in keeping out the personal details. 'I had a great night. Yes, I played a gig at the Coolangatta Hotel. It was very spontaneous; otherwise, I would have let you know, as you asked me to do that. I'm sorry, and yes, I had a wild night. I met some great people to party with.'

Glenn replied with much more openness and normality, making Dalton feel wrong about thinking he was creepy. 'Hey, that's okay. I was busy anyhow. I finished my shift in Surfers Paradise last night, so I checked out a band playing a random gig at the Islander Hotel near the bus depot. I had a quick drink and went home. They were pretty good. Have you heard of an upcoming Aussie band called Powderfinger?'

'Funny you should mention that. I have heard of them just recently. Were they playing a gig last night? I thought the big concert was on Saturday night at the Surfers Paradise Surf Club.' Dalton was interested to know what Glenn knew about this band Powderfinger because apparently Tilly was hanging out with them. He was intrigued to learn more.

'Yeah, they are playing on Saturday night at the Surfers Paradise Surf Club. I heard on the radio that all the tickets are almost sold out, so they must be okay. Last night, they did a spontaneous poolside gig at The Islander Hotel. They didn't publicise it. It's more alluring for a spontaneous night. The Islander Hotel is under new management, and they are trying to get a bit of a regular live music scene happening there. Free entry, cheap drinks and a great atmosphere. I didn't stick around long, but it was a great vibe, and they had a pretty girl on stage with them for a couple of songs.'

Dalton piqued his interest. 'Is that right?'

Glenn continued. 'Well, she was my kind of pretty. I have a thing for dark-haired girls.' He twitched his head and bit into his bottom lip. 'It's a bit of a rarity here on the Gold Coast; all the girls are blonde, or they dye their hair blonde. I prefer dark looks; they are more mysterious if you ask me. The dark-haired girls are more wholesome, somehow. They are more trusting and gentler.' Glenn was going very deep on a tangent to talk about this dark-haired girl, making Dalton feel uncomfortable because he thought it might be Tilly he was referring to since he had heard that she was hanging out with Powderfinger. Glenn continued talking, making Dalton feel more and more uncomfortable. 'This girl wasn't very trusting, though; she had some walls. Even more of a challenge.' He lifted his chin like he was in control of his desired challenge.

Dalton felt a shiver roll down his spine. This guy was a creep. He thought to himself, *Who says that?*

Dalton couldn't stop himself from questioning Glenn, even though he felt weird about it. 'So, this girl on stage with Powderfinger, is she part of their band?'

Glenn replied with the knowledge of a Powderfinger groupie. It was as if he had followed them from the very beginning of their journey. 'Hell no, it's the five boys: Bernard, the main man and lead singer, and then Ian, the two John's and Darren. They don't have a female vocalist; she was just there.'

Dalton questioned a little deeper, interested to learn what Glenn knew about the band and possibly this dark-haired girl that could be Tilly. 'Interesting. How did you know they were playing a gig? I didn't hear about it anywhere?'

'Well, I'll be a bit of a fanboy-namedropper here, but they were on my bus the other day on the way up from Sydney to the Gold Coast. I was excited to meet them. I like their music. As you did, they caught the bus from Murwillumbah Train Station to Coolangatta and then Surfers Paradise. I guess they are staying the week in Surfers, leading up to their big gig on Saturday night. The dark-haired girl was with them, but from what I could tell, I think they had just met on the train. From what I could tell from the vibe, they were all just getting to know each other.'

Dalton nodded, taking it all in. 'Interesting.'

Glenn went into full creep mode. 'I'll tell you what: I'd love to get my powder fingers on that girl.' Throwing his head back in a hideous, creepy laugh.

Dalton felt his blood boiling inside his veins and had to stay in control and not say or do something to this creep. He had to ignore him and just pretend he knew nothing about Tilly. He realised quickly that the less he drew attention to their connection, the safer he and Tilly would be. He didn't trust this guy at all. He was showing signs of being a sociopath or a psychopath. Dalton didn't know the definitions or characteristics of either term, but something wasn't right with this bus driver. He was some kind of "path."

A few other people had boarded the bus, which made Dalton feel a little safer, but he couldn't get to Surfers Paradise quickly enough. Glenn performed the same touristic review over the microphone about the history of the Gold Coast and Surfers Paradise as they drove through the busy streets. He pointed out the famous landmarks and told the story of the Surfers Paradise bikini girls and the Meter Maids. It was creepier this time, as Dalton was more aware of this bus driver's mental state and fascination with beautiful girls, including his beloved Tilly.

The bus pulled into the Surfers Paradise bus depot. Dalton stepped off with his guitar, farewelling the bus driver kindly and hoping he would never see him ever again. 'Bye Glenn, safe travels.' Dalton decided he would no longer travel by bus from Coolangatta to Surfers Paradise, as that seemed to be Glenn's route.

Glenn was busy attending to the female travellers who had boarded the bus, and Dalton was grateful for the distraction. It made it easy for a conversation-free getaway. However, as he was departing the bus, he overheard Glenn offering the young girls to stay at his place if they couldn't find any accommodation in Surfers Paradise. He provided his address and phone number as he did with Dalton upon his arrival on the Gold Coast. It all seemed very friendly, of course. Dalton didn't feel comfortable not to say anything, so he pretended to walk off and waited until the bus had departed.

As he saw the bus move away from the depot and out of sight, he returned to the young girls to offer some kind advice. He felt awkward and intrusive to the young girls who were strangers to him, but he felt the need to say something. 'Hey, I'm sorry to interrupt you, but I just need to say something if you don't mind.'

The girls looked up from their map and smiled. They both said in harmony, one with an accent, 'Sure, please.'

Dalton was very respectful. 'I just wanted to warn you not to take up the bus driver's offer for accommodation. I don't have any accommodation for you, but I don't feel that staying with him would be a safe option.'

The girls both nodded. The shorter one answered with a strong German accent. 'Ja, he was friendly, but a little over-friendly, kind of creepy, over-friendly.' She used her hands to gesture a pinch of creepiness and screwed up her nose in disgust.

Dalton rebalanced his guitar on his shoulder. 'Yeah, that's the best way to describe it. I wouldn't trust him; there is something not quite right about him. Some things he was saying to me: Wow! Creepity Creep!'

The taller girl spoke. She had an Australian accent. 'Thank you for your concern. We have some friends who we are meeting here, so we are okay anyway, but thank you.'

Dalton said farewell and continued on his way back towards the Beachcomber Hotel. He decided he would stop in at the Surf Club for another big breakfast first, and then he thought he might lie by the pool and catch up on some sleep that he didn't have last night. As he made plans for his day, he realised how hungry he was even though he had just enjoyed a BBQ breakfast after his surf. He realised he hadn't eaten much the day before and didn't sleep at all.

Dalton wandered up to the Surf Club and in through the swinging glass doors. Once again, he experienced the waft of Sunflowers perfume, just like he had smelt in the phone booth; it reminded him of Tilly. He could smell her near him. He looked around, hoping to see her, but she was nowhere in sight, just the scent of her lingering in the air.

Dalton walked straight up to the ticket counter and spoke to the lady he had asked previously to reserve his tickets. Her name badge said, Rhonda. He said politely, 'Good morning, Ma'am. You put some tickets aside for me the other day for the Powderfinger concert on Saturday night. I'm wondering if they are still available. I've heard it's almost a sell-out. I just need two of the tickets, thank you.'

She replied, 'Yep, there are just three tickets here that you had on hold. You already have your ticket, right?'

Dalton replied, checking in his wallet as he did so to make sure the ticket was still tucked in the side. 'I do, thank you.'

The lady continued talking. 'I just sold another ticket, about one minute ago. The lovely girl just walked out the door; she was such a pretty girl and so lovely. I could see you and her being a perfect match. You're a musician, obviously, with that guitar hanging over your shoulder like it's part of you.'

Dalton nodded, not understanding who she was talking about. 'Is that right? Thanks for looking out for me.' He laughed.

Dalton was surprised when Rhonda continued talking about the girl as she fiddled around, printing tickets and placing them in an envelope. He had no idea who this girl was, supposedly his perfect match. 'She's doing a surprise performance on stage with the band on Saturday night, but don't tell anyone I told you so. Secret stuff, apparently. She wanted to see the venue and the stage area because she was nervous. She said she usually plays in small pubs, not used to a big stage like this one. I thought it was a cute thing to say because, seriously, this is not a big stage at all. But it's cute that she feels like it is.'

Dalton's mouth dropped open; *It couldn't be. Could it be?*

The lady questioned, 'Are you okay? You look like you've seen a ghost. What's up?'

Dalton shook his head. He had a mouthful of questions, but it wasn't his right to ask this lady to talk about other customers. He felt like he knew the answer to his questions, anyway. That had to be Tilly, who she was talking about. He simply replied, 'No, nothing is wrong at all. I'm all good. I'm just excited about the concert, and I need some breakfast. I didn't get any sleep last night.'

Rhonda looked down her nose, peered over the top of her glasses, and then smiled. 'Well, I hope it was a worthwhile cause.' She winked.

Dalton had some thoughts race around in his mind. *This lady is super friendly, up close and personal, completely different from her demeanour the other day. She was quite standoffish and bossy about the tickets, and now she wants to know why I didn't get any sleep and if it was worthwhile, and she seems to think she's found my perfect match.* He replied. 'It was very worthwhile, thank you. I was surfing at 3 am at Coolangatta, the most amazing sunrise surf I've ever experienced.' He paused. 'What day is it today? Today could be the best day of my life, and it's only just getting started.'

Rhonda replied, looking up at the calendar hanging on the wall. 'It's Wednesday, 23rd of February, and it's still 1994—nothing special about today. I think Saturday the 26th of February might be your special day. I've just got a feeling.'

Dalton adjusted his weight on his feet and re-adjusted his guitar strap as it was falling off his shoulder. He felt goosebumps rise on his arms when she mentioned Saturday was the 26th of February. Dalton replied with gentle scepticism. 'Of course, it's the 26th on Saturday, and you think that will be my special day? Do you know something I don't know?'

Rhonda squinted her eyes together. 'What do you mean?'

Dalton was so confused. 'Well, how do you know that Saturday the 26th will be special for me?'

Rhonda shrugged her shoulders. 'I don't know for sure; I just have a feeling.'

Dalton questioned again. He couldn't help himself. 'So, you know nothing I don't know about that girl and Saturday the 26th?'

Rhonda replied. 'Nope. I know she's a musician like you, and her name is Tilly, and she will be here on Saturday night. She was very polite in introducing herself to me. Small-town manners, I guess. I'm only saying that because it stood out to me. She had beautiful manners, unlike some of the local girls here. Other than that, I know nothing about her, or Saturday. I was just making small talk. Sorry if I've made you feel uncomfortable. I do that sometimes. It's part of my autism. I'm either super friendly, and I talk way too much, or I'm the bitch from hell. You can like me or not? That's just the way I am.'

Dalton almost fell over. 'Oh my goodness, you don't need to be sorry. You didn't make me feel uncomfortable. I'm so grateful for you sharing that secret about the girl and being so open about your autism. Thank you. Saturday the 26th of February is going to be a special day. I'm going to make sure of it. Thanks to you.'

Rhonda was the one who was confused now, but everything was making sense to Dalton. Tilly was here, in Surfers Paradise, and she was playing on stage with Powderfinger on Saturday night, and he had tickets to the concert in his hands. Dalton would soon reconnect with Tilly, on Saturday, if not before.

chapter eighty-five

Joop—Yope

Dalton made his way upstairs and found an empty table on the balcony. It was bizarre that table number 26 was the only table free. Again. This special number was everywhere he looked. Tilly was all around him. He liked the synchronicity of it. It was comforting to him, in some weird and spooky way, a fate and destiny kind of way. He liked it. He wouldn't notice if he weren't taking notice, but now that he *was* taking notice of this special number, it was ironically everywhere. As he thought about this, he looked up at the Keno display television on the wall and pop! Out popped the green number 26. Dalton just shook his head; no one would believe him if he tried to explain this to them.

The young waitress came over and asked if he wanted her to put his guitar somewhere out of the way.

Dalton replied, a little weary now from having no sleep, and his head was in the clouds, thinking about the conversation that had just transpired with Rhonda. 'Yes, please, thank you. I'm so sorry, I wasn't thinking.'

The young waitress replied, 'It's totally okay, no worries at all. I'll just pop it inside the door. There is a safe place near the pot plant stand.'

Dalton replied gratefully. 'I can put it there if you like. It's not a problem. Thank you.' He stood up, carried his guitar inside the restaurant, and placed his guitar up against the wall near the pot plant, as the girl suggested. She took the time to wipe his table down as he did so.

Dalton returned to the table, thanking the girl for wiping it down. 'Thank you.' He didn't question her name as he thought that might be a little creepy. He didn't want to come across as being over-friendly, like Mr GG. It was still giving Dalton shudders, thinking about his weirdness.

The girl extended the conversation first and said, 'Let me guess, a big breakfast and a caramel latte?'

Dalton complimented her. 'You have an excellent memory. Thank you, that's exactly what I need.'

She laughed and replied, 'It's weird. The girl sitting here before you had exactly the same thing, and when you came in and sat down, I remembered that was what you had ordered last time. Is that weird?'

Dalton shook his head and laughed. 'Don't even get me started on weird things today.' Dalton laughed again, throwing his head back, not knowing what else to say that wouldn't sound like he was absolutely out of his mind. So, he said nothing. He was lacking a bit of zest, both hungry and sleep-deprived.

The young waitress waited momentarily to see if Dalton would explain what was so weird. When he didn't say anymore, she simply said, 'I will put your order in, and I'll be right back with your caramel latte.'

'Thank you so much.' Dalton rested back on his chair, putting his arms above his head, noticing that he had a bit of a body sweat odour going on under his arms. Dalton was very particular about hygiene and realised that he had been sweating hard out in the surf and probably should have put on some deodorant after his brief hose-down at Tom and Richie's place. He had some deodorant and aftershave in his daypack, so he reached in and rolled on some Old Spice under his arms. It wasn't his favourite deodorant scent, so he added a splash of Joop aftershave on his face to freshen up a bit and remove the deodorant's scent. He was aware that it might have seemed that he was trying to impress the young waitress, which was not his intention at all. He just liked always to smell fresh and clean.

He sat for a few minutes, people-watching and looking especially closely for anyone resembling Tilly. He had a thought now that he knew Tilly was here. He wondered if the girl he had seen the other day with the big hat might have been Tilly. Even though she said she never wore hats. It looked like her walk. Her beautiful swagger.

Dalton's thoughts drifted off to imagine what it might be like to see her again. If he found her, he wanted their reconnection to be a special and memorable moment. Tilly would be his girl forever from the moment he found her again.

The young waitress returned to the table with Dalton's coffee. She got a waft of his cologne and couldn't resist not saying something about it. 'Mmmm, you're smelling good now. Is that Joop?'

Dalton cheekily replied, 'So, you're saying I wasn't smelling good before?' He laughed. 'I wasn't trying to knock you out with my cologne. I just realised I needed to put some deodorant on my stinky armpits. I went for an amazing sunrise surf this morning, and I really need a shower. I'm hoping the Joop, how do you say it, Yope, might cover up the BO for a moment?'

The waitress felt awful that she had said he smelt good, now. She didn't mean to be rude. She was just trying to compliment him. 'I didn't mean to say that you smelled bad before. I was just saying you smell good now. Anyway, I'm sorry, it is Joop, right?' she pronounced it again, like Yope.

'It's my favourite at the moment, the scent of the new decade, apparently. I like it because no one wears it where I'm from, in the country. My cowboy friends would tease me and say I smelled like a girl. I'm okay with that. Girls smell good, right?' Dalton was nodding, agreeing with himself.

The young waitress replied, 'I think it smells good. Lots of young guys wear it here in the nightclubs. It's quite overpowering, but a very distinguishable scent. Is that the word? Like, you smell it, and you know it's Joop.'

Dalton nodded, 'Yeah, I know what you mean.' He added. 'I like the way you say it, Yope. I always wondered if I was saying it correctly. Clearly, I wasn't.'

The young waitress replied, 'I only know that because I also work in the perfumery section in the pharmacy, just in the mall, across the road, and our boss is always strict on pronouncing the cologne and perfume names correctly. We even have to know the brand designer's name and where they are made. There is a lot to know, let me tell you.

I have to say my favourite cologne is CK One. I can't get that wrong. Calvin Klein from the Bronx in New York City. Do you know it?'

Dalton replied, eager to know more. 'I don't know it. Is it new?'

The young waitress replied with confident wisdom and excitement to share her knowledge. 'It was just released this year, like a month ago. It is the first-ever unisex fragrance. It's really nice, you should try it.'

Dalton nodded. 'Perhaps that will be my next cologne purchase. I'm almost out of my Joop.' He pronounced it Yope.

The young waitress smiled. She wasn't sure what else to say, but she realised she was still holding on to Dalton's coffee. She placed it down in front of him.

As she did, Dalton said. 'I hope it's not rude to ask your name, seeing as you've been so kind to wait on me for the past few times I've been here. Feeding me big breakfast and caramel lattes and now giving me free cologne recommendations.'

The young waitress replied as Dalton sipped his coffee. 'No, that's not rude at all. My name is Madison, but people call me Maddi. I should wear a name badge, but I lost it somewhere. Whoops! They are making me another one.'

Dalton lifted his cup towards Maddi. 'Well, thank you, Maddi, this is lovely, compliments to the barista.'

Maddi replied, proud of her new skill. 'Oh, that was me. I made your coffee this morning. I just finished my barista course last week. I'm still learning. I'm glad you like it. Thank you.'

Maddi returned to her waitressing duties, leaving Dalton to people-watch while he waited for his Big Breakfast.

He looked down from the balcony onto the beach across the road. He noticed the crowds were settling in for the day with their towels and umbrellas all scattered over the beach. It was getting quite busy on the beach. Dalton considered joining the crowd for a surf outside the flags and a sunbake, but seeing how many people were there, it was busy for a Wednesday. He decided he would take his guitar back to the room, grab his surfboard, jump on a bus, and check out Burleigh Heads as he had heard a few different people talking about it, and the swell was supposed to be good for a Burleigh surf today.

Dalton finished his Big Breakfast and headed down the street to call Dan from the phone booth. He had some coins in his wallet, and he promised to call Dan back to check if he and Ariiel were still coming up for the Billabong Pro.

Dalton was careful not to drop Tilly's pick, which he had tucked safely into the zip pocket of his wallet, as he was getting the coins out of his wallet. The phone call was brief, as Dan was heading out for a surf, so there was no time to chat. Yes, he and Ariiel were coming up for the Billabong Pro and the Powderfinger concert. They had already organised some accommodation with Dan's mate in Coolangatta. Dan finished the conversation by letting Dalton know they would drive up on Friday morning and catch him at the Billabong Pro early Saturday. They planned to meet at the information tent at 7 am. It was sure to be a big crowd.

chapter eighty-six

1800-REVERSE

Tilly withdrew some cash and returned to the hotel to put some swimmers on. Then, she had a nothing-to-do day planned. She thought she might finally get to lie in the sun and finish reading her book, The Alchemist. It was a brief read; she just needed a few quiet, undistracted hours.

Tilly packed her shoulder bag, book, sunglasses, Reef coconut oil and Sun-In to spray in her hair for some blonde summer highlights. She grabbed her new beach towel, big-brimmed hat, and umbrella. On her way to the beach, she stopped at the phone booth to call her mum and dad. She had no coins, so she dialled 1800 REVERSE—hoping her mum would accept the charges for the phone call. Tilly wanted to briefly tell her mum and dad that she would be singing on stage with Powderfinger on Saturday night. It was a definite plan.

Tilly pressed the buttons, and she heard the call go through. Then she heard her mum's voice. She was distracted when her mum answered the phone, as she realised that there was a powerful scent of Dalton's cologne inside the phone booth. She sniffed around and then scanned her eyes outside, 360 degrees, to see if he was nearby. No Dalton. No tall, sexiest man alive, blue Bandana boy. She realised that this scent wasn't so unique. Everyone on the Gold Coast was wearing the same scent. It was just a coincidence.

'Hello.' Tilly's mum repeated. 'Hello, is that you, my beautiful girl?'

Tilly smiled, happy to hear her mum's voice. 'Yep, it's me, Mum. How are you?'

'I'm good, I'm good. Your father is good, too. You know we are always good.' Laura was so happy to hear Tilly's voice on the phone. Jack could hear that Laura was talking to Tilly, so he came closer to the phone to be part of the conversation. 'Your father is here, too. We can both hear you, darling.'

Jack chimed in with, 'Hey, my girl.'

Tilly replied quickly, knowing every second was costing money for the call. 'Hey, Dad.'

Jack and Laura both questioned simultaneously. 'How are you?'

'I'm really great. My cast is annoying me on my arm. It's itchy, but I'm getting used to it. I have some exciting news to tell you. I've been invited to sing on stage with Powderfinger on Saturday night. I played a gig with them last night. It was just a little hotel impromptu thing, and it was so fun, but Saturday night, they are playing a sold-out show at the Surf Club here. It's not a huge venue, but the crowd will be bigger than anything I've ever played to.'

Laura was the first to reply. 'That's good to hear, darling. You'll be amazing, I'm sure.'

Jack added, 'Do you know which song you are singing? Is it just one song?'

'Yes, just one song, I think. We are just going to wing it. They will bring me up on stage from amongst the crowd and go from there. So, it's kind of impromptu, but I have sung with them before, so they know me and my voice. I think I'll do Gypsy.'

Laura complimented and encouraged Tilly. 'Good choice, darling. That song suits you perfectly.'

Jack piped in again, trying to be humorous with his weird sense of humour. 'Speaking of gypsies, have you found that Gypsy Boy yet?'

'No, I haven't, but I feel he's close to me. I mean, I can smell him right now in this phone booth. Is that weird?'

Jack replied again. 'It is a little strange, but the world does amazing things to work its magic, you know, just be patient. It'll happen when it should.'

Laura added. 'It sounds like you've got some things to keep you busy in the meantime.'

'Well, not really, Mum. I'm just about to lie on the beach and read my book for a few hours. I like it here. The beaches are nice, but there are just so many people. I prefer our empty beaches, to be honest. But I feel like I'm in the right place, right now.'

Jack added with his fatherly wisdom. 'Just enjoy yourself. It sounds like you are.'

Tilly had one more question. 'So, how are the boys? Please say hi.'

'Well, we haven't seen much of Frankie lately. He's been working, surfing or with his new girlfriend, Chelsea.'

Tilly scratched her head. 'Chelsea?'

Jack replied. 'It's confusing, but it's not Dalton's Chelsea. Like you, that's still a story we don't know, but Frankie's Chelsea doesn't know a Dalton.'

Tilly stopped herself from asking questions. This phone call was costing money. 'Ok, well, that's good for Frankie. I bet she's lovely.'

Laura spoke. 'It's been such a short time, but they seem like they have known each other forever. They are pretty cute together.'

Tilly added. 'And the twins?'

Laura spoke again. 'They miss their little sister.'

'Aww, hug all the boys for me and yourselves. I miss you all.'

The phone started beeping, indicating the charges would increase if Tilly extended the call.

Jack ended the call. 'We will let you go, darling. This 1800-REVERSE thing is expensive, you know. Give us another call on Sunday and tell us all about your gig with the Powderfinger band.'

Tilly acknowledged that the call was expensive. 'Yeah, sorry for the reverse call, but I had no coins left on me. I'll call on Sunday. Big Love you guys.'

Jack and Laura both said together. 'Big Love, baby girl.'

Jack hung up the phone, and Tilly heard a clunk, ending the call.

She grabbed all her stuff that was leaning against the phone booth, trying not to put the weight of her belongings on her broken arm. She walked straight up past the Surf Club and onto the beach on the main strip, where everyone seemed to gather, near the surf club flags, the music, and the action.

chapter eighty-seven

Bird's-eye View

Over the next few days, Tilly did her thing; Dalton did his thing. The number of times they almost bumped into each other was uncanny. If you were a bird watching and circling their movements from above, you would have wanted to swoop down and interfere to align their paths with each other, but it wasn't meant to be. Not yet.

chapter eighty-eight

The Billabong Pro

On Friday night, just before Dalton closed his eyes to rest, he set the alarm clock on the bedside table for 5 am. He had to get on an early bus to get down to Coolangatta and meet with Dan and Ariiel at 7 am. He knew the traffic might have been a challenge because of the big event, so he wanted to give himself plenty of time.

Dalton was excited to see the lady bus driver as he boarded the bus. It was too early in the morning to deal with weird Glen Gaffer.

He sat at the very front so he could easily see the view ahead and around him, with every chance that he might catch Tilly wandering around the Gold Coast somewhere in his path.

He felt lighter and freer because he just had himself and his small daypack on his back. No guitar, no large backpack, no surfboard today. In his daypack, he had a bottle of water, his plaid Stussy cap that he hardly ever wore, his wallet, his sunglasses, his deodorant and his almost empty bottle of Joop!

The bus driver said Good Morning to Dalton and asked if he would mind if she put the radio on.

Dalton wondered why she was asking him that question. She was the bus driver. She could do whatever she wanted. He replied, 'Of course you can. That would be great. I love music. It's part of my soul.'

She explained her reason for asking. 'I just thought I would ask because some people are not morning people, and they like a quiet bus trip.'

Dalton replied sleepily. 'I'm not really a morning person until after I've had a good coffee, but music makes everything better, right?'

'It does,' replied the bus driver. 'What is your name, young man?'

'My name is Dalton, and yours?'

'I'm Sharon. Some people call me Shazza, but that's only when you really get to know me.' She laughed loud and hard, her whole body moving up and down on the bouncy seat as she did.

Dalton laughed with her. She had an uplifting energy.

After the advertisements and news break, the first song that came on the radio was one of Dalton's favourite ever songs—*My Hometown* by Bruce Springsteen. The mood of the song blended in with the time of the day perfectly. It was quiet and mellow. Dalton tuned into the lyrics. *I was eight years old, and running with a dime in my hand, to the bus stop to pick up a paper for my old man. I'd sit on his lap in that big old Buick and steer as we drove through town. He'd tousle my hair and say, "Son, take a good look around. This is your hometown."*

Dalton and Sharon both sang along, lost in the moment of this very emotional song. Dalton's mind returned to Deniliquin and growing up like the lyrics described. His Dad was a decent man, a hard-working farmer. He worked hard for his wife and the three boys to give them the best life he knew how. He provided a roof over their heads, food on the table, and a safe and happy home. Dalton felt selfish about the way he had left home. He had to do it for himself, but he had a little moment of melancholy for his family and hometown. He felt like he had done the wrong thing by his father, with no intention to do that. His family wanted a different life for him. He couldn't help that the life they wanted for him was not the life he desired at all.

When the song finished, Sharon half-turned her head to Dalton, still keeping her eyes on the road. She said, 'You're a country boy, huh?'

Dalton replied briefly, 'I am. Deniliquin. I was born and bred, and I lived every day of my life there until just over a year ago.'

Sharon nodded. 'I'm from down that way, out west in the country, not too far from you, actually. I used to see the signs for Deniliquin when we drove down to Melbourne. I'm from a little town called Yeoval. Do you know it?'

Dalton replied, nodding. 'I've never been to Yeoval, but have heard of it. It's famous for fat lambs, is that right?'

Sharon laughed, 'I guess so.'

They chatted the whole way, from Surfers to Coolangatta, about the differences between living in the city and country life. They only stopped talking to join in with some songs. Sharon had found a country radio station, 4KQ, playing some wholesome country hits. Dalton understood now why she had asked if it was okay that she put the radio on. He imagined that her taste in music wasn't everyone's cup of tea. Dalton didn't mind. He sang along to the hits that he knew. He was excited to hear "*Lady*" by Kenny Rogers and "*Jolene*" by Dolly Parton. His absolute favourite was Neil Diamond's "*Forever in Blue Jeans.*" Sharon and Dalton had an entertaining country bus karaoke thing going on. They were having so much fun.

The bus pulled into the Coolangatta stop, and as the door slowly squeezed open, Dalton was the first to exit. Only a couple of other passengers were on board, and they were at the back of the bus, making their way slowly to the front, still half asleep. It was early.

As Dalton crossed the road, respectfully walking on the crossing even though the roads were still quiet, he heard an old-fashioned horn beep at him. He looked up, firstly thinking, *why is someone beeping at me? I'm on the crossing.* Then he caught sight of The PIE number plate. He saw Dan and Ariel waving at him. *How uncanny, perfect timing!* Dalton was excited to see his Angourie friends. He waved back and shouted, 'Hey guys!'

Dalton continued to cross to the other side as traffic lined up behind Dan. As Dan passed by on the crossing, he called out the window. 'Hey, D. Jump in! We will just park this beast somewhere safe.'

Dalton went to his internal thoughts as he ran back across the road to where Dan had pulled over onto the side of the road. *The PIE. It's such a cool car. And Dan 'Badman', what a great man. I'm so lucky to have met him. It looks like he and his girl are getting along well. They both look so happy. That makes me happy.*

Dalton opened the heavy door and climbed into the back seat. 'How are you guys? So good to see you.'

Dan instigated the polite introductions, knowing that Dalton and Ariiel had not formally met. 'I don't think you have properly met each other. Dalton, this is my beautiful friend, Ariiel. Ariiel, this is the one, the man, the legend, Dalton!'

Dalton slid across to the right so he could reach his hand out. He leaned forward and gestured to shake Ariiel's hand, as it seemed like the polite thing to do. He would rather give a hug, but that wasn't possible from the back seat.

Ariiel reached her hand out and replied shyly, admiring Dalton's presence. Something about him oozed strength, dominance, and friendliness all at once. 'Hi Dalton, are you looking forward to the comp today?'

'I am, and I'm so glad you two could also make it here. I'm definitely missing the Angourie connection. My stay was way too short.'

Dan indicated, pulling back into the traffic, the indicator loudly clicking. 'Well, you need to fill us in on that whole story. We need to know what the fuck happened!? One minute, you and Tilly were fuckin amazing, and the chemistry between you two was sparkling all over Angourie. You were the next best thing that ever happened to the Macallan family, and then there you were, knocking on my door at 5 am.'

Ariiel added to the conversation. 'You don't need to tell us if it's personal, but everyone wondered why you left so suddenly and then why Tilly left the next day. Angourie keeps secrets very well, but the Tilly/Dalton mystery is the talk of the town. You certainly made an impression on the locals.'

'Well, it's hard to explain. It's really, really stoopid, and it's such a mess. Basically, I wasn't upfront and honest with Tilly, and when I tried to talk to her about my past, which Dan knows all about, she wouldn't let me explain. She told me to go. So, me being Mr Vulnerable and laden with guilt, I did. I left as she asked me to. I didn't fight to be heard. I realise I made a big mistake. Our communication at that moment was flawed because I needed her to listen, but she was adamant about me not being controlling because of her past relationship traumas. I just let her walk away when she told me to go. I didn't want to tell her what to do and be like her past relationships. So, I did, I left. The next morning. I hoped she would come back to the room during the night, but she didn't. I left a note for The Macallans and Tilly, and after you dropped me at the highway, Dan, I hitched a ride with a guy to Byron. From there, I've pretty much messed things up even more.' He lowered his head in embarrassment. 'I met a nice girl and spent the night with her in Byron, only to find out from her that Tilly was looking for me. I think. It's so messed up.'

Ariiel asked to get some clarification on the story. 'How does Tilly know where you are?'

Dalton clarified the situation for Ariiel. 'I'm guessing that she doesn't. I don't know where she is, either. But I feel like she's close, and we will find each other soon.'

Ariiel questioned some more. 'Does her family know where she is?'

Dalton replied, 'I don't think so. I called the Angourie Local the other day and talked to Frankie. He hadn't heard from her, and he was worried. But I left him my hotel details so when she calls home, he can pass my details on to Tilly.'

'Oh. That's an idea.' Ariiel nodded and gave some positive feedback.

Dan added. I haven't seen much of Frankie lately. It seems he's got himself a new girlfriend, too. Her name is Chelsea. Did you meet her?

Dalton had a bit of a mind flip hearing the name Chelsea. 'No, I didn't meet her, but I saw Frankie talking to a girl the night I played at The Angourie Local. I was more worried about doing a good gig than anything else and fixated on beautiful Tilly.'

Ariiel continued her investigations. 'So, you talked to Frankie, but not the rest of the family. Perhaps the message didn't get back to the Macallans that you were on the Gold Coast.'

'Yeah, that's a likelihood. It's just a matter of time, I guess.' Dalton was confident that he just had to be patient.

Ariiel added, 'That's true. Time and The Universe. What is meant to be will always be, whether it happens today, tomorrow, or in a year. That's the part we can't control! It's just life.'

Dan couldn't help but add a sarcastic comment. 'Well, that's deep, Miss Ariiel, for this time of the morning, and we haven't even had a coffee yet.'

Dalton replied. 'It's true, though. She's right. The more I live, the more I realise that life is all planned out perfectly for me, and it's up to me whether I have fun and move forward with the good times or stay and dwell on the tough times. I've certainly had spontaneous connections and fun over the past few weeks and met some amazing people.'

As Dan pulled into a carpark, Ariiel finished the conversation with great wisdom. 'I'm sure everything will work out exactly as it is meant to be in the end. Sometimes, it takes a while to get there. That's why it's called the end.'

Dan and Dalton nodded.

They grabbed a coffee before heading to the surf comp to battle the crowds.

As the three amigos sipped on their caffeine and enjoyed the quiet buzz of the Coolangatta streets, Dalton went into a long monologue conversation about his whole travel experiences since leaving Angourie. He talked about his Byron adventure with Travis and Myles and the three girls, Jacki, Adeline, Georgia, and the Spanish bartender, Juan. He spoke about the train station lady and the weird interaction he had on the bus with the psychic lady, Leeroy. He spoke about Trish and her son. He talked, in detail, about Tom and Richie and the gig at The Coolangatta Hotel. He shared the entire story about Cody, the Soul surfer, and their magical sunrise surf. He talked about Maddi, the waitress, and Rhonda, The Powderfinger ticket lady from the Surf Club. He talked about Glen Gaffer with shivers down his spine, as he did. He told them about the Freedom, Friendship and Enough Love cheers. Dan and Ariiel listened with interest and astonishment at the fulfilling interactions Dalton had experienced in such a short time frame. And the final little interesting story Dalton shared was about the guitar pick. He pulled his wallet out of his back pocket and retrieved Tilly's guitar pick from the zipped pocket.

Dan was gobsmacked. 'What are the fuckin chances, man? That will blow Tilly's mind when she sees that again.'

'I know, right? It's unbelievable.' Dalton was excited to tell Ariiel and Dan the complete story, but it wasn't finished yet.

He continued, apologising that he was talking so much.

Ariiel assured him it was okay. 'We don't mind Dalton. It's great to hear what you've been up to. I'm loving this wildly romantic story.'

Dan added. 'Man, this is far more exciting than our lives back in Angourie. This is like a fuckin' Hollywood movie.'

Dalton laughed. 'Not really. It's just how life has happened for me the past few weeks.'

Ariiel took a sip of her coffee and then asked the big question. 'So, what happens now? Excuse my French, but how does this fucked-up love story end?'

Dalton lowered his head and nodded as he thought about the possibilities.

'Well, that's the beautiful unknown. Tilly might be on the Gold Coast hanging out with Powderfinger—the band she met on the train. She may perform with them on stage on Saturday night. I'm assuming all of this information because of bits and pieces of information I've gathered from people I've met over the past few weeks. Life is amazing, huh!? A tapestry of beautiful connections to keep us on the path we are supposed to be on.'

Dan voiced his opinion. 'Well, you know what I think about all of that. Our life is already planned for us. No matter what we do to change it, it will always return to what was meant for us. Whether it's life lessons we need to learn, hard times, challenges or beautiful joy, it's all part of this beautiful thing called the in-between, and one day, it'll all be over, and you can do nothing to change that. It's done!'

Dalton was nodding firmly, agreeing with every word from Dan's mouth. He replied, using his hands to gesture Badman's grand strength and power. 'See. That's why I love you, man. You're so fuckin' wise. Dan "Badman", the Angourie gatekeeper, holder of wisdom and protector of all who enter his ocean.'

They all laughed. Ariiel leaned over and planted a passionate and gentle kiss on Dan's lips. 'See, that's why I already love you, Dan. You're so fuckin' mine until the end.'

They all laughed again.

Dalton wanted to make a romantic comment about Ariiel's expression of love for Dan. He didn't want to be awkward, as he knew Dan had quite a rebellious heart, but he also knew that Dan knew the importance of love. So, he simply said, 'I'm sure you two will work out the beautiful in-between of birth and death now that you've found each other.'

Dan nodded and replied with a comment filled with sarcasm and complimentary at the same time. 'Well, look at you, Mr Romantic, no wonder Tilly had an instant crush on you. You have such a way with words for a country boy.'

Dalton didn't know what to say, keeping it simple. 'Thanks, Dan.'

Ariiel wanted to get back to the end of Dalton's story. She was invested in what the story might look like for Tilly and Dalton. 'So, Dalton, what do you think might happen with you and Tilly?'

Dalton continued the conversation with his take on what might happen. 'Well, I do not know how Tilly and I will meet up again, but I know for sure that when we do, I'm never, ever going to fuck it up again. She's something else. I can't ever stop thinking about her. She's my kind of wonderful in every way.'

Ariiel nodded. 'Well, I hope you can find each other soon.'

Dalton nodded back. 'Me too.'

Dan noticed the crowds were building across the road towards the entry gate. 'Well. Your life path seems to be guiding you back to her now that you've learnt your big lesson. Communication man, it's Number 1. Without it, all that Freedom, Friendship, and Enough Love means nothing.'

Dalton nodded again. 'So true, so true!'

Dan had enough of this conversation and was keen to check out the start of the competition. 'I don't mean to be rude, but let's get amongst it and check out these professionals. I'm not a betting man, but if I were, I'd have my life savings on Kelly Slater for the win.'

Dalton, Ariiel and Dan stood up and pushed in their chairs, thanked the coffee hut staff and headed across the road to join the crowds of the Billabong Pro.

It was a gorgeous day with a beautiful glistening swell, bringing some worthy waves to the competition. The crowds packed in, ready for a day of action in the surf.

The loudspeakers announced that Heat 1 would commence in thirty minutes.

The MC of the event had put some music on to set a bit of vibe for the day, starting with a bit of soft rock and roll from Guns 'N' Roses. Dalton whistled along with the introduction to *Patience* as it trickled through the speakers.

chapter eighty-nine

Patience

She turned on the shower and stepped into the small compartment, thinking to herself, *I think this shower might be the same size as that bloody phone booth. There is no room to save water and shower with a friend in here.* She laughed to herself, thinking that her inner thoughts joke was quite funny, and then reminiscing about Dalton at the same time, making her feel a bit sad. She relaxed, letting the water wash over her face and body, feeling the warmth of the water down her back. She had a good feeling about today. As she lathered herself with soap and immersed her head in a heavy dosage of luscious-smelling shampoo, she started whistling to the tune of *Patience* by *Guns N Roses*. As she did this, she realised how much like her dad she was. He was a whistler, and he was the best at whistling Patience. She had never really tried it herself, realising right now, right here in this shower at The Islander Hotel, that she was pretty good at whistling Patience. She sang as well. *Shed a tear 'cause I'm missin' you. I'm still alright to smile, boy I think about you every day now. There was a time when I wasn't sure, but you set my mind at ease. There. There is no doubt you're in my heart now.*

Tilly dressed in an easy shift dress she could quickly get in and out of and slipped her thongs onto her feet. She was dressed for a day of shopping in clothes and shoes that were easy to remove for trying things on. She had decided to buy herself a nice outfit for tonight's stage performance. She grabbed her shoulder bag, placing her wallet, sunglasses, and a water bottle inside. That's all she needed. She headed downstairs to the restaurant to grab some breakfast.

It was a pleasant surprise when she saw Bernard sitting at a table near the window. He was sitting alone at a small table for two. She figured the rest of the boys were still in bed, and she didn't think Bernard would mind if she asked him if she could join him.

Tilly asked politely. 'Do you mind if I join you for breakfast, Bernard?'

'Of course, I don't mind, Tilly. I would be honoured to have you join me for breakfast. I just got here two minutes ago. I haven't ordered yet.' As he said this, the waiter arrived to take their order. Bernard directed his order to the waiter, hoping Tilly also wanted the full buffet breakfast. It was the only option, other than if you had extra dietary needs, so he couldn't really get it wrong. 'We would like two buffet breakfasts. Thank you, sir.' He paused and then spoke to Tilly. 'Sorry, that was rude of me. Is that what you wanted?'

Tilly replied with a smile. 'Yes, absolutely, the buffet breakfast sounds divine.' Then to the waiter, 'Could I also order a special caramel latte? Thank you.'

The waiter replied. 'Of course, would you also like a coffee, sir?'

Bernard nodded to the waiter. 'I'll have the same as Tilly. It sounds special.'

Tilly turned back to Bernard and said, 'You don't need to pay for mine. I went to the bank, so I have some cash on me now. Perhaps it's my turn to shout you. I'd like to shout you breakfast if that's okay?'

Bernard replied with a hint of frustration. 'Oh, my goodness, let me shout you breakfast, beautiful girl.'

The waiter interrupted. 'I'll leave you two to work out your finances. Meanwhile, I'll put in your order for coffee. Please go to the buffet and help yourselves to everything else.'

They both said in unison. 'Thank you.'

Tilly turned back to Bernard. 'Really? That's lovely, Bernard, but you don't have to.'

Bernard kindly refused. 'No, I want to say thanks in advance for tonight. Having you join us on stage will be a special part of the show. How are you feeling about it?'

Tilly thought for a moment. 'I'm slightly nervous but more excited than nervous.'

Bernard had an excellent way to think about it to settle Tilly's nerves. 'Well, the thing is, it's going to look like it's all on the spur of the moment. Impromptu. Nobody knows that we actually know each other. That's the fun part. That is the perk of show biz, I guess. Once we get on the stage, we are actors, telling stories in our songs and entertaining people. Nothing has to be real life. We can do what we want as long as people enjoy the show. It doesn't matter one bit if something goes wrong, because nothing is planned.'

'Yeah, true, and I'm only singing right, so I don't have to worry about trying to play my guitar with a broken arm.'

Bernard complimented Tilly and made her feel completely at ease. 'Yeah, just singing. Just like the other night, you were perfect.'

Tilly paused and smiled in receipt of the compliment. 'I have thought about which song I want to sing, and if it's okay with you and the boys, I want to sing Gypsy.' Tilly paused. Bernard waited, thinking she was going to say something else. So she did. 'Is that okay?' This was Tilly's go-to, easy song. She felt more comfortable singing it than any other song she knew. She wanted to make sure it was absolutely okay with Bernard because they would have a certain mood in the set lists they were creating, and she wanted to fit in with that.

'That's a perfect song, Tilly. You'll smash it. Best cover version ever. Stevie is going to be so proud of you.'

Tilly smiled. 'I hope so.'

Bernard added. 'I wonder if we can get someone to video record it for you. We will talk to our sound and lighting guy. He's coming down from Brisbane today. I'll ask him if we can get a copy of the recorded concert, especially for you.'

'That would be awesome. Thank you, Bernard, and another reason I am buying you breakfast this morning.'

'Ah, Tilly, I have an idea. The only fair way to solve this. Let's play Paper, Scissors, Rocks to solve the problem.' Bernard held out his fist in the shape of the 'rocks' position.

They both said together as they bounced their hands in time. 'Pa..per..Scis..sors, Rocks!'

Tilly kept her fist as a rock, and so did Bernard. They both laughed and tried again. 'Pa..per..Scis..sors, Rocks!' This time, they both did "paper". Both laughed louder this time. Again, they bounced. 'Pa..per..Scis..sors, Rocks!' They both did scissors. Both cracked up in raucous laughter. It felt good to laugh. Tilly had been having some deep, serious thoughts over the past few days, and she had forgotten the lightness and joy in life. She was so worried about messing up her relationship with Dalton and felt so immature about the whole situation, how she had just walked off on him like a two-year-old, not giving him a chance to explain what he wanted to say. She wondered how they would finally find each other again and what would happen when they did.

Bernard snapped Tilly out of her internal thoughts. 'One more time. Come on!'

They both said together. 'Pa..per..Scis..sors, Rocks!'

This time, Tilly placed her fist as "Rocks", and Bernard landed the "Paper", closing his hand around Tilly's. 'I win,' he said, leaning over and kissing her forehead.

'Okay, you win. Thank you, Bernard. That was fun!'

'Thank YOU, Tilly, it's been so great hanging out with you seriously. You're a beautiful woman, and I wish you all the best in life.' Bernard was sincere in his kind words, making Tilly feel exceptional at this moment.

Tilly looked Bernard firmly in the eyes and said, 'You have to promise you'll keep in touch.'

Bernard replied with a deep and honest stare back at her soul. 'I promise.'

The waitress arrived with a jug of cold water, two glasses, some plates, and cutlery, and he let Tilly and Bernard know that the special coffees were coming soon.

Again, Tilly and Bernard both said 'thank you' in unison.

As they ate breakfast, they sat and chatted comfortably about various things. Towards the end of the conversation and with two full bellies, Tilly shared the story with Bernard about how she had gone to the Surf Club and asked to see the stage. She told Bernard about the lovely Rhonda and assured Bernard that she had purchased a ticket so she would be in the concert crowd, ready for collection up to the stage.

Bernard replied with excitement. 'Oh, lucky you did that. Good idea. We didn't think about that. Yes, you will need a ticket, although plenty should be left.'

'Well, funny you should say that. Apparently, I purchased almost the last ticket. There were only three tickets left, and they had been reserved. So, it's looking like a sell-out crowd.'

Bernard replied, excited that they would have a full house. 'Oh really? That's great.'

Tilly replied with no excitement to bounce back to Bernard. 'Yep, but it's making me even more nervous. You know, I just do little pubs and family stuff. This is a big deal for me.'

Bernard eased her apprehension. 'The way to think about it is this. Just feel the music within yourself. If you're having a great time, everyone else will also be in the moment with you. Just enjoy it. What could possibly go wrong? You're beautiful, you have the voice of an angel, and you know and love that song. The crowd will love you. All the ladies will ogle over me and the boys; at least you can give the men in the audience someone to look at. It'll be fine. Trust me, I promise.'

Tilly leaned in towards Bernard, saying, 'Please, give me your hands.' Bernard wasn't sure what Tilly wanted, thinking she might read his palm. He stretched his hands out towards her, with his palms facing upwards. Tilly placed her hands on the underside of Bernard's, clasping them together towards each other. Her hands were now on the outside of Bernard's hands. She held them together, within hers, in a prayer position. Tilly looked Bernard in the eye, then closed her eyes and lowered her head, saying, 'Thank you, truly and from the bottom of my heart, thank you.'

Pretty Friend

Dalton, Ariiel, and Dan had enjoyed the day and were most impressed with Kelly Slater's win. They had seen impressive surfing from all the competitors, demonstrating high confidence and talent. The ocean and nature provided a fantastic challenge for them all to prove their skills and surf competency. These surfers weren't just good or excellent surfers. They were brilliant and entertaining and had an outstanding skill level far above the general level of surfers who thought they were all that, taking on the sets at Snapper Rocks and Greenmount. These guys were talented professionals.

Dalton had bumped into Cody, Tom, and Richie at different times of the day. Ariiel was interested in meeting these lads that Dalton had told her and Dan all about. She felt she knew them from the stories Dalton had shared about the Flaming Sambucas, the after-party at the den and the CD collection, the night surf with Cody, the soul surfer, and the dolphins in sync. Before Dalton had even introduced any of them by name, Ariiel already knew who Cody was, as Dalton had likened him to Tarzan, and much to Ariiel's amusement, he looked exactly like Tarzan. The only difference was that he was much taller than she had imagined.

When they met, Cody had a bit of a rant about his soul-surfer philosophy and was disgusted that the surfers were getting paid so much for a sport that relied heavily on Mother Nature to provide the playground. He did, however, acknowledge their high level of skill, and once he had shared his opinion, he tried not to make too much of a big deal after that.

Tom and Richie were up to mischief, day drinking with a stash of cold beers in their esky. They had found a perfect spot under a big shady tree to set up their picnic rug. They were more interested in talking to the pretty beach girls in their bikinis and harassing the surfers for their autographs than actually watching the competition. Richie had brought along an old, dinged-up surfboard, and he was collecting as many signatures as she could. He hadn't yet got to Kelly Slater, but it was his number one mission by the end of the day to have Kelly Slater's signature on his homegrown Coolangatta-made surfboard. Coolangatta board-shaper Dane Hamilton had carved it, but it had seen its last days being smashed on the rocks at Snapper one too many times. Richie thought it would make a lovely art piece for the den pool room wall, especially if Kelly's signature was on it.

The lads had invited Dalton, Dan and Ariiel to join them on their hangout picnic rugs under the pandanus palm. They had plenty of beers and snacks to share and a constant flow of humorous banter.

Tom joked with the group gathered on the rugs, including Dalton, Dan, Ariiel, Tom, Cody and some girls they had been hanging out with the night before. 'Did you know if I was batting for the other team and you beautiful girls were not so divine, I'd hit Kelly up for a romantic wedding at Froggies?' Froggies was a trendy wedding venue hidden around the corner from Snapper Rocks. 'He's a bit of everything, that sexy man. He can sing and play the guitar. He's a phenomenal surfer. He's got beautiful eyes, and he'll be a very wealthy man after today. I could settle down, give up my wild, free life and travel the surf scene with him. Do you think he'd say yes?'

He laughed out loud as everyone joined the laugh with him as Richie announced with dissatisfaction. 'You'd miss my hairy back, keeping you warm at night, Tommy.'

Tom laughed and replied with oozing sarcasm. 'True, that is so true, Richie. I wouldn't leave you, mate, don't worry. Who would look after me and cook me mid-week breakfast barbecues like you do?'

The crowd filtered out as the presentations were complete. It was nearing the end of the day as the Coolangatta lorikeets started migrating into the trees to roost for the night. Their screeches and happy tweets were deafening, and it was well known to the locals that this time of day was not the best for a peaceful beach stroll. It was the bird-poopy time of day along the pavement as the Norfolk Pines became the resting place for these screechy birds. Dalton, Dan, and Ariiel used this as their excuse to depart the gang. They had a Powderfinger Concert to get to by 8.30 pm in Surfers Paradise.

Dalton already had the tickets, so all they had to do was go back to the hotel, shower, and walk across the road to the Surfers Paradise Surf Club.

They all said their farewells, knowing it would not be too long before they would see each other again. Dalton had promised Shawn that he would play his gig at the Coolangatta Hotel for the next Sunday session.

As Dalton was departing, he checked with the lads that they could back it up and come and support him the next day. He asked Cody if he would come along as well. Tom and Richie were definite. They always joined in the Sunday arvo session. Cody was Cody. 'I might be there, man. It depends on how the surf is in the morning. I'm thinking of heading down to Sandon for a surf tomorrow or early in the week. You know, I'm not much of a drinker, but I'd love to see you play again. I won't promise you anything, but if I'm there, I'm there. If not, I'll see you around, man.'

Dalton had learned in the short time it took to get to know Cody that no one controlled him. He did only what he wanted. He was the strongest advocate for his own freedom and was adamant that his daily schedule was never planned, especially not by anyone else. Selfish, perhaps, or self-directed, depends on how you viewed it.

Dan had his car, so there was no need to catch a Glenn Gaffer Gold Coast bus, although Dalton wanted Dan and Ariiel to experience the bus ride just to see if they thought Glenn was just as creepy as he did.

Dalton, Dan, and Ariiel were crossing the road near the bus depot to return to Dan's car. Suddenly, they heard a loud voice. 'Hey Mr Music, where you off to, not catching the bus today?' Glenn stood beside the bus as the passengers were loading on. He was smoking his cigarettes as he did, one after the other. He was getting his quick nicotine fix before the long drive to wherever he was travelling, Brisbane, perhaps.

Dalton shouted back, 'Nah, not today. I found some friends.'

Glenn continued the conversation. 'Where are you going?'

Dalton instantly felt invaded and refused to answer honestly, which was not a natural trait for him. There was no way he would mention they were going to the Powderfinger Concert; otherwise, Dalton was sure Glenn would have turned up there. He was that kind of creepy. Dalton answered instead with limited details. 'We are just heading into Surfers Paradise for the night.'

Glenn replied as he stomped his cigarette butt into the ground. 'Enjoy your night, my friend, with your pretty friend there.' With an extended pointed chin, he lifted his head in a tilt to acknowledge Ariiel.

Luckily, Dalton had already told Dan and Ariiel about this bus driver creep-serial-killer-stalker kind of character, so they knew better than to engage in the conversation. They just kept walking. Dan's bristles were up on his back. *How dare he call Ariiel "pretty friend" while I'm holding onto her hand? I mean, that's just asking for it.* His masculine instinct was to lay this creep flat on the ground, but that would do no one any good right now. He maintained self-control. He didn't even look back. He gently grabbed Ariiel's hand tighter and headed toward the car.

Dalton kept walking, too, with his gut churning inside. *How dare he speak about Ariiel like that?* Dalton also knew better than to react to this creep. He replied, trying to control the flare in his nostrils from the anger that had started in his gut. He got out the words incredibly calmly but with so much confined angst. 'Thank you. Have a nice night, Glenn.'

When Dalton, Dan and Ariiel were almost about to reach the car, Dalton said calmly and clearly so that Ariiel and Dan could hear, as they were a few meters in front of him, but not too loud as Glenn was not too far behind them. 'Hey guys, just keep walking past the car. Trust me on this one.'

Dalton had goosebumps down his back, and Ariiel had developed tears and a big lump in her throat, but she had not turned around since she realised it was the creepy bus driver Dalton had told them about. From the moment Glenn shouted hello, her feeling was instant fear.

They kept walking past the car as Dalton caught up alongside them. He could talk to them now without Glenn hearing. 'I just don't trust that guy. You see what I mean, right?'

Dan replied. 'I'm getting serious Ivan Milat vibes, man.'

Dalton replied with a massive shudder going down his back. 'Me too, so it's not just me. He's creepy, right? Let's just keep walking up this way a little further until the bus moves away. If it's on schedule, he won't stay there for long. The buses run on time.'

Ariiel hadn't spoken yet. She was quietly walking beside Dan, feeling completely violated by Glenn's comment. 'The way he said, "pretty friend" was so creepy, it almost made me vomit.'

Dalton suggested they turn left into the next street and wait around the corner until they could see the bus move away. They did.

Dan was thinking deeply and not saying much. He was the kind of guy who usually took matters into his own hands without considering the consequences. He had gotten himself into and out of trouble because of this trait, but his instinct with this guy was not to get involved. Dan wouldn't tolerate disrespect to women, but something deep down in his core suggested this guy wasn't a man of the normal psyche. Something was not right with him, and that was Dan's internal fear. The best thing they could do was walk away calmly.

It wasn't long before they heard the bus engine start and saw it moving off down the highway. Dalton was reasonably sure that Glenn would have been driving that bus. There was nobody there for the driver's changeover. From what Dalton could remember from their conversations, Glenn often did the Tweed to Brisbane trip all the way into Roma St train station. Hopefully, that is where he was going tonight.

They walked back to Dan's car. Ariiel suggested maybe they should report the interaction to the bus depot. The tricky thing was that what he said was not criminal. It would draw attention to them because if the police investigated, Glenn would know to whom he said that. It would also mean they had to hold onto that yucky situation for longer, and what they wanted to do was forget about it entirely and get on with their fantastic day and night. They had all had such a great day so far and were looking forward to the Powderfinger concert.

Ariiel leaned over to Dan and spoke softly in his ear. 'Thank you for protecting me by not reacting. As hard as it was for you not to flatten him, you made the right decision.' She kissed him on the cheek.

Badman, the big tough surfer, turned to Ariiel. 'Thanks for recognising that, babe. You know I would protect you to the end of the world, and sometimes that is all about making the right decision at the right time. The wrong decision at the wrong time could have had us all in shallow graves. There is something not right about that guy.'

chapter ninety-one

The Butterfly Necklace

Tilly headed out of the hotel and wandered into the street, deciding she would spend the day shopping. She wanted nothing too fancy. It wasn't her; she was a jeans and T-shirt girl or a simple dress kind of girl. But tonight, being on stage with Powderfinger, she wanted to go for a smart casual look because it wasn't supposed to be planned, but she also wanted to feel nice. The clothes that she had with her hadn't been washed. She had been living out of her backpack since leaving Angourie and had already worn most of her clothes.

Tilly's first stop was Sportsgirl. She tried on a few things, and they were all lovely. She would have bought them all, but was also aware that anything she purchased had to fit into her backpack for her future travels.

Her favourite item that she tried on was a long black velvet dress. It was simple. It was fitted around the bust with shoestring straps. From the under-bust to the bottom of the dress, it was heavy and flowing to the ground. She imagined it with her boots. It would be perfect. It was a Stevie Nick's vibe. She felt amazing when she was wearing it. *Yep, this is the one.* She felt she needed to spice it up with some lovely jewellery. Tilly took the dress to the counter and grabbed her wallet to pay.

The cashier commented. 'Nice dress choice. What's the special occasion?'

Tilly replied. 'Well, I'm probably not supposed to say anything, but it doesn't matter. I'm getting up on stage tonight at the Surf Club with Powderfinger. I'm just singing one song with them, and it's very impromptu, but I thought I should make some effort rather than pull some dirty jeans out of my backpack.'

The cashier replied, interested in what Tilly was saying and ensuring she finished with the sales pitch, as this was an essential part of her job. 'Oh, that's cool. Perfect choice. You'll look amazing, I'm sure. Do you need any other items, perhaps a funky hat, some nice hoop earrings, or a tattoo choker necklace? They are all the fashion right now.'

Tilly replied with confidence. 'Umm, I'm not a hat girl. I bought one the other day for the beach, but it's not my normal style. I'm not a hoop earring girl, and I have a thing about my neck. I don't think the choker will feel comfortable for me, but thanks for the suggestions. I might try to find some simple jewellery though. That is a good idea. Is there an op-shop somewhere?'

The cashier replied, pointing in different directions as she did. 'There are a few op-shops around the place. Red Cross is on the main street, or you can go to Kleins, which is not an op-shop but a new shop in the mall. They have some affordable options.'

Tilly replied. 'Thank you, that's very helpful.'

The cashier wanted to move off-topic; she had done the hard sell now, and Tilly clarified she had everything she wanted to purchase. 'I hope you don't mind me asking. I've heard a little bit about this band, and my boyfriend bought me a ticket tonight, so I'll see you there, but what kind of music do they play?'

'Umm, I guess you would say alternative Australian rock music. They have some great originals and play some cover songs, too. They will do anything to make sure the crowd is having fun.'

The cashier folded Tilly's new dress. She wrapped it nicely in light paper and placed it in the colourful striped Sportsgirl bag. 'Sounds good. I love a bit of Australian home-grown talent. We don't get a lot of live music here. Most of the bands play in Brisbane, and they never come to the Gold Coast.'

Tilly replied excitedly, wanting to support her new friends. 'Yeah, it's cool, huh? I've been hanging out with them this week, and they are all really nice guys. You'll love them. I suggest you get in early because I heard it's a sell-out show, so if you want to be at the front, you might need to get there before the crowds.'

The cashier passed the bag across the counter towards Tilly, handing it to her like a precious gift. 'Well then, I'll see you in your beautiful new dress tonight. Have a ball.'

'Thank you.' Tilly exited the shop, unsure exactly where she was going next, but happy she had the main thing sorted. She had a lovely new dress to wear.

Tilly wandered into a pre-loved jewellery store and was drawn immediately to a butterfly necklace under the glass counter. She spoke gently to the lady sitting on a high stool towards the back of the shop, doing some knitting. 'I'm sorry to bother you, but could I have a closer look at that gorgeous butterfly necklace?'

The lady spoke and sounded like Bessie from Angourie. Bessie was good at accents and sometimes put on an English accent. This was all part of her disguise tactics. The lady spoke just the same. 'Well, of course you can, dear. It has quite a story, this one.'

Tilly was instantly curious. 'Oooh, do tell.'

The lady replied in an intriguing tone. 'This necklace came to me many years ago, and it has been magical for quite a few customers back in the day, but over the past few years, it has sat in that cabinet, and no one has been brave enough to wear it.'

Tilly was instantly curious. 'May I ask why?'

'Of course you can, dear.' This seemed to be her favourite saying. 'Apparently, it holds special powers. It brings people back together when they least expect it.'

Tilly queried. 'It does? How do you know that?'

The lady continued fiddling through a bunch of cabinet keys. 'The lady who brought it to me said it had worked its magic for her. It was gifted to her by her Great Aunt with the rule that it must be kept moving to keep its power, so she gave it to me, knowing that many people pass through the shop. It's a pay-it-forward gift, waiting for the next lucky person to withhold it. Perhaps that is you, my dear. If you are brave enough.'

'I think I am. I'm Tilly Macallan. I'm pretty brave.'

'Of course, my dear, but you must be certain that the person you want to bring back to you is the person you want to be with forever, because you can't change your mind. That's the power.'

'Well, ah, I think I do. I messed up an amazing love and friendship, and I want it back.'

'Well, my dear, you have to be sure. If you're not sure, I recommend you walk away. Some people go back, and it was never meant to be. They try to force love that is not right for them. This butterfly necklace could be a curse if you have any uncertainty.'

The lady spoke with so much wisdom, yet she gave so much power to this butterfly necklace. It was quite absurd. Tilly doubted this could be true, but in the same way, she was intrigued and curious to learn more.

Tilly didn't know how else to ask without seeming rude and off-putting. She spoke with a hint of unintentional attitude. 'So, how do you know this necklace works? Where is the proof?'

The lady cleared her throat, a little offended but confident in her belief about what she knew about the necklace's history. 'I guess it's up to you whether you believe it.' As she said this, she opened the cabinet and handed the necklace gently to Tilly.

As Tilly held the necklace in her hand, she suddenly had a vision of Dalton, in his blue Bandana, walking across the street to the Angourie Local, followed by a vision of his eyes gazing into hers.

The lady walked around to the same side of the counter where Tilly was standing, holding the necklace. It was like the lady could see what Tilly imagined in her mind, as she said knowingly. 'Is that him? Is that the one you want back in your life?' She paused for quite a long silence, then added. 'Forever?'

Tilly squinted her eyes, furrowed her brow together, and tilted her head curiously. 'How do you know what I'm seeing?'

The lady replied with such wisdom again. 'I don't know what you are seeing, but you do. It's clear as day for you, isn't it?'

'I would give anything to bring him back to me, for me to have a second chance with him. I desperately want a take-two.'

'Of course, my dear.' She repeated those words, moved closer to Tilly, and looked her directly in the eye. 'The butterfly necklace is all yours. On one condition: when you find him, you must return the necklace to me, or pass it on. Its power is strong and ongoing and can't be kept just for you. It's way too valuable.'

Tilly replied with light humour and with the reflected accent of the lady. 'Of course, my dear.'

The lady laughed at Tilly's humour, noticing that she had been paying attention to her accent and the pattern of words. 'You are brave and funny, but you must understand this. Once he is brought back to you, you won't need the necklace anymore. The rest of forever relies on your inner magic that you create together.'

Tilly leaned down instinctively, kissed the necklace, and then clasped her hands together around the necklace, closing her eyes and making a silent wish. *Please bring him back to me.*

The lady patted Tilly on the back and went to walk away, then turned back towards Tilly and said clearly. 'When you're ready, you can place the necklace on and trust in its power with all your heart.'

The lady walked around to the other side of the counter and opened the drawer. 'You might need this for safekeeping.' She handed Tilly a royal-blue suede jewellery tote bag with a bright yellow string. Tilly placed the necklace inside the bag and pulled the string tight. She wasn't ready just yet.

'Thank you so much. Do you mind if I ask your name?' Tilly felt close to this woman, like she had known her for a long time, and it didn't feel right not to have a name to go with the butterfly necklace story.

'My name is Bessie, but people call me Bess.' Tilly instantly felt a stream of goosebumps cover her whole body as this lady reminded her so much of Angourie Bessie, but Angourie Bessie had passed away a few years prior.

All Tilly could do was reply briefly. 'Umm, wow, thank you, Bess. I'm so glad I wandered in here today. You do not know how this moment has possibly changed my whole life.'

'Of course, my dear, but don't thank me yet. Have an amazing night. I hope it's everything you've dreamed of and more.'

Tilly was so appreciative and lost for words. This whole scenario had her mind in a trance. She reached down and grabbed her Sportsgirl bag she had placed on the floor and walked out of the shop, noticing as she did the dangling bells on the door were the same as the dangling bells Bessie had on her shop door in Angourie. Tilly walked out, shaking her head in total disbelief at what she had just experienced. She felt like she was in a dream, but there she was, standing in the street in Surfers Paradise with a butterfly necklace in her hand that was promised to bring Dalton back to her.

The rest of the day couldn't pass quickly enough. Tilly decided she had one more thing to purchase. Tilly was all about smelling good, and she realised after her morning shower that she had used her last drop of Sunflowers cologne. She popped into the mall and found a pharmacy with an entire section dedicated to colognes. Tilly had seen nothing like this in a chemist. In Sydney, she often visited the Myer Store or David Jones and wandered around collecting sample perfume cards. In Yamba, there was not much of a range; hence, the *Sunflowers by Elizabeth Arden* had become her go-to cologne. She was aware of the significance of scent and how it related to memory, so she wanted to create a new scent for this special evening that she instinctively felt was ahead of her.

A lovely young girl came over to the counter and offered to help. A young, sweet voice echoed in Tilly's ear. 'Hi there, can I help you today? Is there anything in particular you are searching for?'

Tilly turned around to the voice and recognised the face of the young waitress from the restaurant in the Surf Club. 'Hi, how are you going? Maddi?'

Maddi replied. 'Yeah, that's me. Where do I know you from? Your face is familiar.'

Tilly said. 'Umm, you served me breakfast at the Surf Club the other day. I'm not surprised you don't remember me; it was so busy,' Tilly continued talking. She questioned politely and complimentary. 'You work here as well? You're a busy girl.'

Maddi replied, eager to explain her story. 'I am. I'm trying to save money for university in a couple of years. I want to be a teacher.'

Tilly assured Maddi that she was onto a good thing. 'Good on you, I have my teaching qualification. I'm not working at the moment. It's a long story, but teaching is a great career, very rewarding, and you can travel anywhere with it. I'd love to get some experience and head overseas to international schools one day. That's my plan.'

Maddi shared more of her plans with Tilly. 'Yeah, I think I'll save up for a couple of years, and then I'll live on campus in Lismore. I've got friends there.'

'That sounds superb. Good on you.' Tilly was interested in chatting, but Maddi was keen to finish her shift.

Maddi cut the conversation short. 'So, anyway, what can I help you with today?'

Tilly replied, realising that other customers had come into the store and Maddi would need to help them as well. 'I'm not sure what I'm looking for, but it needs to be something memorable, something now-ish. I have a special night ahead of me and want to remember it forever.'

'Well, you are lucky to know you have a special night ahead. What's the big plans?'

'Umm, I'm probably not supposed to say anything, but it doesn't matter. I'm playing a secret song with Powderfinger tonight at their concert at the Surf Club. It's an impromptu thing; they will just call me up on the stage and pretend it's all improvised, but I have played with them before, so it's not much of a surprise for me.'

'Ooh, that sounds so fun. Yes, you definitely need a memorable scent. Can I suggest CK One? It's a new cologne by Calvin Klein, and it's non-gendered. It's progressive for the 90s, right? It's the first ever non-gendered cologne.'

'That sounds great. Does it smell good, though? Is it more masculine or feminine? I'm a bit of a tomboy, grew up with three older brothers, so it might be perfect for me.' Tilly liked the sound of the cologne and was keen to try it. She liked the name, too—*CK One, just like my favourite U2 song.*

Maddi explained. 'To be honest, it doesn't have a feminine or a masculine scent. It's completely neutral. Here you go. I'll get you a sample card.'

Tilly took the sample card and fell in love with the scent. She had been wearing *Sunflowers* for so long and was keen for a change. 'Yes, please, that is divine.'

Maddi packed the cologne into a paper bag and added a free *Calvin Klein Eternity* sample bottle. 'I've popped a little sample bottle in there. You'll like that one too. It's fresh. One of my favourites.'

Tilly was delighted. 'Thank you, that's so lovely.'

Maddi had more to say and felt rude that she had cut the conversation short. She loved conversation with her customers, so she loved her job so much. 'Have a super special night. I might see you there. I will be working in the restaurant and the bar tonight at the Surf Club.'

Tilly looked at the time, noticing it was almost midday. 'Wow, you're a busy girl.'

'Yeah, it's not too bad. I love my jobs. I'm finishing here in 10 minutes, and then I'll head home for a nana nap, ready to start restaurant duty at 6 pm.'

'Well, I will most definitely see you there then.' Tilly smiled and thanked Maddi again for help. 'Thank you.'

As Tilly walked out the door, she lifted the sample card to her nose and took a deep whiff of the cologne she had just purchased. It smelt divine on the cardboard. She was excited to return to the hotel and spray it on her fresh-clean-post-shower skin. *Tonight is going to be amazing.*

Tilly took her shopping bags back to the hotel. She still had plenty of time to go to the beach for a walk and a swim to clear her mind and settle her nerves.

The beach radio chimed at 4 pm, telling the people, 'It's time to turn over.' Tilly decided that was her cue to return to the hotel and prepare for the big night.

As she arrived back at the hotel foyer, Bernard was coming back from wherever he had been for the day.

Tilly saw Bernard first and started the conversation as they both headed towards the lift. 'Hey Bernard, how was your day?'

Bernard turned around to see Tilly standing behind him. 'Hey, Tilly. My day was superb. I caught a bus to Coolangatta this morning to watch the Billabong Pro surfing competition. Amaaazing talent! Those guys are seriously something else. Then me and the boys spent the afternoon setting up the stage for tonight.'

'Ooh, that would have been fun. I probably should have come to help.' Tilly replied.

Bernard noticed Tilly's beach bag and towel and saw her bikini strap hanging off her shoulder. 'No, don't be silly. We have a crew to help with all that. I just boss people around and look important. Anyway, it's all set up now. What have you been up to? It looks like you've been to the beach.'

'Yep. I went to the beach. I just had a lovely beach walk and a swim, trying to settle these butterflies.' Tilly gestured swarms of butterflies swimming around inside her belly. She wondered whether to add more detail about her shopping experience and the butterfly necklace.

'Sounds perfect. You'll be fine tonight. You know you will.' The lift arrived, and the door opened as they both stepped in. Another guest ran to catch the lift.

Tilly felt awkward talking to Bernard about her day with a complete stranger in the lift, so she waited until they reached their floor to continue the conversation. Lift rides were always awkward, and there was never enough time for a proper conversation, so there was always small talk or silence.

As they stepped out of the lift and walked towards the rooms, Tilly questioned Bernard. 'What time are you heading over to the Surf Club?'

'We start at 8.30 pm. I've spent the afternoon setting up with the boys, and the sound check was perfect, so we are as ready as we will ever be. We will probably head over and get a meal at the Surf Club just before 6 pm, if you want to join us, and then we can go from there. I think John booked us a table. I'm hoping he did. The good thing is that not many people know who we are, which is nice. We can just blend in with the furniture and have a normal meal. If we were in Brisbane, it would be annoying. People want to come and chat all the time.'

Tilly winked and did a hip tilt to the side, holding up her Sportsgirl bag. 'Sounds like a plan.' I'll be ready, in my new dress, by 5.30 pm.'

'A new dress, huh? Sounds fancy!' Bernard smiled.

'You know me, Little Miss Tomboy, not fancy at all, but I thought I should make an effort outside of my dirty jeans that I've been wearing for the past week or so.' Tilly made a funny little side comment. 'I mean, have you heard the news? I'll be on stage tonight with this amazing band called Powderfinger.' Tilly winked again, and Bernard laughed, a warm-hearty-laugh.

'I heard that; a little bird told me it was a secret.' Bernard winked back.

Tilly held her pointer finger to her lips, making the noise long and loud. 'SSSSShhhhhh!' They laughed together as they unlocked their side-by-side doors. Tilly finished the conversation as they departed company. 'See you in a few hours.'

chapter ninety-two

Chasing Butterflies

Dalton was distracted as they climbed into the car. A bright aqua-blue and black butterfly had landed on the door handle he was just about to open. He didn't want to squash it, so he gently put his hand out for the butterfly to climb on board as he nudged its wings. He moved it to rest on a large green leaf in the garden bed nearby.

'What are you doing?' said Dan, wondering why Dalton was walking away from the car and into the park again. All Dan wanted to do right now was get out of this crazy town.

'I'm rescuing a butterfly, Dan.' Dalton glanced over his shoulder, making sure not to drop the butterfly on the ground as many people were walking along the footpath, heading back to their cars.

'Righto then, you do that, and then let's make tracks out of here.' Dan was antsy to get moving.

All in the car, safe and sound, Dan started the engine with a roar and pressed the horn, making a vibrant melody in celebration of leaving Coolangatta. Dan enjoyed being the centre of attention, but not when psychopathic creeps were around, but he felt safe again now and was happy to celebrate and show off his beloved PIE. Ariiel initially dropped her head in embarrassment, but then she quickly realised this was fun. She laughed with Dan and Dalton, knowing that Dan was doing his best to lighten the mood instantly.

They made their way back through the traffic to Surfers Paradise, arriving at Dalton's hotel, The Beachcomber, in time to have quick showers and make their way to the Surfers Paradise Surf Club for dinner and the concert. They parked the car in the street as it so happened that a perfect empty park was waiting for them just outside the hotel. It was a free hotel guest parking spot with no time limit sign, so they grabbed it. This was a rarity in Surfers Paradise. Dan felt it was a safe place to park his beloved PIE. It was near the hotel entrance and directly beneath street lights, which might deter hooligans from fooling around with it. Dan was fully insured, of course, but he would rather not deal with any damage to his beloved vehicle.

As Dalton climbed out of the car, he went to shut his heavy car door. He noticed again a bright aqua-blue and black butterfly on the door handle. He couldn't help but mention it to Dan and Ariiel. 'Hey guys, how weird is this? The butterfly is back. Do you think it came all the way for the ride? Surely not. Just a coincidence, perhaps.' Ariiel was instantly drawn to the situation. 'Wow, that's uncanny. What does it mean to see a butterfly? Can you make a wish? Are they like ladybugs? If they are, you should make a wish.' Ariiel was nodding, convinced this was some kind of supernatural interaction.

Dan was interested as well. 'Wow, man, that's unbelievable. Do you think it's the same butterfly?'

Dalton reflected on the butterfly on his door handle in Coolangatta. 'Umm. I think so. It was definitely aqua-blue and black. I noticed that, but I mean, there are a lot of blue butterflies.'

Ariiel came in for a closer look. 'I think you should make a wish.'

Again, Dalton rested his hand on the door and nudged the butterfly into the palm of his hand. As he placed it on a large leaf in the roadside garden bed, he made a wish quietly in his mind. *Please bring her back to me.* Dalton shook his head at the circumstance and wondered what the significance of this butterfly was for him, if any. He wasn't usually one to believe in this kind of circumstance, but weirder things had happened lately, and he realised more and more that life was one amazing set of circumstances and an incredible journey. Perhaps this was a sign from Chelsea, an angel alongside him.

They took turns showering and got dressed for the evening. Ariiel was excited about wearing the new Tigerlily dress Dan had bought her on the road trip to Surfers Paradise. It was a gorgeous summer dress that fitted her perfectly, and she felt comfortable in it. She usually wore jeans and an oversized T-shirt, but tonight was special. She even threw on a pair of wedge heels, making her slightly taller. She was excited when she stood beside Dan, realising that she was a fraction closer to his lips. Dan wasn't big on fashion, throwing on a pair of light-coloured jeans and a Billabong T-shirt he had worn for years. It was a faded favourite, but it fitted him well, as his muscular arms and chest filled the space of the T-shirt.

Ariiel snuck over beside Dan while they waited for Dalton to slip on his Blundstone boots. 'You look super gorgeous tonight, Badman. Can I steal a kiss?'

'Well, of course you can, beautiful girl. You look divine, as always. I could devour you right now.' Dan pulled Ariiel close and placed his whole mouth over hers. His strength and warmth encompassed her, and he smelt good, too.

Ariiel blushed, but she returned the flirt all the same. 'Mmmm, I could devour you, too. I bet you taste as good as you smell.'

Dalton instantly felt like the third wheel in this little trio. 'Lucky you two have your own room tonight. I'm feeling the degustation of love from way over here.' They all laughed, and Dan couldn't help but tease. 'You're just jealous Cowboy! Maybe tonight you'll get lucky, too. Maybe we will find Tilly, and you two can sort your shit out.' Dan was a little lacking in manners, but it was the truth.

'Yeah, maybe tonight's the night. I feel like I'm getting closer to her, and there is a massive chance that she will be at the concert tonight if the snippets of random information I've gathered from strangers along the way are true. I just hope that she is happy to see me.'

Dalton was wearing his favourite jeans, the ones he had worn the night he met Tilly. He had also chosen to wear the same white T-shirt he wore the night he met Tilly. He wanted to be typically cliché and pretend they were meeting for the first time again. Like a take-two. But this time, he would not let her walk away. Dalton also put on his blue bandana. It was the easiest way to deal with his curls right now. They were out of control. He had just showered and used the CK One Gift Pack Hair and Body Wash, compliments of Maddi's recommendation and her generosity to throw in the extras. The product had nourished his hair so beautifully that it formed ringlets around his face. The last thing Dalton had to do before they walked out the door was to put on his new CK One cologne. He opened the wrapping and the box and gave himself a liberal spray around his neck and face.

Dan laughed as he slapped Dalton on the bum and grabbed his car keys from the counter. 'Mmm, I could devour you too, Dalton, smelling so delicious like that.'

'It's good stuff, huh? Apparently, it's the latest thing. Gender-neutral cologne. Have you ever heard of such a thing?' Dalton explained the cologne as best he could, using the terminology Maddi had shared to describe the new CK fragrance.

Dan sniffed, interested in working out if it smelt more masculine or feminine. 'I have not heard about it. My little bubble in Angourie doesn't know about French cologne, but I can tell you it smells good to me. What do you think, Ariiel?'

'It smells good to me too.' Ariiel grabbed the bottle, asking if Dalton would mind if she had a spray too.

'Sure, go ahead, we can all smell as one.' Dalton laughed at himself and his quick-witted humour.

'I left my perfume in my car, so I appreciate it. Makes life easy if we all smell the same, huh?'

Dalton noticed Dan had grabbed his keys and thought to mention that Dan was probably best to leave his car here at the hotel, as they just had to walk five minutes up the road. 'Probably best if we leave your car where it is parked and walk. It's not very far from here to where we have to go, and your car is safe where it's parked.'

'Cool man, good idea.' Dan threw the keys back on the bench, and then, on second thoughts, for safety reasons, he grabbed the keys and put them in the top drawer of the TV cabinet. 'To be sure, to be sure.' Making a pun at Shannon's Car Insurance, which had an Irish slogan.

They had planned to have dinner at the Surf Club before the Powderfinger concert, and Dalton was glad that he had made a table reservation for three people at 7.30 pm, with the lovely Maddi. It would most likely be a busy night, and Dalton was guessing many people would have the same plan.

The lineup to collect tickets and go into the concert venue had already started when they arrived. Dalton, Dan, and Ariiel already had their tickets, so they went upstairs to the restaurant.

Dalton was delighted that the first person he saw was Maddi. She smiled and came straight over to them. 'Good Evening. We meet again. You have precision timing, Dalton, right on 7.30 pm.' She tapped her watch. 'I have your favourite Table 26 waiting for you.' She turned and directed them to follow her, looking back as she did. 'You might be interested to know that I cleared this table 10 minutes ago of the famous dirty dishes from Powderfinger, the performing band for this evening were here, and their guest.'

Maddi was keen for a chat, but her duty supervisor interrupted the conversation, letting her know that after she seated these new guests, she needed to clear and separate the large table on the balcony into three tables of four for the next rush of 7.30 pm dinner bookings. Maddi nodded. 'Sure, no worries.' Then she turned back to Dalton. 'I'll take you to your table and grab some menus, and I'll be right back to take your order. It might be an idea to get your meal orders in as soon as possible so you don't miss the show. The kitchen is bustling tonight. Also, if you want drinks, please go to the bar to order those directly.

Dalton smiled his wide, appreciative smile and said, 'Thank you, Maddi, you do your thing.'

As they sat down, Dalton commented that this had been his table every time he had been to the restaurant for a meal. Dan couldn't resist mentioning it, and he hoped Dalton didn't mind him knowing the intricate details about Tilly that only a close friend would know. 'That's a bit of an uncanny circumstance, too. Did you know Tilly's favourite table at The Angourie Local is Table 26?'

'Yes, I knew that. It was one of the first things she told me. Her lucky number and all that.'

Dalton reached to grab the water jug in the middle of the table to pour them all a glass of water. As he did, he couldn't quite believe his eyes. 'Oh my god, you guys, what the fuck?' He pointed to the handle of the water jug where a beautiful blue butterfly sat.

Ariiel couldn't quite see what he was talking about, as she was on the opposite side of the table. 'What is it?'

'It's a butterfly.' Dalton put his head into his hands and circled his face with them, then rested his hands on the side of his face, opening his mouth in disbelief. He had just realised that the butterfly symbolised Chelsea, her favourite T-shirt. He had forgotten all about it, a memory he had cast way back in his mind that he tried very hard not to revisit. The T-shirt Chelsea wore on their last night together and the day she passed had a bright blue butterfly on the front with the word "Believe".

Dan, the big tough Badman, was shaken in disbelief. He said, 'I'm not sure what to make of this. It's just a butterfly, but how many times does it need to be rescued? And why is it following us?'

Dalton shook his head, blinking his eyes. 'I'm none the wiser than you. I have no answers. Let's just go with the fact that "the world is fucking beautiful," right?'

Ariiel was nodding, and her eyes filled with tears. This was a beautiful moment that none of them could explain, and no one would believe it, but they had all witnessed this thing happening, not just once or twice, but now three times. She reached her hand out and placed it on Dalton's on the side of his face, simply saying 'Right?' Dan had told Ariiel all about Dalton's "dark secret" that he had shared with him, so Ariiel was completely aware that perhaps this was an angelic thing that was happening, or maybe just a gorgeous, strange, life circumstance.

Dalton's first instinct was to reach out and take the butterfly to a nearby garden or a plant. A few large palms in pots were scattered around the balcony dining area. But he just let the butterfly stay where it was for now.

After clearing and separating the table she had been directed to, Maddi returned to take their meal orders. She took a notepad from her back pocket to write down the orders. Dan cleared his throat and said, 'We will keep it simple tonight. It's busy, huh? We are just going to order three Chicken Parmys from your specials. I'm happy to go with the chips and salad, but these two are going to be difficult. Ariiel would like chips and mashed potatoes. She loves carbs, and Dalton would like vegetables and salad. Is that okay?'

Maddi replied, smiling. 'That's totally okay; Dalton is one of our regulars here now. He can have whatever he wants.' She paused and changed the subject momentarily. 'I'm getting a strong vibe of CK One. Do you like it?'

Ariiel and Dalton said in unison, 'I love it.' Dalton added, 'Thank you for the recommendation. The extra hair and body wash you threw in the gift pack is playing havoc with my curls, but that's okay. I don't mind.'

Maddi commented, 'I'm actually going to say I like the curls and bandana look. You don't see that look around here often. You'll stand out in the crowd tonight.'

'That's my plan.' Dalton nodded confidently, then added, 'Hey, do you know anything about this butterfly? Is she a regular here?' He pointed to the butterfly on the water jug.

'Oh, that's pretty! What a delightful surprise. No, I've never seen a butterfly here before. It's come a long way from the garden. Shall I place it in the garden bed outside?'

Dalton replied assertively. 'It's fine, you're busy. If it's still here after we eat, I'll take it to the garden bed before we go to the concert. I was just wondering if it's something you see often?'

Maddi replied as she placed her notebook back in her back pocket. 'Nope, definitely, nope.' Dalton nodded, half expecting the answer she had given.

Maddi knew she needed to keep moving to make sure all the restaurant customers had their meal orders in. With the concert starting at around 8.30 pm, they needed to ensure everyone was fed on time. The kitchen was busy. 'I'll get these orders into the kitchen for you; it shouldn't be too long. I'm guessing the bar will be quite busy downstairs in the concert, so maybe get a few drinks in here first.'

All three said at the same time as Maddi departed the table.

'Thank you.'

'Thanks.'

'Will do.'

chapter ninety-three

The Gig - Tilly

Tilly and the boys had finished their meals at the Surf Club long before the crowds started pouring in. Maddi, Tilly's favourite waitress, had placed them at her favourite Table 26 on the balcony. They had managed to get through their entire meal without any interruptions. Either nobody had noticed that they were "the band," or people were politely leaving them to eat their dinner in peace. Probably more the latter because Tilly had noticed a few inconspicuous sniggers and points from onlookers and other diners in the restaurant.

They departed the restaurant after 7 pm and headed downstairs to the concert hall to make the final stage set-up arrangements. Bernard wanted to do a sound check with Tilly on the microphone she would use for her special performance.

The crowds would start rolling in around 8 pm, for the hard-core fans to get their positions up front, near the centre stage. The great thing about this venue was that it was small for a concert venue, so no matter where you were positioned in the room, you would have a good view of the stage and the vocals would be clear.

They had an hour to make sure everything was perfect, and then they would move to the backstage area to get dressed. All the boys had their outfits planned for the evening, nothing too fancy. They all wore black faded jeans and a nice, collared shirt, each to their own taste. Bernard was big on giving the audience a professional show. He was most particular about the perfect sound and lighting, and they had a guy for that job who knew precisely what Bernard and the boys wanted. Bernard also wanted the boys to look professional, as their image was important for the marketing and promotion of their band. If they were going to be super famous, it all started here, at their very beginnings.

Tilly was already dressed in the new Sportsgirl dress that she loved. She had her special necklace in her bag and was ready to start wearing it. She had a feeling that she was prepared for its magic.

After sound check, they all headed backstage to the dressing rooms, where the boys had their outfits hung up. They had also organised a few pre-concert drinks to be placed in their dressing room area. Bernard had ordered a carton of Bundaberg Ginger Beer on ice for the boys and Tilly, and a jar of honey. This was his magic potion to keep his voice smooth before performing. The boys had placed a carton of VB on ice as well, but they all tried to limit their alcohol intake before the performance so they could focus on their craft and give the best performance without cloudy minds.

They always enjoyed a few quiet beverages after the show. The beers would be waiting.

The boys were all dressed and ready. They had created the set list and discussed various aspects of the performance. They talked about extended introductions, extended outros, storytelling moments, crowd involvement moments, and, most importantly, when they would invite Tilly onstage. They had also chosen three songs for their encore, which they knew would inevitably happen. They were ready.

Tilly had brought a few items of make-up to reapply: her eyeliner, mascara and lipstick, and the final piece. She turned to Bernard as he took a long sip from his ginger beer. 'Hey Bernard, do you mind helping me with this?' She handed him her necklace with an opened clasp so he could place it around her neck.

Bernard admired the necklace and the shiny blue colour it was reflecting. 'Wow, Tilly, this is beautiful. Where did you get this?'

'Do you like it? I bought it today at a pre-loved jewellery store. Apparently, it has magic powers.' She nodded convincingly as Bernard placed the necklace around her neck and did up the clasp gently.

'Well, as long as you believe in magic, it will be magical for you.' Bernard kissed the back of Tilly's neck with a friendly kiss. 'Break a leg. You're going to be amazing and magical tonight.'

It was close to 8.30 pm, and the crowds were forming at the front of the stage. Tilly decided she would go to the bar and buy a Macallan's whisky on the rocks for some extra courage.

She made her way out of the side door of the stage and in through the ticketing door, showing her ticket on the way through. She realised she probably didn't need a ticket, as the boys would have let her in and out of the concert venue through the stage door anyway. Still, it felt better that she could go in and out of the public entrance, and she was more than happy to support the band with the small cost of a ticket anyway.

She could feel the energy and excitement building from the crowd as she walked in the door. It was going to be a fun night. As she got to the bar, she could see Maddi, so she put herself in the line leading to her service area.

'Hey, Maddi.' Tilly smiled.

Maddi replied in a high-pitched twang, trying to hide that she didn't remember Tilly's name. 'Hey Girl.' Maddi met many people, and she wasn't good at remembering names. She could tell you details about the person, things she knew about them, their hobbies, the conversation topics they had talked about, but their name.... gone! It was easy for Tilly to remember her name, as Maddi wasn't a common name in Angourie. Tilly didn't know or interact with many people on the Gold Coast like Maddi did in her retail and hospitality jobs. Maddi noticed that Tilly looked beautiful. She was dressed in her new shiny black floor-length dress, and wearing make-up with a cute half-up, half-down-hair-do and a noticeable butterfly necklace hanging around her neck. When Tilly spoke again to order her drink, she suddenly felt nervous, realising a crowd was gathering at the bar, and the room was almost full. When Tilly asked nervously for a Macallan's Whisky on Ice, Maddi remembered that Tilly was doing the gig with Powderfinger tonight. As she handed her the glass of whisky on ice, she winked and said, 'Break-a-Leg, you're going to be amazing tonight.'

'Thank you, Maddi. It's going to be magical. I'm super excited and nervous at the same time.' Tilly replied as she grasped hold of her necklace.

Maddi made one more comment as Tilly passed her a $10 note. 'I love that necklace, by the way. It looks magical on you. You look gorgeous.'

Tilly replied, as she blushed a little, 'Thank you.' Tilly felt beautiful.

Bernard had spoken to the security guards about the impromptu performance plan. They were ready to retrieve Tilly from the audience whenever Bernard required her on stage. Tilly wanted to make it easy for them, so she went through the crowd to the front section. The plan was that when she was called on stage, the security guards would help her through the barriers wherever she made her way to the side or the front. She had a good spot where she could see the stage, but she also had easy access to get out of the crowd. She was ready.

chapter ninety-four

The Gig—Dalton, Dan and Ariiel

Dalton, Ariiel, and Dan finished their meals and went down to the concert hall. Dalton had a job to do on the way. He had captured his precious butterfly in a large glass, safely placing his hand over the top to place it outside in a garden area. As he released it into the garden, he made a special wish, as if wishes on butterflies were such a thing. Ladybugs, sure, everyone knows that; butterflies, why not? He wasn't sure exactly what he wanted to say, so he kept it simple as he didn't have time for long wishes. As he placed the butterfly on a large green leaf, he said, 'I believe, thank you.' The butterfly rested for a moment, then took flight.

Dalton, Dan, and Ariiel joined the line at the concert hall entrance. The place was packed out. They walked in and went to the bar to order a drink before the crowd got busier. Dan was on for the first shout. 'My shout. What's your poison for tonight, D-man?'

Dalton replied, a little distracted as he had noticed a gorgeous dark-haired girl resembling Tilly disappear into the crowd. 'Umm, I'm going to go with a Macallan's Whisky on Ice to get me started. It's an Angourie thing; seeing I'm with you, the Angourie surfing legend, it only seems fitting.'

Dan was excited about Dalton's choice of beverage. 'Perfect, I'll join you with that selection. And yes, it's definitely an Angourie Local thing. We can blame the Macallans for that. Do you know it's the only whisky they stock in the bar?'

Dalton was interested in this fun fact that only a true Angourie local would know about. 'I didn't know that. That's cool, forcing their namesake whisky on their patrons.'

Dan added enthusiastically, 'It is the best whisky, though. You must admit that once you've tried it, nothing else can match its warmth and smoothness.'

They moved closer to the bar, and Dalton noticed Maddi in their service area. Dalton mentioned this to Dan and Ariiel. 'Here is our friend again, the beautiful Maddi.'

Ariiel joined the conversation. 'She said she was working in the concert bar tonight, and she was right; the drinks line is busy. We would have been smarter to have another drink upstairs, but then we would still be back in that lineup to get in here. It's getting packed out. These guys are popular, huh?' Ariiel had never heard of Powderfinger, so she didn't know what the fuss was about but was excited. This was her first-ever concert.

They reached the front of the line. Maddi was excited to serve them again. 'Hey, long time, no see. What can I get for you?'

Dan ordered two of The Macallan Whisky on Ice and a West Coast Cooler for Ariiel. West Coast was the only drink she ever drank. She wasn't much of a drinker, and she liked the sweet melon taste of the West Coast Cooler. She also liked Midori and lemonade for special occasions. It was easy for Dan. He always knew what she wanted.

Maddi spoke to Dan as she prepared the drinks. 'I just opened this bottle and poured a glass of Macallan's Whisky on Ice for another customer two minutes ago. I've never served this whisky here before. Is this a new drink trend that I don't know about?'

Dan replied. 'I'm not sure. For us foreigners, it's an Angourie thing. We can blame it on The Macallan if anything goes wrong or right tonight. Have you ever tried it?'

Maddi replied as she multi-tasked efficiently, making the drinks as quickly as possible, as she could see that the drink lines were continually growing. 'I haven't tried it yet, but I promise to make it my knock-off drink tonight.'

Dalton replied, briefly avoiding chit-chat. She was busy. 'Have a fun night working. We will be in the mix.'

Maddi laughed and replied, 'You have fun, you lot. It's going to be a magical night.'

Dan reached into his wallet and pulled out a $50 note to pay for the drinks. As he did that, Dalton reached over and grabbed Ariiel's West Coast Cooler and passed it to her. He grabbed the two Macallan's drinks and lifted his chin as if to say, follow me. He made a beeline through the crowd for Ariiel and Dan to follow. He was headed in the same direction as he had seen the dark-haired girl disappear into. After Maddi's comment about serving a Macallan's Whisky on Ice, two minutes ago, he was certain it was Tilly. He felt a bundle of butterfly nerves fluttering inside his belly because he did not know what to say to her if he bumped into her, but one thing was for sure. He knew she was in this concert hall. He was absolutely 100% certain of it. He wasn't sure if he should tell Dan and Ariiel that he thought he had seen her, so he kept it to himself for now.

Dan and Ariiel followed along as they walked through the crowd towards the front. Some people were okay with it; others were holding ground, not prepared to give up their floor space or position in the crowd. There were still some gaps in the crowd, so Dalton stopped in a place where there was room for all three of them to stand with a view of the stage.

Dalton, Dan and Ariiel made small talk, as it was hard to hear each other talk while music played through the speakers, and the crowd was buzzing with excitement chatter.

Don Henley's "Boys of Summer" started, and everyone started singing along. It was a well-known song, and everyone knew it. This crowd was going to be fun.

Dalton couldn't keep his secret to himself anymore, so he turned to Dan, standing directly beside him. 'Dan, I think I might have seen Tilly walking into the crowd before. If you see her, make sure you let me know.'

Dan nodded and replied. 'Will do. I wondered why you walked off in such a hurry.'

Dalton lifted his voice above the noise of the crowd and the music. 'Yeah, sorry, I didn't want to be rude, but I didn't want to lose sight of her. It was like a dream. I saw her, and then she was gone, into the crowd.'

Dan was curious. 'What will you say to her when you see her?' Dan was interested in knowing Dalton's thoughts because the last time they had seen each other, she had told him to "go, just go." And now they were in the same place, somehow knowing each other was searching for the other. Maybe. If the tapestry of stories and connections were all true. But Dalton was carrying his guilty conscience about Jacqui and knew that Tilly had been hanging around with Powderfinger. Maybe she had moved on. It was all very unknown. Dalton did know, without any uncertainty, that he wanted a take-two, a do-over, a second chance, and that was what he was going to ask her, if he saw her.

Dalton replied. 'I don't know, man. I'm hoping she'll know what to say. I want to start all over again. I wish I could go back to Angourie, to that Gypsy room. I'd tell her I love her and that I want her to be mine forever.'

Dan smiled and felt warm-hearted, but his reply had to be a tough Badman response. 'So romantic, D-man. Making me look bad in front of my girl.'

Dalton queried. 'How is that? How does my being romantic make you look bad?'

'Well, Ariiel will expect me to talk to her with those romantic words now.' Dan grabbed Ariiel closer under his arm. She was already tucked in. They fit so well together. He smiled at her and gave her a full-mouth kiss, and then he went with the moment and became romantic. This was his chance. He spoke softly to Ariiel, but loud enough so Dalton and Ariiel could hear him over the crowd. 'Did you know I love you and want you to be mine forever?'

Ariiel was shocked and flattered at the same time. 'Really, Dan? But we've only just met. Are you sure?'

Dan was sincere in his reply. 'I'm more than sure. You are my dream girl, Ariiel. You're everything I've ever wanted.'

Dalton felt awkward and didn't know what to say, so he didn't say anything.

Ariiel leaned into Dan and said quietly, 'You're everything I've ever wanted too.'

Dalton finished the awkward moment as the crowd started to cheer loudly. The band was coming out soon. 'You guys are a cute couple. I think life together could work out okay for you both. Angourie needs another clever woman for Badman to look after, and Ariiel, with the little mermaid namesake, what more could a badass surfer dream of? It's a match made in heaven, really.'

Dan and Ariiel laughed at Dalton's humour. They moved closer to embrace each other in this special moment.

The crowd swarmed as the background music quietened, and movement was happening on the stage. Jon, the drummer, took his place first and started a drum beat for the crowd to clap along as the rest of the band members made their way onto the stage and joined in with their musical rhythms. Bernard was last to enter the stage, and the crowd cheered.

They started with a cover of one of their favourite idols' songs, The Rolling Stones' *"Start Me Up."* The crowd went wild.

chapter ninety-five

Pick You Up

Powderfinger had the audience bouncing. They had started with a Rolling Stones cover, then played a few originals, and another few cover songs, feeling the crowd's vibes and energy in the room. They decided to play their favourite new song that hadn't been released yet, but they always received great applause when they played it to live crowds. It was called *Pick You Up.*

Bernard started with the lyrics, and as he did, he searched for Tilly in the crowd. He wanted to direct the lyrics to her and make eye contact with her, to give him the passion that he wanted to give the song for the performance. *"When you are set to throw in your hand. When you are far from home. What you believe is buried in your hands. When you feel outgrown. I'll be the one to pick you up again when you decide you've had enough of it. I'll be the one, I'll be the one."*

He found her amongst the crowd. She had made her way to the second front row, just a little to the right-hand side of the centre of the stage. Bernard continued to sing the entire song to her. When he finished the song, he gave her a nod, and she knew that was her call to be ready to get up on stage. She was ready, but she had to be cool with it all. It was all impromptu, remember?

So, as cool as a cucumber, she clapped like everyone else. There were whistles and shouts from the crowd, 'I love you guys'. She called out loud and clapped along like all the other patrons, wondering how Bernard would introduce her to the stage.

Bernard started telling the story about their travels up from Sydney and how they were returning home to Brisbane. There were quite a few cheers from the crowd when he mentioned Brisbane. He paused with the story to interact with the crowd, saying, 'Oh, hello to our fellow Bris Vegas neighbours; thanks for coming to see us tonight. We appreciate you coming down to the beach here in Surfers Paradise.' The local crowd gave a massive cheer as he mentioned their hometown of Surfers Paradise.

Bernard worked the crowd, grateful for their enthusiasm, and then went back to tell the story that they had been travelling by train, had seen a lot of the Australian countryside, and met some amazing people. This is the part where Tilly started to feel a kaleidoscope of butterflies inside her belly. She knew this was her call.

Bernard continued. 'I have a special surprise for you all tonight. I'd like you to meet a special lady who we met on the train. She's an amazing musician in her own space, but we got lucky to have her join us for a fun gig on Tuesday night at The Islander Hotel. Some of you might remember her if you were there. Let's give her a round of applause as we get her up on the stage. She told me she only does small gigs in her hometown, so be kind...'

Bernard had time to fill in while Tilly made her way onto the stage and took her position near the microphone. While she was getting set up, Bernard continued talking and telling the story as he knew it. 'So, everyone, this is Matilda Macallan, but no one calls her that. You can call her Tilly. She's from Angourie, a place I've never been, about five hours from here.' A few people in the audience gave a cheer. Bernard continued. 'Tilly may or may not remember this, but a short while after we met, she asked for my help, and I promised her I would try to help her with three things.'

Tilly paused momentarily from adjusting the microphone stand and raised her head, looking towards Bernard quizzically, wondering what he would share of their conversations with this crowd of strangers. The crowd clapped at Tilly's reaction and then silenced, intrigued by the story. Bernard had the crowd captivated.

Tilly took it upon herself to become the entertainer alongside Bernard in this compelling performance.

She spoke clearly into the microphone, first ensuring it was switched on. 'I'm intrigued. What three things did I ask you to help me with, Bernard?'

Bernard was delighted that Tilly had joined the storytelling performance. It was going to be so much more entertaining this way. He spoke back to the audience, as this was their show. 'Well, when I first met Tilly, she was travelling around the countryside with a broken arm. So, she's just singing for us tonight. Apparently, she plays the guitar as well, but when I first met her, she asked me if I could get her to a hospital to get her arm looked at.' Tilly held up her cast as if on cue and as if this whole scenario had been planned. Both Tilly and Bernard were winging it.

'The second quest for help, I failed. While travelling from Byron to the Gold Coast, Tilly lost her favourite sentimental guitar pick. We tried to call the Murwillumbah Railway Station, where she thinks it may have fallen out of her pocket, but we had no luck.'

Tilly added her commentary. 'If anyone finds an engraved guitar pick with the band name Have Guitar Will Travel, it's a mouthful, I know. Please return it to The Angourie Local. That's my local. Thank you.' Tilly felt weird. It felt like she was advertising her local pub and her family band name to find a guitar pick that, in reality, would never be found. Still, she provided information so that the guitar pick could be returned should anyone find it. It was worth a try because it was so damn special.

Tilly was thinking ahead, and she knew what the next bit of help was that she had asked from Bernard. She asked Bernard to help her find Dalton. Tilly could feel that Dalton was here, but this wasn't the right place for her to see him again. She closed her eyes and grabbed hold of her butterfly necklace. As she did this, she had a vision of herself, back in Angourie in the restaurant, watching Dalton walk across the road, just as he had the first time she saw him. *That's where I want to see him again*, she thought. *We can start over.* As these thoughts crossed her mind, Bernard's voice came through the microphone again.

'The third thing I promised to help her with was finding something else she had lost, the one that got away. She thinks he might be here in Surfers Paradise, and he might be here tonight.'

There were a few loud cheers from the crowd, men being silly trying to get Tilly's attention.

'That's me.'

'I'm the one that got away.'

As soon as Bernard started talking about Dalton, Tilly decided she needed to interrupt and have her say because even if Dalton was right here, she didn't want this to be the place for them to meet again. The necklace had shown her the vision of where she should meet him again. It was where she first saw him. Way back to the beginning. Now wasn't the right time or place for her and Dalton to start again.

Tilly spoke calmly into her microphone, trying to quell her butterfly nerves so she didn't talk too quickly. She spoke into the microphone but cast her eyes towards Bernard. 'Bernard, thank you. You're the greatest. I'm just happy to be here to share this moment with you tonight, and then I think I will head back to my hometown in Angourie. I hope I'll find my missing piece back there so we can start all over again.' She turned her head and looked at the crowd. 'It's a long story, and I won't bore you all, but to keep it simple, I completely messed up, like seriously "fooked" up something really special. Please excuse my Northern NSW Black Irish accent.'

The crowd clapped as Tilly openly shared this part of herself with an unknown crowd.

Tilly turned back to Bernard and the band. 'You've all been incredible to me. Thank you. You've been more than enough for me over the past few weeks. This one is for you all. I hope you like it.'

Bernard had a few things to say, but he took on Tilly's gesture to move on, and decided to leave the conversation right there. Although the crowd loved the interaction and storytelling, they needed to get on with the performance. 'So, let's give this amazing woman a huge welcome. Tilly, you are amazing.'

Tilly got goosebumps all over. The one thing she had heard all her life was, 'Tilly, you're amazing, but....' This time, again from Bernard, there was no but...

Bernard strummed the D chord as Jon started a gentle tap on the snare drum. 'Matilda Macallan, give us your best ever Fleetwood Mac Gypsy cover.'

The crowd start clapping loudly, encouraging Tilly with excitement and enthusiasm.

chapter ninety-six

Freedom, Love, Enough

Dalton couldn't believe his eyes when he saw Tilly being guided to the stage. He didn't know what to do. Dan and Ariiel were equally shocked.

When Bernard started commenting on Tilly's story, they all felt apprehensive about reacting. They gave a quiet cheer when the name Angourie was mentioned and listened carefully to Bernard's words and the story he was sharing. After all, Dalton had no idea what the connection between Bernard and Tilly had become. Perhaps she wasn't looking for him at all, but then the guitar pick was mentioned. It was safely stowed in his wallet. Then, there was the mention of 'the one that got away'. Dalton felt a sense of calm all over his body. '*Okay, that's me.*' He took on the message from Tilly that he should return to Angourie and start again with her. He had messed it up, too. They were equal on that one.

As she sang, he confirmed that this was the woman he wanted to share his life with forever and ever. It was the first time he had realised that the song Gypsy had three of their Cheers slogans threaded through the lyrics. Freedom, Love and Enough. He wondered if Tilly had also made that connection.

The crowd listened to the entire song, not saying a word or making any comments. The crowd was mesmerised. Dalton was mesmerised. Tilly looked so beautiful up on the stage, her velvet dress shimmering in the stage lights and her smile glowing brightly, covering her face. She was loving every second of this experience. Dalton noticed a blue shimmer from her neck. She was wearing a necklace. He couldn't see exactly what it was, but it was eye-catching. It was shining directly into his eyes. The crowd gave an enormous round of applause at the end. Tilly nervously said, 'Thank you, thank you all, and a special thank you to Bernard and Powderfinger.' When the crowd stopped cheering, she said into the microphone while looking at Bernard. 'I have one more request if that's ok?'

Bernard was not sure where this was going. He tilted his head to the side and narrowed his eyes, trusting that whatever Tilly was saying would be heartfelt and heartwarming because that's just how she was, but he still felt a little uncomfortable in front of this crowd. 'Go ahead, ask away.'

'I want you to promise me you'll always be my friend, even when you're super famous, because I know you'll be super famous. You guys are incredible.' She turned back to face the crowd. 'Let's make some noise for this sensational new Australian rock band, Powderfinger.' Tilly lifted her hands above her head, and although it was difficult with her broken arm, she started a loud clap for Powderfinger.

The crowd went wild, clapping, whistling, and cheering loudly, following Tilly's lead.

As the crowd noise eased, Bernard replied, 'Of course, Tilly. Even when we're super famous.' He continued. 'I like what you've done there, but you can't get away that easily Matilda Macallan. Come on, let's give it up for Tilly from Angourie.'

chapter ninety-seven

The Blue Bandana

Tilly had noticed Dalton in the audience. His blue Bandana was the first thing she saw in the crowd as she started singing the chorus with the lyrics, "*faces **freedom**, with a little fear. I have no fear, I have only **love**, and if I was a child, and the child was enough, **enough** for me to love, enough to love....*" but she didn't make it obvious that she saw him. She saw Dan as well. They were with a girl. The girl was standing between Dan and Dalton. Tilly recognised the girl from Angourie, from the night that Dalton and Tilly went their separate ways. She assumed the girl was with Dan. In the subconscious of her mind, Tilly decided right then and there, as she was concentrating intensely on the lyrics and the tone of her vocals, that she didn't want to speak to Dalton until she was back in Angourie. She closed her eyes and melted back into the depths of the song. She hoped he understood her message and would find a way back to Angourie to start again with her. That was how she felt it would be best for them to meet again. With this idea in mind, as the song finished and the crowd had given their unexpected appreciation, she exited off the side of the stage and into the changerooms.

As Tilly stepped into the small room, she caught a glimpse of herself in the full-length mirror leaning against the wall. Her necklace was gleaming brightly in the reflection, and the velvet of her dress shone in different tones of black and dark silver as it caught the fractures of light. Tilly clutched her necklace and decided she should remove it. She felt its magic had already been cast. All she had to do now was return to Angourie and start again with Dalton. That was the vision. She placed the necklace back in the blue velvet case and tied the yellow string into a small, loose knot. She thought the best thing she should do would be to return it tomorrow to the pre-loved jewellery shop before she boarded the bus back home. That was Bessie's instructions. Once you felt it had worked its magic, you needed to return it or pay it forward. Suddenly, Tilly thought of Maddi. If anyone deserved some luck in love, it was Maddi. She had been so kind to Tilly every time she had been to the Surf Club, and she couldn't think of anyone more deserving of some magic.

Tilly made her way back into the concert hall and she walked straight up to the bar. Maddi saw her walking towards her and reached up to The Macallan whisky bottle, getting it ready to pour a drink for Tilly. As Tilly got closer, she noticed Maddi walking out from around the back of the bar. The next thing she knew, Maddi was in front of the bar, giving her a big hug.

Releasing from the hug, Maddi spoke with excitement. 'Hey girl, you did so well. That was magic. You were a true superstar.'

'Thanks Maddi, you are too.' Tilly was smiling and appreciative of the feedback, but as she received these kind words, she quickly changed her expression to a more serious one.

Maddi sensed it straight away. 'Is everything ok?'

Tilly confirmed everything was fine as she paused and changed the tone of her voice as well. 'I know this might sound weird. I don't want another drink. I'm going to head off and get a good night's sleep. I'm catching the early bus back down south tomorrow, but I wanted to come and say goodbye to you. You've been a good friend, even though we don't really know each other. I want to give you something extraordinary.'

Maddi was confused. Suddenly, in the middle of the concert, Tilly was saying goodbye and giving her something special. They didn't know each other; there were just a few waitress and retail customer interactions. 'What do you mean?'

Tilly explained as best she could over the music. 'I'm going back home tomorrow morning. I have something really important to attend to. Let's call it a take-two, and I will blame it on The Macallan.'

Maddi encouraged more clarity. 'Okay, I'm still confused, but I'm guessing you don't want another drink?'

Tilly fiddled around in her bag. 'Yeah, nah, I'm all good.' She paused. 'Maddi, I want you to have something, but it's magic, and you have to promise me something.'

Maddi didn't know what to say. She replied. 'Okay.'

Tilly was adamant that Maddi followed her instructions. 'I'm giving you this magic necklace—the butterfly necklace I was wearing tonight. Please take it to Bessie at the pre-loved jewellery store and get her to explain its magic. You mustn't wear it until you see her. Promise me?'

Maddi took the small blue velvet pouch in her palm and leaned forward to give Tilly another hug. 'Ummmmm, sure. I promise.'

Tilly released from the hug and smiled a knowing, radiant smile to Maddi, knowing that magic was also coming her way. 'I've got to go now. Thank you for everything.'

'Thank you, Tilly, make sure you visit again, won't you, when you're super famous?'

Tilly laughed. 'It's Powderfinger that will be super famous, not me. I'm going back home to Angourie, where no one knows me. I like it that way.'

'Take care, beautiful girl.' Maddi smiled.

'You too, beautiful girl.' Tilly smiled.

Tilly walked back to the Islander Hotel and packed her backpack. She was on a mission to get back home to Angourie. The bus was due to leave at 8 am, so she would be up early to get moving. The only thing she had to do in the morning was to say goodbye to the Powderfinger boys.

Tilly envisioned how the morning would play out. She wasn't looking forward to it. She knew the boys were packing up and moving on to Brisbane tomorrow, but she wasn't sure when they were leaving. Regardless, it wasn't going to be a fun morning. Farewells were the hardest, never an easy thing to do, especially when you didn't know if you would see someone ever again. It happened all the time in Angourie. It was a transient town, with people coming and going and never returning. It's just the way it was. Tilly was used to goodbyes, but Bernard had promised that he would keep in touch.

chapter ninety-eight

Encore

Dalton, Dan, and Ariiel thoroughly enjoyed the performance. The triple song encore was amazing. Powderfinger finished with a Doors Classic. Love Her Madly. This was a song everyone could join in and sing along to. *Yeah, don't you love her? Don't you love her as she's walking out the door?*

They decided to have one more drink at the bar before returning to their hotel. Dalton had a feeling that Tilly had departed already. The message was loud and clear. Take Two—The Angourie Local. Dan and Ariiel were planning the drive back on Monday anyway, so it made sense that Dalton would catch a ride with them. It was like this whole scenario had been perfectly orchestrated.

Dalton had to fulfil his commitment to Shawn at The Coolangatta Hotel for the Sunday session gig, so that would be a nice way for Dalton to farewell his new mates and let them know where he would be, if they wanted to keep in touch and surf the New South Wales beaches.

chapter ninety-nine

Paper, Scissors, Rock

Tilly awoke and went to breakfast on her own. As she went back to her room to brush her teeth and grab her bags, she heard movement in Bernard's room.

Yes, she thought, *I don't have to wake him. I wonder how the rest of the night went for them.* She knocked gently on the door. 'It's me, Bernard.'

Bernard opened the door, excited to see Tilly. 'Hey Tilly, you off?'

'I am, and you?' Tilly was holding back a few tears. She was emotional about parting ways.

Bernard felt the same, so he filled his sadness with words instead. 'Yep, we are all leaving soon. We are all meeting for breakfast at 8 am, and then we will get on the road.' He continued as the conversation deepened. 'I'm sad to be saying goodbye to you, beautiful girl, but I am happy to be heading home. I'm looking forward to seeing my family. It's been a while. And I'm happy for you. I am.' He reached forward and pulled Tilly in for the warmest hug he had given her since they had met. As he went to let go, he felt her hold a little tighter, so they embraced longer until it felt awkward. Tilly didn't want Bernard to see her tears, so she held them in, taking a big breath and swallowing a big gulp in her throat.

Tilly had some last words to say. 'Thanks for everything, Bernard. You've been such a good friend to me. Promise me you'll keep your promise.'

'I promise.' Bernard smiled.

Tilly changed the subject quickly, assuring Bernard of her plans. 'Thanks so much to you. I've got a good feeling about Dalton. He was there last night. I saw him in the crowd. We will not mess it up this time.'

'I saw him too, Tilly. You two will be fine. I know this, you are amazing, no buts. He's a lucky man.'

Tilly couldn't stop the tears from rolling down her cheek. 'Thank you, Bernard. You have no idea how much that means to me.'

'Oh, yes, I do. I know. I see you.' Bernard moved his hand, signalling the connection from his eyes to hers, and then placed his hand across his chest. 'From the bottom of my heart, I wish you well, beautiful girl.'

'From the bottom of my heart, I wish you well, too. Bernard.' Tilly smiled and put her broken arm across her body, onto the place where her heart would sit inside her chest.

They stood silent for a moment. This was it—the final words.

Tilly had one more thing to say. 'Paper, scissors, rock for whoever has to make the first friendship phone call.'

In unison, they gently pounded their hands onto their opposite palm. 'Paper, Scissors, Rocks.'

Bernard formed a *Rock*. Tilly flattened her hand for *Paper.*

Tilly laughed out loud, pointing a finger repeatedly at Bernard. 'I win. That means you have to call me. The Angourie Local is where you'll find me.'

'Well, Miss Matilda Macallan, I might even come and pay you a visit sometime and do one of your secret sessions when I'm super famous, so that we can blame The Macallan on some Angourie shenanigans.'

Tilly agreed. 'Sounds good to me. The Macallans would love to meet you, and we would love to have you stay and play. Promise me you will?'

Bernard laughed, realising that Tilly needed to get going, or they would keep talking. 'So many promises. You need to go, girl, don't miss that bus. See you in Angourie, beautiful.'

'See you, Bernard.' Tilly leaned in for one last hug, and they both gave each other a goodbye kiss on the cheek.

chapter one hundred

Blame it on *The Macallan*

When Dan turned onto Angourie Road, he instantly felt at home. This was where he was supposed to be. He felt safe, free, and connected to his surroundings. Angourie was home.

Dalton felt it, too.

Ariiel, like Dalton, was a new visitor to Angourie; she had only strolled in a few weeks before, meeting Dan at the Angourie Local. Her little gypsy soul felt very much at ease in Dan's hometown. They had enjoyed their brief trip up north to the big city, but this town was much more her speed. The pace of life was liveable, and Ariiel was utterly smitten with her new man, the godfather of Angourie. If he would have her stay with him, she would be quite happy to roll along and see how things went. There were no expectations or rules. They planned to have some fun and see what happened. So far, that plan was working out well.

It was Monday afternoon, just at dusk, and Dalton had asked Dan if he would be so kind as to drop him back at The Angourie Local. Dan pulled up across the road and sounded his horn. *Barp, bedda, barp, barp, barp, barp.*

Tilly looked over the balcony, knowing exactly what she would see. She had already seen it in her magic butterfly necklace vision.

There he was, Dalton, wearing his blue bandana, T-shirt and jeans, walking across the road with his backpack, guitar and surfboard, exactly the way he did the first time she saw him.

Tilly had already planned how this take-two was going to happen. As he walked in the door, looking directly into her eyes, she put her finger to her mouth and indicated shhh!

Dalton's brow furrowed. *What was she doing?* Every instinct in his body urged him to walk over to her, pick her up in his arms, take hold of her, and never let her go, but he had a feeling that was not how Tilly had this scenario planned. Louis was on duty. The restaurant was busy.

Tilly pointed to a piece of folded paper on the table, and then she disappeared, out of sight.

Dalton put his belongings in the reception area, just out of the way. He knew they were safe there. He walked over to where the note was placed on the table. He unfolded it. It simply said, 'Meet me in the Gypsy Room.'

Dalton checked to ensure his stuff was safe and headed along the pathway to the Gypsy Room.

The door was unlocked. He knocked gently. 'Tilly, are you there?' He remembered her cute trick. 'Housekeeping.'

There was still no answer, so he entered the room. Tilly was in the bed, her body outlined by the sheets as they gently covered her. She was lying exactly how he remembered when he had climbed back into bed the morning after they had made wild and passionate love all night. Dalton instantly felt a rush of euphoria, remembering how it felt to be beside and inside her. He removed his clothing and placed it on the chair beside the bed. He climbed into bed behind her, snuggling into her closely, wrapping his whole body around her and over her, taking in the scent of her aroma and feeling the warmth of her skin against his.

Dalton wasn't sure what to say. This wasn't the way he had planned their reconnection. He wanted this moment to be perfect. He had rehearsed what he wanted to say over and over again because he had so much to say. He wanted to take back his fear of being worried about what Tilly would think about his dark secret. He wanted to apologise to her and tell her everything about his past, because he wanted her to know that he wanted her to be his forever girl. He wanted her to know she was enough; she was amazing with no buts, and she was all he had ever dreamed of in a woman. These are all the things he wanted to say, but the words that came out of his mouth were. 'Let's blame it on The Macallan.'

Tilly took a deep breath, feeling the heaviness of Dalton's arm across her body. Her wrist felt numb from the weight of his hand holding hers. She rolled towards Dalton and said, 'What? What are you talking about? Blame it on The Macallan? Blame what on The Macallan?'

Dalton was still in a dream talk. 'Everything. Let's blame everything on The Macallan.'

'Do you mean the whisky, The Macallan? Or my family? You're not making any sense.'

Dalton shifted and rubbed his eyes.

'Oh my goodness, what time is it Tilly? I'm supposed to be going for a surf with Dan, remember?'

Tilly's eyes adjusted as she tried to focus on the time on the clock radio. 'It's 6 pm, if that clock is right? Yeah, you promised Dan you'd meet him for a surf.'

Dalton was confused because he wasn't sure if it was the soft morning sun shining through the window or the evening sunset glow. 'Did we sleep through the alarm? I set it for 3 pm.'

Tilly had a flashback of being on the stage with Powderfinger and now here she was back in the Gypsy Room at The Angourie Local. She was naked with Dalton wrapped around her, and there was no cast on her arm. It just felt a little numb because Dalton's heavy arm had been resting on hers. 'I'm so confused. Are we okay? I just had the craziest dream.'

Dalton started to shift his body to move himself into a sitting position, then he decided instead to snuggle back in behind Tilly and pull her in close to his chest. 'Me too. I had the craziest dream.'

Dalton shook his head, trying to make sense of what was happening. To make sure, he looked over to the TV cabinet and could see the empty bottle of The Macallan whisky sitting exactly where he had left it after he poured their last drink.

Tilly reached up to feel around her neck, to check that she was still wearing her necklace, the one she had always worn, the small love heart, on a simple chain. Her 18th birthday gift from her family.

Dalton had one more thought. The guitar pick, Tilly's guitar pick. He leaned over to the dresser and opened his wallet. Tilly's guitar pick was zipped inside the front pocket. He scratched his head gathering his conscious thoughts. *Hang on, I picked that up the first night I met Tilly, it's been in my wallet ever since.* Dalton handed the guitar pick to Tilly.

Tilly smiled. 'You found my guitar pick? I wondered where that was?'

They rolled towards each other, their bodies and mouths entangled in a beautiful, warm kiss. They both realised they had woken up from a dream, letting out a breath of gratitude that they were in each other's embrace.

They both paused from their kiss, listening to the silence between them. Tilly spoke first. 'Dalton, I'm so sorry. Please forgive me.'

'Tilly, I'm sorry too. Please forgive *me*.' Dalton paused before saying one more thing. 'Can we promise never to dream like that ever again?'

Tilly replied with a giggle, wondering if she was still dreaming and talking to Bernard. 'So many promises.....'

The sunlight beamed in through the sliding door, shining a golden glow over Dalton and Tilly as they lay naked together in the crisp white sheets.

The butcher birds were singing their morning song in the garden outside.

As Tilly lay with her eyes softly closed as she rested with her internal thoughts, her mind cast back to the conversation Tilly and Dalton had shared after The Macallan afternoon shenanigans. Dalton had asked her to marry him, but since then not another word had been mentioned. *Had he forgotten the conversation, the question?*

Dalton gently rolled Tilly's body towards his, so he could look directly into her eyes. As soon as she opened them, he questioned, 'So Tilly, I do have one more question for you and I'm hoping you know the answer. I want to give you Friendship, Freedom and Enough Love to last you a lifetime. Matilda Rhiannon Macallan, will you marry me?'

The End

Acknowledgements:

This is my first real novel. The first book I self-published was a diary of sorts: Twenty Years An Angel; a tragedy of words, but this, now this.... is a real novel. I hope you enjoyed it. I did my best to put these words together and had so much fun along the way.

I'm so grateful to my beautiful friends and family who have let me go on and on about my novel, for so long, while they listened to my storyline, encouraged, and inspired me in different ways.

Blame It On The Macallan began as Have Guitar Will Travel, when I was on a holiday in 2017 in Angourie with my family. Instead of taking my guitar, I took my laptop and I just started typing. The characters told me the story and their dialogue. Six years later and here I am, writing the acknowledgements. At the time, my two beautiful daughters were thirteen and fourteen. Since the day I started writing this novel, they have encouraged me to take time to myself to write because they know how important it is to me. They would ask me often. 'How is your novel going, Mama?'

My answer. 'I'm getting there my babies, I'm getting there.'

I have worked full-time since the '*age of seventeen*' (good song that by Stevie Nicks) so when I actually started writing when I turned about 40, my novel writing has always been a weekend and night thing or whenever I had holidays from work, whenever I could get windows of time to immerse myself in creativity. I haven't owned a television in six years, so other than not knowing what horrible stuff is going on in the world, I have had a lot of time to be creative. In the past ten years or so I have been working on two novels. This one, Blame it on The Macallan, and Jinx. I do plan to finish Jinx one day, someday. It's a damn good story. Madeline, the main character in Jinx, is me, so I know her story pretty well. I was just trying to figure out a creative way to tell her story rather than a biography, so I started writing a creative novel. The novel is still in a working progress as I continue living my amazing and wonderful, adventurous life. It's going to be way much more fun as a creative fictional novel. But for now, I've been focusing on Blame It On The Macallan.

My first deeply heartfelt thanks are to my beautiful girls, Alijana Josephine and Milla Joelle, two of the most amazing women whom I have ever known. They have always been my constant support in my life, strange I know, as it would normally be the other way around, but these two are special. Beautiful, independent, intelligent, kind women. Our mother / daughter's relationship is unique and special. We are three of a kind. We are all best friends. They are best friends to each other, and we all support each other as a family unit. We've been through A LOT together and have always come out the other side, grateful for what we went through because of what we learned. I am the luckiest mum in the universe because Alijana and Milla are mine. I made them from the best of me, with all my love, constant love, unconditional and true, sometimes tough, but always true. Thank you, my babies. I love you forever, all ways and always. My loves.

I have quite a few friends to be thankful for.

My friend Riz, whom I met in Sydney at a work conference, is legally blind. Riz is one of the most amazing men I have met in my life, and I definitely did not get to spend anywhere near enough time with him to learn more about life from him. Riz is completing his Masters "thesis" on the topic of 'How we come up with ideas!' I mean how interesting is that question? I want to know all of the answers. Riz was excited to hear my story and was the first person to suggest an audiobook version of Blame it on The Macallan. This would be the easiest way for Riz to read my novel. I'm hoping I can do that for him. An audiobook or podcast, something like that would be so fun to do.

Ariiel Gilbert has been invested in my story for so long. I met Ariiel in 2020 through work channels. We became friends, and I somehow became her support person, as she went through some tough stuff, time and time again. What she doesn't realise is that she was equally my support, a true friend always. As our friendship grew, I shared stories about my real life with her and I also shared bits and pieces about my novel with her. She seemed to be interested and invested more than anyone I had shared with. Ariiel was intrigued with the storyline and has always encouraged me and inspired me to twist my story in different ways of thinking. One of my characters changed his name, because of Ariiel. We have come up with a future novel idea. It's called Tigerlily Queeen with a triple e. I need to go back in my phone and find the voice memo and notes as we sketched out the storyline. One day. Some Day. You will meet Ariiel in Blame it on The Macallan. My character Ariiel, and the real life Ariiel have similarities to each other. That was fun. Thank you for weaving your way into my novel, my beautiful friend. I fkn love you.

Maddi Love, my beautiful Maddi, another friend who has woven her name into my novel. Maddi has invested hours of her life into my novel. She has actually listened while I read my story to her, encouraging me to make my novel a podcast, because she doesn't read books. We have spent hours and hours lying around while she listened. We integrated swag camping, beach days, lazy hours in bed or under shady trees while Maddi listened, wondering what happens next. Sometimes predicting it. Sometimes not at all. In some chapters she was hating on my characters. 'Why would he do that?' One day, someday, my novel will be in podcast version, with thanks to Maddi Love for listening. Maddi, I'm so proud of your growth into the amazing woman you are, and I'm so grateful for the spontaneous adventures we shared. Your voice, your laugh and our funny sayings will always stay in my mind. 'I've never tried that before,' and 'You can have it...'. I fkn love you Maddi My Gurl.

Then there is PT Scotty, one of my favourite friends from my Southern Cross University, Lismore days. Scotty and I both studied Sport Science and were mad into exercise throughout our lives. I finished university and followed my career as a PE teacher. Scotty went onto a sophisticated career in the Northern Beaches of Sydney as a PT. Scotty is not only my fastest friend, he also happens to make me laugh more than anyone in the universe. The thought of me writing a novel, a real novel, was a foreign concept for both of us to understand. So, in true Scotty style he went along with it, encouraging me, to the extreme of purchasing himself a pair of classy writer style spectacles, from the op shop in Bellingen, for the times we would meet to hike nature trails together and afterwards discuss how my novel was going. For the novel discussions he would wear the spectacles and look down his nose at me as he listened intently to my plans. He called me one day and left a voice message, on my phone, pretending to be a sophisticated book reviewer with a special eloquent accent, and on many occasions tried to convince me that he was an Australian publisher. He probably should have set his phone to No Caller ID, but it was fun to play along. I was always in hysterics within seconds of answering his phone calls. Thank you Scotty. Imagine that, imagine if my book could actually be published by a real publisher. One day, someday. Scotty has been my most consistent supporter, through my entire book writing journey, making my laugh hysterically, to the point where my abdominal muscles were contracting, as we pondered different concepts for my storyline, or how I could make enough money to get the damn thing published to start with. Now, they were some interesting, preposterous discussions. Scotty's check in chats always motivated me to keep moving with it. He's yet to receive his autographed, gold-embossed copy with the lipsticky kissy thing. Thank you Scotty Rose, you are a beautiful friend and I'm so grateful to you, for always being in my life. Wishing you all the best in health for long-living days as my all-time fastest and funniest friend. I love you.

My beautiful sister, Elisa, has supported me, in her own way, by way of acknowledging my uniqueness, letting me know that my book isn't something that she would like to read, and that's okay. Is any book ever written going to be appealing to everyone in the universe? Of course not. We are all different. And that will be a lesson for me to learn in time, to accept the criticism from readers who don't like the way I write when my novel is something that has taken years of my life and every ounce of my creativity to put together. And that's ok. I'm ready. Bring it on critics, because I hope to learn from your feedback to make my next novels even more amazing. I'm hoping my sister will read my novel, one day.

I'm grateful to Coco Fabry, my beautiful Grafton Big Day Out drinks line up friend. I met Coco in a random chance of synchronicity, and then I was so lucky to meet her again, otherwise we would have been lost from each other forever. Life brought us back together. Thank you for connecting me with Rachael from Secret Sounds, Powderfingers' Manager. This has been a major highlight for me, to have Powderfingers' permission to be fictional characters in Blame it on The Macallan. Coco, I promise to write our jointly created novel, The Butterfly Necklace, someday. I have the storyline in my notes on my phone and when I start writing I'll be in touch for your input. We have the bones of an amazing story. Thank you, Coco. You beautiful woman.

A few of my close friends have accepted PDF copies of my novel as I would have loved to have some feedback before I publish, however no one has got back to me yet. Perhaps they didn't get past Chapter 1. And that's okay. I wish they kept reading to give it a chance. It's hard to read a book from a computer screen, I guess. A hard copy in your hands is so much more fun.

I'm forever grateful to my beautiful property and my quiet space in my caravan where I wrote and slept for a year and half before I moved into my tiny house. In these quiet places, I could immerse myself in my writing. Without my 'soulitude' and 'aloneness', I can guarantee you that my novel would not exist.

I'm grateful to my butcher bird friend, Morrissey, who sat beside me on so many days as I typed thousands and thousands of words. Sadly, he left one day, blown away in an 80km per hour windstorm. I never saw him again after that dreadful, destructive storm. Maybe one day he will find his way back to me. Thank you Morrissey, for all the time we shared, you little cutie.

I'm grateful to my neighbours' cows who chewed on their cud, on the other side of the fence, as I wrote thousands and thousands of more words, and pondered hypothetical plots with them.

I'm grateful to the NaNoWriMo (National Novel Writers Month) challenge that I participated in every November to motivate me to write, write, write, write, write. I encourage all new writers to give it a try sometime. It's a challenge against yourself, and even if you don't complete the challenge, getting anywhere is at least moving forward.

I'm grateful to my beautiful real life, for its extreme challenges and the beauty I have discovered in that. I have been through many life-changing experiences and adventures to draw inspiration from. I've felt the emotions of trauma and grief, immense love and equally devastating heartache, the sadness and the joys of parenthood, the success of hard work and the resilience of failures. I believe that I am one of the luckiest people in the universe, for the simple fact that I have completed this novel. I can't even describe the feeling this gives me. 190,926 words. I created that all by myself. One of my lifelong goals is now complete. How fortunate am I to be able to do that?

I'm grateful also to everyone along the way who has said to me, 'I can't wait to read your novel Mel.' Those simple words have been extremely encouraging, as I imagine these people reading my novel, and I wonder which parts will resonate with their lives. Wow!

Thank you to everyone who has ever been in my life; strangers, acquaintances, lovers, friends, and family members for filling my mind with creative ideas and content while I was simply living my daily life.

My goals for this novel do continue from here. I plan to make this novel an audio version, for anyone who prefers to listen rather than read. It's going to be suitable for a very long road trip, or hours and hours of housework, or hours and hours of exercise. I hope that whatever you are doing while listening, that you will get lost in my story. I've calculated it to be about 16 to 20 hours, of listening. I'm guessing.

I would love to see my novel as a screen version, one day. A movie, or Netflix series perhaps. And I would hope that I could squeeze my favourite celebrity student of all time, Margot Robbie, in there somewhere. Perhaps just a cameo character if she doesn't have enough time. I could see her playing my character Georgia Daniels, so well. I was very lucky to teach Margot when I was teaching Physical Education at Somerset College many, many years ago. Margot is the most beautiful, down to earth woman and she has been incredibly successful through alot of hard work and dedication to her talents. There was always something magical about her.

As for Matilda and Dalton, The Macallan family, and the rest of my characters, I've created these characters and I've brought them to life in my novel, but I'm not sure who would play their characters best. Any ideas?

A belated thank you to my beautiful friend Emma Ocholla who came to the rescue and created my amazing book cover design, and helped me create the audio versions and many other technical things to do with my novel. This is the bio we created for Emma, and this is exactly what he does. Emma is an innovative tech virtuoso with a flair for creativity. Dedicated to empowering the local community, Emma imparts a wealth of digital expertise, encompassing live streaming, web development, software engineering, and multimedia production. With a keen eye for aesthetics, Emma also excels in graphic design, crafting everything from book covers to movie posters, and personalized author images to tailored layouts for independent publishers. Emma's collaborative spirit shines through partnerships, notably with author Melanie Jay, resulting in the striking cover for "Blame it on The Macallan." At the helm of Zatora, Emma's enterprise offers comprehensive support for self-publishing aficionados.

My final acknowledgement is to thank YOU, the reader, for taking the time to read my novel. I really hope you enjoyed the journey of my characters in their daily lives. Life is just that, a journey, between our time of birth and our time of death. The time in-between is all yours to do with it, as you wish. Life can be so simple, yet so rich, if we choose to connect deeply and in kindness, with people and nature, and ourselves. And, if the day doesn't go so well, you can always blame it on The Macallan.

Thank you for your time,

Melanie Jay

References:

Quotes stolen from friends:
Samantha Jane— 'Our strengths are our weaknesses, my darling.'
Annie Lydon— 'Everything in moderation—including moderation.'

Names stolen:
Matilda, well she had to be nicknamed Tilly. The best nickname in the universe. (People who know me, know about my Tilly, Shane Patrick Walsh-Till R.I.P Tilly. I love you forever and always to eternity.)

Laurada May Walton—My little nanny is the inspiration for the name Laura.

Little One—Matilda's nickname, was my nickname when I was younger.

Maddi, the waitress, from my beautiful friend Maddison Elly Love.

Ariiel, Dan the Badman's mermaid 'from my beautiful friend Ariiel Gilbert.

Dan the Badman's character was created from the real live Angourie Godfather Dave 'Baddy' Treloar. He is the original Angourie surfing legend. 'Baddy' died of a heart attack, collapsing on the beach of his beloved Angourie on the 28th March, 2019. 'R.I P Baddy, the point at Anga will never be the same.' Tracks Magazine.

Lee—my beautiful friend Leeroy Paul, if you ever get a chance to meet my Leeroy you'll feel like you've known her forever, she's one of those special women, whom I was lucky enough to share some brief young years of my life with.

'Crystals have largely been dismissed as pseudoscience, although some studies suggest they may offer a placebo effect. Many ancient cultures — including ones in Egypt, Greece, and China — believed that crystals have healing properties. Some people claim that crystals promote the flow of good energy and help rid your body and mind of negative energy for physical and emotional benefits. They believe certain crystals benefit your sleep, help you manifest your desires, and add an additional healing element to reiki. But it's important to note that almost no scientific evidence supports the use of crystals or other forms of energy healing.' https://www.healthline.com/health/mental-health/guide-to-healing-crystals

'Astrology is a range of divinatory practices, recognized as pseudoscientific since the 18th century, that claim to discern information about human affairs and terrestrial events by studying the apparent positions of celestial objects.' https://astrology.com

Book references:

Howard Gardner—America Psychologist, author of 35 books, including *Multiple Intelligences* (1993)

Wayne Payne—*A Study of Emotion: Developing Emotional Intelligence* (1985)

Reuven Bar—On—Israeli psychologist—introduced the concept of EQ (Emotional Quotient) (1985)

The Stonecutter Story—a Japanese folk tale published by Andrew Lang in the Crimson Fairybook (1903) a reworked story from Jeronimus (1842).

The Alchemist—Paulo Coelho, first published in 1988, written in Portugese then translated into 67 languages.

The Giver—Lois Lowry, published in 1993, set in a society which first appears to be utopian but is revealed to be dystopian as the story progresses. A very clever novel.

Movie References:

Greystoke: The Legend of Tarzan, Lord of the Apes. The original Tarzan movie. I was obsessed with this movie in 1984.

Product References:

Monopoly, Cluedo, Scrabble, Chess (my favourite board games as a child.)

Euchre and Canasta (my favourite travelling card games)

Perfect Match TV Show hosted by Greg Evans. *Grundy (1983-1989)*

Palmolive Gold Soap ('Don't wait to be told, you need Palmolive Gold.' Deodorising soap bar famous in the 80's and 90's.)

Blundstone boots— created by John Blundstone in Hobart, Tasmania, in the 1870's.

Akubra—the trade name Akubra came into use on the 7th August 1912, a purpose built factory was created in Kempsey in 1972, worn and made famous by The Man From Snowy River in 1982. Still proudly Australian made in Kempsey, NSW.

Sunflowers—by Elizabeth Arden launched in 1993.

Joop!—by Wolfgang Joop in 1986 (the cologne worn by my first true love—Johnny Woodland)

CK One—launched in 1994, it became a best-seller, making more than $5million dollars in its first 10 days.

Midori Illusion—Midori meaning green in Japanese, created by Suntory in 1964 under the name Hermes Melon Liqueur, changed its name to Midori in 1978. Midori Illusion is a blend of Midori, Cointreau, Vodka, Lemon Juice and Pineapple Juice. Yummy!

1990 Penfolds Grange now sells for $1200.

The Macallan Whisky—1990 The Macallan Fine and Rare Vintage Single Malt Scotch Whisky - Speyside-Highlands, Scotland, selling for around $25,000 per bottle.
Calvin Klein boxer shorts—In 1982, Calvin Klein underwear for men was launched. Calvin Klein Obsession for Men (wedding day cologne 28th September 1996)
Moët—Moët and Chandon, also known simply as Moët first marketed in 1842.
The Rolling Stone Magazine—founded in San Francisco in 1967 by Jann Wenner and Ralph Gleason. John Lennon appeared on the first cover of Rolling Stone Magazine on Nov 9, 1967.

Surfers Paradise Locations:

The Islander is now called The Island.
The Beachcomber is still called The Beachcomber, but they no longer have wild pool parties.
Surfers Paradise Surf Club is still there. Powderfinger actually performed at Surfers Paradise Surf Club in 1989.

Nightclubs in Surfers Paradise in the 90's:
Cocktails and Dreams
The Esplanade

Make sure to scan the QR Code on the back cover or below to download the public playlist that I created on Youtube called Blame it on The Macallan.

Music references:

This novel includes many references to songs and musicians. This is to set the vibe of the era this story was created within. I have created a public playlist on YouTube. It's called Blame It On The Macallan. It includes every song and artist mentioned in this novel. A step back in time. The QR code for the playlist is on the back of my novel.

Blame It On The Macallan Playlist in order of book mentions.
Small Town–John Mellencamp, aka Johnny Cougar, John Cougar Mellencamp (1985) Scarecrow, Riva Records. www.mellencamp.com
Jezebel–Frankie Laine (1951) B-sides, Columbia Records written by Wayne Shanklin.
Fortunate Son–Creedence Clearwater Revival (1969) Willy and the Poor Boys, Fantasy Records.
Matilda–Harry Belafonte (1953) RCA Victor LP, Belafonte, King Radio.
Rhiannon–Fleetwood Mac (1975) B-side Sugar Daddy, Fleetwood Mac, Reprise. Fleetwood Mac (1967 - 1995 * 1995 – present) www.fleetwoodmac.com
Love is a Battlefield–Pat Benatar (1983) B-side Hell Is For Children, Live From Earth. www.benatargiraldo.com
Van Morrison (1967) Blowin' Your Mind, Bang Records, produced by Bert Berns.
Van Morrison (1958 - present) Sir George Ivan Morrison—Van The Man, The Belfast Cowboy, The Belfast Lion. www.vanmorrison.com
Rolling Stones (1962 - present) www.rollingstones.com
David Bowie (1962 – 2016) RIP David Robert Jones, 10th January 2016. www.davidbowie.com
Dolly Parton (1956 - present) Fun Fact: Dolly has 11 siblings and plays 8 instruments. www.dollyparton.com
Kenny Rogers (1977 – 2020) RIP Kenneth Donald Rogers, 20th March, 2020. Kenny was inducted into the Country Music Hall of Fame in 2013. www.kennyrogers.com
Neil Diamond (1966 – retired from touring in 2018) Neil Leslie Diamond has sold more than over 130 million records making him one of the best-selling musicians of all time. An American singer songwriter- three times married (my twin flame). www.neildiamond/#/
Barbra Streisand (1960 - present) Barbara Joan Streisand www.barbrastreisand.com
Billy Joel (1964 – present) William Martin Joel, aka The Piano Man. www.billyjoel.com
Can't Help Falling In Love— Elvis Presley (1961),Blue Hawaii, RCA Victor. www.elvisthemusic.com
Gypsy–Fleetwood Mac (1980) B-Side Cool Water, Mirage, Warner Bros. www.fleetwoodmac.com
One Night–Melanie Jay (2020) inspired by Straalen McCallum.
Tom's Diner–Suzanne Vega (1987) B-side Luka, Left of Center, Solitude Standing, A&M Polygram. www.suzannevega.com
My Girl–The Temptations (1965)B-side Talking 'Bout Nobody but My Baby, The Temptations Sing Smokey, Gordy. www.temptationsofficial.com
Brass in Pocket–The Pretenders (1979) B-side Swinging London, Nervous But Shy, Sire. www.thepretenders.com

Collection of artists on CD shuffle at The Angourie Local.

Frankie Macallan's favourites:
Pearl Jam (1990 – present) aka Mookie Blaylock (1990) www.pearljam.com Fun Fact : Eddie Jerome Vedder (born Edward Louis Severson III) is my favourite voice of all time.
Red Hot Chili Peppers (1982 – present) aka Tony Flow and the Miraculously Majestic Masters of Mayhem (1982-1983) www.redhotchillipeppers.com
Guns N Roses (1985-present) aka GNR www.gunsnroses.com
LIVE (1984 - 2009 * 2012 – present) aka Public Affection (1987-1991) www.freaks4live.com
Aerosmith (1970 – present) aka the Bad Boys from Boston www.aerosmith.com
Nirvana (1987 – 1994) RIP Kurt Cobain 8th April 1994. www.nirvana.com
Smashing Pumpkins (1998 – 2000 * 2006 – present) www.smashingpumpkins.com
Metallica (1981 – present) RIP Cliff Burton 27th September 1986. www.metallica.com

Eddie Macallan's music taste:
Crowded House (1985 – 1996 * 2006 – 2011 * 2016 * 2019 - present) aka The Mullane's (1985) www.crowdedhouse.com
R.E.M (1980 – 2011) aka Hornets Attack Victor Mature, Bingo Hand Job, It Crawled From the South, Twisted Kites www.remhq.com
Counting Crows (1991 – present) www.countingcrows.com
Hunters and Collectors (1981 – 1998 *2009 * 2013 – present) www.humanfrailty.com.au
Hoodoo Gurus (1981 – present) www.hoodoogurus.net
Depeche Mode (1980 – present) aka Composition of Sound (1980) www.depechemode.com
The Cure (1978 – present) www.thecure.com
INXS (1977 – 2012) RIP Michael Hutchence 22nd November 1997 www.inxs.com

Louis' collection:
Alice Cooper (1964 – present) www.alicecooper.com
Stone Temple Pilots (1989 – 2003 * 2008 – present) RIP Scott Weiland 3rd December 2015. www.stonetemplepilots.com
Hootie & The Blowfish (1986 – 2008 * 2018 – present) www.hootie.com
Tom Petty (1976 – 2017) RIP Thomas Earl Petty, 2nd October 2017. www.tompetty.com

All the boys:
U2 (1976 – present) aka Feedback (1976-1977) and The Hype (1977-1978) www.u2.com
Bruce Springsteen (1973 – present) Bruce Frederick Joseph Springsteen—The Boss. www.brucespringsteen.net

John Mellencamp (1974 – present) aka Johnny Cougar, John Cougar Mellencamp
www.mellencamp.com

Matilda's feminine touch:
Sophie B. Hawkins (1990 – present) Sophie Ballantine Hawkins
www.sophiebhawkins.com
Sheryl Crow (1983 – present) Sheryl Suzanne Crow www.sherylcrow.com
Toni Childs (1979 – present) www.tonichilds.com
Tracy Chapman (1986 – present) www.about-tracy-chapman.net
Wendy Matthews (1976 – present) Wendy Joan Matthews. www.wendymatthews.com
Suzanne Vega (1982 – present) www.suzannevega.com
Skid Row (1986 – 1996 * 1999 – present) www.skidrow.com

Dreams–Fleetwood Mac (1977) B-side Songbird, Rumours, Warner Bros.
www.fleetwoodmac.com
Start Me Up–Rolling Stones (1981) B-side No Use in Crying, Tattoo You, The
Glimmer Twins. www.rollingstones.com
Brown Eyed Girl–Van Morrison (1967) Blowin' Your Mind, Bang Records,
produced by Bert Berns. www.vanmorrison.com
American Pie–Don Mclean (1971) B-side Empty Chairs, American Pie Part 2, United
Artists. www.donmclean.com
Big Love–Fleetwood Mac (1987) B side You & I Part 1, Tango in the Night, Lindsey
Buckingham, Richard Dashut, Warner Bros. www.fleetwoodmac.com
Down Under–Men At Work (1981) B-side Crazy, Business as Usual, Columbia.
www.colinhay.com
Devil Went Down to Georgia–Charlie Daniels Band (1979) B-side Rainbow Ride,
Million Mile Reflections. Epic. www.charliedaniels.com
Girls Just Wanna Have Fun–Cyndi Lauper (1983) B-side Right Track Wrong Train,
She's So Unusual. Portrait. www.cyndilauper.com
I Still Haven't Found What I'm Looking For, (1987) B-Side Spanish Eyes, The
Joshua Tree, Island. www.u2.com
Sweet Child O' Mine–Guns N' Roses (1988) B-side It's So Easy, Appetite for
Destruction, Geffen. www.gunsnroses.com
Paint It Black–Rolling Stones (1966) B-side Stupid Girl, Aftermath, Decca (UK) and
London (US). www.rollingstones.com
Listen to the Music–Doobie Brothers (1972) B-side Toulouse Street, Toulouse
Street, Warner Bros. www.thedoobiebrothers.com
Maggie May–Rod Stewart (1971) A-side Reason to Believe, Every Picture Tells a
Story, Mercury. Sir Roderick David Stewart was knighted in 2016 for services to music
and charity, aka Rod The Mod. www.rodstewart.com
Mystify–INXS (1989) Single Release. Kick, WEA. RIP Michael Kelland John
Hutchence 22nd November 1997. www.inxs.com
What's My Scene?–Hoodoo Gurus (1987) A-side Heart of Darkness, Blow Your
Cool! Big time, Elektra, Mushroom. www.hoodoogurus.net
To Her Door–Paul Kelly and the Coloured Girls (1987) A-side Bicentennial, Under
the Sun, Mushroom. www.paulkelly.com.au

I'm Still On Your Side–Jimmy Barnes (1987) Single release, Freight Train Heart, Mushroom/Geffen www.jimmybarnes.com

Road to Nowhere–Talking Heads (1985) B-side Television Man, Little Creatures, Sire. www.store.talkingheadsofficial.com

David Bowie www.davidbowie.com

The Doors (1965 – 1973 * 1978) RIP Jim Morrison – James Douglas Morrison (3 July 1971 – just 27 years old) www.thedoors.com

The Beatles (active from 1960) John Lennon, Paul McCartney, George Harrison and Ringo Star. www.thebeatles.com

Led Zeppelin (1968 – 1980) Robert Plant, Jimmy Page, John Paul Jones, RIP John Bonham.) www.ledzeppelin.com

Big Yellow Taxi–*Counting Crows, such* a great version of *Joni Mitchell's* song (1970) B-side Woodstock, Ladies of the Canyon, Reprise. www.jonimitchell.com Counting Crows featuring Vanessa Carlton version (2002), Single, Hard Candy, Steve Lilywhite. www.countingcrows.com

Jessies Girl–Rick Springfield (1981) Single, Working Class Dog, RCA. www.rickspringfield.com

Welcome to the Jungle- Guns N Roses (1987) B Side Whole Lotta Rosie, Mt Brownstone, Appetite for Destruction, Geffen. www.gunsnroses.com

Bette Davis Eyes–Kim Carnes (1981) B-side Miss You Tonite, Single, Mistaken Identity, EMI America. www.kimcarnes.com

If You Leave Me Now–Chicago (1976) Single Chicago X, Columbia. www.chicagotheband.com

Edge of Seventeen––Stevie Nicks (1981) Single, Bella Donna, Modern. Jimmy Loving www.stevienicksofficial.com

Alright For Now–Tom Petty (1989) Full Moon Fever, MCA. www.tompetty.com

Eternal Flame–The Bangles (1989) B-side Walk Like an Egyptian, CBS, Liberation Australia. www.thebangles.com

Drive–The Cars (1984) B-side My Best Friend's Girl, Heartbeat City, Elektra. www.thecars.org

Waiting For a Girl Like You–Foreigner (1981) B-side I'm Gonna Win, 4, Atlantic. www.foreigneronline.com

Mr Jones–Counting Crows (1993) B-side Raining in Baltimore, August and Everything After, Geffen. www.countingcrows.com

Start Me Up–Rolling Stones (1981) B-side No Use in Crying, Tattoo You, The Glimmer Twins. www.rollingstones.com

Relax–Frankie Goes to Hollywood (1983) B-side One September Monday, Welcome to the Pleasuredome, ZTT. www.frankiesay.com

Free Fallin–Tom Petty (1989) B-sides Down The Line, Love is a Long Road, MCA, Jeff Lynee, Tom Petty, Mike Campbell. www.tompetty.com

1000 Miles Away–Hoodoo Gurus (1991) B-side I Think You Know, Kinky, RCA. www.hoodoogurus.net

Me and Bobby McGee–Janis Joplin (1971) B side Half Moon, Pearl, Columbia. www.janisjoplin.com

Tiny Dancer–Elton John – Sir Elton Hercules John, born Reginald Kenneth Dwight (and I thought I had alot of names, Go Elton!) (1972) B-side Razor Face, Madman Across The Water, Uni. www.eltonjohn.com

Nothing Else Matters—Metallica (1991), B-side Enter Sandman, Elektra. www.metallica.com

I'm On Fire—Bruce Springsteen (1982), B-side Johnny Bye Bye, Born in the U.S.A., Columbia. www.brucespringsteen.net

If You Leave Me, Can I Come Too?—Mental As Anything, (1981), B-side Assault and Flattery, Cats & Dogs, Regular Records. www.mentalasanything.com

Run To Paradise—Choirboys (1988), B-side Struck by Lightning, Big Bad Noise. Mushroom. www.choirboys.net

Miss Freelove '69—Hoodoo Gurus (1991), B-side Stomp the Tumbarumba, Kinky, RCA, www.hoodoogurus.net

Beds Are Burning—Midnight Oil (1987) Diesel and Dust, B-side Gunbarrell Highway, Columbia. www.midnightoil.com

Flame Trees—Cold Chisel (1984) B-side River Deep Mountain high, Twentieth Century, WEA. www.coldchisel.com.au

Need You Tonight—INXS (1987) B-side Mediate, Kick, Atlantic, Mercury, WEA. www.inxs.com

Gypsy—Fleetwood Mac (1982) B-side Cool Water, Mirage, Warner Bros. www.fleetwoodmac.com

Love Shack—B-52's (1989) B-side Channel Z, Cosmic Thing, Reprise. www.theb52s.com

Time After Time—Cyndi Lauper (1984), B-side I'll Kiss You, She's so unusual, Epic. www.cyndilauper.com

Shine On You Crazy Diamond—Pink Floyd (1975) Single. Wish you Were Here. Harvest (UK) and Columbia (USA)

Distant Sun—Crowded House (1993) B-side When You Come, Together Alone, Capitol. www.crowdedhouse.com

Wonderwall—Oasis (1995) B-side Round Are Way, What's the Story, Morning Glory, www.oasisinet.com

Drive—R.E.M (1992) B-side Winged Mammal Theme, Automatic for the People, Warner Bros. www.remhq.com

Black—Pearl Jam (1991) Single. Ten. Epic. www.pearljam.com (Eddie Vedder has my favourite voice in the universe.)

Smells Like Teen Spirit—Nirvana (1991) B-side Drain You, Nevermind, DGC. www.nirvana.com

My Hometown—Bruce Springsteen (1985) B-side Santa Claus is Coming to Town, Born in the U.S.A, Columbia. www.brucespringsteen.net

Lady—Kenny Rogers (1980) B-side Sweet Music Man, Greatest Hits, Liberty. www.kennyrogers.com

Jolene—Dolly Parton (1973) B-side Love, You're So Beautiful Tonight, Jolene, RCA Victor. www.dollyparton.com

Patience—Guns N Roses (1988) B-side Rocket Queen, G N R Lies, Geffen. www.gunsnroses.com

Start Me Up—Rolling Stones (1981) B-side No Use in Crying, Tattoo You, The Glimmer Twins. www.rollingstones.com

Pick You Up—Powderfinger (1996) Single. Double Allergic, Polydor. wwwpowderfinger.com

Gypsy—Fleetwood Mac (1982) B-side Cool Water, Mirage, Warner Bros.
www.fleetwoodmac.com
Love Her Madly—The Doors (1971) B-side (You Need Meat) Don't Go No Further,
L.A Woman, Elektra. www.thedoors.com

Other books by this author, Melanie Jay.

TWENTY YEARS AN ANGEL
(A TRUE STORY)

Twenty Years an Angel
~~*Bee Sting My Bali Diary*~~
~~*Bee Sing My Bali Diary Edit 2022*~~

Author : Melanie Jay

First published in Australia in 2012 and sold on www.lulu.com.

I have recently changed the name of my book to Twenty Years An Angel, as I have found my book being sold on various platforms, unbeknownst to me, and people are making an income for my book that I wrote. Unfair.

My heart, my story.

Copyright Melanie Jay, 2024. All rights reserved

E Book ISBN : 978-1-7635554-9-5
Print version ISBN : 978-1-7635554-8-8

This book is the digitalised true diary of Melanie Jay. The names of most people have been changed for privacy of my friends and family in my story. I wrote this book as a way of sharing my grief and to encourage others to do the same as a way of healing and allowing grief to escape the physical body and the mind. When your grief is out on paper, it's out.

The Bali bombings are unknown in this generation, just something that happened a long time ago, but to me it will always feel like yesterday.

I am open to connect with my readers if it might be a way of sharing grief for the healing of others. Feel free to connect with me on my social media channels through melaniejaybooks @ Instagram, Facebook, Tik-Tok
or email me at melaniejaybooks@gmail.com.
I'm working on my website too. www.melaniejaybooks.com.au

Thank you!

Wherever you are from and whatever languages you may speak, I want to say thank you for reading my novel.

English: Thank you
Maltese: Grah-tsee (Grazzi)
Spanish: Grah-see-us (Gracias)
French: Mare-see (Merci)
Arabic: Shuh-crahn-luh-come (شكرا لكم)
Bengali: Hon-yuh-bahd (ধন্যবাদ)
Russian: Spy-see-bah (Спасибо)
Portuguese: Oh-bree-gah-doe (Obrigado)
Indonesian: Teh-ree-mah kah-see (Terima kasih)
German: Dahnk-uh (Danke)
Turkish: Teh-sheh-coor ed-eh-duhm (Teşekkür ederim)
Italian: Gratz-eh (Grazie)
Ukrainian: Dya-koo-ee-you (Дякую)
Polish: Djen-koo-eh-chee (Dziękuję Ci)
Dutch: Dahnk-hyeh (Dank je)
Romanian: Mool-tsoo-mesk (Mulţumesc)
Czech: Deck-oo-you (Děkuju)
Hungarian: Kuh-suh-nem (Köszönöm)
Greek: Sahs-eef-ha-ree-stow (σας ευχαριστώ)
Swedish: Tack (Tack)
Bulgarian: Boh-gull-dah-ree-ah (Благодаря ти)
Catalan: Grah-see-us (Gràcies)
Danish: Tack-scale-do-have (Tak skal du have)
Slovak: Jah-quee-ehm (Ďakujem)
Finnish: Key-dose (Kiitos)
Lithuanian: ah-chew (Ačiū)
Galician: Grath-us (Grazas)
Slovenian: Huh-vah-luh-vahm (Hvala vam)
Latvian: Pahl-dee-es (Paldies)
Basque: Eh-scare-ee-ask-oh (Eskerrik asko)
Estonian: Ah-ee-tah (aitäh)
Serbian: Hvall-uh-fahm (Хвала вам)
Croatian: Hvall-uh-fahm (Hvala vam)
Welsh: Dee-olh (Diolch)
Irish Gaelic: Gur-uv mee-la mah ah-guth (Go raibh maith agat)
Scottish Gaelic: Tah-puh-lot (Tapadh leat)
Albanian: Fah-lehm-mean-deh-reet (Faleminderit)
Luxembourgish: Mare-see (Merci)
Swahili: Ah-sahn-teh (Asante)
Amharic: Ah-me-seh-gih-nah-leh-hu-ah (አመሰግናለሁ)
Yoruba: Oh-soon (O şeun)
Oromo: Gah-lah-tome (Galatoomi)

Afrikaans: Dahn-key (Dankie)
Hausa: Guhd-ee-ah (Godiya)
Igbo: Dah-loo (Daalụ)
Zulu: Gee-yah-bong-ah (Ngiyabonga)
Shona: Dah-ten-duh (Ndatenda)
Somali: Mah-sen-teh-hey (Mahadsan tahay)
Berber: Ten-meers (ⵜⴰⵏⴻⵎⵎⵉⵔⵜ.)
Hebrew: Toe-dah (תודה)
Kurdish: Su-pas (Spas)
Persian: Moo-shoo-sha-kuh-rahm (متشكرم)
Urdu: Ahv-gah-shoo-pree-ah (آپ کا شکریہ)
Uzbek: Rah-hmat (رحمت)
Baluchi: Mihn-not-wahr (منتوارون شومی)
Zazaki: Bear-who-dar (Berxudar)
Dari: Tuh-shay-curr (تشکر.)
Tajik: See-pose (сипос)
Kurmanji: Su-pas (Spas)
Hindi: Den-yee-niv-ahd (धन्यवाद)
Mandarin Chinese: She-eh She-eh (謝謝)
Malay: Ter-ee-mah kah-see (Terima kasih)
Bangla: Hun-ya-bahd (ধন্যবাদ)
Japanese: Ah-ree-gah-toe (ありがとう)
Punjabi: Dahn-wahd (ਧੰਨਵਾਦ)
Filipino: Sah-lah-maht (Salamat)
Marathi: Dahn-ya-vahd (धन्यवाद)
Korean: Gahm-sah (감사)
Vietnamese: Cahm-uhn-bahn (cảm ơn bạn)
Thai: khop-kuhn (ขอบคุณ)
Kannada: Dahn-ya-vah-dah-gah-do (ಧನ್ಯವಾದಗಳು)
Gujarati: Ahb-har (આભાર)
Malayalam: Nahn-dee (നന്ദി)
Odia: Dahn-ya-bahd (ଧନ୍ୟବାଦ)
Telugu: Dahn-ya-vah-dah-loo (ధన్యవాదాలు)
Tamil: Nahn-ree (நன்றி)
Burmese: Cheh-joo-tchen-bah-ray (ကျေးဇူးတင်ပါတယ်)
Kashmiri: Shoo-kree-ah (शुक्रिया)
Mongolian: Bah-yehr-la (баярлалаа)
Khmer: Sohm ah-kuhn (សូមអរគុណ)
Lao: Kawp-Jai (ຂອບໃຈ)

www.ingramcontent.com/pod-product-compliance
Lightning Source LLC
Chambersburg PA
CBHW070859260626
47162CB00007B/2508